THE
PUSHCART PRIZE, VII:
BEST OF THE
SMALL PRESSES

# THE PUSHCART PRIZE, VII:

## BEST OF THE SMALL PRESSES

# BEST OF THE SMALL PRESSES

*...WITH AN INDEX TO THE FIRST SEVEN VOLUMES*

*An annual small press reader.*

## EDITED BY BILL HENDERSON

with The Pushcart Prize editors

published by THE PUSHCART PRESS
1982-83 Edition

# THE PUSHCART PRIZE, VII:

Library of Congress Card Number: 76-58675
ISBN 0-916366-15-4
ISSN: 0149-7863

First printing June, 1982

Manufactured in The United States of America
by RAY FREIMAN and COMPANY, Stamford, Connecticut

NOTE ON THE ENDPAPERS—The wood engravings used for the endpapers
were engraved by Michael McCurdy of Penmaen Press for the Bieler
Press edition of *Everything That Has Been Shall Be Again* by John
Gilgun. The book will be reprinted in 1982 by David R. Godine Inc.
© 1981 by Michael McCurdy.

The following works are reprinted by permission of the publishers and the authors:

"Release, Surrender" © 1981 Fiction International
"Mercy" "The Witness" © 1981 The Iowa Review
"Getting Through It Together" © 1981 Wickwire Press
"Death and Lebanon" © 1981 The Iowa Review
"Notes on Mrs. Slaughter" © 1981 Mississippi Review
"Détente" © 1981 The Southern Review
"Helping T. S. Eliot Write Better" © 1981 The American Poetry Review
"Harmony of the World" © 1981 The Michigan Quarterly
"Christ Preaching At the Henley Regatta" © 1981 Guy Davenport. Collages © 1981 Roy R. Behrens
"Happy Boy, Allen" © 1981 The Mississippi Review
"The Author Encounters His Reading Public" © 1981 Partisan Review
"A Poetry of Restitution" © 1981 The Yale Review
"Blessing In Disguise: Cross Dressing As Re-Dressing for Female Modernists" © 1981 Massachusetts Review
"On A Drying Hill" © 1981 The Southern Review
"Writing Off The Self" © 1981 Raritan Review
"Poetry In Dark Times" © 1981 Parnassus: Poetry In Review
"El Salvador: An Aide Memoir" © 1981 American Poetry Review
"Mexicans Begin Jogging" © 1981 Revista Chicano-Riquena
"My Father's Martial Arts" © 1981 Antioch Review
"Dear Jeffers" © 1981 Cutbank
"Forever In That Year" © 1981 American Poetry Review
"From My Window" © 1981 The Paris Review
"Turning Thirty" © 1981 Pequod
"My Garden, My Daylight" © 1981 New England Review
"My Father's Desk" © 1981 Ironwood
"What The Gossips Saw" © 1981 Ahsahta Press
"The Journey" © 1981 Logbridge—Rhodes, The Estate of James Wright and Random House, Inc.
"The Snakes of September" © 1981 Antaeus
"A Requiem" © 1981 New Letters
"There Is No Word For Goodbye" © 1981 Blue Cloud Quarterly
"Translation" © 1981 Poet and Critic
"The Eisenhower Years" © 1981 Black Warrior Review
"If Porcelain, Then Only The Kind" © 1981 Mr. Cogito
"The Body" © 1981 American Poetry Review
"And The Scream" © 1981 Antaeus
"Without End" © 1981 Quarterly West
"I Sing The Body Electric" © 1981 Antaeus
"Being With Men" © 1981 Tendril
"From Sand Creek" © 1981 Thunder's Mouth Press
"The Last Straw" © 1981 Tar River Poetry
"Whitman" © 1981 Holy Cow! Press
"A Man of the World" © 1981 by Washington and Lee University, reprinted from *Shenandoah: The Washington and Lee University Review* with permission of the editor
"Tattoo" © 1981 by Washington and Lee University, reprinted from *Shenandoah: The Washington and Lee University Review* with the permission of the editor
"Making A Fist" from *Hugging The Jukebox* by Naomi Shihab Nye © 1982 by Naomi Shihab Nye. Reprinted by permission of E. P. Dutton, Inc. First appeared in *On The Edge of the Sky*, Iguana Press, Springfield, Missouri.
"Poetry In A Discouraging Time" © 1981 by The University of Georgia, reprinted by permission of the author and *The Georgia Review*.
"Roland Barthes, Autobiography And The End of Writing" © 1981 by The University of Georgia, reprinted by permission of the author and *The Georgia Review*.
"The Gardens" © 1981 by The University of Georgia, reprinted by permission of the author and *The Georgia Review*
"Europa" from *The Fortunate Traveller* © 1980, 1981 by Derek Walcott. Originally published in *Antaeus*.
"How Mickey Made It" © 1980 by Jayne Anne Phillips, reprinted by permission of Bookslinger Editions and Jayne Anne Phillips.

*Acknowledgements*

"I Am Learning to Abandon The World", first appeared in *Poetry*, © 1981 The Modern Poetry Association, reprinted by permission of the Editor of Poetry.

"Dusting", first appeared in *Poetry*, © 1981 The Modern Poetry Association, reprinted by permission of the Editor of *Poetry*.

"The Quest" first appeared in *Poetry*, © 1981 The Modern Poetry Association, reprinted by permission of the Editor of *Poetry*.

"From My Window" © 1981 C. K. Williams. Reprinted by permission of the author.

"The Southern Cross" © 1981 by Charles Wright. Reprinted by permission of the author and Random House Inc.

"Shelter The Pilgrim" © 1981 by Fred Licht. First published in *The Hudson Review*.

"Standing By Words" © 1981 Wendell Berry. From *The Hudson Review*.

"Chief" © 1981 Michael S. Harper. Reprinted from *Ploughshares*.

This Book is For
Walter Meade

♨ ♨ ♨

# INTRODUCTION:

## About Pushcart Prize VII

AS USUAL, this edition is very different from other editions in *The Pushcart Prize* series. Many new editors help make selections each year and that may account for our variety. More important, I think, is the imagination, vigor and restlessness of small press editors and writers working in non-commercial freedom.

The poetry this year was picked by Lamont prize winners Carolyn Forché and Gerald Stern. Both poets, after spending months considering thousands of nominations, said they had never read so much poetry in their lives. "A fierce education," said Jerry. Carolyn, who read her share of the nominations while publishing a poetry collection about her experiences in El Salvador, teaching in Alaskan prisons and getting married in Virginia, was amazed to find so many good poets that she had never heard of.

Our thirty-two poems, in a dazzle of styles, moods and thoughts, by both known and unknown poets, are selected from a range of presses including Ahsahta Press, *Black Warrior Review*, *Blue Cloud Quarterly*, *Cutbank*, Iguana Press, *Ironwood*, Mr. Cogito Press, *Pequod*, *Revista Chicano-Riquena*, and publications such as *American Poetry Review*, *Antaeus* and *Ploughshares*.

Some of the essays in PPVII are more political and others are more demanding than in past years. The selections by Christopher Clausen *(Georgia Review)*, Terrence Des Pres *(Parnassus)* and Carolyn Forché *(American Poetry Review)* discuss political and cultural roles for poetry. Essays by Wendell Berry *(Hudson Review)*, Susan Gubar *(Massachusetts Review)*, John Hollander *(Yale Review)* and Richard Poirier *(Raritan: A Quarterly Review—*a brand new publication) will require dedicated reading, but each essay is well worth an evening of the reader's attention. Moving

11

and important biographical portraits are offered by Thom Gunn on his teacher Yvor Winters *(Southern Review)* and by J. Gerald Kennedy on Roland Barthes *(Georgia Review)*.

This year, for the first time ever, *The Pushcart Prize* offers detailed, can't fail, editing and writing instructions by Cynthia Ozick ("Helping T. S. Eliot Write Better" *American Poetry Review)*.

At the very peak of our fiction excitement this year is Barbara Bedway's first-published story "Death In Lebanon" *(Iowa Review)*. Our fiction department also welcomes back Jayne Anne Phillips (Bookslinger editions) and Joyce Carol Oates *(Southern Review)* and we reprint for the first time in this series tales by Charles Baxter *(Michigan Quarterly)*, Richard Burgin *(Mississippi Review)*, Guy Davenport (North Point Press), William Gilson (Wickwire Press), Elizabeth Inness-Brown *(Fiction International)*, Fred Licht *(Hudson Review)*, Amos Oz *(Partisan Review)*, Mary Robison *(Mississippi Review)*, Richard Selzer *(Iowa Review)*, Barbara Thompson *(Shenandoah)* and Edmund White *(Shenandoah)*.

Numbers count for little when introducing such achievement, but each year it is my task to recite some figures. As of this edition, this series has honored work from 227 small book publishers and little magazines. New to the series are Bookslinger Editions, *Cutbank*, Iguana Press, Logbridge-Rhodes, Mr. Cogito Press, North Point Press, *Poet and Critic*, *Raritan: A Quarterly Review*, *Revista Chicano-Riquena*, River Styx, Tar River Poetry, Tendril, Thunder's Mouth Press, Wickwire Press and *The Yale Review*.

To date, we have reprinted 449 selections by 403 authors and honored by citation the stories, poems and essays of hundreds more.

Pushcart Press has managed to do this from a one car garage (the car sleeps outside) on Long Island without any grants for the press itself, but we are always glad when we are able to pay our authors something more than free books and praise. This year The Helen Foundation of Salt Lake City, Utah has provided a $100 award to the lead poem (Charles Wright's "The Southern Cross" *Paris Review)*, the lead essay (Wendell Berry's "Standing By Words" *Hudson Review)* and the lead story (Barbara Thompson's "Tattoo" *Shenandoah)*

We thank The Foundation, and we also once again thank Avon Books for their spirited paperback publications of this series. Our Dedication to Avon's Walter Meade is an inadequate attempt to pay tribute to a man and a company who have supported The Pushcart Prize from the start.

Bill Henderson
Wainscott, New York

Note: nominations for this series are invited from any small, independent, literary book press or magazine in the world. Up to six nominations—tear sheets or copies selected from work published in that calendar year—are accepted by our October 15 deadline each year. Write to Pushcart Press, P.O. Box 380, Wainscott, N.Y. 11975 if you need more information.

# THE
# PEOPLE WHO HELPED

FOUNDING EDITORS — *Anaïs Nin (1903–1977), Buckminster Fuller, Charles Newman, Daniel Halpern, Gordon Lish, Harry Smith, Hugh Fox, Ishmael Reed, Joyce Carol Oates, Len Fulton, Leonard Randolph, Leslie Fiedler, Nona Balakian, Paul Bowles, Paul Engle, Ralph Ellison, Reynolds Price, Rhoda Schwartz, Richard Morris, Ted Wilentz, Tom Montag, William Phillips. Poetry editor: H. L. Van Brunt.*

EDITORS — *Walter Abish, Ai, Elliott Anderson, John Ashbery, Robert Boyers, Joseph Brodsky, Wesley Brown, Hayden Carruth, Raymond Carver, Malcolm Cowley, Paula Deitz, Steve Dixon, M. D. Elevitch, Loris Essary, Raymond Federman, Ellen Ferber, Carolyn Forché, Stuart Friebert, Jon Galassi, Tess Gallagher, Louis Gallo, John Gardner, George Garrett, Louise Glück, David Godine, William Goyen, Jorie Graham, Linda Gregg, Barbara Grossman, Michael Harper, DeWitt Henry, J. R. Humphreys, John Irving, June Jordan, Karen Kennerly, Galway Kinnell, Mary Kinzie, Carolyn Kizer, Jerzy Kosinski, Richard Kostelanetz, Seymour Krim, Maxine Kumin, Stanley Kunitz, James Laughlin, Seymour Lawrence, Naomi Lazard, Herb Leibowitz, Denise Levertov, Stanley Lindberg, Thomas Lux, Mary MacArthur, Daniel Menaker, Frederick Morgan, Howard Moss, Cynthia Ozick, Jayne Anne Phillips, Robert Phillips, George Plimpton, Stanley Plumly, Eugene Redmond, Ed Sanders, Teo Savory, Grace Schulman, Harvey Shapiro, Leslie Silko, Charles Simic, Dave Smith, William Stafford, Gerald Stern, David St. John, Bill and Pat Strachan, Ron Sukenick, Barry Targan, Anne Tyler, John Updike, Samuel Vaughan, David Wagoner, Derek Walcott, Ellen Wilbur, David Wilk, Yvonne, Bill Zavatsky.*

SPECIAL CONTRIBUTING EDITORS FOR THIS EDITION —
*Bo Ball, Jim Barnes, Gina Berriault, Chana Bloch, Michael Blumenthal, Michael Dennis Browne, Frederick Busch, Kathy Callaway, Steve Cannon, Denise Cassens, Kelly Cherry, Naomi Clark, Marilyn Coffey, Andrei Codrescu, Robert Creeley, Susan Strayer Deal, John Engels, Jane Flanders, H. E. Francis, Ellen Gilchrist, Jack Gilbert, Lorrie Goldensohn, Patrick Worth Gray, Lyn Hejinian, Don Hendrie Jr., Michael Hogan, Josephine Jacobsen, Janet Kauffman, Shirley Kaufman, Benedict Kiely, Cinda Kornblum, Marilyn Krysl, Mariam Levine, Gerald Locklin, David Long, David Madden, Clarence Major, Andrienne Marcus, Dan Masterson, Cleopatra Mathis, Colleen McElroy, Michael McFee, Heather McHugh, Sandra McPherson, Douglas Messerli, Paul Metcalf, Judith Moffett, Charles Molesworth, Jennifer Moyer, Lisel Mueller, Carol Muske, David Ohle, Sharon Olds, Joyce Peseroff, Mary Peterson, Robert Pinsky, Jarold Ramsey, David Ray, Michael Ryan, Theodore Roszak, Sherod Santos, Philip Schultz, Lynne Sharon Schwartz, Richard Smith, Elizabeth Spires, Maura Stanton, George Steiner, Pamela Stewart, Barbara Szerlip, Julia Thacker, Stephanie Vaughn, Sara Vogan, Barbara Watkins, Gayle Whittier, C. K. Williams, Harold Witt, David Wojahn, Charles Wright, Christine Zawadiwsky, Pat Zelver.*

ROVING EDITOR — *Gene D. Chipps*

EDITORS AT LARGE — *Kirby and Liz Williams*

DESIGN AND PRODUCTION — *Ray Freiman*

JACKET DESIGN — *Barbara Lish*

EUROPEAN EDITOR — *Andrew Motion*

MANAGING EDITOR — *Helen Handley*

POETRY EDITORS FOR THIS EDITION — *Carolyn Forché, Gerald Stern*

EDITOR AND PUBLISHER — *Bill Henderson*

# PRESSES FEATURED IN THE FIRST SEVEN PUSHCART PRIZE EDITIONS

Agni Review
Ahsahta Press
Ailanthus Press
Alcheringa/Ethnopoetics
Alice James Books
American Literature
American PEN
American Poetry Review
Amnesty International
Anaesthesia Review
Antaeus
Antioch Review
Apalachee Quarterly
Aphra
The Ark
Assembling
Aspen Leaves
Aspen Poetry Anthology
Barlenmir House
Barnwood Press
Beliot Poetry Review
Bilingual Review
Bits Press

17

Black American Literature Forum
Black Rooster
Black Scholar
Black Sparrow
Black Warrior Review
Blue Cloud Quarterly
Blue Wind Press
BOA Editions
Bookslinger Editions
Boxspring
Burning Deck Press
Caliban
California Quarterly
Canto
Capra Press
Cedar Rock
Center
Chariton Review
Chicago Review
Chouteau Review
Chowder Review
Cimarron Review
Cincinnati Poetry Review
City Lights Books
Clown War
CoEvolution Quarterly
Cold Mountain Press
Columbia: A Magazine of Poetry and Prose
Confluence Press
Confrontation
Copper Canyon Press
Cosmic Information Agency
Crawl Out Your Window
Crazy Horse
Cross Cultural Communication
Cross Currents
Curbstone Press
Cutbank
Dacotah Territory
Decatur House

December
Dreamworks
Dryad Press
Duck Down Press
Durak
East River Anthology
Fiction
Fiction Collective
Fiction International
Field
Firelands Art Review
Five Trees Press
Gallimaufry
Genre
The Georgia Review
Ghost Dance
Goddard Journal
The Godine Press
Graham House Press
Graywolf Press
Greensboro Review
Greenfield Review
Hard Pressed
Hills
Holmgangers Press
Holy Cow!
Hudson Review
Icarus
Iguana Press
Indiana Writes
Inwood Press
Intermedia
Intro
Invisible City
Iowa Review
Ironwood
The Kanchenjunga Press
Kansas Quarterly
Kayak
Kenyon Review

Latitudes Press
L'Epervier Press
Liberation
Linquis
The Little Magazine
Living Hand Press
Living Poets Press
Logbridge-Rhodes
Lowlands Review
Lucille
Lynx House Press
Manroot
Magic Circle Press
Malahat Review
Massachusetts Review
Michigan Quarterly
Milk Quarterly
Montana Gothic
Montana Review
Missouri Review
Mississippi Review
Montemora
Mr. Cogito Press
Mulch Press
Nada Press
New America
New England Review
New Letters
North American Review
North Atlantic Books
North Point Press
Northwest Review
Obsidian
Oconee Review
October
Ohio Review
Ontario Review
Open Places
Oyez Press
Painted Bride Quarterly

Paris Review
Parnassus: Poetry In Review
Partisan Review
Penca Books
Penumbra Press
Pentagram
Persea: An International Review
Pequod
Pitcairn Press
Ploughshares
Poet and Critic
Poetry
Poetry Northwest
Poetry Now
Prairie Schooner
Prescott Street Press
Promise of Learnings
Quarry West
Quarterly West
Rainbow Press
Raritan: A Quarterly Review
Red Cedar Review
Red Clay Books
Red Earth Press
Release Press
Revista Chicano-Riquena
River Styx
Russian *Samizdat*
Salmagundi
San Marcos Press
Seamark Press
Second Coming Press
The Seventies Press
Shankpainter
Shantih
Shenandoah
A Shout In The Street
Sibyl-Child Press
Small Moon
The Smith

The Spirit That Moves Us
Southern Poetry Review
Some
The Sonora Review
Southern Review
Southwestern Review
Spectrum
St. Andrews Press
Story Quarterly
Sun & Moon
Sun Press
Sunstone
Tar River Poetry
Tendril
Telephone Books
Texas Slough
THIS
Threepenny Review
13th Moon
Transatlantic Review
Three Rivers Press
Thorp Springs Press
Thunder's Mouth Press
Toothpaste Press
TriQuarterly
Truck Press
Tuumba Press
Undine
Unicorn Press
Unmuzzled Ox
Unspeakable Visions of the Individual
Vagabond
Virginia Quarterly
Water Table
Washington Writers Workshop
Western Humanities Review
Westigan Review
Wickwire Press
Willmore City
Word-Smith

Xanadu
Yale Review
Yardbird Reader
Y'Bird

# CONTENTS

THE
PUSHCART PRIZE, VII:
BEST OF THE
SMALL PRESSES

# TATTOO

fiction by BARBARA THOMPSON

from SHENANDOAH

*nominated by* SHENANDOAH

THE SERVANT WOMAN rolls back the sleeves of her kurta, throws off the flimsy scarf and pours a dollop of oil into her small fleshy palm. Julia is already naked on the cotton mat, her light hair held away from the massage oil by a child's plastic barrette. Her face in company is alert, sharp, foxy, but now in repose, unobserved by anyone, it slips back into the mild formlessness of the time before her marriage.

Kishwar transfers oil to the other hand, automatically invoking the blessing of Allah on her enterprise, falling back on her haunches to gain momentum for the next lunge at Julia's vertebral ridge. Julia tells her friends Kishwar grunts like a sumo wrestler.

Kishwar has been in the household for more than a year. She was hired as Sherezad's ayah, and when the little girl began school last September, she became Julia's part-time masseuse. She is short for a Punjabi, fat and dark, and she has a light merry laugh. Kishwar's husband works somewhere as a driver.

It is mid-May. The foreigners spend whatever time they can manage in swimming suits around the Punjab Club pool. Julia has her massage every day at eleven and goes off, oiled and sleek, to lunch there. Three or four times every month she meets a man. He is Pakistani like her husband, but younger than Julia and still unmarried. His family maintains a huge house on the Canal Bank, but when he can contrive an excuse to come to Lahore from his post in Peshawar, he stays in one of the old-fashioned suites the Club maintains for out-of-station members. This is the first day of such a visit; earlier, after her husband left, Julia spoke with him on the telephone. Smiling, she closes her eyes for what is meant to be a short nap. When she wakens it is well past the hour. Kishwar is still working over her, mindless of time as a water-wheel. Julia jumps up, fumbling for her terrycloth robe on the floor—and sees the tattoos. Kishwar has no time to cover them.

"They're all over her arms," Julia tells Nazir later at the Club. "Hearts and flowers, flying birds. All blue."

Julia lies in a pink bikini at the edge of the Club pool. The day is as hot and dry as if the country were a tandoor, one of the mounded earthen ovens that dot the city. Few people are out, even here: two English children and their doughy mother storing up sun for the summer of home-leave; a crew-cut American who swims ten measured laps and hurries away. Pakistanis are always rare. Only love or lust or cultural alienation would bring a Pakistani to a communal swimming pool at noon in May.

Nazir Ahmad, who possesses all these qualifications, lies next to Julia. He spent ten years in America on a student visa and has sloughed off his origins sufficiently to admire an even tan and be willing to strip to a bit of colored latex in the presence of strangers. He came back five years ago, summoned by a spate of cables warning of his mother's imminent demise. Once he returned her heart condition improved miraculously and his Berkeley Ph.D. in Political Science served to ease his way through the Civil Service Exam. He has become the Deputy Commissioner in Peshawar.

And although he was sufficiently intimidated by his family not to bring back as wife the Jewish graduate student with whom he had been living, for the past ten months he has been seeing Julia. Today, as always, they will drink pink gins, lunch on kebabs and nan, and go up to his room. Julia will go separately, her arms full of brown shopping bags from the Mall, as though she is carrying parcels for some woman friend staying there. No one but the Club servants will know.

"She must have a past," Nazir says. "Your maidservant."

"Why?"

"Respectable 'desi' women don't go in for tattoos. But if one did, it wouldn't be the kind of design you see on British sailors."

"She has a perfectly respectable-looking husband," Julia says.

He is drowsy from the sun and gin and beginning to think of the cool dark room above. He calls the bearer and orders lunch. It is brought to them at the pool by two servants in starched white, their long coats cinched with cummerbands, their pugris stiff and tall above their heads. Julia and Nazir eat with their fingers, their movements quick, expectant.

That night at dinner Julia tells her husband about the tattoos. It is one of her duties as his wife to be entertaining at dinner. She spends a fair amount of time preparing herself—collecting gossip at bridge parties, going to family weddings and funerals and circumcisions, reading the air mail magazines at the Club. *The New Statesman* is best for her purposes, though its politics are not her husband's. He owns a complex of textile mills.

After six years of marriage, her own politics are non-existent, which Julia herself in reflective moments knows to be an odd neutrality in a woman who came here as an officer, however junior, in the U.S. Foreign Service. Lahore was her first overseas post, and nothing in her training or the talk of others had prepared her for the emotions she would feel at the work assigned her, refusing visas to the legion of the hopeless who were trying to emigrate. In time it numbed her: her real life began at twilight on the race course grounds, urging a long-maned polo pony around the perimeter of the field while the men, Pakistanis and a few foreigners, played their games. The horse was lent her by the man who later became her husband, a stocky middle-aged Punjabi from an old family who was at least partially married: his wife lived in the village. The second summer Julia found herself pregnant, and in the lassitude of that state, intensified by the flower-rich monsoon heat, let go of her life of demanding autonomy. With something like relief she let herself be married to him under the polygamous dispensation of Islamic law.

They are dining alone tonight and so her husband summons Kishwar into the dining room. Julia has aroused his curiosity; he will inspect the tattoos himself. The servant woman toddles in raking at the dopatta over her hair, self-conscious at this notice by the Sahib. He is pleasant, hearty, almost flirtatious with her—his habitual manner with women who could not possibly misunderstand.

Because of this manner and its contrast to the strict formality with which he treats the wives of his friends and business associates, Julia believed in the beginning that he had no interest in other women. Then when Sherezad was three, she discovered that every Thursday night, before the ritual bath that purified him for his Friday prayers, he visited a singing woman in a brothel in the Hira Mundi.

When Julia told him she was leaving, he was courteous and calm and offered, with regret at her decision, to take care of the travel arrangements if she was sure that was what she wanted. Of course, she could not take her jewelry, the rubies set with pearls, the heavy kundan earrings with the emerald drops: Customs would search her for any gold illegally exported. And she could not take Sherezad, who was without a valid passport.

Julia, with the wisdom of the weak, gave in immediately and made no terms. She knew he would not relent or be subverted. He loved Sherezad as he loved his Rajput miniatures, rarely looking at them but always conscious that they hung in fine gold frames in an air conditioned room with black cloths over the glass to keep the colors from fading.

They went on as before, but imperceptibly, without any volition on her part, Julia changed. She continued her Urdu lessons with the old Kashmiri ustad who came three mornings a week, but her early proficiency left her; she was lapsing into the kitchen Urdu of the other foreign women who had not been scholars and government officers. And after a time she braved the company of other Americans, steeling herself against a continuation of the coolness they had shown her at the time of Sherezad's birth. But those days and that cadre of diplomats had passed. Julia's husband was rich and clubbable; they were welcomed everywhere.

Her husband rarely accompanied her; he did not want to be officially perceived as a client of the Americans. But he seemed glad that Julia was back with 'her own kind' as though he understood it to mean that she was abandoning the excessive expectations with which she had begun their marriage, and was accepting the compromises her circumstance required.

A summer ago at the Consul General's reception for the Fourth of July, Julia met Nazir Ahmad. If her husband knows about the affair, he has elected to be complaisant. Julia's virtue was never a commodity of great value; he knew there had been men before him. And he knows too, as Julia did only when it was too late, that if he should ever want to do so, he can use this indiscretion to send her back to her own country, cut her off forever from Sherezad.

But there is nothing of that menace in the air tonight as they dine together under the whirring fans while Sherezad sleeps in the adjacent garden in a cocoon of mosquito netting. Julia can see that he is enjoying his interrogation of the maidservant, the flutter into which he has cast her by his courtliness and the range of his questions: Has she sons? What is her village? How does she come to be in Lahore? Kishwar answers in monosyllables, smiling shyly, her eyes downcast. The sleeves of her cotton shirt are tight at the wrists. He has not mentioned the tattoos, and after a while Julia realizes that he never will. That is not his way. He will lead her by indirection to tell him whatever he wants to know, either as an accidental self-betrayal or a free offering. His patience comes of knowing he has, at last resort, the power to command her. Julia feels a chill and goes out into the dark veranda to make sure that Sherezad has not thrown off her covers.

The next morning when she is again naked under Kishwar's kneading, Julia composes her questions in schoolbook Urdu, asking the woman where the markings came from, how she comes to have them. She cannot see Kishwar's face when she asks but she feels the woman's hands tighten. Then with a laugh, Kishwar gives Julia's buttock an affectionate slap. "Meri jan bahaut passand—"

Julia cannot follow the language. "Your husband likes it?" she asks tentatively in English.

Kishwar laughs again, a lazy laugh laced with contempt for the little dark husband about whom Julia could have such an unlikely

idea. "Not husband," she says in English. "Meri jan." My Beloved.
She says it comfortably, companionably.

Julia tells Nazir at lunch: "You can't believe it! She's so ugly.
She's fat and gap-toothed and black as the Ace of Spades. And she
has a lover!"

As she says it she is sorry. Slurs against color are acceptable from
him, not from her. She has heard the tales of British memsahibs
who undressed in front of their servants as they would have their
poodles because, being black, they were not quite men. She is
never sure what Nazir feels; he himself is quite dark, a dull cafe-au-
lait.

"Think of Cleopatra," he says. "Swarthy, short-legged and with a
hooked nose." He congratulates himself on finding an image that is
racially neutral.

"If it's her lover who likes it, I wonder what her husband thinks,"
Julia muses.

That is a line of speculation Nazir prefers not to follow.

In the evening as Julia and Kishwar return from the bazaar,
Kishwar's husband is waiting at the gate. Another man is with him,
a tall lean Pathan with a sharp eye and the clothing of the Peshawar
District. Julia hands over the parcels to the bearer, and Kishwar
goes to her husband. There is a hasty exchange, monosyllabic and
stacatto and then Kishwar comes to ask Julia for leave. Julia gives
her the night but tells her to be back by breakfast time. Tomorrow
is Nazir's last day. She wants to go to him scented and oiled, a sun-
flushed houri. She likes the image of herself as a gift, and she
dresses in bright soft colors—saffron, peach, aquamarine—layers
of cloth to be unwrapped and inside, the firm soft flesh that
Kishwar has prepared.

It is noon when Kishwar turns up. Julia is late already, and still
on the telephone negotiating with her sister-in-law that Sherezad
will be delivered to her house after school. There have been nasty
incidents involving little girls left alone with menservants even in
the best regulated households. Her husband does not permit her
to leave Sherezad without a woman. Julia has explained this more
than once, a little frantically she knows. She has the uncomfortable
feeling that the other woman knows exactly why she is in such a
hurry.

Kishwar looks worn and dirty, and she makes no apology at all for her tardiness, not even the conventional lies about sudden illness or family crisis. Julia has girded herself against the falsehoods but now she finds herself resenting Kishwar's disregard of the forms; it is a little insulting.

Kishwar trails her to the car as though she has more to say. Another request. "Not now," Julia says firmly. Her good nature is being imposed on.

Kishwar goes into halting English. "Memsahib, you speak to Lat'-sahib for me," she says, using the word "lord" that is reserved for governors and high officials. "Nazir-sahib." Her manner is sullen for somebody, especially a Punjabi, asking a favor.

"I can't stop now. I'm late."

Kishwar looks around. The house servants are busy elsewhere. Only two male figures lounging at the gate would see her—if they turn around—as she throws herself at Julia's feet, pressing her little round belly against Julia's shins. She hangs onto them sobbing. The sobs seem real. With a sigh and a glance at her watch, Julia urges Kishwar to her feet, and into the comparative privacy of the veranda.

Kishwar's husband has sent her. His honor is at stake. That much is clear; Julia can follow it even in the mix of Urdu, Punjabi and pidgin English. It is the usual story when some extraordinary request is about to be made. "Safarish," the favor that puts one eternally in somebody's debt, is a way of life here.

The details are difficult for Julia to follow. A Pathan tribesman—an Affridi from the hills outside Peshawar—came to Kishwar's husband yesterday morning. His only son is in jail in Peshawar, charged with murder. The boy is fifteen. He is accused of taking the gold earrings from a three-year-old girl of his village, and, when she said that she would tell her mother, of throwing her into the well. The earrings were knotted in the cord that fastened his baggy shelwar trousers. He said he had found them, but when the police beat him, he confessed. Now he will go to prison for life. The girl's family is willing to accept restitution—the blood-price: she was one of several daughters and the price includes not only gold but animals. But Government says the boy must go to trial. The Deputy Commissioner—Nazir Ahmad—has the power to release him.

"But he's guilty," Julia says. "Why should Nazir-sahib let him go free?" She is about to add, "and why do you plead for him?", when she understands. Of course, this Pathan, the sinewy man with the black moustache here yesterday in the courtyard is Kishwar's lover, the man for whom she had herself tattooed.

"If you want to, you can come with me to the Club. Nazir-sahib is likely to be there and you can speak with him yourself," she says. "I can't take any responsibility for it." She adds that for form; she has already taken on some responsibility just by listening.

The servant woman waits patiently at the edge of the Club lawn, a good distance from the swimming pool, where ayahs are permitted. She squats in the shade of the pink bougainvillea vine, every now and then getting up to look through the servants' gate at something or someone on the roadway. She has wrapped her sheer nylon dopatta over her head and neck, covering herself as much as possible. Near the pool the sahibs, in strength today because of the Friday holiday, lie glistening with sunoil on their bright terry towels. Occasionally a child dives off the board or paddles around the shallow end under the eye of his mother, but the real use of the blue water is to cool the tanning adults who float about on its surface in black trunk inner-tubes, drinks in hand.

Nazir tries to ignore the maidservant. He doesn't like refusing favors and he doesn't want to grant this one. From Julia's report, the boy seems clearly guilty, and any official interference would be not only wrong but conspicuous. So he sucks on his drink, splashing pool water on his shoulders to cool himself. But whatever he does he feels Kishwar's black eyes on him. He may as well hear her out. He throws a towel over his bare torso and walks to the gate.

She stands up and squints over her shoulder as he approaches. He sees two men, one in Peshawari dress, at the end of the servants' walk. "Ji, Mai?" He addresses her in the familiar form of 'mother', glancing without meaning to at her arms. Only the faint blue edge of the tattoo is visible at the buttoned wrist of her shirt.

"I told Memsahib," she says. "I will be beaten if you do not do this thing."

"Why do you plead for this boy? What is the father to you?" Nazir says it in as kindly a manner as possible. He asks not because he doubts Julia's interpretation but out of curiosity, to hear what a traditional Punjabi woman would answer in such a case.

"He did my husband a service once," the woman replies.

Nazir tries not to smile at that way of speaking of it.

She looks him straight in the face as though she reads his thoughts. "This Pathan killed a man for him."

Nazir shouts to the bearer to bring him a chair, slumps into it. He should have known the story was not as simple as Julia said.

Kishwar does not speak again until the bearer is out of earshot. "My husband was in prison," she begins. "It was nothing." She makes a gesture with open palms to indicate the absence of any guilt. "He was innocent. There was a quarrel between families. Someone had to confess. He had no job so he was chosen. He came to prison here in Lahore."

Nazir's work is administering the law; he does not take easily to her assumption that while justice must be served, it need not be served with any precision. For nothing, for his family's convenience, a man will serve seven years Rigorous Imprisonment?

"We were married only a little time. I had no child. I was prettier then. A man saw me. He would wait for me on the paths and give me sweets. He would come to the well and draw water for me. I was weak. I fell.

"When my husband's people came to know of it, they sent me away. I could not go back to my own people as I was, so I went to live with him. He was a good man, he never beat me. He kept me in the inner courtyard and never let me go anywhere, even to the shrine, but he bought me shiny cloth for clothes and pomegranates and wild honey so that I would conceive. Then at the end of the fourth year, he took me to Montgomery to the man who gives tattoos. He said it was so I could not run away. Where would I run to?"

She unfastens the buttons at the wrists of her shirt and rolls back the sleeves. Nazir sees that among the flowers and hearts, the birds in flight, are words in Urdu: a man's name, Asif Magid, and a date in the Islamic calendar. "Memsahib saw this."

"Memsahib can't read the Urdu," he says.

"It was the next year in the dry month before the rains. We were sleeping out on the roof, and on the night of the dark of the moon, someone came and killed him with a knife."

"Asif Magid?"

"Asif Magid, whom I loved. The man who killed him cut his throat so deeply that his head hung loose, and he cut the palms of his hands and his genitals. He must have done all that after he was dead because I did not wake until the flies began to buzz and the vultures circle over him. It was almost daybreak and he had been dead so long his blood was like river mud. I knew my husband had done it, or some of his kinfolk. When the constable came, I told him.

"But word came back that my husband was still in prison in Lahore, and that his kinfolk too had been locked up that night, taken in Lahore on suspicion of planning a burglary. So I went back to my husband's people and lived with them like a slave until my husband came out of prison. He beat me at first to take away the shame, but afterwards he brought me here to Lahore. He swore to me that he had no connection with the killing of Asif-sahib. I believed it because he swore on the heads of our unborn sons."

She smiles a queer smile. "I have no child to this day."

Nazir is impatient. "But what does all this have to do with that other business—the boy, the gold earrings?"

"Yesterday that Pathan came to my husband's quarters. He had shared my husband's prison cell those years ago. He knew—as everything, sahib is known—that I have a place with Memsahib, and that you will not refuse Memsahib's safarish. He asked my husband to obtain his son's freedom."

Nazir is annoyed at the implication that this affair with Julia is generally known. They have been unfailingly discreet. Julia has never even been to Peshawar. "Why should your husband ask you to plead, even if I were able to grant it?"

"This man did my husband a killing once, out of friendship." Her tone is heavy, implying it is something he already knows. "He is the one who came at the dark of the moon and killed Asif-sahib as he lay next to me."

Nazir shouts for another gin. This is like everything else in his official life in this place. He longs for the orderliness of America, where appetites are simple and simply satisfied, where killings are done out of need and anger, not out of duty and friendship.

Kishwar sees his weariness and presses. "This Pathan lived with my husband in his cell. They shared everything, their grief at having no sons, my husband's shame at the dishonor I had brought him. They were closer than brothers.

"He was released from prison a year before my husband. His own village was in the Frontier, a thousand miles away. He had never been to our village, but he knew from my husband's telling that the house of Asif-sahib was the tallest of all, that it stood next to the ruin of the Sikh gurdwara and had wooden pillars carved with flowers.

"He sent a cable to my husband's kinfolk, calling them in the name of their jailed brother to meet him in the bazaar in Lahore. He met them at the tandoor, and while they were eating he went away on some pretext, leaving behind some pieces of luggage. They were filled with burglar's tools. He went to the police constable and told him that he had overheard those men from Montgomery planning a robbery and that their implements would be found with them. They were jailed for two days.

"That night this Pathan killed Asif-sahib as he lay next to me. No one suspected him. He was known to no one. Even my husband"—she spits on the grass—"knew nothing until yesterday."

Kishwar turns her back on Nazir without another word as though now that she has done what she was told to do it is no longer her concern whether Nazir honors her request. She walks slowly, heavily, down the cinder path to the road. Nazir sees that those two men are still there, waiting for her. For the first time he notices that the tall one is carrying a rifle.

"Half the population of Peshawar does," he mutters to himself, wondering why it seems menacing here. He goes back to the pool and lies down on the recliner next to Julia's and tries to unravel for her what the serving woman has said.

"But why on earth should she plead for him then?" Julia says.

He shrugs. Logic is irrelevant. "It's her husband's debt of honor." His tone is ironic: he knows that is what Julia expects of him. He has lost track of his own feelings except an overwhelming desire for tidiness, for a system of justice as clean of speculative mercy as the old Islamic code.

"But the debt he owes the Pathan is for killing the man she loved."

"It could have been worse, Julia. In the villages they don't take these things lightly. The old way was to kill them both and leave the bodies at the well as a warning to others." Nazir hears his own voice; it is so expressionless he cannot tell—so how can Julia?—whether he means to defend these barbarities or only explain them to her.

"You mean Kishwar should be grateful!"

"I didn't say that."

"It's what you meant." Her voice has a hard edge as though it is
dammed against tears. Nazir raises himself to look over at her and
sees that her face is pinched tight. He reaches across to stroke her
arm, but not without first glancing over his shoulder to be sure
they are alone.

Julia has seen that moment of carefulness; she is rigid and still.

"What I meant was that Kiswar sees these things differently than
we do, Julia," he says gently.

She turns away from him, burrowing her face in the jumble of
terrycloth. She knows she is waiting for something, but she
perceives even less than Nazir does that she is waiting for a sign
from him: some proof—an impolitic kiss here in the open, even an
outburst of anger—that what he feels for her is deeper and more
particular than what men customarily feel for women in this place.

He gives what he can: "I'll do whatever you want, Julia. Shall I
let the boy go?"

"I wouldn't ask you that. You're not a 'jungly' to live by these
insane rules."

"This isn't Berkeley, Julia. Maybe it *is* the jungle."

"Do you think that's *right*?"

"What does it matter what I think? Half the witnesses I hear are
perjuring themselves and I know it and they know I know it. The
bazaar rings with the real story and I make my ruling based on
what is brought to my official attention. The British were lucky.
They didn't know. And if that child's father will take some gold
bangles and a mule or two for her life, why should Government
involve itself?"

"You don't really mean that," Julia says.

He feels her relax, and takes his hand away. "Does it matter if
he's guilty if no one cares?"

"You don't really know that he is, of course," Julia says.

"The child was dead. He had the earrings. He confessed."

"He said he found them. The police beat him."

"Julia!"

"If he was guilty there should have been witnesses. There are
witnesses to everything in this country."

Her voice is tart. He can't help wondering if she means witness
to them. Or if someone had whispered to her that his mother is
pressing to arrange a marriage for him. "Julia, what do you want
me to do?"

"Once you start weighing things, nothing makes any sense," she says. "Kishwar gets beaten again, and the boy goes to jail forever—"

"Not forever. And if he's pretty he'll have an easy enough time." He knows this will shock her, will make it even more difficult for her to think in terms of abstract justice. "What do you think these prisons are?" He has lost the thread of his argument, of hers. Which side has he taken?

"Do what you think is right," she says almost primly. She does not want to think about Kishwar's story any longer; it contains a source of pain that she does not want to identify. She stands up and stretches herself. The sun is directly overhead now; it reflects off everything, the enamelled white table-tops, the aluminum frames of the chairs, the river-mica in the concrete.

When Julia comes out of the changing room, Nazir has already gone up. Kishwar is back under the pink bougainvillea and Julia gives her the bag of wet things to put into the car. They do not speak but Julia knows that she is conveying to Kishwar that everything is within her control.

Julia believes it herself. It is a small thing, really, that has been asked of him. Nazir will find extenuating circumstances to justify his action; there are always extenuating circumstances when someone has the will to find them. She wonders fleetingly why it has become so important that Nazir do this for her—do it without her making a direct request. Is it out of sympathy with Kishwar, who tends her daughter and who knows as no one else does her body when it is loose and undefended? Or does she simply crave proof that he will do anything at all for love of her?

Whatever it is, she feels intensely the power she has over him, and borne along upon it, she walks up the wide main stairs to his room without making any attempt at all to conceal her destination. She feels immune from the world's judgment.

It is only afterwards, coming down the stairs in her limp summer dress, that she reflects that Kishwar too must have felt that power, lying on the flat mud roof under the stars with the lover who was so afraid of losing her that he had his name etched in blue arabesques on her skin. And that tiny girl too, angry over the rings torn from her earlobes, reminding the big boy what punishment she can bring down upon him. The moment of power is brief and the danger abiding. Julia knows that and something in her falters, but she can still perfectly remember the elegant tracery of Nazir's ribcage under the wiry hair as he sprawled beside her on the wide bed. She does not yet feel the danger she knows is everywhere.

In the morning, Julia's sister-in-law drops by for coffee. She is a cool woman with streaks of bright henna covering her grey hair. She wastes no love on Julia, but she is invariably correct. This morning, among things of no importance at all, she tells Julia that Nazir Ahmad is to marry Inayutallah's daughter Shams. Julia remains composed but she does not summon the bearer for the usual second cups of Nescafe. When her caller leaves, Julia awards herself a tumbler of gin before she calls Kishwar for her massage.

The strong hands rest her. And as the muscles relax, Julia's mind, too, lets go a little. Nazir will do whatever she wants except—now the perimeters are known—in matters that concern his family.

This wife will not matter. She is one of his own kind and will never understand that part of him that needs Julia. For Julia knows, has known all along, the source of her power over him, and for just a moment she permits herself to think about it, to give it a name.

It has nothing to do with her prettiness, the soft supple body, her cultivated passion. She can age and wither, it will make no difference. He cleaves to her whiteness, the foreign smell—a lifetime of other foods, different rituals of hygiene—and the un-falsifiable paleness of her secret hair. Julia is proof to him that he is not altogether one of these people, that he was changed irrevocably in those ten years away. Nazir never thought to marry her, or to stay free for her, but what she has of him she can keep as long as she wants.

Kishwar sighs as she pours the warm oil onto the soles of Julia's feet. She too moves in a liquid drifting manner as though her mind is far away. Julia wonders if she is thinking of Asif Magid. Did Kishwar love him? And how could she know what love was in a life like that, when she had nowhere else to go? But she must have felt something—pride or power if not love—when he took her to Montgomery to have his name put on her.

The sun has reached the dusty pane of the high window and falls on her back and Kishwar's head. She can smell the pine massage oil and the heavier oil that Kishwar braids into her black hair.

Everything is still. Only Kishwar moves, her heavy rhythms a form of comforting.

Julia is half asleep when she hears her own rough sob like an infant's strangle, and wakes in time to bring back from sleep the image of a pale naked body engraved all over in an intricate calligraphy of fruits and flowers and the indelible names of men.

ჱ ჱ ჱ

# STANDING BY WORDS

## by WENDELL BERRY

from THE HUDSON REVIEW

*nominated by* THE HUDSON REVIEW, *Ellen Ferber and Robert Phillips*

"He said, and stood . . ."
*Paradise Regained*, IV, 561

Two EPIDEMIC ILLNESSES of our time — upon both of which virtual industries of cures have been founded — are the disintegration of communities and the disintegration of persons. That these two are related (that private loneliness, for instance, will necessarily accompany public confusion) is clear enough. And I take for granted that most people have explored in themselves and their surroundings some of the intricacies of the practical causes and effects; most of us, for example, have understood that the results are usually bad when people act in social or moral isolation, and also when, because of such isolation, they fail to act.

What seems not so well understood, because not enough examined, is the relation between these disintegrations and the disintegration of language. My impression is that we have seen, for perhaps a hundred and fifty years, a gradual increase in language that is either meaningless or destructive of meaning. And I believe that this increasing unreliability of language parallels the increasing disintegration, over the same period, of persons and communities.

My concern is for the *accountability* of language — hence, of the users of language. To deal with this matter I will use a pair of economic concepts: *internal accounting*, which considers cost and benefits in reference only to the interest of the money-making enterprise itself; and *external accounting*, which considers the costs and benefits to the "larger community." By altering the application of these terms a little, any statement may be said to account well or poorly for what is going on inside the speaker, or outside him, or both.

It will be found, I believe, that the accounting will be poor — incomprehensible or unreliable — if it attempts to be purely internal or purely external. One of the primary obligations of language is to connect and balance the two kinds of accounting.

And so, in trying to understand the degeneracy of language, it is necessary to examine, not one kind of unaccountability, but two complementary kinds. There is language that is diminished by subjectivity, which ends in meaninglessness. But that kind of language rarely exists alone (or so I believe), but is accompanied, in a complex relationship of both cause and effect, by a language diminished by objectivity, or so-called "objectivity" (inordinate or irresponsible ambition), which ends in confusion.

My standpoint here is defined by the assumption that no statement is complete or comprehensible in itself, that in order for a statement to be complete and comprehensible three conditions are required:

1. It must designate its object precisely.
2. Its speaker must stand by it: must believe it, be accountable for it, be willing to act on it.
3. This relation of speaker, word, and object must be conventional; the community must know what it is.

These are still the common assumptions of private conversations. In our ordinary dealings with each other, we take for granted that we cannot understand what is said if we cannot assume the accountability of the speaker, the accuracy of his speech, and mutual agreement on the structures of language and the meanings of words. We assume, in short, that language is communal, and that its purpose is to tell the truth.

That these common assumptions are becoming increasingly uncommon, particularly in the discourse of specialists of various sorts, is readily evident to anyone looking for evidence. How far they have passed from favor among specialists of language, to use the handiest example, is probably implicit in the existence of such specialists; one could hardly become a language specialist (a "scientist" of language) so long as one adhered to the old assumptions.

But the influence of these specialists is, of course, not confined to the boundaries of their specialization. They write textbooks for people who are not specialists of language, but who are apt to become specialists of other kinds. The general drift of the purpose of at least some of these specialists, and its conformability to the purposes of specialists of other kinds, is readily suggested by a couple of recently published textbooks for freshman English.

One of these, *The Contemporary Writer*, by W. Ross Winterowd,[1] contains a chapter on language, the main purpose of which is to convince the student of the illegitimate tyranny of any kind of prescriptive grammar and of the absurdity of judging language "on the basis of extra-linguistic considerations." This chapter proposes four rules that completely overturn all the old common assumptions:

1. "Languages apparently do not become better or worse in any sense. They simply change."

2. "Language is arbitrary."

3. "Rightness and wrongness are determined . . . by the purpose for which the language is being used, by the audience at which it is directed, and by the situation in which the use is taking place."

4. ". . .a grammar of a language is a description of that language, nothing more and nothing less."

And these rules have a pair of corollaries that Mr. Winterowd states plainly. One is that "you [the freshman student] have a more or less complete mastery of the English language . . ." The other is that art — specifically, here, the literary art — is "the highest expression of the human need to play, of the desire to escape from the world of reality into the world of fantasy."

The second of these texts, *Rhetoric: Discovery and Change*, by Richard E. Young, Alton L. Becker, and Kenneth L. Pike,[2] takes the standardless functionalism of Winterowd's understanding of language and applies it to the use of language. "The ethical dimension of the art of rhetoric," these authors say, is in "the attempt to reduce another's sense of threat in the effort to reach the goal of cooperation and mutual benefit . . ." They distinguish between evaluative writing and descriptive writing, preferring the latter because evaluative writing tends to cause people "to become defensive," whereas "a description . . . does not make judgments . . . " When, however, a writer "must make judgments, he can make them in a way that minimizes the reader's sense of threat." Among other things, "he can acknowledge the personal element in his judgment. . . . There is a subtle but important difference between saying 'I don't like it' and 'It's bad.' "

The authors equate evaluation functionally, at least—with dogmatism: "The problem with dogmatism is that, like evaluation, it forces the reader to take sides." And finally they recommend a variety of writing which they call "provisional" because it "focuses on the process of enquiry itself and acknowledges the tentative nature of conclusions. . . . Provisional writing implies that more than one reasonable conclusion is possible."

The first of these books attempts to make the study of language an "objective" science by eliminating from that study all extra-linguistic values and the issue of quality. Mr. Winterowd asserts that "the language grows according to its own dynamics." He does not say, apparently because he does not believe, that its dynamics includes the influence of the best practice. There is no "best." Anyone who speaks English is a "master" of the language. And the writers once acknowledged as masters of English are removed from "the world of reality" to the "world of fantasy," where they lose their force within the dynamics of the growth of language. Their works are reduced to the feckless status of "experiences": "we are much more interested in the imaginative statement of the message . . . than we are in the message . . ." Mr. Winterowd's linguistic "science" thus views language as an organism that has evolved without reference to habitat. Its growth has been "arbitrary," without any principle of selectivity.

Against Mr. Winterowd's definition of literature, it will be instructive to place a definition by Gary Snyder, who says of poetry that it is "a tool, a net or trap to catch and present; a sharp edge; a medicine, or the little awl that unties knots."[3] It will be quickly observed that this sentence enormously complicates Mr. Winterowd's simplistic statement-message dichotomy. What Mr. Winterowd means by "message" is an "idea" written in the dullest possible prose. His book is glib, and glibness is an inescapable doom of language without standards. One of the great practical uses of the literary disciplines, of course, is to resist glibness — to slow language down and make it thoughtful. This accounts, particularly, for the influence of verse, in its formal aspect, within the dynamics of the growth of language: verse checks the merely impulsive flow of speech, subjects it to another pulse, to measure, to extra-linguistic consideration; by inducing the hesitations of difficulty, it admits into language the influence of the Muse and of musing.

The three authors of the second book attempt to found an ethics of rhetoric on the idea expressed in one of Mr. Winterowd's rules: "Rightness and wrongness are determined" by purpose, audience, and situation. This idea apparently derives from, though it significantly reduces, the ancient artistic concern for propriety or decorum. A part of this concern was indeed the fittingness of the work to its occasion: that is, one would not write an elegy in the meter of a drinking song — though that is putting it too plainly, for the sense of occasion exercised an influence both broad and subtle on form, diction, syntax, small points of grammar and prosody — everything. But occasion, as I understand it, was invariably second in importance to the subject. It is only the modern specialist who departs from this. The specialist poet, for instance, degrades the subject to "subject matter" (raw material), so that the subject exists for the poem's sake, is *subjected* to the poem, in the same way as industrial specialists see trees or ore-bearing rocks as raw material subjected to their manufactured end-products. Quantity thus begins to dominate the work of the specialist poet at its source. Like an industrialist, he is interested in the subjects of the world for the sake of what they can be made to produce. He mines his experience for subject matter. The first aim of the propriety of the old poets, by contrast, was to make the language true to its subject — to see that it told the truth. That is why they invoked the Muse. The truth the poet chose as his subject was perceived as *superior* to his powers — and, by clear implication, to his occasion and purpose. But the aim of truth-telling is not stated in either of these textbooks. The second, in fact, makes an "ethical" aim of avoiding the issue, for, as the authors say, coining a formidable truth: "Truth has become increasingly elusive and men are driven to embrace conflicting ideologies."

This sort of talk about language, it seems to me, is fundamentally impractical. It does not propose as an outcome any fidelity between words and speakers or words and things or words and acts. It leads instead to muteness and paralysis. So far as I can tell, it is unlikely that one can speak at all, in even the most casual conversation, without some informing sense of what would be best to say — that is, without some sort of *standard*. And I do not believe that it is possible to act on the basis of a "tentative" or "provisional" conclusion. We may know that we are forming a conclusion on the basis of provisional or insufficient knowledge — that is a part of what we understand as the tragedy of our condition. But we must act, nevertheless, on the basis of *final* conclusions, because we know that actions, occurring in time, are irrevocable. That is another part of our tragedy. People who make a conventional agreement that all conclusions are provisional — a convention almost invariably implied by academic uses of the word "objectivity" — characteristically talk but do not act. Or they do not act deliberately, though time and materiality carry them into action of a sort, willy-nilly.

And there are times, according to the only reliable ethics we have, when one is required to tell the truth, whatever the urgings of purposes, audience, and situation. Ethics requires this because, in the terms of the practical realities of our lives, the truth is safer than falsehood. To ignore this is simply to put language at the service of purpose — *any* purpose. It is, in terms of the most urgent realities of our own time, to abet a dangerous confusion between public responsibility and public relations. Remote as these theories of language are from practical contexts, they are nevertheless serviceable to expedient practices.

In affirming that there is a necessary and indispensable connection between language and truth, and therefore between language and deeds, I have certain precedents in mind. I begin with the Christian idea of the Incarnate Word, the Word entering the world as flesh, and inevitably therefore as action — which leads logically enough to the insistence in the Epistle of James that faith without works is dead:

> For if any be a hearer of the word, and not a doer, he is
> like unto a man beholding his natural face in a glass:
> For he beholdeth himself, and goeth his way, and
> straightway forgetteth what manner of man he was.[4]

I also have in mind the Confucian insistence on sincerity (precision) and on fidelity between speaker and word as essentials of political health: "Honesty is the treasure of states." I have returned to Ezra Pound's observation that Confucius "collected *The Odes* to keep his followers from abstract discussion. That is, *The Odes* give particular instances. They do not lead to exaggerations of dogma."[5]

And I have remembered from somewhere Thoreau's sentence: "Where would you look for standard English but to the words of a standard man?"

The idea of standing by one's word, of words precisely designating things, of deeds faithful to words, is probably native to our understanding. Indeed, it seems doubtful whether without that idea we could understand anything.

But in order to discover what makes language that can be understood, stood by, and acted on, it is necessary to return to my borrowed concepts of internal and external accounting. And it will be useful to add two further precedents.

In *Mind and Nature*, Gregory Bateson writes that "things' [his quotation marks] can only enter the world of communication and meaning by their names, their qualities and their attributes (i.e., by reports of their internal and external relations and interactions)."[6]

And Gary Snyder, in a remarkably practical or practicable or practice-able definition of where he takes his stand, makes the poet responsible for "possibilities opening both inward and outward."[7]

There can be little doubt, I think, that any accounting that is *purely* internal will be incomprehensible. If the connection between inward and outward is broken — if, for instance, the experience of a single human does not resonate within the common experience of humanity — then language fails. In *The Family Reunion*, Harry says: "I talk in general terms / Because the particular has no language."[8] But he speaks, too, in despair, having no hope that his general terms can communicate the particular burden of his experience. We readily identify this loneliness of personal experience as "modern." Many poems of our century have this loneliness, this failure of speech, as a subject; many more exhibit it as a symptom.

But it begins at least as far back as Shelley, in such lines as these from "Stanzas Written in Dejection, Near Naples":

> Alas! I have nor hope nor health,
>    Nor peace within nor calm around,
> Nor that content surpassing wealth
>    The sage in meditation found,
>    And walked with inward glory crowned —
> Nor fame, nor power, nor love, nor leisure.
>    . . . .
> I could lie down like a tired child,
>    And weep away the life of care
>    Which I have borne and yet must bear,
> Till death like sleep might steal on me . . .

This too is an example of particular experience concealing itself in "general terms" — though here the failure, if it was suspected, is not acknowledged. The generality of the language does not objectify it, but seals it in its subjectivity. In reading this — as, I think, in reading a great many poems of our own time — we sooner or later realize that we are reading a "complaint" that we do not credit or understand. If we fail to realize this, it is because we have departed from the text of the poem, summoning particularities of our own experience in support of Shelley's general assertions. The fact remains that Shelley's poem doesn't tell us what he is complaining about; his lines fail to "create the object [here, the experience] which they contemplate."[9] This failure is implicitly conceded by the editors of *The Norton Anthology of English Literature*, who felt it necessary to provide the following footnote:

> Shelley's first wife, Harriet, had drowned herself; Clara, his baby daughter by Mary Shelley, had just died; and Shelley himself was plagued by ill health, pain, financial worries, and the sense that he had failed as a poet.[10]

But I think the poem itself calls attention to the failure by its easy descent into self-pity, finally asserting that "I am one / Whom men love not . . ." Language that becomes too subjective lacks currency, to use another economic metaphor; it will not pass. Self-pity, like bragging, will not pass. The powers of language are used illegitimately, to impose, rather than to elicit, the desired response.

Shelley is not writing gibberish here. It is possible to imagine that someone who does not dislike this poem may see in it a certain beauty. But it is the sickly beauty of generalized emotionalism. For once precision is abandoned as a linguistic or literary virtue, vague generalization is one of two remaining possibilities, gibberish being the second.

It is true, in a sense, that "the particular has no language" — that at least in public writing, and in speech passing between strangers, there may be only degrees of generalization. But there are, I think, two kinds of precision that are particular and particularizing. There is, first, the precision in the speech of people who share the same knowledge of place and history and work. This is the precision of direct reference or designation. It sounds like this: "How about letting me borrow your tall jack?" Or: "The old hollow beech blew down last night." Or, beginning a story, "Do you remember that time . . .?" I would call this community speech. Its words have the power of pointing to things visible either to eyesight or to memory. Where it is not too much corrupted by public or media speech, this community speech is wonderfully vital. Because it so often works designatively it *has* to be precise, and its precisions are formed by persistent testing against its objects.

This community speech, unconsciously taught and learned, in which words live in the presence of their objects, is the very root and foundation of language. It is the source, the unconscious inheritance that is carried, both with and without schooling, into consciousness — but never *all* the way, and so it remains rich, mysterious, and enlivening. Cut off from this source, language becomes a paltry work of conscious purpose, at the service and the mercy of expedient aims. Theories such as those underlying the two text books I have discussed seem to be attempts to detach language from its source in communal experience, by making it arbitrary in origin and provisional in use. And this may be a "realistic" way of "accepting" the degradation of community life. The task, I think, is hopeless, and it shows the extremes of futility that academic specialization can lead to. If one wishes to promote the life of language, one must promote the life of a community — a discipline many times more trying, difficult, and long than that of linguistics, but having at least the virtue of hopefulness. It escapes the despair always implicit in specializations: the cultivation of discrete parts without respect or responsibility for the whole.

The other sort of precision — the sort available to public speech or writing as well as to community speech — is a precision that comes of tension either between a statement and a prepared context or, within a single statement, between more or less conflicting feelings or ideas. Shelley's complaint is incomprehensible not just because it is set in "general terms," but because the generalities are too simple. One doesn't credit the emotion of the poem because it is too purely mournful. We are — conventionally, maybe, but also properly — unprepared to believe without overpowering evidence that things are *all* bad. Self-pity may deal in such absolutes of feeling, but we don't deal with other people in the manner of self-pity.

Another general complaint about mortality is given in Act V, Scene 2, of *King Lear,* when Edgar says to Gloucester: "Men must endure / Their going hence, even their coming hither." Out of context this statement is even more general than Shelley's. It is, unlike Shelley's, deeply moving because it is tensely poised within a narrative context that makes it precise. We know exactly, for instance, what is meant by that "must": a responsible performance is required until death. But the complaint is followed immediately by a statement of another kind, forcing the speech of the play back into its action: "Ripeness is all. Come on."

Almost the same thing is done in a single line of Robert Herrick, in the tension between the complaint of mortality and the jaunty metric:

Out of the world he must, who once comes in . . .

Here the very statement of inevitable death sings its acceptability. How would you divide, there, the "statement of the message" from "the message"?

And see how the tension between contradictory thoughts particularizes the feeling in these three lines by John Dryden:

Old as I am, for ladies' love unfit,
The pow'r of beauty I remember yet,
Which once inflamed my soul, and still inspires my wit.

These last three examples receive our belief and sympathy because they satisfy our sense of the complexity, the cross-graining, of real experience. In them, an inward possibility is made to open outward. Internal accounting has made itself externally accountable.

Shelley's poem, on the other hand, exemplifies the solitude of inward experience that continues with us, both in and out of poetry. I don't pretend to understand all the causes and effects of this, but I will offer the opinion that one of its chief causes is a simplistic idea of "freedom," which also continues with us, and is also to be found in Shelley. At the end of Act III of *Prometheus Unbound*, we are given this vision of a liberated humanity:

> The loathsome mask has fallen, the man remains
> Sceptreless, free, uncircumscribed, but man
> Equal, unclassed, tribeless, and nationless,
> Exempt from awe, worship, degree, the king
> Over himself . . .

This passage, like the one from the "Stanzas Written in Dejection," is vague enough, and for the same reason; as the first hastened to emotional absolutes, this hastens to an absolute idea. It is less a vision of a free man than a vision of a definition of a free man. But Shelley apparently did not notice that this headlong scramble of adjectives, though it may produce one of the possible definitions of a free man, also defines a lonely man, unattached and displaced. This free man is described as loving, and love is an emotion highly esteemed by Shelley. But it is, like his misery, a "free" emotion, detached and absolute. In this same passage of *Prometheus Unbound*, he calls it "the nepenthe, love" — love forgetful, or inducing forgetfulness, of grief or pain.

Shelley thought himself, particularly in *Prometheus Unbound*, a follower of Milton — an assumption based on a misunderstanding of *Paradise Lost*. And so it is instructive in two ways to set beside Shelley's definition of freedom, this one by Milton:

To be free is precisely the same thing as to be pious, wise, just, and temperate, careful of one's own, abstinent from what is another's, and thence, in fine, magnanimous and brave.[11]

And Milton's definition, like the lines previously quoted from Shakespeare, Herrick, and Dryden, derives its precision from tension: he defines freedom in terms of responsibilities. And it is only this tension that can suggest the possibility of *living* (for any length of time) in freedom — just as it is the tension between love and pain that suggests the possibility of carrying love into acts. Shelley's freedom defined in terms of freedom, gives us only this from a "Chorus of Spirits" in Act IV, Scene I, of *Prometheus Unbound:*

> Our task is done,
> We are free to dive, or soar, or run;
> Beyond and around,
> Or within the bound
> Which clips the world with darkness round.
>
> We'll pass the eyes
> Of the starry skies
> Into the hoar deep to colonize . .

Which, as we will see, has more in common with the technological romanticism of Buckminister Fuller than with anything in Milton.

In supposed opposition to this remote subjectivity of internal accounting, our age has developed a stance or state of mind which it calls "objective," and which produces a kind of accounting supposed to be external — that is, free from personal biases and considerations. This objective mentality, within the safe confines of its various specialized disciplines, operates with great precision and confidence. It follows tested and trusted procedures, and uses a professional language which an outsider must assume to be a very exact code. When this language is used by its accustomed speakers on their accustomed ground, even when one does not understand it, it clearly voices the implication of a control marvelously precise

over objective reality. It is only when it is overheard in confrontation with failure that this implication falters, and the adequacy of
this sort of language comes in doubt.

The transcribed conversations of the members of the Nuclear
Regulatory Commission during the crisis of Three Mile Island[12]
provide a valuable exhibit of the limitations of one of these
objective languages. At one point, for example, the commissioners
received a call from Roger Mattson, Nuclear Reactor Regulation
chief of systems safety. He said, among other things, the following:

> That bubble will be 5,000 cubic feet. The available
> volume in the upper head and the candy canes, that's
> the hot legs, is on the order of 2,000 cubic feet total. I
> get 3,000 excess cubic feet of noncondensibles. I've got a
> horse race. . . . We have got every systems engineer we
> can find . . . thinking the problem: how the hell do we
> get the noncondensibles out of there, do we win the
> horse race or do we lose the horse race.

At another time the commissioners were working to "engineer a
press release," of which "The focus . . . has to be reassuring . . ."
Commissioner Ahearne apparently felt that it was a bit *too* reassuring, and he would like it to *suggest* the possibility of a bad
outcome, apparently a meltdown. He says:

> I think it would be technically a lot better if you said—
> something about there's a possibility— it's small, but, it
> could lead to serious problems.

And, a few sentences later, Commissioner Kennedy tells him:

> Well I understand what you're saying. . . . You could put
> a little sentence in right there . . . to say, were this— in
> the unlikely event that this occurred, increased temper-
> atures would result and possible further fuel damage.

What is remarkable, and frightening, about this language is its
inability to admit what it is talking about. Because these specialists
have routinely eliminated themselves, as such and as representa-

tive human beings, from consideration according to the prescribed "objectivity" of their discipline, they cannot bring themselves to acknowledge to each other, much less to the public, that their problem involves an extreme danger to a lot of people. Their subject, as bearers of a public trust, is this danger, and it can be nothing else. It is a technical problem least of all. And yet when their language approaches this subject, it either diminishes it, or dissolves into confusions of syntax or purpose. Mr. Mattson speaks clearly and coherently enough so long as numbers and the jargon of "candy canes" and "hot legs" are adequate to his purpose. But as soon as he tries to communicate his sense of the urgency of the problem, his language collapses into a kind of rant around the metaphor of "a horse race." And the two commissioners, struggling with their obligation to inform the public of the possibility of a disaster, find themselves virtually languageless — without the necessary words and with only the shambles of a syntax. They cannot say what they are talking about. And so their obligation to *inform* becomes a tongue-tied — and therefore surely futile — effort to *reassure*. Public responsibility becomes public relations, apparently, for want of a language adequately responsive to its subject.

So inept is the speech of these commissioners that we must deliberately remind ourselves that they are not stupid, and are probably not amoral. They are highly trained, intelligent, worried men, whose understanding of language is by now to a considerable extent a public one. They are atomic scientists whose criteria of language are identical to those of at least some linguistic scientists. They determine the correctness of their statement to the press exactly according to Mr. Winterowd's rule: by their purpose, audience, and situation. Their language is governed by the ethical aim prescribed by the three authors of *Rhetoric: Discovery and Change:* they wish above all to speak in such a way as to "reduce another's sense of threat." But the result was not "cooperation and mutual benefit"; it was incoherence and dishonesty, leading to public suspicion, distrust, and fear.

This is language diminished by inordinate ambition: the taking of more power than can be responsibly or beneficently held. It is perhaps a law of human nature that such ambition always produces a confusion of tongues:

And they said, Go to, let us build us a city and a tower,
whose top may reach unto heaven; and let us make us a
name, lest we be scattered . . .
. . . .
And the Lord said . . . now nothing will be restrained
from them, which they have imagined to do.
Go to, let us go down, and there confound their language, that they may not understand one another's
speech.[13]

The professed aim is to bring people together — usually for the
implicit, though unstated, purpose of subjecting them to some
public power or project. Why else would rulers seek to "unify"
people? The idea is to cause them to speak the same language —
meaning either that they will agree with the government or be
quiet, as in communist and fascist states, or that they will politely
ignore their disagreements or disagree "provisionally," as in American universities. But the result — though power may survive for a
while in spite of it — is confusion and dispersal. Real language, real
discourse are destroyed. People lose understanding of each other,
are divided and scattered. Speech of whatever kind begins to
resemble the speech of drunkenness or madness.

What this dialogue of the NRC commissioners causes one to
suspect — and I believe the suspicion is confirmed by every other
such exhibit I have seen — is that there is simply no such thing as
an accounting that is *purely* external. The notion that external
accounting can be accomplished by "objectivity" is an illusion.
Apparently the only way to free the accounting of what is internal
to people, or subjective, is to make it internal to (that is, subject to)
some other entity or structure just as limiting, or more so — as the
commissioners attempted to deal with a possible public catastrophe in terms either of nuclear technology or of public relations.
The only thing really externalized by such accounting is a bad
result that one does not wish to pay for.

And so external accounting, alone, is only another form of
internal accounting. The only difference is that this "objective"
accounting does pretty effectively rule out personal considerations
*of a certain kind*. (It does *not* rule out the personal desire for
wealth, power, or intellectual certainty.) Otherwise, the talk of the
commissioners and the lines from "Stanzas Written in Dejection"

are equally and similarly incomprehensible. The languages of both are obviously troubled, we recognize the words, and learn something about the occasions, but we cannot learn from the language itself exactly what the trouble is. The commissioners' language cannot define the problem of their public responsibility, and Shelley's does not develop what I suppose should be called the narrative context of his emotion, which therefore remains incommunicable.

Moreover, these two sorts of accounting, so long as they remain discrete, both work to keep the problem abstract, all in the mind. They are both, in different ways, internal to the mind. The real occasions of the problems are not admitted into consideration. In Shelley's poem, this may be caused by a despairing acceptance of loneliness. In the NRC deliberations it is caused, I think, by fear; the commissioners take refuge in the impersonality of technological procedures. They cannot bear to acknowledge considerations and feelings that might break the insulating spell of their "objective" dispassion.

Or, to put it another way, their language and their way of thought make it possible for them to think of the crisis only as a technical event or problem. Even a meltdown is fairly understandable and predictable within the terms of their expertise. What is unthinkable is the evacuation of a massively populated region. It is the disorder, confusion, and uncertainty of that exodus that they cannot face. The one is, in Mr. Mattson's phrase, " a failure mode that has never been studied." The other is forty years — or forty centuries — in the wilderness. In dealing with the unstudied failure mode, the commissioners' minds do not have to leave their meeting room. It is an *internal* problem. The other, the human, possibility, if they were really to deal with it, would send them shouting into the streets. Even worse, perhaps, from the point of view of their discipline, it would force them to face the absurdity of the idea of "emergency planning" — the idea, in other words, of a controlled catastrophe. They would have to admit, against all the claims of professional standing and job security, that the only way to control the danger of a nuclear power plant is not to build it. That is to say, if they had a language strong and fine enough to consider *all* the considerations, it would tend to force them out of the confines of "objective" thought and into action, out of solitude into community.

It is the *purity* of objective thought that finally seduces and destroys it. The same thing happens, it seems to me, to the subjective mind. For certain emotions, especially the extremely subjective ones of self-pity and self-love, isolation holds a strong enticement: it offers to keep them pure and neat, aloof from the disorderliness and the mundane obligations of the human common ground.

The only way, so far as I can see, to achieve an accounting that is verifiably and reliably external is to admit the internal, the personal, as an appropriate, necessary consideration. If the NRC commissioners, for example, had spoken a good common English, instead of the languages of their specialization and of public relations, then they might have spoken of their personal anxiety and bewilderment, and so brought into consideration what they had in common with the people whose health and lives they were responsible for. They might, in short, have sympathized openly with those people — and so have understood the probably unbearable burden of their public trusteeship.

To be bound within the confines of either the internal or the external way of accounting is to be diseased. To hold the two in balance is to validate both kinds, and to have health. I am not using these terms "disease" and "health" according to any clinical definitions, but am speaking simply from my own observation that when my awareness of how I feel overpowers my awareness of where I am and who is there with me, I am sick, dis-eased. This can be appropriately extended to say that if what I think obscures my sense of whereabouts and company, I am diseased. And the converse is also true: I am diseased if I become so aware of my surroundings that my own inward life is obscured, as if I should so fix upon the value of some mineral in the ground as to forget that the world is God's work and my home.

But still another example is necessary, and other terms.

In an article entitled "The Evolution and Future of American Animal Agriculture," G. W. Salisbury and R. G. Hart[14] consider the transformation of American agriculture "from an art form into a science." The difference, they say, is that the art of agriculture is concerned "only" with the "how . . . of farming," whereas the science is interested in the "whys."

As an example — or, as they say, a "reference index" — of this change, the authors use the modern history of milk production: the effort, from their point of view entirely successful, "to change the dairy cow from the family companion animal she became after domestication and through all man's subsequent history into an appropriate manufacturing unit of the twentieth century for the efficient transformation of unprocessed feed into food for man."

The authors produce "two observations" about this change, and these constitute their entire justification of it:

> First, the total cow population was reduced in the period 1944 through 1975 by 67 percent, but second, the yield per cow during the same period increased by 60 percent. In practical terms, the research that yielded such dramatic gains produced a savings for the American public as a whole of approximately 50 billion pounds of total digestible nitrogen per year in the production of a relatively constant level of milk.

The authors proceed to work this out in dollar values and to say that the quantity of saved dollars finally "gets to the point that people simply do not believe it." And later they say that, in making this change, "The major disciplines were genetics, reproduction, and nutrition."

This is obviously a prime example of internal accounting in the economic sense. The external account is not fully renderable; the context of the accounting is vast, some quantities are not known, and some of the costs are not quantifiable. However, there can be no question that the externalized costs are large. The net gain is not, as these authors imply, identical with the gross. And the industrialization of milk production is a part of a much larger enterprise that may finally produce a highly visible, if not entirely computable, net loss.

At least two further observations are necessary:

1. The period, 1944-1975, also saw a drastic decrease in the number of dairies, by reason of the very change cited by Salisbury and Hart. The smaller — invariably the smaller — dairies were forced out because of the comparative "inefficiency" of their "manufacturing units." Their failure was part of a major population shift, which seriously disrupted the life both of the country communities and of the cities, broke down traditional community forms, and so on.

2. The industrialization of agriculture, of which the industrial-ization of milk production is a part, has caused serious problems that even agricultural specialists are beginning to recognize: soil erosion, soil compaction, chemical poisoning and pollution, energy shortages, several kinds of money troubles, obliteration of plant and animal species, disruption of soil biology.

Both the human and the agricultural/ecological costs are obvi-ously great. Some of them have begun to force their way into the accounts, and are straining the economy. Others are, and are likely to remain, external to all ledgers.

The passages I have quoted from Professors Salisbury and Hart provide a very neat demonstration of the shift from a balanced internal-external accounting (the dairy cow as "family companion animal") to a so-called "objective" accounting (the dairy cow as "appropriate manufacturing unit of the twentieth century"), which is, in fact, internal to an extremely limited definition of agricultural progress.

The discarded language, oddly phrased though it is, comes close to a kind of accountability: the internal (family) and the external (cow) are joined by a moral connection (companionship). A proof of its accountability is that this statement can be the basis of moral behavior: "Be good to the cow, for she is our companion."

The preferred phrase — "appropriate manufacturing unit of the twentieth century" — has nothing of this accountability. One can say, of course: "Be good to the cow, for she is productive (or expensive)." But that could be said of a machine; it takes no account of the cow as a living, much less a fellow, creature. But the phrase is equally unaccountable as language. "Appropriate" to what? Though the authors write "appropriate . . . of the twentieth century," they may mean "appropriate . . . to the twentieth cen-tury." But are there are no families and no needs for companion-ship with animals in the twentieth century? Or perhaps they mean "appropriate . . . for the efficient transformation of unprocessed feed into food for man." But the problem remains. Who is this "man"? Someone, perhaps, who needs no companionship with family or animals? We are constrained to suppose so, for "objectiv-ity" has apparently eliminated "family" and "companion" as terms subject to personal bias — perhaps as "merely sentimental." By the terms of this "objective" accounting, then, "man" is a creature who needs to eat, and who is for some unspecified reason more important than a cow. But for a reader who considers himself a "man" by any broader definition, this language is virtually meaningless. Because the terms of personal bias (that is, the terms of *value*) have been eliminated, the terms of judgment ("appropriate" and "efficient") mean nothing. The authors' conditions would be just as well satisfied if the man produced the milk and the cow bought it, or if a machine produced it and a machine bought it.

Sense, and the possibility of sense, break down here because too much that clearly belongs in has been left out. Like the NRC commissioners, Salisbury and Hart have eliminated themselves as representative human beings, and they go on to eliminate the cow as a representative animal — all "interests" are thus removed from the computation. With apparently rigorous scrupulosity they pluck out the representative or symbolic terms in order to achieve a pristinely "objective" accounting of the performance of a "unit." And so we are astonished to discover, at the end of this process, that they have complacently allowed the dollar to stand as representative of *all* value. What announced itself as a statement about animal agriculture has become, by way of several obscure changes of subject, a crudely simplified statement about industrial economics. This is not, in any respectable sense, language, or thought, or even computation. Like the textbooks I have discussed, and like the dialogue of the NRC, it is a pretentious and dangerous deception, forgiveable only insofar as it may involve self-deception.

If we are to begin to make a reliable account of it, this recent history of milk production must be seen as occurring within a system of nested systems. This system might be suggested by a sketch of five concentric circles, with the innermost representing the individual human, the second representing the family, the third the community, the fourth agriculture, and the outermost largest representing nature. So long as the smaller systems are enclosed within the larger, and so long as all are connected by complex patterns of interdependency, as we know they are, then whatever affects one system will affect the others.

It seems that this system of systems is safe so long as each system is controlled by the next larger one. If at any point the hierarchy is reversed, the destruction of the entire system begins. This system of systems is perhaps an updated, ecological version of the Great

Chain of Being. That is, it may bring us back to a hierarchical structure not too different from the one that underlies *Paradise Lost*—a theory of the form of Creation which is at the same time a moral form, and which is violated by the "disobedience" or *hubris* of attempting to rise and take power above one's proper place.

But the sketch I have made of the system of systems is much too crude, for the connections between systems, insofar as this is a human structure, are not "given" or unconscious or automatic, but involve disciplines. Persons are joined to families, families to communities, etc., by disciplines that must be deliberately made, remembered, taught, learned, and practiced.

The system of systems begins to disintegrate when the hierarchy is reversed because that begins the disintegration of the connecting disciplines. Disciplines, typically, degenerate into professions, professions into careers. The accounting of Salisbury and Hart is defective because it upsets the hierarchies and so, perhaps unwittingly, fails to consider all the necessary considerations. They do present their "reference index" as occurring within a system of systems—but a drastically abbreviated one, which involves a serious distortion. In a graph of this system, the innermost circle represents the dairyman, the second the dairy, the third agriculture, and the fourth—which contains the first three—represents economics. Two things are wrong with this. First, too much has been left out. Second, the outer circle is too much within the interest of the inner. The dairyman is not *necessarily* under the control of simple greed—but this structure supplies no hint of a reason why he should not be.

The system of systems, as I first described it, involves three different kinds of interests:

1. The ontogenetic. This is self-interest and is at the center.

2. The phylogenetic. This is the interest that we would call "humanistic." It reaches through family and community and into agriculture. But it does not reach far enough into agriculture because, by its own terms, it cannot.

3. The ecogenetic. This is the interest of the whole "household" in which life is lived. (I don't know whether I invented this term or not. If I did, I apologize.)

These terms give us another way to characterize the flaw in the accounting of Salisbury and Hart. Their abbreviated system of systems fails either to assemble enough facts, to account fully for the meaning of the facts, or to provide any standard of judgment because the ontogenetic interest is both internal and external to it.

The system of systems, as I first sketched it, has this vulnerability: that the higher interests can be controlled or exploited by the lower simply by leaving things out — a procedure just as available to ignorance as to the highest cunning of "applied science." And given even the most generous motives, ignorance is always going to be involved.

There is no reliable standard for behavior anywhere within the system of systems except truth. Lesser standards produce destruction — as, for example, the standards of public relations make gibberish of language.

The trouble, obviously, is that we do not know much of the truth. In particular, we know very little ecogenetic truth.

And so yet another term has to be introduced. The system of systems has to be controlled from above and outside. There has to be a religious interest of some kind above the ecogenetic. It will be sufficient to my purpose here just to say that the system of systems is enclosed within mystery, in which some truth can be known, but never all truth.

Neither the known truth nor the mystery is internal to any system. And here, however paradoxical it may seem, we begin to see a possibility of reliable accounting and of responsible behavior. The appropriateness of words or deeds can be determined only in reference to the whole "household" in which they occur. But this whole, as such, cannot enter into the accounting. (If it could, then the only necessary language would be mathematics, and the only necessary discipline would be military.) It can only come in as mystery: a factor of X which stands not for the unknown but the unknowable. This is an X that cannot be solved — which may be thought a disadvantage by some; its advantage is that, once it has been let into the account, it cannot easily be ignored. You cannot leave anything out of mystery, because by definition everything is always in it.

The practical use of religion, then, is to keep the accounting in as large a context as possible — to see, in fact, that the account is never "closed." Religion forces the accountant to reckon with mystery — the unsolvable X that keeps the debit and credit or cost and benefit columns open so that no "profit" can ever be safely declared. It forces the accounting outside of every enclosure that it might be internal to. Practically, this X means that all "answers" must be worked out within a limit of humility and restraint, so that the initiative to act would always imply a knowing acceptance of accountability for the results. The establishment and maintenance of this limit seems to me the ultimate empirical problem — the real "frontier" of science, or at least of the definition of the possibility of a *moral* science. It would place science under the rule of the old concern for propriety, correct proportion, proper scale — from which, in modern times, even the arts have been "liberated." That is, it would return to all work, artistic or scientific, the possibility of an external standard of quality. The quality of work or of a made thing would be determined by how conservingly it fitted into the system of systems. Judgment could then begin to articulate what is already obvious: that some work preserves the household of life, and some work destroys it. And thus a real liberation could take place: life and work could go free of those "professional standards" (and professional languages) that are invariably destructive of quality, because they always work as sheep's clothing for various kinds of ontogenetic motives. It is because of these professional standards that the industries and governments, while *talking* of the "betterment of the human condition," can *act* to enrich and empower themselves.

The connections within the system of systems are *practical* connections. The practicality consists in the realization that — despite the blandishments of the various short-circuited "professional" languages — you cannot speak or act in your own best interest without espousing and serving a higher interest. It is not knowledge that enforces this realization, but the humbling awareness of the insufficiency of knowledge, of mystery.

Applying then the standard of ecogenetic health to the work of Salisbury and Hart, we get a third way to describe its failure: it makes a principle of replacing the complex concern for quality ("how") with the drastically simplifying concern for quantity. Thus motive is entirely "liberated" from method: any way is good so long as it increases per unit production. But everything except production is diminished in the process, and Salisbury and Hart do not have a way of accounting for, hence no ability even to recognize, these diminishments. All that has been diminished could have been protected by a lively interest in the question of "how," which Salisbury and Hart — like the interests they are accounting for —

ruled out at the beginning. They were nevertheless working under what I take to be a rule: When you subtract quality from quantity, the gross result is not a net gain.

And so a reliable account is personal at the beginning and religious at the end. This does not mean that a reliable account includes the whole system of systems, for no account can do that. It does mean that the account is made in precise reference to the system of systems — which is another way of saying that it is made in respect for it. Without this respect for the larger structures, the meaning shrinks into the confines of some smaller structure, and become special, partial, and destructive.

It is this sort of external accounting that deals with connections, and thus inevitably raises the issue of quality. Which, I take it, is always the same as the issue of propriety: How appropriate is the tool to the work, the work to the need, the need to other needs and the needs of others and to the health of the household or community of all creatures?

And this kind of accounting gives us the great structures of poetry — as in Homer, Dante, and Milton. It is these great structures, I think, that carry us into the sense of being, in Gary Snyder's phrase, "at one with each other."[15] They teach us to imagine the life that is divided from us by difference or enmity: as Homer imagined the "enemy" hero, Hector; as Dante, on his pilgrimage to Heaven, imagined the damned; as Milton, in his awed study of the meaning of obedience, epitomized sympathetically in his Satan the disobedient personality. And as, now, ecological insight proposes again a poetry with the power to imagine the lives of animals and plants and streams and stones. And this imagining is eminently appropriate to the claims and privileges of the great household.

Unlike the problems of quantity, the problems of propriety are never "solved," but are ceaselessly challenging and interesting. This is the antidote to the romance of big technological solutions. Life would be interesting — there would be exciting work to do — even if there were no nuclear power plants or "agri-industries" or space adventures. The elaborations of elegance are at least as fascinating, and more various, more democratic, more healthy, more practical — though less glamorous — than the elaborations of power.

Without this ultimate reference to the system of systems, and this ultimate concern for quality, any rendering of account falls into the service of a kind of tyranny: it accompanies, and in one way or another invariably enables, the taking of power, from people first and last, but also from all other created things.

In this degenerative accounting, language is almost without the power of designation because it is used conscientiously to refer to nothing in particular. Attention rests upon percentages, categories, abstract functions. The reference drifts inevitably toward the merely provisional. It is not language that the user will likely be required to stand by or to act on, for it does not define any personal ground for standing or acting. Its only practical utility is to support with "expert opinion" a vast, impersonal technological action already begun. And it works directly against the conventionality, the community life, of language, for it holds in contempt, not only all particular grounds of private fidelity and action, but the common ground of human experience, memory, and understanding from which language rises and on which meaning is shaped. It is a tyrannical language: tyrannese.

Do people come consciously to such language and to such implicit purpose? I hope not. I do not think so. It seems likely to me that, first, a certain kind of confusion must occur. It is a confusion about the human place in the universe, and it has been produced by diligent "educational" labors. This confusion is almost invariably founded on some romantic proposition about the "high destiny of man" or "unlimited human horizons." For an example I turn to R. Buckminster Fuller,[16] here defending the "cosmic realism" of space colonization:

> Conceptualizing realistically about humans as passengers on board 8,000-mile diameter Spaceship Earth traveling around the Sun at 60,000 miles an hour while flying formation with the Moon, which formation involves the 365 revolutions per each Sun circuit, and recalling that humans have always been born naked, helpless and ignorant though superbly equipped cerebrally, and endowed with hunger, thirst, curiosity and procreative instincts, it has been logical for humans to employ their minds' progressive discoveries of the cos-

mic principles governing all physical interattractions, interactions, reactions and intertransformings, and to use those principles in progressivly organizing, to humanity's increasing advantage, the complex of cosmic principles interacting locally to produce their initial environment which most probably was that of a verdant south seas coral atoll — built by the coral on a volcano risen from ocean bottom ergo unoccupied by any animals, having only fish and birds as well as fruits, nuts and coconut milk.

That is a single sentence. I call attention not only to the vagueness and oversimplification of its generalities, but, more important, to the weakness of its grammar and the shapelessness and aimlessness of its syntax. The subject is an "it" of very tentative reference, buried in the middle of the sentence — an "it," moreover, that cannot possibly be the subject of the two complicated participial constructions that precede it. The sentence, then, begins with a dangling modifier half its length. On the other end, it peters out in a description of the biology of a coral atoll, the pertinence of which is never articulated. In general, the sentence is a labyrinth of syntactical confusions impossible to map. When we reflect that "sentence" means, literally, "a way of thinking" (Latin: *sententia*) and that it comes from the Latin *sentire*, to feel, we realize that the concepts of sentence and sentence structure are not merely grammatical or merely academic — not negligible in any sense. A sentence is both the opportunity and the limit of thought — what we have to think with, and what we have to think in. It is, moreover, a *feelable* thought, a thought that impresses its sense not just on our understanding, but on our hearing, our sense of rhythm and proportion. It is a pattern of felt sense.

A sentence completely shapeless is therefore a loss of thought, an act of self-abandonment to incoherence. And indeed Mr. Fuller shows himself here a man who conceives a sentence, not as a pattern of thought apprehensible to sense, but merely as a clot of abstract concepts. In such a syntactical clot, words and concepts will necessarily tend to function abstractly rather than referentially. It is the statement of a man for whom words have replaced things, and who has therefore ceased to think particularly about any thing.

The idea buried in all those words is, so far as I can tell, a simple one: humans are born earth-bound, ignorant, and vulnerable, but intelligent; by their intelligence they lift themselves up from their primitive origin and move to fulfill their destiny. As we learn in later sentences, this destiny is universal in scope, limitless ("ever larger"), and humans are to approach it by larger and larger technology. The end is not stated, obviously, because it is not envisioned, because it is not envisionable. The idea, then, is that humans are extremely intelligent, and by the use of their technological genius they are on their way somewhere or other. It seems to me not unreasonable to suggest that the aimlessness, the limitlessness, of Mr. Fuller's idea produces the aimlessness and shapelessness of his sentence.

By contrast, consider another view of the human place in the universe, not a simple view or simply stated, but nevertheless comely, orderly, and clear:

> There wanted yet the Master work, the end
> Of all yet done; a Creature who not prone
> And Brute as other Creatures, but endu'd
> With Sanctity of Reason, might erect
> His Stature, and upright with Front serene
> Govern the rest, self-knowing, and from thence
> Magnanimous to correspond with Heav'n,
> But grateful to acknowledge whence his good
> Descends, thither with heart and voice and eyes
> Directed in Devotion, to adore
> And worship God Supreme . . .[17]

These lines of Milton immediately suggest what is wrong, first, with Mr. Fuller's sentence, and then with the examples of tyrannese that preceded it. They all assume that the human prerogative is unlimited, that we *must* do whatever we have the power to do. Specifically, what is lacking is the idea that humans have a place in Creation and that this place is limited by responsibility on the one hand and by humility on the other — or, in Milton's terms, by magnanimity and devotion. Without this precision of definition, this setting of bounds or ends to thought, we cannot mean, or say what we mean, or mean what we say; we cannot stand by our words because we cannot utter words that can be stood by; we cannot speak of our own actions as persons, or even as communities, but only of the actions of percentages, large organizations, concepts, historical trends, or the impersonal "forces" of destiny or evolution.

Or let us consider another pair of statements. The first, again from Buckminster Fuller, following the one just quoted, elaborates his theme of technological destiny:

> First the humans developed fish catching and carving tools, then rafts, dug-out canoes and paddles and then sailing outrigger canoes. Reaching the greater islands and the mainland they developed animal skin, grass and leafwoven clothing and skin tents. They gradually entered safely into geographical areas where they would previously have perished. Slowly they learned to tame, then breed, cows, bullocks, water buffalo, horses and elephants. Next they developed oxen, then horsedrawn vehicles, then horseless vehicles, then ships of the sky. Then employing rocketry and packaging up the essential life-supporting environmental constituents of the biosphere they made sorties away from their mothership Earth and finally ferried over to their Sun orbiting-companion, the Moon.

The other is from William Faulkner's story, "The Bear."[18] Isaac McCaslin is speaking of his relinquishment of the ownership of land:

> . . . He created the earth, made it and looked at it and said it was all right, and then He made man. He made the earth first and peopled it with dumb creatures, and then He created man to be His overseer on the earth and to hold suzerainty over the earth and the animals on it in His name, not to hold for himself and his descendants inviolable title forever, generation after generation, to the oblongs and squares of the earth, but to hold the earth mutual and intact in the communal anonymity of brotherhood, and all the fee He asked was pity and humility and sufferance and endurance and the sweat of his face for bread.

The only continuity recognized by Mr. Fuller is that of technological development, which is in fact not a continuity at all, for, as
he sees it, it does not proceed by building on the past but by
outmoding and replacing it. And if any other human concern
accompanied the development from canoe to space ship, it is
either not manifest to Mr. Fuller, or he does not think it important
enough to mention.

The passage from Faulkner, on the other hand, cannot be
understood except in terms of the historical and cultural continuity
that produced it. It awakens our memory of Genesis and *Paradise
Lost*, as *Paradise Lost* awakens our memory of Genesis. In each of
these the human place in Creation is described as a moral circumstance, and this circumstance is understood each time, it seems to
me, with a deeper sense of crisis, as history has proved humanity
more and more the exploiter and destroyer of Creation rather than
its devout suzerain or steward. Milton knew of the conquests of
Africa and the Americas, the brutality of which had outraged the
humane minds of Europe, providing occasion and incentive to
raise again the question of the human place in Creation; and the
devils of *Paradise Lost* are, among other things, conquistadors.
(They are also the most expedient of politicians and technologists:
". . . by strength/They measure all . . .") Faulkner's Isaac Mc-
Caslin, a white Mississippian of our own time, speaks not just with
Milton's passion as a moral witness, but with the anguish of a man
who inherits directly the guilt of the conqueror, the history of
expropriation, despoliation, and slavery.

It is of the greatest importance to see how steadfastly this thrust
of tradition, from Genesis to Milton to Faulkner, works toward the
definition of personal place and condition, responsibility and
action. And one feels the potency of this tradition to reach past the
negativity of Isaac McCaslin's too simple relinquishment toward
the definition of the atoning and renewing work that each person
must do. Mr. Fuller's vision, by contrast, proposes that we have
ahead of us only the next technological "breakthrough" — which,
now that we have "progressed" to the scale of space ships, is not
work for persons or communities, but for governments and corporations. What we have in these two statements is an open conflict
between unlimited technology and traditional value. It is foolish to
think that these two are compatible. Value and technology can
meet only on the ground of restraint.

The technological determinists have tyrannical attitudes, and speak tyrannese, at least partly because their assumptions cannot produce a moral or a responsible definition of the human place in Creation. Because they assume that the human place is any place, they are necessarily confused about where they belong.

Where does this confusion come from? I think it comes from the specialization and abstraction of intellect, separating it from responsibility and humility, magnanimity and devotion, and thus giving it an importance that, in the order of things and in its own nature, it does not and cannot have. The specialized intellectual assumes, in other words, that intelligence is all in the mind. For illustration, I turn again to *Paradise Lost*, where Satan, fallen, boasts in "heroic" defiance that he has

> A mind not to be chang'd by Place or Time.
> The mind is its own place, and in itself
> Can make a Heav'n of Hell, a Hell of Heav'n,
> What matter where, if I be still the same . . .[19]

I do not know where one could find a better motto for the modernist or technological experiment, which assumes that we can fulfill a high human destiny any where, any way, so long as we can keep up the momentum of innovation; that the mind is "its own place" even within ecological degradation, pollution, poverty, hatred, and violence.

What we know, on the contrary, is that in any culture that could be called healthy or sane we find a much richer, larger concept of intelligence. We find, first, some way of acknowledging in action the existence of "higher intelligence." And we find that the human mind, in such a culture, is invariably strongly *placed*, in reference to other minds in the community, in cultural memory and tradition, and in reference to earthly localities and landmarks. Intelligence survives both by internal coherence and external pattern; it is both inside and outside the mind. People are born both with and into intelligence. What is thought refers precisely to what is thought about. It is this outside intelligence that we are now ignoring and consequently destroying.

As industrial technology advances and enlarges, and in the process assumes greater social, economic, and political force, it carries people away from where they belong by history, culture, deeds, association, and affection. And it destroys the landmarks by which they might return. Often it destroys the nature or the character of the places they have left. The very possibility of a practical connection between thought and the world is thus destroyed. Culture is driven into the mind, where it cannot be preserved. Displaced memory, for instance, is hard to keep in mind, harder to hand down. The little that survives is attenuated — without practical force. That is why the Jews, in Babylon, wept when they remembered Zion. The mere memory of a place cannot preserve it, nor apart from the place itself can it long survive in the mind. "How shall we sing the Lord's song in a strange land?"

The enlargement of industrial technology is thus analogous to war. It continually requires the movement of knowledge and responsibility away from home. It thrives and burgeons upon the disintegration of homes, the subjugation of homelands. It requires that people cease to cooperate directly to fulfill local needs from local sources, and begin instead to deal with each other always across the rift that divides producer and consumer, and always competitively. The idea of the independence of individual farms, shops, communities, and households is anathema to industrial technologists. The rush to nuclear energy and the growth of the space colony idea are powered by the industrial will to cut off the possibility of a small-scale energy technology — which is to say the possibility of small-scale personal and community acts. The corporate producers and their sycophants in the universities and the government will do virtually anything (or so they have obliged us to assume) to keep people from acquiring necessities in any way except by *buying* them.

Industrial technology and its aspirations enlarge along a line described by changes of verb tense: I need this tool; I will need this tool; I would need that tool. The conditional verb rests by nature upon *ifs*. The ifs of technological rationalization (*if* there were sufficient demand, money, knowledge, energy, power) act as wedges between history and futurity, inside and outside, value and desire, and ultimately between people and the earth and between one person and another.

By such shifts in the tenses of thought (as sometimes also by the substitution of the indefinite for the definite article) it is possible to impair or destroy the power of language to designate, to shift the focus of reference from what is outside the mind to what is inside it. And thus what already exists is devalued, subjugated, or destroyed for the sake of what *might* exist. The modern cult of planners and "futurologists" has thus achieved a startling resemblance to Swift's "academy of projectors":[20]

> In these colleges, the professors contrive new rules and methods of agriculture and building, and new instruments and tools for all trades and manufactures; whereby, as they undertake, one man shall do the work of ten: a palace may be built in a week, of materials so durable, as to last for ever without repairing. All the fruits of the earth shall come to maturity, at whatever season we think fit to chuse, and encrease an hundred fold more than they do at present; with innumerable other happy proposals. The only inconvenience is, that none of these projects are yet brought to perfection; and, in the mean time, the whole country lies miserably waste . . .

People who are willing to follow technology wherever it leads are necessarily willing to follow it away from home, off the earth, and outside the sphere of human definition, meaning, and responsibility. One has to suppose that this would be all right if they did it only for themselves and if they accepted the terms of their technological romanticism absolutely — that is, if they would depart absolutely from all that they propose to supersede, never to return. But past a certain scale, as C. S. Lewis wrote,[21] the person who makes a technological choice does not choose for himself alone, but for others; past a certain scale, he chooses for *all* others. Past a certain scale, if the break with the past is great enough, he chooses for the past, and if the effects are lasting enough he chooses for the future. He makes, then, a choice that can neither be chosen against nor unchosen. Past a certain scale, there is no dissent from a technological choice.

People speaking out of this technological willingness cannot speak precisely, for what they are talking about does not yet exist. They cannot mean what they say because their words are avowedly speculative. They cannot stand by their words because they are talking about, if not *in*, the future, where they are not standing and cannot stand until long after they have spoken. All the grand and perfect dreams of the technologists are happening in the future, but nobody is there.

What can turn us from this deserted future, back into the sphere of our being, the great dance that joins us to our home, to each other and to other creatures, to the dead and the unborn? I think it is love. I am perforce aware how baldly and embarrassingly that word now lies on the page—for we have learned at once to overuse it, abuse it, and hold it in suspicion. But I do not mean any kind of abstract love (adolescent, romantic, or "religious"), which is probably a contradiction in terms, but particular love for particular things, places, creatures, and people, requiring stands and acts, showing its successes or failures in practical or tangible effects. And it implies a responsibility just as particular, not grim or merely dutiful, but rising out of generosity. I think that this sort of love defines the effective range of human intelligence, the range within which its works can be dependably beneficent. Only the action that is moved by love for the good at hand has the hope of being responsible and generous. Desire for the future produces words that cannot be stood by. But love makes language exact, because one loves only what one knows. One cannot love the future or anything in it, for nothing is known there. And one cannot unselfishly make a future for someone else. The love for the future is self-love—love for the present self, projected and magnified into the future, and it is an irremediable loneliness.

Because love is not abstract, it does not lead to trends or percentages or general behavior. It leads, on the contrary, to the perception that there is no such thing as general behavior. There is no abstract action. Love proposes the work of settled households and communities, whose innovations come about in response to immediate needs and immediate conditions, as opposed to the work of governments and corporations, whose innovations are produced out of the implicitly limitless desire for future power or profit. This difference is the unacknowledged cultural break in Mr. Fuller's evolutionary series: oxen, horse-drawn vehicles, horseless vehicles, ships of the sky. Between horse-drawn vehicles and horseless vehicles human life disconnected itself from local sources; energy started to flow away from home. A biological limit was overrun, and with it the deepest human propriety.

Or, to shift the terms, love defines the difference between the "global village" which is a technological and a totalitarian ideal, directly suited to the purposes of centralized governments and corporations, and the Taoist village-as-globe, where the people live frugally and at peace, pleased with the good qualities of necessary things, so satisfied where they are that they live and die without visiting the next village, though they can hear its dogs bark and its roosters crow.[22]

We might conjecture and argue a long time about the meaning and even the habitability of such a village. But one thing, I think, is certain: it would not be a linguistic no man's land in which words and things, words and deeds, words and people failed to stand in reliable connection or fidelity to one another. People and other creatures would be known by their names and histories, not by their numbers or percentages. History would be handed down in songs and stories, not reduced to evolutionary or technological trends. Generalizations would exist, of course, but they would be distilled from experience, not "projected" from statistics. They would sound, says Lao Tzu,[23] this way:

> "Alert as a winter-farer on an icy stream,"
> "Wary as a man in ambush,"
> "Considerate as a welcome guest,"
> "Selfless as melting ice,"
> "Green as an uncut tree,"
> "Open as a valley . . ."

I come, in conclusion, to the difference between "projecting" the future and making a promise. The "projecting" of the "futurologists" *uses* the future as the safest possible context for whatever is desired; it binds one only to selfish interest. But making a promise binds one *to someone else's future*. If the promise is serious enough, one is brought to it by love, and in awe and fear. Fear, awe, and love bind us to no selfish aims, but to each other. And they enforce a speech more exact, more clarifying, and more binding than any speech that can be used to sell or advocate some "future." For when we promise in love and awe and fear there is a certain kind of mobility that we give up. We give up the romanticism of progress, that is always shifting its terms to fit its occasions. We are speaking where we stand, and we shall stand afterwards in the presence of what we have said.

1 Harcourt Brace Jovanovich, 1975, pages 291-303, 235.

2 Harcourt, Brace & World, 1970, pages 8, 203-211.

3 "Poetry, Community, & Climax," *Field* 20, Spring 1979, p. 29.

4 1: 23 & 24.

5 *Confucius,* New Directions, 1951, pages 89, 191.

6 E. P. Dutton, 1979, page 61.

7 *Op. cit.* p. 21

8 T. S. Eliot, *The Complete Poems and Plays,* Harcourt, Brace and Company, 1952, p. 235.

9 T. S. Eliot, *Selected Essays,* Harcourt, Brace and Company, 1950, page 269.

10 W. W. Norton & Company, Volume 2, 1962, pages 418-419.

11 *Second Defense of the People of England, The Works of John Milton,* Vol. VIII, Columbia University Press, 1933, pages 249-251.

12 I am indebted, for a useful sampling from these transcripts and a perceptive commentary on them, to Paul Trachtman, "Phenomena, comment, and notes," *Smithsonian,* July 1979, pages 14-16.

13 Genesis 11:1-9.

14 *Perspectives in Biology and Medicine,* Spring 1979, pages 394-409.

15 *Op. cit.,* page 34.

16 *Space Colonies,* edited by Stewart Brand, Penguin, 1977, page 55.

17 *Paradise Lost,* VII, 505-515.

18 *Go Down, Moses,* The Modern Library, 1955, page 257.

19 I, 253-256.

20 *Gulliver's Travels,* Everyman's Library, 1961, page 189.

21 *The Abolition of Man,* Macmillan, 1975, pages 70-71.

22 *Tao Te Ching,* LXXX.

23*Ibid.,* XV (Witter Bynner translation, Capricorn Books, 1962, page 33).

*ᕗ* *ᕗ* *ᕗ*

# THE SOUTHERN CROSS

## by CHARLES WRIGHT

from THE PARIS REVIEW

*nominated by* THE PARIS REVIEW, *Carol Muske, Stanley Plumly and
Elizabeth Spires*

Things that divine us we never touch:

The black sounds of the night music,
The Southern Cross, like a kite at the end of its string,

And now this sunrise, and empty sleeve of a day,
The rain just starting to fall, and then not fall,

No trace of a story line.

————

All day I've remembered a lake and a sudsy shoreline,
Gauze curtains blowing in and out of open windows all over
        the South.

It's 1936, in Tennessee. I'm one
And spraying the dead grass with a hose.
The curtains blow in and out.

And then it's not. And I'm not and they're not.

Or it's 1941 in a brown suit, or '53 in its white shoes,
Overlay after overlay tumbled and brought back,
As meaningless as the sea would be
                    if the sea could remember its waves . . .

————

Nothing had told me my days were marked for a doom
                       under the cold stars of the Virgin.
Nothing had told me that woe would buzz at my side like a fly.

The morning is dark with spring.
The early blooms on the honeysuckle shine like maggots
    after the rain.
The purple mouths of the passion blossoms
                      open their white gums to the wind.

How sweet the past is, no matter how wrong, or how sad.
How sweet is yesterday's noise.

————

All day the ocean was like regret,
                 clearing its throat, brooding and self-absorbed.

Now the wisteria tendrils extend themselves like swan's necks
    under Orion.

Now the small stars in the orange trees.

————

At Garda, on Punto San Vigilio, the lake,
In springtime, is like the sea,
Wind fishtailing the olive leaves like slash minnows beneath
    the vineyards,
Ebb and flow of the sunset past Sirmio,
                  flat voice of the waters
Retelling their story, again and again, as though to unburden itself

Of an unforgotten guilt,
             and not relieved
Under the soothing hand of the dark,

The clouds over Bardolino dragging the sky for the dead
Bodies of those who refuse to rise,
Their orange robes and flaming bodices trolling across the hills,

Nightwind by now in the olive trees,
No sound but the wind from anything
                              under the tired, Italian stars . . .

And the voice of the waters, starting its ghostly litany.

————

River of sighs and forgetfulness
                    (and the secret light Campana saw),
River of bloom-bursts from the moon,
                        of slivers and broken blades from the moon
In an always-going-away of glints . . .

Dante and Can Grande once stood here,
Next to the cool breath of S. Anastasia,
                              watching the cypress candles
Flare in their deep green across the Adige
In the Giusti Gardens.
                    Before that, in his marble tier,
Catullus once sat through the afternoons.
Before that, God spoke in the rocks . . .

And now it's my turn to stand
Watching a different light do the same things on a different water,
The Adige bearing its gifts
                    through the April twilight of 1961.

————

When my father went soldiering, apes dropped from the trees.
When my mother wrote home from bed, the stars asked for a
      pardon.

They're both ghosts now, haunting the chairs and the sugar chest.

From time to time I hear their voices drifting like smoke through
      the living room,
Touching the various things they owned once,
Now they own nothing
                    and drift like smoke through the living room.

———

Thinking of Dante, I start to feel
What I think are wings beginning to push out from my shoulder
     blades,
And the firm pull of water under my feet.

Thinking of Dante, I think of La Pia,
                         and Charles Martel
And Cacciaguida inside the great flower of Paradise,
And the thin stem of Purgatory
                    rooted in Hell.

Thinking of Dante is thinking about the other side,
And the other side of the other side.
It's thinking about the noon noise and the daily light.

———

Here is the truth. The wind rose, the sea
Shuffled its blue deck and dealt you a hand:
Blank, blank, blank, blank, blank.
Pelicans rode on the flat back of the waves through the green
     afternoon.
Gulls malingered along its breezes.
The huge cross of an airplane's shadow hurried across the sand,
                         but no one stayed on it
For long, and nobody said a word.
You could see the island out past the orange gauze of the smog.

———

The Big Dipper has followed me all the days of my life.
Under its tin stars my past has come and gone.
Tonight, in the April glaze
                    and scrimshaw of the sky,
It blesses me once again
With its black water, and sends me on.

———

After 12 years it's hard to recall
That defining sound the canal made at sundown, slap
Of tide swill on the church steps,
Little runnels of boat wash slipping back from the granite slabs
In front of Toio's, undulant ripples
Flattening out in small hisses, the oily rainbows regaining their
    loose shapes
Silently, mewling and quick yelps for the gulls
Wheeling from shadow into the pink and grey light over the
    Zattere,

Lapping and rocking of water endlessly,
At last like a low drone in the dark shell of the ear
As the night lifted like mist from the Ogni Santi
and San Sebastiano
                into the cold pearl of the sky . .

All that year it lullabied just outside my window
As Venice rode through my sleep like a great spider,
Flawless and Byzantine,
                webbed like glass in its clear zinc.
In winter the rain fell
              and the locust fell.
In summer the sun rose
Like a whetstone over the steel prows of the gondolas,
Their silver beak-blades rising and falling,
                  the water whiter than stone.
In autumn the floods came, and oil as thick as leaves in the entry
    way.
In spring, at evening, under the still-warm umbrellas,
We watched the lights blaze and extend
                along the rio,
And watched the black boats approaching, almost without sound.
And still the waters sang lullaby.

I remember myself as a figure among the colonnades,
Leaning from left to right,
              one hand in my pocket,
The way the light fell,
            the other one holding me up.

I remember myself as a slick on the slick canals,
Going the way the tide went,
The city sunk to her knees in her own reflection.
I remember the way that Pound walked
                                        across San Marco
At *passeggiata*, as though with no one,
                                        his eyes on the long ago.
I remember the time that Tate came.
                        And Palazzo Guggenheim
When the floods rose
                and the boat took us all the way
Through the front doors and down to the back half
Of *da Montin*, where everyone was, clapping their hands.

What's hard to remember is how the wind moved and the reeds
    clicked
Behind Torcello,
                little bundles of wind in the marsh grass
Chasing their own tails, and skidding across the water.
What's hard to remember is how the electric lights
Were played back, and rose and fell on the black canal
Like swamp flowers,
                shrinking and stretching,
Yellow and pale and iron-blue from the oil.
It's hard to remember the way the snow looked
                                on San Gregorio,
And melting inside the pitch tubs and the smoke of San Trovaso,
The gondolas beached and stripped,
The huge snowflakes planing down through the sea-heavy air
Like dead moths,
                drifting and turning . . .

————————

As always, silence will have the last word,
And Venice will lie like silk
                at the edge of the sea and the night sky,
Albescent under the moon.

Everyone's life is the same life
                            if you live long enough.

Orioles shuttle like gold thread
                    through the grey cloth of daylight.
The fog is so low and weighted down
Crows fall through like black notes from the sky.
The orioles stitch and weave.
Somewhere below, the ocean nervously grinds its teeth
As the morning begins to take hold
                    and the palm trees gleam.

There is an otherness inside us
We never touch,
                    no matter how far down our hands reach.
It is the past,
                    with its good looks and *Anytime, Anywhere* . . .
Our prayers go out to it, our arms go out to it
Year after year,
But who can ever remember enough?

Friday again, with its sack of bad dreams
And long-legged birds,
                    a handful of ashes for this and that
In the streets, and some for the squat piano.

Friday beneath the sky, its little postcards of melancholy
Outside each window,
                    the engines inside the roses at half speed,
The huge page of the sea with its one word *despair*,

Fuchsia blossoms littered across the deck,
Unblotted tide pools of darkness beneath the ferns . . .
And still I go on looking,
                    match after match in the black air.

The lime, electric green of the April sea
        off Ischia
Is just a thumb-rub on the window glass between here and there:
And the cloud cap above the volcano
That didn't move when the sea wind moved;
And the morning the doves came, low from the mountain's shadow,
          under the sunlight.
Over the damp tops of the vine rows,
Eye-high in a scythe slip that dipped and rose and cut down
   toward the sea;
And the houses like candy wrappers blown up against the hillside
Above Sant' Angelo,
       fuchsia and mauve and cyclamen;
And the story Nicola told,
How the turtle doves come up from Africa
On the desert winds,
       how the hunters take the fresh seeds
From their crops and plant them,
The town windows all summer streaked with the nameless blooms . . .

The landscape was always the best part.

----

Places swim up and sink back, and days do,
The edges around what really happened
        we'll never remember
No matter how hard we stare back at the past:

One April, in downtown Seville,
        alone on an Easter morning
Wasted in emerald light from the lemon trees,
I watched a small frog go back and forth on the lily pads
For hours, and still don't know
       just what I was staying away from . . .

(And who could forget Milano in '59
        all winter under the rain?
Cathedrals for sure,
And dry stops in the Brera,
      all of her boulevards ending in vacant lots.

And Hydra and Mykonos,
Barely breaking the calm with their white backs
As they roll over
              and flash back down to the dark . . .)

Places swim up and sink back, and days do,
Larger and less distinct each year,
As we are,
           and lolling about in the same redress,
Leaves and insects drifting by on their windows.

———————

Rome was never like that,
              and the Tiber was never like that,
Nosing down from the Apennines,
            color of *cafe-au-lait* as it went through town . . .

Still, I can't remember the name of one street
                   near Regina Coeli,
Or one block of the Lungotevere on either side,
Or one name of one shop on Campo dei Fiori.
Only Giordano Bruno,
             with his razed look and black caul,
Rises unbidden out of the blank
Unruffled waters of memory,
              his martyred bronze
Gleaming and still wet in the single electric light.

I can't remember the colors I said I'd never forget
On Via Giulia at sundown,
The ochres and glazes and bright hennas of each house,
Or a single day from November of 1964.
I can't remember the way the stairs smelled
                 or the hallway smelled
At Piazza del Biscione.
          Or just how the light fell
Through the east-facing window over the wicker chairs there.

I do remember the way the boar hung
            in the butcher shop at Christmas

Two streets from the Trevi fountain, a crown of holly and
          mistletoe
Jauntily over his left ear.
I do remember the flower paintings
Nodding throughout the May afternoons
                              on the dining room walls
At Zajac's place.
                    And the reliquary mornings,
And Easter, and both Days of the Dead . . .

At noon in the English Cemetery no one's around.
Keats is off to the left, in an open view.
Shelley and Someone's son are straight up ahead.

With their marble breath and their marble names,
                    the sun in a quick squint through the trees,
They lie at the edge of everywhere,
          Rome like a stone cloud at the back of their eyes.

———————

Time is the villain in most tales,
                              and here, too,
Lowering its stiff body into the water.
Its landscape is the resurrection of the word,
No end of it,
          the petals of wreckage in everything.

———————

I've been sitting here tracking the floor plan
                              of a tiny, mottled log spider
Across the front porch of the cabin,
And now she's under my chair,
                              off to her own devices,
Leaving me mine, and I start watching the two creeks

Come down through the great meadow
Under the lodgepole pine and the willow run,
The end of June beginning to come clear in the clouds,

Shadows like drowned men where the creeks go under the hill.

Last night, in the flood run of the moon, the bullbats
Diving out of the yellow sky
                    with their lonesome and jungly whistling,
I watched, as I've watched before, the waters send up their smoke
        signals of blue mist,
And thought, for the 1st time,
                    I half-understood what they keep on trying to say.

But now I'm not sure.
                Behind my back, the spider has got her instructions
And carries them out.
Flies drone, wind back-combs the marsh grass, swallows bank and
        climb.
Everything I can see knows just what to do,

Even the dragonfly, hanging like lapis lazuli in the sun . . .

————————

I can't remember enough.

How the hills, for instance, at dawn in Kingsport
In late December in 1962 were black
                            against a sky
The color of pale fish blood and water that ran to white
As I got ready to leave home for the 100th time,
My mother and father asleep,
                    my sister asleep,
Carter's Valley as dark as the inside of a bone
Below the ridge,
                the 1st knobs of the Great Smokies
Beginning to stick through the sunrise,
The hard pull of a semi making the grade up US 11 W,
The cold with its metal teeth ticking against the window,
The long sigh of the screen door stop,
My headlights starting to disappear
                        in the day's new turning . . .

I'll never be able to.

Sunday, a brute bumblebee working the clover tops
Next to the step I'm sitting on,
      sticking his huge head
Into each tiny, white envelope.
The hot sun of July, in the high Montana air, bastes a sweet glaze
On the tamarack and meadow grass.
In the blue shadows
     moist curls of the lupin glide
And the bog lilies extinguish their mellow lamps . . .

Sunday, a *Let us pray* from the wind, a glint
Of silver among the willows.
      The lilacs begin to bleed
In their new sleep, and the golden vestments of morning
Lift for a moment, then settle back into place.
The last of the dog roses offers itself by the woodpile.
Everything has its work,
     everything written down
In a second-hand grace of solitude and tall trees . . .

---

August licks at the pine trees.
Sun haze, and little fugues from the creek.
Fern-sleep beneath the green skirt of the marsh.

I always imagine a mouth
Starting to open its blue lips
Inside me, an arm
     curving sorrowfully over an open window

At evening, and toads leaping out of the wet grass.

Again the silence of flowers.
Again the faint notes of piano music back in the woods.
How easily summer fills the room.

---

The life of this world is wind.
Wind-blown we come, and wind-blown we go away.
All that we look on is windfall.
All we remember is wind.

———————

Pickwick was never the wind . . .

It's what we forget that defines us, and stays in the same place,
And waits to be rediscovered.
Somewhere in all that network of rivers and roads and silt hills,
A city I'll never remember,
                    its walls the color of pure light,
Lies in the August heat of 1935,
In Tennessee, the bottom land slowly becoming a lake.
It likes in a landscape that keeps my imprint
Forever,
            and stays unchanged, and waits to be filled back in.
Someday I'll find it out
And enter my old outline as though for the 1st time,

And lie down, and tell no one.

🔥 🔥 🔥

# CHRIST PREACHING AT THE HENLEY REGATTA

fiction by GUY DAVENPORT

*Collages by* ROY R. BEHRENS

from ECLOGUES (North Point Press)

*nominated by* NORTH POINT PRESS, *David Madden, Daniel Menaker and George Steiner*

Isn't it lovely, the river, with its flags and barges and laughter and music carrying so far over the water? How curiously the tuba, bouncing like the Bessy in a Morris dance, comes through the windwash, while all the other instruments fade in and out of a deafness.

Henley on such a day has touches of Deauville and of Copenhagen, and the Thames through Oxfordshire gleams as if Canaletto, Dufy, and Cézanne had got at it. Flags of Oxford and Cambridge, Sweden and France, Eton and the United States, of Leander and Thames, Harrow and Bordeaux, rill and snap in our skittish English breeze.

94

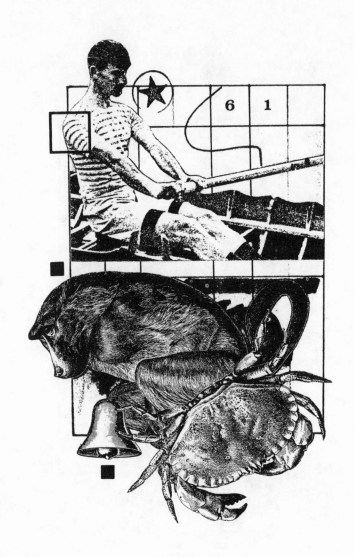

Mrs. Damer's sculpted heads of Thames and Isis look from the posts of the High Street Bridge at Scandinavians smiling and gathering to a clapping of hands before the chantry house and at a file of gypsies of the Petulengro clan moved along by the admonitions of a constable.

Above the noise of automobiles and motorcycles there are pipes and drums playing *Leaving Rhu Vaternish* as they swing with Celtic pluck over the bridge. A county fair at Olympia! And English bells above it all, a course of changes joyously in the air.

—*Sex quattuor tris, quinque duo,* Berkshire calls.

—*Duo tris, quattuor, quinque sex,* the answer falls.

—*Twa threo fower fif six, six fower, threo fif twa,* reply the bells of Oxfordshire.

Through a window, beyond the geraniums on the sill, you can see a photograph of the Duke of Connaught in a silver frame, wearing a leopard skin, head and all. Its jaws fit the duke's head in a yawning bite. The skin of its forelegs drape his shoulders, its tail hangs between his legs, and its hind feet dangle at the duke's tasseled kilt.

— Commander of a bicycle regiment, says Reggie to Cynthia after they have squeezed each other gazing at the duke's photograph. He was returning a salute while wheeling along in review when he wobbled and crashed, engaging himself so intricately in the ruin of his machine that a boffin from the medics had to come and extricate him, don't you know.

— Reggie old thing! screamed Cynthia. Sausage and mashed!

She was as shy and obvious as a rose, but she could stand on one leg, touch her heel to her butt, flip her scarf and laugh like a gasping halibut.

— Cynthia old darling! Pip pip, what?

Her scarf is in the colors of the London Rowing club. Curls crisp as leaves flourish around her neat tam. Having laughed, she skips and hums, and chucks Reggie under his chin.

They throw themselves into each other's arms. The interested eyes observing them are those of the painter Raoul Dufy, who has come to sketch the Regatta. He wiggles his fingers and smooths his hand along the air to see English brick, the tricolor against ash and yew, panamas and blazers, the insignia of barges carved in oak argent and d'or, taupe and cinnamon. Not he but Seurat should be here. And Eakins and Whitman. And Rousseau.

*regardez Georges Seurat ces verts*
*et ces azurs ces outriggers*
*si étroites et si légères*

*cette rivière plus bleue*
*que les yeux saxons*
*regardez cet homme si mystérieux*

He jumps nimbly, Raoul Dufy, out of the way of a Jaquar XKE nosing toward the bridge and gives it a manual sign of French contempt.

*les coups des avirons les étincelles d'eau*
*ces épaules puma ou il y a en marche*
*des souris sous le peau*

*ô filles minces ô garces oiseaux en vol*
*mères truitées autruches milords et morses*
*ô gigue des parasols*

*rameurs grands insouciants et blonds*
*et delà en maillot rouge*
*près de la rive un brave garçon*

*les mains en conque et florentines*
*les joues gonflés et romanesques*
*un triton gosse au chapeau mandarine*

*qui trompete à travers*
*la lumière nordique des après-midis immobiles*
*un son peut-être imaginaire*

*que l'oreille soit la preuve*
*un air moiré et grec et dur*
*et musclé comme la fleuve*

Isambard Kingdom Brunel, spanner of rivers and oceans, pray for us now and at the hour of our death.

A man in an ulster and cloth hat searches the pavements and edges of gardens for the droppings of dogs, which, if the way is

clear, he puts in his pockets, for later inspection in his room above the Swan and Maiden. He is, as Raoul Dufy does not know, Stanley Spencer.

A nanny across the street asks herself whatever is that man doing, and her charge, a boy in a sailor suit, reads her eyes and answers.

— Picking up dog shit and squirreling it away on his person.

— God save the poor sod, says the nurse.

— Now he's pulling his pudding.

— Charles Francis!

An old woman in a plaid shawl has caught Stanley Spencer's attention. She wears gaiters and a fisherman's hat. The crop of white whiskers on her chin pleases Spencer. He imagines her as a girl, as a bride, as a woman getting fleshy about the hips, a woman who would cast her eyes upwards when she laughs. If only he could see her feet.

*Dancing angels know a fire*
*makes this river wind and air*
*seem an iron snarl of wire*

The pipe band returns over the bridge, playing *The Hen Scratches in the Midden*. The melody perplexes a poet who has been dreaming with open eyes. Was it the green of the girl's eyes who was talking with British toothiness to a grenadier in mufti, or the gorgeous quiet of the gardens beyond these ancient walls that loosed his mind into revery? Louis Jean Lumière, pray for us now and at the hour of our death.

*Girlish, vivacious, and brash afternoon*
*That lifts with the wine of its wings*
*From the haunted seasons of yet to be*
*Summer's blond and Illyrian winters.*

Flat light shimmers on the Thames. An airplane drags a streamer through the air, advertising Bovril. A dowager aims her ear trumpet so that a constable can direct her electric wheelchair.

— If Mum will turn left at the pillar box just there at the chemist's and then turn sharp left at the Bird and Baby, you will find yourself right at the royal enclosure. Can't miss it, I shouldn't think.

— Left and left?

Off and away, Spencer's eyes on her Princess Marie Louise hat, she buzzes past tall oarsmen in a row, their fluent sunblenched windblent hair embellished in swirls by limber gusts, Danes in singlets and shorts, with long brown legs and eighteen blue eyes. Louis Jacques Mandé Daguerre, pray for us now and at the hour of our death. Swans ride downstream midriver aloof and alone.

Spencer fixes the old lady and her wheelchair in his memory, the velvet glove at the tiller, the hat that might have been Jacobean, the lace collar spiked out from the back of her neck.

She steers between French oarsmen naked as snakes save for brief white pants and whistles on a string around the neck.

Bugles: a rill and snap of flags. Picnickers look up from their baskets. A couple with loosened clothes behind a hedge look out.

The poet from France adjusts his spectacles.

*Launch the antique swan whose silence began*
*Under Babylon where the wisteria hung,*
*When he should have sung in the red pavilions*
*Passacaglia, toccata, and fugue.*

He inspected shingles, brick, and windows. Bees stitched along the bells of a file of hollyhocks. *Greatly comforted in God at Westchester*, a voice came through a parasol. And *ever so nice, ame shaw*. And from a clutch of gaitered clergy, *nothing but my duty and my sin*.

There milled and trod and eddied a flock of little girls with the faces of eager mice, a family from Guernsey all in yellow hats, Mr. C. S. Lewis of Belfast in belling, baggy, blown trousers and flexuous flopping jacket, his chins working like a bullfrog's, tars from H.M.S. *Dogfish* with rolling shoulders and saucy eyes, pickpockets, top-hatted Etonians chatting each other in blipped English, a bishop in gaiters regarding with unbelieving mouth a Florentine philosopher peeing against a wall, Mallarmé wrapped in his plaid shawl rapt.

*The inward white of radiant space,*
*Cygnus and Betelgeuse and the Wanderers,*

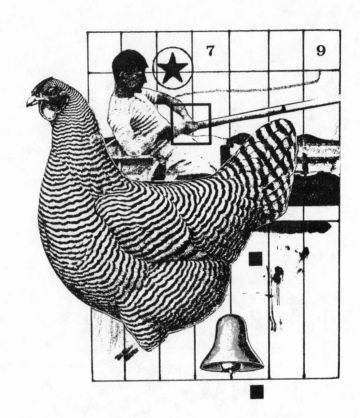

*And swam instead but swan, exile and island and*
*Is now in this utter reality a brilliant ghost,*
*An archangelical, proud, fat bird,*
*Ignorant of what the stars intend by Swan.*

River light wiggles on the ceiling of the Royal Danish Rowing
Club locker room. Oarsmen trig of girth and long of shoulder suit
up in the red and white toggery of their *roningteam.* The illapse of
a Jute foot into a blue canvas shoe, the junt of hale chests under
jerseys, bolled *skridtbinder,* Dorian knees remember, so transparent is time, a tanling foot into a sandal, lynx grace of athletes at The
Shining Dog beyond the harness makers, potters, and wine shops
on the angled and shady street that crooked from behind the Agora
over to the Sacred Way those summers Diogenes made his progress in a wash of curs to the market along the porch.

How foreign and sudden these spare athletes seemed to old men
who remembered William Gilbert Grace and Captain Matthew
Webb. Longlegged rowers file to their boats, carrying oars like the
lances at Breda in Velasquez's painting. Signal flags rise on a mast
frivolling. A trumpet, a pistol shot.

By Stanley Spencer tall oarsmen in shorts and singlets bear their
boat above their windblent vandal hair. He is preoccupied with
another, inward grace.

*Wild Sicilian parsley*
*and wasps upon the pane!*

Old Man Cézanne, he tells himself, was all very well for the
French temperament, going at things logically, vibrating with a
passion for the École Polytechnique, for ratios and microscopes,
precisions and a constant polishing of everything with critical
sandpaper. He was a Poussin run by electricity. But that woman
there shaped like a bottle and her daughter shaped like a churn,
they want to be seen by Cimabue, by Polish buttermold carvers,
by eyes begot of the happy misalliance of stiff northern barbaric
chopped wood sculpture, polychrome embroidery, and beaten
gold with autumnal Roman giant stone: roundly ungainly, stubborn as barrels, solid as brick kilns.

A coxswain light as a jockey clacking the knockers swung around
his neck whistles with Jacobean trills and sweetenings that some

talk of Alexander and some of Hercules, of Hector and Lysander, and such great names as these. To Spencer he is a conceited ass from the continent, the pampered son of a Belgian manufacturer, but he excites the Petulengros who in a fatter time would steal him as merchandise negotiable on the docks.

*There has not a minute been*
*in one thousand nine hundred years*
*twenty months or seventeen*

*But that one Christian or another*
*kissed his image in the mirror*
*standing on his slaughtered brother*

A cousin of Vice Admiral Sir Reginald Aylmer Ranfurly Plunkett Ernle Erle Drax snubs a cousin of Commander Sir George Louis Victor Henry Sergius Mountbatten Lord Milford Haven. Lord Peter Wimsey and Bunter bow in passing to Bertie Wooster and Jeeves. The aging Baron James Ensor of Ostend sweeps the horizon with his ear trumpet picking up the piston click of oars, the barking of coxes, and inflorescence of Scandinavian band music, Romany cheek, an indecent proposal in French to a vicar's sister and her reply in the French of Stratford at Bow as to the pellucidity of the day's air, the freshness of all the foreign young folk, and the silvery azure of the Thames.

Stanley Spencer pockets a nice yellow bit of dog shit and lifts off into a revery to the awful knees of Mont Sainte Victoire and the quarries at Bibémus, green wind awash in Cézanne's trees, fiercely mean old man who orders God about, and shakes his mahlstick at Him, *Seigneur, vous m'avez fait puissant et solitaire: laissez-moi m'endormir du sommeil de la terre.* A shaken fist, a plaintive cry. *I have not painted all of this, and until I do I refuse to die.*

It is the *Grande Jatte*, is it not? There is a lady with a whippet on a leash that will stand for the monkey, and clerks from banks, and little girls in tulle and ribbons, and people picnicking and gazing at the river and lolling on the banks. And those fat women over there with parasols from Camberwell, they make a touch of *The Feast of the Sardine*, do they not? The touts in their candy-stripe trousers and panamas, how they contrast with Sir Charles Parsons on the arm of the Very Reverend Dean Inge, with Margaret Jourdain and

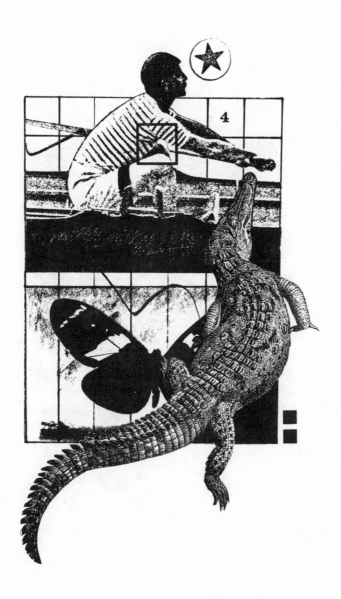

Ivy Compton-Burnett in such an inexplicable mixture of purples and greys, toques thirty years out of date.

Giacomo Antonio Domenico Michele Secondo Maria Puccini, pray for us now and at the hour of our death.

Stanley Spencer anticipates with relish the droppings in all his pockets, the scorched stink of wheat bunt, the dark odor of blight, mealy mildew, the reek of fomes and juniper conk, of black punk rot, potato scald, bruised galls, and scurf.

What gnathion and gullet to the Finns! They sound like foxes talking, and they laugh with their eyes. The American rowers breathe through their mouths and keep their arms crossed, and walk on the balls of their feet.

Pablo Diego José Francisco de Paula Juan Nepomuceno Maria de los Remedios Cipriano de la Santissima Trinidad Ruiz y Picasso, pray for us now and at the hour of our death.

A roopy laugh and: I can't help it I tell you, Alfie, *whoops! Whoops!* it's the little pants they have on, you can see everything they have as plain as cups under a tea towel, *I'll die!* And: Look it, he's vomited all down his front, the poor sod, gorgonzola and beer it smells like. And: Dear chap, these noonings and intermealiary lunchings in air this electric brace me for excesses unknown at the parsonage. Would you believe that I got to pee next to one of those *matelots* with the pom-poms? His caution was. shall I say, ironic. Democracy is so exciting, wouldn't you say?

Auguste Lumière, pray for us now and at the hour of our death.

Spencer pulled his wool bell hat lower over his thatch, getting now onto fat women's elbows, the wrinkles of the tuck, and the sway of loose biceps rolling. What silly treasure of heart and head I would come and steal, soft as the field mouse's white-foot tread. Like the blind bone in Beethoven's ear, I spoke, she spoke, and the drum spoke that could and could not hear. Under Mrs. Damer's eyes of Cotswold stone the Cherwell marries the Thames.

*India and Turkey were in her smile,*
*Madras her breasts, Izmir her hips,*
*That cross-eyed lady of Carlisle.*

Cambridge, and Bob's your uncle! A boy with a bloody nose stands defiantly by a lamp post, answering *no* to every question a policeman puts to him. A woman stung by a wasp is being helped into a pub by a Jamaican and a Hindu. A member of Parliament who has just exhibited his shrivelled penis to three Girl Guides has sunk to the sidewalk, dead.

The crew of the Club Sporting de Marseilles climbs from its boat, victors, gasping, sweating, smiling. Cameras whirr and flash as they toss their coxswain in the river. A toothy official shakes their large hands and acknowledges their Mediterranean smiles with a rabbity scrunch of his lips.

— Good show! he says.

— Sink you! they reply.

Afternoon's long shadowfall across the grass and the garden walls is like music at the end of a day of self-indulgence.

As the crowds milled to the banks for the last race, which was rowed in late level golden light, a peal of Stedmans rang out from churches roundabout.

— *Sex quattuor tris, quinque duo,* Berkshire calls.

— *Duo tris quattuor, quinque sex,* the answer falls.

— *Twa threo fower fif six, six fower, threo fif twa,* reply the bells of Oxfordshire.

*ს ს ს*

# HELPING T. S. ELIOT WRITE BETTER (NOTES TOWARD A DEFINITIVE BIBLIOGRAPHY)

by CYNTHIA OZICK

from THE AMERICAN POETRY REVIEW

*nominated by Robert Boyers, Kelly Cherry, and Sherod Santos*

I<small>T IS NOT YET</small> generally known to the world of literary scholarship that an early version of T. S. Eliot's celebrated poem, "The Love Song of J. Alfred Prufrock," first appeared in *The New Shoelace,* an impoverished publication of uncertain circulation located on East 15th Street. Eliot, then just out of Harvard, took the train down from Boston carrying a mottled manila envelope. He wore slip-on shoes with glossy toes. His long melancholy cheeks had the pallor associated in those days with experimental poets.

*The New Shoelace* was situated on the topmost floor of an antique factory building. Eliot ascended in the elevator with suppressed elation; his secret thought was that, for all he knew, the

103

young Henry James, fastidiously fingering a book review for submission, might once have entered this very structure. The brick walls smelled of old sewing machine oil. The ropes of the elevator, visible through a hole in its ceiling, were frayed and slipped occasionally; the car moved languidly, groaning. On the seventh floor Eliot emerged. The deserted corridor, with its series of shut doors, was an intimidating perplexity. He passed three with frosted glass panels marked by signs: BIALY'S WORLDWIDE NEEDLES; WARSHOWER WOOL TRADING CORP.; and MEN. Then came the exit to the fire escape. *The New Shoelace*, Eliot reasoned, must be in the opposite direction. MONARCH BOX CO.; DIAMOND'S LIGHTING FIXTURES — ALL NEW DESIGNS; MAX'S THIS-PLANET-ONLY TRAVEL SERVICE; YANKELOWITZ'S ALL-COLOR BRAID AND TRIM; LADIES. And there, at the very end of the passage, tucked into a cul-de-sac, was the office of *The New Shoelace*. The manila envelope had begun to tremble in the young poet's grip. Behind that printed title reigned Firkin Barmuenster, editor.

In those far-off days, *The New Shoelace,* though very poor, as its shabby furnishings readily attested, was nevertheless in possession of a significant reputation. Or, rather, it was Firkin Barmuenster who had the reputation. Eliot was understandably cowed. A typist in a fringed scarf sat huddled over a tall black machine, looking rather like a recently oppressed immigrant out of steerage, swatting the keys as if they were flies. Five feet from the typist's cramped table loomed Firkin Barmuenster's formidable desk, its surface hidden under heaps of butter-spotted manuscript, odoriferous paper bags, and porcelain-coated tin coffee mugs chipped at their rims. Firkin Barmuenster himself was nowhere to be seen.

The typist paused in her labors. "Help you?"

"I am here," Eliot self-consciously announced, "to offer something for publication."

"F. B. stepped out a minute."

"May I wait?"

"Suit yourself. Take a chair."

The only chair on the horizon, however, was Firkin Barmuenster's own, stationed forbiddingly on the other side of the awe-inspiring desk. Eliot stood erect as a sentry, anticipating the footsteps that at last resounded from the distant terminus of the corridor. Firkin Barmuenster, Eliot thought, must be returning from the door marked MEN. Inside the manila envelope in Eliot's fevered grasp, "The Love Song of J. Alfred Prufrock" glowed with its incontrovertible promise. One day, Eliot felt sure, it would be one of the most famous poems on earth, studied by college freshmen and corporate executives on their way up. Only now there were these seemingly insurmountable obstacles: he, Tom Eliot, was painfully young, and even more painfully obscure; and Firkin Barmuenster was known to be ruthless in his impatience with bad writing. Eliot believed in his bones that "Prufrock" was not bad writing. He hoped that Firkin Barmuenster would be true to his distinction as a great editor, and would be willing to bring out Elliot's proud effort in the pages of *The New Shoelace*. The very ink-fumes that rose up out of the magazine excited Eliot and made his heart fan more quickly than ever. Print!

"Well, well, what have we here?" Firkin Barmuenster inquired, settling himself behind the mounds that towered upward from the plateau of his desk, and reaching into one of the paper bags to extract a banana.

"I've written a poem," Eliot said.

"We don't mess with any of those," Firkin Barmuenster growled. "We are a magazine of opinion."

"I realize that," Eliot said, "but I've noticed those spaces you sometimes leave at the bottom of your articles of opinion, and I thought that might be a good place to stick in a poem, since you're not using that space for anything else anyhow. Besides," Eliot argued in conciliatory fashion, "my poem also expresses an opinion."

"Really? What on?"

"If you wouldn't mind taking half a second to look at it—"

"Young man," Firkin Barmuenster barked rapidly, "let me tell you the kind of operation we run here. In the first place, these are modern times. We're talking 1911, not 1896. What we care about here are up-to-date issues. Politics. Human behavior. Who rules the world, and how. No wan and sickly verses, you follow?"

'I believe, sir," Eliot responded with grave courtesy, "that I own an entirely new Voice."

"Voice?"

"Experimental, you might call it. Nobody else has yet written this way. My work represents a revolt from the optimism and cheerfulness of the last century. Dub it wan and sickly if you will —

it is, if you don't mind my blowing my own horn"—but here he lowered his eyes, to prove to Firkin Barmuenster that he was aware of how painfully young, and painfully obscure, he was—"an implicit declaration that poetry must not only be found *through* suffering, but can find its own material only *in* suffering. I insist," he added even more shyly, "that the poem should be able to see beneath both beauty and ugliness. To see the boredom, and the horror, and the glory."

"I like what you say about the waste of all that white space," Firkin Barmuenster replied, growing all at once thoughtful. "All right, let's have a look. What do you call your jingle?"

" 'The Love Song of J. Alfred Prufrock.' "

"Well, that won't do. Sit down, will you? I can't stand people standing, didn't my girl tell you that?"

Eliot looked about once again for a chair. To his relief, he spied a high stool just under the single grimy window, which gave out onto a bleak airshaft. A stack of back issues of *The New Shoelace* was piled on it. As he gingerly removed them, placing them with distaste on the sooty sill, the cover of the topmost magazine greeted Eliot's eye with its tedious headline: MONARCHY VS. ANARCHY—EUROPE'S POLITICAL DILEMMA. This gave poor Tom Eliot a pang. Perhaps, he reflected fleetingly, he had brought his beloved "Prufrock" to the wrong crossroads of human aspiration? How painfully young and obscure he felt! Still, a novice must begin somewhere. Print! He was certain that a great man like Firkin Barmuenster (who had by then finished his banana) would sense unusual new talent.

"Now, Prudecock, show me your emanation," Firkin Barmuenster demanded, when Eliot had dragged the stool over to the appropriate spot in front of the editor's redoubtable desk.

"Prufrock, sir. But I'm Eliot." Eliot's hands continued to shake as he drew the sheets of "Prufrock" from the mottled manila envelope.

"Any relation to that female George?" Firkin Barmuenster free-associated companionably, so loudly that the fringed typist turned from her clatter to stare at her employer for a single guarded moment.

"It's *Tom*," Eliot said; inwardly he burned with the ignominy of being so painfully obscure.

"I like that. I appreciate a plain name. We're in favor of clarity here. We're straightforward. Our credo is that every sentence is either right or wrong, exactly the same as a sum. You follow me on this, George?"

"Well," Eliot began, not daring to correct this last slip of the tongue (Freud was not yet in his heyday, and it was too soon for the dark significance of such an error to have become public knowledge), "actually it is my belief that a sentence is, if I may take the liberty of repeating myself, a kind of Voice, with its own suspense, its secret inner queries, its chancy idiosyncrasies and soliloquies. Without such a necessary view, one might eunuchize, one might render neuter—"

But Firkin Barmuenster was already buried in the sheets of "Prufrock." Eliot watched the steady rise and fall of his smirk as he read on and on. For the first time, young Tom Eliot noticed Barmuenster's style of dress. A small trim man lacking a mustache but favored with oversized buff teeth and grizzled hair the color of ash, Barmuenster wore a checkered suit of beige and brown, its thin red pinstripe running horizontally across the beige boxes only; his socks were a romantic shade of robin's egg blue, and his shoes, newly and flawlessly heeled, were maroon with white wing-tips. He looked more like a professional golfer down on his luck than a literary man of acknowledged stature. Which, Eliot mused, was more representative of Barmuenster's intellectual configuration — his sartorial preferences or the greasy paper bags under his elbows? It was impossible to decide.

Firkin Barmuenster kept reading. The typist went on smacking imaginary flies. Eliot waited.

"I confess," Firkin Barmuenster said slowly, raising his lids to confront the pallid face of the poet, "that I didn't expect anything this good. I like it, my boy, I like it!" He hesitated, gurgling slightly, like a man who has given up pipe-smoking once and for all. And indeed, Eliot spied two or three well-chewed abandoned pipes in the tumbler that served as pencil-holder; the pencils, too, were much-bitten. "You know our policy on fee, of course. After we get finished paying Clara and the rent and the sweeping up and the price of an occasional banana, there's not much left for the writer, George — only the glory. I know that's all right with you, I know you'll understand that what we're chiefly interested in is preserving the sanctity of the writer's text. The text is holy, it's holy writ, that's what it is. We'll set aside the title for a while, and put our minds to it later. What's the matter, George? You look speechless with gratitude."

"I never hoped, sir — I mean I *did* hope, but I didn't think—"

"Let's get down to business, then. The idea is excellent, first-rate, but there's just a drop too much repetition. You owned up to that yourself a minute ago. For instance, I notice that you say, over here,

> *In the room the women come and go*
> *Talking of Michelangelo,*

and then, over *here*, on the next page, you say it again."

"That's meant to be a kind of *refrain*," Eliot offered modestly.

"Yes, *I* see that, but our subscribers don't have *time* to read things twice. We've got a new breed of reader nowadays. Maybe back, say, in 1896 they had the leisure to read the same thing twice, but our modern folks are on the run. I see you're quite a bit addicted to the sin of redundancy. Look over here, where you've got

> *'I am Lazarus, come back from the dead,*
> *Come back to tell you all, I shall tell you all'*—
> *If one, settling a pillow by her head,*
> *Should say: 'That is not what I meant at all;*
> *That is not it, at all.'*

Very nice, but that reference to the dead coming back is just too iffy. I'd drop that whole part. The pillow, too. You don't need that pillow; it doesn't do a thing *for* you. And anyhow you've said 'all' four times in a single place. That won't do. It's sloppy. And who uses the same word to make a rhyme? Sloppy!" Barmuenster iterated harshly, bringing his fist down heavily on the next banana, peeled and naked, ready for the eating. "Now this line down here, where you put in

> *No! I am not Prince Hamlet, nor was meant to be,*

well, the thing to do about that is let it go. It's no use dragging in the Bard every time you turn around. You can't get away with that sort of free ride."

"I thought," Eliot murmured, wondering (ahead of his time) whether banana-craving could somehow be linked to pipe-deprivation, "it would help show how Prufrock feels about himself—"

"Since you're saying he *doesn't* feel like Hamlet, why put Hamlet *in?* We can't waste words, not in 1911 anyhow. Now up here, top of the page, you speak of

> *a pair of ragged claws*
> *scuttling across the floor of silent seas.*

Exactly what kind of claws are they? Lobster claws? Crab? Precision, my boy, precision!"

"I just meant to keep it kind of general, for the atmosphere—"

"If you *mean* a crustacean, *say* a crustacean. At *The New Shoelace* we don't deal in mere metonymy."

"Feeling is a kind of meaning, too. Metaphor, image, allusion, lyric form, melody, rhythm, tension, irony, above all the objective correlative—" But poor Tom Eliot broke off lamely as he saw the older man begin to redden.

"Tricks! Wool-pullers! Don't try to tell Firkin Barmuenster about the English language. I've been editing *The New Shoelace* since before you were born, and I think by now I can be trusted to know how to clean up a page of words. I like a clean page, I've explained that. I notice you have a whole lot of question marks all over, and they go up and down the same ground again and again. You've got *So how should I presume?* and then you've got *And how should I presume?* and after that you've got *And should I presume?* You'll just have to decide on how you want that and then keep to it. People aren't going to make allowances for you forever, you know, just because you're painfully young. And you shouldn't put in so many question marks anyhow. You should use nice clean declarative sentences. Look at this, for instance, just look at what a mess you've got here—

> *I grow old . . . I grow old . . .*
> *I shall wear the bottoms of my trousers rolled.*
>
> *Shall I part my hair behind? Do I dare to eat a peach?*
> *I shall wear white flannel trousers and walk upon the beach.*
> *I have heard the mermaids singing, each to each.*

That won't *do* in a discussion of the aging process. There you go repeating yourself again, and then that question business cropping up, and 'beach' and 'each' stuck in just for the rhyme. Anybody can see it's just for the rhyme. All that jingling gets the reader impatient. Too much baggage. Too many *words*. Our new breed of reader wants something else. Clarity. Straightforwardness. Getting to the point without a whole lot of nervous distraction. Tell me, George, are you serious about writing? You really want to become a writer some day?"

The poet swallowed hard, the blood beginning to pound in his head. "It's my life," Eliot answered simply.

"And you're serious about getting into print?"

"I'd give my eyeteeth," admitted Tom.

"All right. Then you leave it to me. What you need is a good clean job of editing. Clara!" he called.

The fringed typist glanced up, as sharply as before.

"Do we have some white space under any of next issue's articles?"

"Plenty, F.B. There's a whole slew of white at the bottom of that piece on Alice Roosevelt's new blue gown."

"Good. George," the editor pronounced, holding out his viscid hand in kindness to the obscure young poet, "leave your name and address with Clara and in a couple of weeks we'll send you a copy of yourself in print. If you weren't an out-of-towner I'd ask you to come pick it up, to save on the postage. But I know what a thrill real publication in a bona fide magazine is for an aspiring novice like yourself. I recollect the days of my own youth, if you'll excuse the cliché. Careful on the elevator — sometimes the rope gets stuck on that big nail down near the fifth floor, and you get a bounce right up those eyeteeth of yours. Oh, by the way — any suggestions for the title?"

The blood continued to course poundingly in young Tom Eliot's temples. He was overwhelmed by a bliss such as he had never before known. Print! "I really think I still like 'The Love Song of J. Alfred Prufrock,' " his joy gave him the courage to declare.

"Too long. Too oblique. Not apropos. Succinctness! You've heard of that old maxim, 'So that he who runs may read?' Well, my personal credo is: *So that he who shuns may heed*. That's what *The New Shoelace* is about. George, I'm about to put you on the map with all those busy folks who shun versifying. Leave the title to me. And don't you worry about that precious Voice of yours, George — the text is holy writ, I promise you."

Gratefully, Tom Eliot returned to Boston in high glee. And within two weeks he had fished out of his mailbox the apotheosis of his tender years: the earliest known publication of "The Love Song of J. Alfred Prufrock."

It is a melancholy truth that nowadays every company president can recite the slovenly unedited opening of this justly famous item—

> *Let us go then, you and I,*
> *When the evening is spread out against the sky*
> *Like a patient etherized upon a table;*
> *Let us go, through certain half-deserted streets,*
> *The muttering retreats*
> *Of restless nights in one-night cheap hotels, etc.*

—but these loose and wordy lines were not always so familiar, or so easily accessible. Time and fate have not been kind to Tom Eliot (who did, by the way, one day cease being painfully young): for some reason the slovenly unedited version has made its way in the world more successfully during the last seventy years than Barmuenster's conscientious efforts at perfection. Yet the great Firkin Barmuenster, that post-fin-de-siecle editor renowned for meticulous concision and passionate precision, for launching many a new literary career, and for the improvement of many a flaccid and redundant writing style, was — though the fact has so far not yet reached the larger reading public — T. S. Eliot's earliest supporter and discoverer.

For the use of bibliographers and, above all, for the delectation of poetry lovers, the complete text of "The Love Song of J. Alfred Prufrock" as it appeared in *The New Shoelace* of April 17, 1911, follows:

## THE MIND OF MODERN MAN
### by
### George Eliot

(Editor's Note: A new contributor, Eliot is sure to be heard from in the future. Out of respect for the author's fine ideas, however, certain purifications have been made in the original submission on the principle that, in the Editor's words, GOOD WRITING KNOWS NO TRICKS, SO THAT HE WHO SHUNS MAY HEED.)

*On a high-humidity evening in October, shortly
after a rainfall, a certain nervous gentleman
undertakes a visit, passing through a bad section
of town. Arriving at his destination, the unhappy
man overhears ladies discussing an artist well-known
in history (Michelangelo Buonarroti, 1475-1564, Italian
sculptor, painter, architect, and poet). Our friend
contemplates his personal diffidence, his baldness, his
suit and tie, and the fact that he is rather underweight.
He notes with some dissatisfaction that he is usually
addressed in conventional phrases. He cannot make a
decision. He believes his life has not been well-spent;
indeed, he feels himself to be no better than a mere
arthropod (of the shelled aquatic class, which includes
lobsters, shrimps, crabs, barnacles, and wood lice). He has
been subjected to many social hours timidly drinking tea, for,
though he secretly wishes to impress others, he does not know
how to do so. He realizes he is an insignificant
individual, with a small part to play in the world.
He is distressed that he will soon be eligible for
an old age home, and considers the advisability of a
fruit diet and of permitting himself a greater
relaxation in dress, as well as perhaps covering his
bald spot. Thus, in low spirits, in a markedly irrational
frame of mind, he imagines he is encountering certain
mythological females, and in his own words he makes it
clear that he is doubtless in need of the aid of a
reliable friend or kindly minister. (As are, it goes
without saying, all of us.)*

# EUROPA

by DEREK WALCOTT

from ANTAEUS

nominated by Michael Harper, Josephine Jacobsen, Dan Masterson, Sherod Santos, and Sarah Vogan

The full moon is so fierce that I can count the
coconuts' cross-hatched shade on bungalows,
their white walls raging with insomnia.
The stars leak drop by drop on the tin plates
of the sea almonds, and the jeering clouds
are luminously rumpled as the sheets.
The surf, insatiably promiscuous,
groans through the walls; I feel my mind
whiten to moonlight, altering that form
which daylight unambiguously designed,
from a tree to a girl's body bent in foam;
then, treading close, the black hump of a hill,
its nostrils softly snorting, nearing the
naked girl splashing her breasts with silver.
Both would have kept their proper distance still,
if the chaste moon hadn't swiftly drawn the drapes
of a dark cloud, coupling their shapes.

She teases with those flashes, yes, but once
you yield to human horniness, you see
through all that moonshine what they really were,
those gods as seed-bulls, gods as rutting swans—
an overheated farmhand's literature.
Who ever saw her pale arms hook his horns,
her thighs clamped tight in their deep-plunging ride,
watched, in the hiss of the exhausted foam,
her white flesh constellate to phosphorous

as in salt darkness beast and woman come,
Nothing is there, just as it always was,
but the foam's wedge to the horizon-light,
then, wire-thin, the studded armature,
like drops still quivering on his matted hide,
the hooves and horn-points anagrammed in stars.

# 🔥 🔥 🔥

# DEAR JEFFERS (A NOTE FROM SHERIDAN TO CARMEL-BY-THE-SEA)

by WILLIAM PITT ROOT

from CUTBANK

*nominated by* CUTBANK

It's a long way from the queer remote silence-making *quawk* of
    that heron
your words snagged on the wing as I
was being born, Jeffers,
decades ago, in a Minnesota blizzard. You were in a squall of rage
near Big Sur in the place no longer your place,
as you foresaw, dragging stone after stone to your tower
    nonetheless
from the live surf and froth of your own sweat. Edged-in now
by homes No-Man built to live in — high priced
suckertraps for men successful in that coming world you shunned
    and decried
poem after bitter poem — your stone tower, Jeffers, even your
    stone tower
raised by hand toward the high blue home
of your beloved hawks
toward whom you turned and turned your falcon of a face for
    evidence
of worthiness, is gone into their hands, their pockets,

enhanced by your famous hatred, the prices rising
with your skydriven fistlike poems exactly
abhorring them.
                          Where I am, in Wyoming still magnificent with
     wilderness
no sea has breathed on for millions of years, the old forces
finding a new grip soon will ream out
ranchers and farmers bewildered by profits sudden as true
     strokes, making way
for holes into which men hungry for the good life will descend
innocent of your hawks, gulls, godlike stallions, and women
with wild eyes will tend them from prefabrications
as some die, most prosper in the ways men do these days, their
     families
dulled by generations of decay
in hearts surrounded by the crown jewels of the age,
appliances and gadgets designed to make
life careless. And they work, dear Jeffers. They do work.

# MEXICANS
# BEGIN JOGGING
## by GARY SOTO

from REVISTA CHICANO-RIQUENA

*nominated by* REVISTA CHICANO-REQUENA, *Steve Cannon and Philip Schultz*

At the factory I worked
In the fleck of rubber, under the press
Of an oven yellow with flame,
Until the border patrol opened
Their vans and my boss waved for us to run.
"Over the fence, Soto," he shouted,
And I shouted that I was American.
"No time for lies," he said, and pressed
A dollar in my palm, hurrying me
Through the back door.

Since I was on his time, I ran
And became the wag to a short tail of Mexicans—
Ran past the amazed crowds that lined
The street and blurred like photographs, in rain.
I ran from that industrial road to the soft
Houses where people paled at the turn of an autumn sky.
What could I do but yell *vivas*
To baseball, milkshakes, and those sociologists
Who would clock me
As I jog into the next century
On the power of a great, silly grin.

# DEATH AND LEBANON

fiction by BARBARA BEDWAY

from THE IOWA REVIEW

*nominated by* THE IOWA REVIEW

OHIO

Mashaya ruins the night for everyone, both aunts say it has to stop. After dinner they find her sitting on our bed already in her nightgown, dark circles under her wide green eyes. Aunt Philamena says tell us, *habibti*, what do you see? Tree shadows? Branches against the window pane?

The dark hair swings no from side to side.

Something you hear, then? The backyard dogs howling, your old aunt here snoring? Maybe Mr. Truskaloski upstairs hacking out his lungs? No?

No.

Mashaya, child, something makes you scream.

118

Sitting in our bedroom window I watch the bonfire in the yard across the alley. With my cheek against the cold pane of glass I see our neighbor wrapped in shawls bringing food on a plate to her dogs. They leap up in their chains. The high-pitched barking goes on and on. If our aunts weren't watching, Mashaya would be in the window with me, watching that fire in the tall metal drum.

You tell me, Ajunya, Philamena says, what can I do now?

At home I am Ajunya and Marcia is Mashaya, but only at home. In the Miner's Supply my aunt calls me Angie; it's Marcia who stocks the shelves. To her customers my aunt speaks Polish, Russian, a little Greek. Her sister Hikmet gets by with just Italian. Everyone here came from somewhere else but my sister and I are the newest: two years here from the Lebanon, because of the events. I was nine and Mashaya eleven when we came with our sita, called grandmother here, to live with her daughters in America. At night I sit in our window and think of Beirut: the flashes of light, the ten-second count to the artillery's boom.

Ajunya, are you listening? *Look* at your room. What can I do that I haven't done? What?

We live with bare walls and a bare floor; all pictures, mirrors, crucifixes got put away and their ghosts with them. Because of Mashaya's dreams our aunts hang up every piece of clothing, never move the furniture when they clean; leave the dresser top, the floor, the chairs bare of anything that in the night could become the head or neck or arm of a stranger. Mashaya told them: his nose is twisted in the crucifix, his eyes shine out of the mirror. Sometimes there is no stranger but something else. Still, Philamena has to open the closet door to poke for hiding strangers, then shut it so the hanging clothes can't shape themselves into the wrinkles on an arm, a face, the back of a huge hand.

Well?

*Xaala,* I don't know.

Mashaya, look at me, even your sister can't tell what it is, she sleeps right next to you. At least she's trying to. Everyone has to sleep, child. Mashaya, can't you *look* at me?

Philamena slaps her reddened hands against her black dress. She is so tired from these interrupted nights that her heavy body sags and her legs and ankles swell. Aunt Hikmet, thin and belted inside her own black dress, tells her beads in the doorway.

Mashaya, Mashaya.

Philamena hugs my sister, whose face disappears in the dark woolen sleeves. Outside the bonfire is low. It will die before Mashaya can watch it.

Aunt Hikmet brings her rosary into our room. She kneels on the rugless floor and we face her. I hear the crack of my sister's bony ankles. She smiles at me and tucks her nightgown under her knees. Philamena leans on my shoulder and groans to her knees. Beads click. We pray.

We pray hail marys for the dead: for our mother, who died having me; and for our sita, whose life gave out once she got us, safe and sound, to America. We pray for who's not dead but dying, the old women Hikmet visits in their homes every week, nuns and widows giving out after years of a life in Christ. We pray for the Lebanon and all the true Lebanese, the believers in Christ, who must not give out until peace comes to the country at last.

Amen, Hikmet says, while my sister's lips are still moving. She's forming silent words to someone, to God or whoever it is, to keep our father from giving out in the Lebanon.

In bed we listen to the sound of our aunt's slippers scuffling down the hallway. We count one minute and hear the creak of their beds. Mashaya reaches for her shoebox from under the bed and I pick up the rosewater bottle by the bedpost. We rub the rosewater into our skin and we sniff each other.

That's good, Mashaya says, and hooking her long hair behind each ear, she bends over her dusty box. Some nights she needs to look and some nights she leaves it alone, but for sleeping she always needs the rosewater smell and the sight of its thick blue bottle.

I hold the flashlight pen while she sifts through her treasures from the Lebanon. There's dirt and broken glass and Sita's hypodermic needle for her insulin. In a rubber band Mashaya keeps strips of posters she tore off the walls of Beirut. She has eyes and hair and lips and shoulders from a hundred different boys, boys whose families plastered their pictures all over the city to honor their sons dead in the events. The boys might have been kidnapped or died fighting in the streets but it's Mashaya who keeps them, their creased smiles and folded eyes.

Hold this, she says, and hands me a strip of wide forehead.

Somewhere in the box she thinks there is a whole face but we haven't found it yet. Once our sita said we were close, we almost had it, but the eyes looked in different directions.

Let's give up, I tell her. Nothing looks right tonight.

Hold the flashlight closer.

The pieces are getting too crinkley to see.

You're not even looking.

I'm tired of looking.

Then we'll never find anything.

She puts back the lid and folds her hands on top of it. I tug at the blanket and wait. She won't look by herself. Sita helped when I wouldn't but Sita died months ago so it has to be me now. I know I should search more but my eyes are too heavy, they close when I tell them not to.

Can we sleep now? I ask her.

I never sleep. She leans down to slide the box under the bed.

You do sleep. You have to. You dream.

I dream with my eyes open.

The dreams began after Sita died. For the week she was sick Mashaya sat beside her next to the trays of pills and needles. It was summer, the hot air thick with unfallen rain, but Sita was keeping us indoors. She watched and worried in her bed damp with sweat. She yelled *y'allah, y'allah,* get inside, and pointed toward the ceiling where she said she saw a locusts' swarm. Hikmet ran for the doctor but Mashaya closed the window and started to shake. Sita called her Melania, our mother's name, and pulled off the cloth Mashaya tried to press to her forehead.

Melania, she said, her gray hair loose and damp across the pillow, get inside. Locusts are the teeth of the wind.


BEIRUT


Papa and his cousin Faisz sit at the kitchen table, talking in French about guns. Both prefer to speak in French. They say the true Lebanese are Europeans by way of the Phoenicians. We have no relatives in France but Papa is proud to have two sisters-in-law who live in America. He sends us there once a year for a month, where he forbids us to speak any Arabic.

Sita laughs at the two men. She calls them *Mughnuuni,* crazy ones, and scrubs her pans viciously. Mashaya dries them and hums to herself over the names and numbers of guns we all know by heart: Katushka, Kalishnokov, Duska; American M-16s, Czech M-58s.

I know Papa is sad he has no sons to help him defend the Lebanon. He is handsome in his olive-green army uniform of the *phalanges libanaises;* his high black boots, the beret atop black hair cropped close to the scalp. He has a plan to get to the teenagers firing a 122-millimeter gun from the Cercle de la Renaissance sportive. The boys fire round after round into the Christian section, then they strut—Faisz gets up to show us their strut, with his hands high on his hips—they strut free as birds across the Avenue de Paris and jump for a swim into the Mediterranean. Faisz says sometimes they pick up rackets for a quick game on the tennis courts nearby.

There are battles all over the city and my father has chosen his. He and Faisz fold up their paper and diagrams and pick up their M-16s.

*Au revoir*, Papa says, kissing Sita.

*Ma issalame*, she answers, facing her dishes.

Papa slams the door.

Remember, Sita tells us, untying the clean white rag from around her grey bun and sinking into a chair, just remember. The French say *merde* for shit but believe me, it still smells the same.

She turns on the radio for Sharif Akhaoui's daily report. He used to give rush-hour traffic reports but now he tells where the roadblocks are and what bridges are safe to cross.

Today, he is saying, you would be mad to go out. The gunmen are everywhere, every street is dangerous. Do not go out. Do not even try to.

Sometimes we listen to Akhaoui for hours while Sita stares at the radio. Today he is naming street after street. No pharmacies opened, no bakeries. *Do not go out*. People telephone him with new sniping in Ashrafiyeh, with kidnappings in Ain al-Rummaneh. He repeats every ambush, every kidnapping.

Sita keeps one hand on mine and an arm around Mashaya. No one touches the dial. Akhaoui's voice gets higher and louder. He screams by the end of the day.

Mashaya's job is to set the trash on fire. Just before curfew at seven o'clock she runs out to the street with a few drops of kerosene and lights the tips of the garbage. While the fire is spreading she tries, quick as she can, to pull what she wants: broken bottles, bloody scarves, twisted pieces of metal. She won't touch moldy bread and she hates the daytime, when flies stay round the piles of trash and keep even the cats away. I don't like the nights when the sky glows red from tracer bullets and we hear rats in the cellar where we sleep on a mattress by the stairs. The rats make a soft, scuffling sound that doesn't worry my sister. She says if you can hear them they're not near you yet.

When our neighbor Mr. Helou left the city, he took a wide glass jar filled with dirt from his home in the mountains. Mashaya keeps bits of crumbling stone from the porch outside in a shoebox beside our mattress. What she pulls from the trash she lines up in a corner and shows me before we sleep. She loves hard things with jagged edges, blackened in parts by fire. In the dark she gives me a sliver of glass and I do what she wants me to do. My fingers curl tight around it; she squeezes my hand with hers. When I open it up my hand is bleeding.

*Mesquina*, poor thing, Mashaya says, and taking back the sliver of glass she covers the cut with her mouth.

Sita says we are going to America. It's early morning and we're sitting in the kitchen where it's still dark. Yesterday the lights flickered out and for the first time did not come back on. When the telephone is working, Sita is busy calling, making her plans. We have to get to Cyprus and we need gold. A cousin's wife's brother is taking a boat in two days and he wants gold. While she's talking, Sita drinks her *arak* with vodka because there's no water and there's no bread either. She won't let us go to the bank building downtown and take water from its oriental fish pond, as certain neighbors have done. But she hands us dried figs to suck on while she cradles the phone to her ear. I chew and chew to make the most juice I can, but the taste is still bitter smoke from the garbage fires and dust from the April *khamsin*.

All week clouds of yellow dust have blown across the city, settling onto the still bodies left in the street and seeping past the newspapers taped over our broken windows. The dust keeps Mashaya moving from room to room, shaking herself and kicking at the choking air. She stops when we hear roosters crowing outside; she says we could be in the mountains if we shut our eyes, listen to those roosters and the quiet of no cars moving in the street. By the living room window we shut our eyes and hear Sita yelling from the kitchen.

It's too early but already there is the crack and whoomph and boom of the fighting from the city center. We hear gunmen scuttling over the walls and into the empty streets. They wear thick ski masks and run with their guns pointing to the sky. Sita slams down the phone and shouts for us to get into the cellar. She stays on the top step because she's never able to make the climb back up from below. With both hands she helps herself sit down near the wall. Missiles fizz through the air. Sita's voice is tired and hoarse.

I think we have a boat for this week-end, she says. Girls, can you hear me? That's two days. You can stand anything for two days.

Your boat is Anthony Quinn's yacht, Papa says, stepping into the kitchen as Sita slams the living room door and stays behind it. You'll go out with *le tout Beirut*. Tell them, Faisz, tell them what a boat that is.

Faisz says that is quite a boat. It's going to have a swimming pool and possibly two. The boat leaves from Jounieh, and in Jounieh all the shops are open and the streets are clean. People dance by candlelight in the Four Seasons Hotel.

I ought to be recuperating in Jounieh, Faisz says, holding up his bandaged hand. He and Papa have dark bristle all over their faces and they smell like the smoke of hashish. It's quiet again, still as mornings used to be. Papa comes back only in the quiet. He's brought bottled water and bread from Damascus. The wooden part of his rifle gleams around the sticker of St. Theresa holding a cross.

When you come back from America, Papa says, Jounieh is where we'll live. He hands each of us a gold coin with a reindeer on one side and tells us to hide it from Sita.

This is to help you come home, in case I can't get there myself you'll have money to get your own tickets.

Pierre, Faisz says, what are you doing that for? They could get stopped and searched on the way to the boat, someone might think they have more somewhere else.

Mashaya starts crying into Papa's shoulder. His uniform is rough but she stays there with her head down and tugs at the buttons. Papa says we won't get stopped, it's taken care of. Faisz reaches for me.

Do you know why you have to go away, *habibti?* he asks, gathering me carefully into his arms. It's because of war, you have to understand war. Everyone looks dangerous now, even children. We were on sentry duty this morning, your father and I, and we saw an old man in slippers alone in the street. Your father looked through his binoculars and said he *seemed* empty-handed, but your father had to shoot him anyway. Now, do you know why he did that?

Mashaya burrows into Papa's uniform. She says nothing and I don't want to.

Tell them, Pierre, Faisz says.

Papa is trying to smoothe the thick tangles in Mashaya's long hair. His wiggling fingers try to work their way through the clumps, but can't.

I know where the man lived, Papa says. He wasn't going to make it anyway.

Be serious, Faisz says, stroking my arm with his bandaged hand.

Papa says, I am.

Papa said we were needed for a maneuver.

He came into the basement with his flashlight and put his face next to ours. He still smelled of hashish and his reddened eyes were large. Mashaya jammed the lid onto her shoebox but our father was not looking there.

Hurry, he said, everyone has to help. Even old women like your sita are helping but Sita's asleep, she's had too much *arak* today.

At the top of the stairs we looked in on her, asleep on Mashaya's bed.

She's out for the night, Papa said.

We stumbled in the dark to the front door and Papa lit a cigarette with one precious match. In the flare I saw Mashaya with her hands in fists staring ahead at the door. There were two soft taps. Papa stooped to kiss us.

This lady is Mr. Helou's aunt, he said. You do what she says and you'll be back before curfew. Ajunya, stop smiling, there's nothing funny about this.

I did feel my mouth stretched wide but I wasn't smiling. I tried to believe my body was nothing, that I could get through the streets like air breathed out of a chest. My chest felt so tight it seemed only the thinnest breath could escape.

Papa opened the door and gave us to the old woman standing

there. She had thick hands like Sita's and dressed like her in a black dress and a rag around her head. She carried a small shovel and told us to say nothing until we got where we needed to be. Papa touched her shoulder and said he had to meet Faisz. He picked up his gun and disappeared into the dark.

The old woman led us down two dark streets where nothing moved. A match flared in an alleyway but no hand seemed to hold it. We stopped at a building site near the corner. Mashaya let go of my hand. More women with children came out of the side streets and alleys; everyone holding shovels, trowels, dust pans.

Do this, the woman told us, pulling a sandbag from the pile of them and holding it out in front of her. We each took a side of the bag while she shoveled dirt from the site into it. I heard her breathing hard and praying in French under her breath. My hands shook and I dropped the bag twice but Mr. Helou's aunt muttered I know, I know, and picked my side up for me. Mashaya's hands were still as she stared at the thickening bag. When it was filled we laid it aside and filled another, then another, until our arms were aching and our breaths were loud in our ears. Two boys pushing a wheelbarrow helped us toss our bags in with others.

Now run, the woman told us. It's one street down and one street over.

People we couldn't see were scurrying into the alleys and buildings. Mashaya and I ran, holding each other's slippery hand and stumbling over the rubble. Behind us we heard the crack of a rifle but we were standing up so we ran on. I thought of invisible things, of a breath that breathes on and a look without eyes. Then my chest was so tight I could think of nothing and held tighter to Mashaya's hand.

We got one street over and our house was easy to find. Sita had put a forbidden candle in the window, and was waiting.

Who told you to go outside?

She pinched me, pulled me through the doorway and yanked Mashaya in by her hair.

Who? Your father?

She cursed and slapped Mashaya, who started to laugh and fell down on her knees, laughing harder. Sita slapped her again and cursed our father, the Lebanon, and Jesus Christ. An explosion too near the back of the house stopped her.

*Y'allah, y'allah,* get downstairs.

She blew out the candle and groped for our hands. Mashaya was still laughing.

Sita is so confused this early morning.

While the taxi waits, she rushes around the kitchen and bed-rooms, swiping at dust with a rag and fluffing up the pillows. She curses the squatters who took over Mr. Helou's house, then says it can't be helped. But they let their goats wander along the balco-nies; they cook their meals on the floor. Enough, enough, it doesn't matter. Get your sister, it's time to go.

After five minutes she finds us in our bedroom, where Mashaya is stuffing strips of paper into the sides of her suitcase. Her blue sweater is grimy and stained and it smells like smoke from the fire she set this morning. She won't brush her hair and she won't take off that sweater.

What, child, is this?

Sita picks among the folded clothes in the suitcase, finding dirt and broken glass and pieces of twisted metal. She takes Mashaya's face in her hands and looks a long time into her eyes.

*Mesquina*, poor thing, she says, but Mashaya pulls away. She runs past me and I brush at the ashes that settled onto her hair.

Don't touch me, she says. I'm burning.


OHIO

Saturdays Philamena works in the store and Hikmet takes my sister to the counselor. I make tea for Mashaya and pour in lots of milk. She stirs it, the spoon goes round and round. Hikmet from the porch yells *y'allah, y'allah*. Mashaya shrugs and brushes past. She leaves her rosewater smell.

Alone in the kitchen I push back the curtains and put three plates in the sink. By the window I say my prayer. *Beirut*. God, let it be like this:

The first time Papa comes back from maneuvers, I say, Don't come in. I say, Father, if you come in, the kitchen chair where you sat with your maps won't sit still for you anymore. If you come back, the table will collapse, the edge where you rest your hand will bend and the legs fold under. Don't try to come in. The door won't let you, the knob that you twist won't turn in to us, won't give us away. God, let Sita be in her place at the sink and Mashaya will be at the window. Let everything here be what belongs, water in jars and bread flat and white on the table. God, God, let here be where Sita does not die, where Mashaya stands wiping our plates in the light of the open window.

## 🔥 🔥 🔥

# POETRY IN A
# DISCOURAGING TIME

by CHRISTOPHER CLAUSEN

from THE GEORGIA REVIEW

*nominated by* THE GEORGIA REVIEW

LIKE A SAGUARO CACTUS from which any desert wayfarer can draw refreshment, the place of poetry in modern civilization flourishes as a palpable, perennially green issue on the frontiers where literary criticism, philosophy, and sociology converge amidst mirages. Nearly every one agrees that poetry in the twentieth century—at least in English-speaking countries—is not so highly honored or widely read as it once was. Few doubt that the rise of science has had something to do with displacing it as a publicly important vehicle for those truths that people accept as

This essay was the lead item in a forum on the place of poetry in our culture featured in *The Georgia Review*, Winter, 1981.

being centrally important. The attempt to persuade the reading public that figurative, ironic, or connotative modes of thought and discourse retain their value in an age of computer language has not been notably successful. Few educated Americans today have any confidence in their ability to understand metaphor or detect irony; most undoubtedly believe that anything of real importance can be better said in prose, which they casually assume to be more natural, direct, and precise than poetry. There is a paradox here, for while English and American prose has become ever more bloated with jargon and tangled in circumlocution, the vocabulary and syntax of most poetry are simpler than they were a hundred years ago. The result may be that poetry is widely distrusted for two contradictory reasons: it is at once too simple in its language to be very important, and too difficult in its figurative qualities to be understood. In any case, nobody who looks into the matter can doubt that some vast cultural change has intervened since the days when Tennyson and Longfellow grew rich, or even the time on the boundaries of living memory when English soldiers carried *The Oxford Book of English Verse* with them into the trenches of Flanders.[1]

Beyond these generalities, the question of what poetry is worth to the modern world and what has happened to its audience remains much as Shelley, Peacock, and Macaulay left it over a century and a half ago.

In this essay I shall restate briefly some of the central arguments of my book, *The Place of Poetry*, (University Press of Kentucky, 1981), recognizing that such condensation inevitably results in important omissions and simplifications.

In 1820, at the dawn of the age of science, Thomas Love Peacock warned (with intentions that remain a matter of dispute): "the empire of thought is withdrawn from poetry, as the empire of facts had been before. . . . A poet in our times is a semi-barbarian in a civilized community. He lives in the days that are past." In consequence, "the poetical audience will not only continually diminish in the proportion of its number to that of the rest of the reading public, but will also sink lower and lower in the comparison of intellectual acquirement. . . ."[2] Thomas Babington Macaulay five years later was still more assertively negative: "In proportion as men know more and think more, they look less at individuals and more at classes. They therefore make better theories and worse poems." Poetry is a form of madness, Macaulay continues; even reading it with enjoyment involves "a certain unsoundness of mind." Since the seventeenth century, language has evolved to the point where poetry is no more than a vestigial survival of credulous times. The age of abstraction and science is upon us; that of particularity and poetry is gone forever.[3]

The predictions of Peacock and Macaulay took about a century to come true. They have come true now with a vengeance, and if we wish to reject the diagnosis on which these accurate forecasts were predicated — that poetry is an inherently archaic mode of understanding and discourse — we must look carefully at the development of Anglo-American poetry since the beginning of the scientific age, and we must not make the assumption that poets and critics are blameless for the ways in which their civilization has evolved. We must also contend with the fact, which would have surprised Macaulay and Peacock, that the poetic audience actually increased for at least half a century after they made their predictions. The leading Romantics and their Victorian successors gave poetry a lease on life that no dispassionate observer at the beginning of the nineteenth century would have been likely to predict. "To an important extent," Walter Jackson Bate declares, "that 'rescue' of the arts through the extension of their public did happen, against all the theoretical probabilities, and was to continue to happen throughout the nineteenth century."[4] The virtual extinction of poetry as a cultural force, though long predicted, is a recent event; it happened within living memory. Whether a second "rescue" is possible remains to be seen, for while the cultural changes attendant on the rise of science undoubtedly altered the position of poetry, they did not make its decline inevitable.

The assumption that scientific knowledge is by itself a complete and satisfying way for a civilization to understand the world has no historical support, and to believe that any large number of English and American readers have ever found it so is to ignore the apprehension that most major scientific advances have occasioned since Sir Charles Lyell's time. It was not only fundamentalist Christians who suffered distress when Darwin established natural selection as the chief means by which humanity came into being; even those who immediately accepted Darwin's verdict set about looking for a new medium of truth and values to replace the Christianity in which they could no longer believe. The compulsive invention of new religions in the nineteenth and twentieth centuries has been one symptom of this widespread need. The expansion of the arts in the same period has been another. Matthew Arnold's assertion that poetry would take the place of religion is well known and often quoted; not quite so well known is the fact that many scientists were in at least partial agreement. Beauty and truth were not to be separated. T. H. Huxley, Darwin's chief defender, praised imaginative literature precisely because it supplemented the truths of science with other truths that were equally vital to individuals and societies:

> . . . the great mass of the literature we esteem is valued, not merely because of having artistic form, but because of its intellectual content; and the value is the higher the more precise, distinct, and true is that intellectual content. And, if you will let me for a moment speak of the very highest forms of literature, do we not regard them as highest simply because the more we know the truer they seem, and the more competent we are to appreciate beauty the more beautiful they are?[5]

To assert that scientific knowledge needs to be complemented by other modes of understanding the world is not to belittle science. A troubled and agnostic age ought to be one in which poetry flourishes. It was, after all, at the beginning of such an age that Wordsworth and the other Romantics found an enormous audience, an audience that had grown even larger by the time of *Origin of Species*. From the 1860's onward, it is true, the *scale* of poetry declined, as few poets felt it any longer possible to grasp the whole of life or to represent it in a comprehensive system. The truths of poetry that seemed to wear best were no longer the "great truths" of which Wordsworth spoke in *The Prelude*, but rather flashes of insight into experience, highly focused clarifications of life (to anticipate Robert Frost's definition of poetry), amalgams of thought and feeling expressed in lyric form. If we divide in half the century between Peacock's "The Four Ages of Poetry" and Eliot's "The Waste Land," we find an instructive pattern. Between 1820 and 1870, the leading poets are the prophetic Wordsworth, Tennyson, Whitman, and Browning—system-makers who thought in book-length units. After 1870, the most important figures are Hopkins, Hardy, Housman, Emily Dickinson, Frost, Yeats, Kipling—lyricists all. The nature of poetic truth had undergone a profound change. Like the men of science, poets had become empiricists.

That very discontinuity, however, suggests a larger continuity. All of the major revolutions in poetry and criticism since the publication of *Lyrical Ballads* in 1798 have been attempts to adjust to the new (and changing) position of science in modern intellectual life, to reassert a place for poetry in a world whose most capacious truths had suddenly ceased to be the doctrines of Christianity and become instead the laws and hypotheses of science. Science never tried to explain the world as Christianity had done; rather than provide a new metaphysic, it implicitly called into doubt the validity of any metaphysical system. Agnosticism has been a characteristic attitude among poets and scientists alike since well before Huxley coined the word in 1869. Far from replacing the certainties of religion with its own, science in the long run made the world seem more mysterious and ambiguous than before. In such a world, the interpreting imagination can never be out of date, and in such a world poetry became very popular — for a time.

## II

It is, Josephine Miles points out,

> characteristic of poets that they are not content merely to make big changes, as from human nature to external nature, and from concept to observation, and from abstraction to imagery . . .; each time they denigrate what has gone before, suggesting that poetry before theirs was not only dull and wrong but especially artificial and falsely poetic. The negative epithet "poetic diction" tends always to be applied to the poetry preceding one's own.[6]

No doubt this succession of movements, each exaggerating its differences from the movement before, has always been with us, but since 1798 — and to a spectacular extent in the twentieth century — the pace of poetic change has accelerated. The Romantics repudiated the poetry of the eighteenth century and begat the Victorians, whose relation to them was always an ambivalent one. Pound and Eliot more drastically repudiated virtually all English

poetry since the seventeenth century and wrought technical innovations that made much of their work nearly unintelligible to most
readers of poetry. (It was the Modernists, as John Crowe Ransom
put it, "in whose hands poetry as a living art has lost its public
support.") Technical innovation has proceeded compulsively on an
almost industrial scale ever since, leading to a fragmentation of
effort today that is unique in the entire history of literature. The
concept of a literary generation has lost its meaning, as each poetic
cell, jealously isolated from every other cell, gives birth to new
cells through mitosis. Meanwhile serious poetry has lost virtually
its entire audience.

As I have already said, the assertion of discontinuity by poets
themselves disguises a more profound continuity of desperation.
The endless innovations in poetic technique are much less important — except perhaps for their effect in further alienating the
poetic audience — than the continuing concern with trying to find
or make a place for poetry in a world that has seemed ever more
hostile or indifferent. Each revolution in Anglo-American poetry
has been an unsuccessful, or at best temporarily successful, attempt to assert the value of poetry itself. Roughly speaking, these
attempts have been associated with two opposed assertions, one
traditional and the other an invention of the nineteenth century:
first, that the poetic imagination provides a kind or kinds of truth at
least as valuable as anything science can give us; second, that
poetry is not concerned with truth at all and represents an
internally self-sufficient system whose entire justification is aesthetic and/or emotional. The first position is that of almost all poets
and readers of poetry before the 1890's. The second is that of many
twentieth-century poets and, in many different formulations, of
most twentieth-century critics from I. A. Richards to the decon-
structionists.

As a body of poetic and critical doctrine, formalism originated in
the mid-nineteenth century and was heavily influenced by the
exaggerated views of science that we have seen Macaulay express.
Implicitly accepting the assertion that referential language and
verifiable knowledge were now the well fenced preserve of the
scientist, such writers as Poe, Wilde, and Pater declared poetry to
be a formal language with its own rules and structures, like logic or
mathematics, autonomous and not to be interpreted or valued by
reference to anything outside itself. This position, ironically akin to

logical positivism, was greatly elaborated in the twentieth century by the New Critics of England and America. The purpose of poetic language was to transmute "emotions and feelings" (T. S. Eliot) into art. The statements that poets made (or seemed to make) about the world were in reality "pseudo-statements" (I. A. Richards) and possessed only "dramatic truth" (Cleanth Brooks); they were not to be read as applying outside the poem. The quality of the thought or ideas in a poem mattered little, for ideas were merely one kind of raw material that the poet made use of. Ignored or denied was Coleridge's assertion that "No man was ever yet a great poet, without being at the same time a profound philosopher."

From the start, the aim of formalist critics was to find a rationale for poetry that no other mode of discourse might claim, a purpose which led them to emphasize constantly — indeed, greatly to exaggerate — the differences between poetic and other uses of language. (In this, ironically, they had again been preceded by the advocates of scientism, as my quotations from Macaulay show.) As to whether poetry could be said in any sense to be cognitive, opinions differed; but all formalists agreed that previous generations had been mistaken in reading poetry for what it could show or tell them about character, conduct, or the world. An emphasis on content was indignantly equated with the reduction of poetry to mere propaganda. One was henceforth to read a poem "as a poem," which on the whole meant confining one's interest to its structural features. Archibald MacLeish's famous lines enshrined the whole doctrine in a single aphorism: "A poem should not mean/But be."

The abandonment of an intellectual role may have seemed at one time to free poetry from what was regarded as a losing competition with science. The drastic decline of the poetic audience during the very period when this doctrine of poetic purposes was becoming widespread, however, casts doubt on the validity of that hope. The attempt to liberate poets from the yoke of detachable meaning more likely had the effect of making their works seem trivial to most potential readers, who like Huxley had been educated on other assumptions about the purposes of literary discourse. Nevertheless, the notion that poetry is at best only peripherally rational or referential is still a widespread dogma among critics. In her recent book on lyric poetry, Barbara Hardy declares as a matter of accepted fact:

> . . . the lyric does not provide an explanation, judg-
> ment, or narrative; what it does provide is feeling, alone
> and without histories or characters. . . . The advantage
> of lyric poetry comes from its undiluted attention to
> feeling and feeling alone, and its articulateness in clarify-
> ing that feeling. . . .[7]

This is not a conception of poetry, lyric or otherwise, that one finds much before Poe's time; if it were correct, the long controversy over the nature and value of poetic truth could never have taken place. If poetry were (or had always been assumed to be) purely emotional, or if it offered nothing more than aesthetic pleasure, few people would ever have taken it seriously enough to attack it. Nor would it have required any defense, except against that variety of puritan who is opposed to pleasure on principle. Poetry would have been as culturally insignificant as pushpin, to which Jeremy Bentham famously compared it around the same time that Wordsworth and Shelley were making prophetic claims for it.

A well-known traditional definition of poetry will show a striking contrast. It is from Sir Philip Sidney's *A Defence of Poetry*, first published in 1595, and for our purposes it has the merit of not having been original even then.

> Poesy therefore is an art of imitation, for so Aristotle
> termeth it in the word *mimesis* — that is to say, a repre-
> senting, counterfeiting, or figuring forth — to speak
> metaphorically, a speaking picture — with this end, to
> teach and delight.[8]

"To teach and delight" — almost every writer on poetry from ancient times until the end of the eighteenth century assumed these to be the purposes of literary art, or indeed of art in general, although poetry had special opportunities and responsibilities because it was so highly articulate. For Sidney and his successors, emotion is only a part of poetry, and it is deliberately subordinated to other things. The combination of emotional power with signifi-cant ideas is what brought poetry into collision with philosophy in Plato's time, with religion on various occasions in the Middle Ages, and — from Sidney's time onward — with scientism.

Literature is valuable for a number of reasons, but one of the most important for a civilization is the insights it provides into whatever problems of thought and conduct people in that civilization are most deeply concerned with. Arnold's definition of poetry as a "criticism of life" and Frost's as a "clarification" are more gnomic than they might be, but they do single out the most important demand that readers have made on poetry past and present. The function of poetry, as of the other literary arts, is not simply to depict the inner or outer life but to interpret it; and the cogency, profundity, and universality of the interpretation (both emotional and intellectual) are important criteria, though not the only ones, of the quality of the literary work that embodies it. The unfashionableness of this doctrine with twentieth-century poets and critics has had much to do with the decline of poetry — and of its audience.

In his study of Romantic theory and practice, *The Mirror and the Lamp*, M. H. Abrams distinguishes five varieties of truth that nineteenth-century poets and critics attributed at various times to poetry. "A frequent dialectical procedure," he declares, "was to allow truth to science, but to bespeak a different, and usually an even more weighty and important kind of truth, to poetry." Of the five categories, three are entirely subjective and have little importance in the cultural debate I am talking about; while they may have helped to maintain the morale of some poets against a hostile environment, they are too slight to function as arguments. The remaining two, however, go to the heart of poetry's claims to a significant place in modern culture. The first is the proposition that "Poetry is true in that it corresponds to a Reality transcending the world of sense." While the claim is an attractive one for poets to make in a time of spiritual uncertainty and has the authority of Blake and Wordsworth behind it, it did not wear well in the nineteenth century, and I am skeptical about its revival in any form that will convince a large or culturally influential audience.

More significant for modern poetry and criticism is the fourth proposition Abrams identifies: "Poetry is true in that it corresponds to concrete experience and integral objects, from which science abstracts qualities for purposes of classification and generalization."[9] Abrams' wording implies what is clearly true, that science offers a highly abstracted knowledge of the world and self that gives us little help in interpreting the endless ambiguities of life in general or our own choices in particular. Viewed in this way, poetry remains an essential form of knowledge because of its unique ability to embody the particular in subtle and powerful form; its comparative lack of generalization is in fact its main advantage. If we are after the truth of moments, situations, relationships, the case of art (and particularly poetry) to elucidate it is a strong one, for such insights are unique and cannot be the subject of theory without being generalized almost out of existence. In a world that takes its truths where it finds them, wishes to be liberated from stock intellectual and emotional responses, and despairs of or distrusts universal Truth, this function of poetry ought to be supremely valued; that it is not so valued in our time may have something to do with the kinds of poems that are being written. The poetry of particulars has a long and distinguished history, from Blake who saw in abstraction the imagination's chief enemy, through Whitman who catalogued the life he saw around him, to William Carlos Williams who postulated "No ideas but in things." As an ideal, it seems particularly congenial to democratic and visionary poets, though in lesser hands than Blake's and Whitman's the visionary contemplation of common particulars has often degenerated into the tedious notation of all life's trivia.

Such a view of poetry contrasts sharply with some of the demands that pre-scientific readers made on the same art, however. It is worth noticing, for example, Samuel Johnson's famous description of the poet's function, placed in the mouth of the sage Imlac in chapter ten of *Rasselas* (1759):

> "The business of a poet," said Imlac, "is to examine, not the individual, but the species; to remark general properties and large appearances: he does not number the streaks of the tulip, or describe the different shades in the verdure of the forest. He is to exhibit in his portraits of nature such prominent and striking features as recal the original to every mind; and must neglect the minuter discriminations, which one may have remarked and another have neglected, for those characteristicks which are alike obvious to vigilance and carelessness."

Imlac's speech represents a synthesis of the prevailing concepts of and clichés about poetry during Johnson's era, and — although it is not usually noted — Johnson distances himself ironically from Imlac's "enthusiasm." In this passage Imlac advises poets to pursue the very aims that most thinkers of the nineteenth and twentieth centuries have ascribed to scientific theorists. It is a notorious fact of literary history that the Romantic poets, Blake most loudly, repudiated this conception of the poetic art. That they and their successors may have gone too far in the opposite direction is less often pointed out, for if poetry is to function as a form of knowledge useful to a diversity of readers, it must generalize more openly than some nineteenth-century and many twentieth-century poets have been willing to do. In doing so it need not make us feel that it has lost touch with the realities of individual experience, nor — the opposite risk — that it has ventured into areas from which the scientific mind might properly seek to displace it.

This series of changes may further suggest that the distinctions so often drawn, from Locke's time to the present, between the purposes of literary and other uses of language are far too rigid. For even science at its most technical is also a work of the knowing imagination. Einstein's theory of relativity, like Newton's early picture of the physical universe, is a brilliant imaginative creation and, like all such creations, subject to the tests of logic and experience. If it ultimately fails those tests, it will not thereby cease to be a great work, either of science or of the imagination. It is also worth remembering that the most significant idea in the whole history of individual psychology — that in memories of early childhood may lie both the source and the solution of adult problems — was laid out in rich detail in Wordsworth's *Prelude* a century before Freud made it the cornerstone of psychoanalysis. There are broad avenues that run between science and poetry, and they are by no means one-way.

That poetry may be true and important by articulating *typical* situations with generalized specificity is perhaps one of the less vulnerable claims that may be made for it. We might make a rough and ready distinction between two kinds of knowing for which there are unfortunately no separate words in English and say that while science is *savoir* — factual and theoretical knowledge about the world, subject to the most formal kinds of verification — poetry is *connaître*, simultaneously the most intimate acquaintance with human experience and its most acute interpretation. It would be rash for an individual or a civilization to dispense willingly with either. Not only are they complementary; at the fringes they become hard to distinguish.

## III

Since I have already made it clear that I think twentieth-century poets share much of the blame for the virtual extinction of their audience, I should emphasize that the very fragmentation of recent poetry makes generalization of any kind perilous. An age in which there are no longer any widely accepted standards of poetic taste or merit will inevitably produce a great variety of poetic intentions and achievements, some of them admirable. To speak only of contemporary poets, A. D. Hope and John Hollander have (in different ways) made praiseworthy applications of seventeenth-century form and tradition to modern subjects. Derek Walcott, one of the most notable regionalists writing today, has effectively married a Yeatsian formal elegance with West Indian materials, while Judith Wright's combination of precision and emotional intensity makes one regret that she is not better known outside Australia. Even Robert Bly's sometimes eccentric blend of nature-mysticism and new-left politics is, at its best, a constructive attempt to reinterest a contemporary audience in poetry without abandoning traditional kinds of poetic significance.

Examples could be multiplied of such attempts in the English-speaking world over the last two or three decades. But the fact remains that all twentieth-century poets in English have come up against the transformations in Anglo-American civilization that have taken place since science began to change people's ways of thinking and living, and none has found a successful way of reintroducing poetry into the mainstream of culture. In the very act of seeking poetic responses to these changes, they have, on balance, merely deepened their own solitude. Literary convention now gives the poet *less* to say—at least less that is important—than a hundred years ago. The much-vaunted expansion of subjects has been an illusory liberation, substituting the private and the ironic for the avowal of sharable insight. The obsessive search by poets for a new poetic language, forms, and subjects is at bottom a search for a context of reference and meaning in which to live and out of which to write, and it is not the poets' alone. The lack of such a context in late-twentieth-century life impoverishes not only poetry but the lives of most people. Confessional poetry, in finding no locus of significance outside the individual self, is a prime symptom of that impoverishment. But what can the self feed on if there is nothing outside itself?

Seven decades have now passed since the first rattling gunfire of the modernist revolution, a longer period than had then elapsed since the death of Wordsworth, and it is time to ask whether the kind of rescue operation the Romantics performed for English poetry is possible again. For in two centuries we have in many ways come full circle, and the late afternoon of the scientific age — if that indeed is where we are — may be no more unpromising a time for poetry than its dawning was. The need for poetry, as I have already suggested, is not less in an era like ours than in any other, contrary to the impression that many twentieth-century poets and their potential readers have conspired to create. The reading public is larger and more restless than ever before, while the cultural fixities of the last century and a half look frailer than they did even a decade ago. The opportunities that the end of the twentieth century offers to poetry will not become fully apparent unless and until more poets take advantage of them, but it would be foolishly pessimistic to maintain that there are no opportunities at all.

The recovery of the balance between thought, feeling, and form, and a less introverted sense of subjects and purposes, will not alone restore poetry to its rightful place; as always, many important factors are beyond the control of poets.[10] Nevertheless, I conclude by suggesting that the effort of such a recovery would be a good start. It is profitable to discover that the stakes are higher than most recent poets in the English-speaking world have been willing or able to recognize. On this issue, we have much to learn from poets whose experience of totalitarianism has forced them to think more seriously about the personal and social consequences of their art. Czeslaw Milosz, the exiled Polish poet who won the Nobel Prize for Literature in 1980, had this to say in his Nobel address:

> There is, it seems, a hidden link between theories of literature as *écriture*, of speech feeding on itself, and the growth of the totalitarian state. In any case, there is no reason why the state should not tolerate an activity that consists of creating "experimental" poems and prose, if these are conceived as autonomous systems of reference,

enclosed within their own boundaries. Only if we assume that a poet constantly strives to liberate himself
from borrowed styles in search of reality is he dangerous. In a room where people unanimously maintain a
conspiracy of silence, one word of truth sounds like a
pistol shot.[11]

Becoming dangerous again, in this sense, might be a start towards
being read again, even in a relatively fortunate society.

[1] Paul Fussell, *The Great War and Modern Memory* (New York: Oxford Univ. Press, 1975), pp. 157–61. Our almost automatic skepticism about the common man's poetic education sixty or seventy years ago is itself a symptom of the cultural changes I am talking about.

[2] Thomas Love Peacock, "The Four Ages of Poetry," in *The Works of Thomas Love Peacock*, ed. H. F. B. Brett-Smith and C. E. Jones (London: Constable, 1924), VIII, 11–24.

[3] Thomas Babington Macaulay, "Milton," in *The Complete Works of Lord Macaulay*, ed. Lady Trevelyan (New York: Longmans, Green, 1898), I, 5–9.

[4] Walter Jackson Bate, *The Burden of the Past and the English Poet* (Cambridge, Mass.: Belknap, 1970), 3.

[5] T. H. Huxley, "On Science and Art in Relation to Education," in *Collected Essays* (New York: Appleton, 1898), III, 179.

[6] Josephine Miles, "Values in Language; or, Where Have *Goodness*, *Truth*, and *Beauty* Gone?" in Leonard Michaels and Christopher Ricks, ed., *The State of the Language* (Berkeley: Univ. of California Press, 1980), p. 365.

[7] Barbara Hardy, *The Advantage of Lyric* (Bloomington: Indiana Univ. Press, 1977), pp. 1–2.

[8] Sir Philip Sidney, *A Defence of Poetry*, ed. Jan Van Dorsten (Oxford: Oxford Univ. Press, 1966), p. 25.

[9] M. H. Abrams, *The Mirror and the Lamp* (New York: Oxford Univ. Press, 1969), pp. 313–15.

[10] It goes without saying, too, that there are many important questions which I have no space to deal with here, like the relations between poetry and such aspects of popular culture as advertising, TV, and rock music; these I discuss more fully in *The Place of Poetry*.

[11] *The New York Review of Books*, 5 March 1981, p. 12.

# FROM MY WINDOW

## by C. K. WILLIAMS

from THE PARIS REVIEW

*nominated by* THE PARIS REVIEW

Spring: the first morning when that one true block of
    sweet, laminar, complex scent arrives
from somewhere west and I keep coming to lean on the
    sill, glorying in the end of the wretched winter.
The scabby-barked sycamores ringing the empty lot across
    the way are budded — I hadn't even noticed —
and the thick spikes of the unlikely urban crocuses have
    already broken the gritty soil.
Up the street, some surveyors with tripods are waving
    each other left and right the way they do.
A girl in a gymsuit jogged by awhile ago, some kids
    passed, playing hooky, I imagine,
and now the paraplegic Vietnam vet who lives in a half-
    converted warehouse down the block
and the friend who stays with him and seems to help him
    out come weaving towards me,
their battered wheelchair lurching uncertainly from one
    edge of the sidewalk to the other.
I know where they're going — to the "Legion"; once,
    when I was putting something out, they stopped,
both drunk that time, too, both reeking — it wasn't ten
    o'clock — and we chatted for a bit.
I don't know how they stay alive — on benefits most likely.
    I wonder if they're lovers.
They don't look it. Right now, in fact, they look a wreck,
    careening haphazardly along,
contriving as they reach beneath me to dip a wheel from
    the curb so that the chair skewers, teeters,

tips, and they both tumble, the one slowly, almost
    gracefully sliding in stages from his seat,
his expression hardly marking it, the other staggering
    over him, spinning heavily down,
to lie on the asphalt, his mouth working, his feet shoving
    weakly and fruitlessly against the curb.
In the store-front office on the corner, Reed and Son,
    Real Estate, have come to see the show:
gazing through the golden letters of their name, they're
    not, at least, thank god, laughing.
Now the buddy, grabbing at a hydrant, gets himself erect
    and stands there for a moment, panting.
Now he has to lift the other one, who lies utterly still, a
    forearm shielding his eyes from the sun.
He hauls him partly upright, then hefts him almost all
    the way into the chair but a dangling foot
catches a support-plate, jerking everything around so that
    he has to put him down,
set the chair to rights and hoist him again and as he does
    he jerks the grimy jeans right off him.
No drawers, shrunken, blotchy thighs; under the thick
    white coils of belly blubber
the poor, blunt pud, tiny, terrified, retracted, is almost
    invisible in the sparse genital hair,
then his friend pulls his pants up, he slumps wholly back
    as though he were, at last, to be let be,
and the friend leans against the cyclone fence, suddenly
    staring up at me as though he'd known
all along that I was watching and I can't help wondering
    if he knows that in the winter, too,
I watched, the night he went out to the lot and walked,
    paced rather, almost ran, for how many hours.
It was snowing, the city in that holy silence, the last we
    have, when the storm takes hold,
and he was making patterns that I thought at first were
    circles then realized made a figure eight,
what must have been to him a perfect symmetry but
    which, from where I was, shivered, bent,
and lay on its side: a warped, unclear infinity, slowly, as
    the snow came faster, going out.

Over and over again, his head lowered to the task, he
    slogged the path he'd blazed
but the race was lost, his prints were filling faster than
    he made them now and I looked away,
up across the skeletal trees to the tall center-city
    buildings, some, though it was midnight,
with all their offices still gleaming, their scarlet warning-
    beacons signaling erratically,
against the thickening flakes, their smoldering auras
    softening portions of the dim, milky sky.
In the morning, nothing; every trace of him effaced, all
    the field pure white,
its surface glittering, the dawn, glancing from its glaze,
    oblique, relentless, unadorned.

# MY FATHER'S MARTIAL ART

by STEPHEN SHU NING LIU

from THE ANTIOCH REVIEW

*nominated by Sandra McPherson and Mary Peterson*

When he came home Mother said he looked
like a monk and stank of green fungus.
At the fireside he told us about life
at the monastery: his rock pillow,
his cold bath, his steel-bar lifting
and his wood-chopping. He didn't see
a woman for three winters, on Mountain O Mei.

"My Master was both light and heavy.
He skipped over treetops like a squirrel.
Once he stood on a chair, one foot tied
to a rope. We four pulled; we couldn't
move him a bit. His kicks could split
a cedar's trunk."

I saw Father break into a pumpkin
with his fingers. I saw him drop a hawk
with bamboo arrows. He rose before dawn, filled
our backyard with a harsh sound *hah, hah, hah*:
there was his Black Dragon Sweep, his Crane Stand,
his Mantis Walk, his Tiger Leap, his Cobra Coil. . . .
Infrequently he taught me tricks and made me
fight the best of all the village boys.

From a busy street I brood over high cliffs
on O Mei, where my father and his Master sit:
shadows spread across their faces as the smog
between us deepens into a funeral pyre.

But don't retreat into night, my father.
Come down from the cliffs. Come
with a single Black Dragon Sweep and hush
this oncoming traffic with your *hah, hah, hah*.

# WITHOUT END

## by ELIZABETH THOMAS

from QUARTERLY WEST

*nominated by* QUARTERLY WEST *and Don Hendre, Jr.*

Now I think of a sleeper in my lap,
your weight round as the slow nest
of summer. Steady as sleep.
My hands smell of feed, of manure,
of everything rising around us.
Do I call you daughter? Lover?
We watch as two people watch nothing:
the afternoon's marriage
of lawn and maples, the grasses'
under-water green, under, under
maple shadow, your hidden face,
your hair, rest.
We keep five roosters, too few
hens. Across the lawn they wake us.
Bug-eyed they cackle and laugh at us.
Their beaks break the day into one long caw,
a riotous beginning. Early, I walk to the barn
to pity the hens. Their backs are scratched
and spurred, I rub my hands
across the worn backs, the featherless
knotted skin as they go for my rings,
my eyes. Twice the dogs get them.
The hens, you say, hung like bright
corsages from their jaws.

Susie and Angel. The dogs' names
you tell me in sleep; I wrap your hair
like wet grass around my thighs.
It's one woman after another. Sweat
in the afternoon rises like a dream.
We make tea before our meal, before
the garden gets weeded. But perhaps
it's only me who watches this day-
dream itself as I turn you around
brush smooth your skirt to your knees.
Behind me the field releases now
and then some crows, some cowbirds.
The afternoon stands patient
as our two horses. From the paper you read,
"Two men have drowned in the Withacahootchie,
in preparation for a baptism." I got out,
deciding to feed the horses for a second time.
The trough had dried to its crusty enamel.
All around me, fields and sky level
into the same rough blue, color a diver
dives into at night, unable to feel
the difference between water and air.

Only the noise of my feet in stiff grass.
The two horses move toward me, but don't move.
Just this presence, *this world,* tonight *without end—*
I can see the two men facing each other
through their mirror world. How we might look
down through the water, through the watery
constellations and see them praying
among thin fish; praying not to return
to heaven or earth but to water.
Seeing not stars, but shiny studded fish.
How they pray! to save two loose, baggy skins
beneath the Withacahootchie as I walk above them
holding the bucket of feed.
I sing my hymn of love, of dusk,
of drier grass at my feet.

♨ ♨ ♨

# RELEASE, SURRENDER

fiction by ELIZABETH INNESS-BROWN

from FICTION INTERNATIONAL

*nominated by* FICTION INTERNATIONAL

THE GI BEFORE HE BECOMES THE GI is an ordinary man; he has a girlfriend and a convertible, and on the day he registers for the draft he takes both with him, and afterwards they go out to dinner, a kind of celebration, and they drink wine and laugh a lot, and later, when he enters her in the back seat of the car, he discovers that she really was, to that moment, what she'd always claimed to be. The next morning a friend is helping him clean the back seat and when he makes a dirty comment, the GI puts a stop to it with his fist, or with the threat of his fist. They clean up the rest in silence, scrubbing at the stains, and then go inside to drink a beer and catch the game on TV.

To the girl, their words snap like jaws, frigid in the winter night air; her nostrils hurt from the cold. She pretends to sleep and they pull her out, reaching hands into the back seat the way her daddy used to when they'd come home late in the car, her daddy reaching into the back seat to fireman-carry her into the house, putting her on the sofa, his heart too weak for the stairs. He took off her shoes and covered her with the afghan her grandmother had made for her; it had her initial on it, a red J in a field of blue squares. This time they are carrying her, up the stairs, to lay her on the bed, and this time they undress her, someone's hands at the buttons of her coat, as if she is a patient. The room is dark until they go because she pretends to sleep; then the moon shines in white and cold like the place, and she sees shadows in the corner and thinks, it's a cradle, the slats bars on the wall; it's a baby cradle, she thinks.

The GI reports for duty, and strips down to his skivvies, as ordered, and stands in line, and is examined and cross-examined, and is judged sane of mind and healthy of body. He feels pride. He feels fear. He feels loneliness. He and the girl make love again, this time in his bed, and afterwards her face is wet with tears, and he flinches when she touches him. "When you come back," she says, and he nods without speaking, and then starts to cry. It is just like in the movies; it is exactly like in the movies; it might be the movies.

Gershwin's "Rhapsody in Blue" wakes the girl, the first few phrases like variegated snakes across the window sill. She lies there and looks at a framed watercolor on the opposite wall, two deer and a huntsman standing in the reeds. The blanket gives off wool and camphor. Frost burns her fingers on the inside of the window pane, a measure of the cold. The watercolor, the huntsman watching, reminds her of summer, of war, of a Bible story, of her mother's green belly of a lawn, of her mother. Later the deer will be split groin to mouth, their viscera will spill out, the red-jacketed huntsman will clean the meat and leave the intestines curled on the trail for wolverines to find, to tear into like sausage.

The GI gives his girl the keys to his car and she leaves him standing at the station, waving good-bye. "Write to me," she says, "think of me." He nods. As he watches her drive away, he feels nothing, nothing at all. He hears his name called, picks up his gear, and turns. In the bus he sits down and shakes hands with another new GI, Mike, who sits next to him. It will be good to have a buddy.

At noon, they play "An American in Paris," and a man in uniform chops at tree limbs in the yard below. She finds bubblegum stuck to the bottom of the seat of the chair, and scrapes it off with her fingernails. A blonde woman brings her a magazine she did not ask for and underwear that is not hers and is stained in the crotch. A girl, about eight months pregnant, brings her a cup of coffee that is not hers. "This isn't my coffee," she says. The pregnant girl turns her back, saying, "How do you know?" and closes the door behind her, leaving the unfamiliar mug painted with blue flowers, coffee too light and sweet. She gets half of it down before the bleached woman reappears. "That isn't your coffee," she says, taking the mug, the magazine, the panties. "How can you drink someone else's coffee?"

She tries to make friends with the pregnant girl. "Are you married?" she asks. The pregnant girl's eyes focus not on her but on the wall behind her. "I hope you like your steak rare," she says.

There is a certain amount of training before the GI can take pride in being a real GI. There is rising before dawn and moving quickly, always quickly, no time for contemplation. There is the study of the body and its limitations ("There is no limit to what you can do"); there is the testing of the mind and its frontiers ("You will not think of anything but the enemy; the enemy will occupy your mind the way he occupies territory"). The body and the mind become equally firm, equally impenetrable, equally calloused. At night, when, if invited, memories might return, the body and the mind are too exhausted to remember anything: he dreams that he is asleep, and he is asleep, and that is all.

Familiar dreams, like old movies to her. A man behind a tree watches her rake leaves which are like burned, curling skins rattling across the yard, the tines of the rake rusty as if with blood. A white curtain blows in and out with moist breezes, clothes on the line, a slip, towels, sheets, white against the grass, the warm blue day. Mother prepares dinner, slapping the fowl on a wooden board, hacking at it with a cleaver. She holds it under running water, the raw meat pale, her hands pink. "There you are," she says. She has a crispy leg in her hand; she gnaws, speaks through the bone with white teeth. "There, wasn't that good," she says, and licks her fingers.

The GI drops into a field from a helicopter that sets down for less than a minute, its blades windstorming. He runs into the field with his gun and drops to the ground. He feels the sweat soaking his fatigues, he smells the putrid smell of the earth and something rotting not far off. He crawls along with his companions, pulling himself forward with his arms. He thinks he sees something but then it is not there. "Hey, Mike," he whispers, to the man next to him. There is a ripping sound and Mike stops, his head split by whatever it was. Mike is dead. The GI moves on, not thinking, not remembering, deliberately not seeing Mike's brain curled like a snake on the ground. The enemy fills his mind though he has not yet seen the enemy. He knows what he looks like. All enemies are essentially the same. You never turn your back on them, no matter what happens.

They pump hot air into her room to keep her from freezing. She wakes from a dream, thinking she is dead, her eyelashes stuck together. When she can't open her eyes she thinks of the stories she has heard, of putting pennies on the eyelids to hold them down. The membranes of her nose and throat are scratchy as she tries to breathe. She asks the girl to bring her a pan of water, a bowl, a glass of water, anything to add to the moisture, but although the girl must hear her she does not answer. Finally, she says, "How about a plant? Something green? To water every day."

"Do you want soup with your lunch tomorrow or not?" says the pregnant girl, taking a short pencil from her pocket.

The doctor is a woman in a white coat and stethoscope. "It seems you won't eat," she says, touching the cold steel to her patient's heart. The patient focuses on the wall beyond the doctor and further on the shadow of a dead moth she sees there. "Do you like your steak rare?" she asks the doctor. "Would you like some soup with your lunch?"

The GI stumbles into a clearing. Inside the roofless building are a man, a woman, and on the table a small boy. Along the walls are beds filled with children, all of them with the silent inscrutable face of the enemy. But they are not the enemy. The GI gets this straight. The boy on the table has half a leg; from what remains extrudes a white bone, raggedly broken off. The doctor looks up from the boy, and says nothing to the GI. The GI looks at the boy, at the doctor, and says nothing. He asks directions. The doctor points, the nurse speaks. "It's not far," she says. Everything seems very far away to the GI. He notices that he has been pointing his gun at the boy on the table. No one has said anything.

The pregnant girl comes in, looking rather limp, her skin the color of eggshells, her hair oily and slipping from its ponytail. She puts the tray down, turns to leave, and faints. The door is open. She sounds like a bag of cement falling from a truck, and the bleached woman appears, tucks her hands into the girl's armpits, and pulls her into the hall. The door closes. Later a thin redhead comes in. She knows nothing of what happened to the pregnant girl.

"What?" says the redheaded one, looking at the patient as if surprised that she can speak. "I don't know — maybe she delivered." She picks up the tray, in a hurry to leave.

The GI has been standing chest deep in a pool of warm water, a camouflaged bay in the river, for ten hours. Long ago he grew accustomed to the constant moisture of the jungle, but this water is like piss, yellow and filled with rotting dead things. Something moves by on the current in front of him: it could be a tree limb, it could be a human arm. He holds his gun above the level of the water for ten hours before he realizes that his arms are tired. He continues to hold his gun above the level of the water. He thinks of his girl, her cool smooth dry skin, the way it would feel to press his fingers into her back with her riding on top of him, on his bed, back home. Suddenly he hears shots, and drops into the water, holding his gun overhead, holding his breath. The water nauseates him. He strains to hear if the shots have stopped. He waves his gun slightly, listening for response. He should never have let the girl enter his mind, because when she came in, the enemy got out.

The frost has taken over all but one pane of the window. Through this she sees white sky, white ground, and green-black trees against a black canvas. The meals, the laundry, the magazines go untouched, but no one has said anything about it. She imagines they snack on her leftovers, stuffing fried potatoes into their mouths on the elevator going down to the kitchen. They wipe their mouths with the backs of their hands, balancing the trays on their hipbones. They smear greasy hands on the black aprons they wear, slip a piece of pie wrapped in paper napkin into a pocket, gulp down the milk, save the apple for later. So no one knows, no one cares. She's glad. She's come to the conclusion that the pregnant girl had not been getting enough to eat; she envies her. She draws a picture of the baby, a healthy boy, a perambulator in a park somewhere. She sits next to the window, careful not to rock the chair, waiting for spring to melt the frost.

The GI and his friends find what was once a village. They think they hear something. They move along as one man until it is louder, a sound like an animal caught in a snap-jaw trap, like a dog whining. The GI tries to recognize the sounds, and when he does, he wants to say leave it be, but they lift what looks like it was once a thatch roof, and find in a hole beneath more than a dozen of them, the enemy, old men, women, children, a baby crying. The GIs laugh and pull the people out, calling them *yellow eyes*, pulling them out of the hole. They are all starving, the people, their ribs perfectly anatomically visible, cages of bone, their arms and legs sticks with swollen joints, their bellies swollen as if each had swallowed a land mine whole. The GIs gesture, saying come on, come on, we'll feed you, and laughing at the way they are saying this with their hands.

"Can you answer a few questions? Can you hear me? Is there some reason you don't want to eat? Does it hurt to swallow?"
    Their walls are pale green; she lies between two cold sheets that stink of chlorine, her knees and heels of her feet peculiarly cold.
    "What is she looking at, can you tell me that?"
    "I'm sorry."
    "Tell us your name, honey." That one, that one sounds like Daddy. The walls are pale green, there is no watercolor, there is a lot of steel glinting like ice. She wonders if they are going to cut her, when they will get the first incision over. It's cold between the sheets, and over her hangs a plastic bag, shiny and full, yellow. "Maybe she just can't swallow. She's too weak to talk, she hasn't

spoken in two days." She looks away from her mother's face. "Don't, baby, what are you looking at?"

"Deglutition? The peristaltic mechanism?"

"No, that all checks out."

"Make her eat, just make her eat."

Mama used to make soup, wasps' nest cookies, golden layer cake, sweetbreads, pear salad, cornstarch pudding, brown betty. Daddy used to spell her name in alphabet letters. J, he'd say, popping it into her mouth. They could never find a U.

The GI helps pull the heavy bag of rice from the metal rations box. They make a fire and fill pots with water and begin to boil it. The people watch with one eye, as a man, all of them together staring at the rice, their hands all bound together so that they form a human fence, standing between the fire and the river. When the rice is cooked, the GIs give it to them in sticky clumps, and at first they eat quickly. Then they begin to vomit, their stomachs having shrunk to the size of walnuts. But the GIs train their guns on them and the old men, the women pick up what they have vomited and eat it again, and feed it to the children, hoping to save them, and then the GIs give them more, more, and they begin to cry as they eat, their tiny faces twisted with pain. They vomit, and eat, and eat more. When the rice is gone, the GIs sit down and watch the people die, their yellow eyes rolling back into their skulls. The baby they leave, silenced, in the river.

The deer stand innocent, the hunter merely observant. She wakes hungry, to "Rhapsody," which today brings to mind a dancing woman in a black sequined dress. Touching the window she melts the frost on the inside but that on the outside remains thick, impenetrable. She licks the cold moisture from her fingers, to taste the ammonia. She imagines what it will be like, to back the car out of the garage, to drive into the country, to find the ocean and lie down on the sand, to find children in a park and push their swings, wax the slide for them, crinkle the paper under her palm. She sleeps well, dreaming of children, of long eyelashes, of tiny seashell incandescent fingernails, of hands with lavender skin.

The GI wanders through the city with his friend Jim. Jim says, "Let's find some cunt," and they wander into that part of town, the

GI not thinking of anything, not the enemy, not home, not his girl, just watching a woman in shiny blue Chinese silk, a slit to her hip, black glossy hair twitching as she walks. Her mouth is a painted red pout. Jim finds another one and the GI takes that one and she shows him to her room. She speaks no English; on his watch he shows her how long he wants her, and says, "All night." They fuck on her thin mattress, cooled by an electric fan in the window. She is considered a rich whore, to have a fan, though the room is without decoration. In English the GI talks freely to her, about the girl, his car, the warm water, his gun, the little yellow-eyed people. He tells her about feeding them to death, about the baby floating for a second in the water. She smiles and nods, encouraging him, doing a good job. He fucks her and talks as he fucks, talking all the time. She smiles and nods all the time. He wants to hit her, even to shoot her, but instead he thrusts and jabs, bites and never kisses her, punishes her for being yellow that way. This is nothing to her but money. In the middle of the night he wakes up, or doesn't wake up, and takes her again up the ass, and says, "Got to learn to starve without dying, damn it. Got to learn, pigs." The whore smiles and nods as if she thinks this is love talk, and afterwards gets up to clean herself, squatting low over a tub of water. At dawn she wakes him, and he dresses and takes out his fat wallet. "Fifty bucks," she says, holding out her hand. "You speak English," he says. She smiles and nods. He slaps her on the face, hard, then drops the money on the floor and turns his back to go. She severs his head neatly from his body with a long knife, takes the wallet from his pocket, and pushes him out of her room and into the river which flows below, and watches as he sinks, quickly, like a stone.

All night long the June bugs hurl themselves at her window with sudden raps until the glass warms in the sun on the sill. Nothing is left of the water but a deposit of minerals around the rim. The shadow of her hand moves on the wall. What has awakened her is a buzzing fly, the kind that comes alive again in the spring.

She hears him crying. Through sheer curtains the sun makes a barred, widening square of light on the wooden floor. There, in the cradle, tiny zippered pajamas, a small hand-knitted sweater soft and blue under the hands. "Hungry?" On the white wall a pastel drawing of parasols, lambs. She sits in the rocking chair, looking out on the green lawn, trees, and the clothesline with its white flags in the breeze, and she unbuttons her blouse, pulls it away, and takes the nipple between her fingers. He moves his mouth blindly, sucking at air.

"There," she says, feeding him. "Is that all you wanted?"

*—for Jean Davidson*

🔥 🔥 🔥

# EL SALVADOR:
# AN AIDE MEMOIRE

by CAROLYN FORCHÉ

from THE AMERICAN POETRY REVIEW

*nominated by Steve Cannon, Kelly Cherry, Maxine Kumin, Miriam Levine, Sandra McPherson, Lynne Sharon Schwartz, and Barbara Watkins*

THE YEAR FRANCO DIED, I spent several months on Mallorca translating the poetry of Claribel Alegria, a Salvadorean in voluntary exile. During those months the almond trees bloomed and lost flower, the olives and lemons ripened and we hauled baskets of apricots from Clairbel's small *finca*. There was bathing in the *calla*, fresh squid under the palm-thatch, drunk Australian sailors to dance with at night. It was my first time in Europe and there was no better place at that time than Spain. I was there when Franco's anniversary passed for the first time in forty years without notice — and the lack of public celebration was a collective hush of relief. I travelled with Claribel's daughter, Maya Flakoll, for ten

159

days through Andalusia by train visiting poetry shrines. The *gitanos* had finally pounded a cross into the earth to mark the grave of Federico Garcia Lorca, not where it had been presumed to be all this time, not beneath an olive tree but in a bowl of land rimmed by pines. We hiked the eleven kilometers through the Sierra Nevada foothills to *La Fuente Grande* and held a book of poems open over the silenced poet.

On Mallorca I lost interest in the *calla* sun-bathing, the parties that carried into the morning, the staggering home wine-drunk up the goat paths. I did not hike to the peak of the Teix with baskets of *entremesas* nor, despite well-intentioned urgings, could I surrender myself to the island's diversionary summer mystique.

I was busy with Claribel's poems, and with the horrific accounts of the survivors of repressive Latin American regimes. Claribel's home was frequented by these wounded; writers who had been tortured and imprisoned, who had lost husbands, wives and closest friends. In the afternoon more than once I joined Claribel in her silent vigil near the window until the mail came, her "difficult time of day," alone in a chair in the perfect light of thick-walled Mallorquin windows. These were her afternoons of despair, and they haunted me. In those hours I first learned of El Salvador, not from the springs of her nostalgia for "the fraternity of dipping a tortilla into a common pot of beans and meat," but from the source of its pervasive brutality. My understanding of Latin American realities was confined then to the romantic devotion to Vietnam-era revolutionary pieties, the sainthood of Ernesto Che rather than the debilitating effects of the cult of personality that arose in the collective memory of Guevara. I worked into the late hours on my poems and on translations, drinking "101" brandy and chain-smoking *Un-X-Dos*. When Cuban writer Mario Benedetti visited, I questioned him about what "an American" could do in the struggle against repression.

"As a *North*american, you might try working to influence a profound change in your country's foreign policy."

Over coffee in the mornings I studied reports from Amnesty International-London and learned of a plague on Latin exiles who had sought refuge in Spain following Franco's death: a right-wing death squad known as the "AAA"—*Anti-Communista Apostolica*, founded in Argentina and exported to assassinate influential exiles from the southern cone.

I returned to the United States and in the autumn of 1977 was invited to El Salvador by persons who knew Claribel. "How much do you know about Latin America?" I was asked. Then: "Good. At least you know that you know nothing." A young writer, politically unaffiliated, ideologically vague, I was to be blessed with the rarity of a moral and political education — what at times would seem an unbearable immersion, what eventually would become a focused obsession. It would change my life and work, propel me toward engagement, test my endurance and find it wanting, and prevent me from ever viewing myself or my country again through precisely the same fog of unwitting connivance.

I was sent for a briefing to Dr. Thomas P. Anderson, author of *Matanza*, the definitive scholarly history of Salvador's revolution of 1932, and to Ignacio Lozano, a California newspaper editor and former ambassador (under Gerald Ford) to El Salvador. It was suggested that I visit Salvador as a journalist, a role that would of necessity become real. In January, 1978, I landed at Ilopango, the dingy center-city airport that is now Salvador's largest military base. Arriving before me were the members of a human rights investigation team headed by then Congressman John Drinan, S.J. (D-Mass.). I had been told that a black Northamerican, Ronald James Richardson, had been killed while in the custody of the Salvadorean government and that a Northamerican organization known as the American Institute for Free Labor Development (AIFLD, an organ of the AFL-CIO and an intelligence front) was manipulating the Salvadorean agricultural workers. Investigation of "The Richardson Case" exposed me to the *sub rosa* activities of the Salvadorean military, whose highest ranking officers and government officials were engaged in cocaine smuggling, kidnapping, extortion and terrorism; through studying AIFLD's work, I would learn of the spurious intentions of an organization destined to become the architect of the present Agrarian Reform. I was delivered the promised exposure to the stratified life of Salvador, and was welcomed "to Vietnam, circa 1959." The "Golden Triangle" had moved to the isthmus of the Americas, "rural pacification" was in embryo, the seeds of rebellion had taken root in destitution and hunger.

Later my companion and guide, "Ricardo," changed his description from Vietnam to "a Nazi forced labor camp." "It is not hyperbole," he said quietly, "you will come to see that." In those first twenty days I was taken to clinics and hospitals, villages, farms, prisons, coffee mansions and processing plants, cane mills and the elegant homes of American foreign service bureaucrats, nudged into the hillsides overlooking the capital, where I was offered cocktails and platters of ocean shrimp; it was not yet known what I would write of my impressions or where I would print them. Fortuitously, I had published nationally in my own country, and in Salvador "only poetry" did not carry the pejorative connotation I might have ascribed to it then. I knew nothing of political journalism but was willing to learn — it seemed, at the time, an acceptable way for a poet to make a living.

I lay on my belly in the *campo* and was handed a pair of field glasses. The lens sharpened on a plastic tarp tacked to four maize stalks several hundred yards away, beneath which a woman sat on the ground. She was gazing through the plastic roof of her "house" and hugging three naked, emaciated children. There was an aqua plastic dogfood bowl at her feet.

"She's watching for the plane," my friend said, "we have to get out of here now or we're going to get it too." I trained the lens on the woman's eye, gelled with disease and open to a swarm of gnats. We climbed back in the truck and rolled the windows up just as the duster plane swept back across the field, dumping a yellow cloud of pesticide over the woman and her children to protect the cotton crop around them.

At the time I was unaware of the pedagogical theories of Paulo Freire *(Pedagogy of the Oppressed)*, but found myself learning *in situ* the politics of cultural immersion. It was by Ricardo's later admission "risky business," but it was thought important that a few Northamericans, particularly writers, be sensitized to Salvador prior to any military conflict. The lessons were simple and critical, the methods somewhat more difficult to detect. I was given a white lab jacket and, posing as a Northamerican physician, was asked to work in a rural hospital at the side of a Salvadorean doctor who was paid $200 a month by the Salvadorean government to care for one-hundred-thousand *campesinos*. She had no lab, no x-ray, no whole blood, plasma or antibiotics, no anesthesia or medicines, no auto-clave for sterilizing surgical equipment. Her forceps were rusted, the walls of her operating room were studded with flies; beside her hospital a coffee processing plant's refuse heaps incubated the maggots, and she paid a *campesina* to swish the flies away with a newspaper while she delivered the newborn. She was forced to do caesarean sections at times without much local anesthetic. Without supplies, she worked with only her hands and a cheap opthalmascope. In her clinic I held children in my arms who died hours later for want of a manual suction device to remove the fluid from their lungs. Their peculiar skin rashes spread to my hands, arms and belly. I dug maggots from a child's open wound with a teaspoon. I contracted four strains of dysentery and was treated by stomach antiseptics, effective and damaging enough to be banned by our own FDA. This doctor had worked in the *campo* for years, a lifetime of delivering the offspring of thirteen-year-old mothers who thought the navel marked the birth canal opening. She had worked long enough to feel that it was acceptable to ignore her own cervical cancer, and hard enough in Salvador to view her inevitable death as the least of her concerns.

I was taken to the homes of landowners, with their pools set like aquamarines in the clipped grass, to the afternoon games of canasta over quaint local *pupusas* and tea, where parrots hung by their feet among the bougainvillia and nearly everything was imported, if only from Miami or New Orleans. One evening I dined with a military officer who toasted America, private enterprise, Las Vegas, and the "fatherland" until his wife excused herself and in a drape of cigar smoke the events of "The Colonel" took place. Almost a *poème trouvé,* I had only to pare down the memory and render it whole, unlined and as precise as recollection would have it. I did not wish to endanger myself by the act of poeticizing such a necessary reportage. It became, when I wrote it, the second insistence of El Salvador to infiltrate what I so ridiculously preserved as my work's allegiance to Art. No more than in any earlier poems did I choose my subject.


The Colonel
*What you have heard is true. I was in his house. His wife carried a tray of coffee and sugar. His daughter filed her nails, his son went out for the night. There were daily papers, pet dogs, a pistol on the cushion beside him. The moon swung bare on its black cord over the house. On the television was a cop show. It was in English. Broken bottles were imbedded in the walls around the house to scoop the kneecaps from a man's legs or cut his hands to lace. On the windows there were gratings as there are in liquor stores. We had dinner, rack of lamb, good wine, a gold bell on the table for*

*calling the maid. The maid brought green mangoes, salt, a type of*
*bread. I was asked how I enjoyed the country. There was a brief*
*commercial in Spanish. His wife took everything away. There was*
*some talk then of how difficult it had become to govern. The parrot*
*said hello on the terrace. The colonel told it to shut up, and pushed*
*himself from the table. My friend said to me with his eyes: say*
*nothing. The colonel returned with a sack as is used to bring*
*groceries home. He spilled many human ears on the table. They*
*were like dried peach halves. There is no other way to say this. He*
*took one of them in his hands, shook it in our faces, dropped it into*
*a water glass. It came alive there. I am tired of fooling around, he*
*said. As for the rights of anyone, tell your people they can go fuck*
*themselves. He swept the ears to the floor with his arm and raised*
*the last of his wine in the air. Something in your poetry, no? he*
*said. Some of the ears on the floor caught this scrap of his voice.*
*Some of the ears on the floor were pressed to the ground.*

El Salvador, May, 1978

The following day I was let into Ahuachapan prison (now an
army *cuartel*). We had been driving back from a meeting with
Salvadorean feminists when Ricardo swung the truck into a climb
through a tube of dust toward the rundown fortification. I was
thirsty, infested with intestinal parasites, fatigued from twenty
days of ricocheting between extremes of poverty and wealth. I was
horrified, impatient, suspicious of almost everyone, paralyzed by
sympathy and revulsion. I kept thinking of the kindly, silver-
haired American political officer who informed me that in Salvador, "there were always five versions of the truth." From this I was
presumably to conclude that the truth could not therefore be
known. Ricardo seemed by turns the Braggioni of Porter's "Flow-
ering Judas" and a pedagogical genius of considerable vision and
patience. As we walked toward the gate, he palmed the air to slow
our pace.

"This is a criminal penitentiary. You will have thirty minutes
inside. Realize please at all times where you are and, whatever you
see here, understand that for political prisoners it is always much
worse. Okay."

We shook hands with the chief guard and a few subordinates,
clean shaven youths armed with G-3s. There was first the stench:
rotting blood, excrement, buckets of urine and corn-slop. A man in
his thirties came toward us, dragging a swollen green leg, his pants

ripped to the thigh to accomodate the swelling. He was introduced
as "Miguel" and I as "a friend." The two men shook hands a long
time, standing together in the filth, a firm knot of warmth between
them. Miguel was asked to give me "a tour," and he agreed, first
taking a coin from his pocket and slipping it into the guard station
soda machine. He handed me an orange Nehi, urging me somewhat insistently to take it, and we began a slow walk into the first
hall. The prison was a four-square with an open court in the center.
There were bunk rooms where the cots were stacked three deep
and some were hung with newsprint "for privacy." The men
squatted on the ground or along the walls, some stirring small coal
fires, others ducking under urine-soaked tents of newspaper. It
was supper, and they were cooking their dry tortillas. I used the
soda as a relief from the stench, like a hose of oxygen. There were
maybe four hundred men packed into Ahuachapan, and it was an
odd sight, an American woman, but there was no heckling.

"Did you hear the shots when we first pulled up?" Ricardo
asked, "those were warnings — a visitor, behave."

Miguel showed me through the workrooms and latrines, finish-
ing his sentences with his eyes; a necessary skill under repressive
regimes, highly developed in Salvador. With the guards' attention
diverted, he gestured toward a black open doorway and suggested
that I might wander through it, stay a few moments and come back
out "as if I had seen nothing."

I did as he asked, my eyes adjusting to the darkness of that shit-
smeared room with its single chink of light in the concrete. There
were wooden boxes stacked against one wall, each a meter by a
meter with barred openings the size of a book, and within them
there was breathing, raspy and half-conscious. It was a few moments before I realized that men were kept in those cages, their
movement so cramped that they could neither sit, stand, nor lie
down. I recall only magnified fragments on my few minutes in that
room, but that I was rooted to the clay floor, unable to move either
toward or away from the cages. I turned from the room toward
Miguel, who pivoted on his crutch and with his eyes on the ground
said in a low voice *"La Oscura,"* the dark place; "sometimes a man
is kept in there a year, and cannot move when he comes out."

We caught up with Ricardo who leaned toward me and  whispered "tie your sweater sleeves around your neck. You are covered
with hives."

In the cab of the truck I braced my feet against the dashboard and through the half-cracked window shook hands with the young soldiers, smiling and nodding. A hundred meters from the prison I lifted Ricardo's spare shirt in my hands and vomited. We were late for yet another meeting, the sun had dropped behind the volcanoes, my eyes ached. When I was empty the dry heaves began, and after the sobbing a convulsive shudder. Miguel was serving his third consecutive sentence, this time for organizing a hunger strike against prison conditions. In that moment I saw him turn back to his supper, his crutch stamping circles of piss and mud beside him as he walked. I heard the screams of a woman giving birth by caesarean without anesthesia in Ana's hospital. I saw the flies fastened to the walls in her operating room, the gnats on the eyes of the starving woman, the reflection of flies on Ana's eyes in the hospital kitchen window. The shit, I imagined, was inside my nostrils and I would smell it the rest of my life, as it is for a man who in battle tastes a piece of flesh or gets the blood under his fingernails. The smell never comes out; it was something Ricardo explained once as he was falling asleep.

"Feel this," he said, maneuvering the truck down the hill road. "This is what oppression feels like. Now you have begun to learn something. When you get back to the States, what you do with this is up to you."

Between 1978 and 1981 I travelled between the United States and Salvador, writing reports on the war waiting to happen, drawing blueprints of prisons from memory, naming the dead. I filled soup bowls with cigarette butts, grocery boxes with files on American involvement in the rural labor movement, and each week I took a stool sample to the parasite clinic. A priest I knew was gang-raped by soldiers: another was hauled off and beaten nearly to death. On one trip a woman friend and I were chased by the death squad for five minutes on the narrow back roads that circle the city — her evasive driving and considerable luck saved us. One night a year ago I was interviewing a defecting member of the Christian Democratic Party. As we started out of the drive to go back to my hotel, we encountered three plainclothesmen hunched over the roof of a taxicab, their machine guns pointed at our windshield. We escaped through a grove of avocado trees. The bodies of friends have turned up disemboweled and decapitated, their teeth punched into broken points, their faces sliced off with machetes. On the final trip to the airport we swerved to avoid a corpse, a man spread-eagled, his stomach hacked open, his entrails stretched from one side of the road to the other. We drove over them like a garden hose. My friend looked at me. *Just another dead man*, he said. And by then it had become true for me as well; the unthinkable, the sense of death within life before death.

## II

"I see an injustice," wrote Czeslaw Milosz in *Native Realm;* "a Parisian does not have to bring his city out of nothingness every time he wants to describe it."[1] So it was with Wilno, that Lithuanian/Polish/Byelorussian city of the poet's childhood, and so it has been with the task of writing about Salvador in the United States. The country called by Gabriela Mistral "the Tom Thumb of the Americas" would necessarily be described to Northamericans as "about the size of Massachusetts." As writers we could begin with its location on the Pacific south of Guatemala and west of Honduras and with Ariadne's thread of statistics: 4.5 million people, 400 per square kilometer (a country without silence or privacy), a population growth rate of 3.5% (such a population would double in two decades). But what does "90% malnutrition" mean? Or that "80% of the population has no running water, electricity or sanitary sevices?" I watched women push feces aside with a stick, lower their pails to the water and carry it home to wash their clothes, their spoons and plates, themselves, their infant children. The chief cause of death has been amoebic dysentery. One out of four children dies before the age of five; the average human life span is forty-six years. What does it mean when a man says "it is better to die quickly fighting than slowly of starvation"? And that such a man suffers toward that decision in what is now being called "Northamerica's backyard"? How is the language used to draw battle lines, to identify the enemy? What are the current euphemisms for empire, public defense of private wealth, extermination of human beings? If the lethal weapon is the soldier, what is meant by "nonlethal military aid?" And what determined the shift to helicopter gunships, M-16s, M-79 grenade launchers? The State Department's white paper entitled *Communist Interference in El Salvador* argues that it is a "case of indirect armed aggression against a small Third World country by Communist powers acting through Cuba." James Petras *(The Nation)* has argued that the report's "evidence is flimsy, circumstantial or nonexistent; the reasoning and logic is slipshod and internally inconsistent; it assumes what needs to be proven; and finally, what facts are presented refute the very case the State Department is attempting to demonstrate."[2] On the basis of this report, the popular press sounded an alarm over the "flow of arms." But from where have arms "flowed," to whom and for what? In terms of language, we could begin by asking why Northamerican arms are weighed in dollar-value and those reaching the opposition measured in tonnage. Or we could point out the nature of the international arms market, a complex global network in which it is possible to buy almost anything for the right price, no matter the country of origin or destination. The State Department conveniently ignores its own intelligence on arms flow to the civilian right, its own escalation of military assistance to the right-wing military, and even the discrepancies in its final analysis. But what does all this tell us about who is fighting whom for what? Americans have been told that there is a "fundamental difference" between "advisors" and military "trainers." Could it simply be that the euphemism for American military personnel must be changed so as not to serve as a mnemonic device for the longest war in our failing public memory? A year ago I asked the American military attaché in Salvador what would happen if one of these already proposed advisors returned to the U. S. in a flag-draped coffin. He did not argue semantics.

"That," he said smiling, "would be up to the American press, wouldn't it?"

Most of that press had held with striking fidelity to the State Department text: a vulnerable and worthy "centrist" government besieged by left and right-wing extremists, the former characterized by their unacceptable political ideology, the latter rendered non-ideologically unacceptable, that is, only in their extremity. The familiar ring of this portrayal has not escaped U. S. apologists, who must explain why El Salvador is not "another Vietnam." Their argument hinges, it seems, on the rapidity with which the U. S. could assist the Salvadorean military in the task of "defeating the enemy." Tactically, this means sealing the country off, warning all other nations to "cease and desist" supplying arms, using violations of that warning as a pretext for blockades and interventions, but excepting ourselves in our continual armament of what we are calling "the government" of El Salvador. Ignoring the institutional self-interest of the Salvadorean army, we blame the presumably "civilian" right for the murder of thousands of *campesinos*, students, doctors, teachers, journalists, nuns, priests and children. This requires that we ignore the deposed and retired military men who command the activities of the death squads with impugnity, and that the security forces responsible for the killings are under the command of the army, which is under command of the so-called "centrist" government and is in fact the government itself.

There are other differences between the conflicts of El Salvador and Vietnam. There is no Peoples Republic of China to the north to arm and ally itself with a people engaged in a protracted war. The guerillas are not second generation Viet-minh, but young people who armed themselves after exhaustive and failed attempts at non-violent resistance and peaceful change. The popular organizations they defend were formed in the early seventies by *campesinos* who became socially conscious through the efforts of grass-roots clergymen teaching the Medellin doctrines of social justice; the precursors of these organizations were prayer and bible study groups, rural labor organizations and urban trade unions. As the military government grew increasingly repressive, the opposition widened to include all other political parties, the Catholic majority, the university and professional communities and the small business sector.

Critics of U. S. policy accurately recognize parallels between the two conflicts in terms of involvement, escalation and justification. The latter demands a vigilant "euphemology" undertaken to protect language from distortions of military expedience and political convenience. Noam Chomsky has argued that "among the many symbols used to frighten and manipulate the populace of the democratic states, few have been more important than terror and terrorism. These terms have generally been confined to the use of violence by individuals and marginal groups. Official violence, which is far more extensive in both scale and destructiveness, is placed in a different category altogether. This usage has nothing to do with justice, causal sequence, or numbers abused." He goes on to say that "the question of proper usage is settled not merely by the official or unofficial status of the perpetrators of violence but also by their political affiliations."[3] State violence is excused as "reactive," and the "turmoil" or "conflict" is viewed ahistorically.

It is true that there have long been voices of peaceful change and social reform in El Salvador — the so-called centrists — but the U.S. has never supported them. We backed one fraudulently elected military regime after another, giving them what they wanted and still want: a steady infusion of massive economic aid with which high ranking officers can insure their personal futures and the loyalty of their subordinates. In return we expect them to guarantee stability, which means holding power by whatever means necessary for the promotion of a favorable investment climate, even if it means exterminating the population, as it has come to mean in Salvador. The military, who always admired "*Generalissimo* Franco," and are encouraged in their anticommunist crusade, grow paranoid and genocidal. Soldiers tossed babies into the air near the Sumpul River last summer for target practice during the cattle-prod round up and massacre of six-hundred peasants. Whole families have been gunned down or hacked to pieces with machetes, including the elderly and newborn. Now that the massacre and the struggle against it have become the occasion to "test American resolve," the Salvadorean military is all too aware of the security of its position and the impugnity with which it may operate. Why would a peasant, aware of the odds, of the significance of American backing, continue to take up arms on the side of the opposition? How is it that such opposition endures, when daily men and women are doused with gasoline and burned alive in the streets as a lesson to others; when even death is not enough, and the corpses are mutilated beyond recognition? The answer to that question in El Salvador answers the same for Vietnam.

## III

We were waved past the military guard station and started down the highway, swinging into the oncoming lane to pass slow sugar-cane trucks and army transports. Every few kilometers, patrols trekked the gravel roadside. It was a warm night, dry but close to the rainy season. Juan palmed the column shift, chain-smoked and motioned with his hot-boxed cigarette in the direction of San Marcos. Bonfires lit by the opposition were chewing away at the dark hillside. As we neared San Salvador, passing through the slums of Candelaria, I saw that the roads were barricaded. More than once Juan attempted a short-cut but, upon spotting military checkpoints, changed his mind. To relieve the tension he dug a handful of change from his pocket and showed me his collection of *deutschmark*, Belgian *francs*, Swedish *ore* and *kroner*, holding each to the dashboard light and naming the journalist who had given it to him, the country, the paper. His prize was a coin from the Danish reporter whose cameras had been shot away as he crouched on a rooftop to photograph an army attack on protest marchers. That was a month before, on January 22, 1980, when some hundred lost their lives; it was the beginning of a savage year of extermination. Juan rose from his seat and slipped the worthless coins back into his pocket.

Later that spring, Rene Tamsen of WHUR radio, Washington D.C., would be forced by a death squad into an unmarked car in downtown San Salvador. A Salvordorean photographer, Cesar Najarro, and his *Cronica del Pueblo* editor would be seized during a coffee break. When their mutilated bodies were discovered, it would be evident that they had been disemboweled before death. A Mexican photojournalist, Ignacio Rodriguez, would fall in August to a military bullet. After Christmas an American freelancer, John Sullivan, would vanish from his downtown hotel room. Censorship of the press. In January, 1981, Ian Mates would hit a land mine and the South African TV cameraman would bleed to death. In a year, no one would want the Salvador assignment. In a year, journalists would appear before cameras trembling and incredulous, unable to reconcile their perceptions with those of Washington, and even established media would begin to reflect this dichotomy. Carter policy had been to downplay El Salvador in the press while providing "quiet" aid to the repressive forces. Between 1978 and 1980, investigative articles sent to national magazines mysteriously disappeared from publication mailrooms, were oddly delayed in reaching editors, or were rejected after lengthy deliberations, most often because of El Salvador's "low news value." The American inter-religious network and human rights community began to receive evidence of a conscious and concerted censorship effort in the United States. During inteviews in 1978 with members of the Salvadorean right-wing business community, I was twice offered large sums of money to portray their government favorably in the American press. By early 1981, desk editors knew where El Salvador was and the playdown policy had been replaced by the Reagan administration's propaganda effort. The right-wing military cooperated in El Salvador by serving death threats on prominent journalists, while torturing and murdering others. American writers critical of U.S. policy were described by the Department of State as "the witting and unwitting dupes" of communist propagandists. Those who have continued coverage of Salvador have found that the military monitors the wire services and all telecommunications, that pseudonyms often provide no security, that no one active in the documentation of the war of extermination can afford to be traceable in the country; effectiveness becomes self-limiting. It became apparent that my education in El Salvador had prepared me to work only until March 16, 1980, when after several close calls, I was urged to leave the country. Monsignor Romero met with me, asking that I return to the U.S. and "tell the American people what is happening."

"Do you have any messages for (certain exiled friends)?"

"Yes. Tell them to come back."

"But wouldn't they be killed?"

"We are all going to be killed — you and me, all of us." he said quietly. A week later he was shot while saying Mass in the chapel of a hospital for the incurable.

In those days I kept my work as a poet and journalist separate, of two distinct *mentalités*, but I could not keep El Salvador from my poems because it had become so much a part of my life. I was cautioned to avoid mixing art and politics, that one damages the other, and it was some time before I realized that "political poetry" often means the poetry of protest, accused of polemical didacticism, and not the poetry which implicitly celebrates politically acceptable values. I suspect that underlying this discomfort is a naive assumption: that to locate a poem in an area associated with political trouble automatically renders it political.

All poetry is both pure and engaged, in the sense that it is made of language, but it is also art. Any theory which takes one half of the socialesthetic dynamic and accentuates it too much results in a breakdown. Stress of purity generates a feeble estheticism that fails, in its beauty, to communicate. On the other hand, propagandistic hack-work has no independent life as poetry. What matters is not whether a poem is political, but the quality of its engagement.

Enzensberger has argued the futility of locating the political aspect of poetry outside poetry itself, and that:

Such obtuseness plays into the hands of the bourgeois esthetic which would like to deny poetry any social aspect. Too often the champions of inwardness and sensibility are reactionaries. They consider politics a special subject best left to professionals, and wish to detach it completely from all other human activity. They advise poetry to stick to such models as they have devised for it, in other words, to high aspirations and eternal values. The promised reward for this continence is timeless validity. Behind these high-sounding proclamations lurks a contempt for poetry no less profound than that of vulgar Marxism. For a political quarantine placed on poetry in the name of eternal values, itself serves political ends.[4]

All language then is political; vision is always ideologically charged; perceptions are shaped *a priori* by our assumptions and sensibility formed by consciousness at once social, historical and esthetic. There is no such thing as non-political poetry. The time, however, to determine what those politics will be is not the moment of taking pen to paper, but during the whole of one's life. We are responsible for the quality of our vision, we have a say in the shaping of our sensibility. In the many thousand daily choices we make, we create ourselves and the voice with which we speak and work.

From our tradition we inherit a poetic, a sense of appropriate subjects, styles, forms and levels of diction; that poetic might insist that we be attuned to the individual in isolation, to particular sensitivity in the face of "nature," to special ingenuity in inventing metaphor. It might encourage a self-regarding, inward looking poetry. Since Romanticism, didactic poetry has been presumed dead and narrative poetry has had at best a half life. Demonstration is inimical to a poetry of lyric confession and self-examination, therefore didactic poetry is seen as crude and unpoetic. To suggest a return to the formal didactic mode of Virgil's *Georgics* or Lucretius's *De Rerum Natura* would be to deny history, but what has survived of that poetic is the belief that a poet's voice must be inwardly authentic and compelling of our attention; the poet's voice must have authority.

I have been told that a poet should be of his or her time. It is my feeling that the twentieth century human condition demands a poetry of witness. This is not accomplished without certain difficulties; the inherited poetic limits the range of our work and determines the boundaries of what might be said. There is the problem of metaphor which moved Neruda to write: "the blood of the children/flowed out onto the streets/like . . . like the blood of the children."[5] There is the problem of poeticizing horror, resembling the problem of the photographic image which might render starvation visually appealing. There are problems of reduction and oversimplification; of our need to see the world as complex beyond our comprehension, difficult beyond our capacities for solution. If I did wish to make poetry of what I had seen, what is it I thought poetry was?

At some point the two *mentalités* converged, and the impulse to witness confronted the prevailing poetic; at the same time it seemed clear that eulogy and censure were no longer possible and that Enzensberger is correct in stating "The poem expresses in exemplary fashion that it is not at the disposal of politics. That is its political content."[6] I decided to follow my impulse to write narratives of witness and confrontation, to disallow obscurity and conventions which might prettify that which I wished to document. As for that wish, the poems will speak for themselves, obstinate as always. I wish also to thank my friends and *compañeros* in El Salvadór for persuading me during a period of doubt that poetry could be enough.

1 (Garden City, New York: Doubleday, 1968), p. 54.
2 "White Paper on the White Paper" (March 28, 1981), pp. 360, 367-71.
3 Noam Chomsky and Edward S. Herman, *The Washington Connection and Third World Fascism* (Boston: South End Press, 1979), p. 6.
4 *The Consciousness Industry: On Literature, Politics and the Media* (New York: Seabury Press, 1974), p. 75.
5 Quoted by Larry Levis in "Some Notes on the Gazer Within," in Stuart Friebert and David Young, eds., *A Field Guide to Contemporary Poetry and Poetics* (New York and London: Longman, 1980), p. 110.
6 *Op. cit.*, p. 79.

# THE QUEST

## by SHARON OLDS

from POETRY

*nominated by Philip Levine*

The day my girl is lost for an hour,
the day I think she is gone forever and then I find her,
I sit with her awhile and then I
go to the corner store for orange juice for her
lips, tongue, palate, throat,
stomach, blood, every gold cell of her body.
I joke around with the guy behind the counter, I
walk out into the winter air and
weep. I know he would never hurt her,
never take her body in his hands to
crack it or crush it, would keep her safe and
bring her home to me. Yet there are
those who would. I pass the huge
cockeyed buildings massive as prisons,
charged, loaded, cocked with people,
some who would love to take my girl, to un-
do her, fine strand by fine
strand. These are buildings full of rope,
ironing-boards, sash, wire,
iron-cords woven in black and blue spirals like
umbilici, apartments supplied with
razor-blades and lye. This is my
quest, to know where it is, the evil in the
human heart. As I walk home I
look in face after face for it, I
see the dark beauty, the rage, the
grown-up children of the city she walks as a
child, a raw target. I cannot

see a soul who would do it. I clutch the
jar of juice like a cold heart,
remembering how my parents tied me to a chair and
would not feed me and I looked up
into their beautiful faces, my stomach a
gold mace, my wrists like birds the
shrike has hung by the throat from barbed wire, I
gazed as deep as I could into their eyes
and all I saw was goodness, I could not get past it.
I rush home with the blood of oranges
pressed to my breast, I cannot get it to her fast enough.

# TRANSLATION

## by MATTHEW GRAHAM

from POET AND CRITIC

*nominated by* POET AND CRITIC

> *Cao Giao flung open the door of room C-2 in the Hotel*
> *Continental where I had just arrived, and we hugged each*
> *other excitedly, both of us happy to be together again in Saigon.*
>
> TIZIANO TERZANI, *Giai Phong*

Not exactly. With its airports and avenues, its awe of the sleight
Of hand and all things misinterpreted — I hated that city.
It reflected only the image of a sleeping thief and liar

And I feared that man because he was a journalist and
     remembered
Everything. Outside the Hotel Continental two ARVN
Officers emptied their automatics into each other's chests

Because they were Catholics and afraid to commit suicide.
I flung open the door of room C-2 expecting a body or a bullet
And received an embrace. It was Sunday, April 27th, 1975

And I had come up from the hard light of the Delta
Into the smoke and confusion the Americans had left
Because the journalist needed a translator; he paid well,

And this was not a time to think of mistakes in judgement.
The shelling stopped two days later and on the early morning
Of the 30th the first tank entered the city. It was covered in palm

Leaves and red mud that turned to dust and smelled of the
   jungle.
Chickens in a wooden cage and bunches of water beets hung from
Its sides. It swung left on Hong Tap Tu Street and stopped a girl

On a Honda. The gunner spread his map on the turret; they were
   lost
And needed to know the way to Doc Lap Palace, please. Later,
While the journalist was climbing on trucks and shaking hands

In the crowd, I thought of the girl. I once knew her when she
Worked nights and was familiar with the Palace and its
   transparencies.
I remembered green tea in bowls pressed with rice grain, the
   small

Half moon scar above her eye, and a time when I woke and saw
A strand of her black hair across the pillow and thought it was
The dark blood of the day old dead. Or the brush stroke

Of an inflection that determines the difference between desire
And fear. Like something she once taught me that I've lost
In translation. Something as clear as a wind chime, a symbol of
   spring

Offensives, that finally arrives, shy and unassuming, asking exact
Directions.

# THE SNAKES OF SEPTEMBER

by STANLEY KUNITZ

from ANTAEUS

*nominated by Michael Ryan*

All summer I heard them
rustling in the shrubbery,
outracing me from tier
to tier in my garden,
a whisper among the viburnums,
a signal flashed from the hedgerow,
a shadow pulsing
in the barberry thicket.
Now that the nights are chill
and the annuals spent,
I should have thought them gone,
in a torpor of blood
slipped to the nether world
before the sickle frost.
Not so. In the deceptive balm
of noon, as if defiant of the curse
that spoiled another garden,
these two appear on show
through a narrow slit
in the dense green brocade
of a north-country spruce,
dangling head-down, entwined
in a brazen love-knot.
I put out my hand and stroke
the fine, dry grit of their skins.

After all,
we are partners in this land,
co-signers of a covenant.
At my touch the wild
braid of creation
trembles.

*♭ ♭ ♭*

# HARMONY OF THE WORLD

fiction by CHARLES BAXTER

from MICHIGAN QUARTERLY REVIEW

*nominated by* MICHIGAN QUARTERLY REVIEW

I

IN THE SMALL OHIO TOWN where I grew up, many homes had parlors that contained pianos, sideboards, and sofas, heavy objects signifying gentility. These pianos were rarely tuned. They went flat in summer around the fourth of July and sharp in winter at Christmas. Ours was a Story and Clark. On its music stand were copies of Stephen Foster and Ethelbert Nevin favorites, along with one Chopin prelude that my mother would practice for twenty minutes every three years. She had no patience, but since she thought Ohio — all of it, every scrap — made sense, she was happy and did not need to practice anything. Happiness is not infectious, but somehow her happiness infected my father, a pharmacist, and then spread through the rest of the household. My whole family was obstinately cheerful. I think of my two sisters, my brother, and my parents as having artificial pasted-on smiles, like circus clowns. They apparently thought cheer and good Christian words were universals, respected everywhere. The pianos were part of this cheer. They played for celebrations and moments of pleasant pain. Or rather: someone played them, but not too well, since excellent playing would have been faintly antisocial. "Chopin," my mother said, shaking her head as she stumbled through the prelude. "Why is he famous?"

When I was six, I received my first standing ovation. On the stage of the community auditorium, where the temperature was about 94°, sweat fell from my forehead onto the piano keys, making their ivory surfaces slippery. At the conclusion of the piece, when everyone stood up to applaud, I thought they were just being nice. My playing had been mediocre; only my sweating had been extraordinary. Two years later, they stood up again. When I was eleven, they cheered. By that time I was astonishing these small-town audiences with Chopin and Rachmaninoff recital chestnuts. I thought I was a genius and read biographies of Einstein. Already the townspeople were saying that I was the best thing Parkersville had ever seen, *that I would put the place on the map*. Mothers would send their children by to watch me practice. The kids sat with their mouths open while I polished off another classic.

Like many musicians, I cannot remember ever playing badly, in the sense of not knowing what I was doing. In high school, my identity was being sealed shut: my classmates called me "el señor longhair," even though I wore a crewcut, this being the 1950s. Whenever the town needed a demonstration of local genius, it called upon me. There were newspaper articles detailing my accomplishments, and I must have heard the phrase "future concert career" at least two hundred times. My parents smiled and smiled as I collected applause. My senior year, I gave a solo recital and was hired for umpteen weddings and funerals. I was good luck. On the fourth of July the townspeople brought out a piano to the city square so that I could improvise music between explosions at the fireworks display. Just before I left for college, I noticed that our neighbors wanted to come up to me ostensibly for small talk, but actually to touch me.

In college I made a shocking discovery: other people existed in the world who were as talented as I was. If I sat down to play a Debussy etude, they would sit down and play Beethoven, only louder and faster than I had. I felt their breath on my neck. Apparently there were other small towns. In each one of these small towns there was a genius. Perhaps some geniuses were not actually geniuses. I practiced constantly and began to specialize in the non-Germanic piano repertoire. I kept my eye out for students younger than I was, who might have flashier technique. At my senior recital I played Mozart, Chopin, Ravel, and Debussy, with encore pieces by Scriabin and Thomson. I managed to get the audience to stand up for the last time.

I was accepted into a large midwestern music school, famous for its high standards. Once there, I discovered that genius, to say nothing of talent, was a common commodity. Since I was only a middling composer, with no interesting musical ideas as such, I would have to make my career as a performer or teacher. But I didn't want to teach, and as a performer I lacked pizzazz. For the first time, it occurred to me that my life might be evolving into something unpleasant, something with the taste of stale bread.

I was beginning to meet performers with more confidence than I had, young musicians to whom doubt was as alien as proper etiquette. Often these people dressed like tramps, smelled, smoked constantly, were gay or sadistic. Whatever their imbalances, they were not genteel. *They did not represent small towns.* I was struck by their eyes. Their eyes seemed to proclaim, "The universe believes in me. It always has."

My piano teacher was a man I will call Luther Stecker. Every year he taught at the music school for six months. For the following six months he toured. He turned me away from the repertoire with which I was familiar and demanded that I learn several pieces by composers whom I had not often played, including Bach, Brahms, and Liszt. Each one of these composers discovered a weak point in me: I had trouble keeping up the consistent frenzy required by Liszt, the mathematical precision required by Bach, the unpianistic fingerings of Brahms.

I saw Stecker every week. While I played, he would doze off. When he woke, he would mumble some inaudible comment. He also coached a trio I participated in, and he spoke no more audibly then than he did during my private lesson.

I couldn't understand why, apart from his reputation, the school had hired him. Then I learned that in every Stecker-student's life, the time came when the Master collected his thoughts, became blunt, and told the student exactly what his future would be. For me, the moment arrived on the third of November, 1966. I was playing sections of the Brahms Paganini Variations, a fiendish piece on which I had spent many hours. When I finished, I saw him sit up.

"Very good," he said, squinting at me. "You have talents."

There was a pause. I waited. "Thank you," I said.

"You have a nice house?" he asked.

"A nice house? No."

"You should get a nice house somewhere," he said, taking his handkerchief out of his pocket and waving it at me. "With windows. Windows with a view."

I didn't like the drift of his remarks. "I can't afford a house," I said.

"You will. A nice house. For you and your family."

I resolved to get to the heart of this. "Professor," I asked, "what did you think of my playing?"

"Excellent," he said. "That piece is very difficult."

"Thank you."

"Yes, technically excellent," he said, and my heart began to pound. "Intelligent phrasing. Not much for me to say. Yes. That piece has many notes," he added, enjoying the *non sequitur*.

I nodded. "Many notes."

"And you hit all of them accurately. Good pedal and good discipline. I like how you hit the notes."

I was dangling on his string, a little puppet.

"Thousands of notes, I suppose," he said, staring at my forehead, which was beginning to get damp, "and you hit all of them. You only forgot one thing."

"What?"

"The passion!" he roared. "You forgot the passion! You always forget it! Where is it? Did you leave it at home? You never bring it with you! Never! I listen to you and think of a robot playing! A smart robot, but a robot! No passion! Never ever ever!" He stopped shouting long enough to sneeze. "You *should* buy a house. You know why?"

"Why?"

"Because the only way you will ever praise God is with a family, that's why! Not with this piano! You are a fine student," he wound up, "but you make me sick! Why do you make me sick?"

He waited for me to answer.

"*Why do you make me sick?*" he shouted. "Answer me!"

"How can I possibly answer you?"

"By articulating words in English! Be courageous! Offer a suggestion! Why do you make me sick?"

I waited for a minute, the longest minute my life has seen or will ever see. "Passion," I said at last. "You said there wasn't enough passion. I thought there was. Perhaps not."

He nodded. "No. You are right. No passion. A corruption of music itself. Your playing is too gentle, too much good taste. To play the piano like a genius, you must have a bit of the fanatic. Just a bit. But it is essential. You have stubbornness and talent but no fanaticism. You don't have the salt on the rice. Without salt, the rice is inedible, no matter what its quality otherwise." He stood up. "I tell you this because sooner or later someone else will. You will have a life of disappointments if you stay in music. You may find a teacher who likes you. Good, good. *But you will never be taken up! Never!* You should buy a house, young man. With a beautiful view. Move to it. Don't stay here. You are close to success, but it is the difference between leaping the chasm and falling into it, one inch short. You are an inch short. You could come back for more lessons. You could graduate from here. But if you are truly intelligent, you will say goodbye. Goodbye." He looked down at the floor and did not offer me his hand.

I stood up and walked out of the room.

Becalmed, I drifted down and up the hallways of the building for half an hour. Then a friend of mine, a student of conducting from Bolivia, a Marxist named Juan Valparaiso, approached, and, ignoring my shallow breathing and cold sweat, started talking at once.

"Terrible, furious day!" he said.

"Yes."

"I am conducting *Benvenuto Cellini* overture this morning! All is going well until difficult flute entry. I instruct, with force, flutists. Soon all woodwinds are ignoring me." He raised his eyebrows and stroked his huge gaucho mustache. "Always! Always there are fascists in the woodwinds!"

"Fascists everywhere," I said.

"Horns bad, woodwinds worse. Demands of breath made for insanes. Pedro," he said, "you are appearing irresoluted. Sick?"

"Yes," I nodded. "Sick. I just came from Stecker. My playing makes *him* sick."

"He said that? That you are making him sick?"

"That's right. I play like a robot, he says."

"What will you do?" Juan asked me. "Kill him?"

"No." And then I knew. "I'm leaving the school."

"What? Is impossible!" Tears leaped instantly into Juan's eyes. "Cannot, Pedro. After one whipping? No! Disappointments everywhere here. Also outside in world. Must stick to it." He grabbed me by the shoulders. "Fascists put here on earth to break our hearts! Must live through. You cannot go." He looked around wildly. "Where could you go anyway?"

"I'm not sure," I said. "He said I would never amount to anything. I think he's right. But I could do something else." To prove that I could imagine options, I said, "I could work for a newspaper. You know, music criticism."

"Caterpillars!" Juan shouted, his tears falling onto my shirt. "Failures! Pathetic lives! Cannot, cannot! Who would hire you?"

I couldn't tell him for six months, until I was given a job in Knoxville on a part-time trial basis. But by then I was no longer writing letters to my musician friends. I had become anonymous. I worked in Knoxville for two years, then in Louisville — a great city for music — until I moved here, to this city I shall never name, in the middle of New York state, where I bought a house with a beautiful view.

In my home town, they still wonder what happened to me, but my smiling parents refuse to reveal my whereabouts.

## II

Every newspaper has a command structure. Within that command structure, editors assign certain stories, but the writers must be given some freedom to snoop around and discover newsworthy material themselves. In this anonymous city, I was hired to review all the concerts of the symphony orchestra and to provide some hype articles during the week to boost the ticket sales for Friday's program. Since the owner of the paper was on the symphony board of trustees, writing about the orchestra and its programs was necessarily part of good journalistic citizenship. On my own, though, I initiated certain projects, wrote book reviews for the Sunday section, interviewed famous visiting musicians — some of them my ex-classmates — and during the summer I could fill in on all sorts of assignments, as long as I cleared what I did with the feature editor, Morris Cascadilla.

"You're the first serious musician we've ever had on the staff here," he announced to me when I arrived, suspicion and hope fighting for control on his face. "Just remember this: be clear and concise. Assume they've got intelligence but no information. After that, you're on your own, except you should clear dicey stuff with me. And never forget the Maple Street angle."

The Maple Street angle was Cascadilla's equivalent to the Nixon Administration's "How will it play in Peoria?" No matter what subject I wrote about, I was expected to make it relevant to Maple Street, the newspaper's mythical locus of middle-class values. I could write about electronic, aleatory, or post-Boulez music *if* I suggested that the city's daughters might be corrupted by it. Sometimes I found the Maple Street angle, and sometimes I couldn't. When I failed, Cascadilla would call me in, scowl at my copy and mutter, "All the Juilliard graduates in town will love this." Nevertheless, the Maple Street angle was a spiritual exercise in humility, and I did my best to find it week after week.

When I first learned that the orchestra was scheduled to play Paul Hindemith's *Harmony of the World* symphony, I didn't think of Hindemith, but of Maple Street, that mythically harmonious piano and write reviews.

## III

Working on the paper left me some time for other activities. Unfortunately, there was nothing I knew how to do except play the piano and write reviews.

Certain musicians are very practical. Trumpet players (who love valves) tend to be good mechanics, and I have met a few composers who fly airplanes and can restore automobiles. Most performing violinists and pianists, however, are drained by the demands of their instruments and seldom learn how to do anything besides play. In daily life they are helpless and stricken. In midlife the smart ones force themselves to find hobbies. But the less fortunate come home to solitary apartments without pictures or other decorations, warm up their dinners in silence, read whatever books happen to be on the dinner table, and then go to bed.

I am speaking of myself here, of course. As time passed, and the vacuum of my life made it harder to breathe, I required more work. I fancied I was a tree, putting out additional leaves. I let it be known that I would play as an accompanist for voice students and other recitalists, if their schedules didn't interfere with my commitments for the paper.

One day I received a call at my desk. A quietly controlled female voice asked, "Is this Peter Jenkins?"

"Yes."

"Well," she said, pausing, as if she'd forgotten what she meant to tell me, "this is Karen Jensen. That's almost like Jenkins, isn't it?" I waited. "I'm a singer," she said, after a moment. "A soprano. I've just lost my accompanist and I'm planning on giving a recital in three months. They said you were available. Are you? What do you charge?"

I told her.

"Isn't that kind of steep? That's kind of steep. Well, I suppose . . . I can use somebody else until just before, and then I can use you. They say you're good. And I've read your reviews. I really admire the way you write!"

"Thank you."

"You get so much information into your reviews! Sometimes, when I read you, I imagine what you look like. Sometimes a person can make a mental picture. I just wish the paper would publish a photo or something of you."

"They want to," I said, "but I asked them to please don't."

"Even your voice sounds like your writing!" she said excitedly. "I can see you in front of me now. Can you play Fauré and Schubert? I mean, is there any composer or style you don't like and won't play?"

"No," I said. "I play anything."

"That's *wonderful!*" she said, as if I had confessed to a remarkable tolerance. "Some accompanists are so picky. 'I won't do this, I won't do that.' Well, *one* I know is like that. Anyhow, could we meet soon? Do you sightread? Can we meet at the music school downtown? In a practice room? When are you free?"

I set up an appointment.

She was almost beautiful. Her deep eyes were accented by depressive bowls in quarter-moon shadow under them. Though she was only in her late twenties, she seemed slightly scorched by anxiety. She couldn't keep still. Her hands fluttered as they fixed her hair; she scratched nervously at her cheeks; and her eyes jumped every few seconds. Soon, however, she calmed down and began to look me in the eye, evaluating me. Then *I* turned away.

She wanted to test me out and had brought along her recital numbers, mostly standard fare: a Handel aria, Mozart, Schubert, and Fauré. The last set of songs, *Nine Epitaphs*, by an American composer I had never heard of, Theodore Chanler, was the only novelty.

"Who is this Chanler?" I asked, looking through the sheet music.

"I . . . I found it in the music library," she said. "I looked him up. He was born in Boston and died in 1961. There's a recording by Phyllis Curtin. Virgil Thomson says these are maybe the best American art songs ever written."

"Oh."

"They're kind of, you know, lugubrious. I mean they're all epitaphs written supposedly on tombstones, set to music. They're like portraits. I love them. Is it all right? Do you mind?"

"No, I don't mind."

We started through her program, beginning with Handel's "*Un sospiretto d'un labbro pallido*" from *Il Pastor fido*. I could immediately see why she was still in central New York state and why she would always be a student. She had a fine voice, clear and distinct, somewhat styled after Victoria de los Angeles (I thought), and her articulation was superb. If these achievements had been the whole story, she might have been a professional. But her pitch wobbled on sustained notes in a maddening way; the effect was not comic and would probably have gone unnoticed by most non-musicians, but to me the result was harrowing. She could sing perfectly for several measures and then she would miss a note by a semi-tone, which drove an invisible fingernail into my scalp. It was as though a gypsy's curse descended every five or six seconds, throwing her off pitch; then she was allowed to be a great singer until the curse descended again. Her loss of pitch was so regularized that I could see it coming and squirmed in anticipation. I felt as though I were in the presence of one of God's more complicated pranks.

Her choice of songs highlighted her failings. Their delicate textures were constantly broken by her lapses. When we arrived at the Chanler pieces, I thought I was accustomed to her, but I found I wasn't. The first song begins with the following verse, written by Walter de la Mare, who had crafted all the poems in archaic epitaph style:

> Here lyeth our infant, Alice Rodd;
>> She were so small,
>> Scarce aught at all,
> But a mere breath of Sweetness sent from God.

The vocal line for "She were so small" consists of four notes, the last two rising a half-step from the two before them. To work, the passage requires a dead-eye accuracy of pitch:

Singing this line, Karen Jensen hit the D-sharp but missed the E and skidded up uncontrollably to F-sharp, which would sound all right to anyone who didn't have the music in front of his nose, as I did. Only a fellow-musician could be offended.

Infuriated, I began to feel that I could *not* participate in a recital with this woman. It would be humiliating to perform such lovely songs in this excruciating manner. I stopped playing, turned to her to tell her that I could not continue after all, and then I saw her bracelet.

I am not, on the whole, especially observant, a failing that probably accounts for my having missed the bracelet when we first met. But I saw it now: five silver canaries dangled down quietly from it, and as it slipped back and forth, I saw her wrist and what I suddenly realized *would* be there: the parallel lines of her madness, etched in scar tissue.

The epitaphs finished, she asked me to work with her, and I agreed. When we shook hands, the canaries shook in tiny vibrations, as if pleased with my dutiful kindness, my charity, toward their mad mistress.

IV

Though Paul Hindemith's reputation once equalled Stravinsky's and Bartók's, it suffered after his death in 1963 an almost complete collapse. Only two of his orchestral works, the *Symphonic Metamorphoses on Themes of Weber* and the *Mathis der Maler* symphony, are played with any frequency, thanks in part to their use of borrowed tunes. One hears his woodwind quintets and choral pieces now and again, but the works of which he was most proud — the ballet *Nobilissima Visione, Das Marienleben* (a song cycle), and the opera *Harmonie die Welt* — have fallen into total obscurity.

The reason for Hindemith's sudden loss of reputation was a mystery to me; I had always considered his craftsmanship if not his inspiration to be first-rate. When I saw that the *Harmony of the World* symphony, almost never played, would be performed in our anonymous city, I told Cascadilla that I wanted to write a story for that week on how fame was gained and lost in the world of music. He thought that subject might be racy enough to interest the tone-deaf citizens of leafy and peaceful Maple Street, where no one is famous, if I made sure the story contained "the human element."

I read up on Hindemith, played his piano music, and listened to the recordings. I slowly found the music to be technically astute but emotionally arid, as if some problem of purely local interest kept the composer's gaze safely below the horizon. Technocratic and oddly timid, his work reminded me of a model train chugging through a tiny town where only models of people actually lived. In fact, Hindemith did have a lifelong obsession with train sets: in Berlin, his took up three rooms, and the composer wrote elaborate timetables so that the toys wouldn't collide.

But if Hindemith had a technocrat's intelligence, he also believed in the necessity of universal participation in musical activities. Listening was not enough. Even non-musical citizens could learn to sing and play, and he wrote music expressly for this purpose. He seems to have known that passive, drugged listening was a side-effect of totalitarian environments and that elitist composers such as Schoenberg were engaged in antisocial Faustian projects that would bewilder and infuriate most audiences, leaving them isolated and thus eager to be drugged by a musical superman.

As the foremost anti-Nietzschean German composer of his day, therefore, Hindemith left Germany when his works could not be performed, thanks to the Third Reich; wrote textbooks with simple exercises; composed a requiem in memory of Franklin Roosevelt, set to words by Walt Whitman; and taught students, not all of them talented, in Ankara, New Haven, and Buffalo ("this caricature of a town"). As he passed through late middle age, he turned to a project he had contemplated all his life, an opera based on the career of the German astronomer Johannes Kepler, author of *De Harmonice Mundi*. This opera, a summary of Hindemith's ideas, would be called *Harmony of the World*. Hindemith worked out the themes first in a symphony, which bore the same title as the opera, and completed it in 1951. The more I thought about this project, the more it seemed anachronistic. Who believed in world harmony in 1951? Or thereafter? Such a symphony would have to pass beyond technical sophistication into divine inspiration, which Hindemith had never shown any evidence of possessing.

It occurred to me that Hindemith's lifelong sanity had perhaps given way in this case, toppled not by despair (as is conventional) but by faith in harmony.

V

For the next rehearsal, I drove to Karen Jensen's apartment, where there was, she said, a piano. I'd become curious about the styles of her insanity; I imagined a hamster cage in the kitchen, a doll-head mobile in the living room, and mottos written with different colored inks on memo pads tacked up everywhere on the walls.

She greeted me at the door without her bracelet. When I looked at her wrist, she said, "Hmmm. I see that you noticed. A memento of adolescent despair." She sighed. "But it does frighten people off. Once you've tried to do something like that, people don't really trust you. I don't know why exactly. Don't want your blood on their hands or something. Well, come on in."

I was struck first by her forthrightness and secondly by her tiny apartment. Its style was much like the style in my house. She owned an attactive but worn-down sofa, a sideboard that supported an antique clock, one chair, a glass-top dinner table, and one nondescript poster on the wall. Trying to keep my advantage, I looked hard for tell-tale signs of insanity but found none. The piano was off in the corner, almost hidden, unlike those in the parlors back home.

"Very nice," I said.

"Well, thanks," she said. "It's not much. I'd like something bigger, but . . . where I work, I'm an administrative assistant, and they don't pay me very much. So that's why I live like a snail here. It's hardly big enough to move around in, right?" She wasn't looking at me. "I mean, I could almost pick it up and carry it away."

I nodded. "You just don't think like a rich person," I said, trying to be hearty. "They like to expand. They need room. Big houses, big cars, fat bodies."

"Oh, I know!" she said, laughing. "My uncle . . . would *you* like to stay for dinner? You look like you need a good meal. I mean, after the rehearsal. You're just skin and bones, Pet — . . . may I call you Peter?"

"Sure." I sat down on the sofa and tried to think up an excuse. "I really can't stay, Miss Jensen. I have another rehearsal to go to later tonight. I wish I could."

"That's not it, is it?" she asked suddenly, looking down at me. "I don't believe you. I bet it's something else. I bet you're afraid of me."

"Why should I be afraid of you?"

She smiled and shrugged. "That's all right. You don't have to say anything. I know how it goes." She laughed once more, faintly. "I never found a man who could handle it. They want to show you *their* scars, you know? They don't want to see any on you, and if they discover any, they just run." She slapped her right hand into her forehead and then ran her fingers through her hair. "Well, shit. I didn't mean to do this *at all!* I mean, I admire you so much and everything, and here I am, running on like this. I guess we should get down to business, right? Since I'm paying you by the hour."

I smiled professionally and went to her piano.

Beneath the high culture atmosphere that surrounds them, art songs have one subject: love. The permutations of love (lust, solitude, and loss) are present in abundance, of course, but for the most part they are simple vehicles for the expression of that one emotion. I was reminded of this as I played through the piano parts. As much as I concentrated on the music in front of me, I couldn't help but notice that my employer stood next to the piano, singing the words sometimes toward me, sometimes away. She was rather courageously forcing eye-contact on me. She kept this up for an hour and a half until we came to the Chanler settings, when at last she turned slightly, singing to the walls.

As before, her voice broke out of control every five seconds, giving isolated words all the wrong shadings. The only way to endure it, I discovered, was to think of her singing as a post-modern phenomenon with its own conventions and rules. As the victim of necessity rather than accident, Karen Jensen was tolerable.

> Here sleep I,
> Susannah Fry,
> No one near me,
> No one nigh:
> Alone, alone
> Under my stone,
> Dreaming on,
> Still dreaming on:
> Grass for my valance

And coverlid,
Dreaming on
As I always did.
'Weak in the head?'
Maybe. Who knows?
Susannah Fry
Under the rose.

There she was, facing away from me, burying Susannah Fry, and probably her own past and career into the bargain.

When we were done, she asked, "Sure you won't stay?"

"No, I don't think so."

"You really haven't another engagement, do you?"

"No," I admitted.

"I didn't think so. You were scared of me the moment you walked in the door. You thought I'd be crazy." She waited. "After all, only ugly girls live alone, right? And I'm not ugly."

"No, you aren't," I said. "You're quite attractive."

"Do you think so?" she asked, brightening. "It's so nice to hear that from you, even if you're just paying a compliment. I mean, it still means *something*." Then she surprised me. As I stood in the doorway, she got down on her knees in front of me and bowed her head in the style of one of her songs. "Please stay," she asked. Immediately she stood up and laughed. "But don't feel obliged to."

"Oh, no," I said, returning to her living room. "I've just changed my mind. Dinner sounds like a good idea."

After she had served and we had started to eat, she looked up at me and said, "You know, I'm not completely good." She paused. "At singing."

"What?" I stopped chewing. "Yes, you are. You're all right."

"Don't lie. I know I'm not. You know I'm not. Come on: let's at least be honest. I think I have certain qualities of musicality, but my pitch is . . . you know. Uneven. You probably think it's awfully vain of me to put on these recitals like this. With nobody but friends and family coming."

"No, I don't."

"Well, I don't care what you say. It's . . . hmm, I don't know. People encourage me. And it's a discipline. Music's finally a discipline that rewards you. Privately, though. Well, that's what my mother says."

Carefully, I said, "She may be right."

"Who cares if she is?" she laughed, her mouth full of food. "I enjoy doing it. Like I enjoy doing this. Listen, I don't want to seem forward or anything, but are you married?"

"No."

"I didn't think so." She picked up a string bean and eyed it suspiciously. "Why aren't you? You're not ugly. In fact you're all right looking. You obviously haven't been crazy. Are you gay or something?"

"No."

"No," she agreed, "you don't look gay. You don't even look very happy. You don't look very anything. Why is that?"

"I should be offended by this line of questioning."

"But you're not. You know why? Because I'm interested in you. I hardly know you, but I like you, what I can see. Don't you have any trust?"

"Yes," I said, finally.

"So answer my question. Why don't you look very anything?"

"Do you want to hear what my piano teacher once said?" I asked. "He said I wasn't enough of a fanatic. He said that to be one of the great ones you have to be a tiny bit crazy. Touched. And he said I wasn't. And when he said it, I knew all along he was right. I was waiting for someone to say what I already knew, and he was the one. I was too much a good citizen, he said. I wasn't possessed."

She rose, walked around the table to where I was sitting, and stood in front of me, looking down at my face. I knew that whatever she was going to do had been picked up, in attitude, from one of her songs. She touched the back of my arm with two fingers on her right hand. "Well," she said, "maybe you aren't possessed, but what would you think of me as another possession?"

# VI

In 1618 at the age of seventy, Katherine Kepler, the mother of Johannes Kepler, was put on trial for witchcraft. The records indicate that her personality was so deranged, so deeply offensive to all, that if she were alive today she would *still* be called a witch.

One of Kepler's biographers, Angus Armitage, notes that she was "evil-tempered" and possessed an interest in unnamed "outlandish things." Her trial lasted, on and off, for three years; by 1621, when she was acquitted, her personality had disintegrated completely. She died the following year.

At the age of six, Kepler's son Frederick died of smallpox. A few months later, Kepler's wife, Barbara, died of typhus. Two other children, Henry and Susanna, had died in infancy.

Like many another of his age, Kepler spent much of his adult life cultivating favor from the nobility. He was habitually penniless and was often reduced, as his correspondence shows, to begging for handouts. He was the victim of religious persecution, though luckier in this regard than some.

After he married for a second time, three more children died in infancy, a statistic that in theory carries less emotional weight than one might think, given the accepted levels of infant mortality for that era.

In 1619, despite the facts cited above, Kepler published *De Harmonice Mundi*, a text in which he set out to establish the correspondence between the laws of harmony and the disposition of planets in motion. In brief, Kepler argued that certain intervals, such as the octave, major and minor sixths, and major and minor thirds, were pleasurable, while other intervals were not. History indicated that mankind had always regarded certain intervals as unpleasant. Feeling that this set of universal tastes pointed to immutable laws, Kepler sought to map out the pleasurable intervals geometrically, and then to transfer that geometrical pattern to the order of the planets. The velocity of the planets, rather than their strict placement, constituted the harmony of the spheres. This velocity provided each planet with a note, what Armitage calls a "term in a mathematically determined relation."

> In fact, each planet performed a short musical scale, set down by Kepler in staff notation. The length of the scale depended upon the eccentricity of the orbit; and its limiting notes could generally be shown to form a concord (except for Venus and the Earth with their nearly circular orbits, whose scales were of very constricted range). . . . at the Creation . . . complete concord prevailed and the morning stars sang together.

VII


We began to eat dinner together. Accustomed to solitude, we did not always engage in conversation. I would read the newspaper or ink in letters on my geometrically patterned crossword puzzles at my end of the table, while Karen would read detective novels or *Time* at hers. If she had cooked, I would clear and wash the dishes; if I had cooked, she did the cleaning. Experience and disappointments had made us methodical. She told me that she had once despised structured experiences governed by timetables, but that after several manic-depressive episodes, she had learned to love regularity. This regularity included taking lithium at the same time — to the minute — each day.

The season being summer, we would pack towels and swimming suits after dinner and drive out to one of several public beaches, where we would swim until darkness came on. On calm evenings, Karen would drop her finger in the water and watch the waves lap outward. I favored immature splashing, or grabbing her by the arm and whirling her around me until I released her and she would spin back and fall into the water, laughing as she sank. One evening, we found a private beach, two hundred feet of sand all to ourselves, on a lake thirty miles out of town. Framed on both sides by woods and well-hidden from the highway, this beach had the additional advantage of being unpatrolled. We had no bathhouse in which to change, however, so Karen instructed me not to look as she walked about fifty feet away to a spot where she undressed and put on her suit.

Though we had been intimate for at least a week, I had still not seen her naked: like a good Victorian, she demanded the shades be drawn, the lights out, and the covers pulled discreetly over us. But now, with the same methodical thoroughness, she wanted me to see her, so I looked, despite her warnings. She was bent over, under the tree boughs, the evening light breaking through the leaves and casting broken gold bands on her body. Her arms were delicate, the arms of a schoolgirl, I thought, an impression heightened by the paleness of her skin, but her breasts were full, at first making me think of Rubens' women, then of Renoir's, then of nothing at all. Slowly, knowing I was watching her, she pinned her hair up. Not her breasts or arms, but that expression of vague contentment as she looked out toward the water away from me: *that* made me feel a tingling below my heart, somewhere in an emotional center near my stomach. I wanted to pick her up and carry her somewhere, but with my knees wobbly it was all I could do to make my way over to where she stood and take her in my arms before she cried out. "Jesus," she said, shivering, "you gave me a surprise." I kissed her, waiting for inspiration to direct me on what to do next: pick her up? Carry her? Make love to her on the sand? Wade into the water with her and swim out to the center of the bay, where we would drown together in a Lawrentian love-grip? But then we broke the kiss; she put on her swimsuit like a good citizen, and we swam for our usual fifteen minutes in silence. Afterwards, we changed back into our clothes and drove home, muttering smalltalk. Behavior inspired by and demonstrating love embarrassed both of us. When I told her that she was beautiful and that I loved her, she patted me on the cheek and said, "Aw, how nice. You always try to say the right thing."

## VIII

The Maple Street angle for *Harmony of the World* ran as follows: SYMPHONY OF FAITH IN A FAITHLESS AGE. Hindemith, I said, wished to confound the skeptics by composing a monument of faith. In an age of organized disharmony, of political chaos, he stood at the barricades defending tonality and traditional musical form. I carefully avoided any specific discussion of the musical materials of the symphony, which in the Schott orchestral score looked over-complex and melodically ugly. From what I could tell without hearing the piece, Hindemith had employed stunning technique in order to disguise his lack of inspiration, though I did not say so in print. Instead, I wrote that the symphony's failure to win public support was probably the result of Hindemith's refusal to use musical gimmicks on the one hand and sticky sweet melodies on the other. I wrote that he had not been dismayed by the bad reviews *Harmony of the World* had received, which was untrue. I said he was a man of integrity. I did not say that men of integrity are often unable to express joy when the occasion demands. Cascadilla liked my article. "This guy sounds like me," he said, reading my copy. "I respect him." The article ran five days before the concert and was two pages away from the religion-and-faith section. Not long after, the symphony ticket office called me to say that my piece had caused a rush of ticket orders from ordinary folk, non-concert types, who wanted to hear this "religious symphony." The woman from the business office thanked me for my trouble. "Let's hope they like it," I said.

"Of course they will," she assured me. "You've told them to."

But they didn't. Despite all the oratory in the symphony, it was spiritually as dead as a lampshade. I could see why Hindemith had been shocked by the public reaction. Our audience applauded politely in discouragement, and then I heard an unusual sound for this anonymous city: one man, full of fun and conviction, booing loudly from the balcony. Booing the harmony of the world! He must be a Satanist! Don't intentions mean anything? So what if the harmony and joy were all counterfeit? The conductor came out for a bow, smiled at the booing man, and very soon the applause died away. I left the hall, feeling responsible. Arriving at the paper, I wrote a review of crushing dullness that reeked of bad faith. Goddamn Hindemith! Here he was, claiming to have seen God's workings, and they sounded like the workings of a steam engine or a trolley car. A fake symphony, with optimism the composer did not feel! I decided (but did not write) that *Harmony of the World* was just possibly the largest, most misconceived fiasco in modern music's history. It was a symphony that historically could not be written by a man who was constitutionally not equipped to write it. In my review, I kept a civil pen: I said that the performance lacked "luster," "a certain necessary glow."

## IX

"I'm worried about the recital tomorrow."

"Aw, don't worry. Here, kiss me. Right here."

"Aren't you listening? I'm worried."

"I'm singing. You're just accompanying me. Nobody's going to notice you. Move over a little, would you? Yeah, there. That pillow was forcing my head against the wall."

"Why aren't you worried?"

"Why should I be worried? I don't want to worry. I want to make love. Isn't that better than worrying?"

"Not if I'm worried."

"People won't notice *you*. By the way, have you noticed that when I kiss you on the stomach, you get goosebumps?"

"Yes. I think you're taking this pretty lightly. I mean, it's almost unprofessional."

"That's because I'm an amateur. A 100% amateur. Always and totally. Even at this. But that doesn't mean I don't have my moments. Mmmmmm. That's better."

"I thought it would maybe help. But listen. I'm still worried."

"Uhhhn. Oh, wait a minute. Wait a minute. Oh, I get it."

"What?"

"I get it. You aren't worried about yourself. You're worried about me."

## X

Forty people attended her recital, which was sponsored by the city university's music school, in which Karen was a sometime student. Somehow we made our way through the program, but when we came to the Chanler settings, I suddenly wanted Karen to sing them perfectly. I wanted an angel to descend and to take away the gypsy's curse. But she sang as she always had — off pitch — and when she came to "Ann Poverty," I found myself in that odd region between rage and pity.

> Stranger, here lies
> Ann Poverty;
> Such was her name
> And such was she.
> May Jesu pity
> Poverty.

But I was losing my capacity for pity.

In the green room, her forty friends came back to congratulate her. I met them. They were all very nice. She smiled and laughed:

there would be a party in an hour. Would I go? I declined. When we were alone, I said I was going back to my place.

"Why?" she asked. "Shouldn't you come to my party? You're my lover after all. That *is* the word."

"Yes. But I don't want to go with you."

"Why?"

"Because of tonight's concert, that's why."

"What about it?"

"It wasn't very good, was it? I mean, it just wasn't."

"I thought it was all right. A few slips. It was pretty much what I was capable of. All those people said they liked it."

"Those people don't matter!" I said, my eyes watering with anger. "Only the music matters. Only the music is betrayed, they aren't. They don't know about pitch, most of them. I mean, Jesus, they aren't genuine musicians, so how would they know? Do you really think what we did tonight was good? It wasn't! It was a travesty! We ruined those songs! How can you stand to do that?"

"I don't ruin them. I sing them adequately. I project feeling. People get pleasure from them. That's enough."

"It's awful," I said, feeling the ecstatic lift-off into rage. "You're so close to being good, but you *aren't* good. Who cares what those ignoramuses think? They don't know what notes you're *supposed* to hit. It's that goddamn slippery pitch of yours. You're killing those songs. You just *drop* them like watermelons on the stage! It makes me sick! I couldn't have gone on for another day listening to you and your warbling! I'd die first."

She looked at me and nodded, her mouth set in a half-moue, half-smile of non-surprise. There may have been tears in her eyes, but I didn't see them. She looked at me as if she were listening hard to a long-distance call. "You're tired of me," she said.

"I'm not tired of you. I'm tired of hearing you sing! Your voice makes my flesh crawl! Do you know why? Can you tell me why you make me sick? Why do you make me sick? Never mind. I'm just glad this is over."

"You don't look glad. You look angry."

"And you look smug. Listen, why don't you go off to your party? Maybe there'll be a talent scout there. Or roses flung riotously at you. But don't give a recital like this again, please, okay? It's a public disgrace. It offends music. It offends *me*."

I turned my back on her and walked out to my car.

## XI

After the failure of *Harmony of the World*, Hindemith went on a strenuous tour that included Scandinavia. In Oslo, he was rehearsing the Philharmonic when he blinked his bright blue eyes twice, turned to the concertmaster, and said, "I don't know where I am." They took him away to a hospital; he had suffered a nervous breakdown.

## XII

I slept until noon, having nothing to do at the paper and no reason to get up. At last, unable to sleep longer, I rose and walked to the kitchen to make coffee. I then took my cup to the picture window and looked down the hill to the trees of the conservation area, the view Stecker had once told me I should have.

The figure of a woman was hanging from one of the trees, a noose around her neck. I dropped my coffee cup and the hot coffee spilled out over my feet.

I ran out the back door in my pajamas and sprinted painfully down the hill's tall grass toward the tree. I was fifty feet away when I saw that it wasn't Karen, wasn't in fact a woman at all, but an effigy of sorts, with one of Karen's hats, a pillow head, and a dress hanging over a broomstick skeleton. Attached to the effigy was a note:

> In the old days, this might have been me. Not anymore. Still, I thought it'd make you think. And I'm not giving up singing, either. By the way, what your playing lacks is not fanaticism, but concentration. You can't seem to keep your mind on one thing for more than a minute at a time. *I* notice things, too. You aren't the only reviewer around here. Take good care of this doll, okay?
>
> XXXXX,
> Karen

I took the doll up and dropped it in the clothes closet, where it stands to this hour.

Hindemith's biographer, Geoffrey Skelton, writes, "[On the stage] the episodic scenes from Kepler's life fail to achieve immediate dramatic coherence, and the basic theme remains obscure. . . ."

She won't of course see me again. She won't talk to me on the phone, and she doesn't answer my letters. I am quite lucidly aware of what I have done. And I go on seeing doubles and reflections and wave motion everywhere. There is symmetry, harmony, after all. I suppose I should have been nice to her. That, too, is a discipline. I always tried to be nice to everyone else.

On his deathbed, Hindemith has Kepler sing:

> *Und muss sehn am End:*
> *Die grosse Harmonie, das is der Tod.*
> *Absterben ist, sie zu bewirken, not.*
> *Im Leben hat sie keine Statte.*

> Now, at the end, I see it:
> the great harmony: it is death.
> To find it, we must die.
> In life it has no place.

## XIII

Hindemith's words may be correct. But Dante says that the residents of limbo, having never been baptised, will not see the face of God. This despite their having committed no sin, no active fault. In their fated locale, they sigh, which keeps the air "forever trembling." No harmony for them, these guiltless souls. Through eternity, the residents of limbo — where one can imagine oneself if one cannot stand to imagine any part of hell — experience one of the most shocking of all the emotions that Dante names: "duol senza martíri," grief without torment. These sighs are rather like the sounds one hears drifting from front porches in small towns on soft summer nights.

🔥 🔥 🔥

# MERCY and THE WITNESS

fiction by RICHARD SELZER

from THE IOWA REVIEW

*nominated by DeWitt Henry and David Wojahn*

## MERCY

He HAS BEEN MY PATIENT for seven years, ever since the day I explored his abdomen in the operating room and found the surprise lurking there—a cancer of the pancreas. He was forty-two years old then. For this man these have been seven years of famine. For his wife and his mother, as well. Until three days ago his suffering was marked by slowly increasing pain, vomiting and fatigue. Still, it was endurable. With morphine. Three days ago the pain rollicked out of control, and he entered that elect band whose suffering cannot be relieved by any means short of death. In his bed at home he seemed an eighty pound concentrate of pain from which all other pain must be made by serial dilution. He twisted under the lash of it. An ambulance arrived. At the hospital nothing

205

was to be done to prolong his life. Only the administration of large doses of narcotics.

"Please," he begs me. In his open mouth, upon his teeth, a brown paste of saliva. All night long he has thrashed, as though to hollow out a grave in the bed.

"I won't let you suffer," I tell him. In his struggle the sheet is thrust aside. I see the old abandoned incision, the belly stuffed with tumor. His penis, even, is skinny. One foot with five blue toes is exposed. In my cupped hand, they are cold. I think of the twenty bones of that foot laced together with tendon, each ray accompanied by its own nerve and artery. Now, this foot seems a beautiful dead animal that had once been trained to transmit the command of a man's brain to the earth.

"I'll get rid of the pain," I tell his wife.

But there is no way to kill the pain without killing the man who owns it. Morphine to the lethal dose . . . and still he miaows and bays and makes other sounds like a boat breaking up in a heavy sea. I think his pain will live on long after he dies.

"Please," begs his wife, "we cannot go on like this."

"Do it," says the old woman, his mother. "Do it now."

"To give him any more would kill him," I tell her.

"Then do it," she says. The face of the old woman is hoof-beaten, with intersecting curves of loose skin. Her hair is donkey brown, donkey gray.

They wait with him while I go to the nurse's station to prepare the syringes. It is a thing that I cannot ask anyone to do for me. When I return to the room there are three loaded syringes in my hand, a rubber tourniquet and an alcohol sponge. Alcohol sponge! To prevent infection? The old woman is standing on a small stool and leaning over the side-rail of the bed. Her bosom is just above his upturned face as though she were weaning him with sorrow and gentleness from her still-full breasts. All at once she says severely, the way she must have said it to him years ago:

"Go home, son. Go home now."

I wait just inside the doorway. The only sound is a flapping, a rustling as in a room to which a small animal, a bat perhaps, has retreated to die. The women turn to leave. There is neither gratitude nor reproach in their gaze. I should be hooded. We are alone. I stand at the bedside.

"Listen," I say, "I can get rid of the pain." The man's eyes regain their focus. His gaze is like a wound that radiates its pain outward so that all upon whom it fell would know the need of relief.

"With these." I hold up the syringes.

"Yes," he gasps, "Yes." And while the rest of his body stirs in answer to the pain, he holds his left, his acquiescent arm still for the tourniquet. An even dew of sweat covers his body. I wipe the skin with the alcohol sponge and tap the arm smartly to bring out the veins. There is one that is still patent; the others have long since clotted and broken down. I go to insert the needle, but the tourniquet has come unknotted; the vein has collapsed. Again I tie the tourniquet. Slowly the vein fills with blood. This time it stays distended.

He reacts not at all to the puncture. I press the barrel and deposit the load, detach the syringe from the needle and replace it with the second syringe. I send this home and go on to the third. When they are all given, I pull out the needle. A drop of blood blooms on his forearm. I blot it with the alcohol sponge. It is done. In less than a minute, it is done.

"Go home," I say, repeating the words of the old woman. I turn off the light. In the darkness the contents of the bed are theoretical. No! I must watch. I turn the light back on. How reduced he is, a folded parcel, something chipped away until only its shape and a little breath are left. His impatient bones gleam as though to burst through the papery skin. I am impatient too. I want to get it over with, then step out into the corridor where the women are waiting. His death is like a jewel to them.

My fingers at his pulse. The same rhythm as mine! As though there were one pulse that beat throughout all of nature, and every creature's heart throbbed precisely.

"You can go home now," I say. The familiar emaciated body untenses. The respirations slow down. Eight per minute . . . six. . . . It won't be long. The pulse wavers in and out of touch. It won't be long.

"Is that better?" I ask him. His gaze is distant, opaque, preoccupied. Minutes go by. Outside, in the corridor, the murmuring of women's voices.

But this man will not die! The skeleton rouses from its stupor. The snout twitches as if to fend off a fly. What is it that shakes him like a gourd full of beans? The pulse returns, melts away, comes back again, and stays. The respirations are twelve, then fourteen. I have not done it. I did not murder him. I am innocent!

I shall walk out of the room into the corridor. They will look to me, holding their breath, expectant. I lift the sheet to cover him. There is a sharp sting in my thumb. The same needle with which I meant to kill him has pricked *me*. A drop of blood appears. I press it with the alcohol sponge. My fresh blood deepens the stain of his on the gauze. Never mind. The man in the bed swallows. His Adam's apple bobs slowly. It would be so easy to do it. Three minutes of pressure on the larynx. He is still not conscious, wouldn't feel it, wouldn't know. My thumb and fingertips hover, land on his windpipe. My pulse beating in his neck, his in mine. I look back over my shoulder. No one. Two bare I.V. poles in a corner, their looped metal eyes witnessing. Do it! Fingers press. Again he swallows. Look back again. How closed the door is. And . . . my hand wilts. I cannot. It is not in me to do it. Not that way. The man's head swivels like an upturned fish. The squadron of ribs battles on.

I back away from the bed, turn and flee toward the doorway. In the mirror, a glimpse of my face. It is the face of someone who has been resuscitated after a long period of cardiac arrest. There is no spot of color in the cheeks, as though this person were in shock at what he had just seen on the yonder side of the grave.

In the corridor the women lean against the wall, against each other. They are like a band of angels dispatched here to take possession of his body. It is the only thing that will satisfy them.

"He didn't die," I say, "he won't . . . or can't." They are silent.

"He isn't ready yet," I say.

"He *is* ready," the old woman says, "*you* ain't."


## THE WITNESS

The boy in the bed is the length of a six year old. But something about him is much younger than that. It is the floppiness, I think. His head lolls as though it were floating in syrup. Now and then he unfurls his legs like a squid. He has pale yellow hair and pale blue eyes. His eyes will have none of me, but gaze as though into a mirror. He is blind. The right cheek and temple are deeply discolored. At first I think it is a birthmark. Then I see that it is a bruise.

"Does he walk?" I ask.

"No."

"Crawl?"

"He rolls. His left side is weak." The mother tells me.

"But he has a strong right arm," says the father. I touch the dark bruise that covers the right side of the child's face where he has again and again punched himself.

"Yes, I see that he is strong."

"That's how he tells us that he wants something, or that something hurts. That, and grinding his teeth."

"He doesn't talk, then?"

"He has never been heard to utter a word," says the mother as though repeating a statement from a written case history.

I unpin the diaper and lay it open. A red lump boils at the child's groin. The lump is the size of a walnut. The tissues around it slope off into pinkness. Under the pressure of my fingers, the redness blanches. I let up and the redness returns. I press again. Abruptly the right arm of the child flails upward and his fist bumps against his bruised cheek.

"You're hurting him," says the father.

The eyes of the child are terrible in their sapphiric emptiness. Was there not one tiny seed of vision in them? I know that there is not. The optic nerves have failed to develop; the pediatrician has told me. Such blindness goes all the way back to the brain.

"It is an incarcerated hernia," I tell them. "An emergency operation will be necessary to examine the intestine that is trapped in the sac. If the bowel is not already gangrenous, it will be replaced inside the peritoneal cavity, and then we will fix the hernia. If the circulation of the bowel has already been compromised, we will remove that section and stitch the ends together."

"Will there be . . .?"

"No," I say. "There will be no need for a colostomy." All this they understand at once. The young woman nods.

"My sister's boy had the same thing," she says.

I telephone the Operating Room to schedule the surgery, then sit at the desk to write the pre-operative orders on the chart. An orderly arrives with a stretcher for the boy. The father fends off my assistance and lifts the child onto the stretcher himself.

"Is there any danger?"

"There is always danger. But we will do everything to prevent trouble." The stretcher is already moving down the corridor. The father hurries to accompany it.

"Wait here," I say to him at the elevator. "I will come as soon as we are done." The man looks long and deep at the child, gulping him down in a single radiant gaze.

"Take good care of my son," he says. I see then that he loves the boy as one can only love his greatest extravagance, the one thing that will impoverish him totally, will give him cold and hunger and pain in return for his love. As the door to the elevator closes I see the father standing in the darkening corridor, his arms still making a cradle in which the smoke of twilight is gathering. I wheel the stretcher into the Operating Room from which the father has been banished. I think of how he must dwell for now in a dark hallway across which, from darker doorways, the blinding cries of sick children streak and crackle. What is his food, that man out there? Upon what shall he live but the remembered smiles of this boy?

On the operating table the child flutters and tilts like a moth burnt by the beams of the great overhead lamp. I move the lamp away from him until he is not so precisely caught. In this room where everything is green, the child is green as ice, translucent, a fish seen through murk, and dappled. I hold him upon the table while the anesthetist inserts a needle into a vein on the back of the child's left hand, the one that is weak. Bending above, I can feel the boy's breath upon my neck. It is clean and hay-scented as the breath of a calf. What malice made this? Surely not God! Perhaps he is a changeling—an imperfect child put in place of another, a normal one that had been stolen by the fairies. Yes, I think. It is the malice of the fairies.

Now the boy holds his head perfectly still, cocked to one side. He seems to be listening. I know that he is . . . listening for the sound of his father's voice. I speak to the boy, murmur to him, hum to him. But I know it is not the same. Take good care of my son, the father had said. Why must he brandish his love at me? I am enough beset. But I know that he must. I think of the immensity of love and I see for a moment what the father must see—the soul that lay in the body of the child like a chest of jewels in a sunken ship.

Through the fathoms, it glows. I cup the child's feet in one hand. How cold they are! I should like to lend him my cat to drape over them. I am happiest in winter with my cat for a foot pillow. No human has ever been so kind, so voluptuous as my cat. Now the child is asleep. Under anesthesia he looks completely normal. So! It is only wakefulness that diminishes him.

The skin has been painted with antiseptic and draped. I make the incision across the apex of the protuberance. Almost at once, I know that this is no incarcerated hernia, but a testicle that had failed to descend into the scrotum. Its energy for the long descent had given out. Harmlessly it hung in mid-canal until now when it twisted on its little cord and cut off its own blood supply. The testicle is no longer viable. The black color of it tells me so. I cut into the substance of the testicle to see if it will bleed. It does not. It will have to be removed.

"You'll have to take it out, won't you?" It is the anesthesiologist speaking. "It won't do him any good now. Anyway, why does he need it?"

Yes, yes, I know. . . . Wait. And I stand at the table filled with loathing for my task. Precisely because he has so little left, because it is of no use to him . . . I know, and I tie the spermatic cord with a silk suture, and I cut off the testicle. Lying upon a white gauze square, it no longer appears mad, threatening, but an irrefutable witness to these events, a testament. I close the wound.

I am back in the solarium of the Pediatric Ward. It is empty save for the young couple and myself.

"He is fine," I tell them. "He will be in the Recovery Room for an hour, and then they will bring him back here. He is waking up now."

"What did you do to my son?" The father's eyes have the glare of black olives.

"It wasn't a hernia," I explain. "I was wrong. It was an undescended testicle that had become twisted on its cord. I had to remove it." The mother nods minutely. Her eyes are the same blue gem from which the boy's have been struck. There is something pure about the woman out of whose womb this child had blundered to knock over their lives. As though the mothering of such a child had returned her to a state of virginity. The father slumps in his chair, his body doubled as though it were he who had been cut in the groin. There in the solarium he seems to be aging visibly, the arteries in his body silting up. Yellow sacs of flesh appear beneath his eyes. His eyes themselves are peopled with red ants. I imagine his own slack scrotum. And the hump on his back— flapping, dithering, drooling, reaching up to hit itself on the cheek, and listening, always listening for the huffing of the man's breath.

Just then, the room is plunged into darkness.

"Don't worry," I say. "A power failure. There is an accessory generator. The lights will go on in a moment." We are silent, as though the darkness has robbed us of speech as well. I cannot see the father, but like the blind child in the Recovery Room, I listen for the sound of his voice.

The lights go on. Abruptly, the father rises from his chair.

"Then he is alright."

"Yes." I nod. Relief snaps open on his face. He reaches for his wife's hand. They stand there together, smiling. And all at once I know that this man's love for his child is a passion. It is a rapids roiling within him. It has nothing to do with pleasure, this kind of love. It is a deep black joy.

# WRITING OFF THE SELF

by RICHARD POIRIER

from RARITAN: A QUARTERLY REVIEW

*nominated by* RARITAN: A QUARTERLY REVIEW, *and Samuel Vaughan*

SINCE THE BEGINNINGS of literature in the West, human beings have wanted to re-present themselves, but they have also wanted to do something nearly the reverse. They have wanted to reduce or even eradicate the human self. Examples can be found in writers so diverse as Virgil, Dante, and Spenser, Bacon, Milton, and Racine, Mallarmé, T. S. Eliot and Artaud, Stevens, Beckett, and Pynchon. Whatever such writers have in common, they are of course markedly dissimilar, and to account for the dissimilarities I would propose that there are three quite different ways in which some of them, and a few others, have suggested that the human self be dissolved or decreated or dispersed or dismissed. Necessarily, then, I am concerned with variations on this topic or idea, and, more specifically, with the problems *in writing* and *in reading* created by passages wherein it is recommended that human beings might just as well erase or exterminate themselves. The problem is that the human self very likely finds it intolerable to remain in a state of impoverishment or incipient extermination even while that self is able to imagine that the very idea of the human is perhaps not an inevitable or preferred alternative. There is no way any writer, no matter how extreme his views on the subject, can be indifferent to this problem. And I say no writer can be indifferent, because to write at all is to salvage, however reluctantly, some part of the existent humanity, the formulae and codes that belong to a shared human inheritance, even if your writing is an invitation to reject and disperse it.

Of the three central modes of self-eradication in literature the first need only be mentioned to be readily understood, which is but one indication of its centrality to Western thinking and of its generally uncritical acceptance as a "good way to go." You wish to bring an end to the self, even at the peril of your physical being, in the expectation of some better life; you surrender the self and the will in order to save the soul, as in Dante, Spenser, Milton, T. S. Eliot, and aspects of Lawrence. But there is always in such instances a re-creative countermovement to self-disposal; it is as if self-erasure were a prelude to a redemptive act. As a result, there is also, always, a presumption of narrative, an expectation that human reality evolves in and through narrative movement. Christ in his death and resurrection is the central example, and it provides an indispensable paradigm for the Western conception of narrative.

This traditional mode will be discussed here only when it helps clarify two other more recent and, to my mind, more exciting ones — exciting, that is, in the kinds of writing stimulated by them. One, which can be called European, will be represented by Foucault and Nietzsche; the other, the American, by Emerson, William James, and Stevens. Neither the European nor the American contingent assumes a creative countermovement to human dissolution, and there is little or no expressed concern in either for the human soul as the projection of the self into an afterlife. Both are implicitly critical of the concept of narrative development, the mythos of narrative. But these two traditions, if they can be called that, exhibit marked and important differences on the issue of voice and of the possible inferences from voice of human presence.

Assume, for instance, that we are listening to a voice — and not all critics bother to listen, even when they are able to hear it — a voice that invites us to do away with ourselves. What can be its possible attractions? On what measure of time, in what measure of space, does this voice ask to exist, when in the same breath it asks that the traditional self be deprived of time and space? the self which is you or I — or the writer? Living in time and space as we read and listen, where and who can we imagine ourselves to be if we assent to the proposition that we shouldn't be at all? that a happier future would be one in which humans like ourselves, and all they have done toward the invention of the self, are assured of irrelevancy? These may seem like primitive or vulgar questions, proper not to literary critics but only to the lost humans of Theodor Adorno, men and women who could not ask them anyway since, in the mass, they have ceased to exist as individuals. For them the question of self-eradication has already been answered. Do the questions even matter, then, except to those, even fewer in number, who are capable of thinking about them?

Perhaps that is the real, the only question. It is not possible confidently to assume that a "voice" allows the inference of a person, a presence, a self behind it. This is not a matter simply of the loss of individual identity to stereotype, to cant. Recent theory, for which Jacques Derrida provides an impetus, has more basically challenged the relative primacy of speech as against writing and, with that, the logocentricism that implies a metaphysics of presence on which claims for the priority of speech, of voice, and of the creative Word are founded. The self who speaks and the self who listens are, in that sense, not real enough even to be obliterated. However, while some English and American readers have a theoretical interest in the nonexistence of the self, few of them can get as genuinely agitated about it as do the French. And for the reason that in the Anglo-American, but especially in the American-Emersonian tradition, there is no one, so far as I know, who has chosen to treat voice as if it were an issue of metaphysical importance or who has given to it such historical reverberation as it gets from being linked to a term like "logocentrism." Deconstruction has been taken for granted in the great line of American literature from Emerson to Adams to Stevens, where the identity of the human self is nearly always problematic. It is a literature which from the outset has already rescinded the authority of the social, ecclesiastical, political institutions that in European literature are strong enough flexibly to define the self and measure its compliant or resistant movements. Where such institutions are recognized in American literature they often exist as Force, "the interpolation of the perverted mind and heart of man," as Hawthorne puts it at the beginning of "The New Adam and Eve." Inklings, fragments of a "true" self are discovered intermittently only in acts of recession from the systems that would define it, in acts of retreat into monologue or landscape or silence. From the "eloquence" of Emerson to the "sound of sense" in Frost, voice is imagined as a species of dramatic extemporization; the self behind voice is contrived for a particular and transient circumstance which is itself, as likely as not, in the process of receding — a myth to be explored for its local or immediate utility, a social demand to be negotiated.

I find it impossible to ignore the sound of the human voice in writing or out of it, but voice never refers me to a self that, to begin with, is ever quite sure of its identity. How could it be? Unless it comes from mad Tamburlaine or Lear or Ahab, the voices heard in Anglo-American literature are never allowed even to pretend that they master the materials, the language, on which their very claim to existence depends. Nor is the English language itself assumed to be stabilized or pure, subject to the rulings of an Academy. In the literature of England and America voice has always struggled with a language which, meanwhile, is often in contention with itself. Hence, the energetic wonder called forth by Shakespeare's language — and by Melville's or Mark Twain's. For a critic like myself, immersed in this literature, voice is therefore not distinguishable from the human will. Writing is a struggle to impose voice or will on the intractable and fluid material of language, language which irresistibly refers to historical, social, and mythological implications that remain very much alive in it. Especially of American literature it can be said that if it confronts the possibilities of self-eradication without a sense of nostalgia for the humanistic and religious traditions being dislodged, it is also without the evident anger or dismissiveness, which is a perverse form of nostalgia, found in the European figures I am about to discuss. American literature is, supremely, the literature that *knows* the distinction between voice and writing, and the problematic relation between voice and presence. It plays with these distinctions not for moral but for mortal stakes — the salvation of voice is nothing less than the salvation of the will. It has altogether less to do with the salvation of the soul.

Ignoring chronology, I begin with Foucault and Nietzsche because to understand the extreme form of self-eradication which they sometimes articulate is to be in a better position to recognize that the radicalism in the Anglo-American examples I will be citing is perhaps more daring and certainly more mysterious. The voice we hear in the more eloquent passages in Foucault is often narcissistically determined that it be admired for the operatic extremity of the cultural role proposed for its author. Take as an example the passage frequently quoted from the end of *The Order of Things*, the title in 1970 of the English translation of *Les mots et les choses*, 1966. I quote in English because, while keeping in mind an admonition from Frost — that poetry is all that is lost in translation — I am satisfied that what I say about the passage, and about a subsequent one from Nietzsche, could be said also of the original:

> If those arrangements [of knowledge] were to disappear as they appeared, if some event of which we can at the moment do no more than sense the possibility — without knowing either what its form will be or what it promises — were to cause them to crumble, as the ground of classical thought did, at the end of the eighteenth century, then one can certainly wager that man would be erased, like a face drawn in sand at the edge of the sea.

These are the accents of someone who feels that he has already exposed and categorized the forces of civilization with extraordinarily tactical prowess. In the test that precedes this passage he has discovered the "arrangements of knowledge" by which man of the present dispensation was brought into being, so that he can now predict — or "sense" — how the arrangements might disappear, and he can confidently "wager" on the apocalyptic results of this disappearance. There is in all this an audible excitement, a Nietzschean excitement. But there is also something from Marx, which, if it delimits the vision of human dissolution, also thereby substantiates, as we will see, the polemical zeal with which Foucault proposes it. Arrangements or structures reveal themselves, as Marx would have it, principally at the moment and in the act of breakdown. Thus the *episteme* of the Classical period—those rules of discursive formation that would govern what can be said even by parties in dispute—became recognizable as such only when, by breaking apart, they revealed how they had been, unnaturally, put together. According to Foucault's calendar, this began to happen to the Classical period around 1790-1810, when it was to be replaced by our present order of things. That new epistemic order is now in its turn, and for the first time, becoming visible to us as it, too, begins to collapse, to expose its design through its fractures.

Though these quite crude periodizations are to be blurred by Foucault's later work, they nonetheless provide here and throughout his writing a license for the rhetorical flourish with which he customarily writes about the disappearance of man, of modern man. Foucault's voice urgently wishes to waste him, to hurry him off the stage, and that he intends the polemical note as a calculated necessity is obvious from some remarks made in an interview a year after *Les mots et les choses:*

> When one is dealing with the Classical period, one has only to describe it. When it comes to the modern period, however, which began about 1790-1810 and lasted until 1950, the problem is to free oneself from it. The apparently polemical character [in his writing about the modern period] derives from the fact that one has to dig out a whole mass of discourse that has accumulated under one's feet. One may uncover with gentle movements the latent configurations of earlier periods; but when it is a matter of determining the system of discourse on which we are still living, when we have to question the words that are still echoing in our ears, which become confused with those we are trying to formulate, the archeologist, like the Nietzschean philosopher, is forced to take a hammer to it.

It was not until *"L'ordre du discours,"* the 1977 Appendix to the American edition of *The Archeology of Knowledge,* that Foucault fully conceived of "event" as the emergence into visibility of subterranean and circuitous discursive formations. But he never, even in *The Order of Things*, chose to think of "event" as simply or as conventionally as his rhetorical use of the word might allow us to infer from the passage at the end of this early book. Which is to say that whether we are reading early or later Foucault, "arrangements of knowledge" emerge only from astonishingly complex and devious movements and never from what is normally thought of as an "event." Since nowhere in Foucault do "arrangements" appear as the result of an "event," a reportable happening, they cannot, except rhetorically, disappear as the consequence of one. The word "event" at the conclusion of *The Order of Things* is knowingly provocative, a come-on. So is the melodramatic suspense induced by a phrase like "at the moment," as if the reader is tensely holding onto the book in expectation of a happening. We are to be rhetorically persuaded that history unfolds with a kind of conventional narrativity, even though he has at this early stage intimated what will be insisted upon in *"L'ordre du discours"* and thereafter: that narrativity is designed to repress the recognition of those movements of force that do not fit into what we are allowed to recognize as narrative. Narrative is a form of repression—and it is also a form necessary to Foucault's polemics.

My intention, again, is not to argue against Foucault's ideas. Rather it is to investigate the status of the writing *at a point* where he has chosen to excite the reader and himself with the prospect that human beings are about to lose the power to recognize themselves as human. It is important to note the oddity and instability of such moments as measured not merely against our ordinary disposition, but even more against the writer's customary procedures. The oddity here is highlighted by the specific trope with which the passage — and the book — is brought to a close: the comparison of a man to a face drawn in the sand. The voice stretches this comparison, doubles it in an accent of lurid gravity, so that the face is not only drawn in sand but at the edge of the sea. Because of certain inescapable connotations passed on to us by writing, the image is close to hackneyed. Is this the sand of Arnold's Dover Beach, allowing for the pebbles? Not likely, but the possibility is there, at least for English readers. Is this the edge of the sea out of which we are supposed to have crawled in an evolutionary movement that is going to reverse itself? Another unlikely possibility, since Foucault is not here, or anywhere else, suggesting the end of man as a physical species. He calls only for the end of human vanity and of the particular organizations of knowledge that are both its creation and its support. But there is some Darwinian echo nonetheless; and it may be stronger, rhetorically, than the more delicate and intended suggestion: what will be destroyed will be a drawing of a man, a self-representation. The drawing, when one thinks of it, is yet another evidence of human vanity.

This is a voice that exults in its own daring; it asks us to celebrate its flamboyance. What is important for our purposes is that, at the same time, its maneuvers with language are outrageously deferential to the "human," to traditional human tastes, including a taste for theatricality. The passage indulges itself in the human vanities it purports to dismiss. A face of man drawn in the sand is of necessity drawn simply, perhaps even childishly. It is far less encumbered with the trappings of human exultation, that is, than is the face of man that emanates from Foucault's sentences, from the presence, the voice, the will that can be heard in them. If the face drawn by Foucault's words were "erased," then with it would go any justification for writing as grandiose as his on this occasion. Indeed, the very scene of erasure, which is made so spectacular for writer and reader, would not, such is the logic of the whole book, ever occur in history, in the sands of time. It could occur only in writing, in some change of discourse.

What is to be said of this? Perhaps we can get closer to the phenomenon by looking now, and more briefly, at a passage in Nietzsche that clearly anticipates Foucault, though without his calendar. The passage is taken from a posthumously published fragment, "On Truth and Lie in An Extra-Moral Sense":

> In some remote corner of the universe, poured out and glittering in innumerable solar systems, there once was a star on which clever animals invented knowledge. That was the haughtiest and most mendacious minute of "world history"—yet only a minute. After nature had drawn a few breaths the star grew cold, and the clever animals had to die.
>
> One might invent such a fable and still not have illustrated sufficiently how wretched, how shadowy and flighty, how aimless and arbitrary, the human intellect

appears in nature. There have been eternities when it
did not exist; and when it is done for again, nothing will
have happened. For this intellect has no further mission
that would lead beyond human life. It is human, rather,
and only its owner and producer gives it such importance, as if the world pivoted around it. But if we would
communicate with the mosquito, then we would learn
that it floats through the air with the same self-impor-
tance, feeling within itself the flying center of the world.
There is nothing in nature so despicable or insignificant
that it cannot immediately be blown up like a bag by a
slight breath of this power of knowledge; and just as
every porter wants an admirer, the proudest human
being, the philosopher, thinks he sees the eyes of the
universe telescopically focused from all sides on his
actions and thoughts.

Spatial images, images of miniaturization, expansion, telescop-
ing abound here. What they suggest is obvious enough: that man,
especially what Nietzsche calls the intellect of man, is no more
significant, in relation to the cosmos, than is a mosquito in relation
to the air in which it floats. Each is solipsistically assured that it is
the center of a flying world. It might be said both of man and
mosquito that they are "wretched," "shadowy," "flighty," "aimless,"
"arbitrary" — and doomed. But anyone should be embarrassed to
offer commentary on matters already made abundantly obvious.
Images so reiterated and redundant call for translation only by
someone so dull-witted as to be beyond reading the passage to
begin with. Instead, the images refer us backward to their source,
to the imperious will and energy of the author. We are free to
decide either that this voice is haughtily contemptuous of its
auditors, or that it assumes auditors who, like itself, do not need to
be persuaded of human insignificance; they want merely to join in
exuberant ranting about it. The energy of the voice owes nothing
to possible dissent. It does not propose even to anticipate it. So
that the spatial images, far from communicating anything important about the ratio of man to universe, refer us instead to a
speaker who, in imagining the end of man, is expansively enthusi-
astic, above and beyond mosquito-man. Rhetorically, he is in a
position much like Foucault's, for while it might be argued that

Nietzsche is far more sweepingly dismissive and that Foucault addresses himself only to the latest in a series of epistemic dispositions, the fact is that neither of them proposes that there is waiting for the species any other form of self-representation. Foucault is no more nostalgic than Nietzsche, and if he sounds more expectant, then his expectations are wholly unspecified.

It is necessary to move carefully at this point. We have been listening to voices that invite us to join in the drama of apocalypse, and as Frank Kermode has shown, in *The Sense of an Ending*, human beings seem always to have found this a thrilling opportunity for advancement. The reasons for finding it so in these instances are especially peculiar, however. That is, with Nietzsche and Foucault we get excited by the drama of self-obliteration as we might with any other writer. But there is something else at work here. There is a kind of cultural and social snobbery. Surely some measure of our excitement comes from the fact that the voice seems to assume that we who listen, like those who speak, are somehow *more* than human. We are being offered some exclusive and exonerating privilege, an inducement to the kind of pride that, on the other side of extermination, would in earlier times have made us ineligible for sainthood. Though the words we hear condemn mankind, the sound of them, the mode of address, clearly exempts the speaker and his auditors. These are not the voices of ordinary mortals speaking to other ordinary mortals.

The phrase "ordinary mortals" or "ordinary man" means no more now by itself than it ever did, and I would explain it by saying that these voices of Foucault and Nietzsche do not, as do the voices we recognize as, say, "George Eliot" or "William James," suggest that we are listening to ordinary mortals who can express themselves at a level of extraordinary articulation and who do so for the good of their fellows. No. These are the voices of genius uninhibited by fellow-feeling or even the pretense to fellow-feeling. More important still, there is no trace of the peculiar fear often exhibited by genius especially in English and American writing — the fear that the price to be paid for it is a barren alienation from ordinary life. Rather, this is genius whose language does not suppose, within the discursive formations of the "modern" period, any specific audience at all. At most, it expects to be overheard by acolytes or aspirants to genius. Ordinary people are not conjured up by this language as its likely audience. Yet even the grandest of us have a few "spots of commonness," as George Eliot might say, and even aspiring Foucaults and Nietzsches are to be included, during their necessarily more humdrum moments, with those who on a given morning or an afternoon are not thinking of the people around them, possibly including their children, as even theoretically expendable no matter how strongly on other occasions it seems advisable to assert that it would be better if they did not exist in the form bequeathed them. What of ordinary listeners, then, or extraordinary listeners in their ordinary moods? How, to repeat, are we to take these passages?

When writing — or any reading of it — arrives at a point of such intransigence, it becomes impossible, even at the risk of digression, to ignore a collateral issue. I am referring to anxiety, especially strong in Anglo-American cultural and literary criticism, about the dangers of modernist or radical or uncompromising rhetoric. Are we now, isn't civility, isn't civilization itself imperiled by this rhetoric? To expedite matters, let me say that, were I voting on this question, I would vote no. And for the reason, in part, that writing, and the reading of it, should be regarded as no more than one kind of experience among many. It has to be said, of course, that it differs from most other kinds of experience because of the extraordinary degree to which, when it is done with any semblance of genius, it calls for examination and for reexamination, the degree, that is, of its calculated solicitation. For that very reason, however, writing on a page reminds us that it is *not* life on either side of it — before we look at it and when we stop looking at it. Writing exists in a mutually modifying but very confused, accidental, and varying relation to other altogether less calculated, usually less examined, and comparatively messy experiences of life. Even while all critics now pay lip service to the fact that literature is not to be taken literally, the vast majority of them have ingenious ways of ignoring obvious facts about the relation of writing and reading to the passage of time. They confuse the passage of time with the passage of history, with time conceived as an already defined pattern of significance or an imagined pattern of events, and they want the materials and activities of their profession, namely writing and reading, to be related to history in an ideal, direct, glamorous, and even potentially perilous transaction. Critics like to worry about what literature will do to "other people," and it seems all the more powerful to those who, despite professional credentials, do not seem to know how writing is written and how writing is read.

Under these circumstances, what to some must seem especially disturbing is that Foucault's or Nietzsche's sort of writing exhibits here a willful indifference to *any* sort of life that might exist in a tangential relationship to it. The mode of address is oblivious to the claims of ordinary, muddled, time-ridden existence. It is equally oblivious to the values of historical inheritance or perpetuation — values nonetheless recognized, usually with a kind of anguish of constraint, elsewhere in Foucault and very beautifully in Nietzsche's "On the Use and Misuse of History for Life." Both Foucault and Nietzsche exhibit a European, as distinct from any comparable American, enthusiasm for self-eradication. The difference, speaking very crudely, is that on the European side is a tendency to express this enthusiasm in terms of historical apocalypse, while, we will presently see, the American tendency is usually more private, witty, more drifting, so that instead of the prospect of historical apocalypse, the reader is offered something like quotidian self-erasure.

One reason for this difference goes back precisely to an Anglo-American distrust of genius, genius that is not organic with life. And this is in turn related to a complicated distrust of literature itself. As twentieth-century examples, T. S. Eliot, F. R. Leavis, and Lionel Trilling, each in a very different way, sound at times as if literature might indeed imperil civilized life, a view which could only result from some prior idealization of literature and of literary tradition, as if these were uniquely the carriers of life ordered and transmitted to us as a potential creative force. It might be objected that a European like Herbert Marcuse is no less an instance of this feeling than is Leavis, its greatest critical proponent in English, but the very similarity would then point to a characteristic difference. Marcuse offers an exorbitant idealization of literature as a sphere of social negation, while Leavis insists that the values of literature ultimately find their source in what he imagines was once the language of an historical organic community of real English people, who find articulation in such a figure as Bunyan.

In the extreme and more pessimistic versions of this Anglo-American mythology, literature can betray its sacred trust nearly to the degree that it becomes prophetic, visionary, apocalyptic — separated or alienated from the daily. Think, for example, of Lionel

Trilling's classroom drama "On the Teaching of Modern Literature": "I asked them to look into the Abyss, and, both dutifully and
gladly, they have looked into the Abyss, and the Abyss has greeted
them with the grave courtesy of all objects of serious study. . . ."
Or Susan Sontag's compelling anger at the social and prejudicial
power of metaphor, an anger which, however poignantly admirable in anyone then in the grip of illness likely to be fatal, proves in
retrospect not only unpersuasive but historically misleading. In
any event, I obviously cannot share such concerns for the perni-
cious power of literature and, at the same time, insist on demonstrating the thwarting problematics of literary or any other kind of
expression. The concern is further objectionable for its implicit
aspersions on the wit, resourcefulness, and common sense of the
"other" people such critics claim to be worried about. Critics
sometimes like to flatter themselves that they are handling explosive materials far more capably than can the average person. In
fact, most people who read do so with an instinctive awareness that
it is reading that they are doing, that it is an activity quite different
from other activities, and that it is not easily translated into "life,"
whether of love or crime or of what Trilling would call "modernism
in the streets." The point of an earlier book of mine, *A World
Elsewhere*, as the source of its title in *Coriolanus* ought to have
suggested, is that literature by its very nature is prevented from
creating such a world except in certain rare moments and only
*while* it is being read. Constraint is implicit in writing and in the
very act of reading.

Thus it is that Foucault and Nietzsche offer, in my view, an
occasion for participating in the only momentarily exhilarating and
cleansing imagination of self-eradication. Indeed, the excess of
rhetorical power and the lack of caution which makes it so enlivening, on occasion, to read Foucault, and especially Nietzsche, is at
the same time the most telling evidence that each is aware of the
resistance in language itself to any persuasive argument for self-
obliteration. It is in the nature of writing that whatever Foucault
and Nietzsche say will be taken as metaphor and subjected to its
constraints. They know this. They also know that, under attack,
almost any adherent will retreat to the position that what they have
written, what anyone writes, is to some degree a fiction. And so it
is. But that is why they try *not* to be taken metaphorically or
fictionally. They ask to be taken literally, and that, of course, is

most difficult to do. A paradox comes into existence in these cases because something needed to be said nearly beyond language, and even while noting its tribulations in language, it is still that "something" with which we should try to be concerned. It is paradoxical that a writer should call for the obliteration of man as we know him even while exhibiting the need for his approval and approbation, and it is paradoxical that a reader should agree to the necessities of self-obliteration using as his guide the mental faculties and educated feelings that are not only objects to be done away with but the provocation for their destruction. But paradox does not neutralize or cancel out any of the possibilities.

What I am intimating is that the effort to talk about the end of human beings should be taken as a clue to one of their astonishing attributes — the capacity to accept, if only for a moment, the argument that their own kind is an impertinence. The effort is a testament to the power of our nonhuman will and explains in part why Nietzsche is a compelling and necessary figure. When he says that with the end of man "nothing will have happened," the "nothing" will include his having said so, his testimony that this is true, his writing. At last, he is really talking, as is Foucault in his sand image, about erasing his own rhetorical discourse. In that sense the writing is, to look forward to Stevens, "Nothing that is not there and the nothing that is."

If we will only elude the inexorable paradox, if we will only literalize, believe what is being said, and take responsibility for the belief — then it becomes possible to recognize what is in fact more significant than the paradox: to recognize the affirmation of human feeling that is *un*sanctified and *un*sponsored. Those who want merely to stop at the paradox would also want, perhaps without even knowing it, to claim that all human feeling about the end of the human should reinvest itself in the humanistic enterprise of preserving and enhancing traditional ideas of the self, like the Christian enterprise of salvation. Getting excited by the prospect of the end of man — the extinction, again, not of a genetic, biological species but of our invention of the human — is no less noble or ignoble than getting excited by projects for the continuation of man in his present form, enhanced or spiritualized. It could be argued that of the two possibilities, the desire for self-obliteration — with no preconceived image ready to receive whatever is left — reveals a more invigorating impatience with the repressive consequences that attend the work of redemption. We are asked, then, to get excited about a future which will be brought about by our own extinction; we are enjoined by a rhetoric of persuasion the power, even the vestiges of which are also to become extinct. ("There have been eternities when [the human intellect] did not exist; and when it is done for again, nothing will have happened.") Those animals which have before called themselves human will in some new form have become immune to this style of persuasion, immune to style itself, deaf to any language shaped by the pressures of a reality which will by then have been discarded.

This is heady stuff, and it could be contemptible to the extent that the expressed desire for human dissolution is programmatic or ideological, a creation precisely of elements said to be expendable. But of course it is the tendency of ideological thinking that it should be ungrateful to its source. If it is agreed that human beings are a consequence of "the arrangements of knowledge," and not the other way around, what then is to be said of the evidence that human beings have the capacity to wish themselves radically other than what they are? to wish themselves evacuated from those "arrangements of knowledge"? and to do so without the comforts of religion? Is that capacity also to be erased? The very source of the longing to be nonhuman? To ask these questions is not to deprive Nietzsche or Foucault (who harbors a profound admiration for the flexibility of human power) of the assent anyone wants to give them. Rather, it is to encourage a degree of consent that can be transferred to those other writers who, without violating the contract with the human invention of life—and also without religious or humanistic pieties—express the desire for entrance into a life alien to what we now call human. If we are willing, that is, to entertain the extremities of Nietzsche and Foucault, we become immediately enabled to appreciate sporadically similar aspects of Emerson or Thoreau, Pater or Ruskin, Lawrence or Stevens, aspects which have been ignored or suppressed in the interest of accommodating whatever they say to the overall humanistic tendencies in their work and, even more, in the work of their interpreters.

Take as one instance a remarkable sentence in a letter written from London in 1889 by William James to his wife Alice, the more remarkable because James, like his father before him, had good reason, in a curiously similar experience of vastation, to be terrified by the loss of self. "The best thing by far which I saw in Brighton," he wrote, "and a thing the impression of which will perhaps outlast everything else on this trip, was four cuttle-fish (octopus) in the Aquarium. I wish we had one of them for a child— such flexible intensity of life in a form inaccessible to our sympathy." We are asked by this voice not to separate the evocation of the nonhuman from the human, not to separate the appreciation of "intensity" from the assurances of "our sympathy," not, so to speak, to exclude the cuttle-fish from the human family. In the tone is a loving complicity, so that the wish to have a cuttle-fish for a child does not need to be explained, needs scarcely to be remarked on, when coming from a husband to a wife whose four children probably called for a sometimes exasperating expenditure of human sympathy. The sentence is appealing because the wishes it expresses are quite strong ("a thing the impression of which will perhaps outlast everything else on this trip") while being in no way grandstanding or provocative. There is an expressed desire for an extraordinary, nonhuman child, but it is expressed by a man firmly committed to the humanly domestic. What is said here depends casually and thus fully on the understanding of the person who shares the speaker's thoughts, as well as his offspring, his life, his writing. It is as if the dazzling image of a nonhuman "flexible intensity of life" was actually prompted by the assured existence of an equally flexible intensity of domestic and family feeling.

In this small and charming instance James is making contact with nonhuman options in a way found also in certain passages of Emerson, Thoreau, Whitman, and Stevens. It may not be an exclusively American way, but it seems more unabashed and austere in the American instances. There are passages in which they look, more aptly stare, at the possibility of self-dissolution, at the stripping away of human attributes. They do this with an impressive indifference to consequences, without apologies or extenuations, without bribes offered to the shocked or disturbed reader, none of those reassurances that Wordsworth feels compelled to give to himself and to us. No matter how wonderfully strange the given moment in *The Prelude*, he tends tiresomely to intrude the cautionary note, as if all the power in the writing were for the utilitarian purpose of building up one acceptable human faculty or another. The American instances are different. American writing is full of compulsive and also inadvertent imitation, of artificialty—Cooper being the exemplification—which exerts a pressure of accommodation on visionary moments. So that passages of the kind I am discussing do indeed carry the sounds and signs of the writer's commitment to human forms already shaped by earlier literature. But it is also the case that those evidences of compliance are, in the Thomistic sense, mere accidents, part of the necessity of writing under the aegis of unavoidable tradition. Or, as in Melville, Hawthorne, Mark Twain, they are a necessity that excites the most sophisticated kind of counterliterary play. These acts of audacity, like the play of vernacular and obscenity against refinement of diction, are gestures that dispel the Wordsworthian fear of genius, of separation, of losing touch with ordinary humanity.

The most obvious example of this American audacity—the famous passage in Emerson's *Nature* where he claims to be transformed into a transparent eyeball—will for my purposes also be the best; it has been made so familiar by literary commentary that it needs to have its strangeness restored:

> Standing on the bare ground—my head bathed in the blithe air and up-lifted into infinite space—all mean egotism vanishes. I become a transparent eyeball; I am nothing; I see all; the currents of the Universal Being circulate through me; I am part or parcel of God. The name of the nearest friend sounds then foreign and accidental; to be brothers, to be acquaintances, master or servant, is then a trifle and a disturbance. I am the lover of uncontained and immortal beauty.

Emerson being who he was and writing when he did, the passage is surrounded by language weighted with the sounds of countervailing social contract. Humans may count as a "disturbance," but the human reader is being socially courted nonetheless. Even so, the passage is uncorrupted by any promise that the experience it describes will be good or useful to the conduct of social arrangements or even to daily life. No wonder Emerson in this mood has resisted all attempts at translation or utility. Some people ice skate, or their children do, and without much trouble at least a few of them can expect to share with the boy in *The Prelude* the whirling out of the self into the world of mysterious sounds and visions. But who expects to repeat the Emersonian experience, or even to imagine the experience, while standing on a plot of bare ground? The passage does not call even for emulation: no metaphoric coordinates are proposed within which this "eye" or "transparent eyeball" could be negotiated into some more familiar or usable shape. Emerson insists that man and not-man are simultaneous states, like the "occult relation between man and vegetable" mentioned a little further on in *Nature,* or like the vision in the later and shorter essay called "Nature": "We talk of deviations from natural life, as if artificial life were not also natural. The smoothest curled courtier in the boudoirs of a palace has an animal nature, rude and aboriginal as a white bear, omnipotent to its own ends and is directly related, there amid essences and billet-doux, to Himmaleh mountain chains and the axis of the globe."

To repeat, this is an inquiry into those passages where human beings are eradicated or temporarily displaced or transformed into shapes not recognizably human; and, more significantly, it is an inquiry into what human readers can make of such passages. So far, I have been concerned with the degree to which writing can register these extraordinary occurrences either with ideological exhilaration, as in Foucault and Nietzsche, or, as in William James and Emerson, with an exhilaration that exists in a kind of gap or interlude within the ordinary, nonideological movement of life—of life imagined, that is, as if it were not less but, because extemporized, immeasurably *more* than the result merely of some "arrangement of knowledge." Emerson and Nietzsche are therefore different from one another, but neither—and this is the important point—will participate in the tradition by which self-eradication is a mere prelude to the reentry of an enhanced self into already existing "arrangements of knowledge." Whether it be Emerson or Nietzsche, a nonideological process or an ideological one, it is presumably possible to experience such an interlude without calling for any of the religious and humanistic sanctions at work in the life around it and without contributing to these sanctions. It is possible to confer value on moments of transformation or dissolution without looking ahead toward a narrative of fulfillment. Instead, the moment is endowed with something as vague as wonder or beauty, cleansed of the desire to translate these into knowledge already arranged or even in prospect of being so.

Why is it important that this aspect in literature be isolated and described? Not, as far as I am concerned, so that anyone may be persuaded one way or another about the desirability of exterminating the inherited self. The issue, rather, is the way in which the human voice, the human presence, affirms itself in literature even in the *act* of imagining the end of it. Literary criticism operates under a still nearly universal assumption that the human presence is a humanistic one. The possibility of being a human while at the same time *not* being one, of looking on a landscape from which the human presence has been banished, and of enjoying all this without even characterizing the enjoyment by such a word as "deprivation"—this is something criticism has never sufficiently recognized in any direct or assertive way. Trained to read books and film and the dance—before the advent of Balanchine and the final acceptance of his unique genius—as if the question of human presence, humanistically and therefore narrativistically enacting itself, was not really a question at all, most critics then respond to the absence of that human presence as something lamentable, or insist, often against the evidence in the writing, that in fact it has to be "there." Though the acquirements of selfhood may be treated with exuberant hostility, as in the novels and poetry of Lawrence, it is nearly always assumed, except by a critic as resourceful as Leo Bersani in *A Future for Astyanax*, that the difficulties this entails for the reader are resolved by translating them into programs for human improvement. And where, as in Stevens, there is an acknowledged reduction to the so-called First or primary or reduced Idea, there has been a reluctance to believe that some of his best poems enact a drama in which the human will remains unactivated by this reduction. Very often in Stevens the human will feels so little menace in reduction tht it does not even exhibit that self-regarding fear which, in Schopenhauer, needs to be overcome if one is to experience the sublime. (In the process of that experience, as Schopenhauer describes it, a human being becomes conscious of objects hostile to the expression of the will. But "through a free and conscious transcendence of the will and the knowledge relating to it," he is then able to contemplate these objects passively and without fear, "raised above himself, his willing and all willing.")

As I read Stevens's poetry, much of it does not finally show the anxieties about the human presence or the necessity for assertions of the human will that are central in Harold Bloom's account of it, both in various essays and in *Wallace Stevens: The Poems of Our Climate*. I bring Bloom into the argument of this paper not primarily to question his readings of Stevens, but because he is a brilliant example of how the idea of the human is more powerfully assertive even in highly sophisticated interpretations of literature than in literature itself. Criticism, with its emphasis on structures that must develop rather than recede, apparently finds it nearly impossible to recognize the quite casual way in which literature calls us sometimes to witness the disappearance of the human. Precisely because Bloom is regarded as an avant-garde critic, he is an especially instructive illustration of the persistence in contemporary theory of the critical problem I have been addressing. His reputation for being difficult, innovative, and courageous obscures the evidence that he is also deeply conservative.

In fact, his exploratory willingness, his avidity in locating points of extreme self-doubt or dissolution in poetry, recoils on itself in the direction of his humanistic, sometimes sentimentally humanistic convictions. So that while he does refer to a stoicism and to a remarkable degree of psychic repression in Stevens, he nonetheless always assumes that, failing the intercession of the human will, the process of reduction will lead inevitably to what he calls "the reductive fallacy": that "the ultimate truth about us is, by definition, the worst that can be said about us," that we arrive at a place of "destruction," "ruin," the "worst." Since this is humanly intolerable, reductiveness is instead imagined as a sort of spring which, pushed down to a point where it touches the root nerve of the will, then recoils, projecting us into a creative upward movement which reconstitutes the self and the world. Most people like to think in this way about literature and about life. It is apparently a necessary way to think, and it unquestionably saves us from despair to be assured that the worst returns to laughter. However, reduction need not be thought of as loss or deprivation but as exploration and gain, and in any case moral suasion has nothing to do with the kind of reduction that promises a world prior to human presence and subsequent to it, a world in which the issue even of dependence so important in Schopenhauer—are we dependent on it? is it dependent on us?—is temporarily annulled.

We catch glimpses of such a world, for example, in Emerson's "Fate," where he observes that "We cannot trifle with this reality, this cropping out in our planted gardens, of the core of the world," or in the *Journals* for 1847 where he says that "we wish to get the

highest skill of finish, an engraver's educated finger, determination
to an aim—and then—to let in mania, ether, to take off the
*individual's interference* [my italics] and let him fly as with thunderbolt." Nor can a process of reduction when inexorably linked to
some form of redemption as both cause and justification embrace
the daring of writers more equivocating than is Emerson, like
Ruskin, with his sporadic desire to see the universe unpeopled and
himself invisible. Disputing a letter addressed by Carlyle to Emerson, he wrote:

> In the beginning of the Carlyle-Emerson correspon-
> dence, edited with too little comment by my dear friend
> Charles Norton, I find at page 18 this—to me entirely
> disputable, and to my thought, so far as undisputed,
> much blameable and pitiable, exclamation of my mas-
> ter's: "Not till we can think that here and there one is
> thinking of us, one is loving us, does this waste earth
> become a peopled garden." My training, as the reader
> has perhaps enough perceived, produced in me the
> precisely opposite sentiment. *My* times of happiness
> have always been when *nobody* was thinking of me. . . .
> My entire delight was in observing without being myself
> noticed,—if I could have been invisible, all the better.

In fact, the tradition Bloom describes, and in which Emerson or,
say, Ruskin would be uncomfortable, belongs a good deal more to
quite other writers than those he favors, writers ranging from
Dante to Eliot who validate the processes of reduction by resort to
terms derived from religious exercises for the salvation of the soul.
Obviously Bloom does not subscribe to this tradition, but his
vocabulary and his procedures implicate him in it. His critical
method is to some extent a trope of the processes of descent-
ascent, and it necessarily prefers poems and interpretations that
reveal a crisis in the spiritual, the psychic, and poetic career of the
writer. The poetic drama of reduction or dissolution to "firstness"
becomes thereby an indication of such a crisis and not, as it easily
might be, an expression—momentary in its effect, exploratory in
its aim, possibly enlivening—of how it is for certain human beings
to envision human disappearance. Bloom is always and everywhere a literary critic dedicated to the energies at work in language, and if he is also a humanist it is to ask that humanism in

poetry be confirmed in the movements of language. When he finds in the language evidences of humanistic crises, he then, inevitably, also expects to find evidences of what he calls a "crossing." "A crossing within a crisis poem, like a poetic crisis, is a process of disjunction, a leaping of the gap between one kind of figurative thinking and another."

In its adduced psychological or aesthetic consequences, however, a "crossing," with all its Freudian implications, is little different from what in an older, religious vocabulary would be described as the struggle for wholeness, for salvation, for the reconstitution of the self. And if this is not found in the particular poem, then the poem is placed by Bloom in the gravitational pull of other poems where it can be found. Such an account of poetic processes is essentially what could be extrapolated from that religious poetry in which, having descended "Into the world of perpetual solitude,/World not world, but that which is not world"—to quote Eliot in one of his more tiresome puns about movement and abstention from movement in a world that whirls— it is imagined that one ascends into a new form potentially salvageable and more worthy. This sequence goes back from Eliot through Milton to Spenser of Book II of the *Faerie Queene* to Dante and the Bible, and it has sexual analogues, again out of Dante, in the treatment of buggery in Lawrence and, both more wittily and superficially, in Mailer. This latter mode could be called, to quote Eliot on Baudelaire, "an attempt to get into Christianity by the back door." Bloom has his reasons for not admiring Eliot, and I link the two only to dramatize how his "crises" and "crossings" commit him to a reading of poetry which, on crucial occasions, is marred by his insistence on a restitutive process little different, in the dogmatic urgency of its phrasing, from what could be expected in the poetry of Christian redemption. This dogmatism emerges most clearly when a poem cannot convincingly be shown to dramatize within itself a "crossing" or an assertion, such as is given in "An Ordinary Evening in New Haven," of the poetic will in response to deprivation. Take, as a conveniently brief example, "The Death of a Soldier":

> Life contracts and death is expected,
> As in a season of autumn.
> The soldier falls.

He does not become a three-days personage,
Imposing his separation,
Calling for pomp.

Death is absolute and without memorial,
As in a season of autumn,
When the wind stops,

When the wind stops and, over the heavens,
The clouds go, nevertheless,
In their direction.

Bloom offers a paraphrase of the poem which adheres strictly to the notion of the First Idea, or rather to this particular version of it:

But what has the First Idea, or an idea of Firstness to do with the poem "The Death of A Soldier"? Stevens seeks what is not possible, in a tradition that goes back to Homer yet never has gone beyond Homer. He seeks to see earliest what the death of a soldier is. His reduction is fourfold:

(1) The soldier falls expectedly, in and by seasonal contraction; this is primal *ethos*, the soldier's character as it is autumn's, and so a limitation of meaning.

(2) The soldier is not and has no part in Christ; he will not rise, after three days, separated from the common fate and requiring celebration.

(3) Any death, by synecdoche, is as final in itself and beyond language as is an autumnal moment of stasis.

(4) That is, any death is also without consequence, in the context of natural sublimity; for us, below the heavens, there is stasis, but the movement of a larger intentionality always goes on above the heavens.

To begin with, this account proposes a clarity of movement that the poem itself does not exhibit. Instead, the voice drifts away, soliciting us as it does so, from the narrative and argumentative assertiveness of the first two stanzas. Beginning with line 8, the poem passes into something like reverie, and though the speaker retains some of his exacting economy, as in his careful "nevertheless," it is by now at the service of developments that cannot be talked about with the finality of such earlier phrasing as "Death is absolute and without memorial." Consider what happens to the phrase "as in a season of autumn." At first it sounds like a clarifying illustration of the inevitable "contraction" of the seasons, of human life, and especially of the life of a soldier. But then the phrase is repeated, and with a qualification that releases it from its initial relatively inert metaphoric function. What was a clarification turns out to have been only a partial glimpse of something, "As in a season of autumn," becomes "as in a season of autumn,/When the wind stops," and then becomes something still more attenuated, "as in a season of autumn,/When the wind stops,/ . . . and, over the heavens,/The clouds go, nevertheless,/In their direction." As if by introspective meandering behind the ostensible forward movement, and prompted by repetition of earlier phrasing, what was a metaphor for the contraction of human life comes gradually to include, really to induce its opposite—a movement in the heavens that has a life of its own. By that peculiar process of reiteration so characteristic of Stevens's poetry, what was a signifier, the season of autumn, becomes the signified of the poem. We thus are encouraged to forget any story of human death as, imperceptibly, we find ourselves within a movement that has no story; we are forgiven time in a prospect of space.

The reader is brought to a change and shift of attention here by the maneuverings of line and by echoings that lull rather than alert attention. If the results can be called powerful, it is a power of restraint on any human urge to *figure* in the scene. Stevens has phased the poem into a mood wherein the human will, instead of registering its supposedly inherent resistance to self-dispersion, simply relaxes into it. Any willful assertion in the second half of the poem would sound merely obtuse, impertinent, and boorish; so would any reminder that we have been reprieved from willfulness. Instead, we experience a stasis on the ground, as the wind stops, and simultaneously the aspect of clouds moving "nevertheless," oblivious to our local sense of things. Bloom objects always to the loss of human will, and where the loss does occur, as here, where the human recedes in the presence of powers independent of it, he tends, as do nearly all critics, to correct the balance by exerting his own will in and on the poem. This often takes the form of engineered readings of particular words. In this case he does odd things with the phrase "over the heavens." It is taken to mean "above the heavens," surely so forced a reading that a larger motive or need impels it. By placing the moving clouds "above the heavens"—whatever that could mean—he is able to ascribe to them what he calls a "larger intentionality" and, more important, to make it inaccessible to the poet and the reader. But it is only a "larger" intentionality for those who want to assume that the human will *should* somehow have been activated by it and competed with it. If the human will really is in recession, then, so far as Bloom is concerned, it may participate in the peculiar effects on the ground but not in anything going on "above" the heavens. This may sound like a small distinction, but it is in fact a central and major one. If the human will is not to assert itself in the poem, then for Bloom it thereby deprives itself, in a "reduced" world, of contact with the sublime. But why cannot the sublime be experienced precisely by the relaxed indifference of the will? That is what the poem, like many others of Stevens, aspires to: a represented and enhanced experience wherein everything on the ground and "over"—that is, "across"—the heavens is occurring all at once, an experience wherein this simultaneity is rendered in a manner beautifully placid, cleansed of contradiction and friction. The clouds need have nothing to do with "the movement of a larger intentionality" but rather with the marvelous absence both of "larger intentionality" and of any dependence on the smaller intentionality of the human will. They move "nevertheless," and it is their freedom from having to mean anything that awes and pleases us. Meanwhile, the human presence, asserted earlier in a phrase like "three-days personage," is, by implication, dissolved into the scene, like the dead soldier.

The poem eschews those anticipatory connotations implicit in all humanistic conceptions of reductiveness—the conviction that it is preliminary to the will's effort at reconstitution. Structurally the poem is identical to "The Snow Man" and the many other poems by Stevens in which, as James Guetti points out, "the exhaustion of the more rational imaginative powers seems always . . . an exercise of mind that readies us to participate in a different sort of perception and energy." In Bloom's account there is a kind of desperation to locate "crossings," evidence of will in the form of rhetorical shifts. To the point, indeed, where he sounds as if he is ready to give up on the poem entirely, though not before hearing an "undersong" which I cannot be alone in finding inaudible. Commenting on his paraphrase, he remarks that it

> omits what matters about the poem, which is rhetorical gesture, tonal *askesis*, dignity of a minimal *pathos*, excluding lament. Yet what it most omits is the poem's undersong, which is its *logos* or crossing. Rhetorically, the poem intimates that any such earliest seeing of the soldier's death is dehumanizing, intolerable, not to be sustained. This brief poem is almost all *ethos*, all contraction; the human in us demands more of a poem, for us, and where pathos is so excluded a death-in-life comes which is more that of the poem's shaper, speaker, reader than it could have been of the fictive soldier before he fell.

From so disciplined a critic, this is a remarkable break in decorum. The soldier is called "fictive," but he is nonetheless suddenly endowed with a real historical life. And why? So that he might testify against the validity of the poem and its author. This is not so much a reading as a plea "for us," on behalf of "the human in us," in the soldier, and in Bloom. His prose answers the plea denied by the poem; it supplies the pathos or will to power over fate to which the poem refuses to rise. In fact, it is to concede too much to say even that the pathos is absent; it is absent only if it is assumed that it ought to be there. Instead, the poem asks us to countenance a refusal of grief; it refuses to grieve for a dead soldier, and, more significantly, it refuses to grieve for our lost selves. We become transparent to the world, Emerson's great eyeball.

Stevens, it need hardly be said, is not finding some benign way to carry out the project of Nietzsche or Foucault. Rather, with Emerson, he shows that freedom is one of the characteristics of Fate. The poem itself is the visible and audible evidence of that freedom. The performance of the poem is a signature of human will and power that affirms its presence in the very act of absenting itself. For him, as for his American predecessors, deconstruction is a given; if it is something preliminary to a reconstituion of the self, it is at others a necessary stage of a process in which the self is a passive observer of its own alternately crescive and transparent possibilities. "I am a victim of neurasthenia and of the sense of the hollowness and unreality that goes with it," William James wrote to his friend G. H. Howison, a professor of philosophy at the University of California, and it could be said that some verison of this, as an enhancement of experience and of thinking, however painful and terrifying, is to be found in the other American writers I have mentioned. James's "will to believe" proceeds from the necessity not for affirmed selfhood and most assuredly not, from the author of *A Pluralistic Universe*, for unity. It comes instead from the more basic desire simply to stay alive, facing into the "pit of insecurity beneath the surface of life." Against the doubt of existence, one does not posture a "self" but only a "belief," and not even a belief in the self so much as in the will to believe in life. "Believe that life *is* worth living," he adivsed, "and your belief will help create the fact." So far as any human self goes, it may be willed into and willed out of existence without loss of consciousness or loss of subjective life, and any act of belief, in the self or in its dissolution, is no more than a modification in the stream of thought. Quoting from Benjamin Paul Blood, an American philosopher, poet, and mystic who, in 1874, wrote *The Anaesthetic Revelation and the Gist of Philosophy*—a book expressing a belief in pluralism based on the use of anaesthetics—James allowed into his own text an eloquence rhapsodic even for him: " 'Reason is but one item in the mystery; and behind the proudest consciousness that ever reigned, reason and wonder blushed face to face. The inevitable stales, while doubt and hope are sisters. Not unfortunately the universe is wild,—game-flavored as a hawk's wing. Nature is miracle all; the same returns not save to bring the different. The slow round of the engraver's lathe gains but the breadth of a hair, but the difference is distributed back over the whole curve, never an instant true,—ever not quite.' " It is fitting that as James came to the end of his life, one of his last essays, "A Pluralistic Mystic," was a tribute to his friend Blood, at the conclusion of which he writes, "let my last word, then, speaking in the name of intellectual philosophy, be *his* word:—'There is no conclusion. What was concluded, that we might conclude in regard to it? There are no fortunes to be told, and there is no advice to be given.—Farewell!' " If this is an echo of Emerson in "The Poet" or "Nature" or "Experience," it is an echo that reaches toward the last poem of Wallace Stevens, a poem called "Of Mere Being," where he celebrates "The palm at the end of the mind,/Beyond the last thought."

# CHIEF

by MICHAEL S. HARPER

from PLOUGHSHARES

*nominated by* PLOUGHSHARES, *Kelly Cherry and Philip Schultz*

*For those who are neither hero of myth nor witness to history:*
*remember all life is holy.*

In the year of the blizzard
in the month of February
I have traipsed up the middle
of Lexington Avenue, a spectacular
middle passage in the snow
to my own poetry reading:
James Wright, Philip Levine,
each having written about a horse,
neither a hero of myth
nor witness to history alone,
nor a palamino looking for a drink.

I could be water, or fire,
and on earth, which is covered with snow,
there is a bar where the air is filled with snow:
the air from my lungs billows  in the fog
of my own friendly breath
as I walk down into the subway
into a labyrinthine holiday of dreams
and a *book of nightmares*
which I carry under my arm
signed by the author, Galway Kinnell,
after his introduction of Etheridge Knight
and me, a high contrast in poetics,
and the politics of light, and the smell
of the one horse I did ride
in Central Park after a girl.

Chief is my hour and my dark horse:
he does not belong to me, or to Crazy Horse,
who was caught by a bullet or a noose
because he was too quick for the camera,
the transcendant Lakota, Enchanted One,
whose name leaps from enchantment
to a horse eating in the snow.
One searches for the meaning of the railroad
and the buffalo, and the hidden names of the horse,

In a blizzard, under martial law, and alone
in Providence, holed up in one office on George St.,
no easy street, and no snowplow, and no horse
to tread the rudders of a delivery truck
on the milk route, or the ice-wagon of my childhood,
or the stubble at the end of my mistress's hand
in the Central Park waterway of the horse.
A mixture of oats and honey, raw carrot
and a moving picture camera of children
riding in the snow. I have loved this image
of a horse running over the plains of Scott
Momaday's "Plainview: 1 & 2"
and the detention of a horse in a mindless barn
of a friend, and once for the ridden part

of a season of horse in a park
where no child was the air of a poetry
reading, or the middle passage of survival,
which put name on the horse,
a camera on the man who rides the image,
and a hero as a witness to the woman
who rides him.

# AND THE SCREAM

by STEPHEN BERG

from ANTAEUS

*nominated by Jorie Graham and Michael Ryan*


The thirtyish, Irish, red-nosed carpenter
who works for Coonan—he rehabs houses up here—
is already half-stoned on beer
before eight and chases his son past my front window,
screaming at him, the kid's glasses
thick as my little finger,
bobbling on his nose.
Thin, steady, grayish drizzle, gray sky,
long smudges yellowing the sky,
clouds darkening the street abruptly,
Pat and Jack Laurent's house gloomy
across from mine (they're away), even the embroidery
of lace curtains, the high-
arched Victorian doors a failure.
That boy, disappearing between houses,
reminds me of when I
punched my whole arm through a glass door
between the dining room and kitchen
(the maid wouldn't leave it open)
and gashed my elbow so it bled on the floor
and kept bleeding big splashes and wouldn't stop
and my mother's or the maid's or my
scream seemed to echo everywhere. That boy.
From this living room one night, in the dark,
I watched his father screaming,
waving a beer bottle, poising it
above his mother who lay in a slip in bed in their bright
  bedroom,

four bulbs in a glassless ceiling fixture making it too bright.
Nobody would call it poetry.
When I leaf through serious books, though, I see
 blindings, suicides, revelations,
families and blood are what we want, as always.
For example, my mother tells me
(we're face-to-face in her living room,
she will not look at me when she speaks)
her mother had to pick lice from her scalp when she was ten,
her Christian Scientist brother, a fine pianist,
refused help from a real doctor so at twenty-six he died of TB,
coughing blood into a bucket, while she watched. Poor. Crazy.
And so on, and so on, and therefore—
incomplete sentences, true,
sketches merely,
like watching a scream through glass, as I have twice lately,
oneself filling-in the detail of hearing,
plus all the other crap: motives, sadnesses,
stupidities, money, sex, someone always dying.
What I need to say now is—
but it's on paper, which can make a man feel silly—
Yes, merely a sketch, that's it,
that's us, not tragic, unredeemable, half-known animals,
and the scream, the scream.

## THE GARDENS

by MARY OLIVER

from THE GEORGIA REVIEW

*nominated by* THE GEORGIA REVIEW *and Mary Peterson*

1

Moon rose
full and without
compromise through the good
garden of leaves,
here and there
stars rode in flickering
slicks of water
and for certain
the burly trees
hunched toward each other,
their dark mantles
like the fur of animals
touching. It was
summer on earth
so the prayer
I whispered was to no
god but another
creature like me.
*Where are you?*
The wind stood still.
Lightning flung
its intermittent flares;
in the orchard
something wandered
among the windfalls
licking the skins,
nuzzling the tunnels,

the pockets of seeds.
*Where are you?* I called
and hurried out
over the silky
sea of the night, across
the good garden of branches,
leaves, water, down
into the garden
of fire.

2

This skin you wear
so neatly, in which
you settle
so brightly
on the summer grass, how
shall I know it?
You gleam
as you lie back
breathing like something
taken from water,
a sea creature, except
for your two human legs
which tremble
and open
into the dark country
I keep dreaming of. How
shall I touch you
unless it is
everywhere?
I begin
here and there,
finding you,
the heart within you,
and the animal,
and the voice; I ask
over and over
for your whereabouts, trekking
wherever you take me,
the boughs of your body

leading deeper into the trees,
over the white fields,
the rivers of bone,
the shouting,
the answering, the rousing
great run toward the interior,
the unseen, the unknowable
center.

# ON A DRYING HILL

by THOM GUNN

from THE SOUTHERN REVIEW

*nominated by Helen Handley*

Yvor winters met me at the Southern Pacific railway depot in Palo Alto on a hot, dry afternoon in early September of 1954. He took me to the room he had obtained for me, where I left my luggage, and then drove me, by way of the Stanford campus, to his home, where I was to have dinner with him, a dinner he would make himself, as he was alone there that day with his young son, Danny.

I had been crossing the country by train for the last few days, and had got little sleep. I was there to start a year as one of the fellows in creative writing at Stanford University, where I would be working directly under Winters. I had just turned twenty-five, and I had published a small collection of poems a few months before, but I was too shy to show it to Winters until the following summer.

He knew nothing about me — and there is no reason he should have — except for the handful of poems I had submitted in my application for the fellowship. As for me, it was not entirely my fault that I knew almost as little about him. Neither his poetry nor his criticism would have been easy to come by in the Britain I had just left (astonishingly little modern American poetry had been published there at that date), and I had read only one of his essays and none of his poems. I had applied for the fellowship more or less blind. Donald Hall, one of the fellows for the previous year, whom I had known in England, had encouraged me to try for it; I had wanted, chiefly, to see something of America; and all I had subsequently learned about Winters was that he had a certain reputation for ferocity, though I did not know what that reputation was based on.

I didn't find him ferocious. He drove me round the Stanford campus in his ramshackle car, briefly identifying certain buildings, and out among the Californian hills of late summer, burned down to a gold from which the heat comes at you harder it seems than it does from the sky, and finally to his home, where he made me comfortable in the yard (half-orchard, it appeared), giving me a drink and then dinner with wine; and I found him merely rather silent, a man of few words. He didn't believe in small talk, whereas I apparently did. My mind somewhat dulled by my journey, I suddenly found myself chattering into a vacancy. I felt at a disadvantage.

He was about fifty-four. He was by now a portly man, and was aware of it: against an assertion in a student's essay that the "thin men of Haddam" were thin because of their wisdom, he wrote that if that were so there was small chance of wisdom left for *him*. He wore glasses and smoked a pipe, and both of these adjuncts served to mask a face that was not in any case volatile. Pleased or displeased, he was most of the time thoughtfully of the same expression; his shabby suit, too, always had the same unpressed demeanor. Almost any photograph taken of him in his last two decades shows accurately what he looked like. It was his voice that was remarkable, though I don't think I noticed it until I started taking his classes. He never played tricks with it, and in fact he habitually used a measured tone in conversation, but it was a voice which an actor would have envied, as you noticed as soon as he started to read poetry aloud. It was deep but capable of great variety in its modulation. It has always struck me that the argument of his essay on the audible reading of poetry is a little weakened by the fact that *he* could read poetry in what from anybody else would have been a monotone but from him was a controlled resonance, suggesting large emotions barely held in reserve.

I don't recollect that he read any poetry aloud that evening. After dinner and my unreciprocated attempts at polite conversation, he asked me what poets I especially liked. I said Yeats and Donne, and added Hart Crane and Robert Lowell, two recent discoveries of mine. He grunted. I wasn't able to interpret the grunt.

What followed I can now see as high comedy. Had I heard of Edward Taylor? No, I hadn't. Well, let's see what I made of this. He set before me the poem beginning "View all ye eyes above." I knew that I was not at my most observant, but I certainly wanted to oblige this mysteriously demanding man while being as honest as I could. I read it through and found it closely written. I had a general impression of something reminiscent of the English Metaphysicals, which in my exhaustion pleased me rather as a panorama of distant woodland might have done. I couldn't make out the details, that is, but I liked the familiar idea of trees. What did I think of it, he asked after a suitable lapse of time. Well, I said lamely, it seems very nice. He grunted. I was beginning to find that the grunt was an ambiguous response, not always of appreciation. Did I notice anything unusual about the third and fourth stanzas? The lines blurred: Well, no. He pointed out that the imagery of the one contradicted the imagery of the other, possibly because one of them was unintentionally preserved from an early draft. I was still a romantic, he remarked as he closed the book. The tone was not disparaging; indeed it was good-humored, but I gathered that a romantic was not what he would have chosen me to be.

He asked me if I had heard of Elizabeth Daryush. No — I searched my memory for poets I might have passed over in anthologies, the Merrill Moores, the Viola Meynells, but Elizabeth Daryush — no, I didn't think so. He presented me with another open page. Good, this poem was much shorter — a sonnet, in fact; it was called "Still Life." I read it through. I read it through again. He sucked on his pipe. The poem did seem a bit lacking in substance. Could he possibly be showing me something he *didn't* like? "I don't really see much to it," I ventured. He took that book from me and closed it too. "It is a very funny poem," he remarked with a certain solid patience. So. It was a very funny poem. I had obviously missed something again. As he drove me back to my new bed, I couldn't help feeling that I had failed a test or two most signally. I imagine he felt I had too.

A couple of days later he held a reception for the new fellows in creative writing. I met his wife, Janet Lewis, and found her immediately appealing. I also met numerous former students and was told on at least three occasions that he was a great man, a piece of information — if that is what it was — that I felt inclined to resist.

My first reaction to Winters, then, was that I didn't know how I was going to get through a year of him. The reaction lasted until about the second or third week of classes.

The term started. It was understood that I was to take Winters' creative writing classes for credit and sit in on the other courses he gave; I was also permitted to sit in on other courses in the English Department.

I had come to California armed with a bunch of conclusions that I had arrived at over the previous three or four years. They derived partly from my decade of the twentieth century, partly from my Cambridge education, and partly from my own observation and reading. Many of them implicitly contradicted one another, but I saw no need to reduce them into consistency, since I wanted above all to keep myself open to books and experience — and in particular to poetry and *its* experience — that might present something to me I had not previously envisaged. The first course of Winters' I attended, on "the criticism of poetry," was an immediate shock to my assumptions, in that he set about the systematic demolishing of my favorite twentieth-century poet, Yeats, in ruthless detail. After Yeats the chosen victim was to be Hopkins, not one of my favorite poets but one I certainly respected. A particular characteristic that he attacked in the poetry of each was that of emotion lacking adequate source or motivation in the context. I couldn't help wondering who was to be the arbiter of what was adequate.

I was angry at first and fought him bitterly. I adored Yeats and was grateful to a career which had seemed exemplary to me in showing how a spirit of romanticism could survive, self-correcting and self-nourishing, into the twentieth century. Moreover, Yeats had not been taught to me as part of any curriculum: he had my special affection because I had discovered him for myself. By way of compensation I was offered Bridges, a poet I had never bothered to examine but whom I had been taught to despise. I was sufficiently able to resist the pictorial prettiness and metrical charms of "A Passer-by" but had to admit that I was impressed by the "passionate intellectuality" of "Low Barometer" and "Eros." I was, too, introduced to the sonnets of Tuckerman, of whom I had never heard, and to a poem by George Herbert, "Church Monuments," which seemed new to me, and which I immediately agreed was as good as Winters might care to claim.

This last example somewhat shook me. I had read through Herbert's poetry more than once, but had never noticed this magnificent poem before. Why not? Why had no anthologist noticed it, either? (That it is now included in many anthologies is a direct result of Winters' influence.) Winters' answer, which I found incontrovertible, was that I had missed it because I was looking for something else, the Herbert style. The Herbert style was thought of in terms of Herbert's idiosyncratic characteristics, which reached high excellence in such poems as "The Collar" and "The Board." In looking primarily for the typical, I had missed the untypical, which I had to admit was perhaps the best poem of all.

Compensations, then, began to appear for the degradation of Yeats. There were also certain immediate agreements. I had long liked the Elizabethans. I knew Nashe's few poems well, Raleigh's, and even some of Greville's; Donne had been, after Shakespeare, my chief teacher. So I already shared some of Winters' tastes, and though I liked the ornate and the metaphysical I needed no persuading to also like the plain style. I had assayed sententiae in my own poetry, after all.

Bit by bit the thoroughness of his arguments and the power of his examples started to win me over to much of his thought. The arguments, however, would have been nothing without the fierce love of poetry that lived behind them. That love knew no antithesis between poetry and the workings of reason, a word he used in a larger Renaissance sense rather than in its more limited eighteenth- and nineteenth-century sense. He did not, as Troilus accuses the politic bishop Helenus of doing, merely "fur his gloves with reason": it was not a genteel defense against the discomforts of passion. If Winters found unreason either destructive or dishonest or both, he did so because he knew its power from inside (see his Conradian story "The Brink of Darkness") and he never made the mistake of dismissing it as trivial. Nor, for him, did reason and passion need to be at odds: he was no Houyhnhnm; he taught from his full experience as a poet and reader. In the poetry he most admired — by Valéry or Jonson, for example — passion and reason were strong collaborators, each partaking of the other.

He was a remarkable teacher, persistent, irreverent, and specific, pressing his arguments, sometimes with considerable humor, until they were accepted. (Questions were seldom left open.) Even though much of his teaching involved the attack on reputations that had seemed to me established forever, the attacks were made so as to emphasize and isolate the really worthwhile. Pound says: "the only way to keep the best writing in circulation . . . is by drastic separation of the best from a great mass of writing that has been long considered of value."[1] Winters must have agreed with such a statement, and for him as for Pound the negations were founded on a feeling for poetry that was jealous, uncompromising, and defensive. His practice too was "drastic." Poetry was an art toward which you had to have responsibility; and it was his sense of responsibility that excited his contempt for those he found betraying it by their slipshod writing, by their incoherent thinking, or by their use of it as an exercising ground for the ego. Poetry could be, he emphasized again and again, a more *exact* and *precise* form of writing than any other. He was fond of Pound's dictum, "Poetry should be better written than prose." Above all, poetry was for him a telling of the truth. Crane's words to the Medicine-man in "The Dance" — "Lie to us" — he found especially reprehensible.

His love, his passion for poetry showed clearly enough in his classes. More than one student commented on the fact that in speaking of some poem or passage he particularly admired he was apt to use the uncharacteristic word "haunting." He used it because his mind was literally haunted by certain bits of poetry, of which the power was greater than the intelligence could practically explain. And all of his students more than once heard his voice crack with emotion while reading other people's poetry, from the sheer wonder, it appeared, that something could be done so movingly well. (This from a man with such a declared antipathy to the histrionic.)

Most teachers and critics, even quite perceptive ones, speak about poetry in terms of its subject matter, its ideas, its "themes," and its imagery, as if it were all just a piece of condensed but tuneless prose. Winters was one of the few people I have ever come across who have spoken — spoken at all, let alone intelligibly — about the way meter works and about the way poetic movement (whether in metrical or in free verse) influences poetic meaning.[2] He would discuss, in fact, what actually happens in the sounds of some famous line in a Shakespeare sonnet, attempting perhaps for the first time to describe what has attracted generations of readers. Meter and verse movement, however, were only a small part of what he discussed. He realized that a poem is the sum of components that bear relationships of almost infinite complexity toward each of the other components; the relationships moreover are not static — they vary in relation to the other relationships; and they continue to vary as the poem moves on from line to line. He was fully aware of why it is so difficult to talk accurately and usefully about poetic technique, and yet he found it worth the effort. But he went further: his was an examination of technique that became, ultimately, also an examination of the way in which knowledge is simultaneously discovered and transmitted.

He was not a bully, though he did not suffer fools gladly. He certainly believed he had come as close to a description of what poetry is and can be, and of the way it works, as is possible. (It is notable that the illogic of the visionary was largely excluded from that description and so was implicitly classed with the work of the charlatan or the self-deluded from which it is sometimes difficult to distinguish it.) But he proceeded largely by means of persuasion and demonstration rather than of dogmatic assertion, and though his arguments were rigorous in detail he was always prepared to discuss the views of the opposition. He respected the alert opposer more than the inert disciple. As I have said, I argued with him from the start and was always ready, often too ready, to disagree. There were times, later, when I half compared myself to the difficult army recruit in the Hollywood movie who earns the liking of the ferocious sergeant in direct proportion to his earlier recalcitrance.

When his friends and students had called him a great man, I had not realized that the word *great* was a favorite term of his. Poetry was divided into individual poems which were either great or not; by extension, their authors were also either great or not. It was a strangely loose word (surely it just meant "very good"?) for such a strict thinker. What is more, though the word would have been clear enough once you became accustomed to its application, in that it was meant to indicate a carefully assembled canon of acceptable poems, the canon became shorter as the years passed, and both individual great poems and great poets got eliminated from it. Of course, it is only human to change one's mind, but Winters' mind-changing was hard on some of those who got demoted and confusing to those who witnessed the demotions.

But this is to look ahead. In the autumn of 1954 I moved, in any case, from extreme distrust to trust, coming to realize, in sudden humility, that I had a lot to learn from the man. (Whether I came to use the word *great* of him I do not remember.) At the very least, he was introducing me to a number of good poems that I had not read, French as well as English and American, and this in itself was enough reason for gratitude. But further, he had a closely worked out conception of the way art fits into the human universe. If you are given the chance of going to school under a man possessing an extraordinary mind, who has attempted to completely assess the consequences of all his assumptions, you would be a fool not to take advantage of it, even if the risk were of ending up a slavish follower.

Perhaps it was the creative writing classes that really won me over to him. The whole notion of "creative writing" and of taking classes in it was new to me. Poetry was something that I, like all the other poets in history, had taught myself up to now. But since I had come here as a creative writing fellow, I was supposed to take the course.

The classes were tiny and informal. They took place in Winters' office, and consisted of the two current poetry fellows and any others he had found promising on the basis of work they had shown him; we were seldom more than seven in all. New poems were usually given in to him earlier in the day, and consisted of single copies which he first read aloud and then passed around the group, an awkward procedure. He would comment on the poem himself first and then the others would add their comments, and the discussion would start. It was a loose arrangement, and sometimes he would ask someone else in the group to open the discussion.

In my arrogance, I was at first astonished at the usefulness of what was said, by him especially. His insights were always useful, whether you were able to work on them or not. He had the knack — the genius perhaps — of divining your intentions, even if the poem was so obscurely or clumsily carried out that those intentions had become hidden. He habitually showed sympathy and patience. His criticism was specific and helpful; it was of the sort that went: "Well, if this part of the poem doesn't work, you could try doing such-and-such," so that if such-and-such wasn't appropriate at least your mind had started recreating something you had assumed you could do no more to.

He would sit facing us in his morris chair, gently sucking his pipe, a genial and informal teacher very little distinguishable from a friend. The informality allowed him a much greater inconsistency than he showed in the more public arena of the larger classes. He would often cite the virtues of poems by people he would seem to have largely repudiated in print — Crane, Frost, or Williams. When he became thus informal, when it came down to poetry in the process of being made, he returned to the more open mind of his youth. Discovering that I had read nothing by Williams, he urged me to read him through as soon as possible. Once, of a poem I wrote about Merlin (we favored that kind of subject in the fifties), he remarked that, much as he liked it on the whole, it lacked in detail both Crane's sharpness of image and Cunningham's sharpness of conceptual language. Crane's line about the mammoth turtles, for instance, had remained for him a touchstone of the alive bright image through over twenty-five years. I even knew his feeling to run completely contrary to his printed statements: he once said to me of Robert Lowell something like, "Lowell *has* it, you know — for all his faults he is a poet; damn it he can write," a remark that any reader and most students of Winters will find nothing less than astonishing. It was perhaps a weakness in his method that he would have been able to find no place for it in his published criticism.

He was, above all, a brilliant teacher because of his knowledge of what is *behind* a poem, what makes a poet want to write in the first place and thus separates him from a prose-writer. It is something many critics cannot grasp, that — what? — sense of urgency and of intensity, of being possessed by the subject, however apparently quiet that subject may seem. For, as he well knew, this intensity (and he might have disliked my word) has nothing to do with melodrama or disproportion of view. He could find it even behind a short piece by Barnabe Googe or an epigram by J. V. Cunningham. They were in the plain style, yes, but they were not just rhyming prose. Thus one of his unkindest epithets was "journalistic." For him, most of Auden's later poems were simply journalistic, neither language nor rhythm raising the writing above that of superficial prose.

Two other words I remember him using to express reservations about poetry were "soft" and "gentle."[3] Not for him "the meek, the white, the gentle," but then he had no wish to be  Tom o' Bedlam either. He had a predisposition on behalf of the hard, the brave, the reticent, and the stoical. Such is not really surprising if you keep his published work in mind, whether poetry or prose.

To such a man, and to such a poet — for I had soon read his collected poems — I was glad to spend a year of apprenticeship, fancying myself as the modern counterpart of some young painter in Florence apprenticed in the workshop of a master painter. Indeed Winters was a master of his workshop too: I think he saw his job in these classes as being not simply to improve the writing of various students but to help us become "great poets."

Since like many another I hoped to join the company of English (and American) poets, I certainly didn't wish to oppose him there. I hoped I was tough enough to use what he had to offer me and still where necessary resist him, that is without becoming an imitator. Many others of his students, before and after, did and were to keep their poetic identities intact — Donald Hall, Edgar Bowers, Philip Levine, Robert Pinsky, Alan Stephens, Scott Momaday, Kenneth Fields, and so on — some even coming in the end to completely reject him. But all of us learned from him, even the most reluctant.

For some of his students his formulations provided a refuge, a harmonious world where everything had already been decided in accordance with certain rules. It became a temporary or lifelong asylum for those who might otherwise have fallen into the arms of a church or a political party. The attraction lay in the logical *completeness* with which he had worked out his ideas, and such students became disciples in a literal sense, limiting themselves to another man's world; but, as my friend Ted Tayler remarked at the time, another man's world, however wonderful, is always smaller than the world you can discover for yourself. I had seen the whole thing happen before, among the students of F. R. Leavis at Cambridge. But on the whole I find Winters' disciples a much humaner and better-tempered lot than Leavis'.

It was not only the ideas of course (it never is), but also the man himself that attracted them, as he did me as well. It is no loose Freudianism to say that for many students he was a father figure. He even told me about one of them who asked his approval of a prospective suitor. He didn't relish such a role at all; it embarrassed him. One thing is certain: he was not interested in having a following, in the acquisition of power; if he had wanted power, he could easily have found some means to get it many years earlier, but it, like reputation, was of no interest to him.

The complete disinterestedness, the modesty, the lack of anything self-serving, only made his character more seductive and his personality more inadvertently charming. It is difficult to explain his diffident sweet-naturedness to those who know his personality rather through the prickly and often eccentric footnotes of *Forms of Discovery*. His manner could be, in Marianne Moore's word for it, "bearish"; it could be brusque, intolerant, even brutal; it could also be generous, good-humored, and relaxed. His wit was quiet and disarming. But he had to feel at ease with you first.

The next summer came round, and I had finished my three terms at Stanford. Some of us asked him out to dinner, but he did not like eating out and instead he and Janet gave a party for us. He showed us his study for the first time: it was  small one-room building across his backyard, with (if I remember rightly) cheap prints of the heads of favorite writers framed on the wall, Emily Dickinson and Herman Melville guarding his desk. His prize Airedale Black Jack was in the freshly hosed-down yard, and muddied the new white ducks of Tom Arp, one of my fellow students. I felt nostalgia already. I had written a lot of poetry during the year, my range was wider, my technique sharper — I had learned so much! I had every reason to feel gratitude. On the train to Texas, where I intended to spend the following year, I drafted a poem to Winters, in which I attempted as a kind of tribute to suggest his own later style. When I came to send him the finished poem later, he merely remarked that he hoped he was worthy of it. I concluded that he didn't like it and it was not until somewhat later that Janet told me he had been pleased and touched by it. He was a shy man, and never knew quite how to receive compliments graciously.

The rest is epilogue. In 1956 I returned to Stanford to do graduate work for the next two years. Winters encouraged me to attend the creative writing classes again, and I went regularly at first, but then I started to become wary. There had been stories of students becoming so dependent on his classes that when they had ceased attending them their source of poetry had dried up altogether![4] I didn't think I was in quite such a bad way as that, but I did conclude that, as I had started writing without help, I should continue without it. I deliberately began to go more seldom and ended by not attending his classes at all.

This was formal contact. Of informal we had for a while more than before. He was, if anything, more generous of his time, his attention, his company, and his house. One Thanksgiving when everybody else was in the kitchen, we were sitting at the hearth of his front room when he announced, with much shyness, that he had lately "committed" two poems, the first in years. They were "A Dream Vision" and (probably) "Danse Macabre," both of which he thereupon recited to me. It may have been at this same time that he talked to me at some length about his parents (I had met his mother, a very old woman, on a similar occasion). I had never felt so close to him as I did that afternoon.

Another time he seriously asked my advice about giving a public reading of his poetry for the Poetry Center in San Francisco. He said that in my poem to him I suggested that he had fenced himself off from the world (it had not been my intended emphasis), and maybe he should consent, for once, to give this reading. I had never heard him give a full formal reading of his work, except on the Library of Congress record, so I encouraged him to do so, as much for the sake of his audience as for himself, and he did indeed give it.

I think it was on my return to Stanford from Texas in 1956 that he asked me to call him by his first name, Arthur. I was moved by the gesture, but on thinking about it was a little depressed. As Allen Tate said to me many years later, when I once met him briefly, "Winters made the mistake of judging people by their poetry." I already knew this; and what was more I knew that my poetry would sooner or later disappoint Winters. He would feel affection for me only as long as he could approve of my poetry and my ideas. So to take up this token of increased intimacy had its ironical aspect. I felt as if I were a partner in some doomed love affair from a French novel: I could see an end in sight even while we achieved the point of greatest symbolic attachment.

I left Stanford eventually without a degree, bored and exasperated with graduate work that seemed to have nothing to do with the reasons I had taken up English in the first place; but of course I continued to visit and write Winters: I kept up with him, though he never liked any poetry I wrote after 1958, the year I left. Once in the sixties when I sent him a group of poems, he wrote back that they were simply journalistic and maybe I should try to learn how to write prose instead. The letter came as no unexpected blow. I had been anticipating something like it for years, and I wasn't going to fight him about it. If he had a streak of brutality in him, I had a streak of sentimentality.

My relationship with him since his death has developed and changed, as my relationships do with the dead. I can see now that in his criticism of me he pinpointed a certain irresponsibility, a looseness, a lack of principle — a promiscuous love of experience, perhaps — which I know I need to keep going, lacking his theoretic firmness. He had been right that first evening: I am still a romantic, thinking with Keats that "nothing ever becomes real till it is experienced—Even a Proverb is no proverb till your Life has illustrated it." Winters rather could believe with Ben Jonson that

> Not to know vice at all, and keepe true state,
>     Is vertue, and not Fate;

that one can evaluate and make choices without physically engaging the actions that one comes to reject; and that the romantic immersion in the life of the senses moreover tends to destroy the power of discrimination, and therefore is to be avoided. (If I appear to be confusing the imaginative with the moral life here, I do so because for Winters at their acutest they were the same thing — the good poem makes moral discriminations.) It is perhaps an argument between two temperaments. I say temperaments because an Olympian wisdom would take neither side: you cannot possibly be "virtuous" (or a good poet) without a degree of undiscriminated experience. On the other hand, a life that was all experience and nothing else would simply wear out the body and the head. The question of *how much* experience to have is one to be judged as you go along; it is a matter of improvisation. What complicates the matter, also, is that experience is always lived for its own sake, not with one eye cocked on its possible usefulness for moral or poetic ends.

Perhaps in this last paragraph I am trying to be the victor in our implicit argument, or perhaps I am being as fair as I can be. I am not sure. Certainly I have peculiar difficulty in recording these memories of Arthur Winters, partly because my recollections of him are jostled and in danger of being replaced by the voice of the books (though I have deliberately avoided referring to them while I write), partly because the man's very forcefulness still arouses my defenses, and partly also because of the disconcerting oppositions between the rigor of his critical presence and what I could almost call the tenderness of his private presence. I have, however, a clear picture of him securely in my mind, which I will keep there till the end. Rather than a single memory, it is probably a composite made from a series of memories. We are sitting in his front room or on seats under the trees, drinking wine and talking; he sucks on his pipe during repeated silences; but he speaks at times, measuring what he says—he speaks of poetry with a peculiar intimacy and dedication for the art about which he had more to tell than anyone else I have known.

---

[1]Ezra Pound, ABC *of Reading*, (New York, 1960) p. 13. Somebody could write an interesting essay about the effect of Pound's early criticism on Winters both early and late. By the 1950s Winters had long repudiated Pound's ideas and practice, though he continued to praise certain poems (with reservations) and continued to quote from the early criticism. But Pound's taste had influenced his own youthful taste, and the coincidence of many of their favorite poems was frequent. Both singled out, for example, Mark Alexander Boyd's "Fra wood to wood," both admired Crabbe, both admired the early Elizabethans (though with a difference of emphasis), both praised Landor, both expressed contempt for the Romantic poets (with a slight occasional exception made for Keats), and both had little time for the famous eighteenth-century poets. Pound too must have been an influence in encouraging by his example both the iconoclasm and the personal search for "the best poems" in the face of the accepted anthology pieces. (I suspect that Pound too had almost as great a dislike for the middle and late Yeats as Winters did.) Since the labors of both Pound and Winters have, ironically, enlarged the canon of those anthology pieces in the last few decades, the similarities of taste between the two men may seem less striking now than they did in the 1950s.

[2]It is worth noting that Brooks and Warren incorporated the gist of the third section of Winters' essay "The Influence of Meter on Poetic Convention" in the third edition of their textbook, *Understanding Poetry*, without any acknowledgment that I can find. That is, they acknowledge their quotation of one of his own poems with his own markings of the stressed

syllables, but they do not acknowledge that they have borrowed his theory of the scansion of free verse as well.

3 I think it was Alan Stephens who pointed this out to him in a class.

4 This makes Winters sound like an addicting drug. But dependence on a strong-minded teacher is one of the greatest dangers to originality in a creative writing class. The opposite danger is the over-permissive teacher: his class sits around liking each other so much that they start to write poetry that aims at pleasing all the other students. Such writing-by-concensus produces the "well-made poems" of our day, homogenized, fashionable, and vapid. (I teach the subject myself nowadays, and have made myself aware of the dangers.)

# MY GARDEN, MY DAYLIGHT

by JORIE GRAHAM

from NEW ENGLAND REVIEW

*nominated by Kathy Callaway and Sara Vogan*

My neighbor brings me bottom fish —
   tomcod, rockcod —
a fist of ocean. He comes out
   from the appletrees between us
holding his gift like a tight
   spool of thread.

Once a week he brings me fresh-catch,
   boned and skinned
and rolled up like a tongue. I freeze them,
   speechless, angelic
instruments. I have a choir of them.
   Alive, they feed

driving their bodies through the mud,
   mud through their flesh.
See how white they become. High above,
   the water thins
to blue, then air, then less . . .
   These aren't as sweet

as those that shine up there,
   quick schools
forever trying to slur over, become water.
   But these belong to us
who cannot fall out of this world
   but only deeper

into it, driving it into the white
   of our eyes. Muddy
daylight, we utter it, we drown in it.
   You can stay dry
if you can step betwen the raindrops
   mother's mother

said. She's words now you can't hear.
   I try to wind my way
between what's here: chalk, lily, milk,
   titanium, snow —
as far as I can say
   these appleblossoms house

five shades of white, and yet
   I know there's more.
Between my held breath and its small hot
   death, a garden,
Whiteness, grows. Its icy fruit
   seems true,

it glows. *For free* he says
   so that I can't refuse.

# A REQUIEM

## by DAVID IGNATOW

from NEW LETTERS

*nominated by* NEW LETTERS, *and J . R . Humphreys*


My father, listening to opera, that's me,
my legs outstretched upon the bed
as I lean back in my chair. I think of him
in his chair, legs crossed carelessly
and with his musing smile recalling his first wish,
to become a baritone, his smile seeking
after his youth or watching it in the distant past,
untouchable. I am alone, and the opera playing
heightens my loneliness, without son, without father,
without my past or present, and my future a problem.

Eh, father, as I listen to your favorite opera
you would have enjoyed my listening and approved
emphatically, while I'd withhold myself,
tentative towards opera, as other matters burned in me,
such as the need to be free,
and so we would argue but soon fall silent
and go our separate ways.

I am alone in my apartment, alone as you were
without me in your last days at about my age.
I am listening to Rossini and thinking of you
affectionately, longing for your presence once more,
of course to wrestle with your character,
the game once again of independence,
but now, now in good humour
because we already know the outcome

for I am sixty-six, going on sixty-seven,
and you are forever seventy-two.
We are both old men and soon enough
I'll join you. So why quarrel again,
as if two old men could possibly settle
between them what was impossible
to settle in their early days?

🔥 🔥 🔥

# DUSTING

## by RITA DOVE

from POETRY

*nominated by Michael Harper*


Every day a wilderness—no
shade in sight. Beulah
patient among knickknacks,
the solarium a rage
of light, a grainstorm
as her gray cloth brings
dark wood to life.

Under her hands scrolls
and crests gleam
darker still. What
was his name, that
silly boy at the fair with
the rifle booth? And his kiss and
the clear bowl with one bright
fish, rippling
wound!

Not Michael—
something finer. Each dust
stroke a deep breath and
the canary in bloom.
Wavery memory: home
from a dance, the front door
blown open and the parlor
in snow, she rushed
the bowl to the stove, watched
as the locket of ice

dissolved and he
swam free.

That was years before
Father gave her up
with her name, years before
her name grew to mean
Promise, then
Desert-in-Peace.
Long before the shadow and
sun's accomplice, the tree.

Maurice.

# DÉTENTE

fiction by JOYCE CAROL OATES

from THE SOUTHERN REVIEW

*nominated by* THE SOUTHERN REVIEW, *Robert Boyers, Josephine Jacobsen, and Robert Phillips*

ALL OF LIFE IS REAL ENOUGH; but it's unevenly convincing.

Begin with a flat blunt bold statement. A platitude, a challenge, a wise folk saying. There are so many wise folk sayings. Hadn't the chairman of the Soviet delegation said, the other evening at the crowded reception, when everyone was being friendly and those who could not speak English were smiling eagerly, hopefully, squeezing their American hosts' hands with a pressure that seemed, well, too intense, hadn't the Chairman, the tall patrician silver-haired Yury Ilyin himself, a former ambassador to the Court of St. James, a former dean of the Gorky Institute, rumored to be an old, difficult, but highly respected friend and rival of the Soviet

270

President — hadn't he said, in impeccable English, with a certain half-lazy irony that chilled Antonia, who had been confused and charmed by the man's social manners: *"Nothing is more distant than that which is thought to be close. A Russian folk saying, very old. Very wise."*

All of life is real but it's unevenly convincing. There are incalculable blocks of time, days and even weeks, even months, that pass dimly, in a sort of buzzing silence; you sleepwalk through your life. Then the fog lifts. Abruptly. Rudely. You didn't realize you were sleeping and now you've been awakened and the sunshine hurts your eyes, the voices of other people hurt your ears, you find yourself astonished at what stands before you.

His name was Vassily Zurov. She rehearsed it, in silence. A tall, slightly stooped man in his mid-forties, lean, cautious, less given to mute strained smiles than his Soviet colleagues, but passionate in his speech, with a habit of widening his eyes so that the whites showed above the dark iris, fierce and glowering. Now he jabbed the air, and struck his chest, his heart, speaking so rapidly that Ilyin had to signal him to slow down, out of consideration for the interpreter. His metal-rimmed glasses had gone askew on his long thin nervous nose. A lank strand of dark lusterless hair had fallen across his rather furrowed forehead. He looked, Antonia thought, with that flash of irony and resentment that always preceded her reluctant interest in a man, like an old-fashioned divinity student. Wasn't there one in Dostoyevsky, in *The Possessed*, hadn't he been one of the demons. . . . If Antonia hadn't been told at last Saturday's briefing that all of the members of the Soviet delegation were probably members of the Communist Party, she would have thought nevertheless, A fanatic of some sort: look at that pale twisted mouth.

His language was, of course, incomprehensible. A massive, intimidating windstorm, a marvelous barrage of sounds, utterly alien. The Russian language: a language of giants, of legendary folk. Like something in a dream. Ungraspable. She stared and listened. She was a woman of some linguistic ability, she could speak fluent French and Italian, and could manage German, but though she had tried to learn some Russian in preparation for this conference she was forgetting it all: the slow stumbling childlike words, the somewhat preposterous sounds, the humble refuge in *Da, da*. She had forgotten everything. In fact it had turned out to

be a perplexing chore for her simply to remember the pronuncia-
tions of the Soviet delegates' names. You must understand that
these people are often quite sensitive, Antonia was told. It's
important that we don't inadvertently insult them.

Vassily Zurov paused impatiently, and the interpreter — hidden
at the far end of the room, inside a glass-fronted booth — said in a
voice that managed uncannily to imitate, or perhaps to mimic, the
Russian's florid style: *What is the function of art? From what does
it spring in our hearts? Why do a people treasure certain works,
which they transmit to the generations that follow? What significance does this have? Is it a human instinct? Is there a hunger for
it, like a hunger for food, and love, and community? Without the
continuity of tradition, what meaning is there in life? As our
Chinese comrades discovered to their chagrin, after having tried
to erase their entire heritage—*

But this was the interpreter's voice, this was another man's
voice; and Antonia was having difficulty with her headphones.
Somehow the mechanism would not work for her. When it
worked, it was seemingly by accident: a few minutes later and the
words sounding in her ears might be flooded by static. . . . *the
writer's mission in our two great nations? Is there a historical
inevitability in art that carries us all along. . . .* Vassily Zurov
hadn't the diplomat's aplomb of Ilyin, or of several of the older,
more distinguished members of the Soviet delegation; Antonia
remembered, or half-remembered, from the briefing that he had
not been allowed to visit the United States before. He had been,
from time to time, in trouble with the authorities. Had he actually
spent some time in a labor camp in the North, or had he been
closely associated with a "liberal" magazine whose editor had been
expelled from the Writers' Union and sent away. . . . Surrepti-
tiously Antonia scanned the official list of the man's credits. It was
part of a lengthy document prepared by the Soviet delegation's
secretary, and listed only achievements that, she supposed, were
impressive in another part of the world. *The Order of the Red
Banner. Two Lenin Orders. Medal for Valiant Labour.* Two medals
for prose fiction, 1971, 1975. Contributor to the journal *Literatur-
noye Obozreniye.* Born in Novgorod, now a resident of Moscow.

How warmly, how guilelessly the man spoke . . .! His voice was
somewhat hoarse, as if he were fighting a cold. During his fifteen-
minute presentation he had led the discussion — "What Are the

Humanistic Values of Present-Day Literature?"—away from the naming of specific authors and titles and dates, which Matthew Burke, the chairman of the American delegation, had initiated, and into an abstract, inchoate region of ideas. Such speculations about life, and art, and the meaning of the universe, had fascinated Antonia many years ago, before she had grown up to become a professional, and surprisingly successful, writer; listening to Zurov now, she felt herself quite powerfully moved. It was all so child-like, so ludicrously appealing. The man's initial caution had fallen away and he was speaking with the urgency of an artist who has come halfway around the world to meet with fellow artists and to discuss matters of the gravest importance.

A photographer for the U.S. Information services was crouching before Zurov, preparing to take a picture. The man's head was hidden from Antonia by his camera: an eerie sight. Zurov paused, and the interpreter translated his words, blasting Antonia's ears in a flood of capricious static. She could not quite decipher what was being said. *Art is political. Art is apolitical . . .?*

The photographer took a number of pictures, rapidly, and Zurov, distracted by him, began to stammer. Antonia blushed. It was an old habit, an old weakness—she blushed scarlet when in the presence of someone who was himself embarrassed. The earphones went silent. Then Zurov mumbled a few more words, now staring down at the microphone before him, and the simultaneous translation overlapped his faltering voice: *Thank you, that is all I wish to say.*

From her attractive third-floor room in the Rosedale Institute Antonia called her friends Martin and Vivian in Chicago. How are the Adirondacks this time of year, isn't June rather early for the mountains, they said, how is the conference going, how do you feel, do you expect to accomplish anything or is it just some sort of diplomatic game. . . . She heard her voice replying to their voices and it sounded normal enough.

How do you feel, Antonia, they asked.

Much better, she said.

After a while they said: Well, he isn't here. And he didn't call.

He didn't call?

One of us has been home the past three nights and he didn't call, are you absolutely certain he was headed this way . . .? You know

Whit sometimes exaggerates. He has such a . . . he has such a surrealistic sense of humor.

I didn't know that, Antonia said.

She spoke so gently, no one could have said whether she was being ironic or not.

They talked for a few more minutes, about the Russians, about the embarrassing political context — the President's highly-publicized stand on "human rights," the recent defection of a Soviet representative to the United Nations — and about mutual friends. As if to console her they offered news of Vera Cullen's divorce: Antonia thought the gesture a rather crude one.

What shall we say if he does call, or if he shows up . . .?

I don't know, Antonia said.

Give us your number there and we'll tell him to call. If he said he was coming here he must be on his way, unless of course something happened. . . . Should we have him call you at the conference?

I don't know, Antonia said, pouring an inch or two of cognac into a plastic glass. The cognac was a gift — a rather premature one, she thought — from a red-faced, gregarious, portly Ukranian who had been very attentive to her the previous evening, and at breakfast and lunch today. *All the way to my homeland,* he said, in careful English, and Antonia had not had the heart to correct him. His name was something like Kolevoy. According to the biographical sheet he was a poet, a writer of sketches, and a member of the board of the Soviet writers' Union. . . . I don't think so, she said.

How long has he been gone? When did he leave?

A few days before I did.

Did he take many clothes, did he take much money . . .?

No, Antonia said. But then he never does.

A pleasantly vulnerable feeling. As if convalescent. But it's been seven years now, Antonia thought reasonably. Surely I have recovered.

Numbness. Emptiness. She was not the sort of woman to refer everything to her femaleness, to her womb; the very thought bored her. Yet something circled, bat-like, nervous and fluttering, about the miscarriage of seven years ago, in the first year of her second marriage. Such things mean a great deal, she thought. Though probably they mean nothing.

It *did* bore her, she would never think of it again.

The problems inherent in a bourgeois existence, she would explain to Vassily Zurov, arise out of idleness. One must think about something in order to fill up time. So we think habitually of sex and death, of loss, of symbolic gestures, dismal anniversaries, failed connections. . . .

She was in retreat from her own life, which she might or might not explain to Zurov. There would be, after all, the problem of language: a common vocabulary. So far they had grinned at each other over glasses of sherry, and talked through one of the several interpreters — You are a poet? No? A writer of prose? Unfortunately your works are not available in my country. . . .

She had not wanted to participate in the Rosedale Conference on the Humanities, though the four-day meeting of Soviet and American writers, critics, and professors of literature did seem to her a worthwhile event. There were the usual promising words, and she liked them well enough to repeat them silently to herself, like a prayer: *unity, cooperation, universal understanding, East and West, friendship, sympathy, common plight, peace, hope for the future*. At the opening session the Soviet chairman Ilyin had even spoken, in English, of the need for Soviets and Americans to resist "our common enemy who seeks to tragically divide us." (The American chairman Burke called his delegation to a meeting room afterward, in order to speculate aloud, with the assistance of a Soviet specialist from Harvard and rapporteur named Lunt, on the possible meaning of Ilyin's carefully oblique words; but the words remained indecipherable, a kind of poetry.) Antonia had not wanted to participate though two friends of hers, or were they perhaps only acquaintances — the poet and translator Frank Webber, and the novelist Arnold Barry — were to be in attendance. In the end she said yes, for no particular reason.

She was a small-bodied woman of thirty-six who looked a great deal younger, mainly because of her shoulder-length, sumptuous brown hair. Which was grotesquely misleading: she did not feel sumptuous, had not felt sumptuous for many years. In fact the word puzzled her. Struck her as faintly comic. Her pale green eyes were slightly prominent and always a little damp. Her skin was an almost dead white: she hated it, and was made uneasy by well-intentioned compliments on her appearance. And by frequent half-accusatory remarks about her "youthfulness" — on the first morning of the conference a young woman journalist told Antonia with a beaming smile that she had pictured her as much older — in fact elderly.

She was the author of two slender novels, both written in her early twenties. They were fastidious and self-conscious, set in the upper-middle-class Catholic milieu of her girlhood in Boston. Obliquely autobiographical, but not stridently so, they were admired by the few critics who took the time to review them, but they were not commercially successful, and were reprinted in paperback only after Antonia achieved eminence for other work — essays on literature, art, and culture in general, some of them iconoclastic and devastatingly critical. Yet for the most part the essays were appreciative; they were certainly methodical, models of unobtrusive research and scholarship. In the world she customarily called "real" — that is, the world outside her imagination, her ceaselessly thinking and brooding self, her book- and music-cluttered apartment on East 72 Street — she was constantly meeting distorted images of herself which came to her with the blunt authority of seeming more real than the Antonia she knew. Though she was dismayingly shy, so quiet at large social gatherings that she might be mistaken for a mute, there was the widespread idea, evidently, that "Antonia Mason" was shrill and argumentative and maliciously — but, so her admirers claimed, *brilliantly* — unfair. She had published in the past decade interpretive and generally positive essays on John Cage, Octavio Paz, Iris Murdoch, Robert Rauschenberg, contemporary German films, contemporary American poetry, and other subjects, but it was for lengthy and perhaps somewhat sardonic assessments of the achievement of Tennessee Williams, Robert Motherwell, the works of Feminist novelists, and those of the "New Journalists" that she was most remembered. It must, she supposed, mean something significant: of six brief reviews she might publish in the New York *Times* in a year it was the one sarcastically negative review that would excite comment. Acquaintances telephoned to congratulate her on speaking honestly, people as far away as Spokane and Winnipeg might write to thank her for having made them laugh, friends alluded to her wit and courage and intelligence — as if these qualities, if they were hers at all, were not present in her more serious work. Even her husband, Whitney, complimented her when she was a "fighter" (his word) in public. If she complained that popular culture seems

to push individuals toward what is most aggressive, most comba-
tive, and least valuable, he brushed aside her remarks as disingen-
uous. "At heart you're really competitive, you're really a hostile
person," he often said, narrowing one eye in a mock wink. "Which
accounts for your astonishing *gentleness* . . . and your exasperating
charity. And your proclivity to forgive."

She could not help forgiving him: he was her husband, after all,
despite his infidelities. And she loved him. Or had loved him. Or,
at the very least, had consoled herself during a rather bad time
some years ago with the thought that she was capable of loving
someone after all — she would devote herself to this new relationship with Whitney Albright, she would meditate upon it, plunge
into it, make the old-fashioned sacrifices now being mocked by her
contemporaries, and thereby save herself. So she was, quite apart
from her promise as a novelist, and her uncontested brilliance as a
cultural critic, a genuine woman: divorced but remarried, once
again someone's wife. She was also someone's daughter and someone's sister. One of the Soviet delegates had referred to her as the
"leading American woman of letters" — or so the translation had
gone. Meanings hung on her like loose clothing.

Someone's estranged wife.

Someone's abandoned wife.

Is it so, Yury Ilyin's secretary, a plump, affable young man with
thick glasses, asked Antonia and several other Americans, that
each year in the United States there are between 700,000 and
1,000,000 children who run away from home . . .? We find this
hard to believe and wonder if the figure was not misreported.

It could not be said, however, that Whitney had "run away." For
one thing adults do not "run away"; they simply leave. And the
circumstances of his leaving were abrupt and dramatic enough to
suggest that the action was going to be temporary — his reply to
her reply, so to speak. (It was not the first time that Whitney had
left her. Several years ago, when driving to the West Coast, where
Antonia was scheduled to participate in an "arts festival" at one of
the state universities in California, Whitney had left her in the St.
Louis zoo, in front of the ocelot cage. The circumstances were
amusing, perhaps, though Antonia had not found them so at the
time. For weeks she and Whitney had been careful with each
other, gentle and solicitous and patient, and the long drive to
California was meant to be a vacation, a sort of second honeymoon;

perhaps the strain of being so unrelievedly nice precipitated a violent quarrel during which each accused the other of being incapable of love and "worthless" as human beings. Antonia had been admiring the ocelots, especially a lithe playful ocelot kitten named Sweetheart, and Whitney had liked them well enough — strolling through the zoo was something to do, after all, a way of killing time until late afternoon and cocktails — but he hadn't Antonia's concern about a penned-up ocelot that was crying angrily and plaintively to be released into the larger cage. The creature was hidden from sight, though by standing on the railing Antonia could *almost* see it. "My God," she said, nearly in tears, "listen to it crying, it sounds just like a child, have you ever heard anything so heartbreaking in your life. . . ." Whitney urged her to come away. After all, the cat must be quarantined for some reason: the zookeepers knew what they were doing. "But it's so cruel. It's so stupidly cruel," Antonia said. The ocelot's enraged full-throated miaows were really quite disturbing. Whitney said something further, Antonia said something further, and then they were shouting at each other, and could not stop. I suppose the goddam ocelot is a symbol of something, Whitney said, I suppose I'm meant to interpret all this in some personal way, a goddam fucking symbolic commentary on our marriage, and Antonia had screamed that it wasn't a symbol, it was a living creature, how could anyone listen to it howl like that and not feel pity and want to help. . . . In the end Whitney had walked away. Antonia did not follow him. An hour later, when she returned to their hotel, much calmer and ready to apologize if it seemed likely that he, for his part, would apologize, she discovered that he had checked out, had taken his suitcases, his share of the toiletries, and the car.)

It might be said that she was abandoned now, and had been so since Whitney disappeared twelve days before, after a quarrel at a friend's apartment; but she did not think of herself as abandoned. Talking with a group of Soviet writers, among them Vassily Zurov, she had answered a question about her marital status by saying with a smile that "such questions were no longer relevant" — she wanted to meet with them as a person, as a fellow writer, not as a woman. Perhaps the translation had been witty: they had all laughed, though not disrespectfully. Zurov said, "That's so, that's right," in fairly emphatic English.

Yet she could not resist, a while later, asking him if he was married. She asked him directly, not through an interpreter; his reply was a dismissive shoulder shrug.

Which, of course, she could not confidently translate, for perhaps he had not understood her question. And she hadn't the ability to ask it in his language.

He sat beside her in the Institute dining room, and hovered near at the cocktail gatherings, and frequently stared at her during the sessions, quite visibly not listening; his hair was bunched and spiky and disheveled by the earphones, with which he had a great deal of trouble. Once when several members of the Soviet delegation were laughing zestfully at a lengthy anecdote told to them by a stout, swarthy man from Georgia — it turned out to be, rather incredibly, about Stalin himself, Stalin as someone's old uncle, gruff but lovable — he pulled her aside and spoke emphatically, half in English, half in Russian, managing to communicate to her the need they had for exercise, for a walk around the lake before dinner, didn't she agree . . .?

She agreed. And halfway around the lake, as they stood on a grassy knoll staring at the glittering water and the Institute's fieldstone buildings on the far shore, he took her arm gently and slipped it through his. She did not resist, though she did not lean against him. "It's lovely, isn't it," she said. "Just at sunset. Just at this moment."

"Yes," he said doubtfully. He was obviously quite excited: she saw a flush on his throat, working its way unevenly up to his face.

At the American delegates' briefing Antonia and her colleagues had been told that the Soviet delegation was, of course, under strict control. They would be watching each other closely, spying on each other. They would above all be intimidated by their chairman and his aides. Yet it didn't seem to Antonia that this was the case. Vassily was his own man: it seemed quite clear that he was no more explicitly subservient to his chairman than the American delegates were to Matthew Burke. Wasn't it all rather exaggerated, Antonia wondered, this drama of East and West, Communists and American citizens, the outmoded vocabulary of the Cold War, the strain, the tension, the self-conscious gestures of brotherhood, the ballet of détente. . . . Walking with Vassily

Zurov she felt only a curious sort of elation. She could not help but be flattered by his interest in her; he was an attractive man, after all.

And it seemed to her that he was rapidly becoming more proficient in English.

At breakfast the next morning they sat together, alone together. She asked him about his stories: would they ever be translated into English, did he think? Were they political?

He asked her to repeat the question.

It would have been difficult for Antonia to determine precisely what, in him, attracted her so powerfully. For some time she had stopped thinking of men as men, she had stopped thinking of herself as a woman in terms of men, the whole thing had come to seem so futile, so upsetting. Adultery appealed intermittently, but only as a means of revenging herself upon Whitney; and as her love for Whitney waned her desire for revenge waned. There was, still, the incontestable value of adultery as a means of getting through a certain block of time: it was an activity charged with enough passion, enough recklessness, to absorb thought, to dissipate anxiety. If she allowed herself to be touched by a man, if she leaned forward to brush her lips against a man's lips, or to allow a man to kiss her, she would have no time to think of the usual vexing questions. Her husband. Her marriage. Her meandering "career." And there were the slightly tawdry, glamorous and melancholy questions of her girlhood: What is the meaning of life? Does God exist? Are we born only to die? Is there a means of achieving immortality . . .? The Russians would not have jeered at such questions. Vassily Zurov would not have jeered.

At last he understood her question about his writing, and labored to reply in English. He leaned forward, gesturing broadly, staring fixedly at her as he spoke. "My stories are political, yes," he said with great care. ". . . As all art."

Antonia felt a sense of triumph.

"All art? Did you say art? . . . But all art isn't political," she said.

She was speaking too rapidly, he begged her to repeat what she had said.

"Art isn't political," she said slowly. "Not in its essence."

He stared at her, smiling, uncomprehending. She saw a dot of blood in his left eye. He adjusted his glasses, still staring. Antonia said, holding her hands out to him, palm upward, in an innocent, impulsive gesture whose meaning she could not have explained, "Of course some forms of art are political. Some writers are basically political writers. But in its essence art isn't political, it's above politics, it refers only to itself. I'm sure you understand, I'm sure you agree. Politics necessitates choosing sides, it excludes too much of life, life's nuances and subtleties, art can't be subservient to any dogma, it insists upon its own freedom. Political people are always superficial people. I couldn't be forced to choose sides — it's brutal, it isn't even human—"

He shook his head, baffled. He asked her to repeat her remarks.

She said only, blushing, that art isn't political. In its essence it isn't political.

He replied half in English and half in Russian, with a barking laugh that startled her. He seemed to be saying that art *is* political.

"Everything," he said firmly. He lifted a glass of water and gestured with it, as if toasting Antonia; he took a sip; he then extended it across the table to Antonia as if he wanted her to drink from it — but she drew away, baffled and a little annoyed. He was so demonstrative, so noisy. "Everything," he said with a queer wide smile, a half-mocking smile, "is political. You see, the water too. In the glass like this. Everything."

She shook her head to indicate that she didn't understand. And now that others were coming to join them, now that their intimate, edgily flirtatious conversation was becoming public, she felt suddenly drained of energy, unequal to his vehemence. She hadn't any appetite: she would have liked to go back to bed.

Vassily greeted the others in Russian and waved for them to sit down. He fairly pulled one of the English-speaking Soviets into the seat beside him, so that he could help with the conversation with Antonia. She looked from one to the other, smiling her strained polite smile, as Vassily spoke in rapid Russian, watching her cagily.

The interpreter — listed as a poet in the dossier, but named by Lunt as an *apparatchik*, a party hack — beamed at Antonia and translated in heavily-accented but correct English: "Mr. Zurov inquires — you do not think that art is political? But it is always political. It seeks to alter human consciousness, hence it is a political act. He says also that a mere glass of water is an occasion for politics. He says — but you see, we were talking about this last night, Miss Mason, some of us were talking about this last night, and Mr. Zurov insists upon bringing it up — perhaps you did not read the local newspaper yesterday? — no? Mr. Zurov refers to the front-page article about the poisons that have drained into the mountain lakes in this area. He says — through the winter, rain and snow have been blown into the mountains from somewhere to the west where there are coal and oil combustion plants, and nitric and sulfuric oxides have been concentrated in the snow, which has now melted, do you see? — and there are now toxins in the lakes — he is not certain of the technical terms, perhaps others here would know — and the fish, the trout, have died in great numbers. And so — "

Vassily interrupted him, speaking excitedly, watching Antonia's face. The man then translated, with a slight bow of his head in her direction: "Mr. Zurov does not mean to distress you on this lovely sunny day. He says — forgive me! But perhaps you did not know, perhaps it needed to be pointed out, that the simple act of drinking a glass of water can be related to politics and to history, if only you know the context in which it is performed, *and the quality of the water*, but of course if you are ignorant and do not know or choose to know, you will imagine it is above politics and you are un-touched. He says, however, to forgive him for being so blunt, but it is his way, it is his only way of speaking."

Impulsively Vassily reached out to seize Antonia's hand, for all to see. His smile was wide and anguished, showing irregular teeth. The gesture surprised Antonia but she hadn't the presence of mind to draw away. "Excuse me, Miss Mason? Yes? It is all right?"

"Of course it's all right," Antonia whispered. But she felt shaken: it was not an exaggeration to say that she felt almost ill. And there was the entire day to get through, the morning and afternoon sessions, and the usual lengthy dinner. . . . Staring at Vassily's slightly bloodshot eyes she knew herself on the very edge of an irreparable act: at the very least, she might burst into tears in public. But how trivial, how demeaning, even to care about such things! She drew her hand out of Vassily's dry, warm, eager grip. "Of course," she said faintly.

A long day of speeches. Prepared remarks. "Allow me to speak, I will be brief," said a thick-bodied swarthy critic and editor from a Soviet journal that translated, according to Antonia's notes, as *The Universe*. He then spoke, not quite spontaneously, for forty-five minutes. . . . Why do United States citizens know so little of

Soviet literature, why is there so much racist and pornographic material for sale in your country, why do you allow a "free market" for the peddling of such trash? Though it was a blatant attack, barely disguised by diplomatic language, the American delegation replied in civil, careful language: one of the novelists, whose books Antonia could never bring herself to read, managed to say something fairly convincing about the First Amendment, human rights, freedom of the press, democracy, the fear of censorship in any form. "And it's important, I think, for us to know, in a democracy, what people seem to want. Pornography disgusts me as much as it disgusts anyone, but I think . . . I think it might be valuable, in a democracy, simply to know what great masses of people seem to want." Antonia's colleague spoke softly but with a sophistication that pleased her.

Yes, freedom is desirable, certainly it is desirable, but racist trash, pornographic trash . . . ? "Such 'literature,' " one of the Soviets said, "strikes us as no more than a means of extracting money from the market."

The issue of dissident writers: tentatively, gingerly, brought up. But Yury Ilyin brushed it aside. Such a matter is not, strictly speaking, a literary or humanistic matter, it has to do with illegal activities, the right of a sovereign state to deal with its criminals, perhaps we will have time to discuss it later. With a chilly, impertinent smile Ilyin said he supposed the Americans were primarily interested in legitimate Soviet writers: otherwise why did the Rosedale Institute extend its generous invitation to this group to visit the United States and to meet with outstanding American writers, their colleagues and equals in the field of literature . . . ?

Vassily was sitting hunched over, peering short-sightedly at the table before him, or at his clasped hands. He had taken off his glasses; with his spiky, rumpled hair he looked like a man surprised in his sleep. Antonia had the impression that he was about to interrupt Ilyin. His pale mouth worked, his forehead was deeply furrowed. He had been, some years ago, a "dissident" writer himself—or at any rate he had gotten into trouble with Party officials. Perhaps he had even been sent away for a while, to a mental asylum or a labor camp. The rapporteur from Harvard, Lunt, hadn't offered much background information for Vassily Zurov, he was one of several "mysterious" members of the delegation, little known in the West, with only a few short stories translated and anthologized. . . . Suppose we become lovers, Antonia thought idly. Then he will tell me everything. Then he will tell me all his secrets.

Prolonged remarks, ostensibly "spontaneous." Frequent references to "the great Mayakovsky" — a poet of mediocre gifts, surely? — and to the concept of "socialist realism," which Antonia had supposed to be outmoded; but perhaps it was not, not entirely. Marxist metaphysics explained succinctly by a youngish Moscow novelist who was also First Secretary of his Writers' Union: we have first matter, there is no contesting that, and then comes spirit, and then comes "spirituality" (but there is no exact word for that concept in Russian) which is the activity of highly organized matter. . . . Antonia tried to take notes, it would be her turn to speak in a few minutes, she was becoming unusually nervous. *The activity of highly organized matter.* But perhaps the translation was only an approximate one? How could one know? How could one be certain?

Maxim Gorky, who is the "father of Soviet literature." Lenin, who stated clearly that the main function of the printed word is organizational. Jack London, Theodore Dreiser, Stephen Crane. Steinbeck. Chekhov. Dostoyevsky, now being reexamined. Vassily, who had spoken little, said a few words about "your great American poet William Carlos Williams." When it was Antonia's turn she spoke briefly of the "post-modern" novel, its movement inward, toward lyricism, toward poetry, away from the statistical world, the objectively historical or political world. . . . She twisted her pen nervously as the Soviets gazed at her with great interest. But when she finished only a single question was directed to her, by the Ukrainian Kolevoy, and it was clearly meant to be courteous, to show his appreciation of her words.

She wondered how those frail words were being translated.

Another photographer was taking pictures, crouching discreetly in the aisle, moving forward on his haunches. He took a number of pictures of Ambassador Ilyin, who gave the impression of ignoring him.

Antonia watched Vassily and wondered what he was thinking. What he had endured. Her delegation had been told that they must not mention certain things to the Soviets — under no circumstances should they inquire about certain books, written by Soviets but published outside the country, nor should they inquire about dissidents whose work they might know. Labor camps, prisons, mental asylums: don't bring the subjects up. Antonia had read that during Stalin's reign several hundred poets, playwrights, and prose writers were murdered by the secret police, in addition to the other thousands, or millions. . . . And in the sixties there was the highly-publicized case of Joseph Brodsky, put on trial for being an idler and a parasite without any socially useful work, sentenced originally to five years of forced labor in the North. And, more outrageous, even, the joint trial of Siniavsky and Yuli Daniel, who dared claim artistic freedom, the right to follow wherever one's imagination leads. . . . If Antonia remembered correctly the men were both sentenced to several years' hard labor in a "severe regime camp." There was also the example of a young man named Galanskov, the editor of a Moscow literary magazine of "experimental" tendencies, first sentenced to a mental institution, then to a concentration camp where he was allowed to die. Perhaps she would ask Vassily about him: it was quite likely that they were acquainted. . . . When she thought of how little she risked, in publishing her essays, even her autobiographical novels, she was stricken with a sense of guilt.

Matthew Burke was speaking, perhaps too slowly, on the "humanistic tradition" in the West. Yury Ilyin then spoke of the "humanistic tradition" in his country. Antonia's head began to ache. She rarely suffered from headaches, this was really quite extraordinary, it seemed to have to do with the simultaneous translation: the phenomenon of hearing Russian spoken and hearing, immediately, its English translation, the words often overlapping, one voice louder than the other and then suddenly subsiding in a buzz of static, only to surface again a few seconds later. And what was the reality behind the words, to what did they refer. . . ? In her world she had grown accustomed to the relative impotence of words: they might have *meaning*, but they rarely had *effect*. But in the Soviet world even the most innocent of words might have an immediate, profound effect. . . .

Ilyin was concluding the morning's "very fruitful discussion." He was speaking of brotherhood, of universal understanding, the hope for global peace. Antonia watched him guardedly, as did the others. One simply could not trust the man. He followed a script, a scenario, possibly prepared in advance; it was clear that most of the members of his own delegation did not know what to expect from him. Though he had proudly identified himself earlier as being the son of "peasant stock" he was clearly an aristocrat in spirit, barely tolerant of his colleagues, and contemptuously formal with the American chairman, whom he challenged often and addressed as "dear Matthew." They had said of him a few days before that he was an anti-Semite. He was a neo-Stalinist. They had said . . . oh they had said wicked things, but Antonia hadn't wanted to listen, she hadn't wanted to believe, after all the conference was designed to bring people together, weren't they all involved in literature, in the humanities, wouldn't it serve the cause of "world peace" if she and Eliot Harder and Arnold Barry sat at the same table in the Institute's handsome dining room with their Soviet friends Vitaly and Boris and Grigory and Vassily and Yury himself. . . . A popular Leningrad poet named Kozanov, whose work Antonia had been reading with admiration, had been withdrawn from the delegation at the last moment and his place given to the mysterious Kolevoy, according to Lunt; an obvious party hack. What this means about Kozanov I wouldn't want to speculate, Lunt said with a conspiratorial drop in his voice, it might mean nothing or it might indicate bad news, very bad news. But I wouldn't want to speculate.

Ambassador Ilyin ended the session by expressing the hope that the United States would someday come to the enlightened realization that total freedom, in the arts as in any other sphere of life, is a very ignorant, one might almost say a very naïve, condition. "We aspire, after all, to the level of civilized man, we wish to leave barbarism behind," he said with a smile.

In Antonia's room she said, far too rapidly, to Vassily: "I'm not here to practice diplomacy, I'm a cultural critic, I think of myself as an amateur even at that, I don't have the stamina, the nerves, for this sort of thing—"

He had come to bring her gifts—a necklace, a slender bottle of vodka, a box of candies with a reproduction of the Ural Mountains on its cover, three slim, rather battered volumes of his short stories, in Cyrillic. Now he stood perplexed and uncomprehending. "What is—? You are angry? You are not—" Here he paused, squinting with effort. "—not leaving?"

"I came here to talk about literature, I didn't come to hear debates about politics, it's very upsetting to me, to all of us, I mean the American delegation — I mean — "

Vassily seized her hands, staring urgently at her.

"You are not leaving?"

He kissed her hands, stooping over. She stared at the top of his head, at the thinning hair at the crown, feeling a sensation of . . . it must have been a wave of . . . something like love, or at least strong affection, emotion. He was so romantic, so passionate, he was an anachronism in her own world, she did love him, suddenly and absurdly. She could not understand his words — he was speaking now in Russian, excitedly — but there was no mistaking the earnest, almost anguished look in his eyes. She felt a sensation of vertigo, exactly as if she were standing at a great height with nothing to protect her from falling.

In an impulsive gesture she was to remember long afterward she reached out to hold him, to bring his head against her breasts. He was crouched over, one knee on the edge of her bed, gripping her tightly, murmuring something she could not understand. She felt him trembling; to her amazement she realized that he was crying. "You're so sweet," she murmured, hardly knowing what she said, wanting only to comfort him, "you're so kind, so tender, I love you, I wish I could help you, you don't know anyone here, you must be homesick, the strain of these past few days has been terrible, I wish we could go away somewhere and rest, and hide, I wish there were just the two of us, I've never met a man so kind, so tender. . . ." He held her close, desperately; she could feel his hot anxious breath against her breasts; he seemed to be trying to burrow into her, to hide his face in her. "I know you've suffered," she said softly, stroking his hair, stroking the back of his warm neck, "you can't be happily married, I know your life has been hard, they've tried to break you, I wish I could help you, I wish we could be alone together without all these other. . . ."

They would be lovers, Antonia thought wildly. Perhaps she would return with him to Moscow. Perhaps she would have a baby: it wasn't too late, she was only thirty-six. It wasn't too late. Stroking his neck and shoulders, embracing him awkwardly (she was thrown slightly off balance by the way they were standing), she felt tears sting her eyes, she was in danger of sobbing uncontrollably. Love. A lover. A Communist lover. Whitney would jeer at her: how can you be so deluded? You can't possibly love this man since you don't know him, you can't possibly love anyone since you're incapable of love. . . .

"You're so far from home," she murmured, confused. "We're all . . . we're all homesick. . . ."

He straightened to kiss her, and at that moment the telephone rang, and it was over. He jumped away from her, and she away from him, as the phone rang loudly, jarringly; and it was over.

Disheveled, flush-faced, Vassily backed out of her room like a frightened, guilty child, muttering words of apology she could not understand.

They were never alone together again.

The next morning, enlivened by a spirit of adventure, she and Vassily and one of the interpreters went for a rowboat ride before the session at nine o'clock, but the wind was chilly, Antonia regretted not having worn her heavy sweater and scarf, and even before the accident — though perhaps it could not be called an "accident," it was simply a consequence of their stupidity — she found Vassily's exuberant, expansive manner jarring. His dark blue shirt was partly unbuttoned, showing graying kinky hair; he looked at her too earnestly, too openly, with a fond broad smile that showed his crooked, rather stained teeth. Quite obviously he was in love with her: the interpreter laughed gaily, shaking his head as if he were being tickled, possibly not translating everything Vassily said. She began to worry about being late for the final session, she brushed her hair out of her watering eyes repeatedly, smiling a strained smile, wondering if this little adventure — there was a notice in the Institute lobby, on the bulletin board, warning against "unauthorized" boat rides on the lake — might get them into trouble.

"We should head for shore," Antonia said. Vassily was rowing, and he was so uncoordinated, so awkward, that the oars were splashing water onto her legs and ankles. Her feet felt damp. "Tell him," she pleaded with the interpreter, "to head for shore. It's getting late."

The interpreter, one of the more genial members of the Soviet delegation, spoke a few words in Russian, and Vassily replied with a gay shoulder shrug, and a torrent of Russian, and the interpreter leaned over to Antonia to translate, somewhat apologetically:

"Vassily says to tell you that we are all running away. An escape into the mountains. Into the woods. He says to tell you that he is very fond of you, he is very fond of you, perhaps you are aware of the fact, previous to this he has traveled in Northern Africa but not in Northern America, this is his first voyage, he is very grateful, he does not want the conference to end. . . . Just a joke, you know, a jest, running away into the mountains, Vassily is known for his humor, perhaps you have noted it."

Then Antonia noticed that her feet and ankles were wet because the boat was leaking.

There was a brief period of alarm, and consternation, though never any panic — for how could the three of them drown, so close to shore, in full view of anyone who chose to watch them from the Institute? The water was very cold. Antonia half-sobbed with the shock of it, and the discomfort, and the absurdity. Despite Vassily's spirited rowing they did not quite make it to the dock: they were forced to abandon the sinking rowboat in about three feet of freezing water, less than a dozen yards from safety. "I will save you — No danger — I will save — " Vassily cried, his teeth chattering from the cold. He tried to make a joke of it, though he was clearly chagrined. The interpreter cursed in Russian, his face gone hard and murderous, his skin dark with blood.

Vassily helped Antonia to shore, and insisted upon taking off his shirt to drape over her shoulders. Some of their colleagues came out to help; Lunt hurried to Antonia with a blanket, and one of the women connected with the Institute fussed over Vassily and the interpreter, who insisted, laughing, that they were all right, it was nothing, they would go change their clothes and that was that.

Antonia, blushing, saw a photographer on the veranda of the main lodge, his camera held up to his face, obscuring his face, as he took pictures. She pulled away from Vassily with an embarrassed murmur.

That was shortly before nine o'clock: by twelve-thirty, when the conference officially ended, her relationship with Vassily had ended as well.

The final session was tense, nearly everyone looked strained, or quite ordinarily exhausted; even Ilyin, taking up a great deal of time with an elegant expression of gratitude for the hospitality of the Institute, looked tired. Then, rather abruptly, certain issues resurfaced: a member of the Soviet delegation insisted upon speaking in response to Eliot Harder's statement of the other day concerning "freedom" of speech and of the marketplace, saying with ill-disguised contempt that one could package and sell human flesh, no doubt there would be some eager consumers, if you hold to a marketplace ideology where everything is for sale, everything is to be peddled, if you believe that in a "democracy" it is valuable to know what people want, what they will buy, why not package and sell human flesh, what is to stop you. . . ?

Another Soviet spoke of racist propaganda he had discovered in the American press. He had visited the United States many times, he said, as a guest of the government and of certain universities, and he had acquired astonishing publications, in order to study the mood of the United States, and it had shocked and disgusted him, anti-Negro propaganda published openly, in fact subsidized by leading capitalists, and there is the notorious instance of the American Nazis, defended by many, and their publications widely distributed, though perhaps it is not to be wondered at, for the United States has not suffered a war, it has not experienced a war like Russia experienced not long ago, when every family lost at least one member and many families of course were destroyed by the Germans under the madman Hitler, and in any case it is widely known, it is a matter of common knowledge, that the United States has no memory, it is the fashion to forget, to forgive and forget as the saying goes, and no doubt members of this American delegation would defend that point of view. . . .

Frank Webber insisted upon speaking, and in a trembling voice asked about the dissident writers, naming several names unfamiliar to Antonia, and going on to say, passionately, not quite coherently, that the humanistic tradition insists upon freedom of expression, freedom of the imagination, the enemy of the spirit is the totalitarian state, the supreme sovereign state, we have no tradition in the West of bowing down to authority, our writers and poets think for themselves, they are never censored, they speak out against the suppression of their fellow artists in all parts of the world. . . . It is complained by the Soviets, Webber went on, gripping his microphone, that we pay attention only to the dissident writers, we ignore the "real" writers, but no one would deny that the so-called dissident writers speak most truthfully, most forcefully, with the greatest aesthetic command, and in any case they would prefer to be published at home, they do not *want* to have their manuscripts smuggled out of their country, they do not *want* to be exiled or jailed. . . .

Matthew Burke intervened, and tried to restore calm, and Antonia sat staring at her hands, wondering why she was here, what pretext had she had for coming here, she remembered Vassily's head gripped against her breasts, she remembered the warmth, the urgency, the incredible unspeakable tenderness of their embrace, but what had it to do with anything else, how could it help them. . . ? Vivian had called to tell her that Whitney had called *them*, he did intend to drop by later in the week, so far as they could judge he sounded in good spirits, he didn't sound at all drunk, or bitter, once he got in Chicago they could persuade him to call her, perhaps she could even fly out, would she be willing, should they raise that possibility to Whit when he arrived. . . ?

Now Ilyin was speaking, now Ilyin had the floor and would not relinquish it. He spoke of Soviet anger over the fact that the American President always surrounded himself with Soviet "authorities" who were anti-Soviet, he spoke with irony of the fact that at the leading American universities contemporary Russian literature is represented by such writers as Solzhenitsyn, who is no longer a Soviet citizen, and Nabokov, who was an American, who is classified as an American, and now — the very latest — they are taking up the cause of the mentally disturbed Sokolov, and the criminal Siniavsky, and others whose works are worthless. . . . There is no genuine feeling of brotherhood between the Americans and the Russians, Ilyin said, or such outrages would not be permitted. Those who are called dissidents are criminals, nothing more. They are ordinary criminals. Why are such matters a concern for the United States, where criminals are dealt with harshly enough. . . ? It is none of your business, Ilyin said, and Antonia looked over to see Vassily staring at his hands, his clasped hands, and all around the table the Soviets sat motionless, silent. At the very moment that Frank Webber rose, not to protest but simply to walk out of the room, Antonia thought weakly, with a sickening certitude, We must leave, we must all leave, we can't sit here listening to this, but of course she did not move, she sat motionless as all the others.

"Problems of human rights are problems of sovereign states," Ilyin said, the interpreter said, droning in Antonia's ears, "not to be dealt with by outsiders. You would think that the Americans, priding themselves on their freedoms, would know enough to allow other states theirs. Why do you imagine that your views of human rights and freedom should be ours? Why do you even want to think so? . . . It is astonishing, I have always found it astonishing, even rather amusing, the tragic misconceptions of my American colleagues."

After Ilyin finished there was a brief silence, and then Matthew Burke repeated, gamely, with a strained courtesy Antonia found touching, a number of the points already made, and there were final remarks having to do with the "communication channels" that had been opened, and with the hope that the conference would be only the first of many. The Soviet chairman, speaking in exactly the same voice he had used a few minutes before, thanked the Rosedale Institute for their gracious and generous hospitality, and the American delegates for their generous friendship, and of course Matthew Burke who had labored to bring all this about, and he believed he spoke for the Soviet delegation in expressing the hope that they would all meet again, perhaps the following year, to discuss literary matters, and matters of humanistic interest, in order to bring together our two great nations, and to work for universal peace and brotherhood, and understanding. . . .

There was silence. Antonia saw out of the corner of her eye how Vassily sat, utterly immobile, still staring at his hands. He was not going to rise to his feet, he was not going to protest, or even to speak calmly and quietly: he was a Soviet writer who had learned his particular lesson.

And what blame could she assign to him, what privileged repugnance had *she* earned. . . ?

Despite her dark glasses the bright sunshine hurt her eyes: the pain was really quite piercing and intense. Yet she managed to say goodbye to everyone. She was sociable, she was unfailingly courteous, one of the friendlier Americans. There was a flurry of handshaking on all sides, and the lively presentation of gifts—mainly books ("Unfortunately I have not yet acquired an English translator") but also bottles of cognac and vodka, and boxes of candy in gaily-colored tins, and, for Mrs. Burke, and Antonia, and the several other women involved in the conference, hand-carved brooches made of walrus tusks. (Antonia, examining hers, thanking the Russians with a broad if numbed smile, wondered if she had heard correctly—walrus tusks? The brooch, approximately the size of a silver dollar, weighed very lightly in the hand and might well have been made of plastic. But it was quite attractive in any case and her admiration was sincere.)

The limousines were waiting. A small contingent to take the Soviet delegation to New York; two airport limousines to take Antonia and her companions away; but it seemed necessary—it seemed unavoidable—that everyone say goodbye yet another time, and repeat how beneficial the conference had been, how marvelous to become acquainted, to establish avenues of communication between like-minded persons. . . . Vassily stood near, smiling at her, though no longer with that hopeful, loving gaze: his expression had gone resigned, even somewhat bitter. He knew how she felt about him: he understood. Certainly he understood, he wasn't a fool, perhaps he wasn't even the amiable well-meaning romantic figure he had presented to Antonia, but quite another person altogether, a Soviet writer who had survived. Antonia smiled at him as she smiled at the others, shaking hands, retreating. Her anger had backed up everywhere in her, it throbbed throughout her body, beat cruelly behind her eyes. She dreaded crying because tears would be misunderstood.

Vassily squeezed her hand roughly and leaned toward her. "You will visit us someday?—soon?" His voice was edged subtly with shame and with anger as well, but Antonia took no notice. "You will be a guest of my government, a week, or a month sometime."

Vassily squeezed her hand roughly. "You will visit us soon? A week, a month in good weather, as a guest of my government?"

"That's possible, yes certainly," Antonia said, edging away. She was smiling her American smile but the corners of her mouth had begun to weaken. "You are very kind to invite me."

She backed away. Already things were shifting into episodes, acquiring anecdotal perspective. Vassily had clutched so eagerly at her, he had pressed his face against her breasts, and she had felt, hadn't she, such immediate, such extraordinary affection. . . . That episode had been genuine. It had really happened. She would remember it, she thought, for the rest of her life.

Vassily was still gripping her hand. He wanted to embrace her— but of course he didn't dare. Instead he pursued the subject of her coming to Russia to give lectures, to meet with fellow writers?— yes?—would she consent? She saw that Vassily chose to interpret

her disdain for him as feminine shyness, or restraint; she understood he would not release her until she gave him the answer he
required, that his companions might overhear. So she smiled and
made an effort to return the pressure of his fingers, she murmured
that helpful word, *"Da."*

# A POETRY
# OF RESTITUTION

by JOHN HOLLANDER

from THE YALE REVIEW

*nominated by* THE YALE REVIEW

THE SOLE ADVANTAGE," said Santayana, "in possessing great works of literature lies in what they can help us to become." Those of us who were nursed by modernist literary and artistic theory find this difficult to assent to. Not only does the "sole" bother us. Modernist aesthetic engaged in a kind of well-intentioned witch-hunt against the didactic, and the very notion that poetry was, should, or even could be of moral importance lay somewhere between the distasteful and the dangerous. That poetry could exercise this moral function in any other than a didactic way was indeed grudgingly admitted, if only in the deep pieties of the idea of a "pure poetry," which found an exemplary, if not an otherwise instructive, virtue in the avoidance of the ethical, even as of the discursive. Robert Frost's wonderful sonnet on the perplexities of heralding the middleness of the journey, "The Oven Bird," carefully conceals the natural folklore that conventionally renders the song of that particularly shrill warbler as "Teacher! teacher!" The moral consequences of myth-making poetry lay ignored in an overview of centrality in poetry which averted its gaze from Spenser, from Milton, from Shelley, from Browning, and which celebrated the sustaining power of irony and purification — or, in the words of Joyce's young poet seeking to escape his backward time and place, "silence, exile and cunning." I shall speak now of contemporary poetry, and, since my subject is its moral dimension, shall refrain from any further revisionist history of our poems and our theories of them. Anyone with an interest in poetic eras rather than in modes may, I suppose, think of my observations as applying to the period of the post modern. I should rather present them as a meditation on three very consequential poems by three of my poetic contemporaries, written over a period of not quite twenty years.

Before we possess ourselves of these texts, however, we might consider a related matter which in the past decade has troubled the American poetic conscience. Let us start with what remains the essential and unimproved formulation of the trouble:

> Though loath to grieve
> The evil time's sole patriot,
> I cannot leave
> My honied thought
> For the priest's cant,
> Or statesman's rant.
>
> If I refuse
> My study for their politique,
> Which at the best is trick,
> The angry Muse
> Puts confusion in my brain.

The evil time is 1847, when "the famous States" are "Harrying Mexico/With rifle and with knife"; the place is Concord (in the only region of the nation in whose dialect *patriot* rhymes with *thought*);

the voice is Emerson's, bridling at the injunctions of poetic vision itself to engage with subjects — the Mexican War, the Fugitive Slave Laws — which are bound to result in bad and possibly even meretricious poems. Like another famous poem of politico-poetical ambivalence written not quite exactly two centuries before, this one commences with its author's somewhat nervous acknowledgment that he can no longer "in the shadows sing/His numbers languishing." Like Andrew Marvell's "Horatian Ode," too, the irregular ode inscribed to the abolitionist William H. Channing (the "sole patriot") concludes not in fencesitting, but in coming down on one side; we learn that the crossing has only been authenticated by the apparent seesawing along the way. In both poems, too, the ironies lead to further ironies — it is hard to believe that Emerson was not thinking of Marvell, whom he so greatly admired and elsewhere echoed — and the very vacillations lead to the resolutions. Emerson rhetorically demands of Channing

> What boots thy zeal
> O glowing friend,
> That would indignant rend
> The northland from the south?
> Wherefore? to what good end?
> Boston Bay and Bunker Hill
> Would serve things still;—

He concludes with an almost apocalyptic formulation: "Things are of the snake" — not just things in the nowadays of an early agricultural-military-industrial complex beginning to tear itself apart. "Things" comprise the very world of material concern and gain within whose interstices meditative and even self-critical vision is afforded. In Marvell's poem, the muses appear to be forsaken at the beginning. In Emerson's, a more complex fiction is needed: the muse, confusing and confused, is angered at having to make a choice between truth and beauty, somehow aware that in choosing either, not the one rejected but the chosen value itself will be thereby betrayed. And yet, at the end of the poem, "The astonished Muse finds thousands at her side"; but we may be sure that Emerson's muse could hardly be surprised that a powerful proclamation would have many adherents — rhetoric, as we know, is very gluey. Her astonishment is somehow at the poem itself, which, by the very act of questioning the relation between moral action and the visionary imagination, has managed to complete itself successfully.

There surely have been great political poems, in which visions of justice, living peace, or unpolluted order have not resulted in epigrams, or even in rhymed essays. (I think that these last should be all the more valuable at a time like the present, when we have no major moral essayists in prose: W. H. Auden wrote our last moral essays in verse.) When a political moment can call forth mythopoeia, the muse is neither reticent nor nervous: one need never have heard of Castlereagh's oppressions to grasp the general moral truth of Shelley's sonnet of England in 1819, with its line about "Golden and sanguine laws that tempt and slay"; nor is the continuing, merely topical applicability of that line to, say, the Harrison narcotics act a test of its truth as poetry, any more than of what we might call its poetry as truth. When morality and poetry are mentioned in learned milieux today, the question of art and political commitment invariably comes up, both as part of the subject and as a cloud in which it is wrapped. During recent decades many morally righteous and politically correct — for the party of what we might call remembered hope to which most American poets belonged — views became incarnated in verse. Epigrams, cabaret satires, pasquinades, exhortations, and editorials proclaimed the injustices, in the late sixties, both of a war and of a peace its wagers envisioned. The authors of these verses must have been of several sorts: first, those who felt that no utterance could be a bad poem if its sentiments were correct; second, those who could not believe any poem of their own to be bad; third — and here we enter a realm of moral seriousness — those who believed with half of Emerson and most of Yeats that thrusting the muse into rusty armor might cripple her and would certainly win no battles. We can be moved, I think, by the notion of a poet who felt that the only way he could expose his "fugitive and cloistered virtue" to an authenticating trial would be in being willing to write badly, if necessary, by way of bearing witness.

But poems have a kind of life of their own. If they — rather than the citizens in whose public being their creators reside — are to bear witness, it must be a figurative bearing and an image of witnessing. I take the poems seemingly called for by crises of political morality only as extreme instances, in recent American poetry, of a more general case. Few poets who responded to the call for an antiwar poem learned much from Emerson's model, but it was a time of demoralizing pressures, and few of those same writers might have responded to public pressures for moral poems of another, more venerable sort — funerary elegies, for example: I cannot see an American poet of the 1960s being urged by his or her fellows to write a dirge for his or her own dead child. Poems mourning one's dead predecessors have always been another matter, and the proliferating sects of poets have always shared this most solemn of liturgical forms.

The response to a call for the imagination's moral power is one thing, and I have wanted to suggest that it is never a simple matter. But it is the poem itself which shall now concern us, the poem which, in whatever its small or cool or tinted mode of glowing, stares sightlessly out at the reader from the page until some voice — although not its own, perhaps — is heard to say what Rilke heard in the presence of his stone poem of antiquity: *"Du muss dein Leben ändern,"* you must alter your life. This is not to say that poets cannot — in verses of some sort and, thereby, putatively as poets rather than generally as exhorting men — do the work that the journalist and the commentator, given the fading away of American literacy, are less and less able exaltedly to do. Sorrow and rage at injustice; or the chill that lasts after the pained smile has gone at ironies which seem now to inhere in events, rather than in the tropes of the writer and thinker — producing these is the bitter work of reportage. The British chaplain De Stogumber, in Shaw's *Saint Joan,* confesses that the burning he had encouraged has altered his life: "I had not seen it [cruelty] you know. That is the great thing . . . It was dreadful . . . but it saved me," to which the poetic ironist Cauchon must respond: "Must then a Christ perish in torment in every age to save those who have no imagination?" The relation between what Yeats called rhetoric and true poetry is in some ways like the relation between the experience of horror and true imagination in Shaw's great question, to which the answer is, alas, probably "Yes." But if we do in fact need both poetry and rhetoric, we should not confuse their functions. Poems do not urge, or propound programs of deportment, or criticize in detail those already propounded. The contemporary poem, like the Renaissance one, must ultimately do its teaching, and be enabled to alter our lives, by mythographic means, even at a late time of myth-making, when instead of moralizing Ovid, it adduces new mythologies in explanation of older ones.

But in order to hear the poem's command to do something about our lives, we must place ourselves directly before it, until there is no place in it that does not indeed see us. Let us start with a beautiful poem of looking and reflecting, written about twenty years ago by a poet only beginning to feel his powers. A dramatic monologue in half-evaded rhymed couplets (the second line, irregular in length, rhymes with the penultimate or antepenultimate syllable of the first one), the poem is also an emblem that reads itself for significance. James Merrill's "Mirror" is truly a speaking picture: the reflecting glass considers itself, and most importantly addresses its pragmatic counterpart, an open window opposite.

> I grow old under an intensity
> Of questioning looks. *Nonsense,*
> I try to say, *I cannot teach you children*
> *How to live.—If not you, who will?*
> Cries one of them aloud, grasping my gilded
> Frame till the world sways. *If not you, who will?*

—The question is not intended as a rhetorical one, but must inevitably remain just that. The mirror of art held up to nature is too wise to attempt an answer, but instead continues:

> Between their visits the table, its arrangement
> Of Bible, fern and Paisley, all past change,
> Does very nicely. If ever I feel curious
> As to what others endure,
> Across the parlor *you* provide examples,
> Wide open, sunny, of everything I am
> Not . . .

(and what a wicked enjambment for a mirror to employ in its treatment of what seems manifestly primary to its mere echoing answer)

> You embrace a whole world without once caring
> To set it in order. That takes thought. Out there
> Something is being picked. The red-and-white bandannas

Go to my heart. A fine young man
Rides by on horseback. Now the door shuts. Hester
Confides in me her first unhappiness.
This much, you see, would never have been fitted
Together, but for me. Why then is it
They more and more neglect me? Late one sleepless
Midsummer night I strained to keep
Five tapers from your breathing. *No*, the widowed
Cousin said, *let them go out*. I did.
The room brimmed with gray sound, all the instreaming
Muslin of your dream . . .

As if to answer her own rhetorical question (and we must recognize
the mirror now, I think, for what she is, gilded and elegant, an
extremely wise old lady, a great Proustian aunt), the mirror
remembers a death. And this is the one point in her meditation at
which the continuing present tense of the verbs, synchronizing all
she has seen in a reflected plane, gives way to preterites. At her
most frighteningly magisterial she asserts, without undue insistence, that it was she and not the window who abandoned the mad
effort of all daughters of memory to eternize human breath. We
notice, too, how she remarks on "all the instreaming/Muslin of
your dream . . ." *Your* dream: the window's dream is that plangent
cliché of reverie, the inblown curtains enshrined in romantic
paintings of meditative room interiors from Adolph von Menzel to
Edward Hopper. The mirror hears the flapping of death in the
darkness; she can read the emblems of consciousness that inhere
even in the objects of conscious perception as no mere window
can. And this is why, and the fact of death is why, they more and
more neglect her.

Years later now, two of the grown grandchildren
Sit with novels face-down on the sill,
Content to muse upon your tall transparence,
Your clouds, brown fields, persimmon far
And cypress near. One speaks. *How superficial
Appearances are!* . . .

—Indeed! But the mirror's depths, her realities, are on, or at most,
she knows, *in*, her surface; she, and the poem itself, shiver at the
callow beauty of the young people's discovery, and when she takes

up her musing for the last time, it is with a brilliant pun, what the French call a *rime riche* on the penultimate syllable of "superficial," at first almost coarsely answering the charge with a flash of *Dasein*, a gross presence, an angel of gleaming surfacing from literal depths. But then, having surfaced, it adds its light to the surface of shining discourse that is the mirror's triumph over mere openness of window, or candor of artificial light:

> *How superficial*
> *Appearances are!* Since then, as if a fish
> Had broken the perfect silver of my reflectiveness,
> I have lapses. I suspect
> Looks from behind, where nothing is, cool gazes
> Through the blind flaws of my mind. As days,
> As decades lengthen, this vision
> Spreads and blackens. I do not know whose it is,
> But I think it watches for my last silver
> To blister, flake, float leaf by life, each milling-
> Downward dumb conceit, to a standstill
> From which not even you strike any brilliant
> Chord in me, and to a faceless will,
> Echo of mine, I am amenable.

Where she—or, rather, perhaps, *it* again, for we are clearly talking of poetry itself—is most transparent, the poem is most blind. It can only reflect—this mirror of art and of our highest consciousness—when its transparency, its Emersonian eyeball, is itself illuminated from within its capacity to know, by a gleaming, a shining from behind. For poetry to be a mirror, after centuries of flaking and dimming belief in its truth, it must at the very least be its own lamp as well. The images, the patches of silvery fiction which project into the broadcasting wind, but down into silent darkness. And when there is nothing to the mirror but the clear glass through which the nothingness of that dark can be read, the imagelessness of that deep truth is preserved even as the truth is presented. In the last darkness which will not be dawned upon, the mirror and the window alike are cold, smooth, unseen glass.

Merrill's mirror reveals itself first as a novelist's figure of wisdom (and why is it that in modern America one encounters more wise old women than wise old men?). Then, radiant beyond the Renaissance emblem of mimetic art, it becomes the modern poem, "the poem of the mind in the act of finding/What will suffice." It is the world mirrored in the most profound way: Hester, alone with her unhappiness and that consoling image that is the legacy of Milton's Eve, cannot but unwittingly confide in the mirror even when she is most alone. We cannot talk about our feelings — and this has been true in the case of all our poetry of love, from Sappho on — without talking about talking about them, without pointing out the peculiar ways in which we must use language in order to tell the truth. Merrill's poem remains shiny, clear, framed in a gilded, semi-antique meter, not in order to be itself — even for Americans, bowed under the weight of history's injunctions to be ourselves, that is not, alas, enough — but in order to mean something. "*I cannot teach you children/How to live.*" But the children's response is our own, and is the poet's own, as he was coming to knowledge of what would suffice. Modernism dictated the refusal to teach, but something at once younger and more grown-up hears the voices of the children: "*If not you, who will?*" It is that enabling climate in which Merrill's poem itself seems to grow older and wiser as we read it; from a modern poem about poetry — and therefore morally pure, unrotted by didactic intention as its surface seems unflecked by expository rhetoric — it emerges as a mirror of life after all. It is in order to reflect what the cheerful, mindless window can only helplessly reveal that the mirror *reflects upon* itself, upon its own mode of reflecting. Less solipsistic than the human children who consult it, the poem comes, by being about itself, to be about everything else outside it. *That* takes something more than thought. The romantics called it Imagination

The lessons we learn are about time, space, and reflections. We are reminded of all the mythology which lies behind the speaking mirror—the looking glasses of both the nude lady who may be Vanitas or Venus, and the one who is surely truth; the mirror into which it is dangerous to gaze, lest, like Narcissus, we inadvertently heed the philosopher's injunction to know ourselves, and thereby lose everything; the strong, enabling mirror held up to the goddess by Amor, an emblem of her own power; the *esoptron* ("glass") of St. Paul, by which we perceive truth "darkly" (*en ainigmati*) in the riddle and puzzle by which all the half-reliable oracles speak; the mirror of modernism, an image of paradox, reversal, self-reference, and schematic mystery; the mirrors of Jean Cocteau's

*Orphée,* all of which are easily unfrozen surfaces covering the many entrances to the poet's hell of self-absorption. But Merrill's poem is also mythopoetic, in that the mirror, the wise old presence, the almost novelistic domestication, and the confrontation with the unanswering window, leave the emblem forever transformed, materially augmented. That augmentation partially exists in the dimension of the work of reflection and memory which we do in our rereading and consideration of it. The images which, Shelley said, enable language to "unveil the permanent analogy of things" can "participate in the life of truth" by making the reader into a kind of poet as well.

Merrill's "Mirror" is by no means his best poem. He went on in subsequent books to move in a Proustian direction which was quite original, and in *Water Street* and afterwards he assimilated the impulses of narrative autobiography to a commanding and continuing mythopoeia. His way has been that of the mirror, not the window. His mature poetry inhabits part of that region of emblematic tale-telling which Elizabeth Bishop for some decades before her death, and Robert Penn Warren more recently, have inhabited for their major poetry. I do not refer, of course, to what has been called "confessional," that shrill and pitiful mode of contemporary verse which, neither window nor mirror, most resembles the sound of breaking glass. We can hear it, but learn nothing from it except that some disaster has occurred and that our lives are full of woe, which it seems shocking to need poetry for to inform us. The first part of Merrill's most recent trilogy mythologizes what is in fact the Spirit of Involuntary Memory as a psychic "control" of a ouija board. This is partially to say that the long, astonishing poem called "The Book of Ephraim" is, in almost every way, in lieu of a novel. But the mirror poem revealed a door, a hallway, down which American poetry of the next two decades would walk, not with the purpose of leaving the house and doing something outside of it, nor indeed on a nervous stroll marked by glances out of the windows in distaste. It was a walk taken indoors in an endless house, continually being added to and restored in some of its older parts, neglected to the point of near-ruin in others. But to explore it, and to map it, was to map heaven and hell, now and then, all the overlays which enable us to read the raw sense of the physical map of life itself.

Now a map of any region may show a way through it, and

perhaps what there is on, and by, the way. But there are times of
terror, times when not merely *things*, but everything, is of the
snake, and when the spirit cries out for rescue. But where there is
no palpable sublime, when there are no summits of nobility from
which the imagination may come in a rush of assistance, where do
we turn? The American Imagination is such a latecomer to the feast
of grandeur! We have no crowns: a top hat marks merely the next
man to take a pratfall. Our mythologies, the tales our grownups
live by, tell of no Founders spawned of Olympus: our mature faith
is in the knowledge of Parson Weems's mendacities. Our com-
memorative statues are bronze gobbets of dishonor: rarely is one
redeemed when the unveiling of morning shows a Chaplinesque
tramp still asleep in its hard arms. For the nourishment of our
minds there is still humor, but for hearts, the momentary beauty:
"Dolphins still played, arching the horizon/But," Hart Crane concluded sadly, "only to build memories of spiritual gates."

So that when "things are of the snake," a second task is set for the
American poem. Let us take for a second text a poem of the 1960s,
one which in its modes of clarity and difficulty is quite different
from Merrill's. It is a poem not overheard, but one which more
dangerously responds to the request for a word at a time of
disaster—a quarrel, a dish dropped and broken, both perhaps
amid the barely heard sounds of distant, rotten warfare. The very
title of John Ashbery's "Soonest Mended" is half the proverb
("Least said, soonest mended") that it tries with self-descriptive
*triage* to follow. It seems aware that we risk more, imaginatively,
by speaking when we are spoken to than by merely being out of
turn. Ashbery's opening flat, public diction, a pitch of the quotidian to which he frequently tunes on setting out, is in this poem
immediately rescued—in the absence of Pegasus, in the loss even
of the hippogriff of romance who replaced him—by the flapping
wings of outlandish allusion. And thereby he takes seriously his
three improbable opening clichés and is off on his poem in lieu of
an apology:

Barely tolerated, living on the margin
In our technological society, we were always having
    to be rescued
On the brink of destruction, like heroines in *Orlando Furioso*
Before it was time to start all over again.

There would be thunder in the bushes, a rustling of coils,
And Angelica, in the Ingres painting, was considering
The colorful but small monster near her toe, as though
    wondering whether forgetting
Might not in the end be the only solution.

Allusion—here, to Ariosto—and secondary allusion (to a problematic illustration of Ariosto, itself poised on the margins of silliness)
have a strange power that keep for the user as much as they give.
One of Ingres's studies for the Ruggiero and Angelica painting (at
the Fogg Museum) is labeled "Perseus and Andromeda," the
foreshadowing types of Ariosto's pair. But for the modern poet, the
later figures are the fallen ones; and the losses are incurred in
moving from myth to romance to gooey illustration to the contemporary moment of remembering all this in a time of need. This
much the poet keeps for himself; what he gives us are the limits to
the possibility of rescue. But forgetting, even in the presence of
the toe of a muse imprisoned in academic painting's *fini*, is not only
not the only solution: it is impossible. Even those of us who
require wisdom seek after a sign. What next for Ashbery?

    And then there always came a time when
    Happy Hooligan in his rusted green automobile
    Came plowing down the course, just to make sure
        everything was O.K.,
    Only by that time we were in another chapter and confused
    About how to receive this latest piece of information.
    *Was* it information?

The hero astride the flying hippogriff or popping out of the rusted
green automobile: unlike the "pagan in a varnished car" which
Wallace Stevens had denied could descend into our lives as a
capable fiction, the Imagination's rescuers dart in and out of the
chapters of our daily story without the fanfare even of the certainty
of their arrivals. This is the residue in major American poetry of
the Wordsworthian view that redemptive vision will be there,
when it is to be there at all, in the light of our ordinariness. The
answer to Ashbery's question is that it *was* information, but could
be authenticated only by having been able to elicit our doubt.

*Was* it information? Weren't we rather acting this out
For someone else's benefit, thoughts in a mind
With room enough and to spare for our little problems (so
   they began to seem),
Our daily quandary about food and the rent and
   bills to be paid?

That daily quandary is the high noon of our usual attention, the
state that W. H. Auden, whose language is indeed suggested in
that last line, invoked as "the time being." It is not that succession
of days from which we are, or desire, to be rescued; at the
beginning of his great later poem, "Grand Galop," Ashbery makes
clear that it is both *through* such a realm, as through an allegorical
surrounding region, and by means of it, that the force of what we
know can become the possible joy of what we do. At the beginning
of a great walk through urban dreck which yields him as many
seeds of light as ever glinted out at Henry Vaughan strolling
through the West Country, Ashbery's vision of desiccated spring
can lead him to the horrendous sequence of days in which poetic
language need only name in order to act: "The weigela," he says,

                does its dusty thing
In the fire-hammered air. And garbage cans are
   heaved against
The railing as the tulips yawn and crack open and
   fall apart.
And today is Monday. Today's lunch is: Spanish omelet,
   lettuce and tomato salad,
Jello, milk and cookies. Tomorrow's: sloppy joe on bun,
Scalloped corn, stewed tomatoes, rice pudding and milk . . .

(not an ecstatic Whitmanian catalogue, but more like a recital by
W. C. Fields, trying to incapacitate further an already nauseated
bank examiner).

   It is through, not from, the time of the dreadful lunches that our
spirits are to pass, perhaps out into sunlight.—Or, at any rate, in
"Soonest Mended,"

> To reduce all this to a small variant,
> To step free at last, miniscule on the gigantic plateau—
> This was our ambition: to be small and clear and free.

In an almost cinematic movement, the poem zooms away from this innuendo of sublimity; and the next strophe of the poem (although unmarked as such typographically) acknowledges its turn away from vision with an allusive touch of older tunes in its diction. Although with a Stevensian exclamation of "Pardie!" as unavailable to him now as a Horatian "Eheu!", the poet must minimize his wail, and move immediately to a confrontation with the difficulty of making poetic arrangements in a late time:

> Alas, the summer's energy wanes quickly,
> A moment and it is gone. And no longer
> May we make the necessary arrangements,
>         simple as they are.

We want to ask, "But how simple *are* they?" What Ashbery elsewhere calls "Using what Wyatt and Surrey left around,/Took up and put down again/Like so much gorgeous raw material," is, after all, simple like the arrangements of the daily quandary from which poetry so differs and yet for which it stands. What is never simple is doing what we have to do at the time, at this time, whenever it is. How can fictions even less than supreme be of any importance now? How can poetry mirror what Shelley calls "the gigantic shadows which futurity casts upon the present" when the covering shade of the past makes such mirrored shadows almost unreadable? Ashbery's answer starts out with a terrifying acknowledgment of the ancestry of all our rhetorical and visionary reticence, and then moves into the central passage of the first half of the poem:

> Our star was brighter perhaps when it had water in it.
> Now there is no question even of that, but only
> Of holding on to the hard earth so as not to get
>         thrown off,
> With an occasional dream, a vision: a robin flies across
> The upper corner of the window, you brush your
>         hair away
> And cannot quite see, or a wound will flash

Against the sweet faces of the others, something like:
This is what you wanted to hear, so why
Did you think of listening to something else? We are
    all talkers
It is true, but underneath the talk lies
The moving and not wanting to be moved, the loose
Meaning, untidy and simple like a threshing floor.

This "meaning," its own chaff and fruit unwinnowed yet, is not only
the meaning of our talk, our poems, our representations to each
other of our lives, neat and complex as such deep structures have
been held to be. It is more significantly the messy meaning of the
word "meaning," the meaning of life. It is as if the poem had come
upon its own central concern at the thirty-sixth of its seventy-one
lines: Ashbery's resolved major theme of Getting On With It.

In "Soonest Mended" the theme manifests itself in its discovery
that significances, moralizations, intentions — all the untidinesses
of meaning — reach out from talking to what is talked about.
Specifically, in the middle of the poem, the postmeridional time in
the history of poetry, in the very chronicle of imaginings, resolves
itself into the time of middle age. This is a poem of being forty-two
or forty-three; what one had set out upon, whether or not in
response to some vocation, twenty-five years or so earlier, will
have been arrived at only in a surprising way. It is not only that the
time of heroic rescues is over and that one finds oneself, in middle
age, in America, awakening to the condition in which all the
available heroisms are part of the predicament rather than the
means of its dissolution. One discovers that acts of consciousness
can be great acts as well:

These then were some hazards of the course,
Yet though we knew the course *was* hazards and
    nothing else
It was still a shock when, almost a quarter of a
    century later,
The clarity of the rules dawned on you for the
    first time.
*They* were the players, and we who had struggled
    at the game
Were merely spectators, though subject to its vicissitudes

And moving with it out of the tearful stadium, borne on
    shoulders, at last.

What kind of action is it, then, to try to grasp the meaning of what
had been overflowing with possible significances? All our modern
kind of poetic knowledge, all of the ways in which, from the major
romantics on, we could possibly be instructed by our moments of
vision as to how to live in between them, preclude the possibility
of direct answers to such questions. The landscape or scene which
is moralized by the very asking of the question, rather than, in the
older poetry, an ultimately anagogic formula, returns in some
hardened or reduced form as if in answer to the questioning. In
Ashbery's poem, "the end of that is past truth,/The being of our
sentences, in the climate that fostered them" brings together our
lives, what we have said of them, what we have — in both senses of
the word — made of them. It is not only that men say things
because they know they have been sentenced to death: what we
say makes up our life sentences. What we could call "the poem of
our lives" is at once the poem *about* our lives and the poem that *is*
the individual life itself. What then, Ashbery goes on to ask, of the
ealy poem when we awaken to our own request for a prose
paraphrase? There is something scary about either refusing the
request or trying to meet it; in any event, the early life affronts
abstraction:

> These were moments, years,
> Solid with reality, faces, namable events, kisses, heroic acts,
> But like the friendly beginning of a geometrical progression
> Not too reassuring, as though meaning could be cast
>     aside some day
> When it had been outgrown. Better, you said, to stay
>     cowering
> Like this in the early lessons, since the promise of learning
> Is a delusion, and I agreed, adding that
> Tomorrow would alter the sense of what had already
>     been learned . . .

"and," Ashbery continues, "probably thinking not to grow up/Is the
brightest kind of maturity for us, right now at any rate."
    The difference between "thinking not to grow up" and pretend-

ing not to have done so is, in a way, the difference between a trivial, reductive reading of Ashbery's lines and the full—and, I hope that I have been suggesting, fully moral—one. Politically speaking, American visions of maturity—particularly during the nineteen-sixties and -seventies—should drive the good man screaming to the cradle. The businessman, the governor, and the soldier, they who represented the potent maturity of being all "balls" and, alternatively, the uncooperating stud who represented the potent maturity of being all cock—these maintained a cloven fiction of manliness, of being grown-up in America, that has always existed, but which the tasks and injunctions of our earlier history put to active use. Poetically speaking, this is the problem of how to get better, how to go on in any art without merely replicating what one can do well, without producing forgeries of one's earlier genuine work. In our losses, in our sense of times promised and time past slipping away from us, we American artists cannot say with Wordsworth in his *Elegiac Stanzas* "I have submitted to a new control"; instead, we move toward a subsequent messiness which we hope will redeem us from our successes.

For Ashbery in this poem, the dilemma about what to do with our beginnings resolves in the very act of contemplating ourselves as we are now. The astonishment at the realization of having arrived makes for a pause, but not a lack of motion. Life and art come together again in the lesson to be learned: our poems must get better, and we must all keep going. "And you see," he continues,

> both of us were right, though nothing
> Has somehow come to nothing; the avatars
> Of our conforming to the rules and living
> Around the home have made—well, in a sense,
> "good citizens" of us,
> Brushing the teeth and all that, and learning to accept
> The charity of the hard moments as they are doled out . . .

Ashbery's continuous clarity makes us overlook the way his poetic surface is occasionally so beautifully wrought—I am thinking here of the precise and powerful definite article in "living/Around the home" (just "home" would give a sense of "hanging around," while "the home" makes it a purposive center of life). Similarly, "brush-

ing the teeth" seems a powerful and delicate alteration of the more
Audenesque "our teeth," the combined "our" of prayer, the editorial, and the nursery. If we think of the "hard moments"—
difficult, windowless, durable in the memory—as being those of
Ashbery's hard poem, we can understand how, in that poem, they
are the moments of life itself. The difficulties of, and in, our fictions
recapitulate those of the rest of our lives. Ashbery's final, firm,
almost measured lines conclude his poem with a substitute for the
traditional openings-out of landscape, or closings-in of shadows,
which the visionary lyric in English derived from Virgil's eclogues
and made its own. The conclusion they draw, in an expository
sense, is a substitute for heroic resolution, or reductive hope, or a
tired, tragic commitment to keeping the inner beasts of disorder
chained up as well as one can. The poem has acknowledged its
response to the truth about lives to be "a kind of fence-sitting/
Raised to the level of an esthetic ideal"; how can it draw itself to a
close? Ashbery's measured appositives to "not being sure" hide
their startling revisions of the ordinary language—even the cliché—of resolution almost until they have themselves drifted by:

> For this is action, this is not being sure, this careless
> Preparing, sowing seeds crooked in the furrow,
> Making ready to forget, and always coming back
> To the mooring of starting out, that day so long ago.

One of these revisions accounts for the deep resonance of
"making ready to forget"—not making ready to forget life, and to
be forgotten, in death, making ready to die; but in fact, making
ready to live and to be living. The other brings about the apparent
oxymoron of "the mooring of starting out." Not only is there an
alteration of the expected "the morning of starting out." There is
also rather a matter of condensation than contradiction; at a more
purely Stevensian rhetorical moment in his work, Ashbery might
have glossed his image more by playing about with the consequences of the metaphor. "It is not that starting out on artistic and,
indeed, generally human courses of wisdom is a matter of cutting
loose from moorings—no complex consciousness could without
the crudest of ironies utter 'I'm adrift, I'm adrift' in avowal of its
uncertainty. It is only that the starting out itself, the vocation, the
initiation of serious life, is all that we can be, or authentically *be*

*said in a real poem to be,* moored to. The trope of moorings and the sea voyage of life can only apply when troped itself." Something like this, in dialectic but certainly not in language, might have provided a passage of an earlier style of American poetic meditation. The very difficulty of this kind of poetry is the difficulty of having it be true of our lives, of having its art unfold in wisdom.

This is a very different kind of poetic difficulty from that of modernism, some of whose obliquities and ellipses of the expository have already become conventional idiom, but whose other mode of allusive elusiveness, of mandarin closure, functioned as a kind of *trobar clus,* as the troubadours called it, a rhetoric which would lock away the expression of perhaps common feelings from the understanding of the vile and the base. There is some deep justification for this hermetic impulse when one is writing of love: announcing a desire for a particular person — or, perhaps even more emotionally dangerous, announcing the condition of one's inner states to the degree of saying "I love you" — both depend upon the same words that *anybody* will use. And yet, Eros being most blind of all to its own lack of specialness, the poetic impulse to say "I don't mean what they, the others, mean by this: I mean *you* and *me*" is one of the most venerable. To extend this to all poetic expression was a different matter. Contemporary poetic difficulty in America (and we are flooded now as always with bad, easy poems, as easy to read as not to read, and probably easy to write — as Karl Kraus said of aphorisms, poems are easy to write when you don't know how), contemporary poetic difficulty in America, at its most important, results from our own critique of our sense of uniqueness, our distrust of the forms of affirmation which belie its continuing necessity. Ashbery has said that all of his poems are love poems, but this is not because the name of a beloved is coded in a pseudonym, or that desires and the sad knowledge we have about desires are clothed in trope or clouded in scheme. He is concerned, as I think all our important poets are now, with what our imagination makes of our ordinariness, with what the possible rescues are actually like. He starts with a rusty old saw which rebukes all poets, all talkers, with the advice to "shut up and then everything may be O.K." He chops it in half, and then says most. Ashbery's poems are full of the unspecial: stretches of banal phrases that stumble against peaks of visionary image, faceted clichés in the ordinarily cheap settings of inverted commas. But to confuse this use of the givens of our lives (as some of his sillier admirers have done) with what has been called "pop art" is a little like confusing Emerson with Mary Baker Eddy. The banalities are hard; the difficulty of the poems as poems is the difficulty of making sense out of our lives. "Reality," noted the young Wallace Stevens, "is so Chicagoan, so plain, so unmeditative" and yet it alone must bear the weight of all our unfancying meditation. In this sense, the truest poetry is New Yorkean, complex, reflective.

But this does not mean that its mode must necessarily be urban: "the need of being versed in country things" is as much a need of being versed, of being mythologically prepared to read any region of experience, as of the mind's hunger for rural truths. In an astonishing little one-line poem, Emerson once implied that poetry associates the extra-urban scene with the broadcasting of knowledge which in the city is kept pent: "A man tells a secret for the same reason that he loves the country." Emerson's image is the exultant yell of openness here, but it must not be mistaken for an echo of the country's own voice, which broadcasts nothing in the way of truth. Like the urban scene, it presents emblems to be read, and it presents the general enigma of emblem — of making sense out of what we know we are amidst. Whether for Whitman's post-initiate consulting the oracle of the sea after hearing the great Ode of the mockingbird's loss, or for the guarded Frost, not even inquiring of his long scythe (in "Mowing") whether it knew the relevant text in Deutero-Isaiah, the voice of nature could only come in a whisper. Straining to hear that whisper has been a major American poetic act always, just as squinting at our scenes for the shadows cast upon them by our lives has been one of the major visions of "that wilder image" (as Bryant called it) of our painting. In one sense, the poet should not want to have nature's voice, for no matter how mighty in decibels the roaring wind, it is a philosopher with laryngitis; the truth of audibly moving water can only be hearsay. And yet the poet's longing for nature's way of making things, and of making things happen (beyond breed to brave Time when he takes you hence), reflects so many of our general longings for authenticity in the manufacture of our lives.

A. R. Ammons is a poet who strains for whispers and squints, not so much for the shadows as for what hides in them and how they appear to lengthen and deepen apart from the time of day. As a poet of nature he walks in the country accompanied by the moving shadow cast by the light of his own consciousness. More than a reader of emblems, more than an epigrammatizing biologist or even a chanting thanatologist, he engages the countryside with the powerful hands of awareness in a working of the land that is also a playing with it. Santayana warned that "if we do not know our environment, we shall mistake our dreams for a part of it, and so spoil our science by making it fantastic, and our dreams by making them obligatory." He was talking of a culture which has gone well on its way toward doing just that; but there is the internalized civilization of the individual imagination which provides us with exemplary states of consciousness, and in Ammons's poetry, the mythology of structure and function in plant and animal flowers all year long.

The last of the poems with which we shall now confront ourselves is perhaps atypical of Ammons's meditations on a site or sample, but representative of the American poem of longing for natural power. It is a text of the 1970s, marked by a somewhat deceptive rhetorical ease and, unlike both "Mirror" and "Soonest Mended," standing clear of the shifting track of memory. It is the set of dedicatory verses to Ammons's long poem, "Sphere." More than some of his rightly best-known meditations on radiance and clarity such as "Gravelly Run" or "The City Limits," it points to the question of our naturalness. The poet starts out from a familiar point: the mountain top from which both classical and biblical visions are vouchsafed:

> I went to the summit and stood in the high nakedness:
> the wind tore about this
> way and that in confusion and its speech could not
> get through to me nor could I address it:

The first *modern* summit is probably that of Mont Ventoux, which Petrarch attained in April of 1336, partially on the original grounds that "it was there and so I had to climb it," partially because of the injunctions of biblical and classical story. He ascended to the very windy summit, accompanied by a beloved brother, ignoring the aged shepherd "in the folds of the mountain" who tried to dissuade him from the climb and, most important of all, carrying with him a pocket-sized manuscript of Augustine's *Confessions*. At the summit, by a kind of *sortes*, he opened his codex to a text which indicated that men go to admire high mountains, the sea, the great rivers, the stars, and thereby desert themselves. What Petrarch discovered on the windy mountain was about the height and scope of consciousness; never again would summits be the same.

Ammons's unnamed, general summit does not afford him the opportunity for discourse, much less communion, that Whitman might have felt there, and having been brought to where he stands by personal history, and by the history of poetic art, he can only examine nature's inability to reflect, or to echo:

> still I said as if to the alien in myself
>           I do not speak to the wind now:
> for having been brought this far by nature I have been
> brought out of nature
> and nothing here shows me the image of myself:
> for the word *tree* I have been shown a tree
> and for the word *rock* I have been shown a rock,
> for stream, for cloud, for star
> this place has provided firm implication and answering
>           but where here is the image for *longing*:

What Ammons, what we all, have inherited from our meditative tradition is a way of reading parts of a world for the whole; his summit-climber finds at the top of contemplation the signatures of the divine words in the things that embody, or image, them. But what had led him to try for heights remains unrepresented in the vision those very heights afford. Neither would natural philosophy afford him that, nor would the most profound caressing of the phenomena themselves, rather than an unpeeling of them in quest of the structures which produce those appearances. Ammons continues, in the next lines, to maintain this, starting with an important echo of Whitman's syntax:

> so I touched the rocks, their interesting crusts:
> I flaked the bark of stunt-fir:
> I looked into the space and into the sun
> and nothing answered my word *longing*:

— And again, his final exhortation to an unlistening nature sings a tune sadly playful in a Whitmanian way at first —

> goodbye, I said, goodbye, nature so grand and
> reticent, your tongues are healed up into their own
> element
> and as you have shut up you have shut me out: I am
> as foreign here as if I had landed, a visitor:

As if the tongues by which nature could speak to Wordsworth, or to Emerson, had been wounds of some sort? The single word "element" is isolated in its verse, free of local syntax, as if thereby to represent its silence. The art which must speak for nature, as, indeed, for all of the rest of our silence, must come from some other, unsublime "element," and Ammons's climber descends to baser ground, to muck around in the Adamic mud and shape a new piece of natural history. It will not be a mere filling of a void, no fantastic substitution for the longed-*for*, but, of necessity, a human image of another sort.

> I took the image to the summit: first
> I set it here, on the top rock, but it completed
> nothing: then I set it there among the tiny firs
> but it would not fit:

Unlike Wallace Stevens's jar that "did not give of bird nor bush / Like nothing else in Tennessee," Ammons's image completes nothing because it answers to no longing of the hilltops, to nothing in rock, tree, stream, cloud, or star that has ever quested after a greater naturalness, or hearkened after a prior voice. This is not the complaint of the First Shaper that His human creation would not fit in Paradise, nor that of some human simulator of forms that his golem would not play properly and quietly in the back yard. I suppose that it is possible to imagine the "image for longing" as a woman, or a beautiful youth — an image *of* (but not, in Ammons's richer sense, "for") a longed-for object of desire. But in this case, it would be the image of an image, and the longing of the poet-climber for the intercourse with mute nature would be troped by the absence of a beautiful body. Nor would a reflexive emblem satisfy the conditions of the poem—a modelled image of a man modelling an image of what — or of whom — he desires. One need only think of the Creator, contemplating his garden with a sense of his distance from his own creation, and setting amid its rocks and trees an image of himself, in order to decide what sort of figure Ammons's image for longing makes.

But its appearance is not in fact the problem. It is a question of the ecology of significance, of what in this poem is spoken of as a setting. Even the poem that would complete the silences of nature must seek out the city of understanding. And "so," says Ammons,

> I returned to the city and built a house to set
> the image in
> and men came to my house and said
> that is an image for *longing*
> and nothing will ever be the same again

—And to do that to everything was why the poet came. Perhaps this ends with the same ambiguity of syntactic closure that makes us wonder, in the absence of canonical punctuation, about who is saying exactly how much at the end of Keats's poem on the urn: despite its present tense, is the last time only what the others say in recognition of the image? Is it not part of the testament of the poem? The time of poetic vocation which lies in the distant past of Merrill's mirror, unremembered or, at any rate, unrecalled, and which Ashbery continually reinvokes, is here memorialized as a bardic anecdote. The image completed nothing in the wild which called forth the need of it; the maker had to return to the ground to gather the element of such an image, and to return to the city to build a house which the image might complete.

In one sense, "I Went to the Summit" is the poem of the First Poem, both in the poet's history and in that of the world. A parody of Creation, it reminds us of the Original Trope (and, perhaps, causes us to linger for a moment over the identity of that trope: is the relation of Creator to Man one of metaphor? irony? synec-doche? metonymy?). But in its parody, Ammons's tale avoids the confusions of the uninspiring winds that tear about the summit. If at a lower altitude they would whisper of death—that message which is our imagination's overload always—at the privileged, high place which seems to point toward transcendence, there is nothing to be understood. In all our general American longings, our uneasy quest for "firm implication and answering," it is so easy to pretend to understand the wind in the high nakedness, and to descend, ever to echo its roaring. But the poet will not have that, nor will, by extension, the unpublishing poet who fills every wise, passionate consciousness. He must make an image for longing, and then build a house of life for which that image will remain the *lar familiaris*, as the Romans referred to it, the household spirit.

Every stage of life has its losses, and every age of culture its own longings. Not to avow these will probably not lead to the making of poems which command us to change our lives, poems imbued with what D. H. Lawrence called "a passionate, implicit morality, not didactic." Much well-intentioned verse which, as we have seen, can respond too directly and too trivially to the violences from without remains, in Ammons's myth, the equivalent of carefully-worked samplers hung on the walls of a house not even built for them, but inherited. (Were I to have been discussing style here, I might have added that during the last decade it even became fashionable for the samplers to present their ABCs and their pieties not in the careful fancywork of long tradition, but over-wrought instead with the *fausse-naïve*, misshapen and tearstained as if by an incapacitated or miserably unwilling child.) But the true poems which embody images for the losses as well as the longing cannot merely *be* homely wisdom. They must reinvent wisdom and even homeliness itself.

To this extent, then — that at the end of every true poem "nothing will ever be the same again" — the problems of American affirmation, of modern heroism, and of the apparent impossibility of wisdom seem part of the same condition. Like the medieval *chansons de geste*, the heroic poems which flowered in times of treasons, strategems, and spoils, and the *chansons d'amour* which filled in with language the space created by absence, our poems of love and deed at once blossom only in our own late aftertime. After the originations of nature, our images of rocks and trees are not enough, and it is only in our poems of awareness of this insuffi-ciency that we can live our imaginative lives. Such poems fill in the spaces vacated by the ever-vanishing hope of our ever *being* our models, our heroes, our images of the good, original life, and aid us to become them, by, and within, ourselves. In an America past the time of its own youth, promise, and capability, it is not for a major poetry to mourn the time of year, but to provide images for *imagining*. If a man, to be greatly good, must indeed "imagine intensely and comprehensively" — if, the more complex his na-ture, the more dialectic, the more historical vision, and the more humor he must be able to exercise — then it must be such poems which will nourish the imagination, if only by forcing the reader to cooperate in their creation. We may want verses to touch, to tickle, to caress, to remind, to wound us: the many modes of sermon, editorial, and epigram contrive to do those and more. In the absence of wisdom, the poetry of modernism informed us, there is only the sad knowledge of that absence and a way of putting what we know in "a series of isolated perfections" perhaps. Our epigrams continue in that task. For the larger questions, our late epics, our derived romances, our scriptures and their commentaries, come more and more to be scattered among the leaves of our meditative lyrics.

It is these poems which have come to be our poetry of restitution — for local and for general losses; for the exhausted powers of private and public language (and when the sword avers the pen to be mightier, let us beware, for that will only occur in a police state); for vanished emblems of wisdom, ever needing replacement; for the vacancies left by modernist poetry's view of its own history; and for the continuing American task of self-invention — a burden as cruel as that of the demand for originality which modernism has thrust upon all poor artisans — if not even half-completed in a summer of national power, then perhaps to be continued in a brave autumn of decline.

# I AM LEARNING TO ABANDON THE WORLD

by LINDA PASTAN

from POETRY

*nominated by Michael Blumenthal, Josephine Jacobsen and Lynne Sharon Schwartz*

I am learning to abandon the world
before it can abandon me.
Already I have given up the moon
and snow, closing my shades
against the claims of white.
And the world has taken
my father, my friends.
I have given up melodic lines of hills,
moving to a flat, tuneless landscape.
And every night I give my body up
limb by limb, working upwards
across bone, towards the heart.
But morning comes with small
reprieves of coffee and birdsong.
A tree outside the window
which was simply shadow moments ago
takes back its branches twig
by leafy twig.
And as I take my body back
the sun lays its warm muzzle on my lap
as if to make amends.

# WHAT THE GOSSIPS SAW

## by LEO ROMERO

from AGUA NEGRA (Ahsahta Press)

*nominated by Ahsahta Press*

Everyone pitied Escolastica, her leg
had swollen like a watermelon in the summer
It had practically happened over night
She was seventeen, beautiful and soon
to be married to Guillermo who was working
in the mines at Terreros, eighty miles away
far up in the mountains, in the wilderness
Poor Escolastica, the old women would say
on seeing her hobble to the well with a bucket
carrying her leg as if it were the weight
of the devil, surely it was a curse from heaven
for some misdeed, the young women who were
jealous would murmur, yet they were grieved too
having heard that the doctor might cut
her leg, one of a pair of the most perfect legs
in the valley, and it was a topic of great
interest and conjecture among the villagers
whether Guillermo would still marry her
if she were crippled, a one-legged woman—
as if life weren't hard enough for a woman
with two legs — how could she manage
Guillermo returned and married Escolastica
even though she had but one leg, the sound
of her wooden leg pounding down the wooden aisle
stayed in everyone's memory for as long
as they lived, women cried at the sight
of her beauty, black hair so dark

that the night could get lost in it, a face
more alluring than a full moon

Escolastica went to the dances with her husband
and watched and laughed but never danced
though once she had been the best dancer
and could wear holes in a pair of shoes
in a matter of a night, and her waist had been
as light to the touch as a hummingbird's flight
And Escolastica bore five children, only half
what most women bore, yet they were healthy
In Escolastica's presence, no one would mention
the absence of her leg, though she walked heavily
And it was not long before the gossips
spread their poison, that she must be in cohorts
with the devil, had given him her leg
for the power to bewitch Guillermo's heart
and cloud his eyes so that he could not see
what was so clear to them all

# SHELTER THE PILGRIM

fiction by FRED LICHT

from THE HUDSON REVIEW

*nominated by* THE HUDSON REVIEW

To MY GRANDFATHER, who was very much a ghetto Jew, charity was one of the exigencies of life. You breathed. You ate. You gave. Steadily and without having to think about it, my grandfather went every week to visit a hospital run by the Orthodox community bringing with him cigarettes, fruit, newspapers and a bit of money.

To my parents who prided themselves on being "advanced Jews" and brought us up to think of grandfather as honorable but picturesque, charity was a duty one performed at a distance. They wrote two checks, one at Passover, the other at New Year and received, in return, a form letter of thanks from the agency that received their donation.

To me, to my brother and to my sister, charity is an equivocal institution designed to keep the poor in their place. We have read Marx and we have read Freud and we can quote chapter and verse about charity as a form of social bribery and self-delusion for the abreaction of social and personal guilt-feelings. We still write and send off checks at regular intervals, but we do so with a good deal of self-irony, as if indulging a quaint but not too harmful superstition. We clearly know that charity is patronizing and shameful and the ugly fruit of uglier injustice. But we are somewhat dissatisfied with our knowledge. We have come to be understanding of our parents and have come to venerate our grandfather and his bag full of cigarettes and oranges with which he set out every Friday after lunch. But we also suspect that we don't know what any of them was all about.

It has always been difficult to think about these things but my brother and my sister and I are convinced that it is the only thing that we ought to think about because if we could come out in the clear in this one simple matter, we could make our peace with all the rest.

When the affairs on my father's firm required our moving from Paris to Berlin in 1937, my mother for all her being "advanced" nevertheless felt that inviting the rabbi over in order to make a donation was as much part of settling into a new home as unpacking the suitcases and spreading the carpets.

The rabbi arrived thoroughly unsettled by the phenomenon of a Jewish family moving *to* Germany in those days of flight and panic. He harangued my parents on the irresponsibility of taking the family into the heart of a dangerous storm but accepted the customary check for the charities of his congregation. Mother, always anxious to win her children over to the outdoor life we despised, asked him whether there was an outing club or sports association in which she might enroll her three children. Patiently, as if speaking to a child, the rabbi explained to her that the community was in chaos and disintegration. Those who had not yet fled took every care to dissociate themselves from anything Jewish in the hope of passing unmolested. For burials, for Bar Mitzvahs and for the High Holidays, he had to hunt and cajole among the remnants of a once proud community sufficient attendance to constitute a *minyan,* the ritual quorum without which services could not take place.

My mother objected that there must be some sort of activity in which her children could contribute so that they would not feel totally disconnected from the kind of religious community which the whole family had always known.

The rabbi, a rather unprepossessing person, as I remember him, with pudgy hands and tiny, perfectly round and staring eyes, thought awhile and then nodded. There was always something to be done but he doubted that we would want to do it. The implication that we were too spoiled and too stupid to understand the situation in which we found ourselves stung us all to the quick and even before he told us what it was he had in mind, we were determined to say yes just to have the pleasure of proving him wrong.

There was, it appeared, a home for retarded orphans still being operated by the community. Most of the healthy orphans had been resettled with the help of Dutch and American and English congregations but, as was only logical, nobody wanted to take in mentally crippled children. There had been fairly generous contributions to keep the institute in Berlin running smoothly, but there was no getting around the fact that they were being abandoned. Among these children there were quite a few who weren't absolutely hopeless. They could dress themselves and do some rudimentary reading and writing. The aunts and cousins who had placed them in the institution had, for the most part, emigrated, and the children were growing more and more despondent as their former contacts with the outside world dwindled to nothing. The nurses hardly dared take them out for walks anymore because there had been violent incidents. Now that Sunday visits to distant relatives had stopped, these children were limited to their dormitory and to the narrow asphalt yard in which they played. For the utterly benighted children, it didn't matter, of course, but for the others . . . In short, would we consider inviting one of these children to our house for weekend visits so that he could have a bit of family life and affection and normal childhood play? It would make an enormous difference.

We children were aghast at the notion and with the healthy brutality of childhood hoped fervently that mother, who usually objected to our bringing school-friends home because they upset her tidy householder's routine, would refuse. We felt absolutely betrayed when, without so much as glancing in our direction, she

said that she would be delighted to receive one of these children
for weekends. Two days later the rabbi phoned to tell her that the
boy he had selected was called Ernst, that we was fourteen years
old, my age, of impeccable cleanliness and that even though he
had the mind of a six-year-old he would amaze us all by a curious
gift he had of doing the most astonishingly complicated mathematical and algebraic problems in his head within seconds.

We children had decided beforehand that the one closest in age
to the impending guest would bear the brunt of the visit while the
others would help out now and then. Ernst, therefore, fell to my
lot and since I didn't have much faith in my sister's and brother's
loyalty in this matter, I didn't look forward to Friday. The mathematical quirk of our imbecile guest was a personal offense.
Arithmetic was my weakest subject, and I toiled over my home-
work in daily bitterness and frustration while my teacher kept
repeating that if only I could understand the mathematical discipline of mind all the rest would come by itself. To have an idiot
crassly expose my weakness enraged me and I went into a wild
tantrum when my mother told me on Friday that I was to fetch
Ernst from his institution after school. Parental orders went un-
questioned in our fairly authoritarian household. But at this I
balked. I would go accompanied by my older sister and by my
younger brother or I simply would not go. My mother found the
scene I made unreasonable but felt, on the whole, that my request,
though silly, was acceptable. At school's end, therefore, I found
Edith and Jonathan waiting for me looking sulky and keeping a
glacial silence. It was a drizzly day toward the end of September
and the orphanage inMoabit was accessible from our school only by
a complicated trip which required changing from the underground
to a bus and then to yet another bus. I tried to make up for the
discomfort that I had imposed on them by offering to buy hot
chocolate at the corner Conditorei. Jonathan who was always
straightforward refused outright. Edith, who was sneaky, accepted
the bribe; but after she had greedily finished her hot chocolate, she
still refused to speak to me.

It wasn't till we were on the last bus, driving through Moabit
that we drew together again. Moabit is an immense and squalid
slum utterly without color or the kind of devil-may-care arrogance
that makes the slums of Latin countries less dispiriting. None of us
had ever seen such wretchedness before. We were too young to

put it into words but involuntarily and silently we put by our
squabble and stood abashed at its triviality. We had suddenly come
up against the extent of our good fortune which had spoiled us and
which we took for granted.

The institution, when we finally found it after losing the way
several times in the mirror-maze of block after block of uniformity
and wretchedness, turned out be a low barracks, sooty and forlorn.
The roof had been mended here and there with tarpaper and
wooden laths; the brick wall which ran clear around it bore patches
of torn advertisements and was topped by a grim run of broken
glass. We were not allowed inside but had to wait in the porter's
lodge which was foul with rancid smells and the fumes of a pot-
bellied stove. The porter stared at us with unconcealed hatred
while we shifted from one foot to the other, avoided each others'
eyes and felt by turns vaguely guilt-stricken and aggressively
arrogant. The door opened and an elderly lady in a white smock
entered resolutely holding on to a recalcitrant boy with a sullen
and peevish look on his round and somewhat beefy face. He was
taller than I and bigger, but in a bloated, unhealthy way. It
occurred to me that if it should come to a fight, I would win
without any great effort.

Meanwhile, with the kind of mechanical cheerfulness that scorns
to hide its artificiality, the woman in the white smock was making
the introductions.

"Don't they look nice, your new friends? You must be Edith, of
course, and which of you young men is Jonathan and who is
Henry? Oh good! Now off with the lot of you before it gets dark.
And remember — be back on Sunday not later than six. Come on
now, Ernst," she cajoled in the same artificially patient tone.
"Come on, there's no reason to be shy! You'll have a marvellous
time."

But Ernst seemed unwilling to budge. I was in an ecstasy of
embarrassment and paralyzed with a surge of compassion such as I
had never felt before. Jonathan, by my side, was also stricken; of
that I felt sure without even looking up. Strangely it was Edith who
saved the situation. As long as Ernst remained a weekend guest in
our house, I never failed to be amazed at Edith's quick and
effective sympathy for him coupled with absolutely cool detach-
ment. Like an efficient but somewhat distraught mother helping
her little daughter with her knitting, Edith would step in when-

ever Ernst and I reached an impasse, set things straight and hand him back to me while she went quickly on her way. Now, rudely and nonchalantly ignoring the nurse, she broke in with one of those algebraic problems that always made me go clammy and weak inside.

"Ernst, if one car starting out here travels at fifty kilometers an hour and another car starts from the same point seven hours later but travels at sixty kilometers an hour, when will the second car overtake the first car?"

"After three hours and ten minutes," Ernst said just as you or I might say "good morning" without the slightest hesitation and without a trace of triumph. Though he towered over her, he took Edith's hand as children do at streetcrossings and without a backward glance turned to leave the porter's lodge. Jonathan and I followed, perplexed beyond the ability to think over what had happened.

Outside, Edith resolutely put Ernst's hand in mine.

"You're going to be Henry's friend from now on," she said.

Ernst looked at her, impassive and stolid, and then looked at me. Unable to fathom what went on in Ernst's round head, I simply stared back, not daring to venture so much as a smile. Then he nodded. His hand which had lain in mine like a passive object closed around mine with a firm grip and he nodded again. Edith, Jonathan and I were seized by the same panic. If we let one minute go by, we would never find the way back to where we belonged. Like children under a spell we would be doomed to wander about in these gray and rank streets forever. Breaking into a run and dragging a puzzled Ernst with us, we made for the bus stop and did not relax till the familiar lights of the Westend gathered about us once again.

At home we were surprised when mother gave Ernst a very summary and hasty reception. Jonathan and Edith disappeared under spurious pretexts, leaving me to show Ernst my room which he was to share with me. I expected him to be pleased. It was a large and comfortable room filled with the oddments that I had collected over the years: a small mineral collection begun and then abandoned; stamps which I had kept at with slightly greater constancy; all sorts of sports-gear; a Tahitian xylophone; books ranging from the Iliad to cowboy tales; a modest collection of records; and a hand-cranked Victrola. Not knowing quite what to do, I put on a record. But Ernst didn't respond one way or the other. He sat in an uncomfortable armchair by the side of his bed and stared at me, patient but obviously expectant, quite oblivious of the Victrola.

"Would you like to play a game?" I asked, wondering secretly what sort of games one could possibly play with Ernst.

His expression didn't change and for an instant I thought he was deaf. Finally, unable to support his steadfast stare any longer, I got out a piece of paper and tried tic-tac-toe. He didn't know the game and I tried to explain it to him. It is difficult to explain very simple matters when one is fourteen, and I was clumsy and self-conscious as I went about the business of x's and o's and how one had to try to line them up. Ernst followed me very seriously and we tried our hand at the game for a few turns. But just as I finally thought he understood the game he unaccountably lost interest. Again he looked at me expectantly. It was many weeks before I realized that his stare was really blank and not at all expectant. He was quite content to sit and watch me even if I did nothing more interesting than read a book. Once I discovered this quirk, things got easier for me, but at that moment I was near the end of my tether.

With the piece of paper between us and a pencil at hand, I decided to try another game: the one in which each participant draws part of an image, folding the paper in such a way as to hide everything but the bottom lines before handing the paper over to the next player. The point of the game is the incongruous, fantastic picture that appears when the paper is unfolded. I remember being fascinated by the game when I was in Kindergarten and thought it would do beautifully for Ernst. He seemed to understand my instructions quite easily this time and turned out to be a very meticulous, painstaking draughtsman. I was delighted to have hit on something that made time pass so agreeably.

"All right now," I said when we had reached the bottom of the page and it was time to unfold the paper, "Let's see what sort of monster we have got here."

Of its sort, the picture was a tremendous success. My sloppy sketches contrasted vividly with Ernst's precise and sober rendering of faces, bodies and landscape. He looked at the page for a long time and seemed to grow perplexed at first and downright angry afterwards.

"Don't you think it's funny?"

He shook his head stubbornly and handed the page back to me visibly agitated, as if he had been tricked in some way and could see no justification for the deception that had been practiced on him. But by then it was time to go into the living room where Edith and mother lighted the Sabbath candles. Ernst was very proud of being given a cap to wear while the prayers were said but didn't seem to have any interest at all in the little ceremony. He kept fingering his hat and later asked whether he could keep it on during dinner.

"Just like in a synagogue," he kept repeating cheerfully.

"Do you often go to synagogue?" mother asked and Ernst nodded and laughed.

"I like going to synagogue." Abruptly he started to mutter a few prayers in Hebrew which he had contrived to learn by heart. But when we complimented him on knowing them so well, he was surprised and started to stare again.

At dinner he behaved better than we could have foreseen. He was clumsy with the silver, holding knife and fork at the very base of the handle and he sometimes lost track of how much he had in his mouth and stuffed himself, but there was a great attention to detail that bore out the rabbi's prediction that he was very tidy and clean. Once when he broke his roll, a few crumbs scattered on the floor and he simply couldn't go on eating without first getting up from his chair and squatting on the floor till he had picked up every tiniest speck. He particularly loved apples and had a way of peeling them in a continuous spiral which pleased him immensely. Father asked him whether he would mind peeling an apple for each one of us and Ernst beamed with gratification. It took almost half an hour before we each had an apple, but because of father's inspiration, we all got up from the table feeling that dinner had been a great success.

Going to bed was what I dreaded most. I hadn't had a chance to get used to my manhood yet and all the family teased me about being exaggeratedly shy. It was excruciating for me to be seen in my pajamas or my underwear, and now I would have to undress with an utter stranger in my room. For his part, Ernst had no qualms at all. With the careful, studied tidiness that marked all his gestures, he slowly got undressed while I sat on the edge of my bed wondering where I could hide and envying Ernst for his nonchalance. As in a trance I watched him take off his sweater, then his shirt, his trousers and his socks. His skin was very white and fine, rather like a baby's; and when he finally stood naked by the side of his bed, I saw that there wasn't the vaguest sign of that change which bedevilled most of my waking and almost all my sleeping hours. The sight of Ernst grown to the full height of a man but childish in every other way overwhelmed me with a sudden, shameful but irrepressible wave of physical disgust. I couldn't get myself to undress in front of him. Mumbling some stupid words meant for an excuse, I grabbed my pajamas, my robe and disappeared into the bathroom.

Returning, I found that Ernst had already turned out the light in my room. I was used to reading in bed before falling asleep; but out of a sense of hospitality I didn't want to turn the light on again even though I could tell from his breathing that Ernst was still awake. I lay in the dark wondering how I was going to live through the rest of the weekend when suddenly his voice broke in on me. He sounded strangely shy and hesitant and like a child that wants something but doesn't know what he wants or how to go about getting it.

"Henry? Please ask me a question, Henry."

"All right. Here's a question: what do you want to do tomorrow?" I spoke more brusquely than I had intended. There was a silence. Then:

"Not that kind of a question," Ernst said timidly and obviously close to tears. "*My* kind of a question." He was almost whispering now. As so often in my encounters with Ernst I felt deeply ashamed and consequently vengeful.

"What's your kind of question?"

"You know — my kind of question. The kind I'm good at."

"All right. But I'm not good at asking them."

"When were you born?"

"On February 12th, 1922."

"Now ask me what day of the week it was."

"All right, Ernst — what day of the week was it?"

"A Saturday. And now ask me what day of the week it will be in the year two thousand and twelve."

"Why don't you just tell me," I said, exasperated.

"Ask me. Please!"

"On what day of the week will my birthday fall in the year two thousand and twelve?"

"Wednesday," he sighed happily. "Thank you, Henry. Thank you for asking me."

Saturday passed easily enough. Ernst liked to stay in bed in the morning, and I sneaked from my room, dressed, had breakfast and sought refuge with Jonathan. It was eleven before Ernst finally got up and since it took him a long time to take his bath and get dressed, the morning was gone without my having to do anything at all. Lunch passed off easily, too. We were all a bit apprehensive about whether Ernst would want to peel apples for all of us but he seemed to have forgotten his triumph of the previous evening. Jonathan promised to take care of Ernst till three when I was to take him to the movies. I had looked forward to having an hour off but when I entered my room alone, I found that I wasn't really in the mood for anything much and just moved about restlessly till it was time to go.

Ernst didn't have any preference where movies were concerned and followed me with great docility to a film about car racing. On subsequent visits our Saturday afternoon at the movies was repeated religiously. In time, I took him to every conceivable kind of film but could never quite make out which sort of movie he liked best. Now and then, especially during sequences that played on a ship or at the beach, he would talk to himself saying how pretty it was but he never seemed to disapprove of anything. Murder mysteries which frightened me to death and love scenes which I thought contemptible went past him without eliciting visible signs of displeasure. And, strangely enough, he always managed to understand the plot when we talked about the movie on the way home even though he could never follow the thread when I tried to tell him of some incident that had happened to me or some story a friend had related to me. Maybe the acting out of the story made it easier for him to grasp the situation while episodes that consisted only of words confused him. I don't know about such things.

If Saturday had been a success, Sunday was a despondent failure. We let him sleep again as long as he wanted to but when he did get up, he was nervous and hurried and got everything wrong and I had to make him undress again and turn his clothes right side out. At lunch he choked on his food; and after the meal, it was obvious that he was already thinking of having to go back to the institution. He just sat there, fidgeting, unable to do anything, just waiting to get it over with. On the bus he hardly spoke a word and kept looking out of the window. He was breathing hard. The window fogged up and he wiped the pane with his hand getting himself all smudgy.

"Why don't you stop wiping the window?" I suddenly said irritably.

He folded his hands in his lap, looking at them with distaste but obviously imposing his best behavior on himself in order to please me. At the porter's lodge, I tried to shake hands with him but he refused because his hands were so dirty.

"I'll be here on Friday again."

"I don't think you will come."

"Yes I will. Of course I will. Why do you say that I won't?"

He was silent, looked down and then turned from me and went through the yard to the barracks at the far end.

After such a gloomy farewell, I expected him to be cheerfully surprised when I came to fetch him on the following Friday. But it was as if he had forgotten all about me in the intervening time, and it was several hours before we were on familiar terms again. The third week he expected me and even though I always resented the duty my parents had imposed on me, I grew used to it. In a way I managed to get a certain amount of prestige out of the situation vis-à-vis my school-friends. It got around that I played nursemaid to Ernst on weekends and gradually some of my more inquisitive friends asked to see him. On these occasions I would sometimes be extra kind to him to impress my friends with my philanthropic tendencies. Just as inexplicably I would sometimes show off before my school friends by being deliberately cruel to Ernst to show my comrades that I had trained him to loyalty as one might train a dog. And either way, Ernst was happy. He clearly regarded these friends who came and went as ephemeral creatures of no account while he was part of the family.

"I'm staying here," he would irrelevantly and abruptly tell these friends at odd moments of the afternoon. "And you have to go home."

He quite willingly put up with my willfulness as if realizing that both my exaggerated kindness and my equally artificial brutality to him were put on only for my friends and had no meaning as far as he was concerned. Once I pushed him so far that we came to blows. My impression that he represented no physical threat to me proved to be quite mistaken. When we began to fight, he was caught off guard. He hadn't noticed my mounting irritation when he remained goodnatured and oblivious to the taunts which I flung at him to show my friend that I was like a ring master with a beast. Taken by surprise, he fought back with far more energy than I expected, and he easily could have got the better of me. But suddenly he stopped fighting and went limp. Looking at me and at my friend he laughed an odd laugh that was cut short in his throat. I managed to free myself and pushed him away so that he staggered against the wall. My friend, awkwardly ashamed for me and of the spectacle I had put on for his entertainment, said he had to go home.

In November my class went on a school trip and to my surprise and also to my disappointment, Ernst gave no sign of sadness when I told him that I would not be back to fetch him next weekend. In December the whole family was to go to the mountains for a skiing vacation and mother decided that we would celebrate Channukah a little early so that Ernst would be able to be with us for the festivities and for the presents. Edith had knitted him socks. I gave him a little box with minerals that glowed in the dark, Jonathan got him some sweets of which he was especially fond and my parents bought him a handsome winter coat. Ernst was beside himself with joy. He was allowed to light the candles and even though you're only supposed to light two candles on the first day of Channukah, he asked to be allowed to light all eight and stood over the Menorah in beatific enchantment torn between looking at the presents and the glow of the chased silver candle-holder.

He had never been demonstrative of his affections. Probably hugging and kissing is something that has to be learned in the cradle and being an orphan, Ernst had never learned it. Now, not knowing how to find release for all the pent-up happiness, he ran from me to mother, from mother to Edith and back to me and to Jonathan. He stood in front of us, tense and tremulous not knowing what to say or do, and when one of us asked him whether he was happy he went visibly rigid with the effort of trying to tell us just how happy he was. It was Edith who again saved the situation by kissing him soundly on both cheeks. Ernst gave a deep sigh after that and went off to sit in a corner with his presents. The minerals

he took to bed with him that night and there was a soft, steady glow
by his bedside when we turned out the lights. In January, when I
fetched him home on our first Friday back in Berlin, he seemed to
have forgotten Channukah altogether — or at least he didn't talk
about it. We picked up our routine again, with Saturday movies
and a walk to a good pastry shop on the Oliva Platz after supper for
sweets gluttonously stuffed with whipped cream. He became so
much a member of the household that we no longer made special
efforts to amuse him. Often I would go out on Saturday mornings
with friends and leave him at home all by himself. He didn't mind
in the least but played with my things or else went into the kitchen
to help peel potatoes for the pommes-frites he adored and always
got at lunch time.

That every farewell brings with it a premonition of death, of the
ultimate farewell, is known to all. Even children have sufficient
experience of that numb, wordless sensation of grief that comes
with goodbyes, a grief that is diluted but never quite dissipated by
time and that surges to the surface ever more strongly each time a
new turning in our lives tears us from old customs and friendships.
But I believe that there is something more important involved
than the mere premonition of death. I believe that there is in our
goodbyes also a prophecy of the manner and the worthiness of our
dying. Are we able to part with friends and with life with conscious
dignity or with a hasty nervousness, anxious to get it over with?
When we come to partings, are we baffled and confused or can we
look steadfastly at what we can't understand and accept it nevertheless? We inevitably show color at such moments and what really
frightens us is the foreknowledge that we will do no better when
the final parting comes. Such moments mark us for life.
I don't precisely know when my parents decided that their
moving to Berlin in such times and under such circumstances had
been an unjustifiable mistake. Or else — my parents have always
avoided the subject — they had come to Berlin with a specific
purpose in mind and having achieved it, they naturally decided to
go home to Paris again. In any case, we children were told late in
April. The school year came to an end in mid-June and shortly after
that we would leave. There remained the business of Ernst.
Mother was of the opinion that it would be best not to tell him
anything. What was the use of burdening him and spoiling the

weekends that remained? For all we knew, his mind was incapable of taking in recurring events. He might miss me for a few minutes when one fine Friday I didn't show up in the porter's lodge to take him home with me but his sense of time was confused in any case. He might not even realize that it was Friday. Father and Edith were against such a plan. Secretly I agreed with them although mother's idea suited me better for I recoiled at the very idea of having to tell Ernst that we were leaving for good. We finally arrived at a compromise. Father was to call the doctor who ran the institution (nominally at least: I don't believe he ever looked in more than fifteen minutes once or twice a week) to put the case before him. The doctor decided that we must tell him and that it would be best to tell him a little bit ahead of time so that he would have a chance to get used to the idea. I know nothing of the clinical side of Ernst's case and cannot tell whether the doctor's advice was sound. But in mid-May, just after Sunday lunch, when Ernst and I were about to get ready for going back to the orphanage, I steeled myself and took the leap.

"Ernst, I have to tell you something that makes me sad and I'm afraid that it might make you sad, too. But pretty soon, all of us, Edith and Jonathan and I and my parents will be leaving to go to Paris."

He looked blank, with his head tilted a little to one side, an attitude he sometimes took when he feared being scolded.

"Paris is very far away. Look, let me show you."

I took out my atlas and showed him where Berlin was and where Paris was and how far it was from one city to the other. But I got tangled in trying to explain the map scale to him and that a tiny millimeter on the map was much, much longer than the trip from the orphanage to our home. I suddenly had the feeling that he could understand if he wanted to — we had managed to get more difficult concepts through to him — but that he simply didn't want to understand what I was saying. I grew curt and told him that sometime in June we would go away and that was that. I gave him his jacket and put my jacket on and headed for the front door.

Outside, of course, I repented having been so short and took his arm as we went off to the bus station.

"You see, we have to go to Paris. That's where our family is. My grandfather and my cousins and aunts. They all live there and we have to go live with them."

He nodded.

"But we won't leave right away. We'll see each other plenty of times before we leave."

He nodded again but I could tell he had fallen into that obstinate silence that was his only weapon against a treacherous world. Those silences were uncanny; you felt that he would endure martyrdom rather than make a sound.

On the Friday after that, I had some business to attend to at home before going off to the orphanage for Ernst. The weather had turned warm, sultry almost, but strong gusts of moist wind blew through the streets and grey clouds, bloated with rain, hung heavy and low above the roofs. By the time I got to the orphanage it was getting dark, but I had telephoned ahead to say that I would be late and didn't feel that I need hurry. At the porter's lodge, I sent word, as usual, for Ernst to come and meet me. Even though I am inquisitive by nature, I had never entered the institution though I had been asked to do so quite often by the nurse who accompanied Ernst to the lodge every time that I called.

I was prepared to wait, as usual, for Ernst. He was slow about getting himself together to go out. But within minutes of my arrival, the woman in the white smock crossed the courtyard alone.

"Maybe he doesn't feel well . . . I don't know what it is, but he doesn't want to come today."

"If he is sick you could have told me when I telephoned."

"Well, I didn't know at the time. But he went to bed. I think he must feel sick. The doctor comes tomorrow in any case. We'll see what he says."

"Does he have a fever?"

"No. I took his temperature first thing. That's why I think we can wait till the doctor comes tomorrow. If you'll call around eleven . . ."

Instinct — or is that just a better word for cowardice? — told me to let it go at that. But I rallied and asked her whether I might come in and see him for a while.

"Of course. Please. I am sure your visit will do Ernst good."

She led me through the asphalted court into a long corridor bleak with peeling paint. Ernst shared a room with four other boys and two of them were in the room with him when I entered. They were mongoloids and grinned at me ingratiatingly, their heads swaying back and forth. The nurse trooped them out but they went unwillingly.

Only one bulb lighted the room from the center of the ceiling. Through the tall windows the evening looked dark and inhospitable, the color of a dark bruise.

"Ernst? What's the matter? Don't you feel well?" I suddenly cursed myself. The artificiality of my tone made everything inside me shrink with a pang of shame. Why had I come?

"I don't know," Ernst said. His voice was surprisingly even. "Turn the light off please."

The room was dark now and I took a chair near his bed. Having started, I vaguely felt that I must go on. I don't know why. But I suppose we all want things to be orderly and tidy. When life frays and threatens to be inconclusive we try out of sheer selfishness to mend things that can't be mended.

"Won't you come home with me? Edith has a surprise for you."

He got up—I could hardly see him, it was so dark—and rummaged under his bedstead for a bit. Then he got back under the covers. In his hands he held the fluorescent minerals I had given him and they shed a soft glow. He didn't cry. My throat tightened with tears and I was sure that from one moment to the next Ernst too would begin to weep. But he didn't. Maybe he felt too sad for the kind of easy tears that were swelling behind my eyes or maybe he didn't feel anything at all.

We sat in silence for a long time. Then suddenly as if inspired he clambered out of his bed again, cumbersomely impeded by the minerals he held aloft. Gingerly and with great affection, he placed the glowing rocks and pebbles on the floor before me and looked up at me invitingly as if he expected me to take part in some ritual that would make everything all right. He had some important idea in the back of his mind connected with the radiant stones I had given him. I racked my brain, seized by a sudden panic because I felt quite clearly that I, too, knew what the ritual was—but this knowledge lay just beyond the reach of memory. For a frantic, paralyzing moment I knew how narrow are the limits of the human mind.

Like an animal I was hard up against the electrified wire that circled my little field. I could either break through the imposed limit by risking the shock or I could retreat. For an instant I thought that I might evade the issue yet by deflecting Ernst's grave and expectant stare by throwing him another algebraic puzzle. But no algebraic problem rose to the surface of my mind. It was for me to find what $x$ was worth — I had been given all the data that the equation demanded. With a little effort I could capture the unknown quantity.

Ernst continued to look at me as if what he expected me to do was the most natural thing in the world. The diffuse, tender glow of the mysterious little stones was matched only by the steadfastness of his inviting smile. Then, slowly only the light of the minerals remained hanging between us as the light of his face subsided under ashen disappointment.

He climbed back into bed then, leaving the little heap of minerals at my feet. Turning on his side he looked unblinkingly at me with every meaning, intent or feeling totally extinguished from his eyes.

I stayed a few minutes and then cleared my throat to say goodbye as normally as I could. But my voice didn't quite obey me and the words were left hanging more as if they were a question, a question apprehensive of inducing silence. Then I swiftly left the room, crossed the courtyard at a run and caught the bus two blocks down the street. I met all my mother's efforts to make another try the next day and then again the next week with a steadfast refusal. Adolescent brutality? Fear of hurting Ernst some more? Cowardice? Good sense? It's too long ago for me to tell. But I suppose that it was a bit of each.

We returned to Paris and resumed the life that had been so unpleasantly interrupted. We were still there in 1940 when Paris fell. Six months later — I was nineteen then — my father managed, by means I'll never know, to arrange a complicated plan first to get us out of Paris, then to obtain false papers for us in Marseilles, and finally to bring us across the Pyrenees to the relative safety of Spain.

At first my father insisted that grandfather come with us. But the old man refused. He insisted that he would only be a hindrance and he produced any number of talmudic quotations that spoke of the necessity of preserving young life even if it is at the cost of the old. Besides, he wanted to be buried by the side of his wife and nothing would stir him from his decision. Late in January we were to leave Paris by a night train. On the evening of our flight mother made a light supper which we carried in bowls to grandfather's house. We sat about in silence after dinner till it was time to go. Then, with tranquil deliberation and with unanswerable assurance, grandfather blessed us one after the other, putting his hands on our heads and speaking a steady prayer over each of us.

During the past two or three years I had grown temperamentally and intellectually into anti-religious attitudes. But even I felt incontrovertibly that this man had the power to bless. I felt at peace but I also felt frightened at losing some small detail because I wanted to remember everything about that moment. It would have to last me to my dying day. Never again would I meet a man who could take the full force of benediction onto himself.

Having given us his blessing, grandfather stepped back from where we were standing and dismissed us with a nod. It was he who was voluntarily going from us even though to others it might look as if we were abandoning him in our flight.

Then we slipped away and found . . . well, safety. Survival. Call it what you will.

As for Ernst and grandfather, details hardly matter. They died and they died alone. But to the end each had retained the power to relinquish what had been his, to say farewell on his own terms. I, on the other hand, have still not learned to say goodbye — nor has anyone else I know. My brother, my sister, and I, left pondering the quick and cheerful way Ernst had with his algebraic equations, are resigned to the fact that the puzzle we shall face during our last moments will be the very one we've never been able to solve.

## 🔥 🔥 🔥

# GETTING THROUGH IT TOGETHER

by WILLIAM GILSON

from THE WICKWIRE PRESS

*nominated by* JOYCE CAROL OATES

CHRISTMAS IS OVER. I bought Anne a sweater, a dark green long sleeved one that looks good on her. I gave it to her on Christmas day when we were at the Saulniers; she put it on, she was wearing her brown skirt, and the combination emphasized her thinness and made her look pretty. I kept hugging her. The rest was the usual sadness, all of us straining to be cheerful and trying to get it over with. The best thing about Anne's family is that there are a lot of them and you can sit somewhere for a while unnoticed with a drink in your hand while the action goes past you. Especially when they get out their fiddles and guitars. But at Christmas even the fast tunes seem sad. The children help, though. My favorite is Willie, Anne's older sister's kid. Anne and I gave him a wagon, and I took

342

him outside and sat him in it and pulled him up and down the street for almost an hour.

Anne's father, skinny Raymond, seemed down in the dumps. A lot of the time he just sat in his chair in the living room, smoking Camels and sipping wine. Something's bothering him but he won't say what. Everyone assumes it's his retirement looming but Anne says there's something else. I wonder if maybe he knows he's sick. Or if he just strongly suspects he's sick and doesn't have the nerve to confirm it.

The usual number of jokes were made about when are Anne and I finally going to have kids. At one point Anne said—she almost yelled it—"Never!" We were at the table, eating, and she was partially smiling and everyone laughed, but I recognized an incipient shrillness and looked at her; we exchanged a very sad glance. We are approaching a point, she and I, but neither of us knows what it means or what will happen.

The worst part of Christmas day was in the afternoon when we went to visit my relatives. First up to Torrington to Betsey and Phil's, then to Coldchester to see Uncle Lou. Uncle Lou wasn't so bad—he never is, really; but Betsey and Phil's is always hard. Poor Anne. I don't know why she puts up with it. I tell her I wouldn't if it was me. But I probably would do it, if it was me. That's what Christmas is like.

My sister is a masochistic coward. But I love her. I don't think there's anything that bothers me about my family, all of the past included, as much as the thought of Betsy making love with her husband. Phil is a newspaper photographer and he has large biceps—the kind where if he rolls up his sleeves he always rolls them halfway up the biceps and the sleeves are stretched taut. His teeth are big white square choppers and he grins insanely, to the point where you haven't the slightest notion what he's feeling. He has large square fingernails. When he asks you what kind of drink you want he's liable to say, "What's your poison?"

"Hydrochloric acid," I said on Christmas day; it's a joke he hates, but he'd been drinking and there were other people there so he let out a big laugh. The others were Hoot and Maureen. Hoot is an old buddy of Phil's and Maureen is Hoot's wife. Betsey and Maureen were in the kitchen, so Anne went right in and joined them, leaving me with the men. Phil handed me a large bourbon and I drank it down and he filled up the glass again.

Hoot said he felt we ought to send the Marines into Iran.

"Absolutely," I said. It was the booze talking. I'd been drinking wine all morning at the Saulniers and the bourbon really seized me. I could feel it razoring back and forth in my brain and I began to experience a familiar crazy euphoria.

"Nuke the motherfuckers!" I said.

"Harrison, you're shut off," Phil said.

"No, seriously. Seriously. Give each Marine a backpack with a baby nuke. The got'em miniaturized now. Then have the Marines tunnel in from the Persian Gulf, all aiming for the Embassy. A division of tunneling Marines. Beautiful!"

Phil and Hoot laughed awkwardly and I could see Anne glance out at me from the kitchen. Then the women came into the living room and Betsey and Phil and Anne and I exchanged presents. We gave Betsey a hand-knitted scarf from a shop in New Haven that sells stuff from Appalachia, and we gave Phil a pair of slippers which Betsey'd told us he wanted. They gave Anne a copper teapot and me a Swiss Army knife.

When I opened the package and saw the knife I started crying. It was awful. I never, ever, cry in front of people. By myself I cry maybe once or twice a year. It was the booze, of course, but it also had something to do with the fact that I liked the present; it was wrapped in white paper, and when I untied the ribbon and tore the scotch tape off, it looked beautiful, red and shiney, and it was the exact model I wanted. I had been looking at them in stores; I'd examined every Swiss Army model, I'd thought it over carefully and decided on the one I wanted. But I hadn't told anyone. I know I never told anyone. I sat there and cried. I put my hands over my face, sobbing. Betsey hugged me and said, "Harrison, are you all right?" She even started crying a little. Anne kneeled in front of me and said, "What's the matter, honey? Are you drunk?"

I managed to nod my head up and down, which made everyone laugh.

"You jerk," Anne said, ruffling my hair. They all relaxed a little then, and I calmed down and blew my nose.

We didn't stay too long after that. I apologized, eyes red, embarrassed. We had to go see Uncle Lou. Betsey gave us a present for him. They'd invited him for Christmas dinner but as usual he'd refused. Everyone made a big deal about insisting that I not drive.

In the car Anne started laughing at me.

"Harrison, what in the world was that all about?"

"Christ if I know," I said, looking out the window. It was a warm wet day, overcast and grey. I started laughing.

"Anne, I love you," I said, and I leaned over and kissed her on the mouth. She was laughing too and our teeth touched.

Uncle Lou is my father's younger brother. Both my father and an older sister, Eunice, are dead. Lou lives alone in a furnished room in Coldchester and wears a toupee, which he calls his "rug." Anne and I both like Lou, we get a kick out of him, but he is not an easy person to visit. He gives the impression that it's irrelevant if you visit him or not. But that's mainly an act. He has found a style that he thinks he can go with for the rest of his life, and he puts a certain amount of energy into pushing away any experiences which might cause him to question that decision. I think most people find him troubling because they can see, in a way, something attractive in his style, but they are mortified by the possibility of it happening to them.

He has lived in his room on Willow Street for an amazingly long time. I have a vague childhood memory of him living in another room, but mostly I remember him right there where he is now. He has a color TV, a double bed, a bureau, a hot plate, an armchair next to the window, a little bedside table with a lamp. He shares a bathroom in the hall with two other guys.

I hope they never tear down Lou's building. Considering how much of Coldchester they have torn down, it's a miracle they've left his alone.

His room is on the second floor and both his windows overlook the street; his armchair is alongside one of the windows, facing the TV; on the windowsill he keeps his ash tray, his cigarettes, his lighter, his waterglass and his cup.

He gets up early in the morning—that's from his years of working at Scovill, where he ran a machine that took the burrs off metal castings. He retired at age 58 because of a bad leg he'd gotten in the Army, but he keeps his old morning schedule. He gets dressed—brown pants with the creases long gone, tee shirt, white shirt without a tie, a pair of old worn brown oxfords—puts on his rug, lights a cigarette and goes down to Lorraine's Lunchroom on Bank Street. At Lorraine's he gets a bowl of oatmeal which he soups up with a lot of milk, just like my old man used to, and a burnt english muffin and a coffee. If they don't burn the muffin enough he sends it back. I've been down there and had breakfast with him, and he hardly speaks to anyone. After all these years you'd think he'd have all kinds of buddies in there, but he just sits and eats his muffin and drinks his coffee. He doesn't even read the paper. He exchanges a few "hellos" or some fragmentary conversation, but not much more. His face has a tired, somewhat bored expression, and he doesn't often look people in the eye.

He has two or three friends, guys his own age, who he now and then goes to visit. He'll say, "I was over to see Frank Sholocki last week. He had another operation, his gall bladder this time." Or every once in a while during the summer I'll see him on the green, sitting on one of the benches with a guy his age. But mainly he stays alone. Mainly you'll see him sitting in his room next to the window, smoking cigarettes and drinking instant coffee.

"Lou is a sad case," my old man used to say, "he never found the love of a good woman." I doubt if he ever found the love of any woman, good or bad. Though you never know.

Lou's main claim to fame is that he knew the Mad Bomber. (Coldchester's main claim to fame is that it nurtured the Mad Bomber.) The Bomber was a thin quiet guy who, according to Lou, always wore a grey suit and a grey tie; he had a wife who almost never spoke, and the two of them lived in an apartment building—since torn down—near Lou's building. The Bomber's name was Herb Turabian, and as a young man he'd worked for Con Edison in New York City and been fired. He felt the company owed him benefits, the company refused, and Herb moved to Coldchester and got a job at Scovill. Secretly—Lou claims Herb's wife didn't even know—Herb began a side career as the Mad Bomber that lasted over twenty years until he got caught. He built pipe bombs in the basement of his building and from time to time he'd take the train to New York with a bomb in a cardboard box and he'd leave it in a movie theater or a phone booth or a bus station with the alarm clock timer ticking. Most of his bombs never went off but the ones that did killed seven people and wounded at least a dozen more. That was his way of taking revenge on Con Edison.

Through chance, the day the law finally caught up with Herb, Lou was visiting him. Herb and his wife and Lou were watching TV in the living room when the cops arrived. There was some confusion over who exactly was the Bomber, and one of the cops put the cuffs on Lou. But Herb told them that Lou was innocent and they released him.

Herb died of cancer in Wethersfield Prison about six years ago, and his wife died a year later in a nursing home in Torrington.

For Christmas we gave Lou the same kind of slippers we gave Phil. I know he won't start wearing them immediately, if he ever wears them at all, because he's already got a pair, all bent over and shaped to his feet. But Anne and I thought that maybe, if he has new ones in his closet when the old ones finally let go, he'll start wearing them. Anyway, he seemed pleased by the present. He was sitting in his chair, as always, smoking cigarettes and watching TV and keeping an eye on the street below. I noticed he has switched cigarette brands again. When I was a kid it was Chesterfields; then it was Pall Malls; then Camels; now it's Vantage.

We brought a little wine and some glasses from Betsey and Phil's—Lou only has one cup and one glass—and we had a Christmas toast. Anne sat on the edge of the bed next to Lou's chair and I sat on the other chair. Lou turned the TV off, thereby acknowledging that the occasion was a special one.

"Here's to you, Lou," I said. "Merry Christmas, and may 1980 be a good year."

"Here's to you, Harrison." He raised his glass. "And to you, Annie."

We drank, and Anne kissed Lou on the cheek.

For some reason the mood was rather solemn, as if we'd all just come from a funeral. We talked about the past, and Lou reminisced a little about his childhood.

"Oh, it was quite a bit different then. You had to fight for a dime back then. Not like today, with welfare and all. Our Dad worked long hours in the shop. And we all worked as kids. No college for us. No thought of college. When Eunice became a nurse, that was quite a thing."

"Was the river clear back then, Lou?" I knew the answer. "Could you swim in it as a kid?"

"The Sewcataug? No, no." He looked out the window. The streetlights had come on. "The river was worse then. Much worse. It was—well, when I was a boy, it had a kind of an orange color to it. Or green. A greenish orange. It's hard to describe. If you put your foot in it you'd get a rash. A boy I went to school with, Gerald

McCann, drowned in the river. They had a closed casket wake. They said it was because of what the water did to his skin. No, the river's a lot cleaner now. The whole town's a lot cleaner."

"That's hard to believe," Anne said.

"Well, it's the case."

Anne touched his arm. "Lou, when are you coming out to visit us?"

"Oh, one of these days, Annie." He smiled and looked into his wine glass. It's amazing how different he is from my old man; he's so quiet, so shy. It's the same insecurity, I suppose, but with opposite results.

"I haven't been out to the country in a long time."

"If you wait much longer," I said, "it won't be country. Actually there's not much country there now."

"How's your job, Harrison?"

"Oh, Lou. Dull. Christ, I'm sick of it. I'm ready for early retirement."

"Too bad you don't have a war wound."

"Yeah."

Lou got his "war wound" in boot camp. He volunteered for the infantry in World War II and as he was crawling through part of a training course, under live machine gun fire, one of the bullets mysteriously hit him in the thigh.

"Harrison's writing a history of Millville," Anne said.

"Oh, really?"

"It's just a pamphlet," I said. "It's not much. I'm doing it for the Historical Association."

"Very interesting. Very interesting. Doing some research, I suppose."

He didn't seem at all interested.

"Oh yeah. Reading stuff—"

"You've always been a reader, Harrison."

"It helps. I guess I picked it up from Betsey."

"And how is Betsey and her family?"

"Oh, they're okay."

And so it went; we talked for about an hour. As usual, Lou's toupee looked ridiculous. From across the street you could tell it's a fake. I think he bought it by mail. It's not real hair—it's some sort of synthetic brown stuff, stiff and shiney, and there's almost no taper to the edges. In spite of his shyness he is strangely out front about it. I've heard him say, "That was back before I got the rug." I remember him before he got it, his baldness was ordinary, a dome with patches of hair around the ears. It's a mystery why he decided he needed the damn thing.

Before we left we had another toast.

Anne said, "Here's to all of us. Merry Christmas."

"Merry Christmas," Lou said, raising his glass.

He thanked us for coming, and for the slippers. I think he was glad we came, but I also think he was glad to see us leave. As we were going down the stairs I heard him turn the TV back on.

In the car, on the way home, she says, "I think he does the same thing to everyone. Makes you wonder if that's what you'll be like."

"I'll never wear a damn rug."

"Don't be so sure."

It's dark, she is driving. We are winding south along the river.

"You could get like that, Harrison."

"I know."

"After you leave me."

"I'm not going to leave you."

"Do you think about leaving me?"

"Of course."

"Then when are you going to?"

"Never."

Silence. Then she says, "When's the last time you thought about it?"

"I didn't think about it once today."

"When yesterday?"

"I don't want to talk about it."

Another silence. That awful silence which is worse than the worst she could say. She is so sensitive. I love the way she's so sensitive, but it infuriates me.

"Jesus Christ, Anne. You're doing that thing again. You want me to say something that'll upset you."

"So what?"

"When I was lying in bed, just after I woke up. I thought, 'I've got to get out of this. I've got to be alone.' "

"Fuck you."

"See?"

"You *are* alone. You're never not alone, Harrison."

"I don't want to be alone. I love you."

"You do so want to be alone."

"I don't want to argue. I already have a hangover."

"Why did you start crying at Betsey and Phil's?"

"It was the knife. I guess. It was the exact model I wanted. The very exact model."

"Really?"

"Yes. Oh, fuck. It was everything. Fucking Christmas. My sister. My stupid godamned sister and her stupid godamned husband. Did you hear him telling how that girl, Darlene, at the paper, broke her shin bone? I bet he's having an affair with her."

"You always think that."

"Well, Christ. Betsey's so homely. I—you're being argumentative."

"I'm sorry."

She puts her hand on my leg. I put my hand on hers.

"Maybe we should get a cat," she says.

"Like Edgar."

"I never knew Edgar."

"You'd have liked him. He—"

"I know. You've told me. A million times."

"Anne, Abe doesn't want a cat. He'd be terrified. You know that. He'd bark all night."

"He could get used to it. He'd have to."

"Maybe we should have a kid."

Silence.

"Let's not fight tonight, Harrison. It's Christmas, that's bad enough."

Back home, she goes to bed while I drink a beer sitting in my armchair next to the record player listening to Thelonius Monk play "Round Midnight." When I get in bed she's asleep. Or pretending she's asleep.

# POETRY IN DARK TIMES

by TERRENCE DES PRES

from PARNASSUS: POETRY IN REVIEW

*nominated by* PARNASSUS: POETRY IN REVIEW *and Kelly Cherry*

TO MOST OF US Brecht's poetry is new. We know him by his plays, and if we come to the poetry from Brechtian theater we shall be, if not misled, then surprised. The two careers ran broadly parallel, but in view of the poems the famous cynicism of the plays looks less savage, less brazenly hard. The whole of Brecht's enormous output, thanks to the poetry now available, needs reading in a different light, not only of genius politically inspired, but of an art directed always to care for how people live.

The one-sided view of Brecht came about because his fame as a playwright came early and lasted; but also because he published a mere fraction of poetry during his lifetime. Events kept upsetting

plans for printings, and what did appear came out in a confusion of
ways, from poems stuck in the plays to those in the small gray
chapbooks, the *Versuche*, which Brecht issued over the years. Of
substantial volumes there were only three: the early *Hauspostille*
or *Devotions for the Home* of 1927; the *Svendborg Poems* published in exile in 1938; and finally, five years before his death in
1956, *A Hundred Poems*. To this last book circumstances attached
which made its occasion an example — usual for Brecht — of politics and art in collision.

John Heartfield designed the book's cover, which featured the
picture of a Chinese tea-root carved in the shape of a lion. Brecht
liked it but his East German (which is to say Soviet) publishers did
not. They argued that the design would brand the poetry as
"formalism" and be condemned by critics spouting the party line in
their pronouncements on the book's merit. The situation was
typically Brechtian. So was the solution. *A Hundred Poems* appeared in an initial edition of 10,000 copies, half with the lion, half
in plain cover. To the critics went the latter, while booksellers
preferred (because it sold better) copies with the design. As a final
touch Brecht put the following poem on the cover of the edition
with the lion:

> The bad fear your claws.
> The good enjoy your elegance.
> This
> I would like to hear said
> Of my verse.

The aggressive element in Brecht's work is well known (people
did fear it, the Nazis burned his books), and the little poem about
the lion, so simple and direct, is Brecht at his elegant best. But to
value the whole of his poetry for its "elegance" is surely odd. In
German the last word of line two is *Grazie*, denoting "grace" or
"charm" or a kind of "suppleness." Graceful and charming Brecht's
poetry is not. He detested decorum and polish, any sort of evident
refinement, preferring instead the rough vigor of the street and
lowbrow forms like the ballad, the popular song, or just "straight-
talk." This turn toward the rude and lowly, as Brecht said of his
early poetry, was less "a protest against the smoothness and
harmony of conventional poetry" than "an attempt to show human

dealings as contradictory, fiercely fought over, full of violence." Such poetry, given its sinewy flex and spring, might possibly be called supple. But for a translator to select the word "elegant" is not therefore perverse.

A lion can hardly be called charming, certainly not the bristly creature of Heartfield's design; and this points to one of the problems reading Brecht. His poetry does not charm, invite, or tease out of thought. It would be heard, not overheard, and does not bank on its status as Art. Its import is in its occasion and it does not, therefore, claim to be transcendent or self-contained, but rather insists upon its place in history, its provisional nature as utterance *in situ*. Most modern poetry posits *a* world, whereas Brecht's responds to *the* world, in particular to events and conditions which determine — to the benefit of some and the harm of many — people's lives. His position is therefore political. In relation to poetry the term "political" may simply refer to poems which bear witness or, going a step further, to poems which confront and defend or, going all the way, to poems which directly speak for and against. The last kind disturbs us most, and that is the kind Brecht principally wrote. He therefore stands as the extreme example of an art which we in America prefer to believe cannot exist in superior form: political poetry, verse openly didactic, aesthetic energy taking a stand.

With Willett's and Manheim's edition of *Poems 1913-1956* before us, there is no denying that Brecht wrote some great poetry, and no denying its political bent. Brecht disliked poets who write solely of inner experience. He did not value poetic vision which cultivates itself only, nor did he think that the poet's main job is to feel and perceive in rarefied ways. Poets ought to *say* something, and what they say should be worth hearing even in a world where global politics — the threat of nuclear wipeout, the terrorist who strikes anyone anywhere — increasingly penetrates private life. History is too much with us, and if we would believe Max Frisch, looking upon the ruins of Europe after the Second World War, Brecht's poetry is of the kind we need: the kind that "can stand up against the world in which it is spoken."

By that standard, almost all poetry being written in America fails, or embarrasses, or leaves us lamenting that nobody takes poetry seriously anymore. Times change, and so do we, and the poetry of self — the Emersonian mandate — has lost its authority.

Our times are not as dark as Brecht's, but they are far from happy and no one, I presume, would predict improvement. Brecht's Marxist vision and his didactic altitude may not be ours but his example still instructs and is potentially liberating, especially if we admit that our lives are more and more knocked about by political forces and that poems worth having are those which can "stand up against" the prevailing climate of violence. Like all political art, Brecht's poetry is unique to a definite time and I do not propose imitation but only some serious thought about ourselves in relation to his *kind* of poetry — poetry which keeps the spirit equal to conditions which, in 1940, Brecht described this way: "When I listen to the news on the radio in the morning, at the same time reading Boswell's *Life of Johnson* and glancing out at the landscape of birch trees in the mist by the river, then the unnatural day begins not on a discordant note but on no note at all."

Speaking of unnatural days, here is Brecht with a kind of poem which, except for the crucial last line, has been epidemic in American verse:

> An oar lies on the roof. A moderate wind
> Will not carry away the thatch.
> In the yard posts are set for
> The children's swing.
> The mail comes twice a day
> Where letters would be welcome.
> Down the Sound come the ferries.
> The house has four doors to escape by.

Entitled "Place of Refuge," the poem might almost be read as a modest portrait — one of those little moments poets celebrate — of the writer setting up for summer on Nantucket or the Cape. The place is quaint, the kids are set, the postal service works. If other writers intrude too much, one can slip out the back and maybe, in a better world, the poem *would* be that. But 1914 was the last golden summer and that sort of innocence, as Brecht put it in another context, is "like having a cloud of dust blow into one's face. Can you imagine that sort of thing ever coming to mean anything again?"

Brecht's poem describes exile, and also illustrates one of the conditions we must allow when reading poetry of this kind. Political poetry addresses itself to a time and a place and is therefore a matter of context. The range of meaning includes a *complex of circumstance* not fully manifest in the poem but which nevertheless functions as part of the poem. Political poetry asks, or rather demands, knowledge of the historical situation and also an outline account of the poet's life. This, presumably, is what infuriates critics who want their poetry pure. But just this fact, that such poems bring history with them, restores to poetry, in our time, a dignity and amplitude not otherwise obtainable.

Brecht left Germany in 1933. His name, although he did not know it then, was number five on one of the Nazi murder lists. In "Place of Refuge" the time is 1937, the place is a fisherman's cottage outside the Danish city of Svendborg. Soon Hitler would invade Denmark, forcing Brecht to use one of the "four doors to escape by." (From there he would go to Sweden, then Finland, then across Russia to the Pacific, and finally to the United States where he would stay until the end of the war.) Much of Brecht's early poetry invents its imagery, in the manner of Rimbaud. But midway his imagery begins to come from the actual situation of which the poem itself is a part. No doubt a paint-peeled oar lay on the picturesque roof. But oar-on-thatch is an image of disorder, of things out of place, and we understand that destructive winds might come. The mail also comes, so do the boats, and in the poem's context these images of things approaching take on sinister tones. The children may play, but not safely. Mail will cause as much pain as gladness. And business as usual — ferries crossing the water — is not to be trusted.

Like many of Brecht's poems, this one is based on personal circumstances, but like his poetry in general, it is not really personal. Of his work he once said: "maybe the poems in question describe me, but that was not what they were written for. It's not a matter of 'getting acquainted with the poet' but of getting acquainted with the world, and with the people in whose company he is trying to enjoy it and change it." To become acquainted with the world, in this case, is to discover that no place is safe, no refuge secure. Political forces drive us into an exile which, like the poet's retreat, cannot be counted on, neither in life nor in art. Brecht takes this theme further in another poem which, except for several lines, is again a type seen in countless numbers. Here the old death-and-rebirth theme stands for a very tenuous and shaky hope, hope edged by hostile facts and brutal foreboding, which is to say hope in its modern, political form. Keeping in mind that the Second World War started in 1939, here is the first stanza of "Spring 1938":

> To-day, Easter Sunday morning
> A sudden snowstorm swept over the island.
> Between the greening hedges lay snow. My young son
> Drew me to a little apricot tree by the house wall
> Away from a verse in which I pointed the finger at those
> Who were preparing a war which
> Could well wipe out the continent, this island, my people,
>    my family,
> And myself. In silence
> We put a sack
> Over the freezing tree.

Brecht regularly pointed the finger, for example in his "Hitler Chorales," written in 1933, which were to be sung to the melodies of famous Lutheran hymns, the first of which begins, "Now thank we all our God/ For sending Hitler to us," and ends:

> He'll paint the filth and rot
> Until it's spick and span
> So thank we all our God
> For sending us this man.

Parody of liturgical forms is one of Brecht's favorite devices; implemented by the ironies of cliché and doggerel, the result is clawlike indeed. Brecht's Easter poem, quoted above, would be a sentimental rerun of the theme of rebirth, were it not for the political references. But now rebirth cannot be counted on; our defenses, like our stock of traditional themes, are pathetically inadequate. Yet there are only the old themes. Brecht gives them new life by allowing politics to intrude; and in consequence, a mythical experience, punctured by history, loses *and* gains in primitive force. Anyone with children, reading the papers, listening for signals of war, knows how poignant that silence is, when with nothing but a miserable sack, a son and father try to save a dying tree. Slight in itself, the poem is like a stone around the neck. It stood up against the time in which it was written, it stands up now.

Political exile, not forgetting Dante, is as old as its ancient Greek and Roman examples. In our time it has become ordinary, a way of life by which to measure our own. Reading American poetry, however, and despite an endless outpour of poems about alienation, we could never guess that exile is a central form of experience in our century. Nor, apart from poems like the one below, could we fathom its peculiar terror. The fifth section of a poem called "1940" goes this way:

> I am now living on the small island of Lidingö.
> But one night recently
> I had heavy dreams and I dreamed I was in a city
> And discovered that its street signs
> Were in German. I awoke
> Bathed in sweat, saw the fir tree
> Black as night before my window, and realized with relief:
> I was in a foreign land.

To fear one's home and prefer a strange place is a mutilating reversal of the ordinary. So is the tree "black as night," ordinarily frightening but here a comfort. And so, above all, is the poet terrified of his own language. The world turns upside down, and by dwelling on this surreal but actual condition Brecht touches the catastrophic heart of our century — the extreme dislocation, geographic and spiritual, forced upon millions of people by wars, coups, deportations, and political brutalities that are, in fact, the surest signs of our time. (I finished that sentence and over the radio came a tape-recording of begging screams, then blunt gunfire, as two boys are pushed to the ground and shot point-blank by military police in El Salvador. Our government supports, with money and arms, that regime, those murders.)
Brecht declared himself a Marxist in 1929, and critics often speak of his "conversion" as if there were two Brechts, the rampaging satirist and then the somber ideologue. Over-simple at best, the distinction is misleading and in the end serves no purpose. Over time, of course, the poetry shows change: it turns less often to rhyme and fixed forms; expansiveness gives way to concentration; more poems are rooted in fact, and Brecht's splendid didactic

mode moves from ironic depiction to straightforward statement as its central vehicle. But what never changes is Brecht's bedrock loyalty to victims — to losers, outcasts, whole strata of society who from birth were doomed to wretchedness. The disposition, not the system, came first. Many early poems take a plural point of view or address collective experience. Images of mass death occur with upsetting frequency. And Brecht's dominant early form, the narrative, is handled with the dedication and authority proper to a poet whose concern would always be with action, with the ways men and women determine, or have forced upon them, basic conditions of life. Which is to say that Brecht's relation to the world was political from the start.

In 1918, for example, while the war was still going and he was serving in a military hospital, young Brecht wrote "Legend of the Dead Soldier" (which is not in the present collection, but available in translations by H. R. Hays and Eric Bentley; the stanza below is by Hays). In the fifth springime of the war, as the poem begins, the soldier dies a hero's death, but—

> Because the war was not quite done
> It made the Kaiser blue
> To think the soldier lay there dead
> Before his time came due.

So the dead man is dug up, revived with schnapps and pronounced fit for service. Soon the stinking corpse is goose-stepping off to a second death, cheered on by patriotic crowds. The ballad, with its cynical clichés, its jaunty rhythms and grotesque imagery, is typical of Brecht's early work. Rimbaud, Villon, and Kipling hover in the background, as does other anti-war poetry written at that time in Germany. The poem rides on the nihilism it mimes, and depicts the horror of perpetual war in terms impossible to stomach (the Nazis *hated* this poem). Brecht always preferred satire to invective; evils were best exposed by letting them display their own disfiguration. And repeatedly, by using emphatic rhyme and barroom rhythms, by exaggeration, repetition, and refrains, Brecht condemns the voice through which the poem seems to speak. This corresponds to his theory of theater, to the way he wanted actors to perform their parts. They were not to identify with, but rather to "quote" the character whose role they played, and in such a way as to show moral judgment.

The following poem, "The Ballad of Paragraph 218," was written in 1930 during the terrible stress of the Great Depression. The number 218 refers to the section of the criminal code outlawing abortion, and the situation of the poem, as the first lines indicate, is that of a pregnant woman begging a doctor to help her:

> Please, doctor, I've missed my monthly . . .
> Why, this is simply great.
> If I may put it bluntly
> You're raising our birthrate.

The three dots are part of the poem; they occur each time the woman begins to give her reasons — her husband is out of work, they have no home, no money, no hope — but she never gets far before the doctor cuts her off with this refrain:

> You'll make a simply splendid little mummy
> Producing cannon-fodder from your tummy
> That's what your body's for, and you know it, what's more
> And it's laid down by law
> And now get this straight:
> You'll soon be a mother, just wait.

The lines are incredibly cruel, as Brecht intends them to be, for the situation is cruel and he wishes the reader to see. Whether a doctor would use such cynical terms is not the point. From the vantage of the State this is the expedient function of motherhood; the poor are there to be used and used up, and their dehumanized plight is expressed exactly by the doctor's brute command. In this way too, Brecht tears away the mystique surrounding the word "mother," revealing woman's role as mere producer. And here, finally, Brecht makes a profound connection, still not understood by many of us: people who oppose abortion on principle never oppose war on principle, and perhaps now we see why.

But back to the doctor's position and the way Brecht sets it forth. This is an example of what Brecht called *gestisch* or "gestic" writing, a technique for exposing the inner logic of a situation in terms of gesture or action at the level of language. The basic unit in Brecht's poetry is not the image or the musical phrase, as in most modern poetry, but the line. Like a Bauhaus beam, each line contributes to some larger structure but at the same time declares

its own shape and strength. To read Brecht correctly we must halt
with subtle emphasis at the line-break. Even enjambment works
this way in his poems, and in his hands, furthermore, the end of
the German phrase or sentence is usually a substantial word, not
the *ab* or *auf* we expect. The rapid pile-up of pointed lines can be
very powerful, especially when further stressed by rhyme. And
this, in turn, can be compounded still more — as in the doctor's
example — by Brecht's habitual use of paratactic syntax ("*And* it's
laid down by law/*And* now get this straight"), which makes of the
poem a sort of inventory for a subjective state which expresses,
through its specific gesture, the political situation.

We might say that Brecht's concept of *Gestus* is an exaggerated
case of what R. P. Blackmur called "language as gesture," the
common property of all poetry. Perhaps so, but what makes
Brecht's usage special is the complexity of meaning he produces by
such bald and deliberate application of the gestic principle — a
technique remarkably suited for jamming pathos and violence
together. Here is a last example from the early poetry, "Of the
Infanticide Marie Farrar," written in 1922. Like many of Brecht's
poems, this one was inspired by an event, here a girl who without
assistance gave birth to her child in the servants' outdoor latrine
and then, senseless with pain and desperation, killed it. The poem
pretends to be an itemized record of the girl's own testimony, a
police report rather than the tragedy it is. Of the poem's nine
stanzas, the following is the eighth. We must also keep in mind that
the last couplet appears at the close of each stanza:

> Between the servants' privy and her bed (she says
> That nothing happened until then), the child
> Began to cry, which vexed her so, she says
> She beat it with her fists, hammering blind and wild
> Without a pause until the child was quiet, she says.
> She took the baby's body into bed
> And held it for the rest of the night, she says
> Then in the morning hid it in the laundry shed.
>> But you I beg, make not your anger manifest
>> For all that lives needs help from all the rest.

Paratactic order (one thing after another) plus the jabbing repetition of "she says" suggests a torment verging on hypnosis. And
indeed, the rest of the poem makes clear that the child's death is

the outcome of a life brutalized beyond endurance, the grim last act of a woman whose existence had been unbearably grim from the start. The irony of "nothing happened until then" is over-whelming but also instructive. Marie Farrar truly does not know what brought her to this awful pass, nor does her ordeal — giving birth alone, in the winter dark of a filthy latrine — seem to her unusual in its degrading pain. The story is horrible, but also matter of fact. Brecht's sympathy is with the servant, and his portrait of a victim is essential to the poem's political character. But that the poem does have a political thrust, and is not merely social criti-cism, depends on how we read the final couplet.

On the face of it, the last lines address those who judged the crime, and then anyone who, upon hearing the story, would be appalled by something so "unnatural" and "inhuman." Part of the irony, then, lies in reversal: Brecht aims for us to see that the child's death follows "naturally" from a life which start to finish could only be called inhuman and unnatural. And further, that those to whom the couplet addresses itself — those whom servants serve — are not as natural and humane as they themselves would like to suppose. By repeating the couplet after each stanza, it gradually takes on the character of a formula, a plea uttered by rote, a useless gesture. And so it is. The plea is genuine but empty. The real message of the last lines is that such an appeal — a Christian appeal made to a Christian society — falls on deaf ears. And if so, then those for whom the message is meant are victims like Marie Farrar, who suddenly see their fate in hers and see also that to beg help from the class which keeps them down will get them nowhere.

The last lines do not, after all, ask forgiveness but state a great truth — "all that lives needs help from all the rest" — which is, or ought to be, the guiding principle for any sound political order. That the appeal is made in earnest but also in vain creates the dialectical perception which gives the poem its political character. As always, Brecht speaks *of* the exploiters and *to* the victims, exposing infamy and instructing the oppressed. And what "Marie Farrar" says finally is said again and again in Brecht's poetry, right up to one of the last poems he wrote:

> That you'll go down if you don't stand up for yourself
> Surely you see that.
>
> ("And I Always Thought")

Brecht was born in 1898 and came of age as a poet and playwright during the ugly years after World War I, when Germany was ruled by defeat and the vengeance of Versailles, by upheaval and paramilitary violence, by resentment, poverty, and rampant profiteering. He witnessed the rise of fascism and when Hitler assumed power in 1933, Brecht went into an exile that lasted sixteen years. From the time of his return, in 1948, until his death in 1956, he lived in East Berlin under a Stalinist regime and the general hysteria of the Cold War. Which is to say that when Brecht speaks of "dark times" he knows what he is talking about:

> Truly, I live in dark times!
> The guileless word is folly. A smooth forehead
> Suggests insensitivity. The man who laughs
> Has simply not yet had
> The terrible news.

Written in 1938, those are the first lines of "To Those Born Later," a poem already known in English as "To Posterity" (in H. R. Hays' translation). The phrase "dark times" occurs often in Brecht's poetry. It refers to half a century during which, by conservative estimate, 100 million men, women, and children were killed in wars, in concentration camps, by bombing and firing squads. Millions more lived out their lives in harrowing dread. To say that civilization collapsed is not to exaggerate, and the great questions, how to stay human, or, as Adorno put it, how to have poetry after Auschwitz, are still very much ours. In "To Those Born Later" Brecht goes on:

> I would also like to be wise.
> In the old books it says what wisdom is:
> To shun the strife of the world and to live out
> Your brief time without fear
> Also to get along without violence
> To return good for evil
> Not to fulfill your desires but to forget them
> Is accounted wise.
> All this I cannot do:
> Truly, I live in dark times.

In an age of terror the old wisdom becomes folly. How return good for evil when genocide and war are the issues? How stay sane

amid madness or bring up children without the desire for a decent
peace? We are embedded in the world's strife and cannot shun it
even if we would. Everything has become political and the "dark
times" prevail. This affects not only how we view the world
morally, but likewise how we see it in aesthetic terms:

> What kind of times are they, when
> A talk about trees is almost a crime
> Because it implies silence about so many horrors?

That was the question Brecht faced, and it remains the question
for poets today. Can poetry keep its innocence? Do poets, like any
of the rest of us, have the right to ignore *what they know?* In one of
his "notational poems," as I would call this form, Brecht offers an
answer. "Reading Without Innocence" was written in 1944, in
response to an entry in Gide's journal for 3 July 1940, immediately
after France gave in to the Nazis, while Gide vacationed in the
Pyrenees:

> In his wartime journals
> The writer Gide mentions a gigantic plane tree
> He's been admiring—quite a while—for its enormous trunk
> Its mighty branching and its equilibrium
> Effected by the gravity of its preponderant boughs.
>
> In far-off California
> Shaking my head, I read this entry.
> The nations are bleeding to death. No natural plan
> Provides for a happy equilibrium.

At least since the Romantic movement, contemplation of nature
has served to console, to divert, to offer a realm apart from human
struggle, something holy and untouchable except through poetic
rapport. In itself, this is genuine and good; but from a political
point of view, poetry grounded in imagery of nature is misleading
because it convinces us, especially through images of the sublime—sea, space, night, mountains—that human strife and pain
are not important; that the cosmos is a timeless whole transcending
hope and fear. And thus an awful conflict arises. In dark times even
nature is suspect. It does not often appear in Brecht's poems, and
when it does, some human element intrudes; the abundant cherry

tree has a thief in it, the spectacular Finnish countryside is viewed by a refugee, or this:

> Fog envelops
> The road
> The poplars
> The farms and
> The artillery.

Brecht sometimes uses nature symbolically, the empty godless sky, for example, or water's inexorable flow. But by disposition he preferred human imagery — tools and utensils, houses, people doing things — and political poetry commits itself to the human sphere in any case. Brecht was appalled by that journal entry because while whole nations and peoples are being wiped out, a famous writer prefers to admire a tree. Gide may have been seeking no more than a moment's relief, but for Brecht something more is at stake. By ending with "No natural plan/Provides for a happy equilibrium," he means that no natural design or governing Providence, but solely the concerted effort of men and women, will bring about a peaceful world. He also means that Gide's aesthetic-mystical awareness induces blindness to history and allows a false feeling of well-being. Almost against its will, poetry promotes acceptance of the world, lyrically through celebration, tragically by leaving us with the feeling that, yes, that's how things *are*. Homer's *Iliad* is truly great and uplifting, but its subject is hideous. That is what Nietzsche had in mind when he said that history is only bearable from an aesthetic point of view. Brecht would have none of this, but if not, how might the aesthetic point of view be used against itself? And at what cost?

One solution, for Brecht, was satire as savage as history itself. Another was reliance on didactic forms, which draw their strength from the conviction that life can be changed. A third strategy was to avoid metaphor, especially insofar as metaphor creates the illusion of transcendence — of being "above" $X$ by seeing it in terms of $Y$. Of his *Svendborg Poems* Brecht said: "From the bourgeois point of view there has been a staggering impoverishment. Isn't it all a great deal more one-sided, less 'organic,' cooler, more self-conscious (in a bad sense)?" One-sided like an ax, cool like metal at night, and thus a poetry which sometimes seems disrespectful of the reader's sensibilities, at other times insisting on a distance between reader and poem, a sort of aesthetic estrangement. Brecht's famous concept of *Verfremdungseffekt* or "alienation effect" applies not only to his theory of theater, but to the central grain of his poetry as well. He will not grant emotional solace, nor catharsis either. The appeal, here, is more to the mind than the heart. We are not to indulge but to see, and to see we must not feel too much at home.

In 1934, in a poem which takes its title from the first line, Brecht set forth his definition of poetry, and not as a theory only, but as the decision which any poet trapped in dark times might make:

Solely because of the increasing disorder
In our cities of class struggle
Some of us have now decided
To speak no more of cities by the sea, snow on roofs, women
The smell of ripe apples in cellars, the senses of the flesh, all
That makes a man round and human
But to speak in future only about the disorder
And so become one-sided, reduced, enmeshed in the business
Of politics and the dry, indecorous vocabulary
Of dialectical economics
So that this awful cramped coexistence
Of snowfalls (they're not merely cold, we know)
Exploitation, the lured flesh, class justice, should not engender
Approval of a world so many-sided; delight in
The contradictions of so bloodstained a life
You understand.

No semi-colon occurs in the German version; the poem is one headlong sentence, a "gestic" enactment of the clarity and conviction with which the poet intends to proceed. In line nine the word translated as "indecorous"is *unwürdige*, which carries the sense of being unworthy, undeserving or, in sum, not respectable. To slam the issue home Brecht puts *unwürdige* in quotation marks, thereby transforming the word into its opposite; and the concluding irony of "You understand" challenges, perhaps even insults. At the same time, we see why Brecht brings the indecorous diction of politics into his poems: it allows him *not* to approve the world as it is, to write poetry which does not inadvertently take "delight in/ The contradictions of so bloodstained a life." And I trust that at least for people living in places like South Africa, or the ghettos of Miami and Detroit, "cities of class struggle" does not sound odd or outdated.

The fact is, political vocabulary seldom appears in Brecht's poems, and when it does it bears a dignity entirely free of jargon. The following example, "A Bed for the Night," was written in 1931 in the depths of the Great Depression when the streets of Europe and America were thick with jobless men:

> I hear that in New York
> At the corner of 26th Street and Broadway
> A man stands every evening during the winter months
> And gets beds for the homeless there
> By appealing to passers-by
>
> It won't change the world
> It won't improve relations among men
> It will not shorten the age of exploitation
> But a few men have a bed for the night
> For a night the wind is kept from them
> The snow meant for them falls on the roadway.
>
> Don't put down the book on reading this, man.
>
> A few people have a bed for the night
> For a night the wind is kept from them
> The snow meant for them falls on the roadway
> But it won't change the world
> It won't improve relations among men
> It will not shorten the age of exploitation.

To call this poem ironic would be misleading. It is, rather, a classic example of dialectical vision. Irony is static, a form of despair; dialectic, on the other hand, is process, a form of disciplined hope. Two conflicting views are not merely juxtaposed and left to mock each other. The older ethic (stanza two) is turned inside out and made to yield its opposite (stanza four), while the latter is seen to emerge from that which it goes beyond through contradiction. Helping people at the local level was sufficient once, perhaps; but in times of great suffering the street-corner approach cannot hope to meet mass needs. The Christian ethic, based on the good deed, now defeats itself; the behavior it promotes is decent, but inadequate and finally sentimental. Also harmful; for as long as we accept face-to-face help (and the good will of passers-by) as the limit of human obligation, we shall not see the magnitude of the problem nor move toward organized solutions. And of course, those who profit from the *status quo* can hide behind strategic charity; they may even persuade those whom they exploit that real care exists — the self-advertised munificence of big oil, for example.

Brecht wrote "A Bed for the Night" at the same time he was writing *St. Joan of the Stockyards*, and in theme the poem and the play are identical. The play, however, depends heavily on pathos and cynicism, whereas the poem is free of both. The difference is instructive and tells us something essential about Brecht as a poet: by using a didactic voice and the dialectical viewpoint within a political framework, he restores in a minimal, no-nonsense way poetry's visionary element, its capacity to reach beyond the actual. This is all the more astonishing in Brecht's case, for no poet ever had a better grasp on the actual than Bert Brecht. Yet in just this way poetry reclaims its integrity, its power to *be*. The simplicity with which he makes this work is amazing. Who would dare think that hope for the future resides in present despair? Who would have guessed that to repeat, word for word, lines in reverse order could provide the literary means for an historical-political vision which might otherwise require volumes of cumbersome argument?

The dialectical process, or rather its poetic enactment, is a good example of poetry and politics working together. The poetic aim is to capture a significant part of the world — a social-political complex — in an instant of time. The political aim is to cut through false pieties and reverse accepted attitudes. Here is a last example:

> The peasant's concern is with his field
> He looks after his cattle, pays taxes
> Produces children, to save on labourers, and
> Depends on the price of milk.
> The townspeople speak of love for the soil

Of healthy peasant stock and
Call peasants the backbone of the nation.

The townspeople speak of love for the soil
Of healthy peasant stock
And call peasants the backbone of the nation.
The peasant's concern is with his field
He looks after his cattle, pays taxes
Produces children, to save on labourers, and
Depends on the price of milk.

The German *kümmert*, translated as "concern," loses its connotations of grief and constant worry, just as *Knechte*, rendered as
"labourers," no longer hints of slavery. Meanings of this kind slip
away in translation, but Brecht's major meanings are carried by
gestures which tend to survive. The poem above depends entirely
on gesture, in particular the collision of romantic generalities with
grim facts, as when "healthy peasant stock" becomes "children, to
save on labourers." The political point is obvious: as with Hegel's
master-slave dialectic, the peasants serve the townspeople while
the townspeople depend on the peasants, and *this* the laborers
should see. The peasants depend on the price of milk, which is
fixed in town, but the town needs the milk. The situation is
dialectical, hence the form of the poem, the way stanza two inverts
stanza one. How the dual act of reversal and repetition contributes
to the poem's success is puzzling. Either stanza contains all the
*visible* information, yet either stanza alone would be trite compared to the mysterious but real power of the two faced off against
each other.

The didactic element is constant in Brecht. He thought of
himself as a teacher, and the point of his work, as he often said, was
to make people see. There have of course been great didactic
poets, Virgil and Lucretius among them, but for sheer formal
inventiveness and for aesthetic effects as powerful as any "pure"
poet might hope to create, Brecht's poetry seems to me the
supreme example of successful didactic art. The didactic mode
served as Brecht's most durable device for bringing poetry and
politics into fruitful union, and if, as Walter Benjamin has argued,
the important artist not only uses a mode but also transforms and
extends it, then Brecht's importance is obvious. Satire is inher-

ently didactic, but the lyric is not, and that Brecht could be didactic *and* lyrical enlarges our idea of poetry in general. And finally, Brecht used the didactic stance to solve perhaps his biggest problem: in radical contrast to the Soviet brand of Marxism, which pretends to speak *for* oppressed peoples, Brecht would go no further than to speak *to* them, propounding no authorities or programs but only insisting that victims everywhere should see themselves in the full sadness of their plight and see also that if politics is part of the human condition, very much of the human condition is a matter of politics.

And yet there is something else, subtler, more delicate, about Brecht's use of didactic forms. They allow him to remain impersonal, they rule out small-talk and self-pity, and where deep emotion arises the didactic stance becomes a technique for restraint, for expression of feeling about world events without splashing the event or the feeling all over the page. And if his role as teacher demanded discipline, it also gave Brecht a certain happy freedom. Consider the following poem, quoted complete:

Refresh yourself, sister
With the water from the copper bowl with bits of ice in it—
Open your eyes under water, wash them—
Dry yourself with the rough towel and cast
A glance at a book you love.
In this way begin
A lovely and useful day.

A love poem, of course; it is addressed to the actress Carola Neher, one of the women Brecht most loved. That she later died in a Soviet concentration camp suggests (I shall need to comment on this) the retrograde impact of future events upon Brecht's kind of poetry. But in the little love poem, his aim is not advice. He wants to preserve a moment of beauty "so that painters could make pictures of it," as he said. The tenderness, in this case, is heightened rather than curbed by the rigor of its expression, and this leads to a general observation about Brecht's style: his severity, his militant push, his sometimes savage irony, these are formal strategies through which, in dark times, care and humanness remain active.

When Brecht started out, in the aftermath of World War One, he, along with Rilke and Gottfried Benn, represented the ways open to poetry in dark times. Rilke retreated into an exalted mysticism which glorified death and said, in effect, that the world is not as it seems. Benn, on the other hand, embraced the abyss, the primacy of slime, and took cold comfort in precise delineation of physical decay as the emblem of man's world. Brecht attacked the nihilism of his age head-on, through satire, and worked toward a political position which would give him the strength, purpose, and scope necessary to confront history without loss of hope or compassion. In retrospect, Brecht's seems the most human option of the three. But to speak of options is perhaps misleading. The poet's commitment is always to his or her vision, or rather, to the relation between self and world which inspires creation. And in Brecht's ease there is no doubt what this relation was:

> The green boats and the dancing sails on the Sound
> Go unseen. Of it all
> I see only the torn nets of the fishermen.

Those are lines from "Bad Time for Poetry," written in 1939. Keeping in mind that Brecht's term of derision for Hitler was "the house-painter," here are the last lines from "Bad Time for Poetry":

> Inside me contend
> Delight at the apple tree in blossom
> And horror at the house-painter's speeches
> But only the second
> Drives me to my desk.

Delight was a privilege Brecht valued but could seldom afford. Not joy, not celebration, but rather compassion and the need to take a stand inform his art. But if poetry arises from the soul's need to sing, how does song survive amid horror? Brecht offered an answer in a little poem, "Motto," which he used as an epigraph in the *Svendborg Poems:*

> In the dark times
> Will there also be singing?
> Yes, there will also be singing
> About the dark times.

In German the last two lines go this way:

> *Da wird auch gesungen werden.*
> *Von den finsteren Zeiten.*

He does not say yes; that would sound too fast, too easy, too confidently thoughtless. With the courage of despair he simply restates the question as its own answer, another example of dialectical form, a crucial reversal. Line-breaks, as I suggested earlier, are central to Brecht's poetry, and that here he should put a period after the second-to-last line not only makes the line stronger and more final. It calls for a halt and a silence before going on to the last line, a halt and a silence which, in a cliché I think Brecht would approve, speaks volumes. *There will also be singing.* How? What kind? *About and against the dark times.* And the cost will be great. The range of vision will narrow, and worse, will focus on unhappy and often terrible things. The obligation this entails will not, once accepted, be lightly cast off. And the poetry itself will be of a kind which many among us would rather ignore as too spartan, too seldom an occasion for delight and happy grace.

Brecht measured these costs and took them for granted. But two things he did not anticipate. The logic of his politics *and* the logic of his poetry would come to dominate his personal fate, leading him — a German, a Marxist, a man returning to his country — to end up in East Berlin. His first travel back and forth, his Austrian passport, his Swiss bank account, all this confirms, in my eyes, Brecht's decision against grave personal doubts to stay in the struggle, despite Stalin, despite the ugliness of life in East Germany. Hannah Arendt missed the central point when she condemned Brecht for his choice; it was the outcome (not the betrayal) of his whole life as a poet, and if living in the Soviet sector did damage to his poetic capacity, that too was part of the cost for one who would sing about and against the dark times.

But the worst cost could not be seen coming until too late. Brecht's poetry embraces a political vision, beautiful in its ideals, which did not survive its totalitarian perversion. The historical failure of Marxism has had enormous consequences for all of us, but for people directly involved the outcome was shattering. Recurring anti-Soviet sentiment and outbreaks of bitterness in Brecht's late poetry reveal the suffering of a man coming to see — as a generation of decent men and women came painfully to see —

that the great moment had passed, that the magnificent dream of human liberation would go unrealized. But if political defeat is the end in actual politics, in poetry the case is strangely otherwise. Brecht's vision was betrayed by history but his poetry does not therefore suffer forfeit or become irrelevant. On the contrary, it gains in retroactive depth, taking on dignity and an import which did not exist when the poems were written but which exists now because of the way events turned out.

Political poetry — at least the kind committed to a cause — possesses a destiny, and when destiny ends in defeat, the result is not failure but tragedy. For this reason Brecht's poetry, as we read it now, bears within it a tragic sense of life which the poet himself could not detect. Or no, in his late years Brecht began to feel it deeply, and in the following poem, one of the last he wrote, the destiny of his poetry — which is the tragedy of hope in dark times — is fully acknowledged:

> At the time when their fall was certain—
> On the ramparts the lament for the dead had begun—
> The Trojans adjusted small pieces, small pieces
> In the triple wooden gates, small pieces.
> And began to take courage, to hope.
>
> The Trojans too, then.

John Willett is second to none as a student of Brecht, and Ralph Manheim remains one of our most dependable translators of European literature. Together — but with the help of many people, including Brecht's surviving friends — they have produced an invaluable book. Brecht wrote more than a thousand poems; but before the appearance of *Poems 1913-1956* less than a hundred were readily available in translation, mainly those in H. R. Hay's *Selected Poems* (1947) and Eric Bentley's *Manual of Piety* (1966). Both books were good but limited; Hays stuck to poems Brecht had selected as a modest first-showing, and Bentley gave us only the early, raucous poet of the *Hauspostille*. Neither suggests even faintly the range and formal variation of which Brecht was master (neither have I in this essay, for example, Brecht's poems uncanny for their closeness to Blake's *Songs of Innocence and Experience*). But now, in any case, we have about half of Brecht in English, and the translators of the new collection — all 35 of them — have done a job worth trusting, work that overall is excellent.

On the one hand, Brecht is "easy" to translate because of his penchant for directness and because he relies on the paratactic syntax of spoken German, as opposed to the hypotactic structure of literary German. No doubt this basic accessibility accounts for the success with which a host of problems have been handled, because on the other hand Brecht offers plenty of resistance. His style is colloquial with a touch of the Bavarian dialect. His language level is that of the street, full of slang and banalities, a sort of calculated crudity given added thrust by the way Brecht absorbed the rude style of Luther's Bible and — stirring all this together — came out with a peculiar syntax and diction which seems demotic to the core, but which in fact is not spoken, or written, by anyone but Brecht.

And yet, a great deal of true Brecht comes through, even allowing for the clumsiness of the rhymed verse, where unexpected successes also occur. What survives best is the later Brecht, the poet for whom "the very simplest words/ Must be enough." What I mean to say is that in *Poems 1913-1956* a voice emerges which is clearly its own, which firmly governs its chosen domain and does not constantly remind us of its status as translation. We might bicker forever over the rendering of certain lines and poems. Brecht's famous *Rückkehr*, which literally means "The Return" and was translated in that manner by H. R. Hays in 1947, has here been rendered as "The Homecoming" and seems a perverse attempt to compete with a prior and adequate translation. Beyond that sort of thing, however, the great point is that a poet of undeniable genius, unlike anyone in America, has been made available.

To the earlier introductions by Hays and Bentley, and to the classic early essays — those by Walter Benjamin, Hannah Arendt, Clement Greenberg, and Max Frisch — must now be added the fine introduction to the present volume, which situates Brecht in terms of his literary and his political coordinates. The book also contains important aids to the general reader, tools not only very useful but which make this edition a model for future editions of political poetry. The editors have arranged the poems in the order they were written, rather than the way they might have been grouped by Brecht for publication; to keep the record straight, however, the editors have also included a section which sorts out all of Brecht's publications. Then they have provided a selection of prose "texts" by Brecht himself about his art. There is an index of all titles in German, and all the poems in translation have been collated with their German originals — pages and volume — in both the German *Collected Works* and in the more manageable *Gedichte*.

For poetry of Brecht's kind, the most important things we need are dates and context. The editors have accordingly assembled 85 pages of "Notes." Every poem is accounted for, sometimes briefly, sometimes at length. The last poem I quoted, which ends "The Trojans too, then," has a whole page of notes, including the poem by Cavafy to which Brecht's poem responds. Personally, I would like to see all poems dated. I would like to know what was happening in the world, and in the poet's larger life, as he or she wrote this or that poem. For political poetry, in any case, dating and historical placement are essential to the poems themselves, which is what I mean by saying that Willett's and Manheim's edition of Brecht is a model of its kind.

CODA: When I read a book like William Shawcross' *Sideshow*, which accounts for the American destruction of Cambodia, or even more heart-rending, a book like Penny Lernoux's *Cry of the People*, which documents in horrid detail the agony of Latin America where tens of thousands of blameless people are "tortured and murdered by organizations funded and trained by the U.S. Government, sometimes with the direct connivance of U.S. agencies" — when I see what these books say I think, my God, how can I *go back* to the next poem in our magazines, the next volume of poetry praised for its sturdy solipsism. I am heartened by the women's movement, poetry by Rich and Piercy for example, which confronts bravely and possesses the dignity of a cause that is real and decent and must sooner or later touch everyone. But then it occurs to me that among the few poets in America worth caring about, at least three, Brodsky, Walcott, Simic, are not native to our tradition and speak partly from another world. And then I am back with the sort of stuff which can be described just as Max Frisch did in 1947: "Most of what goes by the name of poetry looks like irony of the crassest sort when I compare it for even only a single day with my own life."

And so, like Frisch, I find Brecht sustaining, even beautiful, for the way his poems stand up against the world in which they were written. He kept his art open, allowing history its maiming intrusions, making the best of bad prospects. In "To Those Born Later," Brecht said of himself:

> All roads led into the mire in my time.
> My tongue betrayed me to the butchers.
> There was little I could do. But those in power
> Sat safer without me: that was my hope.
> So passed my time
> Which had been given to me on earth.

His hope was betrayed, as hope usually is. And no doubt there was little he could do. All honest vision leads into the mire — Yeats said that, didn't he? — and not just the familiar squalor of selfhood but the bloody, man-created sorrow engulfing the world, from which no one is exempt, about which no one can claim not to know. In a recent poem, half horror, half surreal play, Charles Simic inserts the following lines to suggest how politics grips those innocently swept up, but also the rest of us — those who only behold:

> The act of torture consists of various strategies
> meant to increase
> the imagination of the homo sapiens.

Coleridge never thought of that one. Neither did Emerson. Imagination, for them, was its own sweet prod. But for those born later, the irony of Simic's lines makes terrible sense. Brecht, at least, would think so.

This essay was written in review of Bertolt Brecht, Poems 1913-1956. Edited by John Willett and Ralph Manheim. Methuen 1980.

# HOW MICKEY MADE IT

by JAYNE ANNE PHILLIPS

from BOOKSLINGER EDITIONS

*nominated by Daniel Menaker, David Wilks and Stephanie Vaughn*

THIS BED IS WICKED COMFORTABLE, I mean I sleep like a baby and don't wanna wake up. I guess you OWN a bed like this when you're twenty-eight huh (smile, tawny skin, fine sharp face) and this place is so CLEAN, nothin outa place but your head. Just kidding Darling, don't get hot (lighting his cigarette, frowning over cupped hands). No I mean older women are fine with me, you're fine with me really, a little awesome but I'll call you Mom once in a while just to keep us in line (inhaling, looking up with smoke on his lips). But don't pull any teenager numbers on me, that's all in the past, remember I'm twenty now, that's, uh, TWENTEE — you remember, a week ago when you gave me that book of jokes, those

376

cartoons? In the bar, handed it right over the counter with the little sketch inside of me in my nifty bartender's coat and cardboard bow tie compliments of Savio's what? Yeah, she remembers, signed it WITH LOVE FROM YOUR CUSTOMER HAPPY BIRTHDAY MICKEY. Look, just because we got a little boozed when you took me to lunch that next day, and you said I should call in sick so we could go to the beach, doesn't mean you're RESPONSIBLE for me. I mean if they fired me for that they were going to fire me anyway, I shoulda given them a better excuse but what the fuck it was a suckass job to begin with. I only had it the month I've been back from England, just bread till I get a band together. I've been fired plenty from everywhere without your help, so don't be pent up about it. I'll get another job tomorrow, don't worry about Mickey (shakes his head, black curls cut short on top and long in the back, Galahad punk) I mean I haven't been on my own since I was twelve for nothin, I can get BY you know — I'm a kid but I try real hard. Come here, get closer.

Yeah for a while I was modeling downtown, what a racket that shit is — guys smearing makeup all over your face, three of them at once while you're sitting in a chair (stands up out of bed, pulls on black denim pants, white undershirt) and some other guy is brushing your shoes then, it's Stand up Pull in Turn Stop Splat (flexing his long hard legs, goofing on a Marlboro-smoker stance) HERE's the smile you push GOT IT KID?? You better get it. You see I had this whole whatsis portfolio expensive shit and I walked right in and got the job and the others were pissed, really quite the pisser when they'd been licking ass for weeks to get in the office. But after it was all over—four weeks I did it—I burned the whole thing, the job the pictures the assholes, all of it, and I told that fag to get himself another boy. I mean, can you see it, some chumpy fag drooling over those pictures. Suit, swimsuit, towel around the neck, what bullshit, I never played tennis in my life. I'm a SINGER I don't go for that commercial shit I'LL DO IT MYSELF THANK YOU, Thaaannk Yooooooo!!! Whoo! Jesus.

Doncha like to walk down the street with me, hmmm, doncha? Whoops, somethin tells me you're not amused, not amused HEY well excuse me (dodging passers-by with elaborate swoops and fast two-step skips) I'm part preppie, can't help sliding through crowds, stay close now, we want everyone to know we're TO-GETHER and we're RIGHT and we're COOL, Yoo Hoo, Every-one, This is MY FRIEND, This Girl (pointing, taking off in a sleuth's mince), Here, give HER the prize. Come, Darling. This way darling. And don't drag your feet, I can't AFFORD another pair of Candies this week . . . keeping you in French ticklers keeps food from my mouth as it is . . . Sweetheart, your kicks are killing me, why can't you be satisfied with that Malaysian dwarf I bought you? Ouch, okay, don't kick the shins, need the shins, STAGE-WORK you know, you gotta Stand Up to project, I got the message, I'll shut up, we'll just walk. HEY EVERYONE, we're WALKING here, we're just WALKING. Wow, I love the street. See this lady in front of us with her kid crawling under its own stroller? Hey, she loves the day she loves that kid she loves HER LIFE you can tell. Jesus, look at that face — they ought to lock her up before she walks in front of a truck —

OK, here we are, take a good look, this is CHEAPO'S — Only place to buy records in this town. Darling? Sweetheart? Come back DARLING, Mickey's gonna buy you some MU-SIC, he's gonna pay for his SUPPER, cut you off from that commercial dark ages Stones shit (dancing in doorway, bowing from the waist), Come IN now, don't be shy, never too late for the good stuff, just don't get LOST now that we're on the BRINK (running down aisles in smooth reggae skip) OUH (making faces, doing an imitation clubfoot) I hurt myself, I'm SUING. Now you see that cute punky girl at the counter? She's going to spin some tunes for us, hey, see? (lays out a dollar-a-record tip) here are the imports, the real stuff, there's no real shit over here, it's all happening in England like I told you. Now listen I'm gonna get her to play the Members, oh oh or hmmm (sucking his finger, rolling his eyes) ahhh, the Specta-tor—this cut with the fabulous Moog that drifts off like balloons. You're gonna LIKE IT, it's gonna Change Your Life, you'll be a rock & roll baby — You can't take it in at first, it sounds bitter maybe but when you HEAR it you know what it is all at once . . . and that doesn't mean you go out and buy yourself a string tie and put on some *fashion* pose, just means you KNOW what the real music is and you'll go where you need to go to get it, like, look at these asshole album covers, you can SEE what shit they're playing by the sparkly lights on their jeans and how they hold their fuckin streamline chromeline guitars like giant cocks—it's sickening, man, and people buy this shit. You see these imports. One little rack of singles with penciled-in titles, but this shit is REAL this is REAL music and they don't have to pretend it's sex. Yeah, balls, the family jewels.

I don't know I just never got along with my family, I mean they're not my family really since I'm adopted but they are my family— and it was always weird man, I mean they told me I was adopted from the start but still, all those years it was like, uh, how come *I* got such dark skin and how come I just don't really FEEL it for you. When I was fourteen they gave me the address of the adoption agency and I found out I'm half Comanche and half Spanish. I wrote four letters, four different letters, man, and the agency sent me this long sheet of paper inscribed with the facts, but no names. I was born in Tucson, and my younger sister too, but she's no blood relation. Only the oldest one, my older sister, is their own kid, and Jesus it was always obvious. I mean, who graduated from Barnard, who works for ecology and married a lawyer? Not Mickey, man. Mickey got boarded off at the age of twelve because he was a mean little kid and always in fights. NO, I ain't gonna do it 'cause YOU say so man I mean who the fuck are YOU? And my younger sister, she's a case, she's fat, she sits all day in the easy chair and watches TV like a TV machine. Makes me sick—I tell her, I've told her, get off your butt, it's plain you hate yourself. Not me man. I love Mickey. Who cares if THEY love Mickey—that's why I said I've had it with this shit and I went to England when I was sixteen and lived with Nate. Nate, the kid I played basketball with at Wakefield High, after I came back from correction school where I got CORRECTED ha ha. But Nate, man, he was wonderful. England was really real, I *grew up* over there, I learned about rock& roll. We went out to the pubs and the bars and we had a band and I got into singing. There I was, sixteen and really alive while everybody back here from my old street was asking daddy for the car, oh please daddy can I? Ah come on Dad, I wanna get my hand in someone's pants in the back seat and have her home by 12:30 with her dress buttoned up right so *her* daddy don't ask questions. What? Yeah, I was singing. SINGING, SING-

ING and living with a nice twenty-nine-year-old lady who had a little half-black kid that called ME daddy. Yeah, you see? Quite the difference.

I went to England to stay with Nate and he was living with Clytie, she was going to marry him so he could stay in the country, but I don't know, I just fell for her and Nate moved out with hard feelings but things settled and were cool in a few weeks — Clytie was so smart and hardheaded but crazy enough to put up with me, and had no real set on how anything should be — that's what *smart* is, you know? She shared this two-family flat with her dad and he drove a lorry and picked up scrap to sell. I mean it was two separate flats but her dad was around a lot and she did his meals and he gave her dough. She had grown up with her mother and found her father right after she'd had her baby, this beautiful brown kid she called Feather though his name was really Frederick. Her dad was just a working-class stiff but Clytie could do that, show up after twenty-five years with a half-black baby and make her father love her, and he was cool about her boyfriends. Boyfriends moved in and out and it's not true that kind of number always fucks kids up. Feather was happy, sunny cocoa face, about two and starting to talk. Nate and me took him to the club we worked, he watched while the group played. What a time that was. I'm sixteen and Escaped: school, family, house, and got what I want after *all that time* of bad boy guilt trips. Nothin but YOU GOT NO FEELINGS FOR PEOPLE MICKEY, YR DAD AND I HAVE GIVEN YOU ALL WE CAN BUT YOU DON'T KNOW WHAT TO DO WITH IT DO YOU MICKEY and the day I got them to release me on my own recognizance from the state-ward crap was the luckiest day of my life. I go to England and there's Clytie, pale complexion and black hair cut real short, so she looks like a boy almost, except she's nursing and has these round, heavy breasts. Nothing was dirty to Clytie, nothing was stained or fucked up. She showed me about the feeling of feeding a kid, that it pulled at her inside like a real faint coming and made her wet. Evenings she would be feeding Feather and I would lay down with them and fall asleep from the suckling sounds. I was out at night and she was out in the day sometimes, art modeling, and I took care of the baby. He did, he called me daddy. Now, can you dig how that was for me? I mean, I knew a lot, I'd been OUT THERE a long time, but I didn't know this good stuff, always before I only had glimpses, BAM, quick flash and close the shutter — ah, there, THAT'S REAL — but only for a minute, an hour maybe. I really pushed man, I pushed to get in where the juice was.

The women I've cared about are mostly good women, but I got no illusions about girls in general. You think women don't use men for fucking? Bullshit, plenty of women have used me for sex, just want some big cock to bang their brains out, want you to walk around with them all dressed up because you got a nice hard ass in your pants, they got no feelings for you. Katrin, this other girl I know — the one I met in the bar before I met you, I told you about her — she's not like that, she's a nice little girl, punky and kind of shy under her red lipstick. She lives with her folks, that was her dad's car I borrowed yesterday. Her family has plenty and Katrin wants to pay for an apartment for me, I mean she would still live at home but she would have a place to go at times, you know? What d'ya mean? She knows me, I've been honest with her, she knows how I feel about the jealous maniac number, no, Katrin is cool. Besides, I've got about eighty bucks left and none of the clubs around here are going to let me bartend right off. You got to work up through the ranks just like in a fucking bank — barback and bus and whatever else they want to rankle you with. If I have to spend my dough on just living, rent and that shit, I'll never get enough money to split and do what I have to do. You think I'm wrong? How the fuck can you be me, how can you *do* that? You, with your life all peachy. Just let me be here, okay? Let ME figure it out, I'm experienced.

My first real time was with a neighborhood girl the fall that I was twelve, I got into a lot of trouble over it. She had this big backyard with all these apple trees like a forest and we were back there in the trees, just innocent pushing against each other, feeling pretty loopy, like the first time you're tipsy on booze. She was leaning against a tree and had pulled me against her and her dress was up between us. She had unzipped my pants and then suddenly everything *fit*, you know, sounds like a joke, I mean I wasn't trying to fuck her, I didn't know I could fuck anybody, but she was one of these girls who all of a sudden catches fire and then doesn't know where she is. I mean there ARE such girls. Right then her mother

has seen us from the house through the trees and starts SCREAM-
ING the girl's name across the yard, yelling with this hysterical
warble in her voice, and I was sort of pulling the girl around the
tree so the mother couldn't see us when I slipped inside, really
inside her, almost by accident. I will never forget it, I was amazed,
she came, just in seconds, and I was watching her face the whole
time. I didn't know what coming was and for a long time after that I
thought there was something wrong with me because I hadn't felt
the shaking SHE'D felt, with her eyes wide open but she wasn't
there. Real scary, like the sky cracking open. By the time her
mother got from the second floor of the house and across the yard
to us it was all over—it was the mother who had worked up a
passion and she kept on with it for several days. You might say the
whole mess contributed to my parents' decision to get Mickey
OUT, like once a dog has tasted blood he keeps on killing chickens.
So they packed me off to where there were no chickens they'd
know about — they gave up on me and made me a ward of the
state. I was TWELVE, man, with the whole puberty thing crashing
around my head. I mean, CONFUSED? I was crazy, here was this
totally heavy punishment when SHE was the one who had done
that weird shaking. Had *I* done that to her? I mean I only just
touched her in this softness and she exploded. And really the
PACK HIM OFF gig was already in motion before that, I'd been in
fights with some older boys and I'd done some petty stealing, but
the actual change of residence came right on the heels of magic in
the forest. Magic Mickey, what a laugh, it wasn't any magic I knew
about till it grabbed me. Later I did the grabbing I admit but back
then I was just this hyper wild LITTLE BOY really, big for my age
maybe but not *that* big. It was just this weird MYSTERY, all of
them, all their reasons — Let's do what's BEST for MICKEY
everybody and it felt like jail, like waking up in solitary. I mean it
wasn't like I loved my parents but I thought I was supposed to and
they shoved me off man, they sent me off in the old lifeboat.

Was like they could always say to themselves well we didn't GET
him until he was four years old, he's got things in him we didn't put
there — my mother told me once I had probably been abused as a
young kid which is maybe likely because from the first I knew I was
full of hate, just HATE, hate, a little jet-propelled demon. You
think I'm abrasive now — wasn't that the word, Mickey's new word

from the lady with the big vocabulary?—yeah, *abrasive,* you should have seen me *then.* I did it with dedication, like something was boiling over a fire inside me, you know? I don't have any memory before about age six. No, I DON'T remember any real parents. I mean, my mother is Jewish and my father is Quaker, and they can't have any more kids so they decide to adopt two Indians. Yeah, the liberal American melting pot and what it melted was my head. But that's okay, I dig being runny and hot, I just don't ever want to be dead and I don't give a shit what anyone thinks because I'm not amusing YOU you see I'm amusing MYSELF and whoever digs THAT can stand on my train. I got myself strapped to a big diesel and I got no complaints. I got a lot to do & I'm really HERE, they can all tell and that's why I'm going to make it. I got talent, I got total energy and focus and I can hold a stage. You've never even seen me sing and you can feel it. Just ice, ice and hot white sparks, squeeze it out and control what they feel. It's not how fucking OLD I am or cocktail manners or social skills, it's what I know and no one TAKES that, I GIVE it, *I* give it.

I could always take care of myself, all us kids could, because my mother was sick so much of the time. She has lupus, always had it for years, that's why I'm back from England now. She's not well, she's not at all well. But we kids did our own shit, I mean we washed our own clothes and cleaned up after ourselves and cooked the fucking meals, yeah, casseroles, but still, Mickey is no slouch in the kitchen—that's why it's so funny to me to see these guys who can't wipe their own asses, fucking helpless without a girl to sew their buttons on. I mean that's not what I need a girl for, you know? And the food thing, I always worked in restaurants, those jobs are easy to get and bartending pays if you hang around long enough to get the good shifts. I was doing fifty a night when you met me and don't worry I'll do it again, but Savio's, man, is the craziest place in the Square, all the nuts are in there, the regulars, every night near closing—like that old lady you saw that tried to throw her glass at me. She's in there, sitting on the barstool and talking to herself until she works up a fury. Turns to the other customers with this blitz of curses about whoever serves her DID YOU SEE WHAT HE SAID TO ME THAT UGLY MONKEY LOOK AT HIM PUSHING HIS WHITE TEETH OUT JESUS CHRIST I DON'T HAVE TO TAKE THIS SHIT HE'S AN APE

AN APE MAN A STUPID BABOON. Finally you ask her if she
has the money to pay her bill and she never does, three times the
manager had to help her off the stool and into the street and she's
yelling all the way about how I'd slapped her in the face and ripped
her dress. Then there's Veteran Twitch, this wipeout in army
fatigues who's always there at closing, totally gonzo but very quiet,
stares into his glass and does this endless routine of facial expres-
sions, wound up tight and talking nonstop with no sound. Never
raises his eyes but definitely directs it all to some companion on
the phantom telephone. You don't know how many nuts there are
till you work a bar, I only do it because they don't lay claims, you
do it and get out. And I save all the bucks. I got back from England
and was at my parents' house, couldn't handle it so I was renting
this studio, a sound studio so I could get some musicians together
and do some tapes, $350 a month, that's where all my money went
and I'm sneaking in there at night and sleeping as well and it was
useless as far as the music went, I just couldn't find anyone who
was serious, they're on their way to law school and born cool, they
got to make the cotillion in their MGs. The music ain't going to
come from THEM it's going to come from ME because it's all I
GOT, and then I'm gonna be laughing in their faces which is maybe
a pointless desire because by the time I get there their faces will
have long since been turned to the wall, staring at nowhere,
nothing every minute.

Talk about walls, the rules can do it and women can do it too, put
you on your back unexpectedly. Rules do it over the long haul so
you don't even notice but girls can do it with one punch, like
Giselle, the girl I lived with here between the two times I was in
England. Giselle was a beautiful little girl, man I will always love
her but she was crazy and her life had been shit. She was from the
projects in South Boston and she talked with that nasal flat twang
and was all fashion, living at home with her fucking drunk father
and her drunk brothers and spending all her money from her
boring job on shiny shoes and satin jackets. She was twenty-one
and I was eighteen and I took her out of there like Prince Valiant,
had a good bar job and a place in Allston. Giselle was blond, real
petite, maybe five feet two — I like small girls anyway, so nice and
light to lift and hold in bed — but Giselle had such a way of
*standing*, like a kid with her hands empty. You wouldn't think

much of her, I mean she had nothing to say really, she wasn't so much for brains if you judge by talk, but she had so much heart and would just look at you with everything laid open, like there was nothing she wouldn't give you. Jesus, Giselle — she got to me, I lived with her the longest, about six months, but she had to possess you, surround you. She was a big help to me and I got a lot of work done then on my music, I lost a waiting job during that time and she took over with the money, but later I got a bar thing together and was meeting a lot of ladies. I couldn't lie to her so we broke up and she moved back home. I would still go to see her there though I hated that apartment building, all dark and stale with the TVs going. I called her at work one day to see how she was, I knew she was hassled about me, and they told me she'd been sent home drunk from lunch. Really wasn't like her to fuck up a job. So I went to see her and I find her in her bedroom all juiced and weepy, the room a mess, she could barely talk. I stayed there with her about two hours but then I had to leave to meet Janet, this other girl I was going out with — and Giselle just grabs onto me, begs me not to go, stay, stay with me. I told her I had to split but she could come, I figured I'd take her back to my place and let her sleep it off. But she said no, I had to stay *there* in her bedroom and not move until she was all right. So I'm walking toward the door and she's following, yelling how she's going to kill herself. We're on this falling-down stoop in the projects and she's screaming and I told her not to be stupid, don't be crazy, and she slammed the door in my face. I went off to meet Janet but I was worried, I remembered Giselle's girlfriend telling me how Giselle had tried to kill herself once before over a guy. Tried to phone her but no one home. So that night about three a.m. Janet and I are asleep in my apartment and this tornado blows through the door — Boom Boom Boom — I hear three giant steps as Giselle makes the distance from the door to the bed and then banshee screaming YOU FUCKER I KNEW YOU HAD SOMEONE HERE and fists and I rolled over Janet first to protect her and grabbed Giselle's wrists. I couldn't hold her, she was totally out of her head, kicking and punching me, she kicked me in the balls about three times and bloodied my face. This went on for about twenty full-blown minutes, and then she seemed to calm down and said she was going into the kitchen to wash up. So I'm wiping the blood off my mouth, *tired* man, exhausted, from fighting this tiny girl, and in shock from falling into it out of a total sleep. I mean, I didn't even know she still had a key — she'd given it back a month before when she'd moved out but made a copy on the sly. I found out later she'd been coming over to the place when I wasn't there and just sitting in the rooms, for hours. Anyway, I'm standing there and Giselle walks back in with a butcher knife. She has it in both hands above her head and she's bringing it down into her own stomach and I lunge across the room and grab her — she cut my chest and kept trying to stab me. I couldn't get the knife out of her hands. I yelled to Janet to call the police but I had unplugged the phone earlier and Janet couldn't find the socket to plug it back in, so I'm dragging Giselle around by the arms to show Janet where the phone plug is, blood dripping down my legs from the cuts — really getting scared because this thing doesn't ever seem to be ending, Janet with her clothes on by now and panic-stricken and Giselle like a frozen monster and all three of us crying — I couldn't see anything for crying. It was a nightmare, like getting caught in fast water and you can't tell what's happening, you're just getting beaten from every direction and going under. Janet got the police but there was more blood from somewhere and it really flashed through my mind that Giselle might kill me — it took the fucking cops fifteen minutes to get there and by the time they did I was lying on top of Giselle on the floor, naked and bleeding on both of us, holding her down with my weight and the knife still in her fist. As soon as I got off her she was up and throwing a tape recorder she'd given me through the window, then she picked up a chair — not a great big chair but this was a tiny girl. The cops put her in a straitjacket and when she came to herself she was behind bars, clutching this little suitcase she'd brought over to my place with her. I called a friend of mine to go down and get her out of jail and tell the cops it was domestic and no charges and all that crap, and she went to her girlfriend's and soon after left for Mexico — this trip we'd planned for her when she was still living with me. We'd gotten the air tickets and everything and talked about how getting away would make the transition easier for her. Jesus. This was all about a year and a half ago now and Giselle seems okay, living with some guy who goes home to her every night and lets her cook his dinner. I still care about her, I can't forget the good things about her, but I don't go to sleep now without a chain lock across the door. That was the scariest thing that ever happened to me, and the worst of it was seeing her in that straitjacket. Have you ever seen someone you know in one? She looked amputated, lopped off and exploding, her arms *gone* when I'd felt them *holding* me all that time before.

Holding is a trip, right? The last time my mother was in the hospital, I stayed up with her all one night and couldn't get my head clear for days afterward. She was on chemotherapy then, some drug that was mostly speed because she couldn't sleep at all, and she had these speed raps with everyone in the family. All of us, one at a time, late at night. I'm alone with her in that room, she's the only one of them I love. She told me how hard it was to raise me — I said, shit, you didn't *raise* me, from the age of twelve I was a ward of the state, you call that *raising* me, I mean I was bounced around like a fucking ball and you so-called parents didn't pay for nothing, my clothes, my lodging, my schooling, *nothing* — and no one says you *had* to but then to get on my ass about owing you fifteen bucks, FIFTEEN BUCKS man. Blame me for that if you want to, she says, I'm only trying to teach you to care about someone's rules but your own, and we had to let you go Mickey, you were tearing us up, you were tearing all of us apart, it was you or all the rest of them, I had to decide. Why did you hate us, she says, Why Did You Hate All Of Us coming at me pounding in my head like a drum, christ, in that dark hospital, the halls dark and the nurses' squeaking shoes outside. My legs were shaking, I wanted to get up and run but I couldn't stand up, just her FACE in that bed man — I took her face between my two hands and I YELLED right at her EYES, I didn't hate YOU I hated THEM, I LOVED YOU. Fucking Christ. She's home now and I'm gone, I can't go over there. If I weren't staying with you I'd be staying somewhere else.

All you can do is turn the bad stuff into something else and not flake out on what it costs you — like, I know I'm good, I got metal and breath in my voice and I can hold any space. Use a voice like playing a horn, peeling and slow whines and a good base — like, *I'MWALKin to the STAtion / I'M GETtin ona TRAIN / REAR-RANGEmy LIFE/BUTIT'SALLINVAIN* — hard undercut in the base, that flat BWAABOOM in the lyrics lays down a gut tremor they can't help but give you, give BACK to you. *An DON'T YOU WANT/someone to talk to/an DON'T YOU NEED/someone who really cares*—Yeah, I know I've got it, I sing in the streets and I can hear people pick it up behind me. I'm back in Europe just as soon as I get the bread, there's no rock clubs here, nowhere to do a good band, just posers man, just wearing the fancy leather and the chains and stepping out to masquerade, barns full of sweaty dress-ups, all MONEY, they all got money and no pressure, no push — they don't know shit about music but it doesn't even MATTER, man, the ones doing real music can do it without them and just play them, play them like mongoloid pinball — Nothin fucks music, what is *has*, melts in your mouth and turns to acid halfway down, you don't forget it. AM slosh is no real language. Look, you feel my mouth, you see, we're talking.

Here, I want to keep my face close to your face. You share your pillows with me, okay, darling? I'll be YOUR friend.

When it gets to be night like this, I mean late night — night doesn't start till three a.m. — I like how there's no light and the dark is different from earlier, when they're all out there checking scenes and looking for some flash. About now everyone starts sinking. . . . What do you think? We're not bad roommates — Darling, put those cards away, don't play games in bed. What? Can you tell my fortune with those cards? I believe in that shit, don't scare me . . . turn out the light, I got something for you, do it in the dark if you're going to do it.

# TURNING THIRTY

by KATHA POLLITT

from PEQUOD

*nominated by* PEQUOD, *DeWitt Henry, Josephine Jacobsen and Philip Schultz*

This spring, you'd swear it actually gets dark earlier.
At the elegant new restaurants downtown
your married friends lock glances over the walnut torte:
It's ten o'clock. They have important jobs
and go to bed before midnight. Only you
walking alone up the dazzling avenue
still feel a girl's excitement, for the thousandth time
you enter your life as though for the first time,
as an immigrant enters a huge, mysterious capital:
Paris, New York. So many wide plazas, so many marble
     addresses!
Home, you write feverishly
in all five notebooks at once, then faint into bed
dazed with ambition and too many cigarettes.

Well, what's wrong with that? Nothing, except
really you don't believe wrinkles mean character
and know it's an ominous note
that the Indian skirts flapping on the sidewalk racks
last summer looked so gay you wanted them all
but now are marked clearer than price tags: not for you.
Oh, what were you doing, why weren't you paying attention
that piercingly blue day, not a cloud in the sky,
when suddenly "choices"
ceased to mean "infinite possibilities"
and became instead "deciding what to do without"?
No wonder you're happiest now

riding on trains from one lover to the next.
In those black, night-mirrored windows
a wild white face, operatic, still enthralls you:
a romantic heroine,
suspended between lives, suspended between destinations.

# THE EISENHOWER YEARS

by PAUL ZIMMER

from THE BLACK WARRIOR REVIEW

*nominated by* THE BLACK WARRIOR REVIEW *and Michael Harper*

Flunked out and laid-off,
Zimmer works for his father
At Zimmer's Shoes for Women.
The feet of old women awaken
From dreams, they groan and rub
Their hacked-up corns together.
At last they stand and walk in agony
Downtown to Zimmer's fitting stool
Where he talks to the feet,
Reassures and fits them with
Blissful ties in medium heels.

Home from work he checks the mail
For greetings from his draft board.
After supper he listens to Brubeck,
Lays out with a tumbler of Thunderbird,
Cigarettes and *From Here To Eternity*.

That evening he goes out to the bars,
Drinks three pitchers of Stroh's,
Ends up in the wee hours leaning
On a lamp post, his tie loosened,
Fedora pushed back on his head,
A Chesterfield stuck to his lips.

All of complacent America
Spreads around him in the night.
Nothing is moving in this void,
Only the feet of old women,
Twitching and shuffling in pain.
Zimmer sighs and takes a drag,
Exhales through his nostrils.
He knows nothing and feels little.
He has never been anywhere
And fears where he is going.

# IF PORCELAIN,
# THEN ONLY THE KIND

## by STANISLAW BARAŃCZAK

from UNDER MY OWN ROOF (Mr. Cogito Press)

*nominated by* MR. COGITO PRESS *and Patrick W. Gray*

If porcelain, then only the kind
you won't miss under the shoe of a mover or the tread of a tank;
if a chair, then one not too comfortable, lest
there be regret in getting up and leaving;
if clothing, then just so much as can fit in a suitcase,
if books, then those which can be taken in the memory,
if plans, then those which can be overlooked
when the time comes for the next move
to another street, continent, historical period
or world:

who told you that you were permitted to settle in?
who told you that this or that would last forever?
did no one ever tell you that you will never
in the world
feel at home here?

*translated from the Polish by Frank Kujawinski*

## ὄ ὄ ὄ

# A MAN OF THE WORLD

fiction by EDMUND WHITE

from SHENANDOAH

*nominated by* SHENANDOAH, *Joyce Carol Oates, and Walter Abish*

M Y FATHER WANTED ME TO WORK every summer in high school so that I might learn the value of a dollar. I did work, I did learn, and what I learned was that my dollars could buy me hustlers. I bought my first when I was fourteen.

The downtown of that city of half a million was small, no larger than a few dozen blocks. Every morning my stepmother drove me into town from our house, a fake Norman castle that stood high and white on a hill above the steaming river valley; we'd go down into town — a rapid descent of several steep plunges into the creeping traffic, dream dissolves of black faces, the smell of hot franks filtered through the car's air-conditioned interior, the muted cries of newspaper vendors speaking their own incomprehensible language, the somber look of sooted facades edging forward to squeeze out the light. Downtown excited me: so many people, some of them just possibly an invitation to adventure, escape or salvation.

As a little boy I'd thought of our house as the place God had meant us to own, but now I knew in a vague way that its seclusion and ease were artificial and that it strenuously excluded the city at the same time it depended on it for food, money, comfort, help, even pleasure. The black maids were the representatives of the city I'd grown up among. I'd never wanted anything from them — nothing except their love. To win it, or at least to ward off their silent, sighing resentment, I'd learned how to make my own bed and cook my own breakfast. But nothing I could do seemed to make up to them for the terrible loss they'd endured.

In my father's office I worked an Addressograph machine (then something of a novelty) with a woman of forty who, like a restless sleeper tangled in sheets, tossed about all day in her fantasies. She was a chubby but pert woman who wore pearls to cover the pale line across her neck, the scar from some sort of surgical intervention. It was a very thin line but she could never trust her disguise and ran to the mirror in the ladies' room six or seven times a day to re-evaluate the effect.

The rest of her energy went into elaborating her fantasies. There was a man on the bus every morning who always stationed himself opposite her and arrogantly undressed her with his dark eyes. Upstairs from her apartment another man lurked, growling with desire, his ear pressed to the floor as he listened through an inverted glass for the glissando of a silk slip she might be stepping out of. "Should I put another lock on my door?" she'd ask. Later she'd ask with wide-eyed sweetness, "Should I invite him down for a cup of coffee?" I advised her not to; he might be dangerous. The voraciousness of her need for men made me act younger than usual; around her I wanted to be a boy, not a man. Her speculations would cause her to sigh, drink water and return to the mirror. My stepmother said she considered this woman to be a "ninny." Once, years ago, my stepmother had been my father's secretary — perhaps her past made her unduly critical of the woman who had succeeded her. My family and their friends almost never characterized people we actually knew, certainly not dismissively. I felt a gleeful shame in thinking of my colleague as a "ninny" — sometimes I'd laugh out loud when the word popped into my head. I found it both exciting and alarming to feel superior to a grown-up.

Something about our work stimulated thoughts of sex in us. Our tasks (feeding envelopes into a trough, stamping them with addresses, stuffing them with brochures, later sealing them and running them through the postage meter) required just enough attention to prevent connected conversation but not so much as to absorb us. We were left with amoeboid desires that split or merged as we stacked and folded, as we tossed and turned. "When he looks at me," she said, "I know he wants to hurt me." As she said that, her sweet, chubby face looked as though it were emerging out of a cloud.

Once I read about a woman patient in psychoanalysis who referred to her essential identity as her "prettiness"; my companion — gray-eyed, her wrists braceleted in firm, healthy fat, hair swept up into a brioche pierced by the fork of a comb, her expression confused and sweet as she floated free of the cloud — she surrounded and kept safe her own "prettiness" as though it were a passive, intelligent child and she the mother, dazed by the sweeping lights of the world.

She was both fearful and serene — afraid of being noticed and more afraid of being ignored, thrillingly afraid of the sounds outside her bedroom window, but also serene in her conviction that this whole bewildering opera was being staged in order to penetrate the fire and get at her "prettiness." She really was pretty — perhaps I haven't made that clear: a sad blur of a smile, soft gray eyes, a defenseless availability. She was also crafty, or maybe willfully blind, in the way she concealed from herself her own sexual ambitions.

Becoming my father's employee clarified my relationship with him. It placed him at an exact distance from me that could be measured by money. The divorce agreement had spelled out what he owed my mother, my sister and me, but even so whenever my mother put us kids on the train to go visit him (one weekend out of every month and all summer every summer), she invariably told us, "Be nice to your father or he'll cut us off." And when my sister was graduated from college, he presented her with a "life bill," the itemized expenses he'd incurred in raising her over 21 years, a huge sum that was intended to discourage her from thoughtlessly spawning children of her own.

Dad slept all day. He seldom put in an appearance at the office before closing time, when he'd arrive fresh and rested, smelling of witch hazel, and scatter reluctant smiles and nods to the assembly as he made his way through us and stepped up to his own desk in a large room walled off from us by soundproof glass. "My, what a fine man your father is, a real gentleman," my colleague would sigh. "And to think your stepmother met him when she was his secretary — some women have all the luck." We sat in rows with our backs to him; he played the role of the conscience, above and behind us, a force that troubled us as we filed out soon after his arrival at the end of the work day. Had we stayed late enough? Done enough?

My stepmother usually kept my father company until midnight. Then she and I would drive back to the country and go to bed. Sometimes my father followed us in his own car and continued his desk work at home. Or sometimes he'd stay downtown till dawn. "That's when he goes out to meet other women," my real mother told me at the end of the summer, when I reported back to her what went on in Daddy's life. "He was never faithful. There was always another woman, the whole 22 years we were married. He takes them to those little flea-bag hotels downtown. I know." This hint of mystery about a man so cold and methodical fascinated me—as though he, the rounded brown stone, if only cracked open, would nip at the sky with interlocking crystal teeth, the quartz teeth of passion.

Before the midnight drive back home I was sometimes permitted to go out to dinner by myself. Sometimes I also took in a movie (I remember going to one that promised to be actual views of the "orgies at Berchtesgarten," but it turned out to be just Eva Braun's home movies, the Führer conferring warm smiles on pets and children). A man who smelled of Vitalis sat beside me and squeezed my thigh with his hand. I had my own spending money and my own free time.

I had little else. No one I could meet for lunch and confide in. No one who liked me. No one who wanted to talk with me about books or opera. Not even the impulse to ask for love or the belief that such things could be discussed. Had I known in any vivid or personal way of the disease, starvation and war that afflicted so much of humanity, I might have taken comfort at least in my physical well-being, but in my loneliness I worried about sickness, hunger and violence befalling me, as though precisely these fears had been visited on me by the jealous world in revenge against so much joyless plenty.

I hypothesized a lover who'd take me away. He'd climb the fir tree outside my window, step into my room and gather me into his arms. What he said or looked like remained indistinct, just a cherishing wraith enveloping me, whose face glowed more and more brightly. His delay in coming went on so long that soon I'd passed from anticipation to nostalgia. One night I sat at my window and stared at the moon, toasting it with a champagne glass filled with grape juice. I knew the moon's cold, immense light was falling on him as well, far away and just as lonely in a distant room. I expected him to be able to divine my existence and my need, to intuit that in this darkened room in this country house a fourteen-year-old was waiting for him.

Sometimes now when I pass dozing surburban houses I wonder behind which window a boy waits for me.

After a while I realized I wouldn't meet him till years later; I wrote him a sonnet that began, "Because I loved you before I knew you." The idea, I think, was that I'd never quarrel with him nor ever rate his devotion cheap; I had had to wait too long.

Our house was a somber place. The styleless polished furniture was piled high and the pantry supplies were laid in; in the empty fullness of breakfront drawers gold flatware and silver tea things remained for six months at a time in mauve flannel bags that could not ward off a tarnish bred out of the very air. No one talked much. There was little laughter, except when my stepmother was on the phone with one of her social friends. Although my father hated most people, he had wanted my stepmother to take her place — that is, my mother's place — in society, and she had. He'd taught her how to dress and speak and entertain and by now she'd long since surpassed his instructions; she'd become at once proper and frivolous, innocent and amusing, high-spirited and reserved — the combination of wacky girl and prim matron that world so admired.

I learned my part less well. I feared the sons of her friends and made shadows among the debs. I played the piano without ever improving; to practice would have meant an acceptance of more delay, whereas I wanted instant success, the throb of plumed fans in the dark audience, the pulse off diamonds from the curve of loges. What I had instead was the ache of waiting and the fear I

wasn't worthy. When I'd dress I'd stand naked before the closet
mirror and wonder if my body was worthy. I can still picture that
pale skin stretched over ribs, the thin, hairless arms and sturdier
legs, the puzzled searching face — and the slow lapping of disgust
and longing, disgust and longing. The disgust was hot, penetrating — nobody would want me because I was a sissy and had a mole
between my shoulder blades. The longing was cooler, less substantial, more the spray off a wave than the wave itself. Perhaps the
eyes were engaging, there was something about the smile. If not
lovable as a boy, then maybe as a girl; I wrapped the towel into a
turban on my head. Or perhaps need itself was charming or could
be. Maybe my need could make me as appealing as the woman
who worked the Addressograph machine with me.

I was always reading and often writing but both were passionately abstract activities. Early on I had recognized that books
pictured another life, one quite foreign to mine, in which people
circled one another warily and with exquisite courtesy until an
individual or a couple erupted and flew out of the salon, spangling
the night with fire. I had somehow stumbled on Ibsen and that's
how he struck me: oblique social chatter followed by a heroic death
in a snowslide or on the steeple of a church (I wondered how these
scenes could be staged). Oddly enough, the "realism" of the last
century seemed tinglingly far-fetched: vows, betrayals, flights,
fights, sacrifices, suicides. I saw literature as a fantasy, no less
absorbing for all its irrelevance — a parallel life, as dreams shadow
waking but never intersect it.

I thought to write of my own experiences required a translation
out of the crude patois of actual slow suffering, mean, scattered
thoughts and transfusion-slow boredom into the tidy couplets of
brisk, beautiful sentiment, a way of at once elevating and lending
momentum to what I felt. At the same time I was drawn to . . .
What if I could write about my life exactly as it was? What if I could
show it in all its density and tedium and its concealed passion,
never divined or expressed, the dull brown geode that eats at itself
with quartz teeth?

I read books with this passion, as one might beat back pages of
pictures, looking for someone he could love. The library downtown had been built as an opera house in the last century. Even in
grade school I had haunted the library, which was in the same
block as my father's office. The library looked up like a rheumy eye

at a pitched skylight over which pigeons whirled, their bodies a shuddering gray haze until one settled and its pacing black feet became as precise as cuneiform. The light seeped down through the stacks that were arranged in a horseshoe of tiers: the former family balcony, the dress circle, the boxes, on down to the orchestra, still gently raked but now cleared of stalls and furnished with massive oak card files and oak reading tables where unshaved old men read newspapers under gooseneck lamps and rearranged rags in paper sacks. The original stage had been demolished but cleats on the wall showed where ropes had once been secured.

The railings around the various balconies still described crude arabesques in bronze gone green, but the old floors of the balconies had been replaced by rectangular slabs of smoked glass that emitted pale emerald gleams along polished, bevelled edges. Walking on this glass gave me vertigo, but once I started reading I'd slump to the cold, translucent blocks and drift on ice floes into dense clouds. The smell of yellowing paper engulfed me. An unglued page slid out of a volume and a corner broke off, shattered — I was destroying public property! Downstairs someone harangued the librarian. Shadowy throngs of invisible operagoers coalesced and sat forward in their see-through finery to look and listen. I was reading the libretto of *La Bohême*. The alternating columns of incomprehensible Italian, which I could skip, made the pages speed by, as did the couple's farewell in the snow, the ecstatic reconciliation, poor little Mimi's prolonged dying. I glanced up and saw a pair of shoes cross the glass above, silently accompanied by the paling and darkening circle of the rubber end of a cane. The great eye of the library was blurred by tears.

Across the street the father of a friend of mine ran a bookstore. As I entered it, I was almost knocked down by two men coming out. One of them touched my shoulder and drew me aside. He had a three-day's growth of beard on his cheeks, shiny wet canines, a rumpled raincoat of a fashionable cut that clung to his hips and he was saying, "Don't just rush by without saying hello."

Here he was at last but now I knew for sure I wasn't worthy — I was ugly with my glasses and my scalp white under my shorn hair. "Do I know you?" I asked. I felt I did, as if we'd traveled for a month in a train compartment knee to knee night after night via the thirty installments of a serial but plotless though highly emotional dream. I smiled, embarrassed by the way I looked.

"Sure you know me." He laughed and his friend, I think, smiled. "No, honestly, what's your name?"

I told him.

He repeated it, smile suppressed, as I'd seen men on the make condescend to women they were sizing up. "We just blew into town," he said. "I hope you can make us feel at home." He put an arm around my waist and I shrank back; the sidewalks were crowded with people staring at us curiously. His fingers fit neatly into the space between my pelvis and the lowest rib, a space that welcomed him, that had been cast from the mold of his hand. I kept thinking these two guys want my money, but how they planned to get it remained vague. And I was alarmed they'd been able to tell at a glance that I would respond to their advances so readily. I was so pleased he'd chosen me; because he was from out of town he had higher, different standards. He thought I was like him, and perhaps I was or soon would be. Now that a raffish stranger — younger and more handsome than I'd imagined, but also dirtier and more condescending — had materialized before me, I wasn't at all sure what I should do: my reveries hadn't been that detailed. Nor had I anticipated meeting someone so cross-hatched with ambiguity, a dandy who hadn't bathed, a penniless seducer, someone upon whose face passion and cruelty had cast a grille of shadows. I was alarmed; I ended up by keeping my address secret (midnight robbery) but agreeing to meet him at the pool in the amusement park tomorrow at noon (an appointment I didn't keep, though I felt the hour come and go like a king in disguise turned away at the peasant's door).

The books in the bookstore shimmered before my eyes as I worked through a pile of them with their brightly colored paper jackets bearing photographs of pensive, well-coiffed women or middle-aged men in Irish knit sweaters with pipes and profiles. Because I knew these books were by living writers I looked down on them; my head was still ringing with the full bravura perform-ance of history in the library-opera house. Those old books either had never owned or had lost their wrappers; the likeness of their unpictured authors had been recreated within the brown, brittled pages. But these living writers — ah! life struck me as an enfeeble-ment, a proof of dimmed vitality when compared to the energetic composure of the dead whose busts, all carved beards and sight-less, protuberant eyes I imagined filling the empty niches in the opera lobby, a shallow antechamber, now a home to sleeping bums and stray cats but once the splendid approach across diamonds of black-and-white marble pavement to black-and-gilt doors opening on the brilliant assembly, the fans and diamonds and the raised ebony lid of the spotlit piano.

At home I heard the muted strains of discordant music. One night my stepmother, hard and purposeful, drove back downtown unexpectedly to my father's office after midnight. Still later I could hear my stepmother shouting in her wing of the house; I hid behind a door and heard my father's patient, explaining drone. The next morning the woman who worked the Addressograph machine with me broke down, wept, locked herself in the ladies' room. When she came out her eyes, usually so lovely and unfocused, narrowed with spite and pain as she muttered a stream of filth about my stepmother and my father, who'd tried to lure her to one of those flea-bag hotels. On the following morning I learned she'd been let go, though by that time I knew how to get the endless mailings out on my own. She'd been let go — into what?

That man's embrace around the waist set me spinning like a dancer across the darkened stage of the city; my turns led me to Fountain Square, the center. After nightfall the downtown was nearly empty. A cab might cruise by. One high office window might glow. The restaurants had closed by eight, but a bar door could swing open to impose on me the silhouette of a man or to expel the sound of a juke box, the smell of beer and pretzels. Shabby city of black stone whitened by starlings, poor earthly progeny of that mystic metal dove poised on the outstretched wrist of the verdigris'd lady, sad goddess of the fountain. Men from across the river sat around the low granite rim of the basin — at least I guessed they were hillbillies from their accents, a missing tooth, greased-back hair, their way of spitting, of holding a Camel cupped between the thumb and third finger, of walking with a hard, loud, stiff-legged tread across the paved park as though they hoped to ring sparks off stone. Others sat singly along the metal fence that enclosed the park, an island around which traffic flowed. They perched on the steel rail, legs wide apart, bodies licked by headlights, and looked down, into the slowly circling cars. At last a driver would pause before a young man who'd hop down and lean into the open window, listen — and then the young man would either shake his head and spit or, if a deal had been struck, swagger around to the other side and get in. Look at them: the curving windshield whispers down the reflection of a blinking neon sign on two faces, a bald man behind the wheel whose glasses are crazed by streaks of green light from the dashboard below, whose ears are fleshy, whose small mouth is pinched smaller by anxiety or antici- pation. Beside him the young man, head thrown back on the seat so that we can see only the strong white parabola of his jaw and the working Adam's apple. He's slumped far down and he's already thinking his way into his job. Or maybe he's embarrassed by so much downtime between fantasy and act. They drive off, only the high notes from the car radio reaching me.

A charged space where all eyes take in every event — I'd never known anything like that till now. Maybe in the lobby of Sym- phony Hall, where as a child I'd gone every Friday afternoon for the kiddie matinee, but there little feudal hordes of children, attached to a mother or nurse, eyed each other across acres of marble unless ordered to greet one another, the curtest formality between hostile vassals who might as well have spoken different languages. But here, in Fountain Square, though two or three men might cluster together and drink from a paper bag and argue sports or women, each group was meant to attract attention, every gesture was meant to be observed and transgressed, and the conversation was a pretense at conversation, the typical behavior of desirable types.

That night, however, I had no comfortable assumptions about who these men were and what they were willing to do. I crossed the street to the island, ascended the two steps onto the stone platform — and sat down on a bench. No one could tell me to leave this bench. No one would even notice me. There were policemen nearby. I had a white shirt on, a tie at half-mast, seersucker pants from a suit, polished lace-up shoes, clean nails and short hair, money in my wallet. I was a polite, well-spoken teen, not a vagrant or a criminal — the law would favor me. My father was nearby, working in his office; I was hanging around, waiting for him. Years of traveling alone on trains across the country to see my father had made me fearless before strangers and had led me to assume the unknown is safe, at least reasonably safe if encountered in public places. I set great store by my tie and raised the knot to cover the still unbuttoned collar opening.

It was hot and dark. The circling cars were unnerving — so many

unseen viewers looking at me. Although this was the town I'd
grown up in, I'd never explored it on my own. The library, the
bookstore, Symphony Hall, the office, the dry cleaners, the state
liquor commission, the ball park, my school, the department
stores, that glass ball of a restaurant perched high up there — these
I'd been to hundreds of times with my father and stepmother, but
I'd always been escorted by them, like a prisoner, through the
shadowy, dangerous city.

And yet I'd known all along it was something mysterious and
anguished beyond my experience if not my comprehension. We
had a maid, Blanche, who inserted bits of straw into her pierced
ears to keep the holes from growing shut, sneezed her snuff in a
fine spray of brown dots over the sheets when she was ironing and
slouched around the kitchen in her worn-down, backless slippers,
once purple but now the color and sheen of a bare oak branch in
the rain. She was always uncorseted under her blue cotton uniform; I pictured her rolling, black and fragrant, under that fabric
and wondered what her mammoth breasts looked like.

Although she had a daughter five years older than I (illegitimate,
or so my stepmother whispered significantly), Blanche hummed to
a black station only she seemed able to tune in, and she seemed
like a girl. When she moved from one room to the next, she
unplugged the little bakelite radio with the cream-colored grille
over the brown speaker cloth and took it with her. That music
excited me, but I thought I shouldn't listen to it too closely. It was
"Negro music" and therefore forbidden — part of another culture
more violent and vibrant than mine but somehow inferior yet no
less exclusive.

Charles, the handyman, would emerge from the basement
sweaty and pungent and, standing three steps below me, lecture
me about the Bible, the Second Coming and Booker T. Washington
and Marcus Garvey and Langston Hughes. Whenever I said
something he'd laugh in a steady, stylized way to shut me up and
then start burrowing back into his obsessions. He seemed to know
everything, chapter and verse — Egyptians, Abyssinians, the Lost
Tribe, Russian plots, Fair Deal and New Deal — but when I'd
repeat one of his remarks at dinner, my father would laugh (this,
too, was a stylized laugh) and say, "You've been listening to Charles
again. That nigger just talks nonsense. Now don't you bother him,
let him get on with his work." I never doubted that my father was

right, but I kept wondering how Dad could *tell* it was nonsense. What mysterious ignorance leaked out of Charles's words to poison them and render them worthless, inedible? For Charles, like me, haunted the library; I watched his shelf of books in the basement rotate. And Charles was a high deacon of his church, the wizard of his tribe; when he died his splendid robes overflowed his casket. That his nonsense made perfect sense to me alarmed me — was I, like Charles, eating the tripe and lights of knowledge while Dad sat down to steak?

I suppose I never wondered where Blanche or Charles went at night; when it was convenient to do so I still thought of the world as a well-arranged place where people did work that suited them and lived in houses appropriate to their tastes and needs. But once Blanche called us in the middle of an August night and my father, stepmother and I rushed to her aid. In the big Cadillac we breasted our way into unknown streets through the crowds of naked children playing in the tumult of water liberated from a fire plug ("Stop that!" I shouted silently at them, outraged and frightened. "That's illegal!") Past the stoops crowded with grown-ups playing cards and drinking wine. In one glaring doorway a woman stood, holding her diapered baby against her, a look of stoic indignation on her young face, a face one could imagine squeezing out tears without ever changing expression or softening the wide, fierce eyes, set jaw, everted lower lip. The smell of something delicious — charred meat, maybe, and maybe burning honey — filled the air. "Roll up your windows, for Chrissake, and lock the doors," my father shouted at us. "Dammit, use your heads — don't you know this place is dangerous as hell!"

A bright miner's lamp, glass globe containing a white fire devoid of blues and yellows, dangled from the roof of a vendor's cart; he was selling food of some sort to children. Even through the closed windows I could hear the babble of festive, delirious radios. A seven-foot skinny man in spats, shades, an electric green shantung suit and a flat-brimmed white beaver hat with a matching green band strolled in front of our car and patted our fender with elaborate mockery. "I'll kill the bastard," Dad shouted. "I swear I'll kill that goddamn ape if he scratches my fender."

"Oh-h-h . . .," my stepmother sang on a high note I'd never heard before. "You'll get us all killed. Honey, my heart." She grabbed her heart; she was a natural actress, who instinctively translated feelings into gestures. The man, who my father told us was a "pimp" (whatever that might be), bowed to unheard applause, pulled his hat down over one eye like Chevalier and ambled on, letting us pass.

We hurried up five flights of dirty, broken stairs, littered with empty pint bottles, bags of garbage and two dolls (both white, I noticed, and blond and mutilated), past landings and open doors, which gave men glimpses of men playing cards and, across the hall, a grandmother alone and asleep in an armchair with antimacassars. Her radio was playing that Negro music. Her brown cotton stockings had been rolled down below her black knees.

Blanche we found wailing and shouting, "My baby, my baby!" as she hopped and danced in circles of pain around her daughter, whose hand, half lopped off, was spouting blood. My father gathered the girl up in his arms and we all rushed off to the emergency room of a hospital.

She lived. Her hand was even sewn back on, though the incident (jealous lover with an axe) had broken her mind. Afterwards, the girl didn't go back to her job and feared even leaving the building. My stepmother thought the loss of blood had somehow left her feeble-minded. My father fussed over the blood on his suit and on the strangely similar Cadillac upholstery, though I wondered if his pettiness weren't merely a way of silencing Blanche, who kept kissing his whole hand in gratitude. Or perhaps he'd found a way of re-introducing the ordinary into a night that had dipped disturbingly below the normal temperature of tedium he worked so hard to maintain. Years later, when Charles died, my father was the only white man to attend the funeral. He wasn't welcome, but he went anyway and sat in the front row. After Charles's death my father became more scattered and apprehensive. He would sit up all night with a stop-watch, counting his pulse.

That had been another city — Blanche's two rooms, scrupulously clean in contrast to the squalor of the halls, her parrot squawking under the tea towel draped over the cage, the chromo of a sad Jesus pointing to his exposed, juicy heart as though he were a free-clinic patient with a troubling symptom, the filched wedding photo of my father and stepmother in a nest of crepe-paper flowers, the bloody sheet torn into strips that had been wildly clawed off and hurled onto the flowered congoleum floor. Through a half-open door I saw the foot of a double bed draped like a veteran's grave with the flag of a tossed-back sheet.

In my naivete I imagined all poor people, black and white, liked each other and that here, through Fountain Square, I would feel my way back to that street, that smell of burning honey, that blood as red as mine and that steady, colorless flare in the glass chimney. . . . These hillbillies on the square with their drawling and spitting, their thin arms and big raw hands, nails ragged, tattoos a fresher blue than their eyes set in long sallow Norman faces, each eye a pale blue ringed by nearly invisible lashes — I wove these men freely into the cloth of the powerful poor, a long bolt lost in the dark that I was now pulling through a line of light.

I opened a book and pretended to read under the weak street lamps, though my attention wandered away from sight to sound. "Tommy, bring back a beer!" someone shouted. Some other men laughed. No one I knew kept his nickname beyond twelve, at least not with his contemporaries, but I could hear these guys calling each other Tommy and Freddy and Bobby and I found that heartening, as though they wanted to stay, if only among themselves, as chummy as a gang of boys. While they worked to become as brutal as soon enough they would be, I tried to find them softer than they'd ever been.

Boots approached me. I heard them before I saw them. They stopped, every tan scar on the orange hide in focus beyond the page I held that was running with streaks of print. "Curiosity killed the damn pussy, you know," a man said. I looked up at a face sprouting brunette side-burns that swerved inwards like cheese knives toward his mouth and stopped just below his ginger mustaches. The eyes, small and black, had been moistened genially by the beers he'd drunk and the pleasure he was taking in his own joke.

"*Mighty* curious, ain't you?" he asked. "Ain't you!" he insisted, making a great show of the leisurely, avuncular way he settled close beside me, sighing, and wrapped a bare arm — a pale, cool, sweaty, late-night August arm — around my thin shoulders. "Shit," he hissed. Then he slowly drew a breath like ornamental cigarette smoke up his nose, and chuckled again. "I'd say you got Sabbath eyes, son."

"I do?" I squeaked in a pinched soprano. "I don't know what you mean," I added, only to demonstrate my newly acquired baritone, as penetrating as an oboe, though the effect on the man seemed the right one: sociable.

"Yessir, Sabbath eyes," he said with a downshift into a rural languor and rhetorical fanciness I associated with my storytelling paternal grandfather in Texas. "I say Sabbath 'cause you done worked all week and now you's resting them eyeballs on what you done made — or might could make. The good things of the earth." Suddenly he grew stern. "Why you here, boy? I seed you here cocking your hade and spying up like a biddy hen. Why you watching, boy? *What* you watching? Tell me, what you watching?"

He had frightened me, which he could see — it made him laugh. I smiled to show him I knew how foolish I was being. "I'm just here to —"

"Read?" he demanded, taking my book away and shutting it. "Shi-i-i . . ." he hissed again, steam running out before the *t*. "You here to meet someone, boy?" He'd disengaged himself and turned to stare at me. Although his eyes were serious, militantly serious, the creasing of the wrinkles beside them suggested imminent comedy.

"No," I said, quite audibly.

He handed the book back to me.

"I'm here because I want to run away from home," I said. "I thought I might find someone to go with me."

"Whar you planning to run to?"

"New York."

There was something so cold and firm and well-spoken about me — the clipped tones of a businessman defeating the farmer's hoaxing yarn — that the man sobered, dropped his chin into his palm and thought. "What's today?" he asked at last.

"Saturday."

"I myself taking the Greyhound to New Yawk Tuesday mawning," he said. "Wanna go?"

"Sure."

He told me that if I'd bring him forty dollars on Monday evening he'd buy me my ticket. He asked me where I lived and I told him; his willingness to help me made me trust him. Without ever explicitly being taught such things, I'd learned by studying my father that at certain crucial moments — an emergency, an opportunity — one must act first and think later. One must suppress minor inner objections and put off feelings of cowardice or confusion and turn into a simple instrument of action. I'd seen my father become calm in a crisis or feel his way blindly with nods, smiles and monosyllables toward the shadowy opening of a hugely promising but still vague business deal. And with women he was ever alert to adventure: the gauzy transit of a laugh across his path, a minor whirlpool in the sluggish flow of talk, the faintest whiff of seduction . . .

I, too, wanted to be a man of the world and dared not question my new friend too closely. For instance, I knew a train ticket could be bought at the last moment, even on board, but I was willing to assume either that a bus ticket had to be secured in advance or that at least my friend thought it did. We arranged a time to meet on Monday when I could hand over the money (I had it at home squirreled away in the secret compartment of a wood tray I'd made last year in shop). Then on Tuesday morning at six a.m. he'd meet me on the corner near but not in sight of my house. He'd have his brother's car and we'd proceed quickly to the 6:45 bus bound East — a long haul to New Yawk, he said, oh, say twenty hours, no, make that twenty-one.

"And in New York?" I asked timidly, not wanting to seem helpless and scare him off but worried about my future. Would I be able to find work? I was only sixteen, I said, adding two years to my age. Could a sixteen-year-old work legally in New York? If so, doing what?

"Waiter," he said. "A whole hog heaven of resty-runts in New Yawk City."

Sunday it rained a hot drizzle all day and in the west the sky lit up a bright yellow that seemed more the smell of sulfur than a color. I played the piano with the silencer on lest I awaken my father. I was bidding the instrument farewell. If only I'd practiced I might have supported myself as a cocktail pianist; I improvised my impression of sophisticated tinkling — with disappointing results.

As I took an hour-long bath, periodically emptying an inch of cold water and replacing it with warm, I thought my way again through the routine: greeting the guests, taking their orders, serving pats of butter, beverages, calling out my requests to the chef . . . my long, flat feet under the water twitched sympathetically as I raced about the restaurant. If only I'd observed waiters all those times. Well, I'd coast on charm.

As for love that, too, I'd win through charm. Although I knew I hadn't charmed anyone since I was six or seven, I consoled myself by deciding people out here were not susceptible to the larceny (which I thought grand, they petty) of a beguiling manner. They responded only to character, accomplishments, the slow accumulations of will rather than the sudden millinery devisings of fancy. In New York I'd be the darling boy again. In that Balzac novel a penniless young man had made his fortune on luck, looks, winning ways (since I hadn't finished the book, I didn't yet know where those ways led). New Yorkers, like Parisians, I hoped and feared, would know what to make of me. I carried the plots and atmosphere of fiction about with me and tried to cram random events into those ready molds. But no, truthfully, the relationship was more reciprocal, less rigorous — art taking the noise life gave and picking it out as a tune (the cocktail pianist obliging the humming drunk).

Before it closed I walked down to a neighborhood pharmacy and bought a bottle of peroxide. I had decided to bleach my hair late Monday night; on Tuesday I'd no longer answer the description my father would put out in his frantic search for me. Perhaps I'd affect an English accent as well; I'd coached my stepmother in the part of Lady Bracknell before she performed the role with the Queen City Players and I could now say *cucumber sandwich* with scarcely a vowel after the initial fluty *u*. As an English blond I'd evade not only my family but also myself and emerge as the energetic and lovable boy I longed to be. Not exactly a boy, more a girl, or rather a sturdy, canny, lavishly devout tomboy like Joan of Arc, tough in battle if yielding before her visionary Father. I wouldn't pack winter clothes; surely by October I'd be able to buy something warm.

A new spurt of hot water as I retraced my steps to the kitchen, clipped the order to the cook's wire or flew out the swinging doors, smiling, acted courteously and won the miraculously large tip. And there, seated at a corner table by himself, is the English lord, silver-haired, recently bereaved; my hand trembles as I give him the frosted glass. In my mind I'd already betrayed the hillbilly with the sideburns who sobbed with dignity as I delivered my long farewell speech. He wasn't intelligent or rich enough to suit me.

When I met him on Monday at six beside the fountain and presented him with the four ten-dollar bills, he struck me as ominously indifferent to the details of tomorrow's adventures which I'd elaborated with such fanaticism. He reassured me about the waiter's job and my ability to pull it off, told me again where he'd pick me up in the morning — but, smiling, dissuaded me from peroxiding my hair tonight. "Just pack it — we'll bleach you white win we git whar we gohn."

We had a hamburger together at the Grasshopper, a restaurant of two rooms, one brightly lit and filled with booths and families and waitresses wearing German peasant costumes and white lace hats, the other murky that smelled of beer and smoke — a man's world, the bar. I went through the bar to the toilet. When I came out I saw the woman I'd worked with in a low-cut dress, skirt hiked high to expose her knee, a hand over her pearl necklace. Her hair had been restyled. She pushed one lock back and let it fall again over her eye, the veronica a cape might pass before an outraged bull: the man beside her, who now placed a grimy hand on her knee. She let out a shriek — a coquette's shriek, I suppose, but edged with terror. (I was glad she didn't see me, since I felt ashamed at the way our family had used her.)

I'd planned not to sleep at all but had set the alarm should I doze off. For hours I lay in the dark and listened to the dogs barking down in the valley. Now that I was leaving this house forever, I was tiptoeing through it mentally and prizing its luxuries — the shelves lined with blocks of identical cans (my father ordered everything by the gross), the linen cupboard stacked high with ironed if snuff-specked sheets, my own bathroom with its cupboard full of soap, tissue, towels, hand towels, wash cloths, the elegant helix of the front staircase descending to the living room with its deep carpets, shaded lamps and the pretty mirror bordered by tiles on which someone with a nervous touch had painted the various breeds of lapdog. This house where I'd never felt I belonged no longer belonged to me and the future so clearly charted for me — college, career, wife and white house wavering behind green trees — was being exchanged for that eternal circulating through the restaurant, my path as clear to me as chalk marks on the floor, instructions for each foot in the tango, lines that flowed together, branched and joined, branched and joined . . . In my dream my father had died but I refused to kiss him though next he was pulling me onto his lap, an ungainly teen smeared with Vicks Vaporub whom everyone inexplicably treated as a sick child.

When I silenced the alarm, fear overtook me. I'd go hungry! The boarding house room with the toilet down the hall, blood on the linoleum, crepe-paper flowers — I dressed and packed my gym bag with the bottle of peroxide and two changes of clothes. Had my father gone to bed yet? Would the dog bark when I tried to slip past him? And would that man be on the corner? The boarding house room, yes, Negro music on the radio next door, the co-quette's shriek. As I walked down the drive I felt conspicuous under the blank windows of my father's house and half-expected him to open the never-used front door to call me back.

I stood on the appointed corner. It began to drizzle but a water truck crept past anyway, spraying the street a darker, slicker gray. No birds were in sight but I could hear them testing the day. A dog without a collar or master trotted past. Two fat maids were climbing the hill, stopping every few steps to catch their breath. One, a shiny, blue-black fat woman wearing a flowered turban and holding a purple umbrella with a white plastic handle, was scowling and talking fast but obviously to humorous effect, for her companion couldn't stop laughing.

The bells of the Catholic school behind the dripping trees across the street marked the quarter hour, the half hour. More and more cars were passing me. I studied every driver — had he overslept? The milk man. The bread truck. Damn hillbilly. A bus went by, carrying just one passenger. A quarter to seven. He wasn't coming.

When I saw him the next evening on the square he waved at me and came over to talk. From his relaxed manner I instantaneously saw — puzzle pieces sliding then locking to fill in the pattern — that he'd duped me and I was powerless. To whom could I report him? Like a heroin addict or a Communist, I was outside the law — outside it but with him, this man. He didn't attract me but I liked him well enough.

We sat side by side on the same bench. A bad muffler exploded in a volley and the cooing starlings perched on the fountain figure's arm flew up and away leaving behind only the metal dove. I took off my tie, rolled it up and slipped it inside my pocket. Because I didn't complain about being betrayed, my friend said, "See those men yonder?"

"Yes."

"I could git you one for eight bucks." He let that sink in; yes, I thought, I could take someone to one of those little flea-bag hotels. "Which one do you want?" he asked.

I handed him the money and said, "The blond."

*ፆ ፆ ፆ*

# THE AUTHOR
# ENCOUNTERS
# HIS READING PUBLIC

fiction by AMOS OZ

from THE PARTISAN REVIEW

*nominated by* THE PARTISAN REVIEW, *Daniel Menaker, Cynthia Ozick, Samuel Vaughan, Sarah Vogan, and Patricia Zelver*

THESE ARE THE PRINCIPAL QUESTIONS: Why do you write. What is your driving urge. And why do you write the way you do. What is the function of your writing and what does it achieve. Why do you concentrate so much on the negative aspects and why are your stories always so gloomy. What are you really trying to say. Why did you come along here this evening.

There are polite answers and there are clever answers, but there is no simple, straightforward answer.

Consequently the author lingers in a dingy side street cafe, and tries to concentrate for a little while on these questions. In vain a waitress in a grubby overall tries to wipe the tabletop clean for

414

him: the surface remains sticky. Meanwhile the writer is assailed by the smell of her sweat, a smell of weary womanhood. She notices him eyeing her breasts, her hips, her legs, and gives a snort of naked disgust. Like a cry of despair: A thousand times you've all looked at me like that and a thousand times I've said to you, that's enough, what's the matter with you, a thousand times you've done this and this and this to me and still you haven't had enough, but I can't stand it anymore leave me alone for once let me be you're crazy I've had enough I'm sick and tired of it I tell you.

Politely therefore the writer averts his gaze. He orders an omelette, a roll and a cup of coffee. He extracts a cigarette from his pocket and holds it secreted in his left hand which is propping up his cheek: a thoughtful expression hinting at secret ruminations.

At a nearby table two men are sitting unhurriedly, both about fifty. The principal man is heavily built, tough-looking, and totally bald. He looks like a gangster's stooge in a film. The smaller man looks shabby and worn, his manner is excitable, his face suggests that he will bestow admiration or compassion on anyone who needs it without further reflection. The writer supposes that he is a small businessman, perhaps an agent for a firm of washing machine distributors. They are apparently discussing success, in a general sort of way. The gangsters' stooge is saying:

"And anyway, by the time you've made anything of your life it's all over."

The other replies:

"You're absolutely right Mr. Baghdadi, I agree with you a hundred percent. But you must admit that there's more to life than just living—a man needs to do something for his soul as well. It stands to reason."

"What you are saying," the principal actor remarks frostily, "sounds to me too much like propaganda. Can you give me an example from real life, so that we know what you're talking about."

"Alright why not," the little man concurs. "Take Ovadia Hazzam for instance. You know him, he works for Isratex. He divorced his wife, played around, took out fantastic loans, took no notice of anyone, he even joined the National Religious Party, he lived like a king. Not just like a king, like a lord, even. In the end he caught cancer of the liver and now he's hospitalized in a very critical condition."

and replies indifferently:

"Sure. What do you mean do I know him. Poor sod. But I wouldn't use him as an example if I were you. Everybody knows that cancer doesn't come from loose living. Scientists have proved now that it comes from dirt. They even had a professor explaining it on the radio the other day. You're talking nonsense if you don't mind me saying so, Cohen. Ovadia Hazzam is just plain irrelevant. Leave him alone and get back to the matter in hand."

The author glances at his watch. He gets up, pays the irritable waitress and thanks her politely for the change. He makes for the door, changes his mind and goes down two steps into the stinking lavatory. The burnt-out lightbulb, peeling plaster and stench of old urine in the darkness remind him that he is not really ready for the meeting and how will he answer the questions.

As he goes out into the street he lights a cigarette. Twenty past nine. It is a warm humid summer evening and petrol fumes hang heavy on the air. There is no breeze. It seems a terrible thing to the writer to be lying incurably ill between sweaty sheets on a night like this. In vain have all the windows of the auditorium been opened wide: the bad air solidly refuses to stir. The audience is perspiring. People are greeting acquaintances and sitting down tiredly on hard chairs, youngsters all together, old folk in little groups apart, their clothes sticking to their bodies, each with his own smell and the smell of his neighbor in the fetid air. Meanwhile they exchange opinions about the latest news and the general situation. In vain three ancient fans revolve listlessly above the audience's head: they bring no relief. It is very warm. Insects force their way between collar and neck, as though this were tropical Africa. Outside two streets away sounds the rise and fall and plaintive rise of an ambulance siren or a fire engine. Will the author bring us some new message tonight, will he be able to explain to us how we got into this condition or what we must do to escape from its clutches? Can he see something that is invisible to us? Will he come and tell us about it?

Some have come armed with a copy of the book which is the subject of this evening's meeting, and for the time being they are using it—or the evening paper—as a fan. In vain. We're already late in starting and there's still no sign of him. But anyway there's nothing on the television tonight except a boring quiz. While here the program includes opening remarks by a well-known literary expert, a reading of excerpts from the work itself, a talk by the author, questions, discussion, answers, and closing remarks. Admission is free, and the author has aroused, as is well known, a certain public curiosity.

And now at last here he is.

For the last half hour the local cultural enthusiast has been waiting for him outside, at the foot of the steps, a red-faced balding man twice the author's age, whose cheeks are alarmingly crisscrossed with blue veins but whose soul is still bursting as ever with charm and eager social concern. Immediately he sets to work forging a bond of affection and cheerful respect with the author, a kind of jolly intimacy: after all are we not two priests of the intellect both devoted to the very same ideal, and they are all sitting out there waiting to hear what we shall say. Well well well, welcome my friend. You're a little late. It doesn't matter. Everyone's always late here. How are you? We were beginning to think that the muse had driven us out of your mind. But we didn't give you up, my friend. Not us. We're very stubborn.

The author responds by muttering a feeble witticism: Surely you could have started without me.

"Ha ha, start without you, that's a good one," the cultural enthusiast gives a Russian laugh. "Yes, and you could have started without us somewhere else. By the way," he asks as they are still panting up the steps, "what do you think that fox Kissinger is going to get out of the Russians? Will he achieve anything?"

And he answers his own question:

"No, he won't get anything out of them. Only more trouble for us. Squash or lemonade or something fizzy? Don't worry. Something fizzy for you. That's perfectly alright."

So they both enter the hall.

A hurried whisper runs round the audience. Perhaps because the author is wearing plain khaki trousers, a blue sports shirt and sandals. He doesn't look the least bit like an artist, they are saying, but people say that as a person he's really very nice, they are saying, and look what complicated stories he writes. You can never tell from appearances. Anyway, he looks completely different in his pictures.

The author is placed in the middle, between Ruchele Reznik and the literary expert. They shake hands. The cultural enthusiast opens the proceedings. He requests silence. He apologizes for the delay. He makes a vain attempt, with forced gaiety, to win the audience's sympathy. He even repeats publicly the stupid joke made by the author as they were on their way in: Our guest was surprised to find that we had not started without him, but, after all, for a wedding you need a groom as well as a bride, as Mataniah Starkman puts it in one of his poems. Well, with your permission, I shall now declare this evening's program open. Good evening.

The author, listening to this decides not to smile. He lights a fresh cigarette. He looks thoughtful and even a little sad. The whole audience has eyes only for him, and he, with a refined, faraway look, fixes his eyes deliberately on a picture of the Labour Zionist leader Berl Katznelson on the opposite wall.

Berl Katznelson has a look of kindly cunning on his face, as though he has just this minute succeeded in achieving some fine and noble end by slightly devious means known only to himself. Today he is a king, the author thinks to himself. Not just a king, a lord.

And so, after a slight delay, there finally appears round the author's lips a fine smile which the audience was already expecting while the opening words were being spoken.

At that instant he thinks he catches a kind of titter passing around the hall, and he glances hastily at the zipper of his trousers. But everything is in order. Nobody has snickered. He must have been mistaken. He rests his elbows on the table, leans his chin on his fists, and adopts an air of profundity and humility as the literary expert rises to his feet and in rhetorical tones draws comparisons and parallels, lays bare tangled webs of hidden motifs, indicates the literary artifices employed by the author, casts doubt on the legitimacy of a certain artistic device, without denying the essential relevance of the ironic dimension of the work, etc., until he finally arrives at the problem of the inner meaning. In vain. By now the author is fully immersed in his masquerade: he has stopped listening and is sending acquisitive glances round the hall, snatching here a wry or oafish expression, there a fine pair of crossed legs, a distinguished mop of gray hair, a look of rapt attention, body odors on the close air. As though he were rifling their handbags while they are absorbed in the secrets of his art as expounded by the literary expert. Opposite him, for example, with her thick legs spaced well apart, sits a broad middle-aged woman, who has long since abandoned all efforts and diets, renounced her femininity, her body is soft and swollen like an overripe tomato but she has long given up worrying about appearances and ascended to higher spheres, her eyes fixed now on the celebrated author and her face is set in an expression of supreme cultural rapture. Right behind her is a pleasant-looking lad of sixteen or so, probably a secret poet, his complexion disfigured with acne. A passionate ravenous youth, with curly, dusty-looking hair, eyeing the author through his glasses from the depths of his being with a tortured secret love, your soul is my soul your sufferings are my sufferings you and only you can understand I am the enchanted soul in your stories. From him the author's glance roams to the furious figure of a man with a Labour Party look, probably a senior teacher, forceful and ideal-ridden, in a state school in a well-to-do suburb, perhaps even a deputy headmaster. He has probably come along with the single aim of stating once and for all his adverse judgment on the emerging Hebrew literature which lacks absolutely everything which we need and contains what we have no need of whatsoever.

The author decides to attach to this character the name of Dr. Pesah Yikhat. The waitress from the cafe will be Jacqueline. Messrs. Baghdadi and Cohen can keep their real names. The youthful poet will be Yuval Deutsch or Yuval Dotan. The culture-thirsty woman will be called Miriam Nehorait. The plot will revolve around a scandal: the woman and the boy. Debauchery, remorse and anger. Mortification of the flesh, humiliation of the spirit, the hypocrisy of society and convention, homespun wisdom, ruin, iron of fate. All told perhaps in the first person from the point of view of the shabby culture-fiend, lying awake on solitary sleepless nights in his spartan single-room flat in a block of workers' apartments, scheming how when the day comes he will ruthlessly lay bare the real, the terrible face of life behind all the masks. It may even be possible to incorporate a few traits borrowed from the expert in literature: for instance the half-moon of thin gray hair which crowns his freckled head. His rhetorical delivery, the triumphal tone of a man who has just been attacked with a decisive argument but who, far from giving in, has managed to reply with gentle rage and an argument which is twice as decisive. The author is inclined to allot to this character a marginal role in the action, the part of a sage whom events have proved wrong with unreasonable cruelty.

While these various thoughts are passing through the author's mind, the lecturer comes to his main point, indicating the paradoxical role which is usually played by this author's descriptions of nature. Once again a titter or stifled snigger is heard, which makes the author sweat uneasily in his seat. Disgustedly he lights another cigarette, while the expert concludes his talk with a cunningly ambiguous expression of praise which implies reservations, albeit indirectly.

Now it is Ruchele Reznik's turn to read out two excerpts from the new book. Pretty and nervous, pretty without being attractive, a girl of thirty, old-fashioned, with a single thick plait, wearing an elegant, modest dress printed with a pattern of tiny cyclamens in purple. And she reads as though there were nothing in the book but gentleness and compassion, as though it were about secret yearnings, as though it were the work of a simple sensitive soul seeking to enter similar spirits.

The author is instantly filled with shame and confusion. Why did you come. You should have stayed at home. Shut up safely indoors. What can you say to all these people. Why aren't you an engineer planning railways across difficult terrain, as you dreamed of becoming when you were young. Will falsehood last forever. In a voice transformed by longing Ruchele Reznik is reading from your new book and she is almost a beautiful girl, although she is not attractive.

Among the audience there is a youth — or rather a stiff, lean man of about sixty-five, a strange, angular man, who looks like a party hack who has been dismissed from his post because he has divulged classified information to a rival party. Can it really be that he is the wretch who has just uttered, for the third time at least, a sort of titter or stifled snigger? What does it mean, the author asks himself in alarm, is it spite, or petty stupidity, or envy, or contempt, or is this real suffering?

All these are filling the author's heart. And so, when his turn comes to speak, he appears at his best. He replies wittily to the audience's questions. Makes discreet use of examples drawn from real life. Raises doubts. Delicately trounces the literary expert. Occasionally accuses literature in general and his own writing in particular of shady and even in a sense discreditable motives. Expounds to the audience his well-known view that if only our predicament (human, national, historical, personal) is regarded from a standpoint of despair, it becomes possible to face it with a smile. While he is speaking he bitterly regrets having come to the meeting, agreeing to speak, his own inadequacy, his failure to write what he should really have written, his inability to discover who in the audience is secretly laughing at him, the fact that the mockery is actually justified, and his lecherous glances earlier at the tired waitress in the cafe.

All in vain.

He pauses for a moment. He ruffles his hair with his hand. Otherworldliness, loneliness and sorrow display themselves on his face. He continues speaking, twice as falsely as before.

Afterwards he is surrounded by admirers. He rapidly signs a few copies of his latest book. Accepts compliments with a look of humility. Encourages the shy, secretive youth to send him his first attempts at writing poetry. Takes his leave of the chastened literary expert with a warm handshake and a knowing wink. Then he thanks the cultural organizer who is thanking him for agreeing to come. As they go down the steps he devotes a few warm words to Ruchele Reznik alone.

And then he goes on his way.

For an hour or an hour and a half he paces the darkened streets alone. In vain. He smokes three or four cigarettes, and makes a mental note that he has smoked eight or nine in the course of the evening. Boys and girls pass him with their arms round each other on their way home to bed from an evening out, silent or laughing aloud, and one of the girls lets out a horrified shriek as though someone has just whispered a particularly outrageous suggestion in her ear. Beside an unfinished building a motionless night watchman stands pensively relieving himself. Beyond him there is only a row of streetlamps, and empty pavement, silent walls. And further still the end of the town and the deserted fields. At last you are alone.

On an upturned crate you sit in the dark. You see the shadowy mountains. Stars. There is no breeze. Lift up your eyes and see. At the end of your silence you whisper a plea for pardon. How little that literary expert was demanding, and how arrogantly you denied him even that little. How little was needed to please the cultural organizer who received you so warmly and so self-effacingly. Alone before the mirror in her room Ruchele Reznik is getting undressed now and sadly consoling herself, if only I had breasts my whole life would change for the better. The senior teacher or deputy headmaster was right when he stood up and declared that the function of literature is to provide consolation and encouragement, and that that is precisely where all the modern writers including tonight's speakers have failed miserably. Mataniah Starkman was quite mistaken when he wrote that for a wedding you need a groom as well as a bride. On the contrary, it would be instructive to reflect for a moment on the life of Mr. Ovadia Hazzam for example: he was the man who divorced his wife, led an outrageous life, borrowed enormous amounts of money, threw himself into politics, lived like a lord or a king, and then finally developed cancer of the liver, returned to his former wife, and is now lying sleeplessly in a hot dank hospital corridor dying alone in the dark, perhaps uttering from time to time a stifled chuckle, and this too is in vain. What an insignificant man this writer is, despicable, contemptible, utterly loathsome.

I ought to talk to myself about myself. And if there does come some grace, perhaps it is when I talk about myself to myself that it will happen, and I may produce a good rumor, a gesture of sympathy to the hopeless, a flicker of excitement for the downcast, a partial consolation for some of those tortured souls. Poor Jacqueline. Doctor Pesah Yikhat. Mr. Baghdadi the gangsters' stooge and his shabby sidekick. The young poet Yuval Dotan-Deutsch. The expert in literature. Mrs. Miriam Nehorait. The wretched Ovadia Hazzam. The cultural organizer Yeruham Shda-mati and the reader Ruchele Reznik. It's late at night now, time to go to sleep. I must carefully extract the evening newspaper from their tired fingers. I know a bedtime story and I'll tell it to them all to try to help them sleep peacefully if possible and dream peaceful dreams. Berl Katznelson was a kindly, cunning man who knew how to achieve good and desirable ends even if by somewhat devious means: our condition here is rotten, strange and painful.

And it is still hot and humid in my room and total darkness holds the whole land. Have you ever heard of an old, modest poet named Mataniah Starkman? He was the poet who made the mistake about the bride and groom. And I have just read in the paper which is by my bed that in the early hours of yesterday morning, in Ra'ananah, at the age of 77, of a heart attack, the poet has died. Surely we are obliged occasionally to do a simple sum. Meanwhile it's three o'clock in the morning.

Good night to all of us.

— *translated by Nicholas de Lange*

# MY FATHER'S DESK

by KATE DANIELS

from IRONWOOD

*nominated by* IRONWOOD, *Carolyn Forché, and David Wojahn*

The wrinkles in the taxi driver's face —
I want to lie down there
and make them smooth again.
He might be fifty, my father's age,
everything about him public and accounted for.
He can't hide anything.
I thought I knew my father
because I recognized his big, red ears,
the way he eats his corn.
But this might be my father,
and I, someone else, looking at him.

It's hard to care about the rich girl
who weakens after seeing an old man on Broadway
killed by a car.
She said his cane lay there
like an exclamation mark.
She said the day was so perfect — then this!
She wanted me to make her tea.
I wanted to see the dead man lying in the wet, black street,
and know the place he came from,
where he was going: a chilled flat,
rice boiling on the stove.
He just stepped out to buy a paper.
The dog yaps at the door
awaiting his return,
but he never comes back.
The yellow carpet is just the shade

of the one in my father's office,
worn under the desk where he shuffles his feet.
Like the old man, he wants to get up and walk
out into the rain to buy a pack of cigarettes
or just to look at the waitress with the big soft rear.

Thirty years at the same desk.
I've never looked inside
to find what he might have hidden there —
the funny pack of sugar, a picture
the secretary snapped of him where,
caught in the brief, kind light,
he looks famous! the dark spot
where he lays his head.
The secret note he wrote himself:
"I am fifty now. 50."

The cabbie's voice is loud and tired.
He's just another person with a crummy job.
My father was another lousy
father. But now I can forgive him that.
I know the way it feels
to stay awake and work when all you want
is to lay your head in someone's lap and sleep.

I remember the way he touched me as a child,
the delicate latch of his fingers
on my weakling arm. I was so fresh
he was afraid for me — afriad I would break.
Something the world could never feel for me.

# THERE IS NO WORD FOR GOODBYE

by MARY TALL MOUNTAIN

from BLUE CLOUD QUARTERLY

*nominated by* BLUE CLOUD QUARTERLY

Sokoya, I said, looking through
    the net of wrinkles into
    wise black pools
    of her eyes.

What do you say in Athabaskan
    when you leave each other?
    What is the word
    for goodbye?

A shade of feeling rippled
    the wind-tanned skin.
    Ah, nothing, she said,
    watching the river flash.

She looked at me close.
    We just say, Tlaa. That means,
    See you.
    We never leave each other.
    When does your mouth
    say goodbye to your heart?

She touched me light
    as a bluebell.
    You forget when you leave us,
    You're so small then.
    We don't use that word.

We always think you're coming back,
    but if you don't,
    we'll see you some place else.
    You understand.
        There is no word for goodbye.

*Sokoya:* Aunt (mother's sister)

# FOREVER
# IN THAT YEAR

by HAYDEN CARRUTH

from THE AMERICAN POETRY REVIEW

*nominated by Charles Simic*


Judith, don't you love this great old sound
    Coming at you through the scratches
Of time past? Listen. Prez is blowing.
    Nothing matters, except these snatches

Of humanity, these gusts of sound
    Catching hold of time, moments in his only
Soul. Listen. He is. And he is proud
    And wild, he is unalone and lonely,

And he knows (as I said once in my own sound)
    How "freedom and discipline concur
Only in ecstasy." True, it was true!
    I say it now for you, my philosopher.

Otherwise all is noise, no sound
    Fits in it, only the human horn
Dispels it. Listen. This is Lester Young
    Forever in that year when you were born.

*Coda: une espèce de prière*
Tell me, Thought of my Thought,
Will words try
Ever again to seek what the music sought
Among the people? Can

The language cry
And still be a practical, social art,
A song,
A natural measure that will impart
To woman, child, and man
Their indispensable rightness in the wrong
Of eternity? Thought of my Thought, may
Words cease to fear?
Tell it me in my ear.
Show me the way.

## ROLAND BARTHES, AUTOBIOGRAPHY, AND THE END OF WRITING

by J. GERALD KENNEDY

from THE GEORGIA REVIEW

*nominated by* THE GEORGIA REVIEW, *Robert Boyers and H . E . Francis*

F OR MANY CRITICS and scholars in this country, Roland Barthes came to personify the Parisian menace, the nefarious structuralist plot to turn literature into "writing," works into "texts," and authors into anonymous "scriptors." Barthes, who devoted so much attention to the function of codes and signs within contemporary culture, became himself a symbol of the dehumanization of literary study. How else to account for the gratuitous venom of Hugh Kenner's "Decoding Roland Barthes: The Obit of a Structuralist"?[1] Deftly applying the Five Codes of S/Z to *The New York Times* obituary of Barthes, Kenner manages to demonstrate the self-evident fact that semiotic analysis does not address itself to the uniqueness of the individual. Barthes never pretended that it did; loosely committed to the concept of "the human sciences," he concerned himself in print with the systems and processes of meaning rather than its particular manifestations. He typically regarded the self, the subject, as a locus of confusion, "caught between instinctual drives and social practice within a language that is today divided into often incommunicable, multiple systems."[2] Yet there was — malgré the insinuations of Kenner — a richly human element in much that Barthes wrote, a persistent reflection upon his own memories and desires, antipathies and pleasures, which behind a mask of erudition often disclosed signs of personal struggle. Particularly in the work published after *Sade Fourier Loyola* (1971), one can find a tension between personal confession and implacable theory: Barthes's fetishes comprise a model of the reading experience in *The Pleasure of the Text* (1973); his "autobiography," *Roland Barthes* (1975), presents disconnected fragments of disclosure from a third-person perspective; intimate admissions and literary allusions supply paradigms of desire in *A Lover's Discourse* (1977).[3]

An unpredictable figure, Barthes entered a new phase with *The Pleasure of the Text*. After "social mythology," "semiology," and "textuality" — all more or less empirical phenomena — he turned to the problem of "morality," how the subject functions within a realm of available choices.[4] The actual "subject" of this phase, however, proved to be Barthes himself as a connoisseur of earthly delights, and we note a perceptible change of focus — from objective sign-systems to obsessions and fantasies — which prefigures the announced (but unfulfilled) ambition of his final years: to create a work of fiction. As Max Gallo has noted, Barthes's emergence as a dominant force in French intellectual circles (as signified by his 1977 appointment to the Collège de France Chair of Semiology) was accompanied by the desire to write a novel, "as if subjectivity, pleasure, so long invested in and masked by criticism of great texts or by commentary, dared to express itself."[5]

What sort of work did he hope to compose? What significance attaches to the unfinished, final phase of his writing? From all indications, the novelistic project signaled more than a new "conceptual infatuation"; it marked for Barthes a redefinition of the life of writing. And it prompted a reconsideration of his personal history as well, for he conceived the novel from the outset as a patently autobiographical search for the vanished landscape and lost community of childhood. That quest was not to be completed, but the passion to write a fictive memoir spilled over into other works of his last years. Groundwork for the novel (its conception and content) can be discerned in three sources to be discussed here: his 1978–79 seminar at the Collège de France and two texts composed within a year of his death, "Délibération" (a *Tel Quel* essay) and *La chambre claire: note sur la photographie* (1980).

In October 1978, during a lecture offered as an "apéritif" to the seminar "*Préparation du Roman*" ("Preparation of/for the Novel"), Barthes discussed in broad terms the exigencies of writing. Drawing examples from Dante, Tolstoi, and Proust, he argued that the underlying impulse of narrative is the consciousness of one's own death: we create art both to deny our final fate and to construct our memorials. Hinting at an obstinate interest in the question, Barthes indicated that the seminar would explore the psychology of writing, particularly in terms of the novel and the novelist's apprehension of mortality. Then he made an unexpected confession: he had recently concluded that his previous writing amounted to a betrayal of his true concerns. Saddened by a sense of failure, Barthes expressed the desire to "escape from the prison house of critical meta language" and through simpler, more compassionate language to close the gap between private experience and public discourse.[6] There was a theatricality about the announcement — Barthes loved to defy conventional expectations — but the renunciation spoke for itself, signaling a fundamental change in his relationship to writing.

That fact was confirmed in the first meetings of the seminar in December 1978. Barthes reflected upon his long-held theory of writing (*écriture*) as an action whose end is the satisfaction of its own illogical imperatives: a movement, as he elsewhere remarked, in which "the hand, cut off from any voice, borne by a pure gesture of inscription (and not of expression), traces a field without origin — or which, at least, has no other origin than language itself, language which ceaselessly calls into question all origins."[7] In an earlier version of the argument, he had declared the verb "to write" to be intransitive in its modern designation of literary performance, and he cited as evidence of its objectless, nonreferential status the shifting, illusory nature of the first-person pronoun: "the *I* of the one who writes *l* is not the same as the *I* which is read by *thou*."[8] In exposing the fictionality of the "I" of writing, Barthes found proof of an absolute disjunction between self and text: no matter how "sincere" writing seems to be, its professed innocence is a species of imposture. Over the years, this view — which first surfaced in *Writing Degree Zero* (1953) — had evolved into a complex theory of the artificiality of all discourse and, notoriously, into the concept of *écriture* as a game without players, a self-sustaining system of textual production, in which the writer, far from expressing any originality, functions as "the joker in the pack, a *mana*, a zero degree, a dummy in the bridge game."[9]

But in 1978 Barthes retreated from that position and acknowledged that he was now "less sure" about the status of the verb "to write." His hesitancy sprang from a recognition of the compound infinitive "to want to write" (*vouloir-écrire*) as the signifier of a desire whose object lay beyond the field of writing. Indeed, Barthes was now prepared to suggest — banal apostasy — that the verb "to write" meant "to want to say something," and he described the "phantasm" of writing as the desired union of subject and object, the writer and his fetish. More specifically, he called the phantasm of the novel a vital pleasure, the desire of love: "the novel embraces the world like a lover, . . . it celebrates that which one loves." During this meeting of the seminar (9 December 1978), he made explicit his own relation to the topic: "I am in the process of writing a novel." It would be, he explained, a novel of memory; not a piece of modernist *écriture* at all, but a work inspired by Tolstoi's *War and Peace* and — preeminently — by Proust's *Remembrance of Things Past*. Yet Barthes had no inclination to write a "giant" novel (which he called a denial of the genre); rather, he envisioned "a work which did not intimidate the reader by its language." Alluding to a recent sorrow, which evidently lay behind the novelistic scheme, Barthes mused, "Perhaps the wounds of love can be overcome by the desire to write."

His avowed "preparation for the novel" also arose from a growing anxiety about the approach of death — a predicament he saw metaphorically expressed by Dante's reference to the dark wood, entered in the "middle of life's way." Barthes allowed that he was beyond the actuarial middle of life, but he insisted upon the psychological aptness of the image, which implied for him a sense of the end. He underscored this point at the close of one lecture

(16 December 1978) by relating a deeply personal episode: the circumstances of a "mortality crisis" which befell him at a favorite site near Casablanca in April 1978. Barthes recalled how one afternoon he had visited a waterfall with a few of his graduate students, but feeling increasingly detached and depressed, he returned alone to his apartment and there experienced a powerful consciousness of his impending death. The encounter with this "physical presence" lasted several hours, and afterward Barthes felt a remorse about his career, perceiving an absolute rupture between his emotional life and his mental life (a dichotomy he had often ridiculed as simplistic). He also realized a need to shed his previous conception of writing to produce the novel of memory which would assuage the "wounds of love."

If the incident in Casablanca marked a crucial turn in his work, the retelling of the story produced a bewildering development in the seminar. At its next meeting (6 January 1979), Barthes shifted abruptly to a consideration of the haiku, calling it the act of naming *(nomination)* fundamental to the novel. With this perfunctory transition, he reverted to a familiar topic (discussed in *L'empire des signes*) and for the remainder of the seminar — until early March 1979 — outlined the poetics of the haiku, referring only cursorily in his final lecture to the problem of writing a novel. In one sense this was a typical bit of mystification: as we see in *Roland Barthes* and *A Lover's Discourse*, he was driven to self-revelation yet curiously unable to bare his heart except in formal, oblique ways. As if the narration of his crisis in Casablanca had disclosed too much and had become a source of chagrin, Barthes evaded the whole question of his preparation for the novel and instead retreated behind impersonal critical analysis. But clearly the desire to write a novel remained with him; his last published works, "Délibération" and *La chambre claire* poignantly reveal its traces.[10]

Barthes apparently composed the *Tel Quel* essay "Délibération" during the late spring of 1979, or at about the same time he was writing the book on photography. His ostensible subject is the "malady" of the personal journal: "an insoluble doubt about the value of what one writes in it." The doubt is personal and poses two questions: "Should I keep a journal *with the idea of publishing it?* Can I make a 'work' out of a journal?"[11] At the outset, Barthes avoids closer scrutiny of his own motives and instead ruminates on the "artifice" of sincerity in the journal, the fact that "*I* is a poseur."

(This is, we might note, a subtle but significant modification of the idea—borrowed from Rimbaud—that "*I* is another.") Barthes subsequently tells of three recent attempts to keep a journal and presents passages from two of them. He displays these fragments as writing of uncertain status; their publication has been justified in *Tel Quel*, he implies, only by the generic question they pose: does the journal possess an intrinsic formal value? However, I believe this critical speculation, the "deliberation," actually affords a pretext—a means of securing the immortality of print for material Barthes felt compelled to preserve—for the lengthier of the two segments concerns the period just before the death of his mother. Of this writing he says, "the first, the more solemn because it took place during the illness of my mother, is the longer, perhaps because it satisfied a little the Kafkaesque design of extirpating anguish through writing" (p. 10).

We know from a variety of sources—and perhaps most vividly from the photographic evidence in *Roland Barthes*—that Barthes felt an intense emotional dependency upon his mother, which extended beyond childhood into his later life.[12] In *A Lover's Discourse* he recalled the anxiety of temporary separation: "As a child, I didn't forget: interminable days, abandoned days, when the Mother was working far away; I would go, evenings, to wait for her at the U *bis* bus stop, Sèvres-Babylone; the buses would pass one after the other, she wasn't in any of them."[13] Barthes the theorist derived countless insights from Oedipal myth ("The writer is someone who plays with his mother's body" [*Pleasure*, p. 37]), and he once claimed to suffer from "great Oedipal frustration" at the early loss of his father, who died when Barthes was two (*RB*, p. 45); but one finds no mention of Freudian fantasy concerning his mother. He writes of her lovingly but respectfully; his devotion was extravagant and sentimental, as this excerpt from "Délibération" suggests: "18 July 1977. Mom's birthday. I can give her only a rosebud from the garden; at least it is the only one and the first since we have been there" (p. 12). On 25 October 1977, Henriette Binger Barthes died, and there is every reason to believe that this event precipitated Barthes's own mortality crisis the following April. A few months before his mother's death, he had reflected upon the essential meaning of childhood: "I am still close to the mother and have eternal life before me—in other words, I am immortal."[14] For Barthes, his mother's death entailed a double loss — one immediate and devastating, the other imminent and frightening.

Superficially regarded, the entries published in "Délibération" seem terse and even banal. Their dramatic force resides in the tension between the stated and the unstated, between the restraint of mundane detail and the implied consciousness of his mother's rapid decline. Death was much on Barthes's mind that summer, and his journal indicates its obstinacy as he writes of the new cleaning woman with a fated, diabetic son; his somber thoughts and fears as he foresees "the death of the dear one" (*l'être cher*); the violent emotion prompted by the death scene of old Bolkonski in *War and Peace*. Even the notations describing boredom, discomfort, or the monotony of routine tasks (burning garbage, going shopping) acquire a significance in relation to death: these moments occurred while his mother was dying.

In terms of the turn in Barthes's writing, however, the key revelation of the journal emerges in this reflection on the last days of André Gide:

> The old age and the death of Gide (that I read about in the *Cahiers de la Petite Dame*) were surrounded by witnesses. But these witnesses, I don't know what they have become: doubtless, for the most part, dead men in their turn? There is a moment when the witnesses die themselves without witnesses. History is thus made up of little bursts of life and death, without connection. (p. 10)

Here we discover the essential impulse for the journal and the essay "Délibération": it is writing that bears witness, albeit by implication, to the dear one. As was the case for Proust, the death of his mother affected Barthes profoundly *as a writer*, kindling a desire to recover a lost relationship and a lost time in writing. It also intensified his sense of duty as a survivor; speaking of his intention to write a novel, Barthes once remarked in the seminar: "To portray that which one loves is to immortalize it." Whatever "wounds of love" he had suffered prior to *A Lover's Discourse* (with its discreet references to gay sorrows), the grief animating his last writing was clearly the loss of his mother. This event apparently brought about radical changes in the way Barthes thought about the nature of the self and the purpose of writing.

Such a conclusion becomes inescapable when we turn to *La chambre claire*. By its form alone, this work signals a difference, a basic realignment of writer and subject. Surprisingly, the discussion unfolds not through whimsically arranged fragments but through a sustained, cumulative reflection on the nature of photography. Barthes explains that he has been seized by an "ontological" desire to understand photography; he wants to know what sets it apart from "the community of images."[15] His interest is indeed ontological, but it extends beyond the photographic image to the human subject. He concerns himself with the relationship between photography and reality, between the physical referent and the metaphysics of being. Beyond questions of composition and technique, Barthes explores the photograph as a clue to the mysteries of time, love, death, and the soul. As these observations suggest, *La chambre claire* marks a fundamental break with his past writings.

What sets photography apart from other forms of representation, according to Barthes, is its rapport with reality, for its *noème* (essential idea) is precisely "that-has-been" (*ça-a-été*). His main theoretical insight, in Part I, involves the opposition between *studium* and *punctum*. He defines the *studium* as the range of familiar, conventional associations which a given photograph evokes for any viewer: the culturally coded meaning that expresses the photographer's "intentions" (i.e., a photo of a wedding reception signifies happiness, traditional values, a new life). The *punctum* designates that which literally punctures the *studium*— the unfamiliar or unexpected revelation, the gap in the text, the unintended detail that touches or wounds the spectator and simultaneously displays a field of experience hidden by the *studium* (i.e., a subtle but incongruous aspect of gesture that discloses a desire). Barthes explains the *punctum* through readings of favorite photographs, noting the odd details that skew our response to the human subjects represented.

However intriguing, this analysis has only a tangential bearing on the real task of *La chambre claire* as writing; like his discussion of the journal in "Délibération," the study of photography furnishes a pretext for the introduction, in Part II, of intensely personal material relating to the death of his mother. Written between 15 April and 3 June 1979, the book serves, I think, not as a foretaste of the intended fiction but as a tacit concession of defeat, a recognition by Barthes that the Proustian novel of memory lay beyond his means. At the same time, however, Part II presents the narrative of a search for things past — not a densely symbolic evocation of youth but a spare account of a poignant human situation: Barthes sorting through family photographs just after his mother's death. Here, of course, lies the source of his late obsession with photography: we learn that one evening in November 1977, Barthes went alone to the apartment where his mother had recently died and there tried to put her photographs in order, "looking beneath the lamp, one by one, at these photos of [her], going back in time with her, little by little, searching for the truth of the face that [he] had loved" (pp. 105-6). The quest for the essential image proves disappointing:

> At the mercy of these photos, I sometimes recognized a part of her face, a certain resemblance of the nose and the forehead, the movement of her arms, of her hands. Except in bits, I never recognized her, which is to say that I lacked her being, and that, consequently, I lacked her entirely. It was not she and yet it was no one else. I would have recognized her among thousands of women and yet I did not "find" her. I recognized her differentially, not essentially. (p. 103)

But finally Barthes uncovers the photograph that possesses the missing quality: a picture of his mother, at the age of five, standing on a bridge in a winter garden (*Jardin d'Hiver*) at her childhood home. He writes, "I looked at the little girl, and I recognized my mother at last" (p. 107). The clarity of the face, the naïve placement of the hands, the familiar simpering expression: all produce the idea of a "sovereign innocence," the "affirmation of a sweetness." The picture captures her essence, "the goodness that formed her soul, immediately and forever." Barthes devotes so much attention to the *Jardin d'Hiver* photo because it provides the measure of his loss: "For what I lost was not a Figure (the Mother), but a being; and not a being, but a quality (a soul): not the indispensable, but the irreplaceable" (p. 118). In light of Barthes's previous theories of the subject, his determined effort to explain the irreducible quality of his mother's being signals an immense change in perspective. Note the graphic contrast between his meditations on the *Jardin d'Hiver* photo and this summary of his earlier thought offered by John Sturrock:

> Sartrean existentialism marked him profoundly and traces of it have remained, notably in the extreme distaste Barthes has expressed over and over again for the philosophy to which existentialism was opposed: that of essentialism. Essentialism holds that within each human individual there is some ultimate essence which does not change and which obligates us to behave, as our lives unfold, within more or less predictable limits. . . . Barthes professes a philosophy of disintegration, whereby the presumed unity of any individual is dissolved into a plurality and we each of us turn out to be many instead of one. Barthes will have no truck with oneness, and certainly not with God, the One of Ones; he supports whatever is plural or discontinuous.[16]

In place of his "philosophy of disintegration," one finds in *La chambre claire* a resolute conception of essence, brought into focus by the affliction of its loss: grief. Yet the theory of being adumbrated by Barthes should not be dismissed as a circumstantial response. One of the few continuities in his writing is its radical oppositionism: he initially rejected essentialism because, as John Sturrock observes, it was the facile ideology of the bourgeoisie; he finally arrived at the concept of a soul in defiance of his own theory of the subject, perceiving the insufficiency of the latter to account for the truth of the *Jardin d'Hiver* photo.

The troubling problem of that image plunged Barthes into a protracted meditation on being and nothingness, but it imposed upon the grid of Sartrean thought a disruptive influence: sentimentalism. This emotional self-indulgence was (as he noted in *Roland Barthes*) the "ultimate transgression" of revolutionary praxis; its pervasiveness in *La chambre claire* constitutes a virtual defiance of the *Doxa* of the avant-garde. Nostalgia, sympathy, and filial devotion: bourgeois sentiment reenters the field of writing.

The fetishized object, the *Jardin d'Hiver* photo, aroused in Barthes a wild longing for an irrecoverable past, crystallized the sense of his mother's elemental soul, and sharpened his desire to commemorate her life. That is, the picture led Barthes to the threshold of biography, a genre which (as Sturrock points out) had previously seemed "especially offensive" to him because it entailed "a counterfeit integration of the subject."

In *Roland Barthes* he had exposed the factitiousness of biography with a list of categories suggested by the chronology of his career: "A life: studies, diseases, appointments. And the rest? Encounters, friendships, loves, travels, readings, pleasures, fears, beliefs, satisfactions, indignations, distresses: in a word: repercussions? — In the text — but not in the work" (p. 184). While the text of pleasure accommodates fragmentary glimpses of a life, the biographical work insists upon an illusory ordering of experience, a centripetal conception of the subject. This view of biography as falsification coincides with his theory of subjective multiplicity, but it conflicts significantly with the inherent biographical program of *La chambre claire:* the recovery and reintegration of the subject who was his mother. He discovers her not in the photographs capturing bits and pieces of her nature but in the perfect image of her immanent soul.

Perhaps the clearest evidence of a redefined notion of the subject, however, is Barthes's presentation of himself in writing. In contrast to the method of *Roland Barthes* and *A Lover's Discourse*, where multiple narrative voices imply his "plurality," *La chambre claire* reflects a centering of consciousness in the use of a single voice, a consistent perspective, through which Barthes expresses concerns which are rigorously personal. He avoids any posturing as Writer — as the "dummy in the bridge game" of language — and resists even the inclination to universalize his childhood: "I do not wish to reduce my family to the Family any more than I wish to reduce my mother to the Mother" (p. 116). Instead, he insists upon the essentiality of his mother and the integrity of his own bereavement: "I could say, like the Proustian narrator at the death of his grandmother: 'I care not only about suffering, but about respecting the originality of my suffering'; for this originality was the reflection of that which was absolutely irreducible in her, and consequently lost at once forever" (pp. 117-

18). His ultimate assertion of the "originality" of his situation — its incomparability as subjective experience — is his decision not to publish the *Jardin d'Hiver* photo:

> (I cannot show the Photo of the *Jardin d'Hiver*. It exists only for me. For you, it would be nothing more than an inconsequential photo, one of a thousand displays of "what-have-you"; there is nothing in it to constitute the visible object of a science; it could not establish an objectivity, in the positive sense of the term; at most, it would appeal to your *studium:* period, clothing, photographic genius; but for you, no wound in it. (p. 115)

The omission of the photo attests to the suffering of a subject whose name is Roland Barthes.

His recurrent affirmation of the soul's individuality proceeds from a second general truth inscribed in the photographic text, a truth which relates to the life of the soul as the photographic negative relates to the positive print: I mean the phenomenon of death. For Barthes, the fundamental paradox of the photograph is that in representing life (*ça-a-été*) — and occasionally reflecting back the soul's own image — it simultaneously confirms the inevitability of time and death. Looking at the photograph of a wedding, taken about 1910, he realizes that, necessarily, everyone in the picture is now dead, except perhaps the little children who would now be old ladies or old men. The assignable date of any photo implies calculations of life and death whose ultimate meaning is "the inexorable extinction of generations" (p. 131). Reverting to his theory of the *punctum*, Barthes observes that there is always a second *punctum* in the photograph: Time. The historical photograph (older than a human lifespan) conveys a double message about the crushing effect of time: the subject of the photo, so manifestly alive, is going to die; that subject is also already dead. The discovery of a temporal *punctum* produces a second response to the *Jardin d'Hiver* picture:

> Before the photo of my mother as a child, I say to myself: she is going to die: I shudder, like Winnicott's psychotic, *about a catastrophe that has already taken place.*

Whether the subject is already dead or not, every photograph is this catastrophe. (p. 150)

The photographic print is at once an undeniable proof of existence — "the photo is literally an emanation of the referent" (p. 126) — and an emblem of mortality; it furnishes a "certificate of presence" but likewise signifies an absence: the subject is irrecoverable *as such*.

This perception of doubleness leads Barthes to consider the photograph as the starting point of a true metaphysics:

> Certainly, more than any other art, Photography poses an immediate presence in the world — a co-presence; but this presence is not only of a political order . . ., it is also of a metaphysical order. Flaubert mocked (but did he really mock?) Bouvard and Pécuchet questioning themselves about heaven, fate, time, life, infinity, etc. It is this kind of question which Photography poses for me: questions that belong to a metaphysics which is "stupid" or simple (it is the answers that are complicated): probably the true metaphysics. (pp. 131-33)

What seems extraordinary about this passage, in view of his earlier writings, is the recognition by Barthes of a supernal order of truth beyond the empirical evidence of the photograph. One need only compare this commentary with an early structuralist essay like "The Photographic Message" (1961; *Image* pp. 15-31) to appreciate the revolutionary aspect of *La chambre claire*. This is not to argue that the book represents an emerging religious orthodoxy. Barthes observes disinterestedly that the arrival of the photograph coincided with the decline of ritual (*recul des rites*) in modern society and reflects the displacement of religion as a mode of conceptualizing death (p. 144). Yet his text employs religious metaphors suggestively: "Photography has something to do with resurrection" (p. 129); "for whoever holds a photo in his hand, it is a 'fundamental faith,' an 'Urdoxy,' which nothing can overturn" (p. 165); the photo certifies through a "new order of proof": "the proof-according-to-Saint-Thomas-wanting-to-touch-the-resurrected-Christ" (p. 125). Do these metaphors express a yearning for faith or its irrevocable loss? The answer lies beyond interpretation; it is enough to note that in discerning a metaphysical dimension in the photographic image, Barthes moved beyond temporal, textual questions to confront the "simple" questions of life, death, and infinity. Whether he experienced an illumination is another matter.

The death of his mother, which initiated his search for the true photograph and the truth of photography, induced Barthes to think of his own death as an imminent event. In reflecting on that prospect, he seems to acknowledge a failure of insight, an inability to see beyond the terrible "flatness" of death:

> The horror is this: nothing to say about the death of the one whom I love the most, nothing to say about her photo, which I contemplate without ever being able to fathom it or transform it. The only "thought" I might have is that, at the end of this first death, my own death is inscribed; between the two, nothing more than to wait; I have no other resource than this *irony:* to speak of "nothing to say." (p. 145)

*La chambre claire* represents the effort to make this last paradox intelligible; appalled by the inscrutability of death, Barthes confesses the insufficiency of language and thought to give the problem a dimension of coherency. Yet the unspeakable "flatness" is itself a kind of revelation, through which Barthes perceives ubiquitous images of his own mortality. The click of the camera becomes an instant of dread: a "very subtle moment when, to tell the truth, I am neither a subject nor an object, but rather a subject that feels itself becoming an object: I endure then a micro-experience of death (of parenthesis): I become truly a spectre" (p. 30). Finally Barthes declares that all photographs carry "the imperious sign of my future death" (p. 151), because all bear witness to the "catastrophe" of Time. However, this awareness is far from an understanding of the ontological mystery; the photograph mirrors only "the outrageous confusion of reality" and remains in its depthless *platitude* unfathomable. It evokes in Barthes no conventional leap into faith, only "the suffering of love" (p. 179) — a mad pity for all of the persons whose photographs he has discussed in *La chambre claire:* those who are dead, those who are going to die.

Unhappily, the premonitions of death expressed in the seminar and in *La chambre claire* proved to be correct: on the afternoon of 25 February 1980, Barthes was struck by a laundry van as he crossed the Rue des Ecoles near the Collège de France. To compound the misfortune, he was carrying no identification at the time, and was thus taken, unconscious and unknown, to Pitié-Salpêtrière hospital. Though subsequently identified, Barthes never recovered from internal injuries and died on 26 March. Through this bizarre fatality (at once event and destiny), his writing came to an end, and his book on photography assumed the status of a last utterance. Apart from its critical interest, *La chambre claire* therefore occupies a curious, tendentious position with respect to the uncompleted novel. As the book makes clear, Barthes's memory and imagination were dominated, in the last years of his life, by the figure of his mother. Her loss effected a vast change in his conception of human essence, his consciousness of death, and his understanding of the function of writing. His final discourse is both purposive and referential; it concerns the signified (meaning) embedded in the photographic signifier and constitutes a "work" rather than a "text" in strict Barthesian terms. [17] It possesses an end beyond the play of words: the rediscovery of a soul *(âme)*.

His desire to write a novel was perhaps aroused by the same Proustian experience that produced *La chambre claire:* the sadness of sorting through family photographs, alone, in the apartment where his mother had recently died. Increasingly in his later years, Barthes had fallen under the spell of Proust: "I recognize that Proust's work, for myself at least, is *the* reference work, the general *mathesis,* the *mandala* of the entire literary cosmogony. . . . Proust is what comes to me, not what I summon up; not an 'authority,' simply a *circular memory*" (*Pleasure,* p. 36). The assimilation of Proust coincided with another growing preoccupation evidenced in *Roland Barthes:* the writer's childhood in Bayonne and his adolescent years in Paris. The death of his mother in 1977 completed a parallel he saw between himself and the great novelist, and sometime after his mortality crisis of 1978, Barthes placed *Remembrance of Things Past* before himself as an object of emulation. Despite reservations about the "giant novel," Proust's work became his model of the writer's relationship to his own life.

It is hard to imagine a more perfect formula for failure. Whether or not Barthes had consciously abandoned the novel prior to *La chambre claire*, an awareness of its unwritability emerges in the despair of "nothing to say" — the failure of language to assuage or even explain the "wounds of love." Uncertainty had plagued him from the outset. At the same time that he announced the novelistic project in the seminar, Barthes had wondered aloud about the possibility of writing such a traditional work in the late twentieth century. He confessed doubts about his ability to recall the past; he suffered from a "deformation of memory," intermittent amnesia, which clouded his recollection of key events in his youth. As we see in *Roland Barthes* and *A Lover's Discourse*, Barthes moreover possessed an ingrained reticence about his private life, and despite his verbal exhibitionism, he remained, as Stephen Koch has said, "a very intelligent man for whom the veil of abstraction [was] a reflex, a necessity, a way of life."[18] There was another obstacle Barthes faced, a problem he touched upon in the paper on Stendhal that he was composing the day of his fatal accident: "one always fails in speaking of what one loves."[19] The failure occurs not through a lack of desire but through its opposite, a passion of suffocating intensity. It may be that he recognized in Stendhal's Italian journals precisely the excess of feeling which made it possible for Barthes to write a novel about his mother. There was "nothing to say" because there was so much that wanted saying.

Barthes desired to write a novel both to recuperate the stage of childhood and to fulfill his obligation as the witness of his mother's being. Significantly, he refers to that duty again in *La chambre claire*:

> Before the only photo where I see my father and my mother together, they who I know loved each other, I think: it is love-as-treasure which is going to disappear forever; for when I am no longer here, no one will be able to bear witness to it any more: there will remain nothing but indifferent Nature. (p. 147)

Time oppressed Barthes because of its indifference to human love: yet it is the depth of his love which sets *La chambre claire* apart from his other works as an eloquent commemoration. The author declined to publish a picture of his mother in the book; yet his reflections on the *Jardin d'Hiver* photo transform her physical absence into an enduring presence. That is, his commentary on her photograph bears witness, elucidates "the truth of the face that [he] loved," despite the problem of "nothing to say." In this sense, the book on photography accomplishes the principal task of the never-to-be-written novel.

His narrative of the photographic quest also betrays a covert desire to produce a work of autobiography. In *Sade Fourier Loyola* Barthes had expressed the wish to have his life reduced by "some friendly and detached biographer" to "a few details, a few preferences, a few inflections."[20] This method of isolating "biographemes" informs *Roland Barthes*, a text he described as "totally fictive," the staging of an "image-system" rather than the story of a life; there he playfully insisted that "all this must be considered as if spoken by a character in a novel" (*RB*, pp. 105, 119, 120). Indeed, the book seems a deliberate working-out of the transposition he once attributed to Proust's masterpiece: "By a radical reversal, instead of putting his life into his novel, as is so often maintained, he made of his very life a work for which his own book was the model" (*Image*, p. 144). Like Proust, Barthes had immersed himself so deeply in the life of writing that the work of inscription engulfed the whole of his experience; the "writing self" subsumed the "imaginary person" who retained memories of a childhood in Bayonne. It is one thing, however, to present one's life as an arbitrary fiction and quite another to confront the uncompromising reality of death. As we see in *La chambre claire*, the demise of his mother concentrated his mind wonderfully, produced a sudden appreciation of human essence, and brought him to accept and prepare for his own death.

The thought of his extinction also enabled him to recognize a crucial relationship between writing and death and impelled him toward a novel of memory, a summation (albeit fictionalized) of his own irreducible individuality. That desire never came to fruition, but in certain portions of *La chambre claire*, we can identify an urge to tell his own story, a narrative poignantly intertwined with that of his mother's death:

> At the end of her life, a short time before the moment when I looked at the photographs and discovered the Photo of the *Jardin d'Hiver*, my mother was weak, very

> weak. I lived within her weakness (it was impossible for
> me to participate in a world of force, to go out in the
> evening; all worldliness horrified me). During her ill-
> ness, I took care of her, held for her the bowl of tea that
> she liked because she could drink from it more easily
> than from a cup; she had become my little girl, reunited
> for me with the essential child that she was in her first
> photo. (p. 112)

Here, sentimental rhetoric and simple gesture signify an instinctive tenderness. Yet the act of writing makes the private sense
public, converts it into a moment of pure autobiography, in which
word and image project the human distinctiveness of the writer
and form a memorable emblem of his being. In Part II of *La
chambre claire*, Barthes presents the narrative of a search for
meaning; that pursuit leads him through the general problem of
photography and the mystery of a particular picture toward a
perception of his own elemental anxieties and the revelation of his
innermost self. In this last book, he has become the faithful witness
of his own being, the guarantor of his own remembrance.

As we begin to assess the impact of Barthes's work on modern
critical thought, it seems unlikely that *La chambre claire* will
figure as a major work. Insofar as his career has provided an
accurate barometer of French intellectual trends, the book may
some day mark a general turn from structuralist and post-structur-
alist abstraction toward a more pragmatic and humane discourse.
Nevertheless, his insights into semiology, myth, textuality, and the
erotics of reading will probably be judged his most influential
ideas. And his theory of *écriture*—writing as an end in itself, a
self-sustaining play of fictions — will likely remain the concept
which governs the basic understanding of his work: the texts of
Roland Barthes, from *S/Z* onward, provide perfect instances of
"performative," self-contained language. But as we now know,
Barthes came to see critical metalanguage as a "prison house"; he
hoped in writing a novel to free himself from the constraints of his
own intellectual system. In the seminar, he once described the
novel as a therapeutic activity, a "practice against coldness of
heart." Barthes never wrote his imagined novel, but in *La chambre
claire* he gave the heart its due. He thus accomplished a significant
reconciliation between the writing self and the "I" of writing: the

voice *belongs* to Barthes and the story is self-evidently his own. By example the work restores the intimate and essential reciprocity between the subject and the system of language. No longer is the subject "merely an effect of language"; he is a being whose unique needs and desires may transcend language altogether. Such is the subject who describes this relationship with his mother:

> In a sense, I had never "spoken" to her, never "discoursed" in front of her, for her; we thought, without saying so, that the light insignificance of language, the suspension of images, should be the very space of love, its music. (pp. 112–13)

Through grief, Barthes found that the soul's desire lies beyond the photographic image, beyond the end of writing.

---

1 *Harper's*, August 1980, pp. 68–71.

2 Julia Kristeva, "How Does One Speak to Literature?" *Desire in Language: A Semiotic Approach to Literature and Art*, ed. Leon S. Roudiez (New York: Columbia Univ. Press, 1980), p. 97.

3 I leave out of account here *Sollers, Ecrivain* (1979), which consists largely of essays written before 1973.

4 Barthes suggested this schematic summary in *Roland Barthes*, trans. Richard Howard (New York: Hill and Wang, 1977), p. 145; hereafter cited as *RB*.

5 "Barthes le Français," *L'Express*, 12 avril 1980, p. 91. Translation mine.

6 This and all other references or citations from Barthes's lectures are drawn from my own notes.

7 "The Death of the Author" in *Image Music Text*, trans. Stephen Heath (New York: Hill and Wang, 1977), p. 146; hereafter cited as *Image*. The essay originally appeared in French in 1968.

8 "To Write: An Intransitive Verb?" in *The Structuralist Controversy*, ed. Richard Macksey and Eugenio Donato (Baltimore: Johns Hopkins Univ. Press, 1972), p. 141.

9 *The Pleasure of the Text*, trans. Richard Miller (New York: Hill and Wang, 1975), p. 35; hereafter cited as *Pleasure*.

10 The posthumous collection of notes, fragments, and unfinished writings to be entitled *Les Notations* should provide collateral evidence.

11 "Délibération," *Tel Quel*, 82 (Hiver 1979), 9. This and subsequent citations from the essay reflect my own translation.

12 Speaking of the photos of his mother, Barthes later said the book was "punctuated three times by the image of the Mother: first radiant, designating the only *Nature* recognized by a subject who has not stopped denouncing the 'natural' everywhere; then gratifying, embracing the sad child in the dual relationship, marking him with an eternal 'demand for love'; placed at last beside, before and behind the Mirror and establishing from that moment the imaginary identity of the subject." See "Barthes puissance trois," *Quinzaine Littéraire*, 1–15 mars 1975, p. 5. In his hostile analysis, Philip Thody emphasizes Barthes's "sensitivity to the castrating mother-figure"; see *Roland Barthes: A Conservative Estimate* (Atlantic Highlands, N. J.: Humanities Press, 1977), pp. 76–77.

13 *A Lover's Discourse: Fragments*, trans. Richard Howard (New York: Hill and Wang, 1978), pp. 14–15.

14 *Le Nouvel Observateur,* 9 mai 1977. The remark occurs in a review of Jean Daniel's *Le Refuge et la Source*.

15 *La chambre claire: Note sur la photographie* (Paris: Gallimard Seuil, 1980), pp. 13–14. This and subsequent citations from *La chambre claire* reflect my own translations. The forthcoming translation in English, by Richard Howard, is titled *Camera Lucida*.

16 "Roland Barthes" in *Structuralism and Since: From Lévi-Strauss to Derrida*, ed. John Sturrock (New York: Oxford Univ. Press, 1979), p. 53.

17 See "From Work to Text" in *Image*, pp. 155–64.

18 "Melancholy King of the Cats," *Saturday Review*, 2 September 1978, p. 34.

19 "On echoue toujours a parler de ce qu'on aime," *Tel Quel*, 85 (Automne 1980), 38. One page of this uncompleted essay was found in the carriage of his typewriter after the accident.

20 *Sade Fourier Loyola*, trans. Richard Miller (New York: Hill and Wang, 1976), p. 9.

🔥 🔥 🔥

# HAPPY BOY, ALLEN

fiction by MARY ROBISON

from MISSISSIPPI REVIEW

*nominated by Gordon Lish*

Allen WAS DRIVING HIS FATHER'S DODGE up Light Street, in Baltimore, looking for an empty parking space near Cheshire Towers—the old hotel turned apartment building. As he drove close, Allen noticed an odd-faced teen-ager, who was on the steps of the Cheshire. The boy had an involuntary giggle. He wore shorts and a cowboy hat. He was seated in the white sun, up from the shadows of the mighty shrubs that flanked the Cheshire's entrance doors.

Allen began breathing through his teeth. People such as the teen-ager made him anxious. People who were happy for no clear, visible reason.

The teen-ager bounced from his seat, and threw open the Cheshire's doors for a nurse in pale hose and crisp uniform. Allen pointed his father's car into the far-left lane of the street and kept on driving.

Allen's paternal aunt, Mindy, had a rental suite on the eleventh floor of Cheshire Towers—a creamy, stone building, distinguishable for its many windows and the various drape styles and colors in each. Allen had left his home in Towson that morning on an impulse. He had felt the urge to chat his problems out with someone more mature.

"Aagh," he said, and stamped the brakes for his fourth stoplight. "I hate this damn town. I really do! Row houses, shmow houses. Couldn't they think of something else?" His generator light blinked on. With a little jump and intake of breath, Allen saw the light and snapped off the air conditioner. When the blowers quit, Allen heard the car radio, which was sputtering, forgotten, between stations.

He found a parking slot, at last, on an alley in front of a necktie shop. The shop was open for Saturday business, but empty except for a stout saleswoman, who was planted, angrily, in the doorway.

"Bless you," Allen told the parking meter as he read its orders. He drew a shade with his hand over his eyebrows, and squinted at the façades for his aunt's apartment building. "Please, please be home," he said to the upper-floor windows when he found them. "You must." He adjusted his right foot in its penny loafer, and walked.

The teen-ager in the cowboy hat had come out onto the broad sidewalk, and was watching as Allen approached.

Allen stalled, and got his bearings under a lilac bush. He busied himself with his wrist watch, shaking it, and scowling at its face. It was eleven-forty.

"Guess how much I used to weigh," the teen-ager said. He held open the vest he wore instead of a shirt, and showed Allen his tiny waist and rib cage.

"You're crazy," Allen said.

"Yeah, but just guess," the teen-ager said.

"Four hundred and fifty pounds," Allen said. He headed up the sidewalk, past the teen-ager, toward the entrance doors to the Cheshire.

The cowboy followed, close on Allen's heels. "You belong back in your room at the mental asylum," Allen said. "You're late now, so you better hurry if you want lunch. Let me by, this instant."

"There you go," the teen-ager said. He took his hat, waved it with his hand, and did a low bow. "Monsieur."

Allen looked at the bent-over teen-ager, who had a zodiac pendant dangling from his throat. The boy wore archless sandals of stitched plastic.

"You look about the right weight," Allen said, and swallowed.

"That's what I think," the teen-ager said. He straightened up, and took a soldierly stance. "It took will power."

Mindy was propped on her couch, on foam pillows the colors of Easter candy. She had a crocheted afghan spun twice around the calves of her legs.

The old suite she rented had been restyled with lowered ceilings and a pink-beige carpet. There was a new folding door on the bathroom, and a line of little appliances in the kitchen.

The central room was hushed after the street racket below, and the floor and furniture were striped with light that came through the window blind. Low on a wall, an air cooler was chugging.

"Ooh, thank heavens, you're here," Allen said. "Do you have any idea what would have happened to me if you'd gone out to lunch or something?" He flopped down on the floor in front of Mindy, gripped the back of his neck, and let his head roll back on his hand. "Whew, I'll tell you. I'd be at the police station, right now, filling out reports. That's a tricky downtown, on a good day. But on a day like today — a Saturday, when everything's thronged, the people get irritable enough to kill one another, and they don't even know why. It's because they're hot."

Mindy was watching Allen without interest.

"Aunt Min, I hope you can help me," he said. "I need desperately for somebody to talk me out of doing something stupid."

Mindy creased the pages of the newspaper she had been reading, the *Sun*, and tossed them over her shoulder onto the floor behind the couch. She reached for a glass on the lamp table — a brown drink with a bobbing cherry.

"Give me a minute to get my equilibrium," Allen said. "Then I'll unload the whole problem. Your place sure is coming along. It looks better and better, every time I come. Is that a new painting?"

Mindy lifted herself, and craned her neck to see the wall behind her. "No," she said. She relaxed back into place, and tapped the cherry that floated on the surface of her drink. "I got that at an estate sale, almost a year ago."

"What does it remind me of?" Allen said, thinking. "My head is full of names. I've been taking a course on the history of art — which I love. I was smart, for once, and got the jump on my graduating class. They don't start college 'til fall quarter. Rousseau is the name that keeps sticking in my mind for some reason — in relation to that piece." He nodded at the wall. "Someone, either the textbook or my t.a., says the whole pageant of art history stops right with Henri Rousseau. I think I already knew that, but, anyway, his work sort of reminds you of looking through a magnifying glass. He can take you out into a field or a jungle, say, and leave you standing there. Painting, I found out, is all done with the eyes." Allen straightened his posture, and pulled his feet into a lotus position. "To prove what I mean, we saw these amazing films of Auguste Renoir, in his last and final days, where he was painting with brushes strapped onto the backs of his wrists — which were crippled up with something, but even that didn't stop Renoir."

"No, it wouldn't," Mindy said.

"O.K., you're not interested," Allen said. "But what brought all this up is I really do like your picture, if nothing else, just for the winter theme. I love winter, and I hate summer. You wouldn't believe how lazy I am because of the humidity, recently. I just drop when it gets too bad, and Dad leaves our air conditioner off overnight, so you wake up, already sick. One morning, I was fixing cinnamon toast, or something, and I had to practically lie on the counter to keep from going into a complete faint."

"How is Paul?" Mindy said.

"Fine," Allen said. "So, what I do is I throw a whole tray full of ice cubes into the bathtub with me, first thing, and then I just stay in there until the air conditioner's working enough to make some difference. I know it's not good for you, to go from red hot to freezing cold — it's probably why I'm so hoarse. Dad says I go around coughing twenty hours a day."

"Is Paul still thinking of remarrying?" Mindy said. She untangled her legs from the afghan, stood, and circled where Allen was positioned on the rug.

"That's the whole thing I came to talk to you about, Aunt Min." Allen looked up, and turned slowly on his seat, following Mindy.

"The woman, it turns out — I've never met her. I just heard about her from Dad, and, of course, he left out all the bad stuff. She's older than he is. She's been married, before, at least once. She's got four kids, which're grown, thank God. He wants to move her — Laura Glinnis, is, I guess, her name — into the house with us. You can imagine what that'd do to me. I've never had to live with a woman. Not since we lost Mom."

"You never lived with your mother, Allen. She died in child-birth."

"I know," Allen said, looking sad for a moment. "Everyone always tells me not to blame myself for it."

Mindy said, "Your father never forgave me for missing Margue-rite's funeral. Though I was in Germany then, with Carl. We waited a day too long before flying home. I had no idea they'd bury her so quickly. And then Carl was dead within the year, and I found out how they do things."

"I'm sure Dad forgives you," Allen said. "See, he's forgot all about Mom. That's what gets me." Allen pulled a burr from his sock and threw it onto the carpet. "I had the Dodge out one night, driving around, and thinking over this whole thing. I got off the beltway at some exit, and went to a bar, and had a couple of mixed drinks. No one even asked for an i.d. They just served me the drinks, one on top of another. I was completely exhausted, by then. I didn't care if Dad moved Mrs. Glinnis and her brood right smack into the dining room and fed them T-bone steaks. I started smashing my fist on the table top of the booth they had there. I didn't hurt anything, really. Just my own hand. But I realized I have a capacity to be very destructive. It's like there's some monster inside me, that wants to kill everything in my way."

"Why don't *you* get married, Allen?" Mindy said. She was between him and the couch, snapping at her manicured fingernails with her thumb. "Why don't you get a wife, somewhere, and marry her, and move away? Let your dad find a way out of his loneliness, if he can. Because you'd still have the *idea* of you and your father. I'm sure that'd be better than the real relationship."

"Hmm. Maybe I could," Allen said. He took Mindy's drink, which she had refreshed, and sipped from it. "But you forget I'm underage."

"No, I remembered that, Allen. You could lie. Or you could get permission from your father."

"This is crazy, though, because I don't have anyone to marry," Allen said.

"I know dozens of people."

"That'd marry me?"

"In a minute," Mindy said.

"Yeah, O.K. Only, so many people make me nervous. There was a guy out front, today, for example. . ."

"Tex? Tex is usually out front. You'd delight in him, Allen. He's got just the right touch of. . ."

"You must be thinking of someone else," Allen said.

Mindy was in a bean-bag chair, in the corner, loading color film into her camera. "You know, I bought this camera with money I won in the football pools," she said. "I always win. That's why I love to gamble. I especially like circulating the floors of the office where I work to see who else won, and what teams the poor losers bet on. Oops!"

"What?" Allen said.

"Nothing," Mindy said. "Don't worry." Her chignon had come undone, and the left side of her hair — blonde, though she was fifty-one — had fallen onto the shoulder of her kimono. "I clicked off a couple that I didn't mean to. It'll be all right."

"It will," Allen said, in a low voice, to the cowboy-hatted teen-ager who sat on the couch with him. "She's really more or less a professional. Her work's appeared in a couple of the D.C. galleries — places you'd recognize, if I could remember the names."

"One gallery, and they just showed two of my self-portraits," Mindy said. "A picture of me, at the stove. One of me, petting Abra. . ."

"Cat that ran away," Allen told the teen-ager.

Both young men had been drinking, earnestly. Allen tugged off his cotton shirt and laid it out on the floor. He removed his loafers, and his wrist watch. The teen-ager took off his vest.

"What may I call you?" Allen asked.

The teen-ager puffed his right cheek full of air, then noisily let the air out. "Baker," he said.

"First, or last?" Allen said. The teen-ager shrugged.

"Baker, alone, is fine," Allen said. "Easier to remember."

"One more minute," Mindy said, from the corner. "I'm truly

sorry this is taking so long. It isn't my fault. The spool's in backwards or something. I wouldn't have had Allen get you up here," she said to the teen-ager, "if I'd known this was going to happen."

"These'll be great photographs," Allen said.

"Yeah, if I can. . . . Oops," Mindy said. "Damn."

"Now what's the matter?" Allen said.

Mindy said, "Oh I did something, and now I can't—do you know anything about cameras?"

"I had a basic film theory and technique course," Allen said.

"Loading," Mindy said. "L-o-a-d-i-n-g."

"Not for *any* camera," Allen said.

Mindy struggled out of the bean-bag chair. She came toward them, stepping over the coffee table, and showing one of her legs from the thigh down. She dropped the camera. Its self-timer ticked off fifteen seconds against the floor carpet.

Allen squeezed his forehead and sighed.

"The joke is, I do make good photographs," she said. "Maybe— who's to say?—great ones. But you've got to do daily work to be great, and for that you need a darkroom in your house, and not way across the g.d. town." She sat on the coffee table, with her skirt hitched up.

"That's true," Allen said.

"I had a camera," Baker said.

"Good for you, Tex," Mindy said. "Seriously, I got two rolls of thirty-six people each. . . . What did I just say? Did I say, 'thirty-six people each'? Isn't that a scream? Thirty-six *exposures* each, on each of two rolls. They came up brilliant, brilliant. And the reason was those faces."

"Faces?" Allen said.

"Yes, honey, that's what the world is. There's no world without faces to reflect it. Look at that face."

Allen and Mindy looked at Baker. He was whistling through a cavity in a front tooth. He wiggled his eyebrows at them, hard enough to move the brim of his cowboy hat up and down.

"What's in that face, Allen?" Mindy said.

Allen narrowed his eyes at Baker, and asked him to turn his head left, then right.

"Well?" Mindy said.

"Well, because of the hat, he looks . . . I'd say Western."

"You're a sharp boy," Mindy said.

"I wasn't done," Allen said. "It also looks like a face that's recently lost weight."

"Yeah, I did," Baker said.

"You don't see any pain in those eyes?" Mindy asked Allen.

"Yes. Well, really, no. I don't frankly, Aunt Min."

"Good, because I don't either. There isn't any. How about fear? Do you see fear in his eyes? Never mind." Mindy got up and headed for the bathroom.

"Do you like it hot, like this?" Allen asked Baker. Baker looked around his feet, and then around the apartment.

"I mean, do you like hot weather?"

"Sure," Baker said.

Mindy came back and Allen stood. Baker gathered his vest and stood up as well.

"Here's a face. Sit down, both of you," she said. She showed them a photograph of a young male whose head was shaved, and whose eyes were wild-looking. There were markings, or scratches, on the photo, above the dark eyes. "This one is disturbed. People call him 'disturbed,' but he made perfect sense to me the day I took shots of him. If you look deep enough, you see the calm behind the chaos. It's one reason I wanted to photograph you two," Mindy said.

"Not that you're retarded," Allen said to Baker. "Or me — that I am."

"Oh, you're retarded, all right," Mindy said. "I don't know how, Allen, but you stopped your emotional growth at the age of six."

"Hey, that's the bottle talking," Allen said.

"This was nice," the teen-ager said to Mindy. "I'd like to visit you again, sometime, in the future."

Mindy had felt sick, grabbed up Allen's shirt, and gone swiftly into the bathroom, with the shirt held against her mouth. For a long while, Allen heard faucet water running. Eventually, he tried pushing open the folding door. "Aunt Min?" The door moved a few inches, and caught on Mindy, who lay over the floor tiles, with Allen's shirt balled under her cheek for a pillow.

Allen pulled the door shut. He paced around the apartment, in just his slacks, hissing and swearing to himself. He perched on the back of Mindy's couch, and brought the telephone to his lap. He dialed "one," and then his home phone number.

"Hello," said a woman's voice, startling Allen.

"Is this my house?" he said. "Who is this?"

"I'm Laura Glinnis," the woman said.

"Well, put Dad on, if he's there. I need to talk with him, immediately."

"Just a second, Allen," Mrs. Glinnis said. "Paul?"

"What do you want, now?" Allen's father said into the phone.

"Just to let you know what I'm up to," Allen said.

"Is it serious?"

"I feel that, this time, I'm in deep water, Dad. Things are completely out of my control. I'm sauced, for one thing. There might even be an ambulance case in the bathroom. I'm so messed up," Allen said.

There was a long silence at the other end of the line. Allen heard the whispery scrape of a cupped palm over the phone's speaker. His father's voice came back, slowly, saying, "Relax, boy. Run this thing down for me, step by step."

"O.K., the first thing you should know is I came here to tell Aunt Mindy about what's been happening — my side of the story."

"Who's in the bathroom, hurt?" Allen's father said. "Is it Mindy? Tell me straight. Take it slow now, son."

"Aunt Mindy'll be fine. I'm not worried about her," Allen said. "She's used to being drunk." He laughed once.

"Allen?" the voice said. "Do you know how you make me feel?"

"Yeah, yeah," Allen said, and smacked down the phone's receiver.

He straightened the apartment a little, tidied the kitchen, and perked coffee. He opened the bathroom door the few inches it would go. He hoped the coffee aroma would revive Mindy.

"You know Charles," Mindy said in her sleep.

Allen got the camera off the floor, and sat down, and tried until he was sweating to get the roll of film untangled.

"I feel so . . . regretful," Mindy called.

Allen looked in on her. She was awake, but in the same prone position. Water still splashed from the opened faucet. "This is disgusting, I know," she said. "It must be disgusting for you to see, Allen. A young boy. I'm really so, so sorry."

"You're forgiven," Allen said.

"Do you mean it? You're not really angry?"

"Hell, no. Not at all," Allen said.

Whistling to himself, he borrowed a tailored blouse from a

hanger in Mindy's closet. He rolled the cuffs, where there were pearl, flower-shaped buttons. He turned the collar under, uncomfortably.

In the kitchen, Allen poured coffee into one of his aunt's pretty tea cups. He sat in the tiny dining annex, with his legs crossed, and sipped coffee, and considered his day. He thought he'd drive out around the Baltimore zoo — maybe buy himself dinner.

# THE JOURNEY

by JAMES WRIGHT

from A REPLY TO MATTHEW ARNOLD (Logbridge-Rhodes, Inc.)

*nominated by Logbridge-Rhodes, Inc. and Jim Barnes*

Anghiari is medieval, a sleeve sloping down
A steep hill, suddenly sweeping out
To the edge of a cliff, and dwindling.
But far up the mountain, behind the town,
We too were swept out, out by the wind,
Alone with the Tuscan grass.

Wind had been blowing across the hills
For days, and everything now was graying gold
With dust, everything we saw, even
Some small children scampering along a road,
Twittering Italian to a small caged bird.
We sat beside them to rest in some brushwood,
And I leaned down to rinse the dust from my face.

I found the spider web there, whose hinges
Reeled heavily and crazily with the dust,
Whole mounds and cemeteries of it, sagging
And scattering shadows among shells and wings.
And then she stepped into the center of air
Slender and fastidious, the golden hair
Of daylight along her shoulders, she poised there,
While ruins crumbled on every side of her.
Free of the dust, as though a moment before
She had stepped inside the earth, to bathe herself.

I gazed, close to her, till at last she stepped
Away in her own good time.

Many men
Have searched all over Tuscany and never found
What I found there, the heart of the light
Itself shelled and leaved, balancing
On filaments themselves falling. The secret
Of this journey is to let the wind
Blow its dust all over your body,
To let it go on blowing, to step lightly, lightly
All the way through your ruins, and not to lose
Any sleep over the dead, who surely
Will bury their own, don't worry.

🔥 🔥 🔥

# MAKING A FIST

by NAOMI SHIHAB NYE

from ON THE EDGE OF THE SKY (Iguana Press)

*nominated by William Stafford*

*"We forget that we are all dead men conversing with dead men."*
Jorge Luis Borges

For the first time, on the road north of Tampico,
I felt the life sliding out of me,
a drum in the desert, harder and harder to hear.
I was seven, I lay in the car
watching palm trees swirl a sickening pattern past the glass.
My stomach was a melon split wide inside my skin.

"How do you know if you are going to die?"
I begged my mother.
We had been traveling for days.
With strange confidence she answered,
"When you can no longer make a fist."

Years later I smile to think of that journey,
the borders we must cross separately,
stamped with our unanswerable woes.
I who did not die, who am still living,
still lying in the backseat behind all my questions,
clenching and opening one small hand.

461

# THE BODY

## by MARCIA SOUTHWICK

from THE AMERICAN POETRY REVIEW

*nominated by Pamela Stewart and David St. John*

In my future, there are ashes that control me.
And yet I go on troubling the grass with my footsteps.
I am reminded that this is a *place,*
and that my body will never learn to speak
the pale language of the sun.
I am reminded that the light of each day
will not pass through my personal history
to clarify the events that have changed me.
The night is obligatory,
and there is no point in trying to investigate its origin
in order to alter the state of things.
Outside, the blackbirds will always peck at the seeds
on the tough brown lawns,
or disappear, without worry, into the sky,
which makes me think that the sky must be pure
as a future without sins,
and that one day I would like to go there too,
and be clear and shapeless, without belongings,
because I have had enough of my body
that surrounds me with its blood, hair, and teeth.
I have had enough of this autumn,
which is destined to fail,

as if the leaves contain within them the instructions
for falling, or as if they will whirl into next month,
unamazed at the new season.
If it weren't for me,
the coming night would be a chemistry of perfect shadows.
And as I walk into the open field,
I feel that the shy grass doesn't understand
what it is like to be of solid weight and mass,
to take up space, and to shiver in the cold.

🔥 🔥 🔥

# NOTES ON
# MRS. SLAUGHTER

fiction by RICHARD BURGIN

from MISSISSIPPI REVIEW

*nominated by* MISSISSIPPI REVIEW, *Walter Abish and Anne Tyler*

I'M LIVING WITH MRS. SLAUGHTER in her apartment in Cambridge. She's not a bad housekeeper and now that the Mafia is beginning to leave her alone, she's regained her skill in cooking. Really I can't fault her at all. She doesn't even demand that I work, for example. Money is the farthest thing from her mind. For weeks I lived here without doing a thing, but then I began to feel guilty —I went out and got a job in the library stacking and sorting books. In the early states of this situation I occasionally took walks (although Mrs. Slaughter hated to be left alone) even on the worst days of winter.

I don't wish to rhapsodize unnecessarily about them but these were walks like no others I had ever taken. When you have no direction or specific conclusion in mind your walk is bound to be different. The colors, for instance, you take more note of them. You see that the snow isn't just white, or even predominantly white. You see all the black and grey there is in it, and you also see the blue. And the trees, even the birch trees have orange in them, as if part of them is always on fire. But nothing is so modified for me now as the sky. I would no longer say now that the sky is blue, or the sky is grey. I see too many colors in it that there aren't even words for (for example, what color is the cross between salmon orange, tongue pink, and pebble pink), and so I have stopped talking about the sky.

Of course, if one sense is modified the others change also. For example, the sidewalk began to feel different. Sometimes I had the sensation that I was walking on a river, other times that it was rising over my feet like quicksand. And the buses, the buses seemed to roar past me like tigers.

Once when I went to Harvard Square I began to read a newspaper in front of one of the outdoor magazine stands. Suddenly, I was overwhelmed by the work that went into producing it, the work that was in it. Afraid of bursting into tears, I quickly put it back on the stand.

Maybe there were too many newspapers in Harvard Square. That may be why I started to take the bus out to the suburbs, to Watertown and Newton and Waltham, and do my walking there.

I'll tell you what I saw there once. It was the warmest day of the winter and the snow was melting. A group of very old people, all of them over eighty, were out on their front lawn lining up for a picture. From across the street it was hard to tell how many of them were men, and how many were women. At a certain age the importance of that distinction begins to disappear. One of them, who held the camera, was arguing about how they should pose and soon a yelling match started. Insults were traded back and forth, and even when I inadvertently stopped and stared at them, it seemed to make no difference. No witness could deter them from their fight. Finally, they made a kind of compromise. They lined up in front of an oak tree, and smiling and holding hands, they held their pose, so that the picture was able to be taken. Then all of them began to smile from ear to ear like choir boys. The sun was shining on their white heads lighting them up like crystals. They began fussing over each other and soon they started taking pictures again, as if nothing could stop them, one after another — varying the pose just a little each time, the way an actor takes a screen test.

. . . When I would go to the suburbs I'd naturally come back to the apartment later than when I'd walk around Cambridge. It was during those times that Mrs. Slaughter would really suffer. She'd pace her floor, she'd fill up the bathtub with water only to empty it again, sounds would become amplified, even the air itself seemed to be full of Mafia fingers reaching for her throat.

She couldn't help cross-examining me. She wanted to know where I went on my walks, she wanted to know what I did. When my back was finally to the wall, when she fired one too many questions at me, I'd go to the mantle and take out my pen, and an atmosphere of intense seriousness would suddenly descend.

It was a necessary defense, as well as being convenient. Of course, I couldn't have explained. Silence was the best course, I was sure of it.

So I continued my walks, I continued my rides, soon I began to go all over Massachusetts. Now how can I explain the things that happened? In Marblehead, for instance, as I was walking up and down those sloping roads that lead one away from the water, I stopped to look at a house that was white with dark green shutters and a little petunia garden in front. I looked at the wind blowing the petunias — what can I call those feelings — I've had them before at zoos. I know that real astonishment is our deepest taboo — that even Spinoza would not consider wonder to be one of our emotions.

It was never difficult, after that day in Marblehead, to call up those feelings again. Sometimes it caught me unaware, in the most "incongruous" places. Once it happened in the urinal at the Boston Garden, another time waiting for the train to Park Street, when a man gave me a certain look as he was lighting a cigarette.

Little things, little acts could do it, you see, but still I kept up with my walking, even though it did take a lot out of me.

Now if I ever encountered a woman during my walks it was by pure chance. It would be something that happened to me, rather than something I caused, or even participated in. One of them I met during one of my rare walks through Boston. It was in the Boston Common, as a matter of fact. We met on the bridge, where the boats pass under in the spring and summer. I walked around the park with her for a few hours. She wanted to be something — a singer, a writer — I can't remember exactly what it was.

Probably because I said so little, she assumed that I liked her. She invited me to her apartment, and I followed along dutifully like her dog. I don't remember where she lived. I can't remember that exact location, but I do have a good picture of what her bedroom looked like. In fact, that turned out to be a problem. She was taking her clothes off, she'd gotten down to her bra and panties, and I was still fully dressed and staring at her bureau drawer at the little chips in the thin pink paint. Mistakenly thinking that I wanted her to undress me, she started undoing my belt, but I was already fascinated by the wood on her floor, by its delicate varnish, and its slender cracks.

You see how it was. Finally she lay down on her bed with her legs apart. I watched her cunt for a few seconds, it looked like a miniature violin with a dull finish; to me the bed post proved much more fascinating, there was so much labor in it, so much time in it.

Things were made out of matter but things were also made out of time. Does that sound like a principle? I don't want to convey the impression that I have any. I wasn't trying to prove a thing with my walks, I'm almost positive of that. Supposedly philosophers have stopped asking what things are made of anyway. They want to know how things behave. Behavior is interesting — that's their slogan, apparently directing their lives.

. . . After a week or two of my walks I began to go to some restaurants, simply because as my walks got longer it became necessary to eat. Of course, I can't claim to be a connoisseur of good restaurants. I can't even say that I had a favorite place, but there was one cafeteria near Harvard where I went quite often, because no one noticed anyone else in there, and if I wanted to sit in solitude it was fine, and if I wanted to look at other people I could do that just as easily.

I never saw anything there that made an indelible impression — oh I saw lepers, queens, spastics, impassioned lesbians — but nothing that really left an imprint until I saw this fellow I'll call Mr. Egg. He was very tall, his neck was especially long, and he was thin. He looked as if he'd had a trauma, say in World War II. The remarkable thing about Mr. Egg, who sat in a corner near the water fountain and never dreamed he was attracting anyone's attention, was simply the way he ate his eggs. Or maybe I should say the way he didn't eat them, the way he guarded them. He stared at them reverently as if he were watching twin suns surrounded by a white cloud, then he would bend over them to almost eat them, but at the last moment, he would refrain from touching them, the way a person may stop just short of touching a painting in a museum. How he loved those eggs! And what concentration. He was like a scientist laboring over chemicals, like a worker in a tunnel, or a surgeon studying a heart. Nothing else existed but the eggs on his plate. No other reality was whole for him and he simply couldn't bear to disturb it, he would instead let the eggs grow cold as plastic while he never so much as touched them with his fork.

. . . I don't know why I wrote so much about Mr. Egg. Really, I only saw him there twice. Maybe I want to cling to my picture of him because it was, in a way, the last picture I had before I began to be chased.

I shouldn't say chased, because I was at first simply being followed. As I recall, I left the cafeteria one afternoon after watching Mr. Egg, and I walked a few blocks towards the river, and then I realized that I was being followed — the same steps, the same shadow and sound.

I was surprised that I kept my equilibrium. I didn't even deviate from my course. I didn't, for example, bolt for a bus or else try to hail a taxi. Instead I kept my course straight for the river and my pursuer kept behind me, maybe a half a block behind, stopping to hide behind trees or else a parked car whenever it was necessary.

Quickly I searched myself. I was without any weapons. There was nothing in my pockets but a few small coins. Immediately I wondered why I was going towards the river. Wasn't this just what my pursuer would want? In fact I was sure it was the worst possible thing I could do.

I took a right at the stoplights instead of crossing the street. Nobody was walking on the bridge, but when I looked a second time I saw a little girl leaning over.

Would my change in direction be detected? Would it be discovered that I was walking in a circle? I reminded myself that it was important not to increase my speed. It was necessary to act as if I didn't know I was being followed.

It was very cold out. I hadn't dressed warmly enough — Mrs.

Slaughter had offered me one of her sweaters but I walked out without taking it. The wind picked up. When it blew hard it seemed to go through my neck.

We were like soldiers in a procession, there was always the same distance between us. He is being polite, I thought to myself cynically. Quickly I envisioned a scenario for the pursuer's future actions. Probably it would be weeks, months, before I was taken. There would be phone calls first and no matter what ring I answered on the party on the other end would hang up. There would be perhaps some threats by mail, maybe even a rock through the window, though that seems too barbaric. Maybe this operation would go on only outdoors while I was walking. It would probably consist exclusively of trees and cars and steps and shadows, and nothing so abrasive as a phone would ever be employed.

So the chase by the river never came to pass. Instead I took the bus to Porter Square, as soon as I reached Harvard, and left my pursuer behind. But all the way back to the apartment I wondered if he knew where I lived, if that information was already his property.

. . . Once in the apartment again, it wasn't long before I confessed everything that had happened to Mrs. Slaughter. This surprised me because I didn't think I would ever confide in her. Of course she had her own theory about what had happened. She was sure the Mafia had spotted me and had assigned a man to tail me. I didn't say anything to that. I never paid much attention to her anxieties about them, but in this case, while not accepting her explanation, I was willing to follow some basic rules to protect myself.

For one thing, we agreed to stay inside as long as our food held out. In light of this it was also necessary to keep the door and all windows locked, and to keep all the blinds down. Finally we decided to stay close to each other while we figured out what to do. The argument, such as it was, came down to this: either my pursuer didn't know where we lived and had no way of finding out (in which case we were safe for now), or else he knew, in which case it would do little good to leave town. It was hard, of course, to determine just what he did know. Since we had to stay in the house there was little chance for any real scouting of our own. The only thing we could do was to peek periodically through a few inches of curtain at the street or at the alley in back, and these watches never produced a result.

The other thing Mrs. Slaughter asked of me was to stay in the same room with her all night, since I had developed the habit of pacing the floor at night and sometimes ended up sleeping on the living room couch. But as to what we did then, could one actually call it sleeping? We lay rigid and cold under the sheet with our eyes open like mummies.

Maybe one of us would get twenty minutes or so of sleep on occasion, but then the other one of us felt a special obligation to keep guard. Worst of all, perhaps, we hardly talked at all. Whether from fear of embarrassment I don't know, but we confined ourselves to abortive speculations about what we could do.

The apartment was like a dark aquarium now. In the daytime we moved by each other with our mouths closed like fish. If we opened our mouths it was to suck air rather than to talk. Even the feel of the skin on my body began to drop away from me, as I began to feel more like a fish.

Of course a fish still has a clock in its blood, they know when to swim south, for example, but I had lost the clock too. Consequently, I did everything on impulse. I circulated around and around the house like a fish in an aquarium. Sometimes there would be an obstacle to go around but then I began to master the obstacles. In time I became familiar with every inch of my environment and I kept moving through it, varying only slightly the pattern of my passage each time, and also passing through with a perfect equilibrium — with exactly the same amount of tension, that remained as constant as the fixed temperature in a pool.

. . . At night, the darkness in the house doubled. We would take our food from the cabinets in the pantry because everything in the refrigerator, all the fruits and fresh vegetables, were rotten by then, and we had already run out of meats. We were eating out of cans exclusively. Unfortunately there was no milk or fruit juices. We had to eat dry cereal straight from the box, Cheerios and Sugar Pops without milk, and corn flakes. For our main meals we had tomato soup or ravioli, or canned pineapple, or tuna fish. We had no bread, only a half box of Triscuits.

After dinner we would light two candles and place them on the floor in the middle of the living room. Then we would lay down the game board of Chinese Checkers or Parcheesi on a table and try to get through a game. Not only was it hard to finish our games because we had other things on our mind, but by evening we'd already played each of the games for about an hour in the daytime. There was nothing else to do, you see. Mrs. Slaughter didn't want to play any music. To us, the record player was like a coral reef that cut into our space. It was a kind of intruder.

Once, after we finished our game, we began in a serious way, in quiet measured voices, to account for the time that had passed between my discovery of the pursuer and our present discussion. How much calendar time, for example, had gone by? What had we done in those moments or what were we in those moments we were in? It was like investigating the history of a fish, like compiling the biographies of two fish in two different aquariums. In the aquarium there are no traces. A dog may leave tracks but fish never do. The water is always still, there is never a sign of motion.

No, we had to give it up, it was too much for us. We began instead to discuss our pursuer. When we talked about him he became more astonishing, more real. One could not even say we had any emotions one way or the other towards him, though it would be wrong to say we regarded him as merely a force. But as soon as we got some insights into the pursuer, we ceased talking about him, simply because we could not talk about him without referring to our safety, and the topic of safety was essentially beyond discussion. It was a double-headed monster — for to talk about safety was to talk about danger and we hardly needed to talk about that. It's true, we could make a run for it but we had no place to run to, no money to go anywhere with, and then we didn't want, really, to stick our heads out of the house. We were like termites now — we belonged in the house. If we could have we would have started living between the walls.

Besides, what assurance was there that the pursuer wasn't waiting outside in the alley watching the house, wondering if we were in it or not, looking for a sign, a light, wondering what was going on behind the drapes, wondering if anything could be alive in such constant darkness? No, there was no assurance that that wasn't exactly what he wanted, that he wanted nothing more than for us to make a break for it. And he must have realized that we hadn't called in the police. Even if we had wanted to, there was nothing to show them — for the policeman was a man you had to show something to just like the fireman. He wasn't interested in your stories, he wanted evidence he could see with his eyes, he wanted proof. We had received no letters, no threats on paper or on the phone. To us the policeman was becoming ever less substantial than a rainbow — he had the thickness of dew.

. . . I don't know how long the discussion lasted. At the end of it I suggested that we buy a gun. Mrs. Slaughter moved back a few steps from me when I said that so that I could hardly see her face.

. . . We didn't make any decision on the gun then. But don't think the gun left us. It floated over our heads while we circulated through the house. There were signs of it all over the aquarium. And when we ate, while we picked at our corn flakes or ravioli, the gun was beside it on our plates.

Then one afternoon while I was circulating, Mrs. Slaughter signalled to me with her index finger to come into her bedroom. Somewhat mystified and anxious, I obeyed her. When I was in front of her she suddenly opened her bureau drawer and showed me a pistol lying against a green felt cushion, like a strangely shaped jewel.

She felt compelled to explain why she'd concealed it from me, perhaps to keep my confidence in her strong. It hardly mattered that I told her I wasn't interested in her explanations. Nothing could stop her then. She took it as a trial. She said she'd had it for a long time, a good many months before I'd moved in. But it frightened her. She hated to show it to anyone, to admit to anyone that it was there in her room. Now that she'd exposed it, it would be different, she said, and as if to assure me, she cradled it in her arms.

The gun soon began to preoccupy her. She would keep it beside her plate as she ate breakfast in her underclothes. That, and the food on her plate, were the only realities for her now. She scarcely noticed that I existed. Of course, I could understand. For example, Mrs. Slaughter had gotten quite fond of ravioli, but that's how it is when you don't have much food and you stick to the same diet, you start to have love affairs with your food. They are strange affairs too, they are apt to be cruel, but in the end it is real love and there is no mistaking it or pretending otherwise. That's essentially what happened with Mrs. Slaughter and the ravioli. It began with aversion and from there to ambivalence, and there was even a long period where it seemed they were fighting. But underneath the constant bickering a passion was developing that was bound to surface sooner or later — that simply couldn't be denied.

The ravioli soon became like a theatre to her. The actual eating was only part of it. She seemed fascinated by its form and color and would stare at it intensely for long intervals before placing even her fork on one of the pieces. Then she'd smell it, placing her nose just a few inches above her plate, as if she were inhaling the most exquisite of perfumes. Also, she loved to touch it, and would feel several of the pieces from time to time. In a way I felt bad to merely eat my ravioli, and would have gladly given her some of my share, but I realized it would only detract from her theatre. Part of her enjoyment, I realized, lay in watching me consume my portion. In fact, that was the only time, in those days, when she seemed aware of my existence.

But, you see, there wasn't enough food of any kind left to eat more than twice a day, and since we were still determined not to go out to get any more, the gun was, in a manner of speaking, far more important than the food. The gun she could take with her while she took her hour-long bubble baths, and when she wanted to use the toilet she could hold it like a life saver in her hand.

And then at night while we were under the sheets listening for sounds of the pursuer because she had said she'd heard him singing under our window one night, singing softly like a bird or a lunatic, at night the gun lay between us on the bed and she would periodically slip her hands over it and caress it until it seemed to lull her to sleep.

. . . While Mrs. Slaughter was so fascinated with the gun and the ravioli, I was becoming interested in the drapes. The drapes, I realized in a very intimate way, were protecting me and so I felt a sense of indebtedness to them. Also, at the same time, they were allowing me to investigate the situation, to peek through a few inches of the window and look at the snow on the streets, where I thought I might catch a glimpse of the pursuer.

I don't remember how many times I stared at the drapes, as if to discover the secret of their fiber, I do not know either how many times I parted them as if I were parting a woman's lips, just an inch or two to get a view of the outdoors. It is also difficult to know if the repetiton of my actions increased my anxiety or diminished it.

The one thing I feel certain of concerning my relationship to the drapes is that there came a different stage when I realized rather deeply that while the drapes were in one sense protecting me (since they obstructed the pursuer's line of vision into the apartment) at the same time they were calling attention to me, and maybe they were even tipping off the pursuer.

Just as I began to mistrust the drapes, Mrs. Slaughter in time grew skeptical about the gun. First this showed simply in her reluctance to touch it anymore at night, when there was no light on. She was afraid it would go off, she was afraid it was loaded. It wasn't long before she refused to touch it at all, and so left it on the table without moving it, as if it were somehow sacred. When I suggested that she check to see if it were loaded, she grew petrified and then furious with me. Didn't I know that it might explode in her face while she was checking? Did I want her to go blind, did I want her to get scars like some of the other Mafia women? I didn't say anything to that. I was content to let it stay on the table where she'd look at it with an expression of both fear and intense longing.

. . . But soon she stopped watching it so much. We were beginning to play games again on the living room floor. At first we played Backgammon but soon tired of it, and switched to Chinese Checkers. Chinese Checkers, you see, is not a game like Backgammon where you can outwit your opponent and suddenly move ahead at the end of the game with a kind of O. Henry finish. There is no luck in Chinese Checkers because you do not play with dice or cards. Each marble is an image of your mentality. It advances according to your design. The way we played, with each of us playing for three men, it took as long as a good game of chess.

But here there were also some drawbacks. After fifteen or twenty minutes there would be a big tie-up in the middle of the board. A series of blockades had caused it, and now it was difficult to move any of our pieces more than one space at a time. And somtimes we would have to move sideways or backwards, sometimes at angles that didn't advance a piece but would merely permit a different piece in the near future the chance to advance two places. These are called preparatory moves.

. . . Several minutes later the blockades would multiply. We would be quiet and intense. We were laboring over our moves. Then I'd say, "Do you want to continue this tedium?"

She'd shake her head no, and we'd drink some vodka. Then we'd set the marbles spinning, set them free from their places, disrupting the board, and have a good laugh over it. We'd begin instead to play Parcheesi.

Parcheesi is a game played with dice and four pieces. A piece is always vulnerable and can be sent back to its starting point on any place on the board except the safety places. The object is to get all four men home. You can also form blockades in Parcheesi but they can never last for long because the pieces forming the blockade have to get home too. Parcheesi is a game of running and hiding and searching for safety. Above all it is a game of chance and chance lands on you like a thunderbolt. When you play while drinking vodka it is apt to make you laugh until you are hysterical. But when the hysteria wears off, you may have an empty feeling, you may even feel upset or frightened.

. . . And so we abandoned the games. For a while everything was quiet. Then we discovered, or rather we admitted what we had discovered for a long time, that there was no food left.

"This is the end of reality," I said to myself as I went outside in my overcoat. The walk consisted of two blocks to the nearest grocery store and then back. Except for one turn the walk would be in a straight line.

. . . The light outside was brilliant yellow and white. The cold stung me and the light made me dizzy. My mission was to buy milk, cheese, eggs, bread, and of course, ravioli. I walked briskly, like a man who wants to catch a train but is too dignified to run. I hardly allowed myself to think about what I was doing. It was only later, maybe two hours after we ate that I dared to think about what had happened. Mrs. Slaughter was taking another bath and I was alone on the couch. But it wasn't fear I felt then. Suddenly I had a picture of myself walking through the snow with the bag of groceries. It was so beautiful, why hadn't I looked around and seen more of the outdoors?

True, I did get some reward for my daring venture. Mrs. Slaughter lavished a lot of attention on me. She became suddenly very affectionate and kept kissing me on the neck.

Is it any wonder then, that the next morning I went out on another walk?

This time I saw green and white houses on the snow. I saw a car sputtering out of its driveway like an angry little whale. I saw sand spread out on the sidewalks like caviar and little girls walking to school with their green school bags over their shoulder, and the grey oatmeal colored sky where two dark clouds hung like ships about to converge, over them and over all.

I saw a butcher's shop, a dry cleaning store, a liquor store with its orange neon sign. I saw a shopping center with stores as wide as mountains. I saw the procession of people that passed in and out of the stores like fish in the sea. I examined them closely, as if I expected them to be an hallucination. The woman in the black kerchief who had just bought some lamb chops and was heading towards her car as if it might be on fire, I strained to see the color of the mole above her chin, as if it might lend her some more dignity.

It was stunning, humbling, beautiful and humiliating to walk around. I looked at the Star Market—suddenly so sturdy, so much time in it, a somber and compact paradise. I looked at the sky and back at the ground in front of my feet and then back at the sky again. I felt helpless, dizzy, in the moment I was in the Pursuer was gone! . . . I continued to look, first at the telephone wires as thin as necklaces and I tried to imagine how the signals traveled through them. Then I watched the people on the far corner, so unafraid of each other, so trusting as they waited for their bus.

. . . I began to walk up the sidewalk looking into all the store windows as I passed the liquor store, the drug store, and the camera shop. I turned the corner. In the last window a man was throwing a pizza in the air. I looked at my feet, my black shoes as they walked over the snow.

. . . In the next moment I began to succumb to a strange feeling of helplessness. It was hard to know who I was. Nothing can threaten identity like a flight into ecstasy—no matter how brief. It was almost with relief then, though I was still afraid, that I saw him trailing after me again driving a long black car. I turned a corner heading back to Mrs. Slaughter's and the Pursuer followed after me. I couldn't resist turning around to try and catch a glimpse of him, but the driver was wearing dark glasses, and besides he was too far away.

♨ ♨ ♨

# BEING WITH MEN

by LINDA GREGG

from TENDRIL

*nominated by* TENDRIL, *Jack Gilbert, Heather McHugh, and Sharon Olds*

There are things a man does
that damage a woman. Which are not wrong.
Are even grand and solemn occasions.
Cultivations, seizures of Life from Time.
Treasures which will accompany him
years farther on. The wife grows strange,
but one does not comfort her.
It might look like he is guilty of something.

🔥 🔥 🔥

# WHITMAN

by LARRY LEVIS

from HOLY COW! PRESS

*nominated by* HOLY COW! PRESS

*"I say we had best look our times and lands searchingly in the face,
like a physician diagnosing some deep disease."*
—Democratic Vistas

"Look for me under your bootsoles."

On Long Island, they moved my clapboard house
Across a turnpike, then
Named a shopping center after me!

Now that I'm required reading in your high schools,
Teen-agers call me a fool.
Now what I sang
Stops breathing, like the daughter too high on drugs
To come back, in your arms. Her white dress
So hopeful, & beside the point.
And yet

It was only when no one could believe in me
That I began living again—
In the thin whine of Montana fence wire,
In the transparent, cast off garments hung
In the windows of the poorest families,
In the glad music of Charlie Parker.
At times now,

I even come back to watch you
From the eyes of a taciturn boy at Malibu.
Across the counter at the beach concession stand,
I sell you hot dogs, Pepsis, cigarettes—
My blond hair long, greasy, & swept back
In a vain old ducktail, deliciously
Out of style.
And no one notices.

Once, I even came back as myself,
An aging homosexual who ran a Tilt-a-Whirl
At country fairs, a Mardi Gras tattoo on my left shoulder;
And the chilled paint on each gondola
Changing color as it picked up speed, made me smile.
I thought you caught the meaning of my stare:
Still water, merciless
As my laughter.

A Cosmos. One of the roughs.

And Charlie Parker's grave in Kansas City
Covered with weeds.

Leave me alone.
A father who's outlived his only child.

To find me now will cost you everything.

♨ ♨ ♨

# FROM SAND CREEK
# (selections)

by SIMON J. ORTIZ

from RIVER STYX and FROM SAND CREEK (Thunder's Mouth Press)

nominated by RIVER STYX, THUNDER'S MOUTH PRESS and Ellen Ferber

## Introduction

*November 29, 1864: On that cold dawn, about 600 Southern Cheyenne and Arapaho People, two-thirds of them women and children, were camped on a bend of Sand Creek in southeastern Colorado. The People were at 'peace. This was expressed two months before by Black Kettle, one of the principal elders of the Cheyennes, in Denver to Governor John Evans and Colonel John M. Chivington, head of the Colorado Volunteers: "I want you to give all these chiefs of the soldiers here to understand that we are for peace, and that we have made peace, that we may not be mistaken for enemies." The reverend Colonel Chivington and his Volunteers and Fort Lyon troops, numbering more than 700 heavily armed men, slaughtered 105 women and children and 28 men.*

*A U.S. flag presented by President Lincoln in 1863 to Black Kettle in Washington, D.C. flew from a pole above the elder's lodge on that grey dawn. The People had been assured they would be protected by the flag. By mid-1865, the Cheyenne and Arapaho People had been driven out of Colorado Territory.*

*There was a trip we took once, and we all hid from the street's eyes and townspeople; you wouldn't believe we were this nation's children.*

Toby is sick.

      Closely,
he looks after his shadow.

      Yes,
he is Indian.
He hides and tends
the shape of his face.
In the mirror
of Red & Bill's Cafe.
In La Junta.

He is impossible
to talk with then.
His frozen tongue
is frantic
      with prayer;
he wants to trust.

VA doctors tell him
not to worry.
That's his problem.

      His cough
is not the final blow,
but the glass wall
stares so closely.
Makes him afraid.

      Closely,
Toby tends his shadow.

\*    \*    \*

In 1969
xxxx Coloradoans
were killed in Vietnam.

In 1978
xxxx Coloradoans
were killed on the highways.

In 1864, there were no Indians killed.

Remember My Lai.

In fifty years,
nobody knew
what happened.

It wasn't only the Senators.

Remember Sand Creek.

*   *   *

They must have known.

          Surely,
they must have.

       Black Kettle
met them at the open door
of the plains.

        He swept his hand
all about them.
The vista of the mountains
was at his shoulder.
         The rivers
run from the sky.
        Stone soothes
every ache.
      Dirt feeds us.
Spirit is nutrition.

      Like a soul, the land
was open to them, like a child's heart.

There was no paradise,
but it would have gently and willingly
and longingly given them food and air
and substance for every comfort.
If they had only acknowledged
even their smallest conceit.

*   *   *

Sky is panned
concave,
the eyeballs
             blanch.
Memory
is shriven
clean
as Kansas stateline.
We approached
             winter.

Memory
is stone, very quiet,
like this,
a moment clenched tightly
as knuckles
around gunstock
around steering wheel.

                    *   *   *

Many of them
build their sod houses
without windows.
Without madness.

But fierce, o
with a just determination.

Consulting axioms
and the dream called America.

Cotton Mather was no fool.

A few remembered
Andrew Jackson,
knew who he was,
ruminating, savoring
fresh Indian blood.

Style is a matter
of preference,
performance,

judgement yearning
to be settled quickly.

The axiom
would be the glory of America
at last.
        no wastelands,
        no forgiveness.

The child would be sublime.

                        *    *    *

O Whitman
spoke for them,
of course,
            but he died.

That shed their sorrow
and shame
and cultured their anxiety.
They spoke an eloquent arrogance
by which they thought
they would be freed.
In their theaters,
in their factories,
in their wars.

            They wasted
their sons and uncles
as they came westward,
sullenly insisting
that perhaps, O Whitman,
O Whitman, he was wrong
and had mis-read the goal
of mankind.

            And Whitman
who thought they were his own—
did he sorrow?
did he laugh?
Did he, did he.

                        *    *    *

In the Dayroom,
the Oklahoma Boy sits
sunken into the arms
of a wooden and leather couch
that has become his body.
The structure of his life
an the swirl of his mind
have become lead.

There is beauty
in his American face,
but the dread implanted
by the explosive
in Asia denies it.
The life he now matters by
is pushed away without pity
by the janitors broom
which strikes his shoes.
Only the corners
of his eyes and the edge
of his shoe know the quality
of the couch he has become.

It is the life he has submerged
into, a dream needing a name.
He has become the American,
vengeful and a wasteland
of fortunes, for now.

\*     \*     \*

There should be
moments of true terror
that would make men think
and that would cause women
to grab hold of children,
loving them, and saving them
for the generations
who would enjoy the rain.

        Who are
these farmers,

who are these welders,
who are these scientists,
who are those soldiers
with cold flashing brilliance
and knives.
                    Who struck aside
the sacred dawn
and was not ashamed
before the natural sun and dew?

Artistically,
they splattered blood
along their mad progress;
they claimed the earth
and stole hearts and tongues
from buffalo and men,
the skilled
butchers, aerospace engineers,
physicists they became.
The future should hold them
secret, hidden and profound.

                              *   *   *

The Texan
who takes care of the coffee pot,
who is my vice-president,
is confused by why
I am so mad
with love for these derelicts
who come to us
asking for tobacco, coffee,
shaving cream, shoe laces.

He bludgeons me with his stare.

But I look into his exile eyes,
flaunt my authority,
which he understands,
and I give them what they beg
and apologize for.

Coffee.
Cigarettes.
Shaving cream.
Shoe laces.

I am innocently American afterall,
generous, guileless,
                   but
it is the aboriginal
and the savage that cringes
under his murderous eyes,
and I have to move away
from the invisible gesture
of his hand reaching for my throat.

The derelicts and I
trade poor comfort, receive,
shuffle, and dodge the exile.

\*   \*   \*

Don't fret now.

Songs are useless
to exculpate sorrow.
That's not their intent anyway.

Strive
for significance.
Cull seeds from grass.
Develop another strain of corn.

Whisper for rain.

Don't fret.
Warriors will keep alive in the blood.

# I SING THE BODY

# ELECTRIC

by PHILIP LEVINE

from ANTAEUS

*nominated by Michael Harper and Sharon Olds*


People sit numbly at the counter
waiting for breakfast or service.
Today it's Hartford, Connecticut
more than twenty-five years after
the last death of Wallace Stevens.
I have come in out of the cold
and wind of a Sunday morning
of early March, and I seem to be
crying, but I'm only freezing
and unpeeled. The waitress brings
me hot tea in a cracked cup,
and soon it's all over my paper,
and so she refills it. I read
slowly in *The New York Times*
that poems are dying in Iowa,
Missoula, on the outskirts of Reno,
in the shopping galleries of Houston.
We should all go to the grave
of the unknown poet while the rain
streaks our notebooks or stand
for hours in the freezing winds
off the lost books of our fathers
or at least until we can no longer
hold our pencils. Men keep coming
in and going out, and two of them
recall the great dirty fights

between Willy Pep and Sandy Sadler,
between little white perfection
and death in red plaid trunks.
I want to tell them I saw
the last fight, I rode out
to Yankee Stadium with two deserters
from the French Army of Indochina
and back with a drunken priest
and both ways the whole train
smelled of piss and vomit, but no
one would believe me. Those are
the true legends better left to die.
In my black raincoat I go back
out into the gray morning and dare
the cars on North Indemnity Boulevard
to hit me, but no one wants trouble
at this hour. I have crossed
a continent to bring these citizens
the poems of the snowy mountains,
of the forges of hopelessness,
of the survivors of wars they
never heard of and won't believe.
Nothing is alive in this tunnel
of winds of the end of winter
except the last raging of winter,
the cats peering smugly from the homes
of strangers, and the great stunned sky
slowly settling like a dark cloud
lined only with smaller dark clouds.

# THE LAST STRAW

by PHILIP DACEY

from TAR RIVER POETRY

*nominated by* TAR RIVER POETRY

One minute the camel was standing there,
　　then it was not. I said it was her
straw that did it, she said it was mine.
　　The fact is, if any one
of all those previous straws had been withheld,
　　the camel would not now be dead.
So who can assign responsibility? Better
　　just to say the spine by nature
was defective. I still hear its crack
　　and shudder. I've heard jokes
about the sound, and I've laughed, because
　　they were funny, but unless
you know the experience, you laugh too easily.
　　The camel, as camels go, was a beauty,
less scruffy than most, and we had even begun to admire
　　the hump. It was like a tower
inside which someone noble waits for rescue.
　　If that someone flew
out when the camel fell in a heap before us,
　　I didn't notice.
The mystery to me is why we did it,
　　pile straw like that.
Maybe we thought camels needed a burden,
　　to develop character, or that one
straw plus one straw plus one straw et cetera
　　added up to a good way
to pass the time, our little game. More than
　　likely we did it for no reason

at all, a reflex, a gesture as of the arm
   of a sleeper. What could be the harm,
we must have thought, each piece was so light.
   It's true that now we can see straight
ahead, whereas before we always had to peer
   around, over, or under
that domesticated mass God designed
   not to sink in sand.
Still, I had begun to see patterns, a map
   even, on that skin, when I got up
close enough, though I hadn't figured out where
   North was. And I'll always remember
a look the camel gave me once: those great
   dark eyes wouldn't let
me go until I had translated them into
   this: "I am the master, you
are the beast I prepare for desert-
   duty." I was hurt
into a kind of joy. She, who puts the straws
   on with me, no doubt has
a different camel-story to tell than mine.
   Every day now I see it shine
ahead of me, an oasis of witness,
   the sum of her days,
and watch it, as I approach, disappear
   into the burning air.

🔥 🔥 🔥

# BLESSINGS IN DISGUISE: CROSS-DRESSING AS RE-DRESSING FOR FEMALE MODERNISTS

by SUSAN GUBAR

from THE MASSACHUSETTS REVIEW

*nominated by* THE MASSACHUSETTS REVIEW

> The woman shall not wear that which pertaineth unto a man, neither shall a man put on a woman's garment: for all that do so are abomination unto the Lord thy God.— *Deuteronomy 22:5*

>         Poor mixed rags
> Forsooth we're made of, like those other dolls
> That lean with pretty faces into fairs.
> It seems as if I had a man in me,
> Despising such a woman.
>         —Elizabeth Barrett Browning,
>         *Aurora Leigh, VII*

It was while teaching in Indiana's Women's Prison that I became aware of the truth embedded in so many of Isak Dinesen's stories, specifically her conviction that, while men can and should find in their trials a blessing in disguise, women must make disguise itself a blessing.[1] When I went to the prison for the first time, to teach an English course,[2] I faced an audience ostensibly composed of country and western singers, cover girls, streetwise pimps and lanky cowboys. In spite of their outlandish appearance, as if to confirm the prison as an eerie model of our society's anachronistic system of sex-role socialization, these women had passed through an "Admittance Room" that resembled nothing so much as a Victorian parlor, complete with thin-legged writing desk, mirrors, dainty chairs, and curtained walls. This parlor was consistent with the entire prison structure in which the women were "framed": once they "admitted" belonging in the parlor, the women were photographed, and locked up in prison blocks called "cottages," where they were referred to as "ladies" and written up for such unladylike activities as fighting, cursing or dancing. In this setting how and why had their clothes turned into costumes, and such indecorous costumes as that?

Their pallor and their inactivity, as well as their "rehabilitation," which consisted primarily of cosmetology and laundry, seemed all too reminiscent of the claustrophobic lives of women in the 19th century, just as the elaborate costumes they created with the aid of these feminine crafts recalled the strenuous self-presentation that has obsessed women throughout this century. Not really intending to "pass" for the characters they played, the women in the prison seemed to be involved in an elaborate response to confinement, for their costumes were a survival strategy, even a form of escape: unable to alter their imprisonment, these women transformed themselves; the place stayed the same, but they changed, each of them becoming a succession of different people. The inmates of the Women's Prison in Indianapolis can help us understand how and why costuming has a special place in female consciousness and culture. What the arts of the women prisoners suggest is that clothing plays a crucial symbolic role in the response of women to their confinement within patriarchal structures.

Certainly, at the turn of the century, when the uniform of the lady was undergoing rapid alterations, many women artists were as extravagant in their masquerades as the women inmates: Isadora Duncan posing as a Greek Goddess in the Acropolis and Anaïs Nin dressed up as a caged bird in pasties seem as self-consciously fictionalized as stately plump Gertrude Stein or Radclyffe Hall tempting confusion with Dorian Gray.[3] While male modernists like Hemingway, Yeats, and Eliot were doubtlessly also poseurs, women in the 20th century have had a much greater range of options than men with respect to clothes. In this respect, too, they resemble the elaborately garbed women in the Indianapolis Women's Prison who were taking advantage of the only privilege they have which is denied male prisoners — the right to wear what they please. Just as the women inmates escape confinement by appropriating costumes that define freedom for them, female modernists escaped the strictures of societally-defined femininity by appropriating the costumes they identified with freedom. By the turn of the century, moreover, many identified male clothing with just such a costume of freedom.[4]

Cross-dressing in the modernist period is therefore not only a personal or sexual statement on the part of women; it is also a social and political statement that exploits the rhetoric of costuming to redefine the female self. As in the prison, passing is not the point, although many women did dress to pass in the Paris of the 20's and 30's, as the brilliant photographs of Gyula Brassai illustrate. Among the women artists to be discussed here, however, cross-dressing becomes a way of ad-dressing and re-dressing the inequities of culturally-defined categories of masculinity and femininity. If "man is defined as a human being and woman as a female," as Simone de Beauvoir has argued, "whenever she behaves as a human being she is said to imitate the male."[5] But this means, conversely, that at least one way woman could define herself as human was by determining to imitate man. This is why clothing emerges as a pervasive political issue in the suffrage movement, as well as a persuasive literary image in women's art during the interwar years. Paradoxically the very group who wanted woman to remain feminine might have been responsible for suggesting this strategy to feminists like Alice Stone Blackwell who found themselves constantly reassuring anti-suffragists that "The same fearful prediction, that women would be turned into men, has been made before each successive step of the equal rights movement."[6]

In modernist literature and painting by women, the female cross-dresser figures conspicuously as a heroine of misrule: most simply, this heroine is a woman warrior whose efforts at potency motivate her attempt to prove herself as good as a man; but such presumptuous aspirations can plunge the cross-dresser into a tragic sense of contradiction between her inescapably fallen female flesh and her elegantly and aristocratically masculine attire; sometimes, however, this glamorously Byronic cross-dresser modulates into a being who manages to transcend the dualism of sex-role polarities, calling into question the categories of culture, specifically the category of gender upon which female socialization depends. These three aspects of the cross-dresser — woman warrior, Byronic hero, and androgyne — are what I will trace here. "Inversion" — as the psychologists of the period call it — is most simply an attempt by women to invert the traditional privilege system that lends primacy to men. But inversion goes through a series of displacements, as it is translated into a synonym for per-version and a means of con-version and sub-version.

"What a relief it is to be freed from chignon, extra braids, frizzes, curls, rats, mice, combs, pins, etc., etc."[7] Dr. Mary Walker exclaims in the middle of her chapter on dress in the first of two books she devoted to the political, medical and social situation of American women in the last quarter of the nineteenth-century. Dr. Walker is an important starting point for any consideration of female cross-dressing because, living from 1832 to 1919, she supplies some of the links between this century and the last, even as she points us toward the political origin of this literary subject and strategy for women. In the 1850's, Dr. Walker wore the Bloomer outfit which consisted of a loosely fitted tunic (or coat dress) reaching below the knees over pantaloons. Along with such fellow suffragists and personal acquaintances as Lucy Stone, Susan B. Anthony, and Elizabeth Cady Stanton, Dr. Walker was convinced of the political significance of costuming for women, as her creation of *The Mutual Dress Reform and Equal Rights Association* illustrates.

Like Amelia Bloomer, Mary Walker fought not only for women's right to dress as they please, but also specifically for clothing that would allow freedom of movement, as well as equal distribution of warmth and arrangement so that as little vitality as possible would be expended in carrying it about. In *Hit* (1871) and *Unmasked; or the Science of Immorality* (1878), she argued on hygienic grounds against the dirt of long skirts, the elastics cutting off circulation on the legs, the compression of vital organs by tight-lacing, the fire hazards of large crinolines, the threat to the unborn, and the crippling of feet from small shoes, arguments which had become commonplace in both England and America by this time.[8] But she also reasoned from decency, ridiculing men's notions of modest female dress as the cause of women's vulnerability to sexual attack and abuse. At least one pair of cartoons from *The New York Times* shows Dr. Walker being arrested for an outfit that is far more modest that the hoop-skirt then in vogue. Significantly she even claimed to have invented rape proof underwear that would also discourage (if it could not prevent) seduction.

Harassed by the law and by neighbors, ridiculed by some newspapers for what they euphemistically called her "garmenture of dual form," Dr. Walker was appalled by the weight of unnecessary cloth carried about by the respectable Victorian lady in England and America.[9] She would have agreed with Susan B. Anthony: "I can see no business avocation, in which woman in her present dress *can possibly* earn *equal wages* with men"[10] [emphasis hers]. Dr. Walker believed that fashionable clothing prevented women not only from doing work but from concentrating on it, for women's clothes kept them "unnaturally excited, or in a condition to be easily excited sexually." For this reason,

> While bodies are caged in the petticoat badge of dependence and inferiority, minds and souls are subject to evil, psychologizing wills and cannot command themselves; whereas crowns of strength, joy and sufficiency, with choice of place in the exercise of power await the Unbound Woman.[11]

The issue of work, specifically war work, is what first signals the significance of men's clothing for women. Dr. Walker's trousers were obviously suitable for her medical career during the Civil War, a time which her biographer calls "one of the happiest epochs of her kaleidoscopic career. Rebuffs from top brass did not obviate the fact that she was needed almost anywhere she chose to open her medical case."[12] In *Hit*, Dr. Walker's emphasis on the martial arts of women like Joan of Arc, Margaret of Anjou, Boadicea, and Isabella of Spain matches the taste for danger, exertion and patriotism that won her the only Medal of Honor given to a woman. Actually it is not until the approach of World War I, however, that Walker ostentatiously dressed up in male costumes not just for comfort and dignity, but to appropriate and display conventionally male attainments and status. From the 1890s until her death, Mary Walker dressed herself increasingly in masculine evening dress, in a man's coat and pants, stiff collar and tie, with a tall silk top hat and her Medal of Honor in a prominent position. As elegant as a diplomat's costume or a general's uniform, her outfit had itself clearly become a badge of honor, symbolic of the proud time when she had been traded, "man for man," for a Confederate soldier.

One fashion historian, Lawrence Langner, has argued that men originally devised divided garments to give themselves mobility and undivided skirts to hamper women in their movements, a gender distinction that simultaneously assured the continuity of the race by announcing and guaranteeing that women would be non-combatants.[13] Certainly, like Deborah Sampson in the Revolutionary War, or Emilie Plater, Polish heroine of the 1831 insurrection, or Philis de la Charce, who protected Provence from invasion by the Duc de Savoie in 1692 — all legendary women who dressed as or like men — Dr. Walker was a singular anomoly as a female participant in the Civil War. During World War I, however, a much greater percentage of women worked in the war effort. The Great War furnished a great opportunity to nurse the men at the front and to "man" the coal mines, ammunitions factories, and farm machines at home.[14] It makes perfect sense that the suffragists in England hailed the war, re-dedicating their energies and renaming *The Suffragette* newspaper *Britannia* in 1915, for the war that destroyed so many men supplied women with work and work clothes, as well as the political freedom which both represented.

As if to explain the mystique of adventure and power that associates male clothing so closely with strength born of combat, Anaïs Nin has the heroine of *Ladders to Fire* (1946) explain that the first time a boy hurt her, she went home and dressed in her brother's suit. This "costume of strength" makes her feel arrogant, for "to be a boy meant one did not suffer." Lillian wishes she could find relief from anguish in action:

> "All through the last war as a child I felt: if only they would let me be Joan of Arc. Joan of Arc wore a suit of armor, she sat on a horse, she fought side by side with men. She must have gained their strength."

But all of Lillian's armor lies broken around her. "The mail had melted, and revealed the bruised feminine flesh."[15] A more fantastic and, therefore, more optimistic version of the woman warrior fascinated the most important woman writing science fiction during the interwar period: C. L. Moore published a series of stories from 1934 to 1939 about Jirel of Joiry, a "warrior lady" who is literally "mailed"—both armored and masculinized. A version of *la fille soldat* of folk songs,[16] Jirel of Joiry reminds us that, while such a bid for power is not often allowed women in our culture, it has generally been viewed with a considerable degree of tolerance, when not actually glamorized.

Indeed the attractive figure of the woman warrior reveals that, as Robert Stoller, Deborah Feinbloom, and Natalie Davis have pointed out,[17] the asymmetrical status accorded men and women in our culture is provocatively illuminated by the different attitudes we inherit toward cross-dressing in the two sexes. The goddess Athena, wielding the shield and spear of the male warrior, gains esteem by deriving her identity from her father, as does Ovid's Caenis who chooses to become a man (so as to avoid another rape like that inflicted by Poseidon) and who simultaneously receives the gift of invulnerability that leads her/him to become active in martial pursuits.[18] But when Hercules is dressed as a female and placed before the distaff, he is pathetically weakened, emasculated, because he loses the prerogative and power the male genitals and garb symbolize: authority, primacy, independency, and creativity.

The male cross-dresser is labeled a transvestite, ridiculed as a kind of clown (*Charley's Aunt, Some Like It Hot*), condemned for indulging in irrational anarchistic impulses (*Heart of Midlothian, Bloom in Nighttown*), or judged as a psychopath (*Psycho*), unless he is using his disguise as a con for effecting escape (*Huckleberry Finn*) or for seducing women (Sidney's *Arcadia*). While the male is degraded by imitating a woman, characters like Shakespeare's Rosalind (*As You Like It*) have always delighted male authors and audiences alike, although male actors imitating females obviously had their own reasons for enjoying such roles. Especially after the first wave of feminism in Europe, however, such attractive female characters as Meredith's Bella Mount (*The Ordeal of Richard Feverel*), Hardy's Eustacia Vye and Sue Bridehead (*Return of the Native, Jude the Obscure*), Flaubert's *Madame Bovary*,

Hemingway's Lady Brett Ashley *(The Sun Also Rises)*, and Truf-
feau's "Tomas" *(Jules et Jim)* testify to male fascination with the
female crossdresser, as do the many fans of Sarah Bernhardt, who
played male roles on stage, and Marlene Dietrich, who wore
masculine clothing in a number of popular films.[19]

Clearly such seductive cross-dressers can function as sex symbols for men, reflecting masculine attitudes that range from an
attempt to eroticize (and thereby possess) the independent woman
to only slightly submerged homosexual fantasies. But for women
the inversion of cross-dressing is not always or even primarily
erotic, as we have already seen. Virginia Woolf's inclusion of
photographs of judges, guards, and bishops illustrates in *Three
Guineas* (1938) how male uniforms could become first a symbol
and then simply a strategy for climbing the hierarchical ladder of
sexual stereotyping. From Rosa Bonheur who received authoriza-
tion from the Paris Police to wear male clothing in 1857 to Dorothy
Azner who chose such feminine presences as Lucille Ball and
Merle Oberon for her films in the 1930's, all the while herself
looking directorial and masculine, women have assumed trousers
and ties to facilitate and authenticate their work.[20]

But if cross-dressing implicitly accepts the inevitability of such
stratification, it presents special problems because it simultaneously assumes that, as a female, woman is necessarily condemned
to inferiority. When, for example, Willa Cather spent her youth
dressed in masculine trousers, with her hair cut short, calling
herself "Willie," and proudly displaying herself in a Civil War cap,
she was presumably just a "tom boy," like the Harding girls in *My
Antonia* (1918). For, like her contemporary Dorothy Richardson,
Willa Cather's attraction to male clothes seems well articulated by
the young women in *The Tunnel* (1919): they are exhilarated by the
physical freedom conferred by knickers ("you could knock down a
policeman"), especially by the creative strength knickers seem to
confer (you feel "like a poet though you don't know it"). But
Richardson's heroines are quite sure that they "wouldn't have a
man's — consciousness, for anything."[21] On the other hand, Willa
Cather seems far more aware that male dress could alienate her
from conventionally female roles and activities. Indeed, this complex realization that she dramatized through her clothing in her
youth was profound enough to inform not only the themes but
even the structure of her mature fiction, for she repeatedly cele-

brates maternal characters through the voice of a masculine persona. In *My Antonia*, for example, Cather is both Antonia, the
female Muse, and Jim Burden, the male author, both the natural
world she celebrates and the cultural world that gives her the
language with which to celebrate.

What I am suggesting, then, is that the male narrator is at least
metaphorically a kind of mask worn by the female writer to attain
the trappings of authority. It was, after all, the male pseudonym in
the nineteenth-century that protected the woman artist behind a
masculine public identity. George Eliot, who considered inauthen-
tic women's writing "an absurd exaggeration of the masculine style
like the swaggering gait of a bad actress in male attire,"[22] was
explicitly addressing this dilemma, as were the Bells (the Brontës),
George Egerton (Mary Chavelita Dunne), Michael Field
(Katherine Bradley and Edith Cooper), and Ralph Iron (Olive
Schreiner) implicitly. The woman who associates authorship with
authority and masculinity may feel that in becoming a writer she is
involved in an attempt to disguise herself as a man, whether or not
this is a "vain denial," as Elizabeth Barrett Browning claimed of
George Sand's name.[23] Elaine Showalter has recently shown that
male characters in 19th-century women's novels represent extensions of the female self that had to be disowned as improper or
unfeminine.[24] With more personal freedom in their lives, female
modernists tended to be fairly extreme both in actually playing the
male role and in their reaction against such camouflaging.

When Muriel Rukeyser revised an earlier poem in which she
had portrayed herself as a male god, she condemned her earlier
evasion: "No more masks! No more mythologies!"[25] What her poem
seems to imply is that even male mimicry that presents itself as an
act of assertion can paradoxically, partake of "feminine" self-denial,
even self-hatred, for the male facade or persona may be an attempt
born of shame to deny, hide, or disgrace the female self. This
objection was strenuous enough to yield the title for a popular
anthology of recent women's poetry. But just as influential a group
of modernists accepted the necessity for male masks on female
faces, although such disguises might irreparably filter the timbre
and tone of women's voices.

When we turn to the women painters of the modernist period,
we find two of the most important—Frida Kahlo and Romaine
Brooks—portraying the pain the male costume produces on and in

the female figure. In their different ways, both reveal how—as an erotic strategy—cross-dressing can free the woman from being a sex object for men, even as it expresses the multilation inextricably related to inversion when it is experienced as perversion. For these two artists, the cross-dresser is no longer a woman warrior. Instead she is a self-divided, brooding, Byronic figure who dominates the center of their canvases, hinting at power diminished or fallen. As a Satanic outsider, moreover, this cross-dresser flaunts her perversity so she seems wounded, yet defiant, and glamorous too.

Possibly the most dramatic portrait of the cross-dressed is Kahlo's 1940 "Self-Portrait with Cropped Hair." Against a blood-red background, Kahlo presents herself in a dark suit that is several sizes too big for her, as if she feels unable to fill a man's place. Her delicate hands and feminine heeled shoes look vulnerable and inadequate in this costume. She holds, near her genitals, the scissors that have apparently just been used to cut off her hair, as if to suggest that she has also destroyed herself as a woman. Cropped and seated, she looks like a punished waif. The wisps and tangles of black hair that litter the area around her chair are further evidence that some sort of self-castration has occurred, while they suggest that she is still caught in a maze of pain. Flowing over the chair like tears, these locks also float in mid-space like extra-terrestrial seaweed, the only object existing in her world, but clearly insufficient to tie her to it. The far-flung hairs, no less than the cropped head, make her seem forlorn, as if shorn for sacrifice, not unlike a prisoner of war: she is Rapunzel, forever locked in the tower room now, or a tamed and vanquished Medusa.

Above the seated woman, at the top of the canvas, the words of a popular song appear: "Mira que si te quise, fué pro el pelo,/Ahora que estás pelona, ya no te quiero" (Look, if I loved you, it was for your hair. Now that you are bald, I don't love you any more"). Most simply, the song reflects the biographical background for this self-mutilation, Kahlo's discovery that her husband—Diego Rivera—was having an affair with her best friend.[26] As the writing on the wall which frames her, the song explains her fear that she labored under an illusion when she thought she was loved. As in many of her other paintings, Kahlo's voicelessness (as opposed to her husband's "sentence"), her solitariness, the sterility of the background, and her physical fragility are left to imply how vulnerable and lonely she feels. Again as in her other paintings, however, there is a strong attempt here to exorcise pain through irony.[27] After all, the seated woman has herself produced the man's rejection. Sitting immobile and staring calmly out of the canvas, as if in patient defiance, she says that she does not want the kind of love he is capable of giving. At least the rape of her locks, she seems to imply, will be of her own doing. Refusing to be the object of his admiration, she holds the scissors outward, still open, as if aware of the implied vengeance she could exact against this man who thinks he can walk away from her unscathed.

The figure in Kahlo's painting seems newborn and dangerous, because she knows her own origins. Romaine Brooks' self-portrait is more mysterious about the source of anguish. Yet, while Kahlo's figure denies her female sexuality by dressing as man, Brooks' affirms her ambiguous eroticism through her male clothes. If any single image could call into question the current psychoanalytic argument that there is no such thing as a female transvestite, presumably because women are not genitally excited by their use of clothing, it is Romaine Brooks' self-portrait. Composed in 1923, primarily in her typically dark palette, Brooks' self-portrait displays her wearing a black top hat, black jacket and gray gloves, with an open-necked white shirt. Only the title and a faint redness on the lips give away the gender of this far more androgynous subject, who stands in front of a wasteland composed of crumbling, charred buildings that Brooks' biographer, Meryle Secrest, sees as "the aftermath of a holocaust."[28] The painter's right arm, which is held tightly against her body, and her clenched fist give the impression that she must keep herself together by an act of will. Her shaded eyes have a piercing look, as if she is struggling not to look away from what horrifies her. While, unlike Kahlo's seated figure, she stands up for herself, we sense that she too is caught in the tension between costume and body that reflects some inner self-division. Looking Byronic in her remote melancholy and in her revolt against social conventions, she has turned her back to the world. She is an outsider, marked by her shaded brow like Byron's Cain.

Brooks also resembles Byron's wandering outcast in her seductive glamour. Wan and world-weary, she is exotic and erotic, dashing in her vaguely aristocratic evening clothes. Power and ambiguous sexuality also characterize the other cross-dressers

Romaine Brooks painted, from the boyish "Peter" (1923-24) to "Renata Borgatti" (1919) who sits tensely at the piano, a bent black figure almost like a hawk, shrouded by her cape and as bloodless as all of Brooks' other creations; or "Una, Lady Troubridge" (1924) whose elegant evening clothes and monocle seems as well-bred, if as faintly ludicrous, as the dachshunds who pose with her. Bertha Harris has explained that the international lesbians living in Paris in the 1920's divided the world into two classes: "to be upper class was at its finest to be also gay."[29] Certainly, the aristocratic clothing of Brooks' subject is a sign of their homosexuality. But, for Brooks, homosexuality seems inextricably related to the self-absorption that accompanies the revolt against conventionality: even the most powerful of these figures look lonely, as do the "incomplete beings" of Romaine Brooks' drawings.

Meryle Secrest relates Brooks' obsession with incomplete being to the sense of self created in Brooks when she was dressed in her favored brother's old clothes by a mother who went so far, if we can trust Brooks' unpublished memoirs, as to abandon her. Although Brooks did not especially appreciate the fictional characterization of herself in Radclyffe Hall's *The Well of Loneliness* (1928), Brooks and Hall share this obsession with incomplete being. For both of them, the invert is "grotesque and splendid, like some primitive thing conceived in a turbulent age of transition,"[30] a martyr who is hideously maimed but also a romantic outlaw and rebel. When Hall's heroine in *The Well of Loneliness*, Stephen Gordon realizes she is "flawed in the making," the product of a cruel God, her Bible falls open to "the Lord set a mark upon Cain . . ." (p. 232). Feeling at one and the same time victimized by biological fate and by parents who wanted male children, both Romaine Brooks and Radclyffe Hall identified cross-dressing with lesbianism and lesbianism with physiologically and psychologically masculine traits in women that set them apart as marked.

Known to her friends as John, wearing elegant men's jackets and ties, Radclyffe Hall wrote about the frustration of a girl born to a father who treats his daughter as the son he wanted. Since this is only a slight exaggeration of the psychology of what growing up female can be in patriarchy, it is hardly surprising to find that Hall's analysis of her sense of freakishness repeats itself in the biographies of women whom she would have considered far more normal than herself: Dorothy Richardson, for example, who was called "son" by her father, or Carson McCullers, an inveterate cross-dresser, who considered herself an "invert" because she had been "born a man."[31] Furthermore, like both Richardson and McCullers, Hall's heroine is plagued by doubts over her ability to perform adequately either sexually or artistically: except for a happy interlude—significantly during World War I when she heroically works in The London Ambulance Column—Stephen Gordon feels unable to compete successfully with men for the love of women; "I shall never be a great writer," she further tells herself, "because of my maimed and insufferable body" (p. 246). What Hall implies in *The Well of Loneliness* is that the woman who feels the need to turn herself into a man is haunted by the feeling that, if judged as a man, she is inadequate. If the woman warrior recalls Ovid's story of Caenus, who gained invulnerability to penetration when she was turned into a man, then the Byronic cross-dresser recalls Ovid's Iphis: saved from infanticide by her mother who disguised her in boy's clothes, Iphis longed to wed her intended bride; but she feared "love could never be enjoyed," unless she could be physically changed into a man as well (*Metamorphoses*, X, 229-33).

Radclyffe Hall suffered from bleeding wounds in her hands during the writing of her next book,[32] a symptom that aptly displays her anxiety about writing and her sense of herself as an unjustly persecuted martyr. Certainly, at its most didactic, *The Well of Loneliness* protests against the societally-induced "stigmata of the abnormal—verily the wounds of One nailed to a cross" (p. 280). By fighting prejudice against what she called the "congenital invert," Hall presented her novel as a fictional equivalent of the theories of Havelock Ellis, who was writing the fourth volume of his *Psychology of Sex* (1929) as a plea for understanding how and why women can love one another, a "phenomenon" he traces throughout many different cultures, with special attention to cross-dressers who tried and succeeded in actually passing as men. Not only did Ellis supply the introductory "Commentary" for *The Well of Loneliness;* he advised and helped Hall throughout the legal defense set up after the book was banned in England. Yet he, no less than Hall herself, was confounding lesbianism with what today is called transsexuality. And he, no less than she, implies that the woman born a "congenital invert"—the term alone sounds like an illness— was the helpless victim of a biological tragedy, for "in the inverted woman the masculine traits are part of an organic instinct which she by no means always wishes to accentuate."[33]

Whether or not Ellis actually drove his own wife to "inversion"—that is, to taking female lovers—out of his far less widely published impotence, as one of his biographers suggests,[34] his theory expresses the same sense of biological determinism and freakishness that helped produce the hermaphrodite in Natalie Barney's *The One Who Is Legion* (1930), a "seraphita-seraphitus" figure modelled on Balzac's androgynous hero(ine) *Seraphita* (1835). This same sense of aberration created the atmosphere in which Barney's friend, the poet and cross-dresser Renée Vivien, arranged her anorexic suicide to the dismay of yet another cross-dresser, Colette.[35] It makes sense that Virginia Woolf protested the banning of *The Well of Loneliness*, but even the title might have disturbed her with its equation of female anatomy with tragic destiny. About to write her most feminist criticism, perhaps she would have also been sensitive to the ways in which Hall's and Ellis's notion of inversion actually enforced the sexual stereotypes Woolf sought to evade at least in her most fanciful work, *Orlando* (1928), which was published a few days after the trial and dedicated to her friend, the cross-dresser Vita Sackville-West.[36]

While Orlando's liberation from gender depends on biological, literary and historical transformation bestowed like a gift by the gracious novelist, there is a modernist whose less fanciful analysis of cross-dressing allows us to re-interpret Kahlo dressed in an oversized suit and Brooks' dandies in their inappropriate elegance as clowns. Of course, the elegant masquerades and lavish parties attended by Natalie Barney's guests, including Dolly Wilde who dressed up as her uncle Oscar, indicate how playfully self-conscious lesbian culture continued to be in its perpetuation of the mystique of gaiety throughout the interwar years, regardless of the tragic contradictions explored in some of the art. Isak Dinesen, who actually posed in a Pierrot costume on a number of occasions, suggests in her short fiction that, for all her pain, the invert is in a good situation to di-vert society, for she objectifies the dilemma of all people. In the first of her *Seven Gothic Tales* (1934), "The Deluge of Norderney," one of Dinesen's eccentric spinsters narrates what she presents as a paradigmatic story of growing up female. Her heroine, Calypso, is brought up by Count Seraphina, a man "convinced that no woman was ever allowed to enter heaven" (p. 43). A follower of the strand of Christianity that has surfaced in such texts as the aprocryphal Gospel of Thomas—"For every female who makes herself male will enter the Kingdom of Heaven"—and in such figures as Pope Joan and Saint Pellagia,[37] Count Seraphina recalls again Balzac's *Seraphita*. He also illustrates the link between male homosexuality, theories of androgyny, and misogyny when he dresses his niece up in boy's clothes so as to transform "that drop of blood of the devil himself, a girl, into that sweet object nearest the angels, which was a boy" (p. 43).

This solution becomes inadequate when the girl reaches puberty and consequently becomes invisible to the misogynist men's club of this castle. Resolving to cut off her long hair and to chop off her breasts, Calypso harks back to the mythic Amazons who sliced off their breasts to achieve manly prowess and forward to a character created by Dinesen's most important successor, Carson McCullers. As if acting out Emily Dickinson's call—"Amputate my freckled Bosom!/Make me bearded like a man!" in *Reflections of a Golden Eye* (1941) a rejected woman cuts off the nipples of her breasts with garden shears.[38] Dinesen, however, saves her heroine by supplying Calypso with the unused room of her great-grandmother where she happens on a mirror and an enormous old painting representing three naked nymphs admired for their beauty by the on-gazing satyrs and centaurs. Convinced, by way of comparison with the mirror, of her own physical loveliness, she is paradoxically saved from self-mutilation by yet another image of the effect of the female body on man.

For Dinesen, women's obsession with how they look to men is indistinguishable not only from the fall from paradise, but from the prior fall into gender. Man is born with a memory of the time when he was alone in Eden:

> "But poor Eve found him there, with all his claims upon
> her, the moment she looked into the world. That is the
> grudge that woman has always had against the Creator:
> she feels that she is entitled to have that epoch of
> paradise back for herself" (p. 38).

Having been socialized into asking not "What can I see?" but "How do I look?" (p. 45), women are more deeply enmeshed in costuming and role-playing. Having fallen so much below men from the paradisal nakedness of Eden, women nevertheless gain privileged insight into the duplicities of identity, for the novelist whom Carson McCullers could introduce as Isak Dinesen, the Baroness, Karen Blixen-Fineke, or Tanya[39] authored fictional worlds in which characters even at the very brink of death realize that only " 'By thy mask I shall know thee' " (p. 26). While the women of the nineteenth-century, "living in those tight corsets within which they could just manage to breathe," were a "work of art" (p. 94), Dinesen implies that women of the twentieth-century have liberated themselves not by evading such objectification but by learning how to manipulate costumes so as to become a succession of works of art. Talking of her former self, the artist in "The Dreamers" explains, "Never again will I have my heart and my whole life bound up with one woman, to suffer so much" (p. 345). Dinesen's most highly respected heroines change their identities as easily as they change their clothes. With a number of selves at their disposal, multiple lives to live, such women indulge in the playfulness of impersonation with what seems like Dinesen's complete approval, if only because, within her gothic framework, all faces are finally masks for the skull, all bodies only costumes of the skeleton.

Not a few of Dinesen's characters dream of creating "a being of its own kind, an object of art which was neither boy nor girl!" (p. 43). What they seek is the wisdom of both sexes which led Dinesen to claim that "Moses in trousers could never have brought forth water from a rock." The last two artists I will consider—Gertrude Stein and Djuna Barnes—focus on cross-dressing as just such a dream of prophecy and power. Actually, Gertrude Stein managed to create herself as a "being of its own kind," neither masculine nor feminine. Her inversion is a radical form of con-version, for she seems to transcend not only the limits of gender, but also the confines of humanness. The sculptures of Jacques Lipchitz (1920) and Jo Davidson (1920), as well as the famous photograph by Carl Van Vechten (1934), display Stein looking like a cross between Buddha and the emperor Julius Caesar. Possibly the most expressive illustration of Stein's dramatization of herself as a "being of its own kind," however, is Cecil Beaton's photograph taken at Bilignin Flanked by the seated Alice B. Toklas on her right hand and by the seated Bernard Faÿ on her left, Stein stands serenely in front of what looks like a pagoda or miniature chapel, at the place where the mowed pathways cross, in robes that make her look ministerial as she mediates horizontally between the male and the female, and vertically from the earth upward to the top of the spire and to the sky above.

Earlier in Stein's career, she had exploited the male cover, most covertly in her disguising of herself as Jeff Campbell in "Melanctha"(1909), so as to portray a homosexual relationship in acceptably heterosexual terms. But, in *The Autobiography of Alice B. Toklas* (1933), Stein had overtly adopted feminine Alice's voice in order to portray herself as a "great man." Indeed, Gertrude-masked-as-Alice had first considered writing a book to be entitled "The wives of geniuses I have sat with." It is, of course, because she, Stein, was the genius-husband that she would explain to feminist friends that she did not "mind the cause of women or any other cause but it does not happen to be her business."[40] What *was* her business was fashioning an image of herself through her art: "When this you see remember me," all of her writing insists by virtue of its very eccentricity. But this line, taken from *Four Saints in Three Acts* (1928), implies that the artist is herself a kind of saint testifying to the authority of her experience by speaking in what sounded to many like "tongues." If Stein sometimes used masculine clothing as a clown suit, she always implied that the fool was divine. "Saints talk for me," Stein explained in an earlier piece, "Saints talk to me/ Saints talk with me. Saints talk with saints."[41]

Claiming the right of self-creation with great wit and relish, Stein evaded the gender categories that obsessed so many of her contemporaries. But contempt for the secular classifications of culture also led Stein to create radically innovative art. We can see this as early as *Tender Buttons* (1914), a series of idiosyncratic definitions organized around three subjects: Objects, Food, and Rooms. In fact, as the title illustrates, *Tender Buttons* is (are?) also concerned with clothing, classification, sex, and language: are tender buttons tasty buttons? buttons meant to be tendered? sore buttons? belly buttons? clitoral buttons? Whatever they are, they point to Stein's obsession with the way in which clothing constitutes a sign system that can open or close off meaning.

Consider how many of the objects in the first section are clothes, specifically women's clothes: "Mildred's Umbrella," "A Method of a Cloak," "A Long Dress," "A Red Hat," "A Blue Coat," "A Purse,"

"A Petticoat," "A Waist," "A Handkerchief," "Colored Hats," "A Feather," "Shoes," "A Shawl," and the concluding "This is This Dress, Aider." Most of these common female appurtenances are as mysterious as "A Cloth": "Enough cloth is plenty and more, more is almost enough for that and besides if there is no more spreading is there plenty of room for it. Any occasion shows the best way" (p. 469). The rhetoric of clothing is reduced to non-sense here. But "any occasion shows the best way" also has the ring of some (admittedly mad) fashion magazine blurb. The subsequent sections on Food and Rooms strengthen the possibility that *Tender Buttons* is a daemonic Mrs. Beeton's, a subversive conduct book that copes with traditionally female preoccupations—glamor tips, recipes, interior decorating—in a sybilline manner that ridicules social conventions, even as it defies conventional interpretation. Furnishing her readers with a radically arbitrary set of new meanings for old words, Stein reminds us of the arbitrariness of conventional sign systems.

Published at the very beginning of World War I, *Tender Buttons* sets out to demolish the conventions of nineteenth-century literary realism as systematically as the first World War, in Stein's opinion, "tried to end the nineteenth century."[42] And just as she could characterize the 1914-1918 war as "a nice war," *Tender Buttons* is "nice" in its exuberant certitude that the mimetic, representational function of language and literature could be annihilated. As she explained in her parodic rhetoric *How to Write* (1931), a sentence "Pleases by its sense. This is a fashion in sentences."[43] But, if sense is merely fashion, it is also true that "A sentence is from this time I will make up my mind" (p. 31). Therefore, Stein can be her own and only model, trying on "dress address name" (p. 115) with studied abandon. Supplied with such a resplendently eccentric wardrobe of words, "Think of how everybody follows me" (p. 34). What Stein preaches, then, through exemplification, is that "Grammar is in our power" (p. 73). As a number of critics have suggested, her non-sense functions as a kind of incantation that works to alter consciousness itself."[44] Certainly the operatic sound of this language of her own, so brilliantly perceived by Virgil Thomson, seems to liberate her words from the rigidities of sense. Sometimes what we seem to get in a Stein essay or play are liturgical invocations of the self in praise of what it is in the act of creating, hymns by and about Saint Gertrude, Stein-songs.

If Stein converts the image of the cross-dresser into a kind of icon of herself as a divinity, Djuna Barnes provides what might be called the anatomy of transvestism in *Nightwood* (1936), a novel that focuses on the way in which salvation is possible only through the sub-version preached and practiced by the invert. From baptismal basins described as "loosing their skirts of water in a ragged and flowing hem," to rationalism which "dresses the un-knowable in the garment of the known,"[45] *Nightwood* is a clothing-obsessed book in which we find Dr. O'Connor, who lies in bed wearing a golden semi-circle of a wig with long pendent curls, a man heavily painted with rouge and mascara, and Robin Vote, a girl who habitually dresses as a boy. "What is this love we have for the invert, boy or girl?" (p. 136), the male transvestite asks about the passion the female cross-dresser creates in all who meet her.

Robin Vote is "a tall girl with the body of a boy" (p. 46) whose men's trousers and shoes represent at least initially the physical freedom from feminine constraints that allows her to wander through the streets at night like a libertine, a female Don Juan who enthralls all the women she meets. Robin rejects the dress because it is a symbol in *Nightwood* of feminine vulnerability, specifically women's physical liability of being owned or entered, for the dress—as Mary Walker had warned—allows women to be as easily violated as the "Tuppeny Uprights," prostitutes on London Bridge who for tuppence wait

> "holding their badgered flounces, or standing still, letting you do it, silent and as indifferent as the dead, as if they were thinking of better days, or waiting for something they had been promised when they were little girls; their poor damned dresses hiked up and falling away over the rumps, all gathers and braids, like a Crusader's mount, with all the trappings gone sideways with misery" (p. 130-31).

These "old whore petticoats,"[46] as Sylvia Plath would call them, represent the feminization of women that Robin Vote rejects, much as she rejects motherhood, wifedom, and domesticity.

One of a kind, born and baptized in male garb, Robin is also the invert as pervert, for she is described as sickly, solitary, half-child, half-criminal. Awakened "in a jungle trapped in a drawing room"

(p. 35), Robin is "a beast turning human" (p. 37). Her somnambu-
lism, her inability to remember or fully awaken herself, the fact
that she is lost, with no history and no legitimate place in society,
all of these factors make her seem an emblem of woman as she has
been defined by patriarchy. Sub-human, she aspires to the status
of human being at least in part by dressing as a man. But she is
doomed to fall to the level of the beasts. She is, after all, Robin(g)
Vote: just as her first name illustrates her exclusion from culture,
her last name is at least partially an ironic comment on the limited
potential of the suffrage movement for altering women's fate.

Both Robin and Dr. O'Connor are misfits, neither masculine nor
feminine, belonging nowhere. Like the Jew who longs to be
assimilated, ironically-named Felix, the transvestite is "alone,
apart and single" (p. 10), the object of derision and a marked
scapegoat, as well as the appropriate symbol of a sick, sham society
where everyone feels, as Dr. O'Connor does, as if he "turned up
this time as I shouldn't have been" (p. 91). But the transvestites of
*Nightwood* are also part of a much larger group of characters, all of
whom turn themselves into works of art: the paralyzed man on
display in a box at Coney Island, the "living statues," tattooed
Nikka, Mademoiselle Basquette who looks like a ship's figurehead,
and stitched-together Frau Mann are all living dolls. In Barnes'
world of perpetual circuses and masquerades, the transvestite is
not trying to become or pass for a member of the opposite sex.
Instead, like the minstrel, the dandy, the freak or the clown, the
cross-dresser tends to look like an imitation or artifact — not like a
man, but like a mannikin. As Dr. O'Connor explains, "The last
doll, given to age, is the girl who would have been a boy, or the
boy who should have been a girl" (p. 148).

Used and abused, denied interiority, the perfection of the living
doll nevertheless calls attention to the flawed human being: this is
all a man or woman is, s/he implies, old clothes on a stick. Part of
Robin's allure for her lover, Nora, is that, by turning herself into an
object, she transcends the world of becoming as effectively as the
saint. Perhaps this is one reason why Barnes fictionalizes Natalie
Barney as Saint Musset in the *Ladies Almanack* (1928). In
*Nightwood*, where childbirth only results in death, the invert's
sterility is as precious as the saint's chastity, for both evade the
horror of generativity and successiveness. Taking all punishment,
resembling without containing life, the transvestite-doll becomes a

fetish with magical powers. A remnant of childhood play-acting, the transvestite-doll sustains our trace memories of an androgynous (pregenital?) time when we evaded the trap of gender, or so Dr. O'Connor claims, when he identifies the invert with the romantic character of our childhood dreams:

> "The girl lost, what is she but the Prince found? The Prince on the white horse that we have always been seeking. And the pretty lad who is a girl, what but the prince-princess in point lace—neither one and half the other, the painting on the fan! We love them for that reason. We are impaled in our childhood upon them as they rode through out primers, the sweetest lie of all, now come to be in boy or girl, for in the girl it is the prince, and in the boy it is the girl that makes a prince a prince — and not a man" (p. 136-37).

Yet, by trying to recapture "the living lie of our century" (p. 137), the transvestite only reminds us how far removed we are from the fairy tales of our childhood. Because of this and in direct opposition to the prevailing sanctions of our culture, Barnes actually celebrates the male transvestite in his attempt to tap psychic forces denied or perverted by society. An apostle of darkness, Dr. O'Connor wears a nightgown, the " 'natural raiment of extremity,' " one character explains, because " 'What nation, what religion, what ghost, what dream, has not worn it — infants, angels, priests, the dead; why should not the doctor, in the grave dilemma of his alchemy, wear his dress?' " (p. 80). As a man who would be a prophet, Dr. O'Connor identifies himself with feminine insight and the intuition of the hermaphroditic Tiresias of Dionysus who was also known as "The Physician." A gynecologist, Dr. O'Connor resembles the midwives and shamans of primitive cultures who have traditionally used women's garb, women's medicinal crafts, and even self-castration as a sign of their dedication to female powers.[47] Significantly, Dr. O'Connor calls God "She," because of the "way she made me" (p. 150). Furthermore, there *is* a female god in *Nightwood*: all of the characters are de-voted to Robin Vote who is the votary infusing and epitomizing their lives, for her "flesh . . . will become myth" (p. 37).

Probably the most memorable scene in *Nightwood* is the last vision we have of Robin going down on all fours to play with her lover's dog or to mate with it, a scene curiously ritualized by its being performed in front of an altar of candles and Madonnas, inside the ruined Chapel of Nora's estate. Robin, who represents the night denied by day-time consciousness, is enacting and sanctifying the myth of herself as an invert who recaptures the physical, the bestial, that has been debased by culture. Not only has she rejected a culture shown to be utterly bankrupt; she has herself become Our Lady of the Beasts, for the word "dog" is the word "god" inverted. Robin bows down in a rite of inversion which consecrates the female, not the male, deity. While male modernists like Joyce and Eliot were also fascinated by the heretical power of the woman, they wrote in dread of it. Actually, the crouching, barking woman at the end of Barnes' novel is the "D-o-g" feared as degrading in Circe's whorehouse where Joyce's Bloom-Ulysses is made sensual and effeminate, as well as the Dog Eliot's Tiresias would rather not have exhume the dead corpse in *The Wasteland* (1922), where the Chapel Perilous remains empty. Unlike the grotesque transvestities in modernist literature by men, both of the inverts of *Nightwood* are closely identified with heroic attempts to get back to prehistory. And, interestingly, Berenice Abbott's photographic portrait of Djuna Barnes — reproduced at the front of Louis Kannenstine's *The Art of Djuna Barnes* — presents the artist seated (apparently quite self-consciously) in front of a large clock.

An alternative to historical time, the cross-dressers of *Nightwood* are therefore closely associated with the effort to regain the chaotic, primal forces repressed by the categories of culture. For this reason, both are identified not only with fantasies of childhood, but specifically with the wolf who dresses up as the grandmother in "Little Red Riding Hood,"[48] in part because the wolf is a kind of dog, as Eliot implied in his revision of Webster. Barnes probably would not disagree with Bruno Bettleheim's interpretation of this tale's representation of "the daughter's unconscious wish to be seduced by her father (the wolf)"; nor would she disagree with Erich Fromm's reading of the punishment of the wolf as a "triumph by man-hating women."[49] But what she stresses is the desire of the wolf to be the grandmother, the desire of the girl to make love to her grandmother, and the intimation that the grandmother's love for the little girl is really wolfish in its origin, for she would eat (kill) the girl and eat (savour or love) the girl who is her younger self. By embodying our irrational, secret desires, the cross-dresser for Barnes reflects the savage wildness that can only be hidden, never obliterated, in the forest of the night-wood that is sexuality.

Cross-dressing is, of course, still with us as a symbol in female culture, in spite of the unisex fashions ushered in by the second wave of feminism: in *The Woman Warrior*, for example, Maxine Hong Kingston imagines herself as a swordswoman who actually manages to defend and avenge her people, even as she uses her armor to conceal her pregnancy and protect her baby; Byronic exhilaration in perversity is what lends allure to Patti Smith, the rock 'n roll performer who parodies Mick Jagger, and to the heroines of Jean Stubbs (in "Cousin Lewis") and Ruth Wolff (in *The Abdication*); finally, Iris Murdoch enstates Honor Klein as the androgynous deity of *A Severed Head*, because this philosopher queen wields the Samarai sword as a spiritual exercise and because she has gained savage, forbidden knowledge from commerce with her brother.[50] But all these contemporary artists are elaborating on an image that dominated the imagination of women living between the wars. As a metaphor that flourished when the success of the suffragists paradoxically and tragically marked the temporary destruction of the women's movement, cross-dressing was closely related to lesbianism and expatriation in the art of female modernists. On the one hand a sign of self-division, even self-contempt, on the other an effort at expressing love for other women (and, by extension, for the female self), cross-dressing reflected their anxious sense of transition and uncertainty, even as it demonstrated their remarkably self-conscious experimentation with sexual roleplaying.

One final example, a dream recorded by H.D. during her analysis with Freud in 1933, seems to sum up this uncertainty. She sees herself first dressed in a rose-colored ball-gown and then in male evening dress: "I am not quite comfortable, not quite myself, my trouser-band does not fit very well," she admits; "I realize that I had on, underneath the trousers, my ordinary underclothes, or rather I was wearing the long party-slip that apparently belonged to the ball gown." For H.D. this dream ends on a note of "frustration and bewilderment."[51] But for us this very frustration and bewilderment can be seen as a vital source of women's art, resulting as it does from women's consciousness of their dependence on male-created signs even for the most intimate forms of self-expression. Propelled to discover what would be truly fitting and suitable, as her dance-partner in the dream — Ezra Pound — never had to do, H.D. went on in the next decades to write her great female epics. Her final memoir of Ezra Pound, *End to Torment* (1979), imagines a resolution to their tormented relationship in the appearance of a being, he-her, Seraphitus-Seraphita, who is both their representative and their Divine Child. H.D.'s personal and poetic progress serves to remind us that the women who helped form what we too often consider the exclusively male movement of modernism exploited transvestism only initially to in-vest the traditional forms of patriarchy with authority, for ultimately such artists di-vest conventional forms of legitimacy and, finally, as the etymology of the word transvestite implies, they do this to make a travesty of sexual signs.

A draft of this paper was presented at a conference on Women and Culture at the University of California, Davis, on April 20, 1978 as a companion piece to Sandra M. Gilbert's essay on transvestism as a metaphor in male modernist literature, now in *Critical Inquiry* (Winter, 1980). I am indebted to the insights of Sandra Gilbert throughout, although any inadequacies in the formulation here are my own.

1 Isak Dinesen, "The Deluge at Norderney," *Seven Gothic Tales* (New York: Vintage Books, 1972), p. 24. Subsequent quotations appear parenthetically in the text.

2 Anne Hedin and I taught a Women and Literature course for Indiana University's Department of English at the Women's Prison in Indianapolis in the Fall term, 1977. I am grateful for her generous help in formulating a number of the ideas examined here.

3 See Isadora Duncan, *My Life* (New York: Boni and Liveright, 1927), and Robert Snyder, *Anais Nin Observed* (Chicago: Swallow, 1976), p. 74.

4 For discussions of the appearance of trousers for sports, see Phillis Cunnington and Allan Mansfield, *English Costume for Sports and Outdoor Recreation: From the 16th to the 19th Centuries* (London: Adam & Charles Black, 1969), pp. 225-45. For a discussion of the boyish fashions of the second decade of this century, see C. Willett and Phillis Cunnington, *A Picture Hisory of English Costume* (New York: The Macmillan Company, 1960), p. 140.

5 Simone de Beauvoir, *The Second Sex*, trans. by H. M. Parshley (New York: Bantam, 1961), p. 47.

6 Alice Stone Blackwell, "Making Women into Men, 1893," is reprinted in *The American Sisterhood*, ed. Wendy Martin (New York: Harper & Row, 1972), pp. 108-09.

7 Mary E. Walker, M.D., *Hit* (New York: The American News Company, 1871), p. 69. Jonathan Katz focuses on the relationships between passing women, female transvestism, and dress reform in *Gay American History*, (New York: Thomas Y. Crowell, 1976), p. 243.

8 *Ibid.*, pp. 66-69. See also Helene E. Roberts, "The Exquisite Slave: The Role of Clothes in the Making of the Victorian Woman" and "Dress Reform as Antifeminism: A Response to Helene E. Robert's 'The Exquisite Slave: The Role of Clothes in the Making of the Victorian Woman' " in *Signs* (Spring 1977), 554-79. While one argues that dress reform was a feminist issue, and the other that it was part of anti-suffrage sentiment, both verify the importance of the debate before Walker's formulation of it.

9 Quoted in "Pantsuited Pioneer of Women's Lib, Dr. Mary Walker," by Allison Lockwood in *Smithsonian*, Vol. VII, no. 12 (March 1977), 113-19. "By 1856 a silk dress required 18 to 20 yards of material," writes C. Willett Cunnington, *Feminine Attitudes in the Nineteenth Century* (New York: Haskell House Pub., 1973), p. 163; "when flounces were in style, as they were in the fifties and later, as many as 150 yards of trim" were worn, according to Cynthia Kinnard in "The Women's Movement as Expressed through Dress," Slide Lecture at the Midwest Symposium on the Preservation of Historic Textiles and Costumes, May 17, 1978. I am indebted to the insights of Cynthia Kinnard on the relationship of dress reform to the American suffrage movement.

10 Letter to Gerrit Smith, December 25, 1855, quoted in Robert E. Riegel, "Women's Clothes and Women's Rights," *American Quarterly* 15 (1963), 391.

11 *Unmasked, or The Science of Immortality. To Gentlemen.* By a Woman Physician and Surgeon (Philadelphia: Wm. H. Boyd, 1878), p. 98. This is a quote from a letter written by Mary E. Tillotson of Vineland, N.J. I would like to thank Bernard Horn for making this text available to me.

12 Charles McCool Snyder, *Dr. Mary Walker: The Little Lady in Pants* (New York: Vantage Press, 1962), p. 29.

13 Lawrence Langner, *The Importance of Wearing Clothes* (New York: Hastings House, 1959), pp. 53 and 65.

14 The various ways in which the British suffrage movement dedicated itself to the war effort and found fulfillment in it are documented by Midge Mackenzie, *Shoulder to Shoulder* (New York: Alfred A. Knopf, 1975, pp. 293-317. Women are shown wearing pants both on the front and in the factories.

15 Anais Nin, *Ladders to Fire* in *Cities of the Interior* (Chicago: The Swallow Press, 1974), pp. 37-38.

16 C. L. Moore, *Jirel of Joiry* (New York: Paperback Library, 1969), p. 7. "Jirel Meets Magic" is reprinted in *More Women of Wonder*, ed. Pamela Sargent (New York: Vintage Books, 1976), pp. 3-52. Also see Moore's *Judgement Night* (1943) in which the armored heroine, Juille, fights for her father who had "used to want a son" (New York: Paperback Libray, 1965), p. 6. See my essay on "C. L. Moore and the Conventions of Women's Science Fiction," in *Science Fiction Studies* XX (March 1980), 16-27. Adele Friedman, "Love, Sex and Marriage in French Folk Songs and Popular Imagery," unpublished paper read at a conference on Women, Culture, and Society at the University of California, Davis, on April 20, 1978. According to Tristram Potter Coffin there are "two dozen, British broadside ballads in which a girl, impatient for her lover's return from war or irritated because her parents have pressed her lover to sea, dresses in man's attire and goes in search of him." See *The Female Hero in Folklore and Legend* (New York: Pocket Books, 1978), p. 237. Delores Palomo discusses Margaret Cavendish's plays in terms of female warriors and female sons, i.e., female characters dressed as men who trick not only other characters but the audience as well, in "Margaret Cavendish: Defining the Female Self," in *Women's Studies* special issue on *Women Poets,* (1980) edited by Sandra Gilbert and Susan Gubar.

17 Robert Stoller, *Sex and Gender* (N.Y.: Jason Aronsoh, 1975), 142-58; Deborah Heller Feinbloom, *Transvestites and Transsexuals* (New York: Delta Books, 1976), pp. 10-32; Natalie Davis, *Society and Culture in Early Modern France* (Stanford, Calif.: Stanford University Press, 1975), pp. 124-151.

18 See Ovid, *Metamorphoses*, Book XII, trans. Rolfe Humphries (Bloomington, Indiana: Indiana University Press, 1955). pp. 291 and 299-301. Subsequent citations appear in the text.

19 Photographs of Sarah Bernhardt playing Hamlet, the Duc de Reichstadt and Pelleas appear in Joanna Richardson, *Sarah Bernhardt and Her World* (London: Weidenfeld and Nicholson, 1977), pp. 161, 168, and 179. For a discussion of Marlene Dietrich's exploitation of military uniforms see Alexander Walker, "Marlene Dietrich: At Heart a Gentleman," *Sex in the Movies* (Baltimore, Md.: Pelican Books, 1969), pp. 88-93.

20 Photographs and an interview with Dorothy Azner appear in *Women and the Cinema: A Critical Anthology*, ed. Karyn Kay and Gerald Peary (New York: E. P. Dutton, 1977), pp. 12, 16, and 167. A photograph of Bonheur's "Permission de Travestisement" is reprinted in Karen Peterson and J. J. Wilson, *Women Artists* (New York: Harper Colophon, 1976), p. 77. This permit from the police raises the interesting subject of cross-dressing and the law.

Morton L. Enelow has argued that: "Exhibitionism, voyeurism and transvestism are lumped together by the law and viewed as 'public nuisance offenses' " punishable as acts disturbing or alarming the public. See "Public Nuisance Offences" in *Sexual Behavior and the Law*, ed. Ralph Slovenko (Springfield, Il.: Charles C. Thomas Pub., 1965), p. 278. But a comprehensive history of the law and transvestism apparently still needs to be written. A photograph of Dorothy Sayers, "in a characteristically mannish costume and hat," appears in Janet Hitchman, *Such A Strange Lady* (New York: Avon, 1975), p. 96.

21 Willa Cather, *My Antonia* (Boston: Houghton Mifflin, 1970), pp. 149-50. Dorothy Richardson *The Tunnel* in *Pilgrimage 2* (New York: Popular Library, 1976), pp. 148-49.

22 George Eliot, "Woman in France," *The Essays of George Eliot*, ed. Thomas Pinny (New York: Columbia University Press, 1963), p. 53.

23 Elizabeth Barrett Browning, "To George Sand, A Recognition," in *The World Split Open*, ed. Louis Bernikow (New York: Vintage Books, 1974), p. 113-14.

24 Elaine Showalter in *A Literature of Their Own* (Princeton: Princeton University Press, 1977), pp. 133-52 discusses male characters as extensions of female authors.

25 Muriel Rukeyser, "The Poem as Mask," *No More Masks!: An Anthology of Poems by Women*, ed. Florence Howe and Ellen Bass (New York: Anchor Books, 1973), p. 1.

26 Hayden Herrera, "Frida Kahlo — 'Sacred Monsters,' " *Ms.* (February, 1978), pp. 29-31. Diego Rivera himself describes the pain he inflicted on Kahlo through his infidelities in *My Life, My Art* (New York: The Citadel Press, pp. 225-26 and 284. About himself, he writes: "If I loved a woman, the more I loved her, the more I wanted to hurt her. Frida was only the most obvious victim of this disgusting trait," p. 207-08.

27 Ann Sutherland Harris and Linda Nochlin, *Women Artists 1550-1950* (New York: Knopf, 1977), pp. 335-36. Kahlo underwent some 35 operations resulting from an accident that fractured her spine when she was 15 years old. While both in life and in art, Kahlo usually presented herself in traditionally feminine garb, Bertram D. Wolfe argues that this too was a compensation: "She made up for the accidental crippling of her frail body by turning herself into one of the most effective works of art." See *The Fabulous Life of Diego Rivera* (New York: Stein and Day, 1963), p. 395.

28 Meryle Secrest, *Between Me and Life: A Biography of Romaine Brooks* (London: Macdonald's and Jane's, 1976), pp. 8 and 29-34.

29 Bertha Harris, "The More Profound Nationality of Their Lesbianism: Lesbian Society in the 1920's," *Amazon Expedition: A Lesbian Feminist Anthology*, ed. Phillis Birkby, Bertha Harris, Jill Johnson, Esther Newton, and Jane O'Wyatt (New York: Times Change Press, 1973), p. 79. The identification with aristocratic revolt strengthens the tie with Byron. In this connection, it is worth remembering that Byron himself had a mistress who dressed as a man. See Ethel Colburn Mayne, *Byron* (London: Methuen & Co., 1912), I, pp. 93-94. Byron told Medwin that he used to dress a lover up to pass as his brother Gordon, this at a time when he was also famous for keeping a tame bear for fellowship at Cambridge.

30 Radclyffe Hall, *The Well of Loneliness* (New York: Coucici Friede, 1934), pp. 52-53. Subsequent references appear parenthetically in the text.

31 Showalter, *A Literature of Their Own*, pp. 248-49; Virginia Spencer Carr, *The Lonely Hunter: A Biography of Carson McCullers* (New York: Doubleday & Co., 1975), pp. 159, 167, and 338. Djuna Barnes' portrait of Barney in *The Ladies Almanack* (New York: Harper & Row, 1972), p. 8 explains she had "developed in the Womb of her most gentle Mother to be a Boy," and when she came forth an Inch or so less than this," she had the audacity to explain to her father that she was "more commendable" than the son he desired "seeing that I do it without the tools for the Trade." Susan Sniader Lanser explores Barnes' lesbian humor in "Speaking in Tongues: *Ladies Almanack* and the Language of Celebration," *Frontiers* IV (Fall 1979), pp. 39-46.

32 Jane Rule, *Lesbian Images* (New York: Pocket Books, 1976), p. 60. The stigmata are certainly also related to this novel's Biblical subject.

33 Havelock Ellis, *Sexual Inversion, Studies in the Psychology of Sex*, Vol. IV (Philadelphia: F. A. Davis Co., 1929), p. 222. The trapped soul theory of homosexuality in Ellis, Krafft-Ebbing, and Carpenter is discussed by Barbara Fassler, "Theories of Homosexuality as Sources of Bloomsbury's Anthology," *Signs* V (Winter 1979), pp. 237-51.

34 Arthur Calder-Marshall, *Havelock Ellis* (London: Rupert Hart-Davis, 1969), pp. 138-43 and 180. Not only does Calder-Marshall argue that Edith Ellis felt herself to have been

518 THE MASSACHUSETTS REVIEW

turned into an invert by her husband, he further speculates that she resented being used as a case history and a source of information, as did Olive Schreiner.

35 Renée Vivien, who is also analyzed by Ellis in *Sexual Inversion*, p. 200, is discussed in relation to male masquerading by George Wickes in *The Amazon of Letters* (New York: Popular Library, 1978), p. 71. Background information on Barney and Vivien appears in Jeannette Foster, *Sex Variant Women in Literature* (Baltimore, Md.: Diana Press, 1975), pp. 154-73.

36 Phyllis Rose, *Woman of Letters: A Life of Virginia Woolf* (New York: Oxford University Press, 1978), pp. 192-93. Many historians of lesbianism in this period focus on the difference between *Orlando's* frivolity and the tragic dimensions of *The Well of Loneliness*. See, for example, Dolores Klaich, *Woman + Woman* (New York: Simon and Schuster, 1974), pp. 189 and 199-201. For a discussion of Woolf's love of women, see "Women Alone Stir My Imagination: Lesbianism and the Cultural Tradition," *Signs* IV (Summer 1979), pp. 718-39.

37 The quotation from Jesus to Simon Peter who wants Mary to leave because "women are not worthy of the Life" is quoted and discussed by Carolyn G. Heilbrun, *Toward a Recognition of Androgyny* (New York: Harper Colophon, 1973), p. 20. The story of Saint Pellagia who was "the archetype for the female transvestite saint" is recounted by Vern L. Bullough and Bonnie Bullough, *Sin, Sickness, and Sanity: A History of Sexual Attitudes* (New York: New American Library, 1977), p. 78. For a modern rendition of the Pope Joan legend, see Lawrence Durrell's *Pope Joan*, adapted from the Greek *Papissa Joanna* (1886) by Emmanuel Royidis (New York: Penguin Books, 1974).

38 *The Complete Poems of Emily Dickinson*, ed. Thomas H. Johnson (Boston: Little, Brown, 1960), J. 1737. Carson McCullers, *Reflections in a Golden Eye* (Cambridge, Mass.: Riverside Press, 1941), p. 40. Significantly, McCullers dedicated this book — which is about at least one character who "obtained within himself a delicate balance between the male and female elements" (p. 13) — to Annemarie Clarac-Schwarzenbach, a Swiss writer and cross-dresser with whom she was in love.

39 Carson McCullers, "Isak Dinesen: In Praise of Radiance," *The Mortgaged Heart*, ed. Margareita G. Smith (Boston: Houghton Mifflin, 1971), p. 271.

40 *Selected Writings of Gertrude Stein*, ed. Carl Van Vechten (New York: Vintage, 1962), p. 13. Unless otherwise indicated, all citations refer to this text. See the interview with Berthe Clevrergue (Natalie Berney's housekeeper) where she says of Stein: "She frightened me. She dressed very strangely with long skirts that trailed along the ground and with her short cropped hair. I took her for a man. When I learned that she was a woman, I said: 'That's not true.' " "The Salon of Natalie Clifford Berney: An Interview with Berthe Clevrergue" by Gloria Feman Ornstein, *Signs* (Spring 1979), p. 489. Also see Catherine R. Stimpson, "The Mind, the Body, and Gertrude Stein," *Critical Inquiry* III (Spring 1977), pp. 489-506.

41 Gertrude Stein, "Talks to Saint or Stories of Saint Remy," in *Painted Lace* (New Haven: Yale University Press, 1955), p. 111. I am indebted here to conversations with Tom Boll.

42 Gertrude Stein, *Wars I Have Seen* (London: B. T. Batsford, 1945), p. 48-49.

43 Gertrude Stein, *How to Write* (Paris: Plain Edition, 1931), p. 27. Subsequent page references from this edition appear parenthetically in the text.

44 Several critics have worked with the idea that Stein's language must be viewed as magical or incantatory. Allegra Stewart argues that mystic religiosity lies behind the seemingly trivial in *Gertrude Stein and the Present* (Cambridge, Mass.: Harvard University Press, 1967); Michael Hoffman argues that Stein's "image of herself [as a saint] provides an interesting metaphor with which to interpret so simple and primitive an art of the surface and of the celebration of the ordinary as we find in *Tender Buttons*." See *Gertrude Stein* (Boston: Twayne, 1976), p. 66. Norman Weinstein discusses "word mysticism" in *Gertrude Stein and the Literature of the Modern Consciousness* (New York: Frederick Ungar, 1970), pp. 53-67.

45 Djuna Barnes, *Nightwood* (New York: New Directions, 1961), p. 88. All quotations are parenthetically included in the text. The best critical treatment of this novel appears in Louis F. Kannenstine, *The Art of Djuna Barnes* (New York: New York University Press, 1977), pp. 86-127.

46 Sylvia Plath, "Fever 103," *Ariel* (New York: Harper & Row, 1961), p. 55.

47 Wolfgang Lederer, M.D., *The Fear of Women* (New York: Harcourt Brace Jovanovich,

1968), pp. 144-46. Olive Schreiner also celebrates a man who wears women's clothing in *The Story of an African Farm* (New York: Schocken, 1976).

48 See p. 79 of *Nightwood* where Dr. O'Connor in bed causes Nora to realize that children actually "like Red Riding Hood and the wolf in bed," and p. 63 where Nora dreams of her grandmother (a surrogate for Robin), "dressed as a man, wearing a billycock and a crooked moustache, ridiculous and plump in tight trousers and a red waistcoat, her arms spread saying with a leer of love, 'My little sweetheart!' "

49 Bruno Bettelheim, *The Uses of Enchantment* (New York: Vintage, 1977), pp. 166-83; Erich Fromm, *The Forgotten Language: An Introduction to the Understanding of Dreams, Fairy Tales and Myths* (New York: Rinehart, 1951), p. 241.

50 Maxine Hong Kingston, *The Woman Warrior: Memoirs of a Girlhood Among Ghosts* (New York: Vintage), pp. 42-63; Iris Murdoch, *A Severed Head* (New York: Avon, 1961); Jean Stuggs, "Cousin Lewis," in *Women and Fiction*, ed. Susan Cahill (New York: New American Library, 1975), pp. 269-87; Ruth Wolff, *The Abdication* in *The New Women's Theatre*, ed. Honor Moore (New York: Vintage, 1977), pp. 341-454.

51 H. D., *Tribute to Freud* (New York: McGraw-Hill Book Co., 1974), pp. 80-81.

# CONTRIBUTORS' NOTES

STANISLAW BARANCZAK was born in Poland in 1946 and currently teaches at Harvard. He is the author of two books published by Mr. Cogito Press.

CHARLES BAXTER has published two books of poetry with New Rivers Press and his essays and fiction have appeared in *The Georgia Review, Boundary 2, The Antioch Review,* and elsewhere. "Harmony of the World" received The Lawrence Foundation Prize as the best short story to appear in *The Michigan Quarterly* in 1981.

BARBARA BEDWAY is working on a cycle of stories about Lebanon before and after the civil war. This is her first published story.

STEPHEN BERG is a founding editor of *American Poetry Review.* His books include *Grief* and *With Akhmatova At the Black Gates.*

WENDELL BERRY is the author most recently of *Recollected Essays, The Gift of Good Land* and, in the fall of 1982, *The Wheel,* all from North Point Press.

RICHARD BURGIN is editor of *The New York Arts Journal.*

HAYDEN CARRUTH is an editor with *The Hudson Review,* the author of numerous collections of poetry and a professor at Syracuse University.

CHRISTOPHER CLAUSEN's *The Place of Poetry: Two Centuries of an Art in Crisis* was published in 1981 by The University Press of Kentucky.

PHILIP DACEY's most recent collection was published by John Hopkins University Press.

KATE DANIELS has published in *Ironwood, Massachusetts Review, New England Review* and *Poetry Now.* She is co-editor of *Poetry East.*

GUY DAVENPORT is the author most recently of *The Geography of The Imagination* (North Point) and several other books, including two collections of short stories. In 1981 he was given The Morton Dauwen Zabel Award for fiction by The American Academy and Institute of Arts and Letters.

TERRENCE DES PRES is the author of *The Survivor: An Anatomy of Life In The Death Camps.* His book on poetry and politics is forthcoming from Viking Press.

RITA DOVE has published chapbooks with Penumbra Press, Porch's Inland Boat Series, *The Ohio Review* and Carnegie-Mellon University Press. She received a National Endowment for the Arts grant and served as Pittman Fellow at Tuskegee Institute.

CAROLYN FORCHÉ is a winner of The Lamont poetry award. Her most recent collection of poetry has just been published by Harper and Row.

WILLIAM GILSON lives in Cambridge, Massachusetts. The Wickwire Press will publish his chapbook, *Old Poems*.

JORIE GRAHAM's poems have appeared in *Ironwood, Antaeus, The Paris Review* and elsewhere. She lives in Arcata, California.

MATTHEW GRAHAM was a member of The New York Collective in the mid-sixties. He now lives in Baltimore.

LINDA GREGG's first book of poems *Too Bright to See* was published last year by Greywolf Press.

SUSAN GUBAR teaches at Indiana University.

THOM GUNN's publications include *Selected Poems* (1979), *The Passages of Joy* (1982) and *Occasions of Poetry* (1982). He lives in California.

MICHAEL HARPER is the author of seven volumes of poetry and teaches at Brown University.

JOHN HOLLANDER teaches English at Yale University.

DAVID IGNATOW, the author of eleven books of poetry, is the winner of The Bolligen Prize, a Wallace Stevens Fellowship and The Shelley Memorial Award.

ELIZABETH INNESS-BROWN's collection of stories, *Satin Palms*, was published by *Fictional International* in 1981. She teaches at The University of Southern Mississippi in Hattiesburg.

J. GERALD KENNEDY directs graduate studies in English at Louisiana State University and is the author of *The Astonished Traveller*, a biography of William Darby.

STANLEY KUNITZ's most recent collection, *Collected Poems of Stanley Kunitz 1928-1978*, was awarded The Lenore Marshall Prize by *The Saturday Review of Literature*.

PHILIP LEVINE's most recent book is *One For The Rose*.

LARRY LEVIS won The Lamont Poetry award in 1976 and teaches at the University of Missouri.

FRED LICHT teaches Art History at Boston University.

JOYCE CAROL OATES is the author most recently of *Invisible Woman: New and Selected Poems 1970-82* (Ontario Review Press) and *A Bloodsmoor Romance* (Dutton). She teaches at Princeton.

SHARON OLDS lives in New York and is the author of the collection, *Satan Says*, published by The University of Pittsburgh Press.

MARY OLIVER's fifth book of poems, *American Primitive*, will be published by Atlantic-Little Brown. She lives in Provincetown, Massachusetts.

SIMON J. ORTIZ is a 1982 NEA Fellowship winner and the author of several books.

CYNTHIA OZICK is the author of the novel *Trust* and three short story collections.

AMOS OZ's most recent story collection was *Where The Jackals Howl*. He lives on Kibbutz Hulda in Israel.

LINDA PASTAN's forthcoming book, *PM/AM: New and Selected Poems*, will be published by Norton.

JAYNE ANNE PHILLIPS is the author of *Sweethearts* (Truck Press), *Counting* (Vehicle Editions) and *Black Tickets* (Seymour Lawrence), which won the Sue Kaufman Prize for First Fiction in 1980.

RICHARD POIRIER holds the Marius Bewley Chair in English and American Literature at Rutgers University and is the author, most recently, of *Robert Frost: The Work of Knowing*.

KATHA POLLITT has published poetry in *The New Yorker, Nation, Paris Review* and elsewhere. She lives in New York.

MARY ROBISON is the author of *Days*, a short story collection, and *OH!*, a novel, both published by Knopf.

LEO ROMERO teaches in the Poetry in The Schools program in New Mexico and is completing work on an M.A. at New Mexico State University. He also exhibits his etchings and lithographs at art shows in the Southwest.

WILLIAM PITT ROOT has published poetry collections with Atheneum, 4 Zoas, Moving Parts, and Full Court. He lives in Arizona.

RICHARD SELZER is on the faculty of The Yale Medical School and is the author of three books about his profession of surgery.

NAOMI SHIHAB NYE is the author of two poetry collections, *Different Ways to Pray* (Breitenbush Books) and *Hugging the Jukebox* (E. P. Dutton). She lives in San Antonio, Texas.

STEPHEN SHU NING LIU was born in China and now lives in Nevada. His poems have appeared in many magazines and a book of poems, *Dream Journeys To China*, has just been published in China.

GARY SOTO is the author of three poetry collections and has been awarded the Discovery-The Nation Prize, The Bess Hokin Prize from *Poetry*, a Guggenheim Fellowship and a grant from The National Endowment for the Arts. He teaches in the department of Chicano Studies and English at the University of California, Berkeley.

MARCIA SOUTHWICK is a visiting lecturer at The University of Iowa Writer's Workshop. Her poetry collections have been published by The University of Georgia Press, and Pym-Randall Press. She is co-editor of an anthology of women writers to be published by *The Iowa Review* and Macmillan.

MARY TALL MOUNTAIN is a member of the Koyukons, Indians of the Alaskan Athabaskans. She currently lives in San Francisco and is working on an Athabaskan novel.

ELIZABETH THOMAS teaches at The University of Alabama and is poetry editor of *The Black Warrior Review*.

BARBARA THOMPSON's "Tattoo" is one of a group of stories she is writing about foreigners—especially foreign wives—in Pakistan. She has also done interviews for *The Paris Review*'s Writers At Work Series.

EDMUND WHITE is the author of two novels, *Forgetting Elena* and *Nocturnes for the King of Naples*. "A Man of the World" is, in a different form, a chapter from his third novel, *A Boy's Own Story*, to be published by Dutton.

CHARLES WRIGHT is the author of five books of poems, most recently *The Southern Cross*. He lives in Laguna Beach, California.

JAMES WRIGHT won the Pulitzer Prize in 1972. His poetry appeared in *Pushcart Prize V* shortly after his death in 1980.

PAUL ZIMMER has published five books of poetry with Dryad Press, one with Slow Loris Press, and is currently the director of the University of Georgia Press.

DEREK WALCOTT was born in St. Lucia and now lives in Trinidad and Boston. He is an honorary member of the American Academy and Institute of Arts and Letters.

C. K. WILLIAMS is the author of *Lies, I Am The Bitter Name* and *With Ignorance*. He lives in Brooklyn, New York.

# OUTSTANDING WRITERS

(The editors also wish to mention the following important works published by small presses last year. Listing is alphabetical by author's last name.)

## FICTION

Mariana — Ines Arredondo (Fiction)
Bodily Harm — Margaret Atwood (Paris Review)
Jogger's Reef — Will Baker (CoEvolution Quarterly)
Walkie-Talkie — John Balaban (New England Review)
Politics — Russell Banks (Shenandoah)
Smoke — Djuna Barnes (Sun & Moon)
Unabstract Pictures From Border Guards — Jonetta Barras-Abney (Black Scholar)
Magic Castle — Frederick Barthelme (Fiction)
Angel's Laundromat — Lucia Berlin (Turtle Island)
Spiller and Leakey — Beverly Brown (Chicago Review)
Paris Visitation — Michael Brownstein (Rocky Ledge Cottage Editions)
Angels — Fred Bruning (Intro)
On the Emperor's Birthday — Jerry Bumpus (Carpenter Press)
Shame — Jerry Bumpus (Epoch)
Wide Open — Jerry Bumpus (Vagabond Press)
Lieberman's Father — Francois Camion (Missouri Review)
Childhood — Janine Canan (Conditions 7)
excerpt from *Twisted Kicks* — Tom Carson (Entwhistle Books)
Why Don't You Dance — Raymond Carver (Paris Review)
The King of Pango Pango — Carl Clatterbuck (North American Review)
Points of Origin: Where My Mind Comes From — Arthur Cohen (Fiction)

524

Smithsonian Depositions — Clark Coolidge (Vehicle Editions)

Confessions of a Solipsist — Denis Corish (Kenyon Review)

Work — Doug Crowell (Crazyhorse)

Good Skin — Michael Cunningham (Shankpainter)

Green Thumb — Jack Curtis (Capra Press)

Said — Stephen Dixon (Boundary 2)

The Doctor of The Moon — Harriet Doerr (Ark River Review)

Ul'Lyu, Ooo Ooo Ooo — John Domini (Ploughshares)

Widow — Pam Durban (The Reaper)

Bijou — Stuart Dybek (Ploughshares)

Household — Susan Engberg (Ploughshares)

The Creator of One Fingered Lily — David Evanier (Chelsea)

Bruno The Carver — William Ferguson (Calliope)

Dancing Ducks and Talking Anus — James Ferry (The Literary Review)

Lovers of Today — Maria Flook (Northwest Review)

Stenburg's Refrain — Edward Fortner (Antioch Review)

A Disturbance of Gulls — H. E. Francis (Missouri Review)

Sable's Mother — Pat Therese Francis (North American Review)

Through The Walls — Pat Therese Francis (Kansas Quarterly)

Notes From The Bloodwell — Thaisa Frank (North American Review)

Dad and The Kids, 1989 — Bill Franzen (The New Satirist)

Like Dragons — Catherine Gammon (Shankpainter)

Night Vision — Catherine Gammon (Missouri Review)

Revenge — Ellen Gilchrist (Prairie Schooner)

Pie Dance — Molly Giles (North American Review)

Everything That Has Been Shall Be Again — John Gilgun (Bieler Press)

Heart Failure — Ivy Goodman (Ark River Review)

White Boy — Ivy Goodman (Ploughshares)

Possession — DeWitt Henry (Ploughshares)

Sophie — Linda Hogan (Conditions 7)

1968: The Fifth Day Robert Kennedy Is Shot — James Houston (Quilt)

Save One for Mainz — David Huddle (Mid-American Review)

American Dad — Tama Janowitz (Paris Review)

My Poor Prisoner — Roberta Kalechofsky (Micah Publications)

They Tore Down The Polo Grounds in 1964 — W. P. Kinsella (Descant)

My Last Drugstore — Michael Knoll (Antaeus)

Son — Claude Koch (Four Quarters)

The Kleber Avenue Communion — Hans Koning (Paris Review)

Four Circular Stories — Richard Kostelanetz (North American Review)

Eagle — David Kranes (Red Earth Press)

I, The Realtor, Spy — Peter La Salle (Kansas Quarterly)

Imagination — Gordon Lish (Antioch Review)

The Man Who Had Maps — Barry Lopez (North American Review)

The Girl With The Scar — Arnost Lustig (TriQuarterly)

The Visitor's Blue Movie — Ian Macmillan (Hawaii Review)

Etheleen's Collection — Bobbie Ann Mason (Epoch)

Likerish — Dennis Mathis (Ploughshares)

Lovely Things That Should Not Pass Away — Jack Matthews (Georgia Review)

Why Billy Jordan Crashed and Burned — Walter McDonald (Clarity)

The Unknown Kid — Joseph McElroy (TriQuarterly)

The New Automaton Theater — Steven Millhauser (Canto)

Crossing — Kent Nelson (Sewanee Review)

The 7th Room — Jay Neugeboren (Rendezvous)

A Wild Lens — Catherine Petroski (Fiction International)

Mister Mercury — Robert Phillips (New Letters)

Coyote Goes Upriver — Jarold Ramsey (Georgia Review)

The Brute — Roger Rath (Green Mountain Review)

Drifting Out — Mary Elsie Robertson (New England Review)

Tea Party — Sarah Rossiter (Ontario Review)

Garden In Twilight — Yoshiko Shibaki (Western Humanities Review)

The Smoke In The Mountain Valley — Yoshiko Shigekane (Mississippi Review)

Oral History — Lee Smith (Carolina Quarterly)

The General — Mark Strand (Antaeus)

Sophistications — Danielle Swanson (Ploughshares)

Above The Bay — Barry Targan (Southwest Review)

Jesse James Betrayed — Robert Taylor, Jr. (Quarry West)

Photograph — Calvin Thomas (Georgia Review)

Remembering Sonny — Jean Thompson (Kansas Quarterly)

Under The Swaying Curtain — Robert Thompson (Missouri Review)

Aftermath — Marian Thurm (Mississippi Review)

The Woman In The Moon — William F. Van Wert (Denver Quarterly)

The Mermaid — David Wagoner (Western Humanities Review)

Early Snow — Irene Wanner (Antaeus)

Kafka: In Oklahoma & Other Strange Places — Winston Weathers (Kansas Quarterly)

Parker Lacrimans — Gordon Weaver (Georgia Review)

The Accompanist — R. R. Weisbrod (Sewanee Review)

Next Door — Tobias Wolff (Antaeus)

Passengers — Tobias Wolff (Triquarterly)

A Compassionate Leave — Richard Yates (Ploughshares)

Unglued — Patricia Zelver (Ohio Review)

excerpts from Dine Bahane: The Navajo Creation Story — Paul Zolbrod translator (Georgia Review)

Modern Madonna — Edward Zorensky (Mississippi Review)

## NONFICTION

Down the River with Henry Thoreau — Edward Abbey (Peregrine Smith)

The Genius of Jan Geertghe — Steve Arata (William and Mary Review)

The Feminine Bildungsroman: Education Through Marriage — Elaine Hoffman Baruch (Massachusetts Review)

The Body and The Earth — Wendell Berry (North Point Press)

Ladies & Monsters: On American Women's Poetry — Ellen Marie Bissert (13th Moon)

A Liberal Education — Janet Lindquist Black (Kenyon Review)

What The Signs of Promise Are — Paul Breslin (Ploughshares)

The Poetry and Thought of Octavio Paz: An Introduction — Kosrof Chantikian (Kosmos)

Freud and God — Robert Coles (Virginia Quarterly)

Chinua Achebe: At The Crossroads — Jonathan Cott (Parabola)

Robert Penn Warren, aet. 75 — Malcolm Cowley (Georgia Review)

Two Views of *The Bridge* — Malcolm Cowley (Sewanee Review)

Finding — Guy Davenport (North Point Press)

Leavis and Eliot — Denis Donoghue (Raritan)

from The H. D. Book — Robert Duncan (Montemora)

Hot Spicks Versus Cool Spades: Three Notes Toward A Cultural Definition of Prizefighting — Gerald Early (Hudson Review)

High Minds, Low Thoughts: Popular Culture and Intellectual Pastoral — Thomas Edwards (Raritan)

What I Did Last Summer — Betty Eppes (Paris Review)

The Galilean Sayings and The Sense of "I" — Erik Erikson (Yale Review)

Introduction to *The International Bill of Human Rights* — Tom J. Farer (Entwhistle Books)

Headless, With Flares — Ross Feld (Parnassus)

Talking Back to Walt Whitman: An Introduction — Ed Folsom (Holy Cow!)

Robert Bolt and The Marxist View of History — William Free (Mosaic)

On "Reading" Rooms — B. H. Fussell (Ontario Review)

My Father's Love Letters — Tess Gallagher (American Poetry Review)

A Sharp Enquiring Blade — Reginald Gibbons (Parnassus)

Careerist and Casualty: The Rise and Fall of Canada Lee — Glenda Gill (Freedom Ways)

Northumberland The Unknown County — Penelope Gilliatt (Grand Street)

Ellen's — Albert Goldbarth (Kenyon Review)

Naipaul and The Voices of Negation — Eugene Goodheart (Salmagundi)

The Undeciphered Audience: An Inquiry Into Small Presses and Related Matters — Jaimy Gordon (Open Places)

Listening and Making — Robert Hass (Antaeus)

Paschal Matters — Robert Hass (Ironwood)

Kafka and The Mice — Ronald Hayman (Partisan Review)

Beyond Categories — William Hellermann (Benzene)

The Amazing Mets and Structuralist Activity — Jerry Herron (Antioch Review)

The Poetry of Everyday Life — John Hollander (Raritan)

Philosophy and Black Fiction — Charles Johnson (Obsidian)

Feminist Press, Feminist Poetry In 1980 — Suzanne Juhasz (Open Places)

Androgyny, Old and New — Robert Kimbrough (Western Humanities Review)

The Meaning of Lives — Berel Lang (Western Humanities Review)

The Tenth Symphony — David Lavery (Georgia Review)

Herring Oatmeal, Milk and Salt — Mari MacInnes (Quarterly Review)

For A U.S. Peace Academy — Milton Mapes (East River Anthology)

Revolt and Faith: Nat Turner and the Myth of Sisyphus — Manning Marable (Black Praxis Press)

Painting and Primitivism: Hart Crane and the Development of an American Expressionist Esthetic — Robert Martin (Mosaic)

Those — Rosemary Mayer (White Walls)

The Mysteries At Bly — John Harmon McElroy (Arizona Quarterly)

Lily Briscoe: A Self Portrait — Mary Meigs (Fireweed)

On Innovative Writing — John Mella (Chicago Review)

On Illustrating Dante — Barry Moser (Fine Print)

No-Good Self-Righteous Bragging Boasting Chickenshit Character — Marvin Mudrick (Hudson Review)

Solzhenitsyn *versus* the Last Revolutionary — Marvin Mudrick (Hudson Review)

Working For A Living — Alice Munro (Grand Street)

Tenants — Ann Nietzke (Capra Press)

The Intellectual Odyssey of Martin Luther King — Stephen Oates (Massachusetts Review)

The Bewildered Equilibrist: An Essay On Buster Keaton's Comedy — Gilberto Perez (Hudson Review)

The Poetry of Yvor Winters: The Achievement of a Style — Douglas Peterson (Southern Review)

Poetry and the World — Robert Pinsky (Antaeus)

Letter to Peter Wood — Harold Pinter (Kenyon Review)

And Die In Dixie — David Roediger (Massachusetts Review)

Insisting On Love — John Rosenthal (The Sun)

The Z-D Generation — Edward Sanders (Station Hill Press)

On American Humor — Neil Schmitz (Partisan Review)

Lines I Dare to Write: Lesbian Writing in The South — M. Segrest (Southern Exposure)

A Farewell to Poetry — Robert Shaw (Yale Review)

The Human Image in Sterling Brown's Poetry — Clyde Taylor (Black Scholar)

Five Caviar and Cabbage Columns — Melvin Tolson (New Letters)

Wisdom and the Magic of the Extreme: A Meditation — Eric Voegelin (Southern Review)

Preface to O.ARS — Don Wellman (O.ARS)

The Ghost of the Matter — Michael Wood (TriQuarterly)

Body and Soul: Coleman Hawkins, 1939 — Al Young (Black Scholar)

Regarding Recorded Literature — Nicholas Zurbrugg (Precisely)

## POETRY

I Know What The Small Girl Knew — Anya Achtenberg (Sez)

Song of Our Last Meeting — Anna Akhmatova (Poetry Now)

The Four Elements — Rudolfo Anaya (River Styx)

They're Used to Putting Things In The Ground — Jimmy Santiago Baca (Revista Chicano-Riquena)

Her Elegy In Harvest Season — David Baker (Ahsahta)

Who Says Words With My Mouth — Coleman Barks (Yellow Moon Press)

Eulogy: Adios, Adios — George Barlow (Antaeus)

Wee Hours — George Barlow (Callaloo)

Good Friday At The Laundromat — Richmond Behm (Midwest Quarterly)

Little Story — Marvin Bell (Ploughshares)

Black — Stephen Berg (Yale Review)

Seizure — Richard Blessing (Poetry Northwest)

Night and Sleep — Robert Bly translator (Yellow Moon Press)

One Way or Another — Roo Borson (Fireweed)

The Burning of Books — Bertolt Brecht (Poetry Now)

Traveling Light — Christopher Buckley (Missouri Review)

Notes Upon A Hot Streak — Charles Bukowski (The Spirit That Moves Us)

Smooth — Charles Bukowski (Tendril)

The Only Thing Worse Than The Terror Itself Would Be The Silence Afterward — Christopher Bursk (Poetry)

Woman Ironing — Olga Cabral (Croton Review)

Spider Reeves — Henry Carlile (Running Lights)

At The Stone of Losses — T. Carmi (Kenyon Review)

Nocturne — Nathan Cervo (En Passant)

Ornithopilous — Michael Collier (Sonora Review)

The Lament of Cratylus and His Wife — Robert Cording (Tar River Poetry)

The Seventies — Gerald Costanzo (Minnesota Review)

The Admiral Byrd Poem — James Costello (En Passant)

In A Southern Cemetery — David Craig (Piedmont Literary Review)

The Spring At Diana, Tenn. — Jacqueline Crews (Tendril)

Essays In Criticism — Philip Dacey (Kansas Quarterly)

Red Feather — Glover Davis (Pacific Poetry and Fiction Review)

Daguerreotype VI — Drought — Susan Deal (En Passant)

A Prayer For My Father's Flight — Emilio De Grazia (Dacotah Territory)

On This Table Land of Malwa — Chandrakant Deotale (Sez)

Scion — James Dickey (Deerfield Press)

Larchant — Stephen Dobyns (Pequod)

Six Poems After Balthus — Stephen Dobyns (Poetry)

Coming On — Stephen Dunn (Georgia Review)

Images of China — Paul Engle (Poetry)

Atlantis — John Engman (Sonora Review)

Born In The Afternoon — Gretel Erlich (Ahsahta)

Mark Stern Wakes Up — Frederick Feirstein (Countryman Press)

Giving In — Elliot Figman (Confrontation)

Little Fingers — Elliot Figman (Choice)

How Old Man Stone Entered Into Heaven — Mike Finley (Poetry Now)

Bread and Roses — Aaron Fischer (Plum)

The Eyes of Amanda — David Fisher (Choice)

Poison Cloud — Maria Flook (Shankpainter)

When I Didn't Shout In Dulles Airport — Jack Forbes (Freedomways)

Upland Birds — James Galvin (Sonora Review)

Wheat — Gary Gildner (Georgia Review)

Ode To Failure — Allen Ginsberg (River Styx)

Blue Flowers — Albert Goldbarth (Poetry)

Thish Beelya — Albert Goldbarth (Carolina Quarterly)

Mist — Jorie Graham (Iowa Review)

Two Paintings by Gustav Klimt — Jorie Graham (American Poetry Review)

Children Among The Hills — Linda Gregg (Columbia)

The Color of Many Deer Running — Linda Gregg (Sonora Review)

Marriage and Midsummer's Night — Linda Gregg (Ironwood)

Gerda In The Eyrie — Marilyn Hacker (Poetry)

Motown/Smokey Robinson — Jessica Hagedorn (Momo's Press)

Describers — Mark Halliday (Ploughshares)

Dear Old Stockholm — Michael Harper (Georgia Review)

Hooking — Michael Harper (Field)

Upon Seeing A Cocoon On A High Branch Of A Sycamore After Stafford's Reading — Judith Harris (Sou'Wester)

Russia In 1931 — Robert Hass (Antaeus)

Spring Drawing, II — Robert Hass (Ironwood)

The Snow Hen — William Heyen (Ontario Review)

The Clean People — Jim Heynen (Copper Canyon)

Uncle Jack and Miss Paraffin — Jim Heynen (Poetry Now)

Tenant — Brenda Hillman (American Poetry Review)

The Elements — John Hollander (River Styx)

Songs and Sonnets — John Hollander (Georgia Review)

The Legend — Garrett Kaoru Hongo (Black Warrior Review)

Off From Swing Shift — Garrett Kaoru Hongo (Kayak)

I Am Idi Amin — David Ignatow (Choice)

Of That Fire — David Ignatow (New Letters)

Another Country — Ron Ikan (Croton Review)

Songs From My Father's Pockets — Llewellyn Ivory Giles (Sez)

Cells — Phyllis Janowitz (John O'Hara Journal)

The Black Globe In The Captain's Quarters — Mark Jarman (Cumberland Poetry Review)

Caprices — Mark Jarman (Sonora Review)

What Child Is This? — Mark Jarman (Field)

Addenda To The Papal Bull — June Jordan (13th Moon)

Taking Care — June Jordan (The Little Magazine)

The Double Helix — Mary Karr (Tendril)

My New Diet — Mary Karr (Poetry)

Catching Skies — Judy Katz-Levine (The Sun)

A Pact With Spirits — Gary Kessick (Xenophobia Press)

Everyone Loves Children — Milton Kessler (Poetry)

Memory of Wilmington — Galway Kinnell (Three Rivers Journal)

A Father and Mother — Sandra Kohler (Poetry Now)

The Hearts Graveyard Shift — Yusef Komunyakaa (Shankpainter)

Ele'Ele — Laurie Kuribayashi (Three Rivers Journal)

The Imaginary Tree — Thomas Lavazzi (En Passant)

For Marina Ivanovna Tsvetayeva — Irving Layton (Poetry Canada Review)

Her Destiny — Denise Levertov (Countryman Press)

Talking To Oneself — Denise Levertov (Copper Canyon)

The Doctor of Starlight — Philip Levine (Michigan Quarterly)

I Wanted You to Know — Philip Levine (Missouri Review)

Plea From The Angel of Good Luck — Philip Levine (Hudson Review)

Poem for My Brother — John Logan (BOA Editions)

Cartography — William Logan (Agni Review)

Tatiana Kalatschova — William Logan (Sewanee Review)

The Evening News — Audre Lorde (Woman Poet-East)

Early On, The Decade's Light Smelled — Thomas Lux (Pequod)

Flood — William Matthews (Georgia Review)

Unsparing — William Matthews (Columbia)

Salt — E. L. Mayo (New Letters)

People Who Deserve To Live In Light — Mekeel McBride (Zephyr Press)

The Bread of This World (Praises II) — Thomas McGrath (Copper Canyon)

Letter to An Imaginary Friend — Thomas McGrath (Sez)

Fishing for Horn Pout — Michael McMahon (Tendril)

Aunt Sylvia — Molly McQuade (Croton Review)

Parable of The Fish — Gary Metras (En Passant)

Native Dancer — Sara Miles (Woman Poet-East)

6 a.m. — Jane Miller (Woman Poet-East)

Duplication — C. Mills (Croton Review)

Field Theory — Robert Morgan (Iron Mountain Press)

Lenore — Erin Moure (Fireweed)

Prisoner Aboard The S.S. Beagle — Calvin Murry (Sez)

Enlistment — Carlos Nejar (Quarterly Review)

The Rusted Pail — Mark Nepo (En Passant)

Flannery O'Connor's Train — B. E. Niditch (Piedmont Literary Review)

Billy—Sherry Noethe (Ohio Review)

Drunkwalk — John O'Brien (Poetry Now)

Firelight — Diana O' Hehir (Poetry Northwest)

The Signal — Sharon Olds (Poetry)

A Poem For The Winter Nights — Mary Oliver (Western Humanities Review)

We Come To Silence — Linda Pastan (Georgia Review)

Nocturne of San Ildefonso — Octavio Paz (Kosmos)

Afloat With Robert Mitchum — Robert Peters (Sombre Reptiles Press)

From The Portugese — Constance Pierce (John O'Hara Journal)

It Breaks — Marge Piercy (Croton Review)

After Whistler — Stanley Plumly (Antaeus)

On Robert Bly — David Ray (Poetry East)

Portrait of a Mexican Barber — David Ray (Kayak)

Bat — Liam Rector (The Reaper)

Express — James Reiss (Kenyon Review)

Madre Sofia — Alberto Rios (Ironwood)

True Story of the Pins — Alberto Rios (Dooryard Press)

Fragmented — Yannis Ritsos (Antaeus)

Wax Images — Yannis Ritsos (Willow Springs Magazine)

The Encouraging Sea — Len Roberts (Quarterly West)

Justification of The Horned Lizard — Pattiann Rogers (Iowa Review)

Suppose It's Wednesday Morning — Norman Russell (Piedmont Literary Review)

Terra Incognita — Sherod Santos (Antaeus)

9:00 A.M. At Broadway and Walnut for Your Birthday — Ripley Schemm (Dooryard Press)

Finding The Way — Denis Schmitz (Tendril)

The Messenger — Grace Schulman (Antaeus)

The Stars and The Moon — Grace Schulman (Hudson Review)

Balance — Philip Schultz (Choice)

The Russian Doll — Jane Shore (Ploughshares)

White: A New Version — Charles Simic (Logbridge-Rhodes)

The Little Room — William Stafford (Copper Canyon)

Walking With Your Eyes Shut — William Stafford (Plainsong)

Elegy For Ralph Eugene Meatyard 1925-1972 — Sue Standing (Pale Fire)

Shooting Pool — Sue Standing (Ploughshares)

The Lion's Eyebrows — Maura Stanton (American Poetry Review)

Visiting Florida Again — Gerald Stern (Poetry East)

Staircase — Pamela Stewart (Vegetable Box)

Pears — Mary Swander (Iowa Review)

In The Darkness of the Body — Stephen Tapscott (Missouri Review)

In An Arab Town — Susan Tichy (Antioch Review)

The Woodcarver's Song To A Tree — Margot Treitel (Minnesota Review)

Pennsylvania Summer — John Unterecker (Poetry Now)

The Black Messengers — Cešar Vallejo (Sachem Press)

Bloodsong — H. L. Van Brunt (West Branch)

Letter From Vermont — Ellen Bryant Voigt (Antaeus)

For Clint on The Desert — Diane Wakoski (Tendril)

Little Tricks of Linear B — Diane Wakoski (Plowshares)

Letter This Far — Derek Walcott (Antaeus)

Family Of — Alice Walker (Freedomways)

Between Words — Bronwen Wallace (Fireweed)

Northern Lights — Emily Warn (Copper Canyon)

Letter to Abiah From Emily — Elizabeth Weber (Columbia)

Staying Up For England — Miles Wilson (The Reaper)

The Will To Fail — Miles Wilson (Southern Poetry Review)

Clear Lake — John Witte (Ontario Review)

For The Girl Drowned Off the Provincetown Breakwater — Ellen Wittlinger (Zephyr Press)

Above Palm Desert—David Wojahn (Shankpainter)

As It Happens — Susan Wood (Missouri Review)

Elegy for My Sister — Susan Wood (Missouri Review)

The Failure of Language — Susan Wood (MSS)

Miranda Lives The Examined Life — A. J. Wright (Piedmont Literary Review)

Dying In The Veritas Ditch . . Charles D. Wright (Clearing Away)

Lost Bodies — Charles Wright (Field)

Lost Souls — Charles Wright (Field)

The Sumac In Ohio — James Wright (Ohio Review)

The Summers of James and Annie Wright—James and Annie Wright (River Styx)

The James Cotton Band At Keystone — Al Young (Black Scholar)

# 🔥 🔥 🔥

# OUTSTANDING SMALL PRESSES

(These presses made or received nominations for this edition of *The Pushcart Prize*. See the *International Directory of Little Magazines and Small Presses*, Dustbooks, Box 1056, Paradise, CA 95969, for subscription rates, manuscript requirements and a complete international listing of small presses.)

Abbey, 5011-2 Green Mtn. Ctr., Columbia, MD 21044
Abratas, 426 W. 23rd St., New York, NY 10011
Academia, P.O. Box 7266, Albuquerque, NM 87194
Accessories, University of Colorado, Boulder, CO 80709
Acheron Press, Bear Creek At the Kettel, Friendsville, MD 21532
Adastra Press, 101 Strong St., Easthampton, MA 01027
Agni Review, P.O. Box 229, Cambridge, MA 02138
Ahsahta Press, Boise State University, Boise, ID 83725
Akiba Press, Box 13086, Oakland, CA 94611
The Alchemist, P.O. Box 123, LaSalle, Quebec, Canada
Aldebaren, Roger Williams College, Bristol, RI 02809
Alice Jones Books, 136 Mt. Auburn St., Cambridge, MA 02138
Alta Napa Press, P.O. Box 407, Calistoga, CA 94515
Alternate Publishing, 15 Harriet St., San Francisco, CA 94103
Alternate Review, 826 W. Huron, Ann Arbor, MI 48104
The Alternative Press, Grindstone City, MI 48467
American Arts, 570 Seventh Ave., New York, NY 10018
American Poetry Review, 1616 Walnut St., Philadelphia, PA 19103
Angst World Library, 724 Forest Creek Rd., Selma, OK 97538
Annex 21, University of Nebraska, Omaha, NB 68182
Another Chicago Magazine, 1152 S. East Ave., Oak Park, IL 60304
Antaeus, 18 W. 30th St., New York, NY 10001
Antenna, P.O. Box 16074, San Diego, CA 92123

Antioch Review, P.O. Box 148, Yellow Springs, OH 45387

Anyra Publishing, 12077 Wilshire Blvd., West Los Angeles, CA 9002

Applezaba Press, P.O. Box 4134, Long Beach, CA 90804

Ariadne Press, 4817 Tallahassee Ave., Rockville, MO 20853

The Ark, Box 322, Times Square Sta., New York, NY 10108

Ark River Review, W.S.U., Wichita, KS 67208

Artful Dodge, 110 S. Roosevelt, Bloomington, IN 47401

Art Ink, 716 11th St., NW, Washington, DC 20001

Ascent, University of Illinois, Urbana, IL 61801

Ashford Press, RFD 1, Box 182-A, Willimantic, CT 06278

Asphodel, 613 Howard Ave., Pitman, NJ 08028

Associated Writing Programs, Old Dominion University, Norfolk, VA 23580

Asunda Publications, P.O. Box 158, Harris, IA 51345

Atlanta Art Papers, Inc., 28 Sixteenth St., N.W., Atlanta, GA

August House, 1010 West Third St., Little Rock, ARK 72201

Aura, 117 Campbell Hill, University Sta., Birmingham, AL 35294


Bad Henry Review, P.O. Box 45, Van Brunt Sta., Brooklyn, NY 11215

Ball State University Forum, Muncie, IN 47306

Baltic Avenue Press, 1027 South 30th St., Birmingham, AL 35205

Bankers Press, 8019 So. State St., Chicago, IL 60619

R. L. Barth, 14 Lucas St., Florence, KY 41042

Beacon Review, 2511½ E. Yesler, Seattle, WA 98122

Bear Claw Press, 1039 Baldwin St., Ann Arbor, MI 48104

Belleridge Press, P.O. Box 970, Rancho Santa Fe, CA 92067

Bellevue Press, 60 Schubert St., Binghamton, NY 13905

Bellingham Review, 412 N. State St., Bellingham, WA 98220

Beloit Poetry Journal, P.O. Box 2, Beloit, WI 53511

Bennington Review, Bennington College, Bennington, VT 05201

Benzene, P.O. Box 383, New York, NY 10014

Berkeley Poets, P.O. Box 459, Berkeley, CA 94701

Bernwood Press, R.R. 2, Box 11 C, Daleville, IN 47334

Bibliotheca Press, Box 98378, Atlanta, GA 30359

Bicentennial Era Enterprises, P.O. Box 1148, Scappose, OR 97056

Bieler Press, P.O. Box 3856, St. Paul, MN 55165

Big "O" Publications, 103-39 103 St., Ozone Park, NY 11417

Bilingual Review, Eastern Michigan University, Ypsilanti, MI 48197

Bitterroot, Blythebourne Sta., P.O. Box 51, Brooklyn, NY 11219

BKMK Press, 5725 Wyandotte, Kansas City, MO 64113

Black Buzzard Press, 8508 Hempstead Ave., Bethesda, MD 20817

Black Market Press, 1516 Beverly Rd., Brooklyn, NY 11226

The Black Scholar, 2670 Bridgway, Sausalito, CA 94965

Black Sparrow, P.O. Box 3993, Santa Barbara, CA 93105

Black Swan Books, P.O. Box 327, Redding Ridge, CT 0687

Black Warrior Review, P.O. Box 2936, University, AL 35486

Blue Cloud Quarterly, Marvin, SD 57251

Blue Harbor Press, P.O. Box 1028, Lomita, CA 90717

Blue Unicorn, 22 Avon Rd., Kensington, CA 94707

Blueline, Blue Mountain Lake, New York, NY 12812

BOA Editors, 92 Park Ave., Brockport, NY 14420

Bogg Magazine, 2010 N. 21st St., Arlington, VA 22201

Book Emporium, 768 Main St., Willimantic, CT 06226

Book Forum, Hudson River Press, Rhinecliff, NY 12754

Book Promotions Unlimited, P.O. Box 122, Flushing, MI 45433

Books of A Feather Press, P.O. Box 3095, Terminal Annex, Los Angeles, CA 90051

Bozeau of London Press, 87-89 Leonard St., New York, NY 10013

Briarpatch, Box 2482, Davidson, NC 28036

Brook Farm Books, Glassville, New Brunswick, Canada E0J100

Brown House Studios, Rose Valley, PA 19065

Buckles, SUNY, 1300 Elmwood Ave., Buffalo, NY 14222

Burning Deck, 71 Elmgrove Ave., Providence, RI 02906

Byls Press, 6247 N. Francisco Ave., Chicago, IL 60659


CSS Publications, P.O. Box 23, Iowa Falls, IA 50126

Caislen Press, Box 28271, San Jose, CA 95157

Calyx, P.O. Box B, Corvallis, OR 97330

Cambium Press, P.O. Box 147, Stone Ridge, NY 12484

Canadian Encounter, 406 Elizabeth St., Sault Ste. Marie, Ontario, Canada P6B3H4

Canadian Fiction Magazine, Box 946, Stn. F, Toronto, Ontario Canada M4Y2N9

Canadian Literature, 2075 Wesbrook Mall, Vancouver, BC Canada V6T1W5

The Cape Rock, SE MO State University, Cape Girardeau, MO 63700

Capilaro Review, 2055 Purcell Way, N. Vancouver, Canada, V7J3H5

Capra Press, P.O. Box 2068, Santa Barbara, CA 93120

Carolina Quarterly, University of North Carolina, Chapel Hill, NC 27514

Carolina Wren Press, 300 Barclay Rd., Chapel Hill, NC 27514

Carpenter Press, Rt. 4, Pomeroy, OH 45769

Catalyst, Memorial Union, Durham, NH 03824

Cat's Eye, 4425 Westlawn Dr., Nashville, TN 37209

Cedar Rock, 1121 Madeline, New Branfels, TX 78130

Central Park, P.O. Box 1446, New York, NY 10023

Chanteau Review, Box 10016, Kansas City, MO 64111

Chariton Review, Northeast Missouri State University, Kirksville, MO 63501

Charnel House, P.O. Box 281, Stn. S, Toronto, Ontario Canada M5M4L7

Chelsea, Box 5880, Grand Central Sta., New York, NY 10017

Chicago Review, 5811 S. Kenwood, Chicago, IL 60627

Choice Magazine, Box Z, SUNY, Binghampton, NY 13901

Chthon Press, 10 Mark Vincent Dr., Westford, MA 01886

Cimaron Review, Oklahoma State University, Stillwater, OK 74074

Cincinnati Poetry Review, University of Cincinnati, Cincinnati, OH 45221

Cleis Press, P.O. Box 8281, Minneapolis, MN 55408

Coevolution Quarterly, P.O. Box 428, Sausalito, CA 94965

College English, Dept. English, Indiana University, Bloomington, IN 47401

Cologne Press, P.O. Box 682, Cologne, NJ 08213

Columbia, Columbia University, New York, NY 10027

Conceptions Southwest, Box 20, Albuquerque, NM 87131

Concerning Poetry, Western Washington University, Bellingham, WA 98225

Conditions, Box 56, Van Brint Sta., Brooklyn, NY 11215

Confrontation, Long Island University, Brooklyn, NY 11201

Connecticut Quarterly, P.O. Box 65, Enfield, CT 06082

Consumer's Advisory Press, P.O. Box 77107, Greensboro, NC 27407

Continuing Saga Press, 1822 Main St., San Francisco, CA 94113

Copperhead, P.O. Box 271, Port Townsend, WA 98368

Copper Canyon, P.O. Box 271, Port Townsend, WA 98368

Coraddi, University of North Carolina, Greensboro, NC 27412
Cornfield Review, Ohio State University, Marion, OH 43302
Cotton Lane Press, 2 Cotton La., Augusta, GA 30902
Countryman Press, Woodstock, VT 05091
Crawl Out Your Window, 4641 Park Blvd., San Diego, CA 92160
Creative Arts Book Co., 833 Bancroft Way, Berkeley, CA 94710
Cross Country, P.O. Box 21081, Woodhaven, NY 11421
Crosscurrents, 2200 Glastonbury Rd., Westlake Village, CA 91361
Croton Review, P.O. Box 277, Croton-On-Hudson, NY 10520
Cumberland Journal, Box 2648, Harrisburg, PA 17105
Cumberland Magazine, College P.O. Box 2, Pikeville, KY 41501
Cutback, University of Montana, Missoula, MT 59812
Cypress Review, Box 673, Half Moon Bay, CA 94019

Dacotah Territory, P.O. Box 775, Moorhead, MN 56560
Dancing Crow Press, P.O. Box 362, Larkspur, CA 94939
Dandelion Magazine, 922-9 Ave. SE, Calgary, Alberta, Canada
    T26-054
Dark Horse, P.O. Box 36, Newton Lower Falls, MA 02162
Dawn Valley Press, P.O. Box 58, New Wilmington, PA 18142
Dayspring/Black Bart, P.O. Box 48, Canyon, CA 94516
Deerfield Press, Deerfield, MA 01342
Delaware Today, 206 E. Ayre St., Wilmington, DE 19804
Denver Quarterly, University of Denver, Denver, CO 80201
Descant, Box 314, Ste. P., Toronto, Canada M55 258
Design Enterprises of San Francisco, P.O. Box 14695, San Fran-
    cisco, CA 94114
Devil's Millhopper, University of South Carolina, Columbia, SC
    29208
Dialogue, Bard College, Annandale, NY 12504
Dog Ear Press, Hills Cove, ME 04644
Doggerel Press, 417 Sea View, Santa Barbara, CA 93108
Dooryard Press, P.O. Box 221, Story, WY 82842
Dovetail Press, 250 W. 94th St., New York, NY 10025
Downtown Poets Co-op, G PO Box 1720, Brooklyn, NY 11202
Dragon Gate, Inc., 508 Lincoln St., Port Townsend, WA 98368
Duck Down Press, P.O. Box 1047, Fallon, NV 89406
Duck Soup, North Lake College, 5001 N. MacArthur Blvd.,
    Irving, TX 75062
Duir Press, 919 Sutter St. No. 9, San Francisco, CA 94109

Earthwise, PO Box 680-536, Miami, FL 33168

East River Anthology, 75 Gates Ave., Montclair, NJ 07042

Edition Heliodor, 2071 Salisbury Park Dr., Westbury, NY 11590

Elpenor Books, Box 3152, Merchandise Mart Plaza, Chicago, IL 60654

En Passant/Poetry, 4612 Sylvanus Dr., Wilmington, DE 19803

Entwhistle Books, P.O. Box 611, Glen Ellen, CA 95442

Epoch, 243 G.S., Cornell University, Ithaca, NY 14853

Equity Publishing Co., 1850 E. 17th St., Santa Ana, CA 92701


Fablewaves Press, P.O. Box 7874, Van Nuys, CA 91409

Farming Uncle, P.O. Box 91, Liberty, NY 12754

Fedora, P.O. Box 577, Siletz, OR 97380

Feminist Studies, University of Maryland, College Park, MD 20742

Fiction, CCNY, Convent Ave at 138th St., New York, NY 10031

Fiction International, St. Lawrence University, Canton, NY 13613

Field, Rice Hall, Oberlin College, Oberlin, OH 44074

The Figures, 2016 Cedar St., Berkeley, CA 94709

Fireweed, PO Box 279, Sta. B., Toronto, Ontario, Canada M572WZ

First East Coast Theatre and Publishing Co., P.O. Box A244, Village St., NY 10014

Ford Press, P.O. Box 615, Corte Madera, CA 94925

Floating Island, PO Box 516, Point Reyes Station, CA 94956

Focus, 1151 Massachusetts Ave., Cambridge, MA 02138

Format, 405 S. 7th St., St. Charles, IL 60174

Four Quarters, LaSalle College, Philadelphia, PA 19141

Freedomways, 799 Broadway, New York, NY 10003

Friends of Poetry, University of Wisconsin, Whitewater, WI 53190

From Here Press, Box 219, Fanwood, NJ 07023

C. J. Frompovich Publications, Chestnut Rd., Coopersburg, PA 18036

Frontiers, University of Boulder, Boulder, CO 80309

Fullcourt Press, 228 N. Broadway, Edmond, OK 73034

Full Deck Anthology, 515 E 6th St., C-8, New York, NY 10014


Galileo Press, PO Box 2117, Iowa City, IA 52244

Gallery Press, 19 Oakdown Rd., Dublin 14, Ireland

Gamut, Cleveland State University, Cleveland, OH 44115

Gargoyle, 40 St. John St., Jamaica Plain, MA 02130

Garden Publishing Co., 6833 Greston Rd., Edina, MN 55435

Gazelle Publications, 20601 W. Paoli Ln., Colfax, CA 95716

Georgia Review, University of Georgia, Athens GA 30602

Ghost Pony Press, 2518 Gregory St., Madison, WI 53710

Gondwana Books, P.O. Box 407, Calistoga, CA 94515

Grand Street, 50 Riverside Dr., New York, NY 10024

Grapetree Productions, 600 Graptree Dr., Key Biscayne, FL 33149

Graywolf Press, P.O. Box 142, Port Townsend, WA 98368

Grean City Review, P.O. Box 413, University of Wisconsin, Milwaukee, WI 53201

Great River Review, P.O. Box 14805, Minneapolis, MN 55414

Great Society Press, 451 Heckman St. (308), Philipsburg, NJ 08865

Green Mt Review, Johnson State College, Johnson, VT

Greenfield Review Press, R.D. #1, Box 80, Greenfield Cent, NY 12833

Green's Magazine, P.O. Box 313, Detroit, MI 48230

Grey Whale Press, P.O. Box 1758, Florence, OR 97439

Greywolf Press, Port Townsend, WA

Guavionex Press Ltd., 201 W. 77 St., New York, NY 10024

Guernica Editions, P.O. Box 633, Sta. N.D.G., Montreal, Quebec, Canada H4AJR1

Gull Books, 657 E. 26th St., New York, NY 11210

Gusto Press, P.O. Box 1009, Bronx, NY 10465


Hampden-Sydney Poetry Review, P.O. Box 143, Rice, VA 23966

Hand Press, 12015 Coyne St., Los Angeles, CA 90049

Hanging Loose Press, 231 Wyckoff St., Brooklyn, NY 11217

Hard Press, 340 E. 11th St., New York, NY 10014

Hard Pressed, P.O. Box 275, Port Arena, CA 95468

Harian Creative Press, 47 Hyde Blvd., Bellston Sps, NY 12020

Harpoon, P.O. Box 2581, Anchorage, AK 99510

Hartmus Press, 23 Lomite Dr, Mill Valley, CA 94940

Heldseff Publications, 4000 Albemarle St. N.W., Washington, D.C. 20016

Helicon Wire, 5920 Mission Dr., Mission Hills, KS 66208

Hemlocks and Balsams, Lee-McRee College, Banner Falls, N.C. 28604

Hermes House, 6384 Hillegess Ave., Oakland, CA 94010

High/Coo Press, Rt #1, Battle Ground, IN 47920

High Rock Review, Box 614, Saratoga Springs, NY 12866

Hiram Poetry Review, Box 162, Hiram, OH 44234

Holmgangers Press, Star Route, Shelton Cove, Whitehorn, CA 95489

Holy Cow! Press, P.O. Box 618, Minneapolis, MN 55440

Home Planet News, P.O. Box 415, Stuyvesant Sta., New York 10003

Hope Tracks, 109 South Walnut, Hope, AK 71801

Hong Kong Publishing Co., 43-55 Wyndham St., Hong Kong

Hop Nod Annual, 715 Dorsey Rd., Lancaster, PA 17601

House of Anansi Press Ltd., 35 Britain St., Tornoto, Ontario, Canada M5A1R7

The Hudson Review, 65 E. 55th St., New York, NY 10022

Hyena Editions, P.O. Box 121, Water Mill, NY 11976

Hygenia, P.O. Box 4048, Santa Rosa, CA 95402


Images, Wright State University, Dayton, OH 45435

Indiana Review, 216 N. Jordan Ave., Bloomington, IN 47405

Imprint, 6360 N. Guilford, Indianapolis, IN 46220

Ins & Outs Press, P.O. Box 3759, Amsterdam, Holland

Interstate, P.O. Box 7068, University Sta., Austin, TX 78712

Intro, Old Dominion University, Norfolk, VA 23508

Invisible City, P.O. Box 2853, San Francisco, CA 94126

Iowa Review, University of Iowa, Iowa City, IA 52401

Ironwood, P.O. Box 40007, Tucson, AZ 85717

Ithaca House, 108 N. Plain St., Ithaca, NY 14850


John Bart Gerald, Books & Co., 939 Madison Ave., New York, NY 10002

Journal of Canadian Studies, Trent University, Peterborough, Ontario, Canada


Kansas Quarterly, Kansas State University, Manhattan, KS 66506

Kayak, 325 Ocean View, Santa Cruz, CA 95062

Kenmore Press, 3317 Thornhill Rd. SW, Winter Haven, FL 33880

Kenyon Review, Kenyon College, Gambier, OH 43022

Phil King Publishing, c/o Carters Beach, Erie, PA 16510

Konglomerati Press, P.O. Box 5001, Gulfport, FL 33737

Kosmos, 381 Arlington St., San Francisco, CA 94131

Lake Street Review, Box 7188, Powderhorn Sta., Minneapolis, MN 55407

Lancaster-Miller Publishers, 2165 Adeline St., Berkeley, CA 94703

Laughing Waters Press, 1351 Washington St., Denver, CO 80203

Lemon Creek Gold, 11120 Glacier Highway, Juneau, Alaska 99803

Laurel Review, West Virginia Wesleyan University, Buckannon, WV 26201

Light Living Library, P.O. Box 190, Philomath, OR 97370

Lightworks, P.O. Box 1202, Birmingham, MI 48012

Lips, P.O. Box 1345, Montclair, NJ 07042

The Little Apple, P.O. Box 429, Federal St., Worcester, MA 01610

Little Balkans Press, 601 Grandview Heights Terr., Pittsburg, KS 66760

Little Free Press, 715 E. 14th St., Minneapolis, MN 56404

Little Light, 52 E. 7th St. #10, New York, NY 10003

Limberlost Review, P.O. Box 1041, Pocatello, ID 83201

The Literary Review, 285 Madison Ave., Madison, NJ 07940

Logbridge-Rhodes, P.O. Box 3254, Durango, CO 81301

Long Island Poetry Collective, P.O. Box 773, Huntington, NY 11743

Long Pond Review, 533 College Rd., Selden, NY 11784

Lotus Press, P.O. Box 21607, Detroit, MI 48221

Lowlands Review, 6048 Perrier, New Orleans, LA 70118

Low-Tech Press, 30-73 47th St., Long Island City, NY 11103

Luna Bisonte Prods, 137 Leland Ave., Columbus, OH 43214


M. N. Publishers, Rt. 2, Box 55, Bonnersdale, ARK 71933

M.O.P. Press, Rt. 24, Box 53C, Fort Myers, FL 33908

MSS, SUNY, Binghampton, NY 13901

Magic Changes, 1923, Finchley Ct, Schaumburg, IL 60194

Magical Blend, P.O. Box 11303, San Francisco, CA 94001

Main Trend, Box 344 Cooper Station, New York, NY 10003

Madness Network News, 1744 University Ave., Berkeley, CA 94703

Manhattan Review, 304 Third Ave. 4A, New York, NY 10010

The Massachusetts Review, University of Massachusetts, Amherst, MA 01003

Matrix, Box 510, Lennoxville, Quebec, Canada, J1M126

May-Murdock Publications, P.O. Box 343, Ross, CA 94957

Maze, P.O. Box 8251, San Diego, CA 92102

McKettren Publishing, P.O. Box 12067, Seattle, WA 98102

Metacon Press, 31 Beaver St., Worcester, MA 01603

M'godolim, 7541¹/² E. Yester Way, Seattle, WA 98122

Micah Publications, 255 Humphrey St., Marblehead, MA 01945

Michigan Quarterly Review, University of Michigan, Ann Arbor, MI 48109

Mid-American Review, BGSU, Bowling Green, OH 43402

Midwest Quarterly, Pittsburg State University, Pittsburg, KS 66762

Mill Hunk Herald, 916 Middle St., Pittsburgh, PA 15212

Minnesota Review, Box 211, Bloomington, IN 47401

Mississippi Mud, 3125 S.E. Van Water St., Portland, OR 97222

Mississippi Review, University of Southern Mississippi, Hatties-burg, MS 39406

Missouri Review, University of Missouri, Columbia, MO 65211

Mr. Cogito, Pacific University, Forest Grove, OR 97116

Modern Haiku, P. O. Box 1752, Madison, WI 53701

Mole Publishing Co., Rt. 1, Box 618, Bonners Ferry, CO 83805

Momentum Press, 512 Hill St. #4, Santa Monica, CA 90405

Moonfire Press, 3061 N. Newhall St., Milwaukee, WI 53211

Moonlight Publications, P. O. Drawer 2850, La Jolla, CA 92038

Moosehead Review, Box 169, Ayer's Cliff, Quebec, Canada JIM 2A

Mosaic, 208 Tier Bldg, Univ. Manitoba, Winnipeg, Canada

Mothering Publications, P. O. Box 2046, Albuquerque, NM 87103

Mothers of Mud, 152 Forsyth St., New York, NY 10002

Mountain Cat Press, 14 Washington, Denver CO 80203

Mountain State Press, University of Charleston, Charleston, WV 25309

Moving Parts Press, 419-A Maple St., Santa Cruz, CA 95060

Muscadine, 1111 Lincoln Pl., Boulder, CO 80302

Muse-Pie, 73 Pennington Ave., Passaic, NJ 07055

Museum of New Mexico Press, P. O. Box 2087, Sante Fe, NM 87501


NR6, 703 N. Forest, Pellingham, WA 98225

Naiad Press, P. O. Box 10543, Tallahassee, FL 32302

New America, University of New Mexico, Albuquerque, NM 87131

New Directions, 80 Eighth Ave., New York, NY 10011

New England Review, Box 170, Hanover, NH 03755

New Letters, 5100 Rockhill Rd., Kansas City, MO 64110

New Mexico Humanities Review, New Mexico Institute, Socorro, NM 87801

New Oregon Review, 537 N. E. Lincoln St., Hillsboro, OR 97123

New Renaissance, 9 Heath Rd., Arlington, MA 02174

New Rivers Press, 1602 Selby Ave., St. Paul, MN 55104

North American Review, University of Northen Iowa, Cedar Falls, IA 50614

North Country Anvil, P. O. Box 402, Winona, MN 55937

North Point Press, P. O. Box 6275, Berkeley, CA 94706

Northwestern University Press, 360 Huntington Ave., Boston, MA 02115

Northwest Review, University of Oregon, Eugene, OR 97403

Northwoods Press, P. O. Box 249, Stafford, VA 22554

Not Guilty Press, Box 121, Water Mill, NY 11976


OARS, Box 179, Cambridge, MA 02208

Oboe, 495 Ellis St. San Francisco, CA 94102

Occident Magazine, 103 Sproul Hall, UC, Berkeley CA 94720

Oconee Review, P. O. Box 6232, Athens, GA 30604

Odd-Moment Press, P. O. Box 31702, Seattle, WA 98103

John O'Hara Journal, P. O. Box 106, Potterville, PA 17901

Ohio Review, Ohio University, Athens, OH 45701

Old Plate Press, P. O. Box 219, Fanwood, NJ 07023

Ontario Review, 9 Honeybrook Dr., Princeton, NJ 08540

Open Places, Box 2085, Stephens College, Columbia, MO 65215

Osiris, Box 297, Deerfield, MA 01342

Outerbridge, 715 Ocean Ter., Staten Island, NY 10301

Owl Creek Press, 2220 Quail, Missoula, MT 59802


Pacific Poetry and Fiction Review, San Diego State University, San Diego, CA 92182

Painted Bride Quarterly, 314 Marvin Rd., Elkins Park, PA 19117

Pale Fire Review, 162 Academy Ave., Providence, RI 02908

Pandora, 3721 Barcelons St., Tampa, FL 33609

Parabola, 150 Fifth Ave., New York, NY 10011

Paradise Press, 875 Ocean Front Walk #1, Venice, CA 90291

The Paris Review, 541 E. 72nd St., New York, NY 10021

Parnassas: Poetry In Review, 205 W. 89th St., New York, NY 10024

Partisan Review, 128 Bay State Rd., Boston, MA 02215

Passage North, Fire Arts Center, Escanaba, MI 49829

Paycock Press, P. O. Box 57206, Washington, DC 20037

Penguin Review, Youngstown State University, Youngstown, OH 44555

Penumbra Press, Rt. 1, Lisbon, IA 52253

Pequod, 536 Hill St., San Francisco, CA 94114

Peregrine Associates, P. O. Box 22292, Ft. Lauderdale, FL 33311

Peregrine Smith Inc., P. O. Box 667, Layton, UT 84041

Periwinkle Press, P. O. Box 1305, Woodland Hills, CA 91365

Permanent Press, Sagaponack, NY 11962

Pheasant Run Publications, P. O. Box 14043, St. Louis, MO 63178

Philadelphia Poets, 21 Concord Rd. Darby, PA 19023

Michael Joseph Phillips Editions, 430 E. Wylie, Bloomington, IN 47401

Philosophy Press, P. O. Box 1600, Uniontown, PA 15401

Piedmont Literary Review, P. O. Box 3656, Danville, VA 24541

Pikestaff Publications, P. O. Box 127, Normal, IL 61761

Pinchpenny, 4851 Q St., Sacramento, CA 95819

Pin Prick Press, 2664 Green Rd., Shaker Heights, OH 44122

Pipe Dream, P. O. Box 252, Storrs, CT 06268

Piton Publications, 67 Templets Pkwy, Watertown, MA 02172

Placebo Press, 4311 Bayon Blvd., Pensacola, FL 32503

Places, Box 810 Gracie St., New York, NY 10028

Ploughshares, P. O. Box 529, Cambridge, MA 02139

Plowshares 8, 168 W. 100th St., New York, NY 10025

Plumbers Ink Books, 127 E. Water St., Sante Fe, NM 87501

Poem, P. O. Box 919, Huntsville, AL 35804

Poet & Critic, Iowa State University, Ames, IA 50011

Poet Tree, 2701 24th St., #8, Sacramento, CA 95818

Poetry, P. O. Box 4348, Chicago, IL 60680

Poetry Canada Review, P. O. Box 1280 Stn. A., Toronto, Ontario, Canada M5W167

Poetry Center, Cleveland State University, Cleveland, OH 44115

Poetry East, 1909 Jefferson Park Ave. #3, Charlottesville, VA 22903

Poetry Miscellany, University of Tennessee, Chattanooga, TN 37402

Poetry Northwest, University of Washington, Seattle, WA 98105

Poetry Now, 3118 K St., Eureka, CA 95501

Poetry Project Newsletter, 10th Street and 2nd Ave., New York, NY 10003

Poets On, Box 255, Chaplin CT 06235

Point Riders, P. O. Box 2731, Norman, OK 73070

Poly Tone Press, 16027 Sunburst St., Sepulveda, CA 91343

Porch, 5310 E. Taylor, Phoenix, AZ 85008

Portland Review, P. O. Box 751, Portland, OR 97207

Potto Publications, 201 Bowie #2, Nacogdoches, TX 75961

Poultry, P. O. Box 727, Truro, MA 02666

Prairie Publishing Co., Box 264, Postel Station C, Winnipeg 9, Manitoba, Canada

Primivara, P. O. Box 371, Oconto, WI 54153

Primavera, 1212 E. 59th St., New York, NY

Prisim Press, 11706 Longleaf La, Houston, Tx 77024

Prototype, 155 George St., Toronto, Ontario, Canada A15A2MB

Pteranodon, P. O. Box 229, Bowbannais, IL 60914

Pterodactyl Press, 770 Joost Ave., San Francisco, CA 94127

The Public Press, 423 West 46th St., New York, NY 10030

Puerto Del Sol, Box 3E, New Mexico State University Las Cruces, NM 88003

Pulp, 720 Greenwich St., New York, NY 10014

Quarterly Review of Literature, 26 Haslet Ave., Princeton, NJ 08540

Quarterly West, University of Utah, Salt Lake City, UT 84112

Quicksilver Press, Box 171, Baltimore, MD 21203

Quilt, 2140 Shattuck Ave., Berkeley, CA 94704

Rainbow Publications, 1493 S. Columbia Way, Seattle, WA 98144

Rainy Day Press, P. O. Box 3035, Eugene, OR 97403

Rara Avis Magazine, P. O. Box 3095, Terminal Annex, Los Angeles, CA 90051

Raritan: A Quarterly Review, 165 College Ave., New Brunswick, NJ 08901

Red Cedar Review, Michigan State University, E. Lansing, MI 48824

Red Earth Press, P. O. Box 1741, Corvales, NM 87048

Red Hand Books, 74 13th St., NE, Atlanta, GA 30309

Reflect, 3306 Argonne Ave., Norfolk, VA 23509

Reinfecter Press, Box 831, College Park, MD 20740

Release Press, 411 Clinton St., Brooklyn, NY 11231

Revista Chicano-Riqueña, University of Houston, Houston, TX 77004

Rhiannan Press, 1105 Bradley Ave., Eau Claire, WI 54701

River Styx, 7420 Cornell, St. Louis, MO 63130

Riverfront, P. O. Box 3777, Omaha, NE 68103

Riverrun, P. O. Box 4915 Main Station, Vancouver, BC Canada

Rower Tree Press, 124 Chestnut St., Boston, MA 02108

Rundy's Journal, 217 Elizabeth St. #7, New York, NY 10012

Sachem Press, Old Chatham, NY 12136

St. Andrews Review, Laurinburg, NC 28352

Salmagundi, Skidmore College, Saratoga Springs, NY 12866

Salt Lick Press, P. O. Box 1064, Quincy, IL 62301

San Fernando Poetry Journal, 18301 Halsted St., Northridge, CA 91324

Sands, 17302 Club Hill Dr., Dallas TX 75248

Saturday Press, P. O. Box 884, U. Montclair, NJ 07043

Schola Satyrica, University of South Florida, Tampa, FL 33620

Scop Publications, P. O. Box 376, College Park, MD 20740

Seal Press, 310 S. Washington, Seattle, WA 98104

Seattle Pacific University Press, Seattle, WA 98119

Seattle Review, University of Washington, Seattle, WA 98195

Second Coming, P. O. Box 31249, San Francisco, CA 94131

Sedna Press, 1409 Twining, Anchorage, AK 99567

Seed-In-Hand, P.O. Box 88, Blackstock, SC 29014

Seems Lakeland College, Sheboygan, WI 53081

Samisdat, Box 129, Richford, VT 05476

Seven Buffaloes Press, Box 249, Big Timber, MT 59011

Seven Woods Press, P.O. Box 32, Village Sta., New York, NY 10014

Sewanee Review, University of the South, Sewanee TN 37375

SEZ, P.O. Box 8803, Minneapolis, MN 55408

Shankpainter, 24 Pearl St., Provincetown, MA 02653

Shearwater Press, P.O. Box 417, Wellfleet, MA 02667

Sheep Meadow Press, 145 Central Park West, New York, NY 10022

Shenandoah, Box 722, Lexington, VA 24450

Silverfish Review, P.O. Box 3541, Eugene, OR 97403

Sing Out, 505 Eighth Ave., New York, NY 10018

Singular Speech Press, 507 Dowd Ave., Canton, CT 06019

Sky Publications, 210 Skylands Rd., Ringwood, NJ 07456

Small Pond Magazine, P.O. Box 664, Stratford, CT 06497

The Smith, 5 Beekman St., New York, NY 10038

Smoke Shop Press, 38 New Hampshire St., Cranston, RI 02920

Snapdragon, University of Idaho, Moscow, ID 83843

Snowy Egret, 205 S. Ninth St., Williamsburg, KY 40769

Society Ordo Templi Orientis in America, P.O. Box 90144, Nashville, TN 37209

Solo Press, 7975 San Marcos Ave., Atascadero, CA 93421

Sombre Reptiles Press, P.O. Box 9147, Berkeley, CA 94709

Some, 309 West 104th St., #9D, New York, NY 10021

Some Other Magazine, 47 Hezer Ct., Wayne, NJ. 07470

Sonora Review, University of Arizona, Tucson, AZ 85321

Soundings East, Salem State College, Salem, MA 01970

South American Explorers Club, 2239 E. Coltex Ave, Denver, CO 80206

Southern Exposure, P.O. Box 531, Durham, NC 27702

Southern Poetry Review, University of North Carolina, Charlotte, NC 28233

Southport Press, Carthage College, Kenosha, WI 53141

Southwest Review, SMU Press, Dallas, TX 75275

Southwestern Review, S.M.U., Dallas, TX 75275

Southwestern, Southern Illinois University, Edwardsville, IL 62026

Space and Time, 4-B, 138 W. 70th St., New York, NY 10023

Spirit That Moves Us Press, P.O. Box 1585, Iowa City, IA 52240

Spoon River Press, P.O. Box 1443, Peoria, IL 61655

Spoon River Quarterly, Southwest State University, Marshall, MN 56258

Starlight Press, Box 3102, Long Island City, NY 11103

Station Hill Press, Barrytown, NY 12507

Stone Country, 20 Lorraine Rd., Madison, NJ 07940

Stonehenge Books, Parker Plaza, 1582 So. Parker Rd., Denver, CO 80230

Stony Hills, Weeks Mills, New Sharon, ME 04955

Story Press, P.O. Box 10040, Chicago, IL 60610

Story Quarterly, 820 Ridge Rd., Highland Park, IL 60035

Street Bagel, 147-156 Roosevelt Ave., Flushing, NY 11354

Studio Mystica, 6000 J St., Sacramento, CA 95819

The Sun, 412 West Rosemary St., Chapel Hill, NC 27514

Sun & Moon, 4330 Hartwick Rd, College Park, MD 20740
Swamp Press, 320 Pelham Rd, Amherst, MA 01002
Swift River, Box 264, Leverett, MA 01054

Tamarind Magazine, 200 W. 83rd St., New York, NY 10024
Tamarisk, 319 S. Juniper St., Philadelphia, PA 19107
Tar River Poetry, East Carolina University, Greenville, NC 27834
Taurus, Box 28, Gladstone, OR 97027
Tejas Art Press, 208 Morningside Dr., San Antonio, TX 7820
Telephone Books, 109 Dunk Rock Rd., Guilford, CT 06437
Temenos, 47 Paulton's Square, London, England
Tendril, Box 512, Green Harbor, MA 02041
Texas Review, Sam Houston State University, Huntsville, TX 77340
13th Moon, Box 3, Inwood Sta. New York, NY 10034
This, 2020-9th Ave., Oakland, CA 94606
Threepenny Review, P.O. Box 335, Berkeley, CA 94701
Thunder City Press, P.O. Box 11126, Birmingham, AL 35202
Thunder's Mouth Press, 242 W. 104th St., New York, NY 10028
Timberline, P.O. Box 397, Fulton, MO 65251
Time Capsule, G P.O. Box 1185, New York, NY 10116
Tinderbox, 334 Molasses La., Mt. Pleasant, SC 29464
Tompson & Rutter, P.O. Box 297, Grantham, NH 03753
Toothpaste Press, Box 546, West Branch, IA 52358
TriQuarterly, Northwestern University, Evanston, IL 60201
Truly Fine Press, P.O. Box 891, Bemidji MN 56601
Turkey Press, 6746 Sueno Rd., Isla Vista, CA 93117
Tuumba Press, 2639 Russell St., Berkeley, CA 94703

Uncle Magazine, Rt. 1, Box 1134, Springfield, MO 65803
Unicorn Press, P.O. Box 3307, Greensboro, NC 27402
United Artists, 9B, 172 E. 4th St., New York, NY 10009
U.S. Catholic, 221 West Madison St., Chicago, IL 60606
Universal Black Writer, P.O. Box 5, Radio City Sta., New York, NY 10101
University Press of Mississippi, 3825 Ridgewood Rd., Jackson, MS 39210
Uzzano Press, 511 Sunset Dr., Menomonie, WI 54750

Vagabond, 1610 North Water, Ellensburg, WA 98926

Valhalla, 59 Sandra Circle A-3, Westfield, NJ 07090

Vanderbilt Review, 911 W. Vanderbilt, Stephenville, TX 6401

Vanguard Books, P.O. Box 3566, Chicago, IL 60654

Vanity Press, 160-6th Ave., New York, NY 10013

Vegetable Box, 135 Madison La. #1, Charlottesville, VA 22903

Ventura Press, P.O. Box 1076, Guerneville, CA 95446

The Virginia Quarterly Review, One West Range, Charlottesville, VA 22903

Visible Language, P.O. Box 413, Milwaukee, WS 53201

The Volcano Review, 142 South Creek Canyon, Volcano, CA 95689


Washington Review, Box 50132, Washington, D.C. 20004

Washington Writers' Publishing House, P.O. Box 50068, Washington, D.C. 20004

Water Mark Press, 108 Arbor Glen Cresc., London, Ontario, Canada N5Y129

Waves, 79 Denham Dr., Thornhill, Ontario, Canada L4J1P2

Webster Review, Webster Groves, MO 63119

West Branch, Bucknell University, Lewisburg, PA 17837

West Coast Poetry Review, 1335 Dartmouth Dr., Reno, NV 89509

West Southwest Book Publishing Co., P.O. Box 4064, Redding, CA 96099

Western Humanities Review, University of Utah, Salt Lake City, UT 84112

Western Publishers, 204, 10711-107 Ave., Edmonton, Alberta, Canada T5H0W6

Westwood, 1610 15th St., Denver, CO 80202

W. Whimsy Press, 1822 Northview, Arnold, MO 63010

White Ewe Press, Box 996, Adelphi, MD 20783

White Pine Press, 73 Putnam St., Buffalo, NY 14213

White Walls, P.O. Box 8204, Chicago, IL 60680

Whitmarsh and Co., 6342 Ivarene Ave., Hollywood, CA 90068

Wickwire Press, 290 Harvard Yard, Cambridge, MA 02139

William and Mary Review, Williamsburg, VA 23185

Willow Springs Magazine, P.O. Box 1063, Eastern Washington University, Cheney, WA 99004

Wind, Rt. 1, Box 809K, Pikeville, KY 41501

Windless Orchard, Purdue University, Ft. Wayne, IN 46801

Winesburg Express, 624 Duane, Glen Ellyn, IL 60137

Wings, R2, Box 325, Belfast, ME 04915

Women-In-Literature, P.O. Box 12668, Reno, NV 89510
Woodrose Editions, 524 Larson St., Waupaca, WI 54981
Works In Progress, P.O. Box 188, Edgewater, NJ 07020
World University Press, 31 High St., New Haven, CT 06511
Wormwood Review, P.O. Box 8840, Stockton, CA 95208
Wot, 657 Ardmore Dr., RR2, Sidney, B.C., Canada U8L351
Writ Magazine, 2 Sussex Ave., Toronto, Canada M5S1JF
Write to Sell, P.O. Box 706, Carpinteria, CA 93013
Writers Forum, University of Colorado, Colorado Springs,
   CO 80907

Xenophobic Press, 95 Mission St., Wailuku, Maui, HI 96790

Yale Review, 1902A Yale Station, New Haven, CT 06520
Yellow Moon Press, 6 Shepard St., Cambridge, MA 02138
Yellow Silk, P.O. Box 6374, Albany, CA 94706
Yellow Umbrella Press, 501 Main St., Chatham, MA 02633

Zartscop Inc., 267 West 89th St., New York, NY 10024
Zephyr Press, 13 Robinson St., Somerville, MA 02245

# INDEX
# TO THE FIRST SEVEN
# *PUSHCART PRIZE*
# VOLUMES

The following is a listing in alphabetical order by author's name of works reprinted in the first seven *Pushcart Prize* editions.

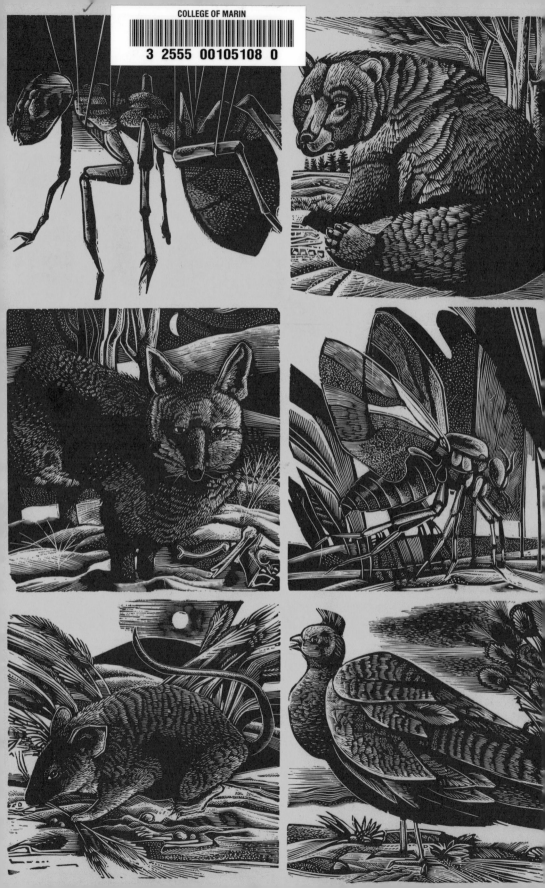